MW01193461

Medieval

Book of Blood

Dallas S. Paskell

Book 3 of the Medieval Series

authorHOUSE®

AuthorHouse™
1663 Liberty Drive
Bloomington, IN 47403
www.authorhouse.com
Phone: 1-800-839-8640

Published by AuthorHouse 12/19/2014

ISBN: 978-1-4969-6012-2 (sc)
ISBN: 978-1-4969-6011-5 (e)

Personal thanks to:
My mother first and foremost always: Tillie Paskell,
for always believing in me and my crazy dreams from
professional wrestling, to fighting to writing!
My amazing family
My father: Fred Middlebrook Paskell Jr. without
which, I'd probably have been homeless
My brother: for always being there.
There are too many people to name here, so all of my friends that
helped me see this book through. Kevin Duke for always lending
his services and ability and ear to the projects. (the illustratior of my
novels) Marian Ashline for taking on the role of my new editor.

Personal Thanks:
Paradigm Training Center, Fight Lab, Rilion
Gracie, Old School Combat Gym,
#1 Jeremy Loflin, the best kept secret in MMA
Sam Hoger
Coach David Kelly
Professor Romulo Reis Pereira
Coach Grant Johnson
And all of my teammates from then to now.

To:

James "Bubbie Nugent, Winston Webster, William House, Cory Molloy, Tieng Ho, Kacey Weinkman, John Dingman, Robert Garlic, Nick Cryer, Joshua Flynn, James Nichols, Drew Hays, Erica Flint, Kerry Ashline, Craig Lewis, Alex Lewis, Michael Hiner, Pablo Tamargo,

Also:

to Natalie Cawthorne… The journey has only just begun…

And lastly:

I want to give a personal and sincere thanks to John Mccreary and Ayman Jarrah, my two bosses and friends in the real world. They have given me the ability to work, write and fight. You guys are the greatest! Thank you both for everything!

Safeguard Home Security

Rebels Honky Tonk (Houston, Texas)

Gaslamp (Houston, Texas)

Contents

Prologue

Failure or postponement, that question was worth pondering, wasn't it? Falling Star's first attempted march ended with a halt, at least in one place, Burning Brook. One of his strongest soldiers, Lithil, had been beaten. No matter, Falling Star's forces continued to scourge the land. He needed that artifact, that relic of power, the Pact Stone.

The Pact Stone was the one thing that, if in the right hands, could potentially halt or even end his push into the plane of Thedia. Falling Star's senses gave him a strong feeling about the might of Lithil's victor and his allies. Luckily, the shadow forces did enough to split them. The city of Burning Brook was finally taken, but at what cost?

Lithil was still unaccounted for. Meanwhile, Falling Star dwelled in his own satisfactions knowing Malagant, his strongest soul, had taken his area with ease. Malagant, a soul who'd been around perhaps as long as any, smashed into this land's mightiest forces head on and prevailed.

The world knew his name. Soon all of Thedia would belong to him. Then the mighty Soul Dragon of Shadows would be able to Return to Gemini's plane of conquered verses and take it for himself. Yes, that was the plan. Gemini failed. Failure meant weakness. He'd never failed before, so weakness must surely be the reason why, he thought. The land, the pantheon of Corvana was in shambles already and yet, he hadn't really done anything. His promise, his promise would forever be remembered.

"A thousand mortals shall burn for every scale scratched. For every day imprisoned, a hundred cities will perish."

Lithil bled. His blood mixed the colors of red and a dark milky black. Who was this Taj? He heard something call out his name. His name was Taj. Taj was fantastic! He would make a great host for perhaps Malagant. The city fell and its inhabitants fled. They would be found and usurped accordingly. Lithil was too weak. He hadn't been in Thedia long enough to recover if he was to die. Death was acceptable and never permanent, unless killed too soon upon crossing over. And that's where he was. He was second only to Malagant, the true champion of Gemini. Lithil knew his homeworld was dying. He knew his mission was critical. In order to keep those alive that he loved, he had to lead the armies along with Malagant into the taking of other worlds.

Geminus, Gemini's homeworld, had been dying for an untold amount of time. In order for it to maintain stability and life, it had to feed on the essence of other verses. And Lithil and Malagant were the driving forces behind keeping Geminus alive.

He hurried. He pushed his body as fast as his wounded feet would carry him. Looking back every so often, the dying elf saw nothing but his trail of blood. He could smell the burning soot and ash in the air. Not all of his enemy's allies survived. It had been so long since anything had put up a fight such as Taj did. His swords, Lithil felt an impressive amount of power coming off his swords. Was his power in the swords? Maybe, but there was also something else about him; great entities attached themselves to him. At least one was inside him and two or three others were around. His soul was impenetrable. Something(s) already had it.

The shadows never liked the night. However, it was where they were forced to exist. It didn't mean they had to like it. Older than the blood feud of elves and orcs, the shades never cared for the undead, and likewise. And this Taj, though not undead himself, certainly had a strong connection to them. Lithil's ability to sense the undead was second to none and Taj's body was very much alive and well, but something inside him was not. Who was this Taj or better, what was he?

The human died. How was another Eternian here? Who was he and why was he here? What was this new thing they were facing? His life was getting worse and worse. It was becoming increasingly complicated. Sevok and Warryn were both dead. Their bodies lay scattered amongst the blanket of death. The wizards who started the defense of the city were also dead. The paladin was dead. Helios broke rank and luckily ended up with Danth. So far, his body hadn't been found. Hopefully, he made it. Talon was missing. Did he make it back with Danth to? Only a wounded Taj, Malakai, Giovanni, Rhoeve, and Halo remained. The team had been split. Blood had been spilled. Somehow, during the disarray, Malakai ended up with the Pact Stone. Malakai was virtually untouched. His powers were spent. Legions of the infected had been obliterated, laid to waste by the now seemingly invincible elf, Malakai Downing.

Chapter 1

T aj returned from the valley where he faced Lithil to the ruined village of Burning Brook. Taj was pleased. He singlehandedly defeated the mighty elf. Unfortunately, he was unable to finish him before his shadowy powers saved him from his blades. Lithil's shadow stepped back out of the valley and into a small legion of the infected. As humor was on Taj's side, it was the same Legion Malakai had just turned his focus to.

Taj sheathed his blades, knowing they were both happy. He could hear Froth speaking to him from the inside now. That voice was too clear not to recognize it. It was Froth. Froth was growing inside him. His body was strong yet weak. It was living but something inside him was very much dead, or undead.

Coming from the smoking remains of what was one of the city's walls, Malakai came first. Taj looked to his right. Halo was sitting down, quietly meditating in what used to be the town square. Rhoeve was finishing a few barely living infected off at the far side of the city while Giovanni pulled the dead to a pile.

"There's no need for that Gio," Malakai said.

"We have to give them a proper burial," he answered defensively.

"We're going to burn the whole thing. Everything here will become ash and return to the earth from whence it came," said the multi-innate sorcerer.

Taj knew. His swords first recognized it. There were four main types of sorcerers. Each type drew its power from a different source. Certain powers were unique to that specific type. Taj had marked it down every time he'd seen something different. So far, Malakai had covered Draconic, Chaotic,

1

Storm, and even Cosmic, the most rare of sorcerer types. Lastly and in secret, he'd even utilized powers only known to the shadow elves and the outcast sorcerers that came from them.

"Burn the whole thing, to nothing?" Giovanni asked.

"This is your legendary friend you told me so much about? I spent time with you two in the war, Giovanni, and the whole time Taj reminded me of how great you were. You know why, because of your inability to feel mortal compassion. Has that changed?" Malakai laughed as he spoke words of aggravation to the Sylvan.

"No Malakai, but these were the only real people that ever accepted me."

"They would understand, they do understand, old friend. You're lucky we have someone as powerful and in tuned as Malakai. Otherwise, we'd just have to leave them."

"What's Halo doing? Oh by the dead Gods, you've got to be kidding me."

"Easy Mal, I'm sure there's an explanation." Rhoeve had finished off the last of the infected and had made his way back to the regrouping three.

"Find what you can that's flammable and not already burning and spread it. I'm not sure if these things will come back," said Malakai.

"I doubt it. Usually the shadow and the undead don't work together. The shade is a different form of existence. It's different from the undead," Taj added.

"These things fought like rabid zombies infused with a high dose of magic if you ask me," Rhoeve replied.

"Sevok and Warryn are both dead. I'll be the first to say it," Rhoeve continued.

"They weren't part of our real crew anyway. We found them along the way. I'm not sure if I really trusted them anyhow," Taj said with no concern for his dead allies.

"Nonetheless, they were still allies. I thought I saw Talon heading off somewhere toward the retreating group over there," Giovanni chipped in; pointing toward the direction Danth and the others had fled. "Has anyone seen him?"

"I'm not sure where he is. The good news is, his race his powerful and plentiful in those mountains. If he did get that far out, he'll be fine. He should be fine. I hope he is," Rhoeve answered.

"It doesn't matter. Halo, Gio, Malakai, and you Rhoeve are all I've got left. Danth and the others should be safe and secure."

2

"Taj, what about the others? You can't simply be that heartless," Giovanni questioned.

"I gave my word I'd stop this thing and make that territory inhabitable by Corvana in order to save my land. My world, at least what I know of Thedia, is in my hands," Taj said.

"I don't think Corvana's concerned about the war right now. I don't think you should be either." Rhoeve challenged.

"What's with Halo?" asked Giovanni. He kept looking back to her as the conversation continued. "I'm going to see to her." He rushed off to see how Halo was and why she was sitting Indian style, meditating calmly.

"I'm not sure if I like the new Giovanni," Taj said, for the first time showing legitimate concern in his voice.

Malakai laughed. They had a lot to do. They hadn't a plan. Their team had been split. Even unified, they really didn't stand a chance against the godlike creature from the foreign world. What was the plan? Thedia itself had let the Tarrasque loose. There were so many stories as to what that could even be. In all the ancient tales, it was something so vicious it annihilated civilizations and everything else in its wake to once again purify Thedia.

The group agreed no one really knew enough about the Tarrasque to worry about it. The focus was Falling Star.

"We have the Pact Stone. Falling Star is free and Corvana is dying. What now?" Rhoeve asked.

"The Pact Stone sealed Falling Star. Something in it must be a weakness for him. Or, it at least reveals or opens up a weakness that he has. We have to get to Falling Star." Even while speaking, Taj knew how preposterous his words sounded.

"We're supposed to fight a God, a Dragon God?" Giovanni asked. His words were abstract even as he said them. "Exactly how are we supposed to go about doing that?"

"I don't know," Taj answered.

"At least I know I have one true ally here, Taj," Rhoeve said, finally sheathing his bastard sword.

"And what's that supposed to mean, sir?" Malakai's tone told Rhoeve of his anger. He was quick to anger and everyone knew it. He had absolutely no problem killing anyone for the slightest reason.

"It just means I feel like Taj and I are on the same page about getting rid of this problem."

3

"Rhoeve, I've been here the whole way. I'm still here and I killed more of those damned things than any of you. I kind of feel like your words should've been directed at me as well."

"Mal, he's just saying I want to see this through because of the word I gave and he wants to see this through because this is his homeland," Taj said, trying to cool down his friend.

"What about my home, Taj? My homeland is your homeland. Whenever this place is nothing, Falling Star isn't just going to quit."

Rhoeve smiled. Now he knew he had another true ally. "Yes, you're right, sorcerer, and I stand corrected. You are also a trusted ally and well met. I'm lucky to travel with such a sorcerer."

Malakai sat back. He didn't want to admit it. He liked the praise and appreciation of Rhoeve's words.

Taj laughed.

"What's up, Halo?" Giovanni crouched next to the small creature before sitting down beside her. Though he'd changed, his affinity for women hadn't. Of course, he wasn't the man who slept with every girl he wanted anymore, was he? Seeing Giovanni with Halo comforted Taj. It made him remember back to when Giovanni was really himself.

"Just like old times," he said thinking back to times he watched Giovanni conquer so many beautiful women.

"Oh sorry," she said. It was obvious he interrupted her. "I was just trying to…" She stopped.

"What?" he asked pleasantly. This time, there were no ulterior motives. He was truly concerned and curious.

"My sister and I, it's just that…" she started again before pausing.

"What about your sister and you?" he persisted.

"Well, we have this link."

"Link?" he questioned.

"We're able to stay in touch. We're able to communicate, telepathically. She's okay. They made it to the hold in the mountains. Teraxius and Danth are fine as well. Danth is trying to connect to one of his old guilds. I'm not sure the name though. He's trying to unify all of his old guilds into one. What's left of them anyway, from what Eve told me." She seemed more like her sister than herself. She was different. Maybe it was the fight or the fact her sister was gone for the time being. Either way, she wasn't as bubbly as she normally was.

4

Medieval

"That's magnificent! Why didn't you tell us that? We'll be able to keep in touch with them. We'll be able to work together while not together," Giovanni said excitedly. He reached over, leaning into and on top of Halo, hugging her tightly.

"What's going on over there?" Rhoeve asked.

"There's no time for that!" Taj barked.

Malakai just mumbled, "How does he do that?" to himself.

Giovanni informed them it wasn't anything like that at all. Halo and the Sylvan quickly reunited with the rest of their party. He was quick to inform Taj of Halo's ability with her sister. Of course, Taj and Rhoeve were both equally pleased.

"Do you know of Talon? Is he all right?" Rhoeve asked.

"I don't know. His name didn't really come up."

"Well, ask her," Malakai said sarcastically.

"No, it doesn't work like that. I can only do it every so often. Once, maybe twice in a week's time. I mean it's something we've rarely done together but we always knew we could. Somehow, the powers that be just never wanted us apart," she said happily.

"Hmmm." Malakai gestured.

"Very well, we'll have to seek shelter and figure out our next plan of attack from there." Taj was clear in his words and his motives.

"How are those things taking over our people?" Rhoeve asked. "I just can't figure it out."

"I don't know. Lithil used the powers of both a Paladin and a wizard. He was crafty. I'm thinking he was both and I don't mean the type to just know a few things here or there. I mean, he was doing all sorts of things not typical for a paladin."

Rhoeve heard his words, as did the rest. Halo was the first to pitch back a reply. "Maybe whatever these things are, they take over your mind as well as your body. I mean there are many different explanations for these infected. It was said to us by your people, Giovanni, that these things do operate in such a manner, correct?"

"Aye," he answered.

"What are they attaching themselves to?" Taj asked.

The answer came from inside him. Deep within his very own chest and heart rested the answer he asked for. It was clear. Froth had answered him. They were right. These shadowy specters from the other world had the ability to implant and infuse themselves with living beings' souls. From there, everything would be taken over by the being. Taj relayed his message to the team and went over what the others had said before.

The remaining five spoke of the infected and how they worked. They spoke of the Tarrasque and how to possibly go about locating it and/ or possibly stopping it. They'd been over it several times. It had been discussed, exactly what the infected were. Now they were dealing with it, fighting it, living against it. To speak of something of such power is one thing, but to experience and defend against it something else.

"First thing's first. As soon as you are able, find out if Talon is okay," Taj ordered.

Halo nodded. "I'm sure he's fine."

"All the same, just confirm it," he ordered again.

"I will."

"We should make camp," Malakai said, laughing. "I'll start the fire." Not too many of his group delved into his dry humor. It wasn't too funny to the rest of them.

He made true on his promise. The team spent a few days hiding in and out of the city ruins, mostly in the underground sewage tunnels. Within a few days, everything was set up and Malakai burned it all. The blaze was massive as the village was the size of a few city blocks. Halo had the Pact Stone. Somehow, she managed to carry it gracefully.

Malakai did desire the orb of power. It was possibly the most powerful weapon in the world. It carried powers from the mortal realm, the lost Gods, the dragons, demons, devils, angels, the elements, and even some of the shadow that was left behind during the Final War of the Shadow.

"We need knowledge. None of us carries the religious knowledge needed to continue forward. In fighting something such as this, as foolish as it is already, it would possibly be even more foolish, to say we would do it without the aid of a priest, preferably one of the Draconic faith." Giovanni wasn't always right but this time he was dead on.

"Danth is in the mountains at the hold. I know of no other priests of his stature or greater. We need the oldest and most knowledgeable priest in Corvana," Giovanni seconded.

"I know a little about the faiths," Halo chimed in, trying to make light of the situation.

"There is one," Rhoeve said hesitantly.

"A priest?" Halo asked.

"Why exactly do we need a priest? Why can we not take care of this?" Taj asked.

"Because with what we're dealing with, Taj, we're going to need all the help we can get. And secondly, a great cleric or priest might know little details that could make the difference in life and death, victory and defeat," Rhoeve replied.

Taj didn't like it but he understood it. Another new face. All his life he'd continually added new faces to his memory. There were very few worth trusting. As always, he knew it was coming. He figured he'd go ahead and break the ice.

"Who is this priest?"

"Golric Firesoul," announced Rhoeve.

"Golric, what kind of name is Golric?" Halo asked.

"He's what they call a goliath. They descend from giants, mostly hill giants and such, and ogres and humans and things like that."

Rhoeve had just told them he wanted to enlist the help of a half-giant, or goliath. Back in Myasuna, Taj remembered seeing a few. There were even a few in Eternis here and there. They were rare, extremely rare.

"Do you know how to get to this Golric Firesoul and do you know if he'll help us?" Malakai asked.

"To be honest, we don't know who is alive and who isn't. What I can tell you is his burning Redlands are far Northwest of here. Mountains and caves and badlands and everything in between block his people from the rest of Thedia."

Giovanni turned to Rhoeve, who seemed to know so much about Golric and his land. "So you were just going to let them keep it, right?" He said, allowing the emotional past of Burning Brook to get the better of him.

"Absolutely, Golric's people are remote and quiet. They don't bother anything and they live in the nearly uninhabitable burning territories, or at least one of them. Corvana has no business in that territory," he replied.

"They do now," Giovanni said, whipping right back at Rhoeve, saying that Rhoeve, who was of Corvana now had business in the Redlands because it was in fact for the safety and future of Corvana.

"The Redlands are a series of four territories in the Northwest past the Dripping Mountains. The volcanic activity is beyond measure. Geysers and volcano eruption is as common as dirt. It's said there are waterfalls of fire in those lands." Rhoeve did know his land. After all, he was an ambassador for Corvana.

"Then why or how would anybody live there?" asked Halo.

"Golric isn't a Draconic priest. There are some beings of the others faiths he's come to respect and appreciate as higher powers. Every one of those beings is of the fire domain. Golric Firesoul is the High Priest of the Elemental Church of Fire. It was a title handed down to him by his father. And the title belonged to his father before him."

"How do you know so much about him?" Giovanni asked.

"Let's just say his presence in Corvana has been known for quite some time. His family's presence has been known for millennia. The outside border cities and kingdoms all know to remain far from the Redlands borders. The Burning Kingdom, as he calls it, does not take well to intruders."

"Well then, let's not intrude," Taj said kindly.

Chapter 2

The trek to the Redlands was the most grueling of Taj's life. Even with his hosts, he was hurting. His insides, his abdominals, felt as if they were going to fall out of him. He couldn't explain it. It wasn't a pain he could keep ignoring. It was getting worse.

More and more of the infected came. From atop hillsides and mountain slopes, the team watched as cities fell and turned. This army was different. The more adversaries you brought against them, the more hosts they seemed to claim. Fighting them at the front was a losing battle. How could they fight this army, much less, the head of it?

"We have quite a bit to go through here before we can even think we're going to make it. We have to hope to make it without being seen in the first place. I'm not sure how you'd fend off one of those things against your soul," Rhoeve said to the group while taking a big step over a large boulder.

The first portion of their hike would take them through the burnt and destroyed remains of several borderland villages and cities. It was all too new and fresh to worry about unexpected surprises. However, stray infected could be anywhere and they were. Every so often, the crew of five would have to end another unfortunate soul's life.

"These poor innocent people," said Giovanni, saddened.

"It has to be done," Rhoeve announced peeling his sword out of yet another hiding infected.

"Yes it does," agreed Taj.

"I don't like it any better than you do, Gio. For the greater tomorrow, it has to be done." Rhoeve felt strong in his words though he wasn't even sure if he believed them.

"So what do we do in the event one of these things comes after one of our souls? I mean, will we even see it coming? How do you fight something that targets your soul?" Taj asked.

"You don't, old friend. You run. You run as fast as you can. I have a few tricks up my sleeve to get rid of some. You'll see them. I'm sure of it." Something about Malakai's words told Taj he knew more than he was letting on.

"Do you know something that I don't?" Taj asked.

"You mean that we don't," reminded Rhoeve.

"No, I'm just saying you'll probably see them coming. They'll probably look like shadow people, or something," the sorcerer answered, halfway confused, or perhaps he was just pretending to be.

"I don't know. If we see something that doesn't sit well with us, we run."

"No Rhoeve, you all run and point it out to me and I'll fight it off while you all get to safety," suggested Malakai.

"LLLEEEETTT'S just cross that road when we get there." Giovanni started off saying the word let's really loud and long, intensifying it in order to get the team back on track.

City after city, village after village, the team of five carried itself onward. Finally, Halo was able to tell her friends that Talon was in fact unaccounted for. Danth assumed he'd returned to Taj. Halo informed Eve that Talon was in fact not with them and presumed gone.

On a good note, Danth's old guild Reforged had been found. Actually, Reforged found them. The old mountain stronghold was done for. It was gone, all but obliterated. Several Reforged scouts stations inside the old hold found them and brought them back to their sanctuary.

Immediately after the Soul Dragon of Shadows was released, Reforged began renovating an ancient underground citadel that had been lost to the archives through the marches of time. One of their members had stumbled across it years prior.

Wyoman was a clerical servant of the Rivermortal and the current leader of Reforged. He was nothing but a name to Taj after Halo relayed the information. Taj cared not for this Wyoman or his guild. He didn't care for any guild for that matter. What he did care for was victor. Victory at all costs was his goal.

He often scolded Halo for using her time with her sister to navigate through useless things rather than critical matters that could, in fact, be the difference between life and death.

It had been a few weeks since their journey began. Halo was doing her best to keep in contact with Eve. Reforged's underground citadel was prospering. It was growing. More and more survivors were being rescued by Reforged's scouts.

Taj couldn't wrap his head around the time distortion. How long had the Soul Dragon of Shadows truly been awake before they returned? From the time they took the Pact Stone until the time they made it back to Corvana, how much time had passed? Why did this guild just magically happen to have an underground citadel ready and in place?

"Halo, has Eve told you why this guild somehow managed to have an underground citadel in place and ready? How did they know this was going to happen?" Taj asked, getting angry. The more he thought about it, the more hate filled he became.

"No, I will ask for you next time," she replied submissively. She wasn't the same as before. Ever since Eve left, her whole demeanor changed. She was different. Actually, she was more like Eve now.

Taj pondered on Eve's demeanor. Was she the same or was she more of a wild and free spirit? Froth comforted Taj reinforcing his confidence by saying his soul was impenetrable. Had Froth been inside him this whole time? That explained many things to Taj. Way back when, so long ago, when Froth first bit Taj, was it to truly save him or create an insurance policy for himself? Or, was it both?

"Isn't it odd how Reforged had a hidden citadel ready and in place?" Taj questioned aloud to the group.

"Guilds can be funny. Some stay ready for anything," Rhoeve said.

"It's all a blur. I remember getting the Pact Stone and then returning, meeting back up with you, Gio." Taj pointed to his Sylvan friend. "When we appeared back in front of Burning Brook... Well... To us, it was as if we just reappeared. Time had passed. The Dragon had been released for a while. He had to have been."

"So, you want to know how long Falling Star's presence was felt before you came to Burning Brook?" asked Giovanni.

"It would answer a lot of questions," added Malakai.

"Aye, it would," seconded the Eternian.

"That territory began acting strange—" started Giovanni.

"The territory acted strange?" Taj interrupted.

"Aye, let me finish," said Giovanni.

"That storm happening, or whatever it was, I remember that thing," Rhoeve said under the tone of Giovanni, not wanting to interrupt him.

"Storm?" asked Halo.

"Let me finish!" Giovanni said again, laughing but seriously wanting to get it out.

"Yes, let him finish." Taj unsheathed his blades and rested the crossing point on the back of his neck.

Giovanni just looked at Taj and smiled. The rest of the crew waited patiently for Giovanni to continue.

"It had been one third a year of the coming of Falling Star, to the day, that you arrived—that you came back, returned." Giovanni knew it down to the day. The suffering pressed upon his people and others by Falling Star was immeasurable.

"We were gone for that long?" Taj asked, almost lost. He couldn't believe it. Nearly one hundred and sixty seven days of his life were missing, gone from his memory.

"I guess. I don't know how long you were gone or where you were., We counted the days. The day of his arrival was the worst in Corvanian history. Nothing documented ever did so much as Falling Star did the day of his awakening. You appeared at Burning Brook one hundred and sixty six days later."

The others listened to Giovanni. He knew what he was talking about. Halo, Rhoeve, Malakai, and Taj just walked, oblivious to their surroundings. Giovanni kept a vigilant eye. He knew he had to. Halo spent most of her time thinking about Teraxius and her sister. She'd never been apart from her sister before.

Giovanni spoke again of the promise of Falling Star, reiterating to his teammates just what was out there and what was to come.

The five traveled through the broken towns, the abandoned borderland cities, and through the rough terrain for days, weeks and even months with minimal encounters with the infected. Giovanni's keen eye located a survivor.

The team had come up through the back end of an old city. Giovanni and Halo both knew the city, the grand city of Wyndemere. Wyndemere was known for its glamorous buildings and structures. Even the Corvanian inner council would venture out to Wyndemere to purchase special relics and one of-a-kind treasures for their spouses, family, and other loved ones.

It was Halo's idea to search the city. Compared to the others, it looked to be in remarkable shape. It was desolate however with no signs of life, no dead bodies, no skeletons, rotting corpses, no nothing.

There were four entrances into Wyndemere, a gate entrance on each side. A fifth entrance existed with only a select few ever gaining knowledge of it. As luck would have it, Halo was one of those people.

"So you know the hidden entrance?" Rhoeve asked.

"I do," she replied.

"The gates are open. Why not just walk in through the front gate?" questioned Malakai boldly.

Taj thought back to that conversation before they entered the city. Halo informed them that they were nearly out of rations and their armor needed mending. Some weapons needing fixing. Wyndemere looked good from afar. It was a no brainer to search the city for supplies, rations, and such.

Malakai's concern was that the infected would scour the cities for life. Wyndemere was one of the premier cities. Upon entering through the back alleyway, they noticed nothing seemed out of place.

A decent walk took the team from a hidden alleyway surrounded by old warehouses and stores to the center of town, the town square. An old fountain still springing water stood in the center. It was made of stone and in a circular fashion. In the center of the circle was a structural masterpiece sculpture fashioned as a five-layer abstract piece of artwork filled with fountains and ducts for all to see. The water was stained with gold. It was beautiful.

Typically, Halo was more fascinated than the others. She already liked nice things, and more than that, she was a woman. Taj laughed seeing the little Halo fascinated. Giovanni looked around, keeping his eagle eye out ready for any and everything. Rhoeve was tired. The elven ambassador turned to line his back up against the fountain. The elf hit his butt, exhausted. Malakai looked about and was the first to approach the golden-laced water and fountain.

The sorcerer looked down at the perfect water. It reminded him of better times. For a fleeting moment, he wasn't where he was. He was back in his homeland appreciating what he had.

"Malakai, Malakai…" Taj said his name louder and with more meaning the second time. It was to get his attention.

"Yeah," Malakai said still half out of it. "Sorry." He snapped back into reality and turned around to see his team. Their eyes were scanning the city's walls and for good reason. If the infected were present and got the drop on them, they would certainly be done for.

"We can fight the physical infected. The ghost ones are a problem," Rhoeve said.

Halo pulled her hair back with one hand and scratched the top of Rhoeve's head with the other. "Let's not worry about the infected right now. Let's get our supplies and rations and anything else this town can offer and get out of here." Rhoeve's head was buried in his hands but he did appreciate the head scratch.

"That's foolish Halo. We should always be ready in case the infected are near. They're a type of enemy you can never take lightly. We're not even sure what they are or how to fight them," Giovanni said.

"I guess you're right," she replied

"Of course he's right," Taj said haughtily while pulling blades.

Taj's hand and eye signals told the team he was looking at something. Rhoeve was the last to stand and ready himself. They were ready and Taj's eyes had found something.

From afar, on the other side of town square heading toward the front of the city, a single being exited an old abandoned warehouse. It was human, or at least half human. She wore tattered clothes and her short brown hair down. She was dirty, as were her weapons. She looked like a traveling scout or adventurer. Dried blood splotches also covered her outfit. It was mostly the color of brown leather but with black boots.

She walked closely toward the team. The team mirrored her movements, advancing closer to her. Giovanni yelled out to the girl, "Hey, are you okay?" but the woman said nothing in return. "Stop moving and answer me," Giovanni said, giving her a second chance.

"He said stop moving!" Malakai ordered ferociously. His hands garnered a glowing green energy instantly. His eyes mimicked his fists.

"Malakai," Taj yelled, "hold."

"Not a chance," he replied, psychotically laughing at what would soon become his next victim.

"Mal," Halo yelled, concerned.

"What's with you all? Kill her!" The sorcerer made his stand clear. He wasn't taking any chances.

"We don't know who she is—" Rhoeve started to say but was interrupted.

Malakai let loose a series of intertwining green and white missiles at the woman. The woman just walked unconcerned with the sorcerer and his attempts to end her. Seeing the whistling bolts of energy zoom toward her, the woman peeled her weapon, a black maul with ancient inscriptions gleaming with magic, necrotic magic.

The missiles refocused their attention and headed toward the maul and soon after were absorbed. Malakai laughed. "Oh she blushes," he said; ready to have at her again.

Rhoeve rushed to the right side as Giovanni made his move to the left.

Taj laughed to himself. "Perfect, I'll get her head on," he said, seeing Halo pull her short bow.

Malakai was readying another spell. This time, he was entrenching himself in a white smoky power. It was a different type of energy, one his team hadn't seen before. Malakai was known for his rays, bolts, and missiles more than his area-of-effect spells, zones, and blasts. His trickery magic was non-existent, as far as his allies knew.

Suddenly, screaming bombs of cloudy smoke rocketed themselves toward the woman. This time, they hit. The woman's aura quickly filled with the smoky power of Malakai's choosing. It wasn't a radiant energy but still energy unknown to the others. Halo should have known the energy type. She knew magic and power.

Halo's bow was readied. It carried miniscule magical prowess. The woman fell helpless and the clouds of smoke covered her. The remnant remains of the bombs dug themselves deep into the ground around her. They were still empowered and electrical lines danced across them.

"Ha!" Malakai laughed.

The woman's maul fell away from her. Giovanni kept a vigilant eye out. He knew if it were the infected, she wouldn't be alone.

"Everyone okay?" yelled Rhoeve.

"No, I'm dying over here. She got me," Malakai said, laughing.

"Knock it off," Taj ordered still in militant mode.

"What was she?" Halo asked.

"Your guess is as good as mine," Rhoeve answered nearing the wreckage of the woman's body. Looking up, he saw Giovanni following.

Taj, Malakai, and Halo also closed their distances to the woman as well. The five surrounded the dead creature. She was a woman with both human and elven origin. Malakai's magic destroyed her. What if she wasn't one of them? What if she was a survivor? Why did she pull the maul?

Giovanni couldn't help but notice. The city was different. There was something different about it. It was in perfect shape, immaculate, and yet not a single solitary sign of life. Until the woman of course, and then, who was she and why was she there alone?

"That maul looks like it has some power in it." Rhoeve picked up the dead woman's weapon. It was heavy, but not as heavy as it should have been. It was the magic of the maul that lightened its load.

"I think you got a new toy," Taj said, laughing.

"Aye, I do," Rhoeve answered.

Giovanni was zoned out. He was scanning the area, the upper windows of the buildings, the entryways, and the like for anything else that could have been a threat.

"What are you looking for?" Halo asked Giovanni while still looking down at the remains of the woman. Remarkably, Malakai's powers didn't mutilate the woman, burn, or char her. She didn't seem to have too much damage at all, minus her eyeballs, which were no longer present.

"It's a power source you wouldn't understand. It's a power not too many practice anymore," Malakai said, seeing Halo confused at the woman's remains and how she died. "It was a trickery magic mostly. It tricks the insides into turning on themselves. I infused it with minute electricity to speed up the process."

"I wasn't aware your arsenal consisted of trickery magic as well," Halo said.

"There's a lot about me you don't know. It was the only type of magic I trusted to penetrate her defenses," Malakai stated. "Something protected her initially from my first blast,"

"Maybe it was the particular spell or the type of energy," Taj said.

"I know necrotic energy works, radiant energy works, and usually anything I do works," Malakai boasted.

"How do you know what works?" asked Rhoeve.

"Because it worked at Burning Brook," answered Malakai, aggravated. The sorcerer with innate powers felt frustration and rage. Why would anyone ask him how he knew his powers worked? The answer was simple, because they worked before.

"Search the city. Don't leave a single rock unturned. Collect all supplies. Make sure nothing else is here. Giovanni, you go with Malakai, and Halo, you stay close to Rhoeve," Taj ordered.

"Hmmm, I guess you don't want her with me for obvious reasons. Who could blame her? I wouldn't be able to hold myself back if I saw me either." Malakai's arrogance poured out with his words.

Halo just rolled her eyes. "You know, of all the men I've met in my life, I don't know if I've met one I'd choose you over."

The team oohed and ahhed, laughing and joking at the little oddity's comment to the sorcerer. Malakai didn't think it was funny. He didn't like being challenged, especially by a woman. "Move." Malakai, Halo, Rhoeve, and Giovanni all heard the word echo again from Taj's mouth. Immediately, they obliged.

The promise of the Falling Star was one Thedia would soon learn. It would first fall upon Corvana. It already had. Corvana was in ruins. Soon, those isles to the Southwest would also belong to the Soul Dragon of Shadows. The wreckage and carnage was already too much for any kingdom to come back from. Corvana was finished.

Another vermin trap proved successful, thought the ancient deity. Everything was in place. Something to the West, yes, it was the West calling. One of his baited had been taken. Yes, that meant life was there. Life non-belonging to the shadow existed in an area where his army had already marched. They had failed. They had overlooked something. Lithil was too far away as was Malagant.

It was time for a new soul to shine. Grismuth. Grismuth's legions were near. Lithil's bait host was killed. Falling Star wasn't foolish. They were rushing for the Northwest. Those Burning Lands, the Redlands, and the Burning Kingdom were still a threat. Fire was a weakness for the Shadow.

The undead were always a force coinciding and colliding with the shadow. Neither necrotic nor radiant energy was strong or weak against the shadow. everything was vulnerable against the shadow, everything.

Fire, those burning lands were going to be a problem and many of the armies would succumb to their burning prowess. Perhaps it was an area better suited for Falling Star himself. Fight their strongest asset head on, that was the way of Falling Star.

Soon, those living bodies walking alongside the borderlands heading Northwest to the Redlands would be taken. Their bodies were strong. Their souls were strong. They would make fine members of the Shadow's Army.

Falling Star blissfully serenaded himself in his own splendor. The thought of his shadowy essence ousting the fires of the burning kingdom brought him great pleasures. The pantheon of Corvana now belonged to him, as if he were the god of the realm. He could see just about everything. Everything already in his shadowy palm and everything warm enough to stand out, he saw. Perhaps only the undead were safe from his vision.

He laughed, thinking back on his promise. It was one he knew he would forever keep. He reminisced, thinking of Thedia before Gemini the invader invaded. Thedia was a dumping ground. It was a place some lost gods found and came together on. It was a perfect plane for farming a new existence.

Then they cut themselves off from the rest of the multi-verse, keeping its splendor and magic for themselves. At one time, Thedia had enough astral resources to keep Gemini's world alive indefinitely. The constant wars and battles and the deaths of the gods had taken their tolls on the plane. It would still be plenty to take with him to conquer Gemini's world for what he did to him. Yes, Gemini, his former liege would soon be his slave and his pet.

He remembered when his people first announced his promise. His words etched indefinitely.

> "On the deepest night, and darkest hour,
> When blood is sweet, and sugar is sour,
> Shadows will rise, and light will fall
> For this is the deepest and coldest night of all.
> When the might of Thedia breathes her last sigh
> Rivers will bleed and mountains will cry,
> Tonight's the night we're destined to die.
> And no matter how hard we strive to survive,
> The deepest death is impossible to revive.
> And when the Lord of Shadows hits his final wave
> To Falling Star, we'll all be slaves."

Chapter 3

The city was searched and nothing was found. It was cleared for resting. Toward the end of the search, Halo and Rhoeve came across something truly impressive. Rhoeve was still wielding the woman's maul. It had officially taken the place of his sword. An old merchant's shop had a hidden chamber underneath it filled with magical weapons, armor, items, jewelry, rings, wands, staves, etc.

Taj, who initially kept watch while the other four searched, couldn't believe the find. Nobody just hoards magical items like that. Especially when items such as those were so rare, and even if they did, why weren't they taken when the town was abandoned?

The team reconnected and made their way into the magical stash. Taj knew certain things could be picked up on certain creatures' radar. Magic was one of those things. He made it clear. Take what you want and need and get out.

It was late. It took forever to search the entire city. They were going to have to rest and soon. Taj didn't pick up anything. The three entities in him wouldn't let him. Then again, he didn't need anything. Some things didn't hold up along the way. Some things were destroyed along the way, and still other things even lost. He couldn't even really remember how they were lost. Then again, with the three beings being inside him, he felt as if a lot of his time had been lost and blurred.

Giovanni grabbed a short blade and a chakram. The Chakram was sonically infused and the short sword was one of the Red Wyrm, giving it the magical fire property. Like everybody, he found two rings of protection and a circlet to wear. Magical protection was absolutely the best in most cases. It wasn't as encumbering as heavy armor but worked just as well, if not better.

Rhoeve chose to keep the woman's necrotic maul. He picked up a magical longbow as well. Most of the weapons down there were infused with a particular type of magical energy. The longbow was not. It was simply just magical.

Recently, Halo was becoming increasingly a ranged fighter. An amulet of eternal throwing daggers found its way into her possession, as did a magical short bow. Again, like Rhoeve's longbow, it was of no particular type. Two rings of protection as well as a circlet also found their way onto her body.

And lastly, Malakai, the elven sorcerer, picked up something he believed never existed, an arch mage's staff of the high council. He also took up a few wands, a rod, and other countless pieces of magic. He, more than the others truly loaded himself down. He knew a goldmine when he saw one.

"Okay, we've got to get out of here," Taj said.

"Wait, why can't we just sleep in here? I mean, it's hidden," Halo asked, still playing with her short bow.

"Because if the find us, they'll be able to swarm us and lock us in from moving or escaping," Taj replied.

"I agree. Grab javelins, missiles, bows, arrows, bolts, crossbows, and everything else," Rhoeve said. "We need to find the high ground here,"

"I come equipped with enough to annihilate an army. I proved it at Burning Brook," Malakai bragged.

Halo just snarled. "We're all getting tired of your cockiness. Your arrogance has run its course."

Malakai just laughed at the little thing.

"Get in touch with your sister. We're going to need them just in case," Taj said. "If all goes well, we'll wake to a sunny morning with this town being just as desolate as it is now."

"How do you know something's going to come?" asked Halo.

"I don't. I'm just assuming," answered Taj.

Giovanni was silent for the conversation. He was too busy digging in and around the magical treasury for anything that could possibly help them in the event of an ambush. "Guys."

The other four turned around to see the crafty Sylvan going to work. He was defusing and reworking all kinds of magical instruments into each other.

Not even Malakai could decipher his agenda. "What are you doing," asked the elven sorcerer.

"I'm building traps, perimeters, something to scatter around the outside of town. If something enters, we'll see it coming."

"Do you think it's going to work?" Rhoeve asked.

"I don't know but it's worth a try. It won't take me long. If you all could just watch my back while I finish this thing, I'll set it all up and then we can get some sleep."

The other four all quickly complied with Giovanni's wishes and within the hour, his gadgets were done. Some looked like basic wands, others were trip wires; each one was very unique and crafty. And with the help of his four comrades, the giant perimeter surrounding Wyndemere was as close to being fully protected as possible.

When it was done, Giovanni pointed high to the front gate's guard tower. "There, there we shall rest."

"No," challenged Malakai, pointing toward an extremely tall structure toward the center of town. "That has to be a wizard's tower. We searched the lower levels of it earlier. It has all the signs. It gives us the best defense in the event of an attack."

"If we need to escape the city, we'll be high up and can just jump over the opposition to safety from there," Giovanni barked back, still pointing toward his choice.

"I'm not one for running," Taj said loudly.

"This isn't exactly running. It's more like avoiding the minor stuff to take out the major stuff," Halo added.

"I just don't know about this. This whole thing seems foolish. We're hiding from an invincible army. The more you send against it, the stronger it becomes. We need a healer. We're hoping that the Burning Kingdom will provide Golric Firesoul to us. Who's to say he'd even join?" Rhoeve was losing faith in it all.

"We have to try," Giovanni muttered. "At the very least, the Burning Kingdom and the Alabaster Isles are the only two things really still decent since his coming,"

"And the Alabaster Isles only take care of their own," said Rhoeve, barely above a whisper. He was down, really down and losing faith by the minute.

"It will be too difficult to get to the Alabaster Isles. We need the strongest right now. The fire people are known for their powerful clergy.

In Corvana, there is no priest worth his weight like Golric Firesoul. Stories of Golric surpass that of any priest I've ever known or heard of. He even surpassed the stories of his father. There's a reason the Burning Kingdom hasn't been attacked yet and Corvana has already been all but decimated." Giovanni was really trying to piece it all together.

"I don't know the reason, but I'll soon find out. We'll all find out soon enough. Our path is to the Burning Kingdom in the Redlands. The Burning Territory is our sanctuary for now. I'm not turning around to head to the Isles now." Taj was determined and he trusted Giovanni's judgment. Not to mention, it was Rhoeve's decision to head to Golric in the first place.

"Rhoeve, it was your decision to head to Golric in the first place, remember?" Giovanni asked, convincingly reminding Rhoeve that heading for Golric and the Burning Kingdom was in fact his decision.

"Yes it was. Thanks for reminding me," he replied, laughing. He was lightening up, his spirit rising again. The maul was filled with a type of energy neither Malakai nor Halo could figure out. It wasn't one native to Thedia. Rhoeve continued with his maul. He'd never used one before.

Everything was set. It took a bit but everything was in place. Halo felt it was a little much to do for a place they weren't planning to stay in too long. Halo commented she would try to get ahold of her sister and check the status of Danth and Reforged.

After another brief argument, it was decided. Giovanni conceded allowing Malakai's choice of resting locations to win. To Taj, Halo, and Rhoeve it didn't matter. They just wanted to get away from the unusual hidden room of magic and to a place that would be safe in the event of an attack. The wizard's tower provided all such protection.

It was a long walk up the winding stairs to the upper living levels of the tower. Just as Malakai promised, books and wands and materials of all such were in the highest room. No beds though, just chairs and tables made of wood—and vacant areas left open for those young apprentices trying out their new spells. An old book of rituals found its way into Malakai's hands.

"Strange, you don't see this every day." He opened the book to skim through it.

"What's that?" Halo questioned, grabbing a few knick-knacks of her own.

"This book has two forbidden rituals."

"What are they?" Giovanni questioned, looking down out of the highest level's only window.

"A resurrection type of ritual called Raise Dead and another one called Create Undead, wow." Malakai muttered the word wow to himself but barely loud enough for everyone else to hear. "These were once simple spells for seasoned priests. Now, they're rituals and even arcane casters can summon back the dead to life."

"Resurrection is looked down upon because the powers that be and the powers that were all have a plan for us. If we return to life after our time is up, then we're spitting in the eyes of our creators." Halo was sincere in her words. With each day, she was sounding more and more like Eve.

"Who's to say the powers that be and the powers that were didn't grant us the power of a second opportunity?"

"Do not mock the Gods!" Rhoeve yelled, enraged at Malakai's comment.

Malakai just laughed at the Ambassador's ill-opened mind. "The Gods are dead," Malakai reminded.

Giovanni wanted to lighten the mood and get the crew back on track on what was important. "If something comes, we should know it. We should know before they even get close to an entrance."

Malakai laughed. He knew what Giovanni was trying to do. Taj was staying out of it all. He was thinking. He was thinking about a lot. That woman alone and refusing to speak or drop arms was just too odd for Taj.

The deeper night came and the party all succumbed to sleep. Usually, there would be an order and at least two would be awake at a given time. This night, the entire team was exhausted and Rhoeve, though trying to stay positive, was losing face and turning ill. His body was succumbing to something. Whatever it could be was still queer to the team.

Even Taj fainted from exhaustion. They'd been pushing hard and, like Rhoeve, he was ill and getting worse. Though he tried and tried to ignore and it and keep it from his comrades, they all knew he was hurting. And like Rhoeve, the reason why was still a mystery.

Taj knew why. It was Froth. Froth was inside him and now he was strong enough to get out. In his dreams, he often spoke to Froth. He often questioned his dark father. On that day, so very long ago he spared Taj from a vile death in the Broken Lands. What else did he do? He kept himself from dying.

"Froth."

"Yes, my son. It's almost time."

"Time for what?"

"Time for me to return, of course."

Taj looked around. There they were. Starius, Gunnar, and the rest of his old team; they were all there on the Broken Lands where Taj first and lastly saw the true Xavius Froth. He knew he was dreaming, but his dreams were open for Froth's communication.

"You're the father of the undead, are you not?"

"Aye."

"Then why not die on the Broken Lands. Thousands of memories race through my mind everyday. Memories I never had come to me and haunt me. They're your sons and your sons' sons. And so on. And—"

"If I let myself expire there on those lands, something else would form to take my place. Something else would grow into something like me. Everything ranks up a little, Taj. All forms of undead would become forever stronger and the strongest would take my throne. I cannot have something like that Death Knight that carried LORE taking it, or perhaps Giorgio? I planted a seed in you. That seed was my essence. My body expired still. The undead grew stronger for it. I still am. It was something I never had to do before and your body has worked magnificently. However, it's not going to hold up. I need a new host. Something I can keep."

"I will not let you take a life for your own. You've had too many already."

"Boy, it's not a choice. If I so choose, I'll take you. I do not wish to do that. I like you and have taken you as my son. Your body has hosted me during my roughest stages and soon your body will weaken. You will die soon enough. I need something stronger."

"I must see this through, Froth."

"And I will help you. You must help me."

"What is it you want?"

"I want victory. I want Falling Star defeated and my homeland spared from the might of Corvana."

"I don't think Corvana is a threat to anything right now. What will you have me do?"

"I am the keeper of our pantheon. The shadow has always fallen to fire and fire to shadow. This pantheon is as new to me as it is you. I've known of its existence yes, but never touched it. I can tell you this. As of now, you'll never make it to Golric's and if you do, you'll fail still," Froth said.

"What, why? Why do you say that?"

"The shadow ghosts do not infect the body but the soul. You are safe as your soul is protected by my essence. Your friends however are doomed. They're all going to fall to this infected army. I witnessed it during the Final War of the Shadow some thousand years ago or so."

"What do you want from me?"

"They're going to die. Blood restores my body. My body is no more. Souls restore my essence. I need souls, empowered souls. Convince them all to hide their souls in a phylactery with my essence. I'll grant you the ritual and raise the proper beings needed to do it. From there, just carry the phylactery. I will use their souls sparingly and will not use any of them until the time is right. They may even live out their entire mortal lives'. Eventually, as I've always done before, I will reform from the very phylactery and their bodies will fall. I will be again. They're just mortals. They come and they go."

"You want me to betray everything I have left," Taj said.

"Yes, and I want you to do it for everything that you remember is good."

"What's that supposed to mean? You're not good my dark father."

"Think of your time at war, my son. Do you think it was you that kept you alive? How many times did your 'subconscious' override your consciousness and undead spring forth from your fingertips right in the nick of time? I couldn't very well have my vessel killed on me."

"I thought you were helping me that day there on the Broken Lands."

"I was," Froth replied. "I did. If not for me, you would have surely died."

"I was to become even greater than my father. Not a cursed monster, subservient to you and your undead."

"If not for me and my undead, son, you'd have fallen long ago, long before achieving anything like your father. You couldn't put it together. You couldn't figure out why the undead and necrotic forces were coming to you, for you, from within you."

"It was you," Taj said partially as a statement and partially as a question.

Froth came to full appearance then. The Froth from old returned. His hair was a stringy white and his body was shriveled and more than pale. Blue veins peeled out his skin and in some places, even seemed to break through. His eyes matched his veins. Vampire eyes were usually yellow, but not his. No, his were just gray. As the powers beneath them had faded, so did their color. It would return. It was going to come back and it was coming sooner than later.

Taj's dreaming presence was stunned into amazement. His elongated teeth out and gleaming, with every second more flesh grew and pushed/pulled in the veins. It was him. It was really him. He seemed more terrifying and all-powerful here than he did while dying on the Broken Lands.

"You tell me, as you've done so many times before, but then say my host was the first time you've ever had to do it... Which is it?"

"My young and naïve son, of course I've had to manipulate the essence of existence, the fabrics of time and space, and the immortal weave to keep myself alive. Especially during my earliest years, beings were built more fiercely. Might and magic filled the lands. Sometimes it was which being got the jump on the other, and fights rarely lasted long. I can't even remember my beginning right now. Through time and with your help of feeding me the right beings' essences, I will remember my past and I will relay it to you."

"These people, they're all I have, Froth."

"Every vampire goes through it."

"Vampire, I—"

"Yes, every vampire's first hundred years are hard. Until everything you knew as a mortal dies off, it's hard. Only then can you begin your real life."

"What?"

"Yes, of course you knew this was coming," Froth said. "The price of your survival wasn't free, my son. Now, as your family, I need you as you once needed me."

"What If I could get you more souls or souls that weren't them?"

"We'll start with them. If you add more using the ritual, I'll spare your friends. Empowered souls are rare these days, my son, and I cannot, I will not feed upon feeble souls."

"I'm not a vampire, Froth!"

"Denial," Froth said.

"What do you mean denial? My blood is as warm as any human's."

"Yes, but you are a host to me now, that means your soul is not—not anymore."

"My soul is corrupted?"

"Advanced. Corrupted is a horrible word," Froth replied. "You're better than you were. I'm the only vampire with an inner essence, a being beyond physical. Vampires exist both in the positive and negative plane believe it or not. Their essence somehow is cast as negative. It's all very complicated."

"Just please, give me the opportunity to spare my friends. And Malakai and Giovanni, their souls will be protected but under no circumstances are you to devour them."

"I will say this only once. You are to never demand anything of your dark father. No vampire ever demands anything from his maker. And nothing will ever DEMAND anything of me? Do you understand?"

Taj's presence was broken. The dark father put him in his place. He was weak, puny, and putrid to Froth. Froth was seemingly the most powerful being ever to be. Memories told Taj he'd faced Diemos, Gemini's highest priest during the Final Year of the Shadow. Other memories also crowded Taj's memory, bringing him to his knees.

"You'll do what you're told. I am the reason you survived Raino Shadowblood, the Forsaken. I am the reason you survived the war. Not a vampire, and yet you bit Marko Kane to maintain life. My son, your blood is warm but your soul is as cold as mine. I was your conscience telling you to bite him. Though my presence was gone and it took so long, you still fed. It kept you alive. You're an anomaly, Taj Odin Xavier, but my son nonetheless. You'd have died had you not fed. They're no such things as half-vampires. Either your blood is cold or it's not. You Taj, your blood is warm. Your soul is cold. You're a first of your kind. You're a living vampire, maybe even a half. At the very least, my blood will forever run in your veins. Your soul has forever been dipped in my essence.

Halo fell fast asleep. She too had the connection of dreams. Though Taj's was through Froth's power, Halo's was a joint effort with Eve. Eve was their only connection to Danth and Reforged. Teraxius and Helios were also among them. Not to mention the countless people they saved that day on top of the others that had come since then. As far as the outside crew knew, Danth and Reforged were fine inside the confines of the underground citadel built nearest the mountains and partially underneath it. Its exact location was still a mystery, but if put to the test, Halo could find it.

"Halo," Eve said, waking her sister into the dream world.

"Hey gorgeous," answered Halo, waking up as her usual self with her usual attitude.

"I felt a change in you recently."

"And I in you," Halo replied, smiling.

Everything around them was black, yet not dark. It was beautiful in its own way. It was as if time was flying by them and yet they were standing still.

"The citadel has become quite full with survivors. We're no longer able to fight them. Danth has ordered everything secured to its best ability. I don't feel safe here anymore. I don't think Danth is telling us everything."

"Has security been breached?" Halo questioned curiously.

"No, but something tells me there's a chaos amongst us."

"You mean Falling Star?"

"No, something internal, something here at the citadel."

"You look beautiful."

"As do you," responded Eve.

"How is Teraxius?"

Eve hesitated. She knew she had to contact her sister this night. She wanted to. She also knew she would ask of Teraxius. Teraxius was good. In fact, he was amazing, brilliant in so many ways.

How could she answer her sister? She'd never lied to her before. How could she begin now?

"He, uh, he is good," she stuttered.

"Oh, there's something in your voice. I can tell when you're hiding something," Halo said, getting excited.

"No, Teraxius, Helios, they're all fine. I think Helios was dipped in anger. It shows often." Eve tried to pull the conversation away from Teraxius.

"So, has he said anything about me?" Halo was curious. She had to know. She kept her feelings to herself mostly but she yearned for the gladiator. His verve for life was extraordinary. He was a magnificent specimen of a man.

"Yes, of course he has. Danth says your name daily, making sure I am keeping in touch with you. I walk alongside him as his shadow now."

Halo knew something was wrong. Eve was trying too strongly to avoid the questions and current conversations.

"Eve, has Teraxius mentioned my name?"

"I've never seen you so trying for a man. You sure do fancy him," Eve said in a friendly tone.

"I do. I don't know why, Eve, but I love him. I love him very much."

"Love, wow Halo, have you ever used that term before? You don't even know him."

Eve was becoming defensive of Teraxius. Halo could sense it. Halo's heart broke right there in that dream. Somewhere in her words, she spilled the truth.

"Eve, You… You… and he… you…." Halo couldn't even speak, it hurt so much. Eve lost her words in trying to salvage it. The dream connection disconnected with the two sisters reaching for each other. The connection was lost when the… connection was lost.

Chapter 4

The citadel was locked and secured. Wymon had actually taken over. He was the head of Reforged and had been since Danth stepped down. More than that, Danth was the man who handed him the position. Rightfully so, Wymon's clerical talents were second to few; perhaps Golric Firesoul being one of those few.

Three people walked with Wymon at all times: Alihaedra - his wife, Danth, and Peni, a gnomish scout and current leader of the search parties. Peni was an elder gnomish woman, wise with age and dipped with a sense of humor.

Danth followed closely behind the man behind it all, Wymon—the same man he put in charge. He was pleased with his decision. Wymon was a good leader. He was older than Danth but Danth was the reason he was where he was. He was the reason Wymon was who he was.

Wymon was an average looking man with short brown hair and green eyes. His story was a love fable. Alihaedra was born with stature. Wymon was born to the same borderland kingdom as Alihaedra. Alihaedra was born with a name. Her family would have never accepted Wymon. Wymon never called to her. He knew his place. Then Danth granted him the power of Reforged and the stature that came with it.

Soon after, Alihaedra was his and within the year they swore their vows to each other. Alihaedra wasn't gorgeous but she was certainly beautiful in the average kind of way. She was a mother to several small children. Before motherhood, her shamanistic powers were world-renowned. Unlike Wymon, Alihaedra had a name backing her and quickly earned the powers to go along with it. Alihaedra's powers as a shaman far exceeded Wymon's as a priest of the Rivermortal, but it was his gift of leadership that drew Danth to handing him the reins to Reforged, his most favorite guild ever.

Peni was just a longtime member who earned her way to her position the old fashioned way. Secretly, she adored Wymon and Wymon knew it. Alihaedra had his heart and he would never betray that.

Danth had changed since they'd last seen him. He was bigger, stronger, and filled with more divine power than ever before. He was a walking beacon for those that followed dragons and the Draconic Order.

Helios spent the majority of his time as a common man. His swords were rarely drawn. Training or keeping vigilance was the last thing on his mind. Teraxius, on the other hand, was different. Just as he'd always done, he trained. He ran every morning and kept steady with every weapon and form of fighting.

Eve actually became very close to Alihaedra, as her shaman powers rivaled Wymon's wife. Though Eve's didn't truly measure up to Alihaedra's, she had powers that Alihaedra did not. Unlike the wizards of old, powers weren't just transferable other than through rituals. Powers still could be learned and taught. More so, Alihaedra was just pleased to have another dedicated to her craft with capabilities equal to hers.

Peni was just steps behind Wymon as he walked out of a military structure somewhere inside the citadel. Waiting on them, a strong-willed rising name among the wizards of Reforged, an eladrin named Ereven.

Ereven wasn't built very well. He was short, even by eladrin standards. His hair was light blond and somewhat shaggy in a straight-combed kind of way. His eyes were a beautiful green. They burned of ambition and desire. There were questionable actions documented on Ereven in the past with Reforged, but he always had an answer for them. "Lady Peni." He dropped his head slightly to show his customary respect.

Wymon stopped and looked back. He'd heard the stories of Ereven and didn't care for the backstabbing eladrin. The alleged backstabbing eladrin. Danth stopped too. Ereven looked at the lot of them, dropping his head to them, keeping his sign of respect active for them all.

"Yes Ereven, what is it?" Peni answered.

"The shadow armies have moved again. They're not pushing anymore."

"How do you know this?" Peni questioned.

"They've turned. They're heading away, to the north."

"I wonder why they've stopped their push?" Wymon said to Danth, Peni, and/or Ereven.

"I think I know why," Ereven replied.

"How would you know?" Wymon asked, taking over for Peni.

Ereven seized the opportunity to speak directly to Wymon, the leader of Reforged. He hoped to one day have Peni's position and possibly the one above it. Peni didn't think anything about it. She wanted to handle it. Ereven was assigned to one of her scout groups. Wymon wanted to take over the conversation so she was going to oblige him.

"Because we engaged them," answered Ereven. "Their actions in that battle told me."

"So you know how these shadows think now?" Peni asked. She was aggravated but she didn't want to admit it, to herself or anyone else. Ereven answered to her. Why was he speaking directly to Wymon about scout business?

"No, but their actions told me everything I needed to know."

"Where's Drago?" Peni asked quickly. She just remembered. Drago was Ereven's indentured servant. He was a paladin of the Rivermortal and indebted to the conspiring eladrin. He was a well-known holy champion of the Rivermortal and a decorated ally to Reforged. Drago was not an official member but the members of Reforged treated him as such.

Ereven bowed his head as if he were saddened by the thought. His eyes spoke the truth. Wymon and Danth assumed he was as he appeared. Peni knew the truth and one day she would right all the wrong Ereven did. She would make him pay for his dreadful actions.

"He was hurt badly in the fight."

"He is alive?" Peni quickly asked.

"Our clerics have him now," Ereven replied.

"I'm glad he's okay. Now tell me how their actions spoke to you," Wymon said, taking control of the conversation.

Peni was happy and disgusted all at the same time. Drago was always getting hurt. Secretly, others had told Peni of Ereven's actions toward Drago. Ereven's inattentive approach toward fighting the opposition constantly proved deadly to his allies, primarily Drago. Drago had been caught in his blasts and area-of-effect spells more than once.

"They moved in an organized way. Half of their units split off. The remaining units regrouped and the retreating groups reset themselves. Something alerted them. I don't know what, but something alerted them. Clearly, enough of them weren't where they needed to be so they reorganized and regrouped. That means they're not of nil intelligence.

They're smart. Something is controlling them. Whatever it is, if we kill it.… Well, kill the head and the body shall fall. Catch my drift?"

Wymon, Danth, and even Peni listened to the crafty Eladrin as he spoke. Though none present really cared for him, his words cut them like knives. Wymon could tell something was dishonest about the wizard and Danth had heard the stories. Not to mention, Danth really liked Drago and had worked alongside him before being Ereven's indentured servant.

The three looked at each other." We've known they're not simple. The shadow is a complex being," Wymon said.

"If given the opportunity and the right manpower, I could finish it," Ereven boasted.

"No," Peni screamed quickly, and quickly remembered it wasn't her place to answer.

Danth kept his cool. Wymon had a flaw. He sometimes felt as if others didn't view him as they did Danth. He thought some didn't see him as their true leader, but they did. He was the one who couldn't see it. It was a character flaw in him. Sometimes, his frustration and flaw caused him to act hastily and without caution.

"Ereven, take what you need. Head them off at the pass. Take the paths of Broken Hearts behind the Blue Cliffs and stop them from heading to their destination. If you feel the need, stalk them. Find out where they're going."

Danth didn't like that idea. Ereven was reckless already as a member. Giving him leadership powers could turn disastrous and he quickly told the Reforged leader what he thought. Wymon wouldn't have it. To prove his leadership powers to those around him, who already knew he was a leader, he kept his motion.

Ereven grinned with excitement, dirty excitement. "Why would stalking them be dangerous?"

"I know there is life out there, Ereven, but right now we can't save it all. We have to fight their armies any way we can. Keep a distance and the radiant powers vibrant."

"Wymon, we don't know what kind of power these things will turn away from."

"I'm going to assume it's radiant," he said.

"Not wise," whispered Danth.

Wymon pretended not to hear it. He knew what Danth meant. Danth meant no one knew what the shadows were vulnerable to, none in the citadel anyway.

Ereven nodded, understanding what Wymon wanted. Peni was already upset. She knew Ereven's greed and ambition was dangerous. Unfortunately, Wymon didn't see it. Danth felt it, but Wymon was too busy. He had too much on his mind.

Once Ereven successfully finished off the retreating shadow forces, the people of Reforged and the citadel would see him as an even greater Leader. Eventually, with more successes like that under his belt, the people of Reforged would come to love him as they did Danth. Eventually, they would come to love and adore him even more than they did Danth.

Ereven took his leave. Unusually, Peni did the same. Danth looked closely at Wymon. Wymon knew he wasn't pleased. That didn't matter anymore; Wymon was the leader of Reforged now. Alihaedra looked softly at her man. She felt a softness for him she hadn't felt before. That leadership flaw bled out of him like a dying man impaled on three stakes.

Danth knew the position of leadership would either make or break Wymon. Danth believed in him enough to think it would make him before it would break him. Sadly for Wymon, something queer and world threatening approached not long after his coronation.

Wymon kept his wits about him, though he was the face and head of Reforged, he still felt as if Danth was the true leader. He still looked at him as such. "You're not pleased with my decision."

Danth was a massive man now. His body never moved. His face told Wymon all he wanted to know and more.

"And you Alihaedra," he asked to his loving wife.

Like Danth, she felt a mistake would come from his actions. Wymon tried so hard to please her. Lately it was becoming more and more difficult. She still loved him. At night, she counseled him, suggesting perhaps he step down, as the position possibly was too much for him at such a crucial time. She even recommended asking Danth back.

Insecurities birthed from her words. Wymon was now more heartset on pleasing her and proving her wrong than ever. He was the man for the job. Danth saw it in him. He saw it in him, didn't he? Wymon adored Danth and secretly he knew Reforged needed him. In his defense, Danth stepped down. His heart wasn't in it. That was his flaw in regards to the guild.

Wymon's loving wife stepped closer to her man, rubbing his shoulders. The musty underground air filled her nose as she dropped her head to his shoulder and pressed her lips to his neck. Without saying a word, she knew, as did everyone else, these were hard times. These were very hard times.

Malagant's link to Falling Star was the strongest. The leader was in Shangri-la fermenting his powers. Everything was as planned; Falling Star bathed in his own powers while Malagant commanded his armies from the Material. The Prime Material Plane of Thedia was fading and the Corvanian Pantheon would be the first to fall. Once taken, Thedia's life essence would serve as a prime feast to awaken the proper beings needed to invade and destroy Gemini and his shadow world.

Malagant moved his mightiest legions to Corvana's First Regent. The strongest essence of life came from there. Malagant knew of the citadel. The survivors and escapees of his armies fled to it. Those that didn't fled to those damned isles. Something in those isles was repelling his shadows. Something in those isles was powerful enough to hold off his legions.

Only the strongest of the shadows would be able to penetrate it. It was no wonder Corvana had never invaded the isles. The level of power of the isles was second to none save Falling Star and the shadow.

The Burning Lands had also never been attacked. Why? Unfortunately for Malagant, his shadow was weak to the fire, but the fire was also weak to the shadow. It was another war setup for catastrophic events. The Alabaster Isles to the south and the Burning Territories to the northwest would both be wars plentiful with casualties.

Malagant smiled. The end was near. And with the end would come the beginning. The beginning to a new war; everything was in place and a New War of the Shadow was coming. The flaws of the Corvanian Pantheon had been exposed and the entire realm had already been taken. What was left would just succumb to the greatness and power of Falling Star. Everything was perfect. Nothing could stop them. This time, Thedia would be taken and Malagant would lead the charge.

Chapter 5

The vacant city of Wyndemere was long behind them. Days, weeks, even months passed before the team really stopped again. They pushed onward harshly, rarely stopping but to rest every so often. Rhoeve was nearly gone. He'd faded so much since Wyndemere. Nothing ever came, but their sound awoke them. Something very big was coming and it wasn't far behind them.

Sporadically, the team came across small groups of infested. Usually, Malakai alone would end them. Occasionally, more was needed. They pushed through the ruins of borderland cities until finally reaching the Badlands.

The Badlands were a rough, rocky, terrain that led to the Blistering Hills. The Blistering hills were more like mountains. They were certainly more dangerous than any known mountainous regions. The weakened Rhoeve knew of a trail off the beaten path and far more safe. Taj was also still sick. Most of the time, he was out of it. He often spoke to himself asking what to do and where to go. He tried to keep to himself as much as possible.

"The Path of Broken Swords lies just there," Rhoeve said, coughing violently. He pointed through a small patch of Blistering Hills. "From there, we can find our way around the entire set of hills as well as the Barbican Peaks."

"Barbican Peaks?" Taj asked.

"Barbican is a mountain range, very steep and very dangerous. It's the only known way to Bird's Eye." Rhoeve knew the team was curious now of Bird' Eye, so he continued. "Bird's Eye is an ancient natural structure linking the center pieces of Barbican together. It also links three or four other mountain chains. Somewhere in Bird's Eye lies one mortal-made bridge of unknown origin. It will let us bypass the steep and dangerous alternatives. It's narrow but it will take us directly into the Burning Territories. The four most connecting parts of the Burning Territories is where the Redlands exist. The Redlands is where Golric Firesoul's Burning Kingdom lies."

Epic fights left the team scarred but more aware of the various types of infected. They passed through it all. Flying creatures left them all but dead while near the Barbican Peaks. Finally, through trial and error, Rhoeve Manduwalker brought them to the mortal-made bridge that would lead them to the Burning Territories.

A giant bridge, carved of stone and rock extending some three to four hundred feet, connected two old rocky mountainous openings. Below the bridge were darkness, water, fog, and death. The lot of them were deep in the mountains and the Path of Broken Swords got them to where they needed to be.

They'd skidded down a sidewall of a mountain to the hidden opening that bled the mortal made bridge across a giant canyon in the mountains. Going back the way they came was not an option.

"So this is why Corvana never invaded the Burning Kingdom – ha, ha, ugh!" Taj said, trying to laugh. His cough caught up with him. Like Rhoeve, his words lessened. Malakai engulfed in laughter with Taj's words. Halo was questionable. More and more, she resorted back to what she was. They'd been cut off from Eve and the others for months. Halo claimed her powers were being blocked and Eve's were unable to connect to her.

In truth, Halo refused to speak to her sister. Eve betrayed her. Didn't she? Halo adored Teraxius and she hoped to one day bed him and more. Eve came to discover why and hoped to take the gladiator for herself. Why, why would her own sister do that to her? Their origin, was it in their blood to deceive? Some believe they descended from demons, others said angels. Devils were also a popular guess among those questioning their origins. Only Halo and Eve knew the truth. They descended from the fey, nymphs to be exact. Nymphs were creatures native to the feywild with little known about their behavior and societies other than they absolutely despised and hated ugliness and evil.

The other side of the mortal made bridge opened to another opening with a climbing texture and terrain. Their trek had been brutal with some close near misses, but the Burning Territory was close. The air was getting harder to breath. The humidity was gone. Even the air was dry enough to cut with a knife.

Rhoeve breathed heavily, holding his stomach, halfway doubled over. "If Corvana wanted this place, it would have sent airships." His words were to both Malakai and Taj.

"Corvana destroys, conquers, or breaks down everything that grows. If it's a threat, they nip it in the bud early. Either these fire people aren't worth the trouble or something's missing here." Giovanni was good at putting two and two together.

"Golric is a good leader. He probably just made allies in the right places," answered a sick Rhoeve.

"How do the Alabaster Isles feel about the fire people?" Halo asked.

"They're allies," Rhoeve answered.

Malakai smiled. Taj did too. Giovanni looked around to make sure everything was all right. He didn't trust anything. He signaled his people to commence searching as well.

"That's far enough," a voice said.

It was unfamiliar and hailed from the darkness behind several rocks pressed up against a mountainside. A humanoid looking creature arose from the darkness. Its body was towering. At first, it resembled Talon but a second take proved it to be yet another true gargoyle, or wargoyle.

His body stemmed out from the darkness. First, his limbs and head came into sight. Following came the beast's torso. It was clad in bones and irons. A horned creature's skull dressed as a helm covered the majority of the true gargoyle's head.

"Who are you?" Taj rubbed his stomach, hoping it would somehow ease the pain inside.

"That's not important. What I am, however, is," answered the winged beast.

"And what are you?" Malakai demanded.

"I belong to the Aedigis Bone, a gargoyle tribe here in the mountains. We guard this last pass to the Burning Territory. It's part of a pact. I'm afraid the Burning Kingdom isn't accepting new visitors."

"We've come a long way," Halo said.

"I don't care how far you've come. Your journey to the Burning Kingdom ends here." The wargoyle was in full sight. He stood just over seven feet. He carried no weapons save his own body and claws.

"Wargoyle, we've come to ask Golric Firesoul for his help. We need the help of the greatest priest and the help of his fire." Giovanni pleaded with the wargoyle. It was to no avail. He wasn't budging.

"We're passing this bridge, with your blessing or not." Taj had heard enough. His hands were at the hilts of his weapons.

"I warn you human," barked the gargoyle.

Malakai was with Taj. They'd had too many encounters already. They were too close to deal with another one now. Giovanni, Rhoeve, and Halo hoped to end the dispute diplomatically.

Rhoeve yelled, startling everyone, including Taj. "I'm Golric's ally on the inside!"

What? That changed everything. Rhoeve was such a diehard Corvanian. How could he have secret alliances with outside countries? Were the Alabaster Isles connected to him as well? Was Rhoeve keeping the Burning Kingdom and the Alabaster Isles safe? Why would he do that?

"Golric has no alliances on the inside. You do mean Corvana, right?"

"Yes, we had a pact and I kept his people out of war. Now, I need that favor returned."

"Golric's doesn't take well to beggars."

The air was musty. The sound of something moving all around was present but not loud. The shadows were coming. They all knew it, even the gargoyle.

"My friend, Golric will be pleased to see me," Rhoeve said, still coughing horribly.

"We're not beggars you—" Malakai started. Taj waved him silent.

The gargoyle stood and smiled. It was clear. His people guarded the fire people. Or, were his people part the fire people? In time, it would all be out. This gargoyle wasn't wanting them to pass. Taj listened as the conversation between his people and the gargoyle continued. Malakai's words drowned out the rest when he spoke. At first, it seemed as if the gargoyle was being truthful. More and more told Taj something to the gargoyle was foul.

Alas, Taj pulled his blades. His lightning reflexes and movements sent both LORE and SOUL cutting through the gargoyle before any knew what happened. Blood spewed from the behemoth's mouth. Again, a foe fell to the blades of Taj Odin Xavier.

"No more," he said, watching the life of the beast strive to sustain. "We move."

The lot of them made their way onto the mortal-made bridge. Halo remarked of the height. It was clear she wasn't fond of them. Giovanni took the lead. Taj took Rhoeve's weight on his shoulder. Malakai picked up the rear. Behind them, the gargoyle lay in a puddle of his own blood.

As the team made their way across the antediluvian bridge, more and more of its history came about. Carvings of statuic gargoyle faces made their presence known. Taj had a feeling the gargoyles and the bridge had a history. Halo couldn't stop looking down below. She was terrified. Heights had always been her biggest fear, her only fear.

Rhoeve was sick. His cough was getting worse. What was causing his sickness and why was it getting worse? He didn't figure he was long for the world. He had to live long enough to see his old friend, Golric Firesoul, face to face.

Giovanni kept a strong lead and a fast pace, never taking so much as a step without uncovering every single, solitary rock. Malakai's stroll at the rear was the only one not keeping pace. He didn't care to keep pace. He was appreciating the architecture all around him. More than the others, he saw the sculptures, even the hidden ones.

A flying bullet screamed through the air. The night around them lit up with gleaming white eyes. A shoulder of one of the seven-foot wargoyle beasts crashed into Taj's gut, forcing out fluids and solids. The mixture of foods, fluids, liquids, and other inside gunk spewed from Taj's mouth. The creature wrapped him up and tackled him before any of them had any idea something was present. Before he knew it, he was in a downward spiral with a behemoth of a wargoyle. Taj lost grip of his swords. They refused to lose grip of him; the chains once again reappeared reattaching themselves to him through his wrists.

Punches, kicks, scratches, and headbutts forced the two to entangle themselves in each other. The wargoyle wasn't even able to keep flight because of Taj. More came out of the woodworks. Malakai again surprised the party by casting wind wall on the eastern side where the beasts seemed to be coming from.

One by one, the creatures slammed into the wall disorienting them a bit, knocking them off their desired courses. Another came from the other side clipping Malakai's right leg and crippling him. Something in these beasts wasn't right. They were different. Malakai had faced and fought alongside true gargoyles, or wargoyles before.

Giovanni sprinted. He made it to the other side, evading several attempts on his life by the constantly aggressing creatures. Some of the creatures weren't wargoyles; they were the gargoyles. Gargoyles and Wargoyles hated each other. Ever since the old war, they'd never gotten along. Here they were working together.

Halo let loose daggers like those that they'd never seen. She was the first to fire back. Taj knew there was something up. Looking up and around, Giovanni saw openings. He sent his chakram screaming across the mountainous ledges, knocking boulders, rocks, and dirt free.

Sadly, Taj was still down and falling with that first wargoyle. Finally, Taj took the top position over the wargoyle with his sword, SOUL, in hand. His left hand was choking the creature while LORE dangled from it. One after another, thrust after thrust, SOUL pierced the body of the winged creature.

Malakai refused to fall. Instead, he chose to push his staff downward upon the ground. The staff helped the sorcerer keep himself up.

"You cast walls now!" Halo screamed still throwing the daggers from her straps. Her straps became endless once she donned the amulet of endless weapons.

"I do what I need to get the job done!" the sorcerer barked back.

Giovanni was stunned. Taj fell from sight. The fog below clouded him out. He was gone. Looking down from the other side and seeing his old friend gone completely dropped his heart. Malakai knew his old friend was in trouble. Rods, staves, and wands were on his side. Moreover, they were on the side of Taj Odin Xavier. One of the rods Malakai grabbed was of Ally Recall and it had more than one charge left. Within seconds, Malakai's wall was gone but Taj was back. As if preparing, both SOUL and LORE were in hand and ready.

Something stopped and took out the sorcerer's wall. What had that kind of capabilities? From the other side, Giovanni hid. His chakram was still humming through the air. Rocks, dirt, and boulders came atop the encircling gargoyles and wargoyles. The dirt was too much for their wings. The rocks and boulders also assisted in their downfall. Occasionally, one would slam into a party member. Taj made sure to cut them down before anything could come of it.

Rhoeve was virtually useless for the fight. He fell feint face down upon the dirt of the bridge. Blood trickled from his mouth. He didn't have anything left and none of them had the ability to call upon the powers of healing. Healing, that was the main reason for going to the Burning Kingdom. They needed another strong priest. Danth was the strongest they knew and he was back at the citadel with Reforged. Halo hadn't been able to reach Eve for a spell. Hopefully, that would all change soon.

Two of the quicker gargoyles flew in unison interchanging fly routes while heading straight for the newly recovered Taj. Taj moved exquisitely perfect; his nimble body fit just between the two creatures' routes, giving his blades the perfect opportunities to gash open his adversaries' faces.

Several daggers also found their marks compliments of Halo. Rhoeve's sickness got the better of him and it couldn't have come at a worse time. Giovanni's chakram finally came back to him. From a crippling stance, Malakai's rods blew craters in the sides of mountains. The after effects of the spells as well as their initial damage did more than enough to finish off the coming gargoyles.

"I kind of figured that wargoyle was lying," said Taj.

"Is everyone okay?" Halo questioned loudly.

"Perfect, we're all perfect," replied an arrogant Malakai, hobbling toward Giovanni and the other side of the bridge.

Taj sheathed his weapons, closing the distance between him and Rhoeve. The Eternian hoisted the Ambassador over his shoulder. "Let's go," he said sickly. His eyes told the story of the war his body was fighting. It was a war he couldn't win. Every day he lost a little more.

Halo kept a vigilant eye from near the rest of the team, minus Giovanni, who kept a vigilant eye from the other side of the bridge.

"Gargoyles, Wargoyles," Malakai complained. Conversation lightly sparked up about the fight. It wasn't too much of one, but things could have gone much differently.

"Malakai, sorcerers don't have all the capabilities you seem to have," Taj said, taking his final steps on the bridge and then off it.

"Rods, staves, and wands can make a caster appear much different. If it weren't for these things found in Wyndemere, you'd have been lost." Malakai spoke softly. He'd calmed down a bit already. His right ankle hurt and was still bleeding. One of the horns atop the creature's wings along with the wing itself did a number on him and he was paying for it.

"Just be sure no bad surprises come our way. Is there anything we need to know about?" Taj asked.

"I'm on your side," he answered with a cocky grin.

By the day's end, the team had passed the last few obstacles. Finally, they were in the Redlands of the Burning Territory. The ground was hard and dry. Most of the plant life had either died or been mutated magically to oblige the land. It was as if a desert had gotten too hot and burned to death. Odd little creatures scurried about the hard red dirt.

The final cliff was steep. Scaling it sent the team to a whole new world. The Burning Territories were something different than they'd ever seen. Nonetheless, the journey was still not over and they were hurting.

Rhoeve finally came to. Like the sorcerer of many talents, Halo popped out a few of her own—light healing capabilities. Rhoeve was steady enough to keep the team moving and in the right direction. It took two more weeks, but finally the Burning Kingdom was in sight. The landmarks Rhoeve spoke of before the journey began were all around them. Like every mortal bunch, they still needed to rest. Even though they made quick work of the gargoyles, their wounds still lingered with pain.

It was dawn. Giovanni had watch with Halo. Taj and the others were fast asleep. Rhoeve didn't take shifts watching anymore. Those awake tended to their hurting comrade. In the distance the blazing sun rose and silhouettes of men riding horses were coming at them.

"Taj, Taj," Halo said.

Giovanni turned to wake up Malakai. Rhoeve still slept soundly. Seconds later, Malakai, Taj, Halo, and Giovanni were all up and ready.

Taj was the quickest to awaken. He looked down. Rhoeve was in no position to fight. "Halo, whatever happens, protect Rhoeve. Guard him with your life. Right now, he's our lifeline to this Golric and his people." Taj made himself abundantly clear. Rhoeve was the reason they journeyed to the Burning Kingdom. Golric was the reason they were headed to the Burning Kingdom and Rhoeve was the driving force behind it.

The silhouettes were slowly taking shape. Bugbears, orcs, giant humans, tieflings, and the like were heading their way. It wasn't the heat playing tricks on their minds. They were real. Funny, no humans, elves, or even dwarves were present, mostly just the monstrous type.

The creatures they rode were big and not horses. They appeared to be bipedal with massive trunk-like legs extending down into star-shaped, four-point claws. Their heads were narrow and pointy and their rough, thick skin color ranged from a light brown to a dark red. Each one carried one, two, or sometimes even three humanoids atop them. They were large, very large. Their faces came to a point and looked to be built for tunnel digging.

Rhoeve opened his eyes barely able to speak. "Bullettes."

"I'm not sure I know of bullettes," Taj replied.

"They're… They're…" Rhoeve tried to speak, but his voice wouldn't come out. Finally, "They're creatures who thrive underground and usually attack by shooting up from the underground. They're not known to be steeds."

The riders came in fast, surrounding the five. Taj was the first to raise his hands hoping his team would catch on and do the same. Giovanni quickly followed his lead, followed by Halo. Rhoeve rolled over, taking a deep breath. His glazed eyes opened and closed quickly, as if smashing them and extending them open would somehow ease the pain.

The first to approach carried only one passenger. A funny hat and light loose clothing covered the half-giant's body. The half giant, or goliath, was the dominant race present, roughly by sixty percent or so. The first one pulled his reins on his beast.

"Whoa Nelly," he yelled.

Dirt and dust kicked out from under their massive clawlike hooves. The team covered their faces. Halo knelt down, positioning her body over Rhoeve's.

Malakai looked down and smiled. "I wish you'd put your body on mine like that."

"Who might you all be? We don't get too many visitors around here," said the massive, haughty goliath.

"My name is Taj Odin Xavier."

Giovanni chimed in, taking over. "And we represent Ambassador Rhoeve Manduwalker of Corvana. He's come here to seek an audience with the high priest Golric Firesoul."

"Ah, we always welcome new visitors, but I can't guarantee Golric will see you." The goliath seemed pleased with them, not at all what Taj or the others expected.

"Wait a minute, you're always welcoming new visitors? That's not what the gargoyles and wargoyles said," Malakai stated.

"Gargoyles, wargoyles?" said one of the goliath's people.

"Yes, we just killed a few and knocked a whole bunch senseless," said Halo.

"And something there killed my wind wall," added Malakai.

"Hmmmmm, I bet it was Gor-ram." The goliath sounded pretty certain about it.

"Gor-ram?" Taj asked.

"Just a bandit Wargoyle allying what he can between his species and his counter species. He leads a band of misfit outcasts. His numbers have been growing lately. They're eternally at war with an allied tribe of ours, the Aedigis Bone."

Malakai laughed, so did Taj. The Wargoyle claimed to be of the Aedigis Bone. Taj looked down at Rhoeve. He was in bad shape and in desperate need of medical attention.

"Well, they're light a few members now. I'd love to keep this conversation going, but our friend… Golric's friend is in desperate need of divine help. Can we continue this in the walls of your country?" Taj asked.

Two of the goliath's men jumped off their steeds and made their way to Rhoeve. The lead goliath looked at him closely, muttering something underneath his breath. "I believe that is Ambassador Rhoeve Manduwalker." Giovanni read his lips. He was the only one who heard what he said. Quickly, he relayed the message to the others.

The monstrous beings seemed more friendly that some normal societies. Within a few moments, they were all on bullettes heading back toward the goliath's kingdom, the Burning Kingdom. Deep inside, Taj felt pleased.

Another stepping-stone had been passed. They were clear and free. Nothing was going to fight them before they made it to the Burning Kingdom. Hopefully, Rhoeve had enough left to make it to the Burning Kingdom where his "old friend" Golric Firesoul and his people could heal him.

Chapter 6

It was a small village, not at all what the party expected. It was days before they were acknowledged. In that time, Taj saw the vastness of the people. Several villages scattered all around made up one great, big, massive city—a city of monstrous beings, yet civilized. Goliaths walked around commonly.

Rhoeve was taken in and removed from the group. Taj trusted it was with the best intentions. Malakai also removed himself from the bunch, choosing to keep himself company while researching the rituals he'd come across while in Wyndemere.

Giovanni kept close to Taj. Halo found the festivities. Sanctuary, she thought. People dancing around campfires and singing songs made her feel like a child again. The team couldn't really hold it together. Only Taj, Giovanni, and Malakai truly had the mission in mind at all times.

Finally, the day came when Golric Firesoul agreed to meet with the team. It was the day Rhoeve Manduwalker was healed. He would never be the same. He would never be the fighter he once was but nonetheless, his time in the world wasn't quite up.

The coming days saw the people of the Burning Kingdom saddened and brokenhearted. The four were told Rhoeve would meet them there. A guide put the other four on horseback and led them to the back of the villages. The entire set of villages and towns backed up to a vertical mountainside wall. Built into that wall was the grandest temple of fire ever built, the Forbidden Flame.

"Well, there it is," said the guide. Shortly after, the human took his leave.

The four made their way into the grand temple. No doors were present. It was built with massive, kiln-burned bricks built upon and carved into the mountainside. No doors or window shutters were present at all.

It was not a day of worship for the fire people. No one was in the temple. Taj wasn't even sure where to go, once entering. The guide made it perfectly clear; he would know where to go once he got there.

Inside, satin silks and red velvets melted across the place. Bizarre gold and blue designs were stitched into every piece of fabric. On the inside, not a single piece of brick could be seen. The building held plenty of windows, seemingly on every floor.

"He said we'd know where to go." Malakai's voice seemed sure but also aggravated, possibly at the idea of the guide saying they would know exactly where to go in a place such as the Forbidden Flame.

"A fire is hottest at its core," Halo mumbled.

"What?" asked Giovanni.

"When a campfire dances for its guests, blue flames spark up every so often, right?" The nymph descendant questioned.

"Yeah, so?" said Taj.

"Blue flames are much hotter and burn much more pure than the red and orange."

"Halo, I think you might be onto something. You know, you might be more useful after all. I mean, other than just your looks and body." Malakai snickered.

Halo grinned back. She was starting to catch on to the cocky sorcerer's ways. Something about him was also repulsive. Something about him was demanding and hot. Something about him was catching her eye, whether she wanted to admit it or not. In fact, the thought of talking to Eve now excited her more than ever. Why was she like that? Why did she have to have something to throw in her sister's face just in case? No, she was not wrong. She liked Teraxius and Eve stole him from her; not that she could steal him under normal circumstances, but they were all separated.

Giovanni looked around. Seemingly, the girl had a point. It was a good assumption.

"Now how did you come up with that?" Giovanni jokingly asked.

"I don't know. It just kind of, well, came to me," she replied with a smile.

"Sometimes I think you have more than just five senses. Something innate… is in you." Malakai rubbed the playful little Halo's head.

Taj started first. The others quickly followed in line. Halo never said it, but Taj knew what she was thinking: follow the deeper and more plentiful colors of blue. The place was desolate on the inside and the outside inhabitants were all in a state of mourning. What was going on?

The crew traveled through the massive church following the blue velvet drapes and designs more than the other colors, as if the blue designs and colors actually headed to something. Just then, after about an hour of searching, the team came across the first inhabitant of the church.

He was an elder man, bald and dressed with burning brands all across his upper body. He wore only a long pair of pants. No shoes, no shirt, or any other kind of clothing piece touched the man's body at all. He was just strolling along. He was a half-orc and peculiarly short for one. His body wasn't in the best of shape either. His stomach was protruding and hanging over his belt line. Brands of lines and other fiery symbols strategically formed a great fire design covering the most of his front and left side and lower back.

"Are you here for the funeral?" he asked. "The high priest has declared this church vacant of all people until the ascension is complete."

"Then what are you doing here?" Malakai asked.

"Ah, the keepers of the temple are forever keeping it. The great Golric did not mean to clear this place of us."

"Us?" questioned Taj.

"The keepers," the man said.

"Ahhh," said Giovanni, and then the rest of the crew each made their own understanding noise.

"In fact, we're here to see Golric Firesoul," Halo said.

"Yes, the people of this land ordered us here," Taj said, taking the leadership persona back.

The half-orc bowed his head. He wasn't very pleased and seemed distracted.

"Is something troubling you? Can you take us to Golric? He is here, isn't he?" Taj asked.

"Yes, he is in the room of the Infernal Ardor of the Burning."

"Infernal Ardor of the Burning, I like the sound of that," Malakai said, thinking it had something to do with magic.

"It's where one tells their loved ones goodbye and the final transformation to the afterlife is completed."

"Can you take us to Golric?" Giovanni asked.

"I'm not sure now is a good time."

"Who in the hells is he saying goodbye to?" Malakai asked, aggravated.

"His brother," answered the half-orc slightly disgusted with Malakai's attitude.

Taj fell back for a moment. Adrian Paschal Xavier, his one true brother came to mind. What was Adrian doing? For that matter, what was Destiny doing, and his child? What about the child Sasha gave birth to? Was it okay? Who was taking care of it? Was Legion, his son doing well? Surely, Adrian would oversee his children in his absence.

"I'm sorry sir. Forgive our intrusion," Taj said out of nowhere. The other three hadn't a clue on how to take it.

"Huh," Halo mumbled.

The others did the same, all mumbling curiosities on Taj's quick change of character.

"Well, if the people sent you here then it wasn't malicious. High priest Golric's younger sibling has perished. It was a good death."

"What?" asked Halo obviously rubbed the wrong way. Did he just say good death? What in the hell did that mean?

Malakai and Giovanni both kept silent. Neither of them understood a word of it either. Where they came from, there were no such things as good deaths—well, in their line of work anyway.

"Their faith is strong. Surely, it'll see them through this tragedy." Taj spoke up again, bowing his head.

Inside yes, inside him brewed the devious being, the father of the damned, Xavius Froth. Froth took the backseat for the moment, giving Taj his much-needed emotional breakdown. Taj connected with the stranger Golric Firesoul. It was every second of every day that Taj thought of Adrian and his life back home. He tried not to but he couldn't. His brother and family were constantly on his mind.

Perhaps that was one of his reasons for his actions. Froth fought to keep Taj focused. Whether focused on pain or other areas, the ancient surely didn't want him thinking of home. Reminiscent thoughts caused hesitation and hesitation could get a man killed. Again, there was no way Froth was going to allow his vessel to die, not yet.

"We will go," Taj said, turning to head back to the stairwell from which they came.

"We will?" asked Malakai again confused.

Giovanni looked at Halo and Halo looked back at him. Neither of them knew what to do or what to say.

Just then, two thundering trunks rang out climbing up the stairwell. The sound startled the four and the keeper. Boom, boom, boom, boom, it sounded like the brick and stone would soon give out. A matching voice bellowed out from the stair's hallway catching the attention of Taj, Giovanni, Halo, Malakai, and the keeper.

"Golric's expecting them," it said.

Every single member of the crew drew their weapons and readied their positions. The keeper yelled vivaciously for the team to stand down. They did no such thing. The monstrous voice and hammering footsteps continued its upward movement. They were getting closer.

"Stand down!" yelled the keeper.

"Get ready!" Malakai screamed.

"Calm yourselves," the voice spoke up again. This time it wasn't nearly as loud or as booming as it was the first time. It was still a deep and commanding voice, but its meaning was not to grab everyone's attention the second time it spoke as it was the first.

A beast of a man came up from the walkway. It was another one of those goliaths. Just as the others, it was bald, but this one carried deep, sickening scars across its head. His right eye was missing. Instantly, Taj thought back to the old paladin that died at Lithil's hands.

No patch, no cover, no nothing. It was just another hole in the giant's head. The team saw several goliaths when they were first approached and then again, when they arrived at the fire people's city.

Two leather straps draped crossways across the goliath's torso. His brown leather pants had seen better days. No boots, only bare feet; come to think of it, the crew were the only ones with any type of footwear on.

The goliath's one good eye glared down upon their shoes. Giovanni's perception kicked in and he immediately commenced removing his footwear. Halo caught on and quickly did the same. Malakai didn't understand, nor did he really care as to what they were doing or why.

Taj saw the man's feet and like Giovanni, his intuition kicked in. Within seconds of the monster entering the wide room of the second floor where he met the party and the keeper, all four members of the crew had bare feet. Even Malakai, though he groaned and complained, his shoes too came off.

The second floor opened up to wide red flooring. Only giant pillars carved to look like burning fires stood. The brick became large tile on the second floor. Several hallways opened up unmethodically throughout the giant room obviously leading to other areas of the temple and/or other floors.

He hated to say it, but the monstrous goliath had their attention. Taj had seen giants before. The troll of the Myasuna's sewers was much larger than the goliath. The goliath was much more fearsome.

"We're not meaning to intrude." Taj cautiously put his swords away.

One by one the team followed, all except Malakai, whose staff was out and ready just as it had always been.

"I know," said the goliath, clearly aware of why they were there.

"Are you—" Giovanni was cut off from asking the very same question everyone was wondering.

"I am Olric, Olric Firesoul. I am the eldest of the Firesoul brothers."

Walking behind him was another; this one was a familiar face. He wasn't so sick anymore, but his sunken in face and eyes told the others he wasn't completely out of the woods yet. It was Rhoeve. How did he get to Golric's brother before they did?

"Rhoeve!" Halo said excitedly.

That's how women were. She was more excited to see Rhoeve than she'd ever been. Why, because they'd been separated just for a bit. Wow, women, Malakai thought still thinking devilishly of taking the woman from behind.

Giovanni wasn't the same. He knew he wasn't. He was more like the Brick character he created to blend with the people of Burning Brook. Who was Giovanni Vandren? Nothing more than a series of cowardly personas blended together, he thought to himself. The old Giovanni would have been all over Halo already. He wasn't the old Giovanni. No part of that man still existed, save the debt he felt he owed Taj Xavier. And for that, he would continue. Ridden with guilt, the Sylvan would still carry on.

"Olric?" Giovanni asked puzzled.

"I'm the Champion of the element of Fire. I am a paladin of the element. You may have heard stories of the Red Knight or the Burning Knight of Plateaus?"

Rhoeve kept walking up. Taj, Malakai, nor Halo had ever heard of him. Giovanni knew of him. He'd heard of him many times before. He was a legend among the outer rim kingdoms and borderlands.

"I know of you," Giovanni said, mustering up again.

"Forgive us. We're not from around here," Taj said.

What had gotten into Taj? The others didn't understand it nor could they put their fingers on it. He was acting different, subtle, and friendly. He was being human. None of them save Giovanni knew him to be human.

Too many entities were fighting over Taj. SOUL, LORE, Froth, and his own self were all fighting over body supremacy. It was more like Froth was constantly battling SOUL and LORE for hosting benefits to Taj. SOUL and LORE were connected to his body. Froth had his very soul. Taj was locked down in so many ways.

"Rhoeve, you're looking dapper. You look to be feeling better as well." Halo was so happy the team was all back together again. She'd come to appreciate the Corvanian Ambassador.

Malakai's inner jealousy got the better of him. He snarled a bit at the woman's remarks but not enough to catch the attention of the others.

Olric Firesoul waved off the keeper and soon it was just the five of them and Olric. A huge circular indention covered most of Olric's belly. Olric was built very well with big arms, legs, and trunk. Like the orc, his stomach was big. The orc's stomach however was soft and flabbier than Olric's. Olric was destined to be big. His stomach protruded but unlike most, his was solid. Even the veins of his gut stuck out like muscles. He was just all around a very solid, thick man.

"My brother did want to see you. Now is as good as a time as any. He's not going to be any better anytime soon," Olric said.

"Who runs this place, you or Golric?" asked the sorcerer.

Olric smiled. He didn't answer the question. He just moved and waved for the lot of them to follow him. The crew welcomed Rhoeve back and were pleased to see he'd been healed somewhat. Malakai was acting funny. He walked carelessly and stumbled very occasionally. His eyes wandered, not at all like the Malakai of before the Burning Kingdom.

Halo noticed his eyes. They'd changed. They'd blackened over. She watched as he closed them to fight off whatever was going on. Something now in Malakai was sick and different. Halo panicked but Malakai's signals instructed her not to say and word.

"I'm going to get outside. I need some fresh air. It's too stuffy in here," Malakai said while following Olric.

Olric just kept walking. Halo announced that she'd accompany him. Giovanni, Taj, and Rhoeve kept forward, following the champion of fire step for step. He was moving with haste. From behind, Taj admired the seven-and-a-half foot man. The indention on his gut told a story of a ball and chain or some other bludgeoning weapon of that sort. His back told a story of a thousand lacerations. The man had seen his fair share of war and more. He was to be respected. SOUL, LORE, and Taj all agreed. Froth not so much. His essence was sill harvesting in Taj's soul. Soon it would be time.

Froth had planted the seed already and Taj watered it. His companions knew the time would come and their souls would be offered a place among his in the new phylactery of Xavius Froth. Vampires having phylacteries, Taj had never heard of such. Then again, Xavius Froth wasn't just a vampire. He was an irreplaceable essence. He carried the powers of many forms of undead, including the lich.

Taj had spoken many times of once reaching the Burning Kingdom, possibly executing the ritual to transport Froth's essence, Taj's soul, and the souls of all the others into the new phylactery, if that's what it could be called.

Halo trusted him. Malakai constantly laughed it off claiming he was too powerful to worry about the infested getting to him. Giovanni was weary but trusting. Rhoeve didn't like the idea one bit, but he knew from their previous battles and experiences that walking openly with a soul was a death sentence. Their journey this far told him so.

Now, it was just Taj, Giovanni, and Rhoeve. Malakai and Halo took their leave of Forbidden Flame. Malakai breathed heavy all the way to the outside. Even still, the heavy breathing continued.

"Mal, why the heavy breathing, are you okay?" she asked.

"I'm fine," he said with his hands on his knees, doubled over. The pain was too severe to ignore. Something was hurting him. Malakai used fire many times so it couldn't have been the fire. Could it?

"Then why the sickness. Why the pain." she asked, legitimately concerned.

"I uh, I don't know. Maybe I got what Rhoeve's got," he suggested.

"Rhoeve's cured."

"He's still a little sick, huh?"

"Yeah, I think so but he's a lot better. Maybe you should see their healers here?"

"No. I'll be fine. Just tell the others I had to rest for a while. My innate calls for it."

"I will," she said softly.

Malakai reached. Halo fell into his arms. The two embraced as friends, as true close friends. They were family now. Their time together could never be taken away. Never before did they understand that until now, neither of them.

"Where will you go?" she asked with her face buried in his chest.

"I'm not leaving the village. I'll be around. Something here is affecting my innate. I'm not sure why, Halo. I swear to the dead gods and those that have replaced them I don't know."

"Okay Mal. Please sorcerer, be careful and tell me if you need anything."

"Something in this temple is eating at me. What I'm not certain. Why does this church bother me painfully? I've thought of Taj's offer."

"And what offer's that?"

"It's pretty deep when you think about it. Our souls aren't safe. We've fought those infected one too many times already. Those soulish things fly like banshees screaming through the air. If one of those crashed into us, we'd be done for. We've just been lucky. I'm strong. My soul is strong. I'll be fine. I trust Taj, little one, and you should think deeply on encasing your soul until this is over. I'd even connect to Eve. I know you haven't stayed connected to her, but I know you can. It'd be best you saw her soul and those with her protected as well, as many as can fit. Danth, Teraxius, and the others, they should all be given the opportunity to take advantage of Taj's protection."

"I'm going to take him up on it. Why aren't you?"

"I'll be fine. I don't want to hold up a place of a decent person. I'm just a scary old man Halo. Are you sure you want to be alone with me out here?"

Halo laughed. Malakai laughed with her. They'd seen their share of blood. They'd spilled their blood together and for one another. A bond was made with them. They'd had their differences but something recently had bonded them. She couldn't explain it and neither could he.

The remaining three members of the team made their way to the sacred room on nearly the highest floor of the church. The room was built extending over the ledge with massive window openings strategically placed to overlook the village of the fire people down below.

In the center of the oval room rested an altar and directly above it a circular opening in the curved ceiling of the room. On the altar rested a similar looking Goliath. Its plated body covered the majority of the holy area. It was so intensely high up, thought Taj. Olric took his place kneeling beside the altar next to his brother. A similar looking man actually much larger than Olric was already present in the room and kneeling before the dead goliath. Red plated armor covered the dead goliath's body. His head was covered by a beautiful open-faced helm. In the center of his torso rested a great wound. A thick laceration extending from the right collarbone to the left hipbone; it was wide and deep, all the way through.

Pools of blood dripped from his lifeless body. Beside the altar rested a great warhammer, perhaps the biggest any of the non-Firesouls had ever seen. It was the color of hot lava and taller than any of the Firesouls so far, and Golric was at least a foot taller than Olric.

"He was the favorite little brother," Olric said, kneeling next to Golric.

Golric wore nothing. Unlike the others, his body didn't carry the deepened scars and lacerating stories. His smooth bald head carried no war wounds. No brands or marks of any kind touched this goliath at all.

"He was destined to be great." Golric wiped the tears from his eyes.

It was clear. Olric was slightly older than Golric, but Golric wasn't too far ahead of the dead brother in the race of age.

"Golric Firesoul, I've come a long way to see you," Taj said. Something in his voice told the others he'd resorted back to his old self. The self that cared not for emotion or anything human but only to get the job done; and right now the job was Falling Star and the infected shadow army.

Golric ignored Taj's verbal advance. His focus was his dead little brother. His mannerisms told the others he was truly hurt. Olric seemed to be taking it better than Golric. Finally, Golric spoke. The team was more than ready to get through the uncomfortable silence.

"He fought well," Golric said, trying more to please himself than anyone else with his words.

"Yes he did." His older brother threw his left arm around Golric to comfort him, as he knelt before the youngest Firesoul to Golric's right side.

"How did he die?" Rhoeve asked.

Rhoeve was smart and he knew the Firesouls and their people. Right now, their focus was on the youngest sibling. The fire people were a peaceful yet aggressive people. The way of fire was a fierce one. Rhoeve knew Golric's mind was on his little brother, as it should have been obviously.

"He fell against the shadow," Golric answered.

When Olric first saw Rhoeve, he knew Golric would be pleased to see his old friend. Rhoeve kept the Burning people out of war with Corvana for many years. Corvana, a mighty kingdom known for ousting other countries coming into power, let the fire people be—solely due to the efforts of Rhoeve.

"Wait a second, the shadow?" Rhoeve asked quickly. Golric's words concerned him deeply.

"The shadow... How did he fall against the shadow? Have the shadow attacked your people here?" Golric's words concerned Taj. Taj quickly let his questions flow.

Golric stood. Olric followed his oldest, youngest brother. Simultaneously, the two brothers turned to face the team. Taj, Rhoeve, and the others all stood opposite Golric and Olric.

"No, our alliance with Alabaster cost him his life," Golric replied.

"Alliance?" Rhoeve questioned.

"We'd formed an alliance long ago. It was a pact really. In the event of an attack on either of our people, we would come together against the mighty beast... Corvana." Golric replied with a smile. It was a half-smile but still a smile. It was the first positive sign Golric had given out.

"We longed to keep our friendship with you, secret or not Rhoeve, but you're still Corvanian. Corvanians are almost always out for themselves." Olric was friendly, sincere, and yet honest. He meant what he said.

"You didn't trust me?" Rhoeve asked.

"Of course we did. In the event of a change, we had to be secure against your people," Olric answered.

"Do not take it personally, old friend, but I had to keep the interest of my people at hand, even over my own instinct. And it cost my little brother his life." Golric was sulking and falling back into his depressing stupor.

"It's not your fault," Rhoeve said, trying to comfort the legendary priest.

"Lawtor died because I sent him to help fight against Alabaster's enemies alongside them. Albaster's enemies united against them and the kingdom had some difficulty pushing them all back. Lawtor and his company left to assist them. They were slaughtered."

Olric's head dropped hearing his last brother speak of Lawtor's death. Olric added on after his brother's words stopped. "Three Kingdoms, a rising lich with an army, and then the shadow all came at them at once. For the Burning Kingdom, Lawtor and his men answered the call."

"How did they get all the way to the south? That must have been quite a hike. Were they impending attacks? Were they at war?" Taj asked, now seriously curious.

"No, no one has attacked the Alabaster Isles in over two hundred years. Golric knew Corvana's plan to put them down," Rhoeve said, unimpressed with Golric. His previous feelings of Golric Firesoul had instantly changed.

"Now's not the time to discuss this old friend," Golric said to Rhoeve.

Rhoeve was upset. Corvana was utterly destroyed. And right now, Alabaster and the Burning Kingdom were all that remained to help stand against Falling Star and the shadow. "Golric, you have my sincerest condolences, but we certainly have business to discuss."

"What business—" Golric started, but Rhoeve interrupted him screaming.

"The business of betraying your allies! I kept you all out of war! I risked everything to forge an alliance with you. You know the Alabaster Isles were enemies of Corvana. The unspoken war of Corvana and the Albaster Isles is one everyone in the realm knows of. How could you forge an alliance with me and Corvana, and let me risk everything for your people and then do the same with Corvana's only real threat, if you could even consider them as such?"

"Not anymore," Golric said. "Be gone."

"Not anymore?" Rhoeve questioned.

"Pshhh," Golric sighed waving the lot of them off.

"Golric please, we've come here to seek your aid. You're the greatest priest in all the land. We need you!" Rhoeve pleaded. "I spoke highly of you. I gave my word on your behalf, Golric Firesoul. We go back too far. Your father would hear me out!" Rhoeve screamed, pleading for Golric's attention. He got it.

Golric made sure to set his body and eyes uniform to Rhoeve's. His eyes dug deep within the elf's. He walked slowly toward him. Olric watched his little brother. Olric was the eldest and like his father, chose the path of paladinhood. Lawtor the youngest also chose the path of the holy champion. Golric was different. He had the body of the physical champion but swore the fire spoke to him differently. It spoke of a more divine path.

He spoke to Rhoeve with the intention of filling the ears of all present with his words. His words reeked with conviction. "Little brother, I believe they're ignorant of the happening," Olric said to his little brother just before he started.

Golric hesitated, listening to his brother first. Afterwards, he carried on as he intended to. His eyes told of desire, burning ambition, and conviction. "Old friend, do not speak of my father as if you knew him."

Rhoeve wasn't having it. He did know him. He did know the elder Firesoul. "I did know your father. My pact with the fire people began with him."

Golric let him finish and then continued. He patiently waited while Rhoeve spoke. His feet never ceased carrying him onward. His lips immediately commenced once Rhoeve's stopped.

"My words were taken mistakenly old friend. Not anymore will the Alabaster Isles rival or even threaten Corvana. Falling Star annihilated the kingdom just days ago. Lawtor, my little brother, and his company were all among the casualties. Yes, the shadow has fallen upon us. They fell upon us without breaking ground. Not trusting my instinct sent my little brother to the isles. There, I was punished for my disloyalties. Do not mistake my words for weakness. I will have my vengeance upon the shadow and Falling Star will know the name Firesoul. The fire people will burn bright even in the darkest night."

His words were music to their ears, especially Taj's. Taj was forged of war now. It was all he knew. The human in him was virtually gone. SOUL appreciated this Golric Firesoul. LORE did as well but for different reasons. SOUL appreciated the desire for war that burned in his heart. LORE acknowledged his blood loyalty, his love for his people and desire to oust Thedia of the shadowy evil. It all truly caught the attention of the blade.

Taj's last host, Xavius Froth, knew of the fire that lurked in Golric's veins. It was a fire he'd faced many times many lifetimes ago. It was a strong force and one they'd need if they'd hoped to be victorious against the shadow, albeit Falling Star was amongst it.

"That is why we are here old friend," Rhoeve pleaded. The sickness inside him was still present, just not as active. Sickness does not escape a good priest. Rhoeve was still very ill, although since the priests had tended to him, he'd been doing much better. All the screaming, yelling, and getting worked up had his sickness acting up. Pain stretched out, forming in his abdominals.

"We seek to strengthen our team." Taj added, speaking over his old ambassador.

"By adding Firesoul to it," Giovanni finished for Taj.

"I was born with greatness, to greatness. I was destined to be magnificent and mighty. Lawtor connected with fire as I do. He sought the path of the defender, to uphold the weak against the strong. To shield those in need of shielding, all because it was the path of our father; it was what our father wanted," Golric said.

"Golric and myself remain of the Firesoul family." Olric joined the conversation while still looking over his dead brother's body.

"It's not what you're born with. It's what you do with it," Malakai said, chiming in for the first time.

The sorcerer's words hit home somewhere for Golric. Before he could counter them, Taj, Halo and the others quickly asked about his words of the Isles; surely, something was missing in his story.

"We've come because we're to face Falling Star and his shadow, whether it be alone or with the aid of fire." Malakai wanted Golric to understand their position, his position.

Golric looked at the crew. One question after another, they all wanted to know what he meant about Falling Star and the Alabaster Isles. Golric knew what they were thinking: Surely, this is exaggerated and will all be cleared up soon enough. He wasn't exaggerating; the Alabaster Isles were gone from Thedia forever.

Golric backed away from the team. Halo was the most curious of them all. Taj's curiosity was kept silent by his lips. Olric answered all their questions.

Olric spoke up for his brother. "Falling Star sent no army against the mighty kingdom."

"I thought Corvana was the greatest of all kingdoms. And I was told Alabaster was the only thing ever to pose a legitimate threat," Giovanni stated curiously.

"It was. Something inside the walls of the isles kept it highly guarded from magic, all magic. Its navy was second only in quantity. The quality of their ships was second to none."

"Corvana—" Rhoeve started.

Golric took back over for Olric, cutting his old ally off. "Lawtor died because I failed to trust my pact with you and the power of the fire people. Lawtor suffers for my insolence. He's gone now. Nothing will change that. The borderland kingdoms trembled at Alabaster's powers even more than they did Corvana's. Corvana was destroyed in a matter of days by both Falling Star and his shadow armies. His armies marched against Alabaster but were unable to break ground. They couldn't pass."

"So what happened?" Halo asked excitedly.

"They just left," Olric answered softly.

"So why is Alabaster no longer a threat?" questioned Rhoeve angrily. He wanted to know the fate of Alabaster. Corvana was in shambles. Alabaster and the Burning Kingdom were the only two kingdoms left in the pantheon worth mentioning. Corvana hadn't allies, but only kingdoms subservient to them. Rhoeve knew in order to be successful against the shadow, the fire, Alabaster, and what was left of the five regents; Corvana would have to come together.

"BECAUSE FALLING STAR DESTROYED IT!" Golric screamed louder than he'd ever done before.

"Destroyed it?" Halo questioned, nearing tears.

"People across Corvana claimed when Falling Star took to the sky, he blacked out the sun," Golric answered.

"As if Thedia wasn't dark enough in these times," said Olric.

"People flocked to the isles once the infected armies spread. The people of Alabaster claimed they were protected from the shadowy presence. Falling Star proved their words false." With every sentence, Golric furthered Falling Star's powerful presence to the team.

"We long to find the dragon of shadowy souls, the Soul Dragon of Shadows, or whatever name he goes by. Whatever he was before, it doesn't matter. We long to put an end to the bastard creature and end his reign of terror. And I shall bring a reign of terror of my own to fight him with." Malakai sadistically laughed as he spoke.

Halo fell to her knees, completely devastated by the news of Alabaster's crushing annihilation.

"What's left of the islands?" she asked, wiping the streams of tears from her face.

"Nothing. When the clouds of darkness unveiled his doing, even the islands themselves were gone. Whether swallowed by the sea or his own darkness, Alabaster is all but a memory," Olric concluded.

"And our little brother gone with it," finished Golric.

"I do remember days when the sun seemed vanished from our sky," Giovanni said.

"I am grateful your people are still safe," said Rhoeve sincerely to the Firesoul brothers.

"What is it you ask of me?" Golric hadn't really taken in anything said to him thus far. He wanted the team to reiterate everything for him and they did.

The team explained thoroughly and counted their lucky blessings for Rhoeve's persuasive manner in insisting they head to the Burning Territories. Had Rhoeve not convinced them, they would all surely be dead. He did convince them and now they were standing before the greatest priest in all the land, and perhaps all the world.

"All right, I'll send my vengeance with you, but on one condition."

"Wait a second little brother. I will not lose…" Olric quieted down as soon as Golric signaled for him to.

"I will take Magmarok and we will join you on this quest. My vengeance is better served alongside others on this particular day. Olric will stay and lead these people. Rhoeve will stay and help train the men here in the event of an attack."

"Attack, doubtful, fire hates shadow and shadow hates fire," Malakai said

"Rhoeve stays. He's too weak. He'll better serve training others."

"Golric no, I came here for you. I—"

Golric didn't have to interrupt him. Taj did. "He's right, and if these are his conditions, then so be it."

"Taj," Rhoeve pleaded.

"Do not argue. Let him finish. He's right," Taj continued.

"Agreed," said Giovanni.

Halo was still in shambles. She didn't say a word. Her people, so many of her people were in Alabaster and now it was gone, just gone. What was next? Who was next? Her old lover Tol was there. He was surely among the dead.

As the conversation continued, Taj fell from consciousness. He stood as if normal, but his mind was elsewhere. Something else had to be done and before they left. The souls of the people had to be brought together in common ground for Froth.

"I've seen this army and they infect good people. They will not infect me."

"You're surely right, Golric," Malakai quickly said.

Golric just stood there in silence staring at the elf.

"Your link to fire is one they'd assume never feel… I assume of course. I on the other hand am just clearly too powerful to be possessed. We are among great men here."

Taj broke from his inner consciousness, snapping back into reality. "The others, we're all in grave danger. These are a people of spirit and power. Gather them all. Eve, connect to Eve little Halo. Wipe your tears and connect to your sister. I have something inside of me that can protect us. It came to me before."

"Oh?" Olric said curiously.

Taj quickly explained the essence inside him, not his true goals, but what he was told to explain. Rhoeve had nothing to lose. Halo trusted Taj.

Giovanni trusted Taj, not so much as the others, but he did. It was just in his nature to second guess.

"You want me to put my soul in what?" Giovanni asked.

And it began. It was a long and drawn out conversation but Taj finally did it. All but Golric and Malakai agreed. Once Halo reconnected with Eve in the evening, every member of their crew in the citadel also agreed. Taj explained the ritual could protect many of them but the infected would focus on mainly the strong. The strong, those that could protect the others, they should be given sanctuary in the phylactery first.

Danth, Teraxius, Helios, and Eve all gave their souls through Eve and Halo's connection to the phylactery. Taj, Giovanni, and Rhoeve all did the same. Olric was also among the protected, as were four of his most powerful followers.

In the coming days, Taj birthed powers never before seen by the team and, further, by the Firesoul brothers as well. Taj called forth liches, revenants, and other necromantically infused beings, mostly undead, to take part in Froth's ancient ritual. Golric admitted he cared not for the ritual or the energies it brought. Taj's words of not surviving long enough to see their vengeance through kept Golric and Olric quiet and cooperative.

The entire colony of people was used in the ritual. An old diamond the size of a walnut was taken from the Burning Kingdom's treasury. It was the center point of the ritual. Another part of the ritual was the simultaneous funeral of the fallen champion of fire, Lawtor Firesoul.

The ritual took days and time preciously needed by all. It was necessary. Golric was convinced he could protect himself against the shadow, as was Malakai. However, the others weren't so magically inclined or infused to protect their souls as the sorcerer and priest were. Taj explained that it was the soul that was attacked and not the body.

When it was done, the partaking members would walk soullessly. Their souls protected by the undead entity Froth. Taj explained how his soul was safe as the shadow faired ill against the undead. With Froth leaving his body he would have to transport his soul as well, otherwise he'd be open game for the shadowy banshees. It was his closing argument to get the others to do as he needed, for himself and for Froth.

Lawtor's funeral, Halo and Eve's meditation, and the ritual consisting of over a hundred participants all went on at once. It was a magnificent sight. Three prisoners of the Burning Kingdom had their blood spilled to fulfill the destiny of the ritual.

The hosts of the phylactery felt no different. Their souls were hidden in a safe place. Froth told to keep the diamond hidden for the time being inside the treasury of the Burning Kingdom. Taj declined silently. He fastened a necklace with the diamond, giving it to Malakai to hold.

Malakai happily took it. Golric didn't know what to make of Taj's necromantic powers. After Froth's exit from his body, Taj assured the others his unique and unusual powers were gone. The fire people feared his powers and the creatures he summoned. They feared he could easily turn on them. Golric knew better. More, he cared not if the quasi-dead anomaly tried to turn. Golric carried a lot of weight, especially with his own people. He carried power, political knowledge, courage, and many more things. Fear was not any one of the things that burned inside him.

The great kingdom of fire was the only place where any one creature was truly safe. The citadel was no longer safe. In the days to come, the infected move more fiercely than they'd ever moved before. Eve's pleas for help cut deep into Halo's ears. Before long, she'd almost forgotten why she was upset with her dear sister.

Malakai's arrogant ways and reckless behavior had somewhat of an effect on the nymph descendant. Their blood carried more than just that of a legendary fey creature of beauty. It also held a lineage to Celeste, the late god of magic, creator of arcane and keeper of the divine powers. Even still, more powers of demons, devils, and angels brewed in their bodies. The sisters were truly special, gifts from the gods. Their bloodline was singular in origin and the only left descending from the gods themselves. Neither Halo nor Eve knew the extent of the powers in their bloods. The nymph ancestry was all he knew.

Eve was given order by Golric Firesoul to give word to Danth; the people of the citadel are to move to the Burning Territory inside the walls of the Burning Kingdom. It was too risky as of now but it would happen soon, very soon.

The ritual took days but it was done. The old enemy of the fire and all of life, the undead, were now distantly allied with Taj, Golric, and all those that defied Falling Star. Their souls were safe and held tight by the magnificent Malakai of Lyneth, sorcerer of sorcerers.

All were coming together for a common cause. Those summoned by Taj or perhaps the entity, were sent away. What became of them still queer to those of the Burning Kingdom. Liches walked amongst the living upon Taj's word, powers such his hadn't been seen since The Sundering of the world.

It was agreed Rhoeve would stay back with the eldest Firesoul. He felt a coward for it. He truly wished to die in the service of Corvana. Corvana was nothing but a ruined kingdom, buried in its own ash and dirt.

At first Halo was ordered to stay back as well. More discussions and debates led the men to believe the mobile team would need the connection to Eve and the citadel. If all was to fall into place, the citadel and the Burning Kingdom would soon be one.

Golric would join Taj, Halo, Giovani, and Malakai on their quest to end Falling Star. One remained of the five champions sent by Corvana to aid Taj, six considering both sisters. Taj was proud, pleased to fight alongside her. Once long ago, Arakros felt the wrath of the forsaken. It was a force he'd soon feel again.

Danth gave word back just before the team's departure. Thankfully, the citadel now knew of the isles' demise. In case the people of Reforged hoped to make it to their walls, Halo informed them that no such walls still stood. Reforged, the Citadel, and its people all knew the Burning Kingdom's burning land was now possibly safest place in all of Corvana. Marching so many to the Burning Kingdom was too risky; for now, they would defend their underground citadel at all costs.

Taj's swords were excited, of course for different reasons. Golric cared not for the others. He wore nothing special. His thick leather crossed straps forged by the fires of Thedia and dipped in broken down residium. His leggings were done the same, as were his boots. A half-leather half-metallic mask covered the majority of his face. The lower right jaw-line and side of his mouth was visible, nothing else. On his back rested a series of looped leathers, straps, and metals. It was the hangar for Magmarok; his fire-forged warhammer was two times the size of any warhammer or any two-handed weapon ever seen by any of the members of the party.

"Come, vengeance awaits," said Golric, smiling ready to take on the quest.

"I've been speaking with my sister, great priest. The scouts of Reforged have granted information on the movements of the infected. I know where they're moving. You know where they're moving here. We can fight this. We have to lure them here. These lands are too much for them. The fire is too much for them. Golric, you and I, we must have words."

Golric smiled. Why wouldn't he? The little girl was a beauty. Malakai snarled under his breath. Even with Falling Star and the shadow all around them, the capable sorcerer still thought of bedding the nymph-blooded bitch. The term applied. She was ferocious and playful, honest yet deceitful, but something in her was deep. Something in her matched her own darkness.

Chapter 9

Three days of fighting, the citadel was under attack. The infected really showed their potential against the underground stronghold. A higher ranking infected known as a corrupted led the attack. It was a bugbear named Throxar.

Wymon felt the pain of his trust in Ereven on the edges of thousands of the infected. The infected moved more than Ereven expected. The army double backed before Ereven could even reach them. Unfortunately, Ereven and his men fell victim to a pincer attack.

Throxar knew the citadel would give chase. He found his instinct to be true only because Ereven proved it so. Drago pulled Throxar away from his minions, soldiers, and protectors, to include one guardian. Guardians were similar to paladins but rather than connecting to the divine powers, they were linked to the arcane.

Ereven's direct team members charged forward, hoping to save Drago from a vicious and violent death at the hands of the infected bugbear. Drago was built, trained, and prepared to isolate powerful members of the infected and he did so with ease. Sadly, Throxar was among the strongest of all the infected. He was one of the few known to the shadow as a corrupted.

Corrupted were exquisite. They were powerful souls native to Thedia corrupted by an evil, more powerful shadow. Throxar lived deep in the mountain caves. His collected tribe of kinsmen was taken and the majority still fought under his banner.

Drago's sword and shield were no match for the shield and axe of Throxar. Throxar's iron tower shield stood decorated with the limbs and bones of his fallen victims. His great axe slammed into Drago's medium iron shield as if it were a weapon twice its own size.

Drago lay beaten and battered but he'd done his job. Just before his final breath was taken from him, more swords, staves, bows, and shields crashed down upon the giant bugbear, halting him in his tracks.

The attacks were no use. Just as Drago, every other member of Ereven's party was thrown around and off just the same. One, two, three, four, and finally five; five hammering strokes of Throxar's axe splintered Drago's shield.

A series of bolts and rays cried out from a distance, compliments the eladrin Ereven. The streams of energy stumbled Throxar. "Now," yelled Ereven hoping his team would get up and seize the advantage he'd just given them.

Danth and his crew stood tightly together. Even Helios' blades were present for the battle. As of late, his faith in his swords had faded. His desire to carry them, use them, and serve the common cause had faded as well. On this day, for this battle, he rang out with soaring dedication. Perhaps the entire citadel's fate riding on one battle captured his curiosity.

One corrupted is enough to change the tides of any war or battle. With the armies regrouping and doubling back, another found itself in the presence of the underground citadel. An elven man named Lithil, paladin, also walked with the ranks of the two armies of Infected. He was much stronger than Throxar.

The elf doused in the darkness of Gemini stalked the battlegrounds for legitimate threats. Others present during his fight with the mortal–Taj they called him? They were here! He weeded his way through the array of bloodshed, chopping down all that stood at him. Each one fell within just a swing.

There he was. His armor was metallic and light, an iron pair of short breeches with linked chain pieces wrapping all across his body. It was a setup he'd never seen before and it carried residium. Residium, the broken down dust made from the breaking down of magical weapons, it was a food worthy of sustaining life to Gemini. An entire plane the size of Thedia had enough residium to keep the Gemini's world breathing for a long time. That was a different life and a different war. The motives were different. The players were different. His liege was different.

He fought differently than he'd done in the past. He carried a small iron shield on his back. Under it rested another two-handed greatsword.

In his right hand, Teraxius held a gleaming trident. It must have caught his eye while in the citadel. The trident was long and dripped with radiant powers. In his right hand another iron shield, and under it yet another short blade, Teraxius was a gladiator. He knew the day's battle would call for a variety of weapons.

Teraxius moved magnificently through the ranks of the infected. He spun, twisted, ducked, and jumped precisely when needed. Aiding him were three others from all angles. None were close to him. A shaman, a priest, and another melee fighter wielding two blades fought alongside him. The priest stood a good distance away, protected by several normal mortals. The shaman stood close to the priest. The other melee fighter was just a few feet away. They both took advantage of their caster allies, yet, they each fought alone.

Danth and Eve stood close, Eve summoning spirits to guard the backs of Helios and Teraxius while Danth kept them healed and helped fend off the oncoming hoards of infected. Danth was a healing priest and he was good at it. His Draconic powers were better suited for enhancing his allies and fighting himself. Nonetheless, he was not without healing powers.

Lithil felt their presence once before, when he faced that "mortal" at Burning Brook. Undead and other entities surrounded that damned being. He wasn't there. He wasn't among the numbers fighting against his shadow. Malagant will surely be pleased, he thought anxiously.

Alabaster was built upon more powers than Corvana. Though hidden, the isles did carry more threats than the massive five regent kingdom. Now both were gone. Only the Burning Kingdom could hope to prove worthy against them. The fire always pushed them back and those infused by it were nearly impossible to take. After today, only the Burning Kingdom would remain of enemies of worth to Falling Star. Corvana was gone. Alabaster was gone. Today, the citadel would be gone. As easily as it was found, it would vanish.

The mortal who most caught his attention was laced with necrotic energy and wrapped in chain-linked armor. It was the gladiator! Looking around, the savage lower ranking infected scoured the surrounding lands.

The gladiator was killing his people swiftly and beautifully. Oh but what was to come? Those already taken by the shadow were in rank and present. However, his daemons would come soon. Daemons were his men in spectral form. They could blacken the sky and raise an army in a matter of moments. And best of all, they weren't killable by anything of this world.

Lithil sparked the gladiator's attention. The peaceful manner in which Teraxius agreed to engage was pleasant; a simple nod and smile. Thick and wide green colored scars raced around his body. *It's amazing he still breathes*, thought Lithil.

Both Lithil and Teraxius cut down enemies on their way to each other. Lithil now held but a single blade in his grasp. He swung it with both hands with a force questionably material. Was something else aiding the possessed elf to swing with such force? Teraxius wondered. Teraxius' shield dented upon first contact. Had it not been for the shield, Teraxius' head would have surely been split by the over-the-top swing of Lithil.

Teraxius was forced to a knee from the blow. From his position, Teraxius' trident found openings in Lithil's game, slashing open the armor and skin just above his feet.

"Ahhhh," Lithil roared out in pain, letting loose one hand to counterbalance his body while swinging downward wildly at Teraxius. Teraxius was quick witted and used to battle. The clever gladiator rolled over his left shoulder atop his head, popping back up to his feet and reengaging the possessed elf.

Teraxius popped up. His shield was causing difficulty. The damage done by Lithil's sword was too great and now a burden to keep. The experienced fighter released his grip from it, sliding it down and off his arm. Where the shield bent in, it dug a little into his forearm; Teraxius kept the sword that had been tucked underneath a secondary weapon. He knew the short sword would act as a shield and nothing more. No matter how great the opening, defense was still necessary. In large battles, defense was far more useful than offense. One cannot utilize their offensive skills if dead, he thought.

"No!" Helios screamed, seeing Teraxius against the possessed elf. They knew him from his battle with Taj. They felt his presence. Helios charged angrily toward his brother in arms. Eve summoned wolf spirits to assist in the attack. Danth called forth an empowered circle to be centered on Teraxius. All in the circle allied with the gladiator would be granted divine protection as well as swiftness and strength, albeit for a short time.

The axe of Throxar had all but ended Drago and his team. Thankfully, Ereven's precision bolts and blasts lured him to a nearby cliff. Just past the valleys, hills, and opposite the mountains rested a small cliff leading downward to a strong river. Not far down from where the cliff overlooked it, the river opened into a waterfall. The geography outside of that was unknown to them all.

Drago and the others fought with Throxar to get him near the cliff. From there, with Ereven's help, they hoped to force him from the cliff's ledge. Throxar's shield bash sent one of their own over the side. Ereven's team was losing. He was out of bolts and rays. He did have a few area-of-effect spells left. The ground beneath them was shaking. It was loose. Throxar saw his adversaries fall helplessly. Drago was the most difficult. The possessed bugbear peeled him from the earth and held him from it by only his neck. He laughed, seeing victory in hand. Looking around, he knew all before him that was lost would be replaced upon the arrival of Lithil's daemon army. Those fallen to the citadel would be replaced by those taken from it.

A slamming power burned Throxar's arm. All around him, everything was engulfed in radiant energy. An ancient and powerful wand of the old world existed in Ereven's clutch. It sent a transmute rock to mud spell at the rocky cliff edge where Ereven's surviving team members faced the bugbear.

Ereven's final spell was a radiant barrier engulfing all those within it in a sheer force of radiant energy. It was equivalent to using a fireball but with radiant power and also a lasting one. With fireball, after discharge it faded, unless materials caught fire of course. Ereven's radiant barrier created a wall of radiant energy imbedding all those who stood where it began. It was a type of a wall.

The lot of them became encased in Ereven's radiant barrier. Immediately following, the strong and solid rocks that held the area from which they were fighting dissolved into slippery mud, sending all five to their pitted deaths, including both Drago and Throxar.

Ereven was out of breath and out of spells. He hadn't a single ally around him. The infected were still coming. Throxar was dead and the beast's blood as on his hands. He grinned with satisfaction. He cared not for those lost. Casualties, he thought.

Helios charged in, engaging Lithil the same second Teraxius popped back up. In unison, as a team, the two fought the crafty elf. A cloud of darkness ability enveloped Lithil in darkness, throwing both of his adversaries off guard. Teraxius being the more knowledgeable immediately retreated to safety while Helios' temper saw him still trying to fight through it.

"Get back," Teraxius bitched angrily.

"I'll kill him myself!" Helios barked back.

Helios' words finished. A sword cloaked in darkness came from within its confines, finding its mark behind the scale armor of Helios. As instructed, Helios fell back, unintentionally dropping both swords. His knees touched the ground. His hands held the wound.

"No!" Teraxius yelled, leaping over his ally in a wind sprint.

His trident met Lithil's sword, still only being held by a single hand. The attack nearly disarmed the elf. With haste, he quickly doubled his grip again. Once again, the two faced off. Teraxius was skilled in the art of disarming and every time the corrupted's blade landed between the forks of his trident, Teraxius would quickly spin and twist it, hoping to peel the weapon from its wielder.

Helios fell to his side, fading to darkness. Death would come soon. Another pinch sparked him. A soothing force came over the dual-wielding ranger. It was Danth. Danth's divine power sealed the wound mostly, giving Helios yet another chance at life, and better, another crack at that damned elf.

The ensuing battle continued for days. Lithil survived both Helios and Teraxius, even with the aid of Danth. And the two fighters survived Lithil just the same. In the days to come, Lithil slew many, believed to be hundreds, all on his own.

With the end of each day came the realization that the infected were growing stronger and that more continued to come. So far, none of the spectral creatures had arrived. All of the infected pushing against the citadel were in physical form, meaning they'd taken over the souls and bodies of mortals native to Thedia. The shadow specters were believed to be untouchable by anything of the known world. Once a shadow's essence took over a soul, the true power of that essence would come into full form.

It was dawn of the fifth day. The first four days and nights were in the bag. Lithil was the archetype soldier of the battle. He killed more than any by many. Every single day, Helios and Teraxius would search for and engage the possessed elf hoping to stop him from killing others. Every day Danth would make himself ready to aid them with healing.

The scouts returned. Peni wasn't pleased with the news. How was she going to tell Wymon? She wasn't. Ereven was still healing from his epic dual with Throxar. More and more drizzled out of the realm of lies in regards to the eladrin; it was all but concrete that he'd killed his own men to kill Throxar.

Peni had a tough job on her hands. The citadel secured all its doors. Only the hidden trap doors remained for entry and exit. More than enough scouts and hidden guards kept watch at all times. The fifth day started smoothly. The surviving combatants of the citadel were still well within its walls even after the sun was set in for the day. Usually, fighting commenced in the early morning and carried on late into the night. Somewhere, sometime in the night the infected would flee and scatter. Just like clockwork, they resumed their ravenous duties the following morning. When the infected were spotted, the citadel would sound its horn. The horn never sounded this morning.

Wymon and the others knew of the spectral shadows. They'd heard stories and some had even seen them. There was no clear way on how to fight them or what to do in the event of their presence. Wymon and the citadel didn't care. They were going to hold. They had to hold. They had to hold to the last man; too many innocents were at stake. It seemingly stood as the final outpost for survivors. Constant scout teams continuously searched for survivors and spread the word of the safe haven. It wasn't about saving anything anymore but about rebuilding in the event they defeated the shadow. It was now about having people left to rebuild and something to rebuild on.

Wymon was smart. His scouts worked double time. Half watched while the others built and set traps. Magical devices and everything else was used to forge traps strong enough to dent their numbers. Another experienced guild member, a scout, rushed to Peni. She was too late. Another had already told Peni of the unfortunate news.

The citadel was absent of several. Hundreds already gone at the hands of the infected, some charged with relentless pursuit like savage zombies. Others fought quasi-intelligently with kills being more of a concern than surviving. More, even others fought above their grade and battled with intelligence beyond understanding. They were smart, dedicated, and patient. Lastly, there were those even greater than those of high intelligence. These not only possessed a strong intellect and prowess, they were capable of fighting as more than one being, warriors slinging magic missiles and wizards casting heals. How was the citadel supposed to compete?

Throxar and Lithil stood greater and above all other physical shadow thus far. Throxar was killed already. Ereven took his life. His own words claimed it was a do-or-die situation. He spoke of his team as if they were already dead by the time he separated the ledge of the cliff from the rest of the connecting soils.

Since Throxar's death, Lithil clearly took the reins of the army. After the first day's end, Eve didn't return to combat. She sat in solitude, meditating, training on mind, body, and soul on what was to come. Alihaedra joined her after the second day. They were given a room, religious items, residium, and several other ritualistic necessities.

Then on the fifth day, doomsday came in the form of a dark storm. The ravenous wave of mindless cretins was gone. The second wave had been pushing since the end of the second day. They were smarter. They fought harder and with more discipline but weren't above self-sacrifice to get the kill.

Helios' body was battered and upon hearing the news of the fifth day, the ranger gave up his swords. He'd hung them on the wall of the small barracks unit he was staying in. The morning of the fifth day, after the news was handed down, he laughed and returned to his cot, assuming the worst was yet to come.

He was right. The fifth day's wave came in two forms: the usual physical led by the newly growing legend, Lithil, and the phantasmal form of spectrals. Somewhere in the downtime of the battle, a Reforged shaman attained the name Daemon. Daemon was the proper title for the shadowy soul infecting creatures.

The sun was cloaked by the number of daemons in the sky. Their banshee like screams cut through the air. The citadel was now completely outmatched and most of their more experienced combatants were already dead. They'd been killed in the days prior.

A human named Luka was among the dead and already sorely missed. Others preceded him and even more succeeded him in death. And worse, more was still to come. One, two, three, four, five, six… the hidden trap doors of Reforged's citadel all came open, while the daemons came and blocked out the sun. The shadowy storm was among them and when it came, it blacked out the sun.

Eve and Alihaedra returned to their respected places among the active members of the citadel. Wymon felt all was lost. He'd done magnificently but sometimes, no matter how perfect the plan is or how well it goes, it just isn't enough.

Teraxius walked affront with Danth and Wymon. Alihaedra made her way to her broken-hearted husband. Lithil led an unstoppable army.

Smoldering ash and smoke filled the skies. Blood bathed the dirt beneath them. Everything around them was a complete wreck.

Lithil walked casually as if nothing was wrong. Teraxius, alongside Helios and others, couldn't fell the mighty possessed elf. How would he do it today without any help at all? Wymon looked back at his brave guild. His members filled the majority of the ranks. Still, some that had come and others that began and fled to the citadel also walked among them. Wymon smiled, looking back at his guild climbing from the iron trapdoors. The iron doors were secured by two sets of chains on opposite sides of the rectangular doors. The door hatches slung open and lines upon lines of his men poured out.

This was it. The storm of daemons was coming. The infected physical force was just ahead of them on the ground ready to complement their every action. Wymon knew this was it. This was where he and his guild fell. Alongside him walked the "true" leader of the guild, Danth Craven. Alihaedra walked close behind him. She loved him, yet she felt sad for him.

Wymon positioned himself to gain the attention of his rising men. An old tree provided a large enough stump for Wymon to jump on. The stump was to act as a stage and it served its purpose well. The citadel was built around the mountains just before the elevations began. On one side were cliff edges. Throxar met his end being dropped from one, as did most of Ereven's party.

"Reforged... People of our citadel... When we built this place, it was never truly given a name. What's in a name? Everything is in a name! Names carry meanings and meanings carry memories! Today, we're of Reforged, of the citadel, and of THEDIA!" Wymon emphasized the name of the world.

The people fighting alongside him slowly changed their routes to end at him. Wymon was an orator. Danth had just discovered. Wymon could speak well. That was something Danth could never get out. Rarely, could the great priest of the dragons put his thoughts into words, real words that others could understand.

The leader of Reforged continued. "An army never before seen by our eyes is among us. There's no way to kill it. We have no hope in success here. We can hold them off and give them hell long enough to see our brothers end this. Some of you know of this Taj and some of you don't. We have allies in high places and forever it grows higher."

The men clapped and cheered; roars of the men matched the screams of the daemons.

"Whatever happens today, fear not. Thedia will prevail. She's always seen it through. Today, wherever we came from means nothing. We fight as one, not as Corvanians, Alabasterians, or even as borderland people. Today, we fight as Thedians. If we fail, all we know dies. We must remain like the cockroach. It refuses to die out. WE MUST DO THE SAME!"

Again, the people cheered. Alihaedra looked at Danth. The two smiled. A chemistry silently brewed. Neither would dishonor nor betray the leader of Reforged, their true friend and lover, Wymon.

Peni now made it to the ranks of Wymon. She stood with her back to the enemies. She looked back at them one more time before turning back to see her fellow guild members. Peni fell into deep thought. She was the one who first broke the news to Wymon of the daemon army accompanying the infected one. The people of the citadel were doomed. An undefeatable army was approaching along with another that was far superior in age and experience. The blank-minded crazy creatures had all been killed off. Now, the real threat approached. An experienced and more cool-minded army of infected walked in the shadows of the daemons.

"Reforged, we're the reason these people are still here. The shadow's come before. Thedia ousted it then and we'll do so again! Death is a natural part of life. Embrace it!"

Again, the roaring members of Reforged and the citadel cried out, weapons and helms in the air to give praise to their leader and all of their accomplishments. Wymon felt a gentle touch upon his lower back. His loving wife touched the area of his body that neared her face from his standing upon the stump.

Secretly, Wymon instructed certain high-ranking members to hide among the citadel and disappear from their ranks. Once the battle was underway, their mission would be to lace the entire citadel in oils of all kind. From there, should the shadow find themselves within their walls, they'd soon find hell coming with it.

Ereven was also amongst the ranks opposite the infected army. Ereven's tongue was smooth. Several younger members of the guild jumped at the idea of fighting alongside a "well-respected" wizard of Reforged.

Lithil's units swarmed strategically in a left push. The left would push the defenders toward the cliff ledges. Pushing them to the right would back them up into the mountains, giving them at least some chance of escape. While the first wave pushed, the second wave would infiltrate the underground citadel and finish off any who chose to stay behind and/or hide. Meanwhile, the daemons would take new hosts, refilling the spots in the legions where their soldiers had already fallen.

The push went according to plan. The ledges were a little farther back than expected but useful just the same. Teraxius held strong against the oncoming aggressors. Lithil sought him out. He had old business with the scarred human.

Eve found her place close to Teraxius. She felt safe and warm with him. Eve also had a plan. She knew her blood was special. She was going to give it all to protect the people of the citadel. Alihaedra too found herself standing close to the man she loved.

Wymon's speech was cut short by the persistence of the pushing aggressors. A secret unit stationed by Wymon came from the mountains and flanked the forceful infected. Wymon's tactic encased the aggressors. The daemons took from Wymon what he so rightfully deserved. The flying shadow ghosts, or daemons, smothered the battlefield, taking with them nearly sixty percent of Wymon's army. They didn't instantly turn. The shadows would slam into them, as a boy would dig into mud. Then, as a squirrel digging into a hiding place, so did the shadows dig into the souls through the bodies of their targets. They fell convulsing on the ground as if possessed. They were possessed.

Wymon saw his people dying. He saw his people fighting but for no greater glory. For Wymon and the citadel, there was no light at the end of the tunnel. Peni was among those taken. None were safe. Ereven blew up scores of areas with his bombing evocation spells. It got the attention of some even Ereven hoped to avoid. Between the charging, barbaric infected and the chasing aerial daemons, Ereven found himself in quite a pickle, racing and rushing to evade his would-be killers. The mountains he thought, the mountains would be a splendid place to escape this battle.

Teraxius' trident found Lithil before Lithil's two-handed weapon found him. The seasoned gladiator cut him up early. Lithil smiled. The fully plated elf had armor for days. His full plated armor was absent only of the helm.

"Would you like me to try?" he asked, laughing.

Teraxius just continued pushing forward. Every single day the two engaged. Every single day, Teraxius lost a shield to him. The fifth day was no different. Lithil's powerful swings eventually shattered yet another shield, the sword being held beneath it, and lastly the magical trident he fought with so splendidly.

Teraxius had yet to bleed this day, but bleeding wasn't Lithil's goal just yet. Teraxius stepped back, seeing he was defeated. Lithil stalked forward slowly. Lithil made a move. Amazingly, so did Teraxius and the human gladiator was quicker. A diving forward roll found Teraxius with two more short swords, compliments of the defenders who died wielding them before. Immediately, Teraxius flipped the sword in his left hand upside down.

Lithil laughed. "The little human has some fight left in him yet," he said, devilishly grinning from ear to ear.

Cling! Teraxius' aggressing sword found itself in a defensive posture from just a single lash from Lithil's blade. Teraxius had to move flawlessly. To hesitate or falter meant instant death to the gladiator. A solid combination of swings and thrusts, Teraxius leaped back, pulling his stomach back and throwing his hands in the air to further his evasive jumping posture.

Still, Lithil held enough reach with his one-step-forward attack to graze and bust the chain-linked armor of Teraxius. His sword was something special. It was some dark and different. Teraxius reengaged sending his swords one after another overhead only to be caught time after time by precision defense. It was exactly what Teraxius wanted. After a brief pause, Lithil hesitated to look for his next action. The gladiator ducked and spun counterclockwise, preparing himself to cut into, through, and possibly even sever Lithil's legs.

"Ugh," Teraxius groaned.

Somewhere in the spin, he caught an iron boot/leggings across the left side of his face. Everything around him went black. An evil laughed echoed in the background. His weapons were no longer in his hands. Did he let them loose? He could feel the warmth of his blood soothing the outer skin of his face. Some of his teeth were broken. He'd been in so many battles, fights, duels, and the like. Was he really defeated so easily? Inside, he laughed. So this was it? He thought. When you are hit just right by the one that has your number, well, it's your time. It was a phrase an old guide of the arenas once told him. May the powers that be protect those I love; he silently prayed seeing the blackness grow even dimmer.

Lithil's cloud-of-darkness ability surrounded both himself and his adversary in complete and total blackness. He could see. Teraxius could not. His armor was laced with shadowy magics and residium of the same kind. Teraxius wasn't beaten down. His vitality hadn't burned out. He was merely knocked from consciousness. His mind drew blanks. Everything was fuzzy and fading. A sharp edge broke the first layer of skin at his throat. The laugh echoed out again, this time louder than the last.

Teraxius' mind fell back, bringing him back to one of his most favored times as a gladiator. It was early in his career, long before they knew his potential. The people of Corvana threw him in a scenario battle. The scenario was based on the Battle of Stolen Arrows; an epic fourteen day battle with a united Borderland force facing the Fifth Regency of Corvana.

The united outside forces fought and conquered several cities and kingdoms of the borderland before rising up against the sleeping giant, Corvana. The scenario first saw the raiding forces of the borderlands killing and conquering the final city of a mighty kingdom. From there, the saviors of the realm, Corvana, would take the field uniting and unifying all under their banner. The wars would stop. The pain and hurt of the realm would stop with the ceasing of the wars. Corvana would unite all who stood against them and make them allies. A common motto of a Corvanian: What better way to get rid of an enemy than to make them an ally?

It was one of his first times before the roar of the crowd. At first, he loathed them for their very existence. He hated them for their bloodthirst. He'd escaped slavery and treachery in his own kingdom only to have it handed to him again at the hands of another. Teraxius was a hated life by the higher-ups of the Regent. He was made to be one of the common, unarmed villagers of the beaten down city left to the mercy of the raiding united outsiders.

Teraxius made quick work of those that came at him, quickly arming himself with the weapons of his fallen foes. The reenactment didn't go as planned. Teraxius yelled for formation. Some knew what the new slave spoke of while others just stood ready to defend themselves. Those that understood hastily armed themselves as Teraxius felled their aggressors.

At the last minute, several masters of the arena offered more slaves to fill the ranks of the Corvanians for the duel. Luckily, the arena's promoters carried extra slaves and workers for all kinds of business. Freedom was offered to all if success was secured. Teraxius concreted his fate by brutally mauling through every single member of the Corvanian regiment with only minimal help from the others.

Teraxius awoke. The sword was piercing slowly into his throat. The laugh was still present. Darkness still covered his mind and vision alike. The sounds of aid were too far to instill hope into. His end was now. His time had come.

Eve's summons kept her protected as well as Danth. Danth focused on keeping the key members strong and healthy. His zones of empowerment filled his men with strength, power, and courage. Alihaedra knew Eve's plan. It was an ancient plan and one too far gone from Thedia to instill hope into.

Eve's blood covenant with the ancient powers that be and the great spirits lost in time imbued her with such convoluted powers from a world long gone that even she hadn't a clue as to how to use them. She couldn't hold them. Controlling them wasn't optional. They weren't to be controlled. The night before the fifth day and even before that, Eve focused with the help of an even greater shaman to create a shamanistic martyr in order to call to the old spirits.

Some claim the dragons took the place of the dead gods; others believed it was the angels who stepped up and took up the task. The Rivermortal was said to govern the world by itself, while even more thought it was being governed by the dragons, demons, devils, or angels. Speaking of demons and devils, they too found large groups of worshippers.

The great spirits of the lost world had long been forgotten. Those of elements were still faintly remembered by the scarce few who followed them. Religious organizations of the elements fire, earth, wind, life, and even death sprang from the death of the gods at the hands of Gemini, the taker.

It was believed the ancient gods were granted their power by the oldest of essences, the great spirits of the lost world. The term "lost world" was as old as time and the term referenced many ancient beliefs.

Eve tapped into a power source too great for a mortal to withstand. It was going to kill her. The ancient spirits granted their powers only to the blood of the gods. Divine blood of the highest level was the only thing worthy of their powers.

Looking around, Eve saw her people falling. Danth charged in at a last ditch effort to dent the citadel's impending doom. He was safe from the daemons, as his soul had been sent through the link of her and her sister and into the phylactery of Taj's inner undead essence.

The daemons tried to take him only to find out there was nothing to take. The body was absent of the soul. The infected still swarmed him. Dozens fell to his flailing morning star. A cry from Danth secured Eve's feeling. She was doing the right thing. A blood omen, a cast from which she could never regain herself, blood casters were of the rarest kind and lowly were they among the ranks of mortals.

Prismatic colors predominately green, white, and black orbited around her. More colors came to be and the peculiar shaman became consumed by the powers. Her people were utterly annihilated. Her eyes lastly fell upon a dark aura of clouds. It was where Teraxius met Lithil. She was doing the right thing. How could she be certain the spirits of the lost world were who contacted her? What if it were just demons or devils playing malicious tricks with her mind?

"No!" She screamed. Her legs opened to a wider stance. Her elbows were near her ribs with her forearms stretched out. The streaming colors came together as one engulfing the shaman in an electrically charged looking orb of bright light.

The aura of darkness vanished. The gladiator's throat was half slit. Lithil's sword just barely missed the important part. What happened? Where was the darkness? Where was Lithil? Teraxius' eyes were blinded with blankets of forceful power. The blanketing powers consumed the entire battlefield. The last image in the gladiator's eyes was of a gigantic apparition of a dog, also primarily appearing in white and black; not a Dalmatian but a Great Dane of similar color. The image spawned from ground above where Eve stood. A whirling tornado of winds encircled the dog.

All daemons, even those whom recently had taken a new host, were annihilated. The majority of the infected were obliterated. The blinding white energy smothered the battlefield.

Lithil was still present. His body still existed somehow. His armor broken and washed away in the winds of power, his weapon was also taken and swept away into the forceful power of Eve's doing.

Preparing to take his last breath, Danth opened his eyes only to be blinded by the same light that blinded Teraxius. Peni also awoke. The daemon inside her was gone, pushed away by Eve's powers.

Lithil's body screamed out. It convulsed and sprayed spit from the mouth. Tears of blood ran from its eyes, nose, mouth, and ears. The possessed paladin fell to his knees and then to his face. His body still shaking from the convulsions, it muttered something before stopping dead still.

The survivors of the citadel arose; even those nearly taken by the daemons were well. Some were already too far gone and they faded into nothingness along with the shadowy specters. The citadel was saved. Eve was the cause. When the people of Reforged and the citadel finally came to, Eve still stood strong with whirling winds wrapping high above her. Inside the loose tornado-like winds rested the Great Dane dog-like apparition.

Wymon was among those still fighting when the blinding power surrounded them all. Alihaedra was far off in a different place. Her part in the ritual was to synergize with Eve, keeping her mind, body, and soul focused on the job at hand and to deliver more essence and power if need be. Their powers became one and linked for the duration of the ritual.

A scholar of the old ways, Wymon knew the essence she summoned. "That's Enad, greater spirit of loyalty. Their existence has never been proven. Their powers never summoned. How is that little girl able to do such magics?" Wymon spoke aloud to himself and those around him.

Alihaedra was still unaccounted for. Peni was pulling herself off the ground. Ereven was safe in the mountains at the time of power blanket. He felt the energy hit him hard. Unlike most energies, this one wasn't reckless; no mountains or earth of any kind was moved or damaged in any way.

Eve held the apparition in place long enough for everyone's eyes to return to normal. After, she kept it strong for all to see. Then, she disbanded the summon and the energies and winds around her left as well.

"Yes Wymon, Enad, greater spirit of loyalty." She spoke stronger than she'd ever spoken before. Wymon approached her. Alihaedra made her presence known through the crowds of men retaking her place by her man.

"Not in a thousand eons have powers such as that been heard of. What lurks in your mind, soul, what's in your blood little one? What are you?"

"Your wife spoke of simple spirits. Not one of us shamans or any other has been able to summon anything better than simple or in rare cases lesser, spirits since the beginning of time. Some believe the spirits higher than the lesser are what gave the gods their powers. Where they came from is not known. Their origins not known; your wife assisted to assure my survival." Eve finished her piece holding out her left forearm. It was sickening. A giant tear in her flesh from her elbow at the bend twisted around to the back of her wrist.

The hole was black, with color diluted with deep shades of fading reds. Eve revealed herself as a blood caster. Blood casting was long forgotten and always forbidden. One caught spilling blood for the sake of magic, or worse rituals, was forever cast out from civilization. In time, their own calloused bodies and magically infused scars proved their true nature.

"How many times have you done this?" Wymon asked.

Danth and the others leading members of Reforged stepped up as well. The defenders cheered for Eve. For once in her life, she got as much recognition as her sister and even more. For once, Eve accepted it with open arms. She loved it. Finally, after all these years, she understood why Halo desired such admiration and attention. It felt good! She felt appreciated and needed. It was a feeling worth having.

Teraxius stood, barely. His mind was still fuzzy. His body wasn't finished. His vitality hadn't failed him. It probably wasn't even the magic, poison, or residium on Lithil's armor that felled him. It was just a precise a shot to the perfect spot. His head felt faint and his body fell. He was knocked nearly unconscious.

Lithil lay stretched out among the earth. Looking up, Teraxius saw a happily walking Ereven heading his way. Eve was the center of attention, the reason for it all. Nothing in this world was supposed to be able to fight the daemons. Perhaps she wasn't of this world.

"I only learned and performed the ritual last night. It was something I've longed for. I've only held off in fear. I've lost all reasons for fear now. I've given up everything for you all. Once you link to a spirit of higher than lesser stature, you're dedicated to him. Enad is the greater spirit of loyalty and is forever linked to me. That essence will forever flow in my blood." (Enad, pronounced Enade)

"Should I expect more shamans to do this in the future? Will my wife be linked to Enad? Will my wife forever have him in her blood?" Wymon asked.

"Wymon, you speak to her as if she's done something wrong," a soldier chiming up.

"She called upon powers long forgotten from this world. She did so with a blood covenant, of a ritual no less. If we were meant to fall then…"

Danth heard enough. He'd had enough. Wymon was wrong. He looked to make it right. Eve did what she had to do to save the citadel and possibly the entire world. Thedia was in her debt. "That's enough!" Danth ordered.

Wymon turned around, seriously aggravated at the remark. "I beg your pardon," he snarled.

This time, Danth was a little calmer, "I said that's enough."

"I believe Reforged is under my command and this citadel belongs to me."

"It does. Eve did what she had to do to protect us. She kept us alive and stopped us from being utterly slaughtered. Without Eve, not only would we be gone, many of our bodies would be used to reinforce their enemies. As a follower of Hellwing and the Draconic Order, you saved my life and therefore, I am forever in your debt." Danth stepped to be just before the little lady. He bowed courteously and then stepped back.

Wymon sighed. Though it was still hard to take in, acknowledging and accepting a blood caster just wasn't going to be easy for the cleric leader of Reforged. No one had ever summoned a greater spirit before. The greater spirits again were believed to be what first granted the gods their powers. They were beyond worlds or pantheons.

Enad saved them. He wasn't of this world, perhaps a key to origin of Eve her sister. The surviving Infected fled off or died shortly after. Only Lithil remained remotely intact. Teraxius signaled to his lifeless body and made his way through the soot and ash toward Eve. The little halfing creature smiled.

He stood exhausted. His body was bruised and bloody with wounds from the days prior now reopened. Wounds acquired before his encounter with Lithil were also still present. He tilted his head back and wiped the black ash and dirt from his eyes. "My lady, you're the reason I'm still breathing. And breathing in itself is its own reward. I am forever in your debt. What can I do to repay a debt of infinite gratitude?"

Eve smiled, pleased with herself and the power that lay within her. She thought for a moment. She had fallen for the combatant, but her sister also loved him. Her sister was gone and could have any man she desired. What to do? Initially, she backed off, knowing the gladiator fancied her back. Now, she had the right to get what she wanted. After all, if not for her, the entire citadel would have fallen.

Danth, Wymon, Peni, and the others thankfully survived. Other heroes were lost. Ereven found himself accounted for as well. In the days that passed, the citadel rebuilt itself with what it had. The light of Eve's power drew more survivors to them. Another presence finally made itself known; traveling informants, survivors, and seasoned Reforged scouts all came to the citadel telling of a great beast. It stood over fifty feet, bipedal, and looked like a mixture of a thousand dinosaurs. Its teeth cut through buildings, allowing its massive mouth to swallow large portions of them whole. Its tail lashed and whipped around, leveling city blocks and wards in every direction it went.

All of Reforged as well as the entire citadel came to appreciate Eve. She became a hero amongst the heroes. The holes in Ereven's story gave reason for Wymon to research. He wanted to know the whole thing and talk to every single person who'd touched, talked, or witnessed anything the wizard did while on the battlefield.

Wymon knew his distant scouts would return soon. He'd kept a keen eye on the beast once it awoke. Which direction would it head after Eve summoned Enad? After all, that power caught the attention of every other living being in world. Eve's continual reports of her discussions with her sister told Wymon the beast was still heading straight for Falling Star. That was a blessing. As long as the Tarrasque aimed for Falling Star, it would remain advantageous for the citadel, Reforged, and all of Thedia.

Chapter 8

Three strong plans came into fruition in the Burning Kingdom. Even with Golric Firesoul now notably at the helm of the crew, the Burning Kingdom's plans' had to change. A happening far south, somewhere in the area of the citadel caused a realm-wide ruckus.

A power rivaling even Falling Stars' and any ever present in the realm materialized; the Burning Kingdom only felt its power, visually blind to whatever it was. Taj informed the others that Eve carried the Pact Stone and the Pact Stone was what released Falling Star.

The shadows would be after it. What was the cause of all the power? Was it the Pact Stone? Golric believed it to be a possibility after taking in all the information. Giovanni put the blame/credit on the Pact Stone as well. Malakai and Taj claimed it to be something different. Rhoeve was comatose. His opinion wasn't voiced.

Golric, Olric, and the Burning Kingdom put their initial plans on hold. They had to march to the grand presence of the power source to the south. No matter what decoy beacon they created, the shadow would still be drawn to the greater power. The power source, even though very briefly, clearly caught the attention of the realm. It even caught Golric and Olric's attention.

Sacrificing the entire land in order to sink it while filled with the shadow army was no longer feasible. At one point, Golric was willing to sacrifice the Burning Kingdom and feed it to the liquid fires below in order to help the realm by devastating the shadow army.

Just before their plans were put into place and the crew was to head off, the presence was felt and blinding white light erupted in the south filling the sky with the very force that now had the attention of every living soul in the realm.

Now, the link between Halo and Eve was even more important. Immediately, Taj and the others ordered Halo to make the connection. She quickly obliged. Well, she quickly commenced to the meditation process.

When the two finally connected, Halo saw a difference in Eve. Her eyes were different, filled with the black of night and touched with the stars that lit up in the black. Something was different with her.

"Sister," she started excitedly. She was happy and thankful. Her sister was still alive. It was never believed she'd fallen. As blood always does, it worried.

"Halo, we're at odds." Eve still wasn't completely sure how her sister felt or what she even knew.

As always, their surroundings floated by ever so quickly as the two kept still, unmoved.

"I was hurt Eve. I am hurt. We're not what's important now." Halo acted under Taj's orders.

"I disagree, sister. You have to let me explain everything to you, please. I beg you," Eve pleaded.

"There will be time for that later."

"No Halo. You have to listen to me."

Halo tried to ignore it. She didn't want to discuss her sister's situation with Teraxius. She knew it would cut too deep. Eve was different and she was even more different now. She wanted everything out. Halo was more with Taj at this point. She wanted the situation taken care of and a clear plan laid out in front of them. "Fine," she conceded.

"I saved Teraxius' life. I look at him the way men have always looked at you. We are what's important. I tried something I've always believed. I found it to be true. The old legend claims but a string of the old gods' blood still exists. We are that string and I proved it so."

"I don't understand," said Halo.

"We are what's important. I carry the Pact Stone. The spirits talk to me as they always have. Just now, a greater spirit speaks. It was once believed that spirits ranked from simple to greater to over. This is true, but what we once believed to be intermediate and greater were still only simple and lesser. The older legends claiming the great spirits and over spirits, not of this natural earth but before, are what granted the gods life. I now believe this to be true as I summoned the greater spirit of loyalty, Enad. He is the reason we still breathe. He is the reason we're still here. He's come to me again. Falling Star will march everything he has against us now. Alabaster is gone. Corvana is in shambles. The Burning Kingdom means nothing now. I have the Pact Stone and, even more, I spilled the blood of gods to bring forth the first greater spirit of the beyond to Thedia. Even when Thedia was at its peak—"

Halo finished her sister's words. "No such presence ever made itself known."

"Exactly. I have the Pact Stone and the blood of the gods. My blood is linked with powers ascending higher than the lost gods. Falling Star senses yet a single obstacle in his way to victory."

"We descend from Gods sister?" Halo asked to confirm.

"The only way for me to perform the ritual is with the spilling of a God's blood."

"And the ritual brought down Enad, the greater spirit of loyalty?"

"Yes, and with it, I destroyed an army of the infected and the daemons that followed them," Eve said.

"The daemons cannot be hurt by anything of this world. We've had to hide from them many times. Taj's inner power created that phylactery to protect us from them."

"Yes, and now Enad has granted me the ability to face them effectively."

"How?" Halo asked.

"I've been blessed with the ability to grant things his power, temporarily of course. Summoning the great Enad is too great to do regularly. However, I can grant a circle of power to my allies. Those loyal to me will have their weapons and belongings protected and laced with Enad's power."

"And therefore those who fight closest to you will be able face the daemons?"

"Precisely!" Eve said.

"We're the aggressors and you're with the defenders?"

"The shadow will be coming to us. This will be the opening you all need to get in and get to Falling Star. I am the single, solitary thing Falling Star feels can hinder his progress. I have the Pact Stone. I have the power of Enad, a power that exceeds even his. He'll want to kill me before I educate myself more on this power. The ritual is done. It is required only once to perform the ritual. The bond is made. Enad is on our side."

"And what of you and Teraxius?" Halo couldn't help but ask. She'd attained the information she was ordered to get. Now, she wanted to know about her sister and the man who'd caught her eye. She loved the gladiator, or at least she believed she did.

"Halo…" Eve started.

Halo shushed her. She was uncertain as to whether she wanted to hear it or not. Finally, she let her sister continue.

"I love Teraxius as I love Danth, Taj, and the others. We've grown close, finding sanctuary in each other in your absence. We both speak of you regularly. We both miss you dearly and we are all looking forward to our reunion."

Halo smiled. She believed her. She trusted her sister, though something still felt different. She wanted to know more but there was more left to do, too much left for the groups and too little time to do it.

In the days that came, the Burning Kingdom kept strong to Golric and Olric's orders to hold. More traps were set for impending attacks. Olric took charge of the kingdom while Golric "allegedly" took charge of the crew.

Rhoeve would stay behind. He was in no shape to continue. He took it harshly but knew he was in no condition to push forward. For better or worse, he would only slow them. Golric took his place and added a healing cleric loyal to the eternal flame to the party.

Eve's information kept the team on guard. The information of the Tarrasque still heading for Falling Star was keen. Wymon and the others knew of the awakening of the Tarrasque even before Taj and the others returned with the Pact Stone.

The stage was set. The Burning Kingdom would stand as a last hold against the shadow with inner secrets, guards, and wards set in place in the event the worst came to be. The citadel would act as a secondary hideaway for survivors, escapees, and any other who would stand against the shadow. The two would have to work connectively and in unison if they were going to be successful.

Olric led the Burning Kingdom now and Wymon stood as the head of the citadel. The Tarrasque was a creature allegedly created to protect and/or cleanse Thedia of anything capable of knocking the plane off balance. Falling Star was such a creature.

The Pact Stone also represented plane-breaking power. It was formed to guard and keep imprisoned the Soul Dragon of Shadows. Various powers came to a truce, realizing Falling Star was a threat beyond all threats.

Taj, Golric, Giovanni, Malakai, and Halo set off for Falling Star. The Soul Dragon of Shadows made his home in a demi-plane created somewhere around the Third Regent. Why the third Regent, the team wondered.

Months into their journey, after fighting hoards of the infected and dodging legions of daemons, Taj and the others looked over the edge of a plateau. They were close. Far below, an army marched, larger than any army they'd ever seen and stretching as far as the eye could see. Golric's inner power led the team to the shadow demi-plane.

"Thedia was formed separate of the weaves," Golric said, looking down at the army.

"What in the hell are we to do with that?" Giovanni questioned.

"Eve said more and more shadowy regiments continue to attack them. Ever since she summoned Enad, they've hammered the citadel, focused on it even." Halo spoke with Eve regularly now. As much as she didn't want to ponder about her sister and the gladiator, she couldn't help it. By now, she should've forgotten the man. She hadn't. She couldn't. He was special and unique.

"The only reason we've made it this far is because Froth gave us a way around the daemons," Taj said broken-heartedly.

"Yes, and we still bypass them every single time," Malakai charged. "Why" he asked.

"We're still not sure you and Golric are safe from them," answered Halo.

Malakai groaned angrily. Looking down, he wanted nothing more than to show his team what he could do and just what he was made of.

Over the course of their journey, they'd learned of the name Lithil. Eve spoke frequently of the captured elven man. When Giovanni first heard of Lithil's safe return, he became ecstatic and hopeful. The two were actually good friends at one point.

Lithil was an elven man taken by the daemons and then saved at Enad's hands, Eve's hands. Since her summoning of the greater spirit of loyalty, Lithil's true self and spirit became the sole captain of his body. However, the lingering effects were still present. His body was now deteriorating. He couldn't move as he once could. Staying honest was a day-to-day feat. The once revered paladin now had to battle every day to remain a fragment of his former self. Nonetheless, he was a new addition to the resistance fighting against the empowering Falling Star.

"There's no reason to take up arms against adversaries we can avoid," Taj scolded Malakai.

Malakai knew his friend was right. Daemons had charged them before. None were able to penetrate Golric, and Malakai's secret would keep him safe indefinitely. A shadow's soul cannot be taken by shadows.

More and more the team pushed on, seeing the giant Malagant lead his team through the quickest passes. He was heading to the citadel. Falling star wanted the Pact Stone and the bringer of Enad slain. Hope that the Burning Kingdom's heat would at least lure some of them was gone. The citadel was the primary target.

That night Halo connected to her sister again. Eve already knew what was coming. They all did. The entire shadow force planned to rain down upon them showing no mercy, killing and taking whatever they could. Falling Star wanted Thedia, the purest of realms.

The five finally made it to the shores of the Third Regent. The waters were abnormally calm. Froth explained to Taj, "Just like the Broken Lands back home, son, even the waters fear washing ashore here now."

He was right. The beasts dwelling deep below stayed there. Nothing sane wanted any part of Falling Star.

As the team trekked through the beach toward the nearby forest, Golric started the obvious conversation. "So what exactly is our plan once we get to Falling Star?"

"Golric, I'm thankful Rhoeve led us to you. Without you, we'd probably have never found him. I don't rightly know, but I'm sure we'll secure victory one way or another," answered Giovanni.

Malakai signaled for a quick rest. Something was bothering him. His gear wasn't right. He needed to readjust. The elven sorcerer of unusual innate powers revealed his bare body while adjusting his belongings. His upper chest, biceps, shoulders, and back told a story unique in its own right. On his left side, an army of demons charged forcefully. At his right, angels came to answer the call. In the center, a beautiful female angel held a kneeling, weeping demon. A number of devils made their appearance on the side of demons, at least one did anyway.

"What in the hell is that?" Golric asked.

"A story," he answered, laughing casually while preparing to reequip his gear.

"Wow, amazing, such beautiful work," Halo said, astonished.

"Don't start acting like you appreciate this perfect body now little one," he said, laughing.

Halo didn't even respond to his perverted comment. She immediately moved to trace her hands around his body to fully inspect and appreciate the detail of the work. His tattoos were the best she'd ever seen.

Golric didn't know what to think of it. To each their own he thought. Malakai knew there were questions.

"Finer details tell of the weave. I believe the angels and demons; with the devils of course, are what governs our world. Each day we are at a struggle. This work relates that struggle."

"I can respect that," Golric said. He paused and then began to laugh. "The fire surrounding the demons is perhaps the pinnacle of your work."

Malakai laughed. "Your braggart, boastful ways are appreciated and respected. Don't think I don't appreciate fire as much as you do or more."

"How dare you!" Golric yelled.

"Fire's killed more of my enemies at one time than any other power in existence."

Golric stalled but then laughed. The others joined in as well.

"Well played sorcerer, well played." Golric doubled over with his hands on his knees.

The air was dry and stale. Everything about the atmosphere was changing. The clouds were forever dark. The five of them had hopes for rain. Even Golric, even a priest of the element of fire understood the importance of water. Those loyal to the elements understood the need for balance more than any.

Malakai and his infected, along with the daemons, eventually marched to and through all obstacles. Strategically places assassins, scouts, and bombardiers fought valiantly for as long as they could. Malagant's armies were like a snowball rolling downhill. It marched and moved. With every encounter, they seemed to get stronger. The once hope-inspired resistance found their chances growing more dismal by the second.

More encounters left more infected slaughtered. The team finally came across it. There, where the castle of the Third Regent once stood rested a great entropic portal. The portal was the size of ten castles and hovered over the ground far out of the reach of any mortal.

The road to the Third Regent's capital, where the castle once stood, was still long. They were still a few days away. Even though a phylactery separated the two now, Froth's essence still managed to connect to Taj, possibly because of the time it spent inside of him.

The five stood on the giant rock overlooking the road and lower ground level that led to the capital. Everything around the city was grim and dark. The clouds overhead seemed to be filled with more darkness than most. Rain fell around the area. The droplets appeared darker than normal, as if almost tainted themselves. Plant life had all but either died or transformed. Mutations of things spawned everywhere. It was like a horrible nightmare.

All around the capital walked legions of infected. The present ones clearly more powerful than those previously faced. Infected with mutations were far stronger and far more advanced than the simple ones.

"Daemons lurk across the sky," Taj said, pointing to the floating menaces circling the portal.

"We're going to have to go into that portal," Golric said.

"We don't have any idea where it goes," Halo blurted out confused. The portal gave an aura of raw power that didn't sit well with her.

"We don't have to get into it. We just have to destroy it. Falling Star is inside resting and bathing in his own greatness. That portal is his last link here. If we can seal it, it'll be done," Malakai barked.

"How in the hell would we seal something like that?" asked Taj.

"Taj old friend, there's something I need to tell you. In order to seal a shadow's portal, one must begin with shadow magic."

"What?"

"How do you know?"

"What are you speaking of?"

Question after question birthed from the mouths of his allies. Malakai looked about. He knew what he had to do.

"Golric represents the earth."

"I represent fire!"

"I know Golric, and fire comes from the earth. I didn't mean the force earth; I simply meant you bring forth from our mother earth's plane the element of fire. I bring the Shadow. Halo, your powers will be needed here. My ritual will help spring them from you." Malakai spoke as if he'd done something like this before.

"I don't know what you're talking about. I have no real powers as you and Golric. Mine come differently as my origin is lost to even me."

"It's ok Halo. I know a ritual, but I will need your help. I will need everyone's help. Taj and Giovanni will offer a diversion when we begin. It's the only way."

"Wait a second, what do you mean diversion?" Giovanni wasn't keen on blatantly putting himself in danger.

"I'll just walk down there and kill them all." Taj laughed arrogantly. Part of him sounded as if he was joking while the other half told his teammates he was more than being honest.

"We may need you to be super human tomorrow, Taj." Malakai was calmer than he usually was. Something in him was different. He knew this was their only chance.

"Tomorrow?" Halo asked.

"The ritual is going to take quite a while to complete, little one." Malakai stroked his hands through her hair trying to calm her.

The five of them were nervous. There was no denying it. Malakai prepped the crew on what needed to happen from each person. Everyone was in unison and the ritual commenced. Malakai spoke in a lost language. His eyes weren't really there. He was somewhere else, but still there with them.

The phylactery glimmered with new power. It felt stronger. Malakai knew something in it was brewing stronger and deeper than before. It wasn't the ritual. Perhaps maybe it was Froth? He had to be careful, they all did. Froth held their souls in his grasp. Without Froth, they would be sitting ducks for the infected.

Malakai laid out the ritual's components: a circular ring of bloodstones, quartz, and four diamonds, one at each point of the circle. Broken pieces of magical relics of times past were strategically scattered and setup for the ritual as well. Malakai himself stood in the center. Halo stood opposite him. Golric was to the left and the phylactery itself held the last position on its own.

Taj and Giovanni patrolled from just a few feet down on the hill with the thousands of infected just waiting and patrolling below them.

As long as they weren't sensed, Malakai's plan should work, Taj thought. The second the ritual started, Taj felt every ounce of undead and link to Froth taken from him. Even Froth knew what was going on.

The team knew of Eve now and her powers, of Enad and her ability to summon it. The ritual would allow Eve to help Halo dig out her powers and assist her in the using of them. Eve would also be able to attack the portal, channeling it all through her sister. Malakai took it upon himself to act as Froth's channel. When the time came, Malakai would channel both his powers and Froth's necrotic energy. Golric would send his melting fires and Halo her unknown force. Four totem poles were set behind each one of them. The poles were crafted by Giovanni and Malakai earlier in the night. The poles would help stabilize the forces in order for their casters to utilize them more potently.

"Do you think it'll work?" Giovanni asked, peering down at the legions of creatures.

"It has to. They're talking magic. That's not our field of study, old friend. I do trust Malakai as I trust you."

Giovanni quickly crouched down and signaled Taj to do the same. The two looked about. The Infected noticed them, or noticed something. In unison, they regrouped and started to march. Their numbers were in the thousands. The ritual was not yet complete. Taj thought fast. They had to do something.

Chapter 9

Up, down, left, right, they were coming from everywhere. Where was Giovanni? Taj was too far in the fray to worry about it now. He had their attention. SOUL and LORE were helping him once again do his job. With every swing, a throat opened. With every thrust, an abdomen became disemboweled. With every slash came the severing of a limb. His swords glowed with fury and anger.

Something got him! The soft ground was at his back. All around him were infected, grabbing, biting, and yearning for his life, like zombies feuding for the last living morsel. A rolling maneuver sent ten or twelve more to the earth a bloody mess.

Finally, he was able to get to his feet. Oh by the dead Gods, he thought. The hovering portal was just overhead. How did he get so far into the fray and not even know it? A rapturous blast came from behind. It was elevated. Boom, another blast rang out, then another! Finally, a fourth blast shot out. The lights seemed to having a blinding, dazing effect on the infected. Red, black, green, gray, and white streaming rays of energy slammed into the portal. Immediately, it seemed to have an effect. The red was fire. The green was Froth's necrotic. The white was probably a radiant power from Halo. What was the gray? Shadow powers often seemed gray and/or black. Other forces could visually be seen as those colors as well.

Taj felt it. He'd felt it before. They gray was shadow and the black was Malakai's own mixture of necrotic and force powers. So many types of power out there, how did Taj know what they were? A deepening roar echoed out killing many of the infected, even the stronger ones. Something was close though, something else—not the roar.

His eyes finally reopened. He felt like they'd been open, but yet, he just couldn't see anything. The portal was still open; the legions of infected were dead. Did he kill them all? Wait, there was a blinding light, he remembered. Where was Giovanni? Was he all right?

The ground was beneath his feet again. He was standing. He could stand! His swords never left his hands. He arched his body back to look overhead. Something was different in the lightning-like streams. They didn't seem quite as strong, but Taj felt as if more was still to come.

Giovanni's eyes opened. He was alive! His body was bloody and beaten, but alive. He too looked up to see the giant lightning-like bolts streaming from where Malakai started his ritual. Footsteps: one, two, one, two, Giovanni dropped in a spinning motion to his left knee. His body kept spinning planting one dagger in the creature's moving leg. Momentous motion kept his body moving, spinning all the way back up and around, planting a series of knives linearly down the creature's spine. It fell lifeless. He laughed. Still, nothing surprised Giovanni.

"Taj," he cried out, hobbling over toward his friend.

Taj was still a little out of it. How many did they kill and what killed the rest of them? Taj was in better shape than Giovanni. Finally, the Eternian sheathed his blades. And the Sylvan noticed he was completely out of knives other than his magical vestment.

"You're still alive?" Taj asked.

Giovanni smiled shaking his head. Just then, the bright lightning forces dimmed. Taj and Gio both looked up. The white source was gone. Nothing made it past them so what could have happened? Malakai didn't promise everyone would survive.

Taj sensed another. He was right. This one was massive. In his ear, he heard his old friend order the blasts to continue. "Keep going," said Malakai loud enough that both Giovanni and Taj heard him.

Giovanni shook his head. He smashed his palm to his left ear. It was bleeding badly and he couldn't seem to make the ringing stop.

Walking alongside the Third Regent's castle, Taj noticed a massive man; he stood just over seven foot and was a barrel of a man. His long black hair flowed down almost rivaling his body in length. His black metallic armor was made of an ore not of this world. His silver sword glowed with an aura queer to Taj. Taj nudged his friend. Giovanni took a step back in awe of the man. What was he?

His face was worn with time. Vertical scars lined the right side of his face. Other than his face, not a single piece of flesh was visible. Tattoos crawled up from his neck giving the assumption his body was covered. He carried his sword single-handedly and yet it was larger, longer, and seemingly heavier than a fullblade. His eyes were black and gray, a man completely submerged in the powers of the shadow.

"Get to them," Taj said.

"No, what about you?"

"You're going to be no good to me dead, old friend"

"I can fight."

"You'll die."

"How do you know? Maybe he's just another one."

"I don't know how, but I can sense these things. This one is strong. He's the strongest I've ever sensed."

"I have to—"

Taj cut him off. The monster of a man was closing the distance and there just wasn't time. "Go!"

Giovanni didn't argue anymore. He turned to head back up the hill. His body was failing him. Maybe he was hurt more than he thought. His leg was hurt badly. He carried on, dragging it all the way until he was back with his team.

Something was wrong. Something was different. How could it be? Had they lost an ally? Was the body absent a soul? A new being was present and this one he knew. How could he forget? His very aura was spoken with reverence. What happened?

Just as he sheathed his swords, it appeared he would need them again. SOUL and LORE were again out and ready. A second roar came from the portal as the forces of Taj's allies continued to blast it. From the looks of it, they weren't doing very much. Hopefully, Malakai knew what he was doing.

"What are you..." Taj started almost seemingly engaging.

The man just roared back swinging his first wing. Taj crossed his blades to reinforce them on the defensive posture. He felt something he'd never felt before, a raw brute force greater than any he'd ever encountered. Taj's feet lifted from the ground and before it was finished, he was flat on his back sliding through the dirt and grass that lay beneath him.

How was he going to fight this thing? Even with SOUL and LORE it seemed impossible after just a swing. The creature kept marching forward. Taj quickly reset himself. His squatting position suited him just for the moment while his thoughts clicked around in his mind. He grinned. He had an idea.

Once again, he engaged the monster. Another downward lash by the man. Taj calculated the attack and rolled forward, resetting his footing just to the man's right flank. A backward slashing of LORE cut through the man's armor and into his flesh. A thick, black blood began to ooze.

Just as he thought, not naturally mortal. He didn't stop there, however, another twisting motion toward the man' body allowed SOUL to cut into his left lower ribcage. The humanoid monster turned angrily to finish him. The elusive Eternian willingly went to his back, this time only to backflip up several feet away from him.

The monster smiled devilishly. "Not bad kid, shall I begin?"

"Who are you? What are you?"

"I am Malagant. I am your killer."

"Many have died hoping for that title."

"I've killed more men than days you've breathed, son. Today is the day you die."

"Strong words from the mighty wounded!"

Malagant angered at Taj's words. He charged, as did Taj. Taj eluded every single swing of Malagant's. He couldn't allow their swords to meet. Malagant was too strong. The roaring started up again and it was getting closer.

"Hurry," Taj cried trying to keep the man busy.

A clear coating finally seared the portal shut. It was the new being's necrotic/radiant, and other forces working in unison that was getting the job done. Malakai's forces were also working better than they were before. Golric's fire did its job. It opened the essence of the portal from the inside. Now, his fire was no longer needed.

"Golric help Taj!" Malakai ordered.

Now wasn't the time to argue. Giovanni still knelt beside the lifeless body of Halo. Her flesh and bones sucked for every ounce of verve they once held. She was dead. Halo was dead. The phylactery was shattered. Every single one of them felt their souls reenter their bodies. Standing where the phylactery once lay was a tall, thin being; his long white hair was fluffy and beautiful. His naked body outlined and chiseled and full of color; his eyes shimmered with a yellow color proving his vampiric heritage. Prismatic colors rang from him into the portal. When his powers transcended into the prismatic colors, the roaring on the other side dimmed out.

He didn't speak. He didn't have to. Taj knew what he wanted him to do. Malagant flipped his sword as if it were made of nothing. He moved like Giovanni but faster. He flickered cantrips like a wizard, throwing Taj completely off. Luckily for Taj, SOUL's experience kept him in the game. Malagant's known sweeping strike threw Taj's legs high into the air. Head first he landed on the hard ground below.

Immediately, Malagant forced his sword downward at a forty-five-degree angle. SOUL's unchallenged reflexes forced Taj to quirk his body to its left side. Taj rose, using his left hand for support and planting his palm over the hilt of SOUL. LORE on the hand went upward at a forty-five-degree angle, implanting itself into the beast's abdomen. Malagant's sword cut through Taj's right collarbone and shoulder so deep it nearly severed the arm.

Another booming roar and a forceful gust of wind came down on both Taj and Malagant. Something unknown to Taj hit Malagant hard, hurling him far, far into the portal, actually breaking the thin seal Malakai and the others had just started.

Taj's eyes closed when the wind hit him. He worked his way down and off the sword. It was stuck deep into the ground. Taj felt the magic radiating from it. His right arm was useless now. In the air, he couldn't believe it.

A dragon had come to aid them. It was hovering over where his party was. It wasn't gargantuan or colossal but it was still a good-sized dragon. Its scales were golden with tints and shades of black and purple. What the hell was it? Did a God actually come down to aid them? Taj knew dragons and something was different about this one. It looked like a cross between a giant wyvern and a gold dragon. This one had deformities to it. In some places it appeared more evolved. It was staring down hard at his team up on the elevation. He was still down at the bottom of the hill.

Taj cried out in pain—his arm. He used his left hand to sheathe LORE and then to sheathe Soul. He wasn't afraid. Hellwing was on his side after all! This wasn't the time for it. They had to seal the portal. Without warning, the dragon turned! A breath of golden dragon breath along with an arsenal of spells pushed forward, finally sealing the portal for good. Or did it? The portal closed. The dragon finally landed.

Taj stumbled but kept going. Then, another roar stronger and more potent than the previous bellowed out, and as if it never left, the portal reopened. Alas, a creature far larger than any known to Thedia emerged. Each scale measured approximately the size of the unique dragon that had somehow come from nowhere to aid them.

How it came from that portal was a mystery. It did and it was free! It was Falling Star. Its very aura weakened the surviving members, even Froth. They each gazed upon his greatness as he soared into the sky. It was over. They'd lost. Their one chance at Falling Star was to seal him in his own domain. Now he was free to do as he pleased. He'd already decimated the mightiest nation in the world.

Taj fainted. When he awoke, his arm was healed and he lay next to Giovanni on a soft pallet. It was dark and a fire was roasting fresh meat. Where was Halo? Malakai and Golric were there. And, and he was there. It was he. He'd freed himself from the phylactery. He freed himself from the phylactery.

Also, another was present. He was average sized and hairy. He was lycanthropic, a werewolf to be precise. His hair was polar white, however, and he sat relaxed and calm as if a normal person.

Taj's eyes gleamed down at his right shoulder. A thick and colorful scar nearly smothered out all of his flesh. It seemed as if Golric poured a healing coat of lava into the gaping wound in his shoulder and somehow it settled in, keeping its shining color of both orange and red.

Halo was nowhere to be found. Giovanni knew what his friend was thinking. "She's dead," he said, confirming Taj's suspicions.

Taj dropped his head. Another lost, he thought. "How" he asked. "And what is that?" He tried to point at the werewolf.

Xavius Froth, the first...the true keeper of the night and once ally of Taj spoke up. In times past, Froth was never one for words. Usually, his meanings were understood mentally without the use of a voice. "He's Liam, king and keeper of the night." His voice was dark and cold, yet smooth enough to take in quasi-comfortably. It was different than before. He was stronger than before. His presence told it. It proved it. Taj knew Froth's powers had never been greater. Somehow, he could sense it.

"I thought you told me Gaiyrmynceth was the king of the night. I thought the Gargoyle King was the keeper of the night?" Taj asked.

"He capitalized on a wounded adversary."

The werewolf sat quietly and patiently as Froth spoke to his old friend/host. Malakai and Golric also took advantage of their patience while the vampiric entity spoke.

"The portal sealed, Taj, but Falling Star got out before it was done," Malakai said, finally breaking his silence.

"What happened to Halo? What killed all those things out there? Where the hell did the dragon come from and what the hell was it doing here?" Taj was filled with questions. Everything just wasn't adding up.

Froth started to answer. Malakai and Golric started to say something as well. Finally, the werewolf spoke, interrupting them all.

"I am the dragon you saw, human. Your friend made his presence known and I came to finish it."

Froth took over trying to clarify, "I've always known Liam lived. After everything, the war, the forsakers, just everything, I hadn't the power or the ability to face him. I had to keep my existence off his radar."

Liam took back over, "…and in order for me to survive that bite I took so long ago, I had to find something stronger and I did. My most potent form is that of a half dragon/draculich if that is fathomable to you. I've come to end this fight between Froth and me."

"And knowing the situation, he chose to put his feud to the side while we finish this thing with Falling Star and the shadow realm," Golric finished. Froth and Liam already explained it all to him and Malakai.

"Without my powers, Liam's newfound powers, Malakai's, Golric's, and the godblooded, we'd have failed. To close a portal of shadow origin, shadow must be present," Froth concluded.

"Who here is of the shadow, Liam?" Taj asked.

Froth and Liam both looked to Malakai. Taj stepped back readily waiting for something to happen. An awkward silence surrounded the campsite. "Taj, I wanted to tell you. One half of my blood descends from the shadow realm. I am as much on your side as any."

"Halo is dead now. Malakai, what happened to her?" Taj grew angry.

"I needed her blood to refuel my essence. With her essence inside me I will be able to become what I once was. Without her death, a victory would be impossible. Her and her sister's powers channeled together helped finish off what you could not. Her death was necessary. She died for a cause," Froth said standing directly opposite Taj.

"They trusted me, Froth. They trusted me to trust you."

"And you knew what it was."

Taj dropped his head. Golric made it clear he knew better than to trust the undead. Giovanni couldn't believe what he was hearing. Malakai used it to justify his own actions.

"It looks like I'm not the only one with a deceptive secret, old friend. I didn't entrust my soul because shadow cannot infect shadow."

"Fear not the daemons now, my presence will keep them at bay. I assure you."

"You're a lot more vocal than you once were, master vampire," said Taj.

Taj couldn't believe it. He was the reason Halo was dead. Froth assured him it was necessary for their success. More conversation told him it wasn't clear whether Eve was okay or not. Sending the power of something like Enad through a channel via a ritual was unknown to the common world.

Now, it was down to Froth, Liam, Taj, Giovanni, Malakai, and Golric. Falling Star was free and Liam seemed to think he knew where he'd go. Liam explained he was the closest thing to a demi-god the world had ever seen, though his powers and Froth's far exceeded the demi-gods of old now. Froth's godblood came directly from the ancient deities. Liam's godblood came from the new age of gods, the dragons.

"The bringer of Enad will die. She carries the Pact Stone as well. Everything Falling Star wants and needs is within or on the single body of Eve. We have to get back to the others. Falling Star will destroy them all. We have to help them. He's probably summoning his Legions to march on them as we speak." Malakai and Liam took turns saying what they both already knew.

"At least my Burning Kingdom will be safe," Golric said sarcastically.

"For now," Liam replied not so sarcastically.

Liam dallied between the land of the mortals and the land of the dragons now. What would happen when this was all over? Would he defeat Froth? Did Taj want Liam to win? He felt linked and connected to Froth but Froth killing Halo, whether for the good of the world or not, still stabbed him like a dagger of cold steel. Part of the journey was complete.

"With the portal closed, Falling Star's power source is weakened. In the coming days he'll feel it. He'll reopen the portal once he usurps the power of the Pact Stone. Now is the time to strike. Now is the time to finish it," Froth stated.

Liam transformed back into his draconic self. Taj noticed something he hadn't noticed before. His eyes were hollow, only a white burning fire rested in his sockets. In the wolf form, his eyes were fine. He'd not yet completed the fine-tuning of transformation and the undead of Froth's blood still plagued his body.

The others knew what he wanted and they all climbed on. Froth couldn't even believe he summoned Liam. His essence reformed with the powers of the godblood and became so strong that Liam was able to sense him. Now, they would work together for the first time in order to prevent the entire world from collapsing and falling victim to Falling Star and the shadow realm.

Liam soared into the air at speeds surpassing that of normal golden dragons. Sparks and flames of white popped out of thin air as they flew. While in dragon form, he was clearly in between the realms of the living and the dead. They would soon make it back to the citadel and hopefully with enough time to warn them. Hopefully, they'd have the time needed to prepare them for war.

Chapter 10

L iam and the others arrived just in time to see the citadel withstand Falling star's very first strike, an abhorrent cloud made of a thousand colors, a thousand gases, and several forces, some not even known to this world.

Eve stood affront, nearly alone. Wymon and Teraxius were both close by. The remaining soldiers of the citadel hit Falling Star's legions of infected head on. Daemons scoured the sky. The shadow dragon of souls himself blacked out the sun; Liam touched down dead center his back. Taj and Golric both leaped off.

"Liam go!" Malakai screamed.

Giovanni rolled off, tactically rolling end over end, carefully planting one dagger after another in the giant winged beast's scales. Froth dove up from Liam. The ancient vampire hovered directly over the weredragon, if Liam could be called such a thing.

The Infected pushed hard. A counterstrike was in place. Olric and the fire people charged out of their hidden locations, encasing the vile creatures. Thedia drank the blood of its own as well as the blood of the shadows. Falling Star was truly outraged. His power source had been cut off and sealed. Only the Pact Stone would grant him the powers he needed to reopen it. His powers were great but linking planes took specific powers. In all his infinite powers and wisdom, Falling Star's ability to link worlds died with his portal to his own domain.

Eve utilized her godblooded powers to hold Enad on the battlefield. Falling Star did battle with the Great Spirit. Powers far beyond mortal comprehension burned the sky. Explosions went off every second. Giant magical bombardments went off as if great militaries were present. Liam and Malakai managed to escape Falling Star's back before Enad's powers engulfed him.

For a second, Falling Star was prone. Giovanni launched himself from the back of the creature just in time. A wing slapped Giovanni, launching him high in the air. The entrenching powers of Enad and Eve just barely caught the Sylvan.

Secretly, Giovanni crafted special daggers meant to explode when tampered with. The crafty Sylvan added secondary injuries, though minute, to the massive dragon. His nearly lifeless body fell to the earth a bloody mess, a simple sack of bones.

Liam and Malakai flew circles around Falling Star keeping the foreign dragon deity as distracted as possible. Malakai blasted the creature with everything he had. Searing rays of burning white light came forth from Liam's eyes. From his mouth, a burning gold dragon breath charred just a scale of the monstrous entity.

Nothing was working. Falling Star wasn't even fazed by the force of Wymon, Taj, Liam, Froth, and his resistance. From hovering overhead, a third force rose up. Some appeared out of the very sky while others pulled themselves from the soil—reapers! Cloaked skeletal creatures each armed with its own magical scythe came to Froth's calling. They were believed to be Death's direct army and soldiers.

The reapers ripped into the Infected, slaughtering them by the second. At first, Wymon and the others didn't know whether to fight them or befriend them. Froth summoning the army of reapers did turn the tide just a bit. However, their real mission was to face the daemons and that's what they did. The reapers all took to the sky, seeing the citadel's people retaking the advantage. Their scythes cut through the daemons like hot knives through butter.

Falling Star had enough. For the first time since his coming, he unleashed a physical strike, biting the Great Spirit in half. The bite alone wouldn't have been enough to even touch the Great Spirit. However, his body was so infused with power that each tooth itself could be considered a legendary artifact or relic. A single bite from the monstrous deity sent Eve's strongest force back to where it came from. The destruction of Enad in summoned form wounded the godling, dropping her to the earth nearly lifeless as well.

Taj still climbed through the scales, sheering them off one by one. By the time Enad's enveloping started, the crafty Eternian was already deep inside the beast's body, hidden and guarded by the creature's own scales.

He wasn't hurting the beast too terribly but he was irritating it enough to at least slightly knock it off its game. Lithil was present as well; the elven paladin carried a new shield with an old sword. Falling Star noticed him when he took the brunt of the force for Eve when her body fell limp. He was shattered now. No matter, he'll die soon enough, thought the great deity.

These pathetic cretins truly thought they could rival the Soul Dragon of Shadows. Only the Great Spirit could even hope to harm him and the being above the god's was already destroyed. Falling Star couldn't wait to have it all finished. All he needed was the Pact Stone and Eve had it.

Lithil swiped his giant steel circular shield around, batting away most of the Infected. A sneaking slash from his sword even felled a few of them. Looking down, the quick-witted paladin pulled the Pact Stone from Eve's belongings, leaping forward, and shadow-stepping out of the way. Lithil's time infected earned him new abilities.

A straight line of scalding hot, boiling water shot from Falling Star's mouth. Lithil and the orb were luckily out of its way. Wymon and Teraxius were not. Nearly forty defenders cooked alive. Daemons evading the reapers managed to take their now weakened and dying bodies. Wymon was one of the ones taken. Teraxius somehow managed to escape it.

Wymon stood again calmly. His weapon was nowhere to be found. The newly infected priest peeled an old mace from a dead man's hands. Eve's body was boiled and burned, but oddly enough already healing? No matter, thought the infected Wymon. I'll just end her now. Wymon found himself stinging with bludgeoning and piercing pains. He'd been knocked to the ground, to all fours. What hit him?

The last thing the great leader of Reforged saw was an upward coming spiked ball on a chain smashing into his face. Wymon was dead. Danth stood over him. There was no time for hesitation. Danth picked up Eve's body and rushed back to the citadel. He'd killed enough but he did have to get back. They needed him. He knew something about Eve the others didn't. Her situation was dire and delicate.

Teraxius' body was steaming but the gladiator kept moving. Falling Star was dealt another crippling blow as Malagant's armies, now led by the last of his corrupted, fell to a trap in the Burning Kingdom. Falling Star hoped to squash the last of the Corvanian realm's resistance all at once. A trap was left by Olric Firesoul encasing the entire kingdom and the armies of Falling Star. The great plateaus that once held the ancient kingdom of fire plummeted deep into the cavernous openings beneath them. Quakes erupted, spreading the ground beneath them, swallowing it all like the ocean smothering the sands of the beach during high tide.

Rapid spells burst everywhere. Scores of Reforged fell to them. Some burned, some necrotically melted, and others just disintegrated. More breaths killed even more. Giovanni took Halo's vestment of endless throwing daggers. His eyes were opening but his body refused to move.

Teraxius' movements were slower than usual but with a sword in his left and a hammer in his right, the gladiator kept the death coming. Arrows flew overhead. One, two, three, killed off by the unknown sender of the arrows.

Coming freshly into sight, Rhoeve and a small team of the Burning Kingdom's inhabitants also joined in the fight. On the ground front, the citadel was winning. Even severed from his domain powers, Falling Star's presence was too great to go unnoticed. With Falling Star on the battlefield, every single one of them was going to die.

Froth and Liam charged down into Falling Star. Taj had all but cut his way through the creature. Alas, the lower abdominal scale fell and Taj was free to fall helplessly down to the ground. The fall was too far.

Something hit Falling Star, knocking his great body back through the air. Taj lost his balance. The quick-witted Eternian sheathed his blades, simultaneously grabbing the nearest scale to him. His body dangled below the great deity helplessly. He could barely see but what was visible was Liam and Froth working in unison using powers never before seen by Thedians. Where was Malakai?

Taj saw him. He'd been dismounted somehow. His body fell. He was a sorcerer. He had ways to ease his fall.

"MAALLLAAAKAAAIII!!!!!" Taj screamed at the top of his lungs hoping his friend would hear him. He didn't. Taj's grip weakened. The Eternian plummeted to the ground. Just before Taj's end was met, Malakai's supernatural senses kicked in and blessed Taj, granting him a feather fall for his last fifteen or twenty feet; the force of the fall was still great and the Eternian still hit hard.

The fight continued until finally Teraxius, Lithil, and Eve regrouped. They stood opposed to a vile threat. Throxar, the corrupted lizard had arrived. His once green scales now tinted and dripping with a shadowy black. Shining metallic armor pieces strategically covered his abdomen, half his face, and his right shoulder and arm. More metallic-like plates ran down his tail, coming to an end with a series of chain whips. In his left hand rested a beautifully decorated circular shield and in his right hand a great mace. The shadow essence of his weapon and board penetrated the very souls of his adversaries.

Malagant had been defeated and sent back to the shadow world. Lithil had been saved, partially. He'd been shattered. His body would fail eventually. The shadow in him would eat at his very soul until he was done. In the meantime, he'd be able to use both his shadow powers as well as his Paladin powers to fight against the shadow.

Lithil managed to somehow keep Eve alive. The two regrouped with Teraxius and now the three would face the greatest threat of the battlefield, save Falling Star. Teraxius was in and out of weapons. His weapons changed with every second. A double-bladed, double-sided two-handed weapon was his current weapon of choice. On one end, it was a giant hammer and the other a double-bladed axe.

Seeing his friends stand against the leader of the shadow army, Rhoeve made his way to join the fight as well. He and his team of fire people charged toward Throxar hoping it wouldn't be too late before they arrived.

Throxar began with a swift whipping slash of his tail, turning his back toward Eve only to face Lithil. Eve flew up hard and landed even harder. Rain began to pour. The mud and blood mixed together nicely. The ground was getting slick. Lithil shadow stepped to land at Throxar's flank. Teraxius came in engaging the lizard, taking Lithil's place.

Teraxius actually moved quite nicely with the giant weapon he'd just taken from a dead half-giant. One block with the mace, a second with the shield, then a spinning whipping attack from the tail and its chain whips forced Teraxius on the defensive. Even still, the gladiator found blood spilling from his face and stomach.

Lithil reappeared just as he desired, shield-bashing Throxar from behind. The mighty lizard went with the momentum, allowing the shattered paladin to roll off and over his shoulder to the flat of his back. Turning the mace upside down without hesitation, Throxar implanted it nearly through the body of Lithil.

Teraxius came over the mace, catching Throxar in the face with the maul side of his weapon. The giant lizard would have toppled but his tail was there to keep him straight. The blow angered Throxar. A backing slap with his shield forced Teraxius' own weapon into him. The rain was coming hard now. Teraxius lost his footing and fell.

A roaring groan of two cats came into fruition. Eve sent two phantasmal panthers at her enemy. They did a little more than irritate and postpone Throxar's next move. It worked. They did their job only to be annihilated within seconds.

Eve was on her way back up. She was hurt. Losing the phantasmal panthers cut into her life even more. More and more ghost bolts and phantasmal blasts and rays came his way. Throxar shielded them as best he could with his iron shield. No, he was forced back from his weapon! His weapon was still implanted in the shattered paladin!

Rhoeve and his crew arrived just in time. Bites, tail whips, and even punches and frontward kicks put Rhoeve's new team in shambles. A sword caught the lizard from here and there but usually ended up costing the attacker his/her life.

Finally, even Rhoeve was beaten. The lizard's shield was gone. He held the elf by his throat high in the air. Teraxius was still barely coming to. Hurling his shield to put Eve out of commission now seemed like an even greater idea than it did when he did it.

Rhoeve surely couldn't last long against the great lizard. Throxar brought him in for a closer look. After a quick smell and taste with his tongue, he extended his arm back out. Licking his chops, Throxar was anxious. This fight, this battle, was all coming to a close.

Teraxius regained his footing. Rhoeve's swords were now in his grasp. A long sword and a short sword, both with magical properties. Teraxius grinned as he hadn't grinned in a decade. Fire-based weapons were in his grasp and his adversary's flank was to him. He launched the first short sword, catching Throxar directly in his back. The sword ran deep. Throxar's grip on Rhoeve broke and the elf fell to the ground.

Throxar flicked his tail, knowing the gladiator was charging him. The chain whips caught him every which way but not before Teraxius planted Rhoeve's other blade through the back of Throxar's head.

The creature screamed out in pain. The gladiator fell to the ground, a bloody mess. Tiny iron and stone balls equipped with short spikes buried themselves in the gladiator's already marred flesh. Rhoeve found the shaft of a broken sword and took it into his hands. Rising up from his knees, he gutted the creature, from stem to sternum. As he stood, the creature fell lifelessly to the ground.

Meanwhile, Danth, Alihaedra, and several others regrouped together to channel their powers against the unbeatable Falling Star. Even Ereven returned to fight; he stood alongside Danth and the others coming together. Where'd he come from, Danth pondered? However, questioning the morbid wizard was the last thing on the great priest's mind.

Lithil's eyes opened. He knew his time was running short. He'd taken the orb from Eve's unconscious body. He had one last trick in him. He knew what he had to do. Malakai and Taj came to the gladiator's aid, seeing Eve, Lithil, and Rhoeve near him.

Lithil didn't say a word. He used the last of his powers to open a portal back to the shadow world. Falling Star felt the presence of his world when it opened. The Pact Stone was spotted too. The great shadow dragon deity raged on, seeing Lithil's foolishness. Falling Star was no longer able to access his world because of godly complications. A mortal, or half mortal, did it for him. Now his powers would truly come and he would finally reach full potential.

Malakai's powers once again surprised the surviving members of the citadel. A shadowy force as great as any ever seen rang forth from his near-dead hands, slamming into the very eyes of the great beast; Danth, Alihaedra, Ereven, and a score of others joined Malakai from all over the battlefield, giving the now empowering Falling Star everything they had left.

"Lithil's a traitor!" Rhoeve said.

Teraxius laughed from the ground, speaking barely loud enough for his own ears to hear. "I don't think so."

Lithil leaped through the portal with the Pact Stone in his grasp. Falling Star answered the surviving fighters with a force of a thousand elements. A force strong enough to annihilate the entire landmass shot forth from his great orifice.

Malakai's shadowy powers cloaked him, protecting him from the deity's blast. Taj's eyes opened just in time to see the sky blanketed with thousands of elemental powers. A light brighter than even Falling Star's rose from the ground, meeting the breath of a thousand elements; Eve's body had taken too much but Enad was linked to it now.

Enad once again broke ground, using the helpless Eve as his channel. Without Enad, the great spirit of loyalty, Falling Star would have surely ended the battle. Falling Star did rip into Lithil's portal, tearing it open like a fire on clothes. The Pact Stone was on the other side. He had to retrieve it. He had to fend off the great spirit.

Falling Star gave his all, pushing back against Enad's incredible powers. Enad pushed at him with both radiant and fire energies. Falling Star countered solely with shadow. The infected were instantly annihilated by Enad's powers. The daemons were also obliterated by Enad's powers. It was a power source unlike any he'd ever faced.

The two greatest forces Thedia had ever seen were colliding and the land below was paying for it. Danth and the others now secured their regrouping survivors with every form of protection spell, guard, and ward they had. Alihaedra possessed tricks that truly blessed their protections as well.

Falling Star felt the presence of the Pact Stone fading. It was falling farther and farther into his own shadow realm. If Gemini managed to acquire the stone before him, his plans for unifying the realms under his own rule would be gone.

Alas, the great deity did what he had to do. He sent the forces he had remaining at the orbiting powers of Enad, all the while jumping through the portal himself. In his absence, ghost powers left behind, as remnants of him would fight in his place. Slowly but surely, they ate at Enad as Enad at them. They were harder and more difficult to fight and were purely outmatched by the overbearing powers of Enad. They'd do their job and hold it off until Falling Star could get back.

Taj, Malakai, Giovanni, Rhoeve, and Teraxius managed to make it back to Danth, Ereven, Alihaedra, and the others.

"Falling Star created ghost forces of himself and his breaths to fight off Eve's spirit while he goes and gets the Pact Stone," Malakai said.

"I knew Lithil wasn't a traitor," Teraxius said, coughing up his last lung.

"We have to close the portal. It's our only chance. I knew what Lithil was doing," Malakai said.

"How?" Taj asked.

"Because I am of the shadow and more than you think. I can feel the Pact Stone like I feel my own heart beating. We all can. We have to seal the portal," said the shadow sorcerer. "Ever wonder why I possess the powers of storm, chaos, draconic, and cosmic sorcerers? It's what my shadow gift grants me."

Danth was probably in the best shape of them all. They were all near death. Danth smiled. He knew their powers weren't keeping them alive. It was Enad through Eve. Alihaedra called forth spirits of all kinds to swim through Enad's awesome powers to help finish off the stronger daemons.

Two more blasting powers poured out. What were they and where was it coming from? Taj's swords glimmered greater than they'd ever done before. SOUL was especially thrilled. It had been here before, back when it, as Arakros Awestrike, sealed the great shadow portal during the First War of the Shadow.

LORE also gleamed in excitement. It was once again going to be able to assist in the securing of Thedia. LORE's inner being, the former king of the lost empire Esgaria, Goddimus Ryven had been yearning for the opportunity to redeem himself for the damages he'd caused so many millennia ago.

"I can help seal the portal, Taj," said SOUL.

"We have to help secure Thedia," added LORE. For the first time, the two swords were working together.

With SOUL and LORE Taj would be able to seal the portal, right? Malakai wouldn't have to. Taj still felt Froth's presence and through Froth's presence; he felt the aura of Liam as well. They were still out there, outside of the bubble of protection fighting to and through the unchallenged power of Enad. How was Eve? Would she survive?

Taj couldn't wait around any longer. He charged out, leaving the safety and security of the bubble. Everything around him had gone completely white and blank. His swords guided him. He raced to the portal solely on faith.

"Taj no!" Giovanni's bloody scream curdled out. Again, he watched as his only true friend made out for the ultimate sacrifice.

"Fear not, Giovanni, he won't make it," Malakai said laughing.

"Wait, what?" asked Danth, confused at the shadow sorcerer's response.

With that, Malakai vanished, leaving Thedia with but a few words. "To close a shadow's portal, one must be of the shadow and it must be done from the shadow's realm. For 'tis the work of Gemini who created the shade portals in order to keep them from closing on their destination's side."

Danth, Alihaedra, and the others couldn't believe how fast Malakai was gone. Of them all, perhaps he was the least hurt. Looks can be deceiving, thought the Draconic priest.

In a flash, Enad's bright light of power was gone. The infected were also gone. They'd been annihilated. Some had even been saved. Giovanni spotted his old friend Lithil lying not too far from where their protection bubble had been. The milky white light that surrounded the entire area for the short time left them blind from their ally that had lain just a few feet from them.

Danth's powers told him Lithil was cured. His body would never be the same but the paladin was cured. The shadow was now absent from his body. The survivors came together. Eve, where is Eve? thought Teraxius, who darted off after his secret love.

To his dismay, his secret lover had passed, her body unable to withstand the incalculable powers of Enad. Enad and his power were gone. Liam and Froth stood tattered sided by side not too far from where the portal was. SOUL and LORE couldn't believe it. They'd been robbed of the ultimate victory. And yet, they were still victorious.

"Falling Star is no more," Danth said.

"We must rebuild," said Rhoeve.

"With what?" asked an arrogant Golric Firesoul coming up from the way; he'd been standing with Liam and Froth blasting the portal with his fire powers, hoping to keep it from expanding and/or letting anything and everything else come in.

Liam and Froth's splintered frames fell, completely drained of everything they had. Collectively, they simultaneously shielded Golric so as a trio they could blast the portal. Froth resorted back to his withered pale white frame with long platinum hair, cracking gray eyes— the yellow was gone again—with blue veins visible throughout his entire body.

Liam's draconic frame was missing a wing and scales ripped from every part. He wasn't long for the world. Then again, neither was Froth. Somehow, they spared Golric. For what and for what purpose was the fire priest spared?

"Golric, you're alive!" Rhoeve yelled excitedly.

"Well done," said Danth. He wasn't happy with the cost but the outcome was still more than he could ask for.

One was pleased more than the others. Ereven the eladrin wizard was ecstatic. Now, he'd be able to rank up through several positions in Reforged. "Danth, I'll assume the responsibility of the arcane in Reforged," he said, almost too happy to hold back his grin.

"No Ereven, you'll spend the rest of your days imprisoned for your actions," Danth replied.

"What?" he yelled, angrily whirling about his powers.

Without hesitation, Alihaedra cast totems and phantoms to disable the wizard as quickly as he mustered up his powers.

Giovanni took it upon himself to bind the wizard.

"He's killed too many heedlessly. It'll not happen again, nor will it go unpunished." The Draconic Priest was stern in his decision. After today, Ereven the eladrin wizard would never see the light of day again.

The survivors took up salvageable supplies and returned to the citadel. Giovanni, Rhoeve, and Taj spent several days in the sanatorium. The active priests with healing powers focused on the civilians of the place. They focused on the survivors that came to the citadel everyday looking for a new beginning.

Teraxius ignored his wounds. He found something near Eve's body he couldn't turn from. He knew what it was and how it happened. Enad sped up the forming process and birthed his child. The host would have to die. He knew that. Enad spared and even saved his little boy. The secret love life of the two became a folktale around the citadel.

Golric organized his people in the citadel. He hadn't anything left to go back to. Corvana was in for a hard tomorrow. It was completely laid to waste. The people of Corvana would come out again. The people would come together and reform, rebuild, and start again. Danth would lead Reforged and the driving force behind it all. He would do it with Alihaedra at his side.

Malakai was gone. From the minute he left the safety of the protection bubble, he'd not been heard from since. In a sense, he saved Taj from making the ultimate sacrifice. Froth and Liam fell to the marred ground beneath them. They too spent many days recovering in the sanatorium.

Their room was separate of the other. The phylactery was no more of course and other than Halo; none had to feel the wrath of Xavius Froth. Liam used his divine powers to protect the three of them during their trio blasting of the portal. Froth defended himself as well as Golric and Golric simply focused on the portal.

Liam took far more damage than Froth for it. He was hurt. He'd never be the same. His wing, though, as a lycanthrope could possibly grow back with time. Froth thought back to that day of their first encounter. He thought back to how, because of that bastard Gaiyrmynceth became the king of the night.

Their room was just big enough for the two of them. Reforged dressed it with drapes of cotton and silk with two made up beds built precisely for their bodies. Froth's eyes opened. His head fell to the side seeing a sleeping Liam. He thought back to that dreadful day so long ago. Liam was the reason for everything he'd lost and worst, not attained.

He laughed. The ageless vampire pulled himself up and off the bedding. His was built in the design of a coffin to a suit him. It certainly didn't do its job, he thought. Froth carried his destroyed body to the remnants of Liam. Liam was barely alive. He would be able to sustain life and eventually, his body would begin to regenerate. Then, it would be too late.

Froth looked around the beautifully colored room. Stains of blood decorated the decorations. Those ancient orbs locked onto Liam's face. Only he knew how long he was forced to hide from the beast. All this time he knew. He knew exactly how to locate Liam. In order to prevent Liam from finding him, he had to remain hidden and keep his aura weakened and cloaked.

Now the table had turned and it was Liam who was desperate, whether he knew it or not. Froth's tongue lapped at his fangs. He'd devoured the soul and essence of a godborn. Now, he'd take the blood of the master lycanthrope who'd evolved into nearly a god from feeding on one of the more powerful dragons. Excitement, his dead heart pumped faster and faster, harder and harder.

His veins burned with temptation. Nothing around seemed to matter. The strongest blood was before him and helpless. The psychotic Liam who'd never been known to be controllable was helpless before him and his blood would send the vampire into something he'd never been before, a god. He'd own the blood of himself, the godborn, and now that of the first Lycanthrope. And that lycanthrope was now even more of a god than he was the first time they met.

He remembered back to when Liam took in his blood. So many questions sent through the years from that fight. Was Froth playing possum or did Liam truly defeat him? Did Froth allow him to take in his blood or did Liam take it on his own? And more so, what happened after?

Froth knew what happened. His mind took him back immediately to that place. At the time, Liam was too much for him to face singlehandedly. His blood was enough to hold him off and stun him, if only for a little while. It worked! It worked better than he'd planned! Liam fled. Then, the gargoyle king arrived and Froth had nothing left to offer him in terms of a fight.

It was a unique trio between the three. Gaiyrmynceth could've handled Liam with relative ease but stood no chance against Froth. Liam's physical force and ability to withstand Froth's tactics made him too much for Froth, at the time. Froth secretly faced the gargoyle king before and proved to be the better being. It was just an oddity of a situation. Now the gargoyle king was dead, Froth was empowered, and Liam was helpless.

In the final moment, the king of the lycanthropes peeled open his eyes. Liam's eyes held a story of disgust but acceptance. His many children would one day avenge him. Liam spent so long in Nevermore, the core center of Thedia. Very few knew of its existence other than its natural inhabitants. Only Froth, Croste, and Liam had ever made it to it. Croste was dead and Liam would soon be dead. And Froth would never spill his knowledge of that place to anyone or anything.

Froth hadn't placed his pallet upon the flesh of anything in over two thousand years. Now Liam would be the first to feel it. Unlike Liam, whose body was warm and filled with life, Froth's body was cold and lifeless. When Liam took in the dead blood of the most potent creature, it chilled his body almost to nothing. Reversed, Froth's body would only warm a bit, possibly too much for him to withstand. After, would he be able to do what Liam had hoped for then? Would he be able to venture into and out of the realm of the living and the dead at his leisure?

Froth's fangs pierced the scales of the half-dragonoid looking creature. Liam almost looked like a half-wyvern of some kind in his current form. Blood filled eyes stretched open farther than they'd ever opened before. Thick claws buried themselves into the still wounded vampire's body. Liam's scales christened with death modifying the body into a more a decrepit shell of its former self. His scales began to shed their color. His eyes now drained of all life. In a last ditch effort, Liam rose to sink his teeth into the empowered being.

The two continued to feed on each other waiting for the other to die. Liam's body was more damaged and closer to death. Froth's body was wounded but still filled with the blood and soul of the godborn. In the end, it was Liam whose grip lessened. It was Liam's eyes that closed. Froth's body began to change as well. His flesh grew a new type of humanoid looking scale. His body grew in height and size. Though taller, the shriveled being was still sickly thin. The scales colored themselves both black and white with both radiant and necrotic energies.

Liam shriveled to nothing more than a pile of bones, scales, and ash on the floor. Froth looked something more like a fallen angel that had been dipped in the depths of the hells. Two large bone structures popped out from his shoulder blades. Feathers, scales, and blood dripped and spurted out from his body. The bastard was growing wings.

Taj awoke to healing hands of many clerics and priests rubbing down his body. His eyes etched a vision of damage, pain, and death to his mind. His body subconsciously sat straight up and without thinking, he was already walking through the halls and the corridors of the citadel. Taj's gut told him it was his link that wanted him. Xavius Froth wanted to see his warm blooded son one last time. After all, it was Taj that convinced his own people to trust the essence of a vampiric being with their souls.

Taj's mind raced. He couldn't take it in. Where was Malakai? He wasn't in the sanatorium. He would've seen him, right? No matter, he had to get to Froth. Only by faith and presence would Taj find him. He hadn't a clue of what had been going on. He'd been out. Very occasionally, his eyes would open to see Giovanni next to him. Malakai was probably a closer and more dear to him than even Giovanni now.

Alas, Taj made it through the people and the corridors of the citadel to a room draped in silks and bathed with blood. On the floor lay a large pile of bone, ash, and scales. A being he once knew as Froth stood before the pile. The being looked to be something out of a folk tale, a cross between a master vampire, an angel, and a demon or devil. Its eyes were black like its heart. Its withered body outlined with beautifully crafted crimson black and radiantly white scales. Great wings born from its back extended outward laced with bloody red feathers and scales similar to its body.

Instantly, Taj knelt before him. He knew nothing else. Immediately, the creature's actions filled Taj's mind. He knew what he'd done and the missing parts and times of the epic fight against Falling Star filled Taj's mind.

His wits glistened. Now, he remembered passing Helios in the corridors. The bastard was still alive, Taj thought. He automatically knew Ereven the eladrin wizard was imprisoned on the bottom floor and Danth, with Alihaedra had taken back control of Reforged.

In that same thought Froth was gone, vanished. Taj stood back up. Something else had come over him. He felt different. He felt hopelessness and contentment all at the same time. He stood there, mind adrift, contemplating everything. His entire life flowed through his eyes like a string of portraits laid down before him. Never would any have thought he'd come so far and yes, he was his father's equal. Wasn't he?

Chapter 11

In the coming days Taj, Giovanni, Golric, Helios, Rhoeve, Teraxius, and Lithil led by examples for Danth and Alihaedra. Golric even served as the presiding priest over their wedding ceremony. Helios found new life in this new beginning and he wanted to do something more than he'd done before. He quickly became Danth's number one captain of the still-rebuilding guild.

Teraxius focused much of his time on Tera, his son. Lithil's body was broken down but the way of the Paladin would be taught on through him. Giovanni engineered new structures, platforms, and plans. His ingenuity was much needed and appreciated.

Taj led teams in search of survivors and supplies. Rhoeve shared Taj's mission with a company of his own men. Days became weeks. Weeks became months. Months became years. Rhoeve never fully recovered from his sickness and/or the wounds from that last battle. Throxar even managed to bite him before dying. The bite mark never faded and Rhoeve's condition continued to worsen.

Malakai, the shadow sorcerer whose powers far exceeded any mortal they'd ever known, was gone but not forgotten. Images of the sorcerer continued to haunt Taj, mostly in his dreams and upon first waking. Occasional visions of the sorcerer even plagued him during search missions.

Eventually Rhoeve succumbed to his sickness, dying the day Golric found his surviving family members. Teraxius took up his position after his comrade fell. Helios even enlisted his services to Teraxius. Golric began riding with Taj. The others continued to remain at the citadel. Tera was now seven and a star pupil. Hundreds of small cities, towns, civilizations, etc. began to pop up all over the scarred surfaces of the Corvanian lands. Most immediately fell subservient to the citadel of Reforged hoping to conscript their aid in the event of conflict.

Reforged became the centerpiece of the growing civilizations and Danth was its head. Everyday Taj found more and more resources and helped build and structure more and more cities. Taj located the areas in which cities would most prosper. The battle with Falling Star was over, but the war was not. One final battle was left.

It had been seven years to the day since Falling Star was sealed from Thedia. Teraxius and Taj sat upon their great white steeds overlooking a new valley of beautiful resources with their men standing tall behind them. It was an Edenic garden, perfect, pure, and without fault. It had never felt the touch of mortality; it's resources never harnessed before.

"Secure the valley," Taj ordered.

The people of Taj's companies strategically set out down the hills and across the mountains that made the beautiful valley what it was. Teraxius gave the order and his men followed as well.

"Rejoice Taj, we just saved Corvana!" Teraxius was ecstatic. He'd been concerned about the well-being of his son for some time.

"I know you've been haunted to ask me," Taj replied. He didn't seem as thrilled about their find as Teraxius was. His body was still burned and marred but the former gladiator trooped on always as a king to his people.

"With this find I feel my ghosts will go away."

"I trust your instincts will have you ask me anyway. So go ahead old friend," Taj said, keeping his keen eyes open and vigilant.

Teraxius leaped from his horse onto Taj's instantly. The former gladiator pulled two magically enchanted arrows from the air. They came from nowhere and would've been direct hits had the gladiator's instincts not sensed them.

The horse's body toppled Teraxius over, forcing a backward flip and fall to the back of his head. He didn't hesitate. He rolled back to his feet, dropping the arrows and pulling his newly fashioned falchion from his sheath. The falchion was Teraxius' true weapon of choice, and though few could wield it singlehandedly, this gladiator was one of those people.

Taj dismounted ripping SOUL and LORE out before another sound was made. The surrounding mountainous regions enveloping the valley blackened out with darkness. SOUL, LORE, and Taj knew what had come. Teraxius just knew it was trouble.

As the shadows of the coming threat swallowed the ground, the screams of their men and women filled the sky.

"Go," Taj ordered.

"Not likely," Teraxius yelled back.

The two charged side by side to the left side of the mountainous terrain toward the shadowy black that had apparently come for them. Suddenly Taj stopped. Teraxius followed his ally but just a few steps ahead.

"Hold Teraxius."

The gladiator did as instructed. He'd already come to a complete stop.

"I told you, you should've left when you had the chance. You have a son to think about."

The mountainous terrain was blocked and hidden by a circular forest growing all around it. The valley was in the center of the great forest. The forest was mostly bleak and dead but something kept a lot of the green from ever dying. It was an anomaly and the reason Taj and Teraxius wanted to investigate it to begin with.

Now, shadows came from the forest. The shadows became humanoid creatures drenched in a gray substance. Their very skin was dim with the gray and their eyes mostly dark, sometimes darkened to a true black.

"And you one day hope to return to your family. That's what you told me, isn't it?" Teraxius questioned, still breathing heavily from the hard run he'd just done.

"Indeed Teraxius, but I'm not the man I once was. I am no longer the man linked to that family. I'm a monster. I'm a monster that fights monsters. I've ascended. I'm different and I can never go back."

A familiar face emerged from the forest. A seven-foot humanoid frame came from within the ashy-skinned people. His long black hair flowed evenly and perfectly down his stone and bone armor. He was the dark knight out of a folk tale and a massive hangar rested on his back. Archaic and alien symbols of gold decorated his outfit. His cold black eyes stared straight toward Taj Odin Xavier.

"Malagant," Taj said, barely above a whisper.

They'd met before and Taj knew his name. It was Falling Star's champion. He'd returned. How long had they been back from the shadow world? How long had they been upon Thedia's surface?

The man nodded, hinting to Taj that he was indeed correct. Malagant didn't say a word. Taj knew what he planned to do. Taj's military genius told him to the tee what was to come. Daemons would be sent to infiltrate their souls. Then, as hosts of the daemons, they'd be forced to infiltrate the citadel for Malagant.

Malagant turned his back to the two, showing no signs of concern whatsoever for the living legends. Taj and Teraxius' names were growing, as were the names of the other heroes who'd helped bring down Falling Star. Golric, Taj, Danth, and Teraxius' seemed to have attained the greatest amounts of recognition for their services.

Just as Taj predicted, ghostly humanoids slithered through the cracks of the forest, past the shoulders of the ashy skinned men, to very area where both Taj and Teraxius stood.

Dozens of arrows sung through the air, all naissance from the same source. One, two, three; precision shots sent one shadow mortal after another to the ground, lifeless. The arrows were catching the shadow people either through the right eye or in the heart, all fatal shots.

Taj's peripheral caught Helios charging up the mountainside, letting loose three and four arrows at a single time. Directly behind him came Golric Firesoul and from the looks of the fire whirling around, he was preparing something much worse for the shadowy army.

The carefree tactics of the Shadow Army allowed one fatal mistake. Malagant departed without assuring the weapons of Taj Odin Xavier and Teraxius were taken. Malagant didn't want them taken. He wanted his daemons to be able to utilize them once their bodies were assumed.

The daemons jumped, hoping to get the new vessels before the fire came their way. Fire had a nasty effect on the shadow. Too late, Golric Firesoul's conflagration spell discharged, paving its way through masses of the shadowy soldiers.

Just as the flames engulfed the shadow folk, it shrouded around the four, protecting them from not only the in cinerary flames but also from the shadows' hostile retaliations. Golric led the escape through the forest; slipping directly past daemons, shadow folk, and even Malagant.

The four rushed back away from the shaded as fast as they could. As figured, Malagant ordered small units to give chase. As creatures neared the group, they would smite them.

The four ran for days. Golric finally demanded the group stop to rest. Taj didn't want to but he knew the goliath was right. Teraxius also knew that in order for the crew to make it back to their citadel, a decent rest was a necessity.

Helios scouted the area. The light forest became thick. He discovered a perfect area for the crew to lie low. A small hillside birthed a decent valley filled with dips and rocks for the crew to hide. Helios' intuition led the group to a small tucked away indention inside the hillside.

Days passed. Once the crew succumbed to their own fatigue, it took days for them to regain their strength and recuperate. Golric naturally took it upon himself to keep the team warm with fire. His campfires were special. Something about them was different. His fires kept the team filled with warmth and something about them helped regenerate their bodies.

Taj's keen intellect saved the four from a vile death at the hands of Malagant and the Shadow Army. They made it all the way back to the citadel, fighting any and everything off that came their way. Golric was hurting badly and so was Teraxius.

Just ahead, the four saw the entrance to the stronghold now sitting atop the entrance to the main citadel. They could've made it to other cities but Taj knew Danth needed to hear about this. The leader of Reforged and the person in charge of the strongest fighting unit going needed to know Falling Star's champion was back.

The stronghold's gates opened. The portcullis was just about completely raised as the bloody bodies of the four approached. The guards knew Taj, Golric, and Teraxius by sight. The name Helios was known but his physical appearance wasn't as easy to pick out.

Taj blew off the celebrating guards and civilians of the stronghold. It was built mainly of stone, wood, and iron. Few families resided in the prison-like fortress, only those families whose husbands or wives were legitimate soldiers or guards.

The clerics took both Teraxius and Golric away.

"Helios," Taj started.

"I'll get on the wall and get with the gate captains. I'll make sure everything's prepped. I'll get this hold ready for action." Helios answered the question Taj hadn't even asked yet.

Taj was alone again, rushing the crowds of people, waving off their pleas and thank you's and other notions that were all out to get his attention. He needed Danth. At last, a local guard finally gave him the information he needed. Danth was atop in the stronghold itself. He and Alihaedra were seeing to new strategic plans brought forward by scores of leaders.

Taj made it to the General's Quarters, a square building fortified with soldiers, scattered papers across desks, and the like. Danth was present. He was eye deep in a series of documents with a few of Reforged's gate captains.

"Danth," he said as strongly as he could.

"What is it, Taj? Welcome back, brother. Where are the others? Everything is well, I take it?" he asked.

Then he stopped. Taj was battered and bloody. Open wounds still poured blood from his body. His swords still glowed as they always did when enemies neared their wielder. Danth looked at the swords and then gave Taj another once over.

"Malagant's back," said the Eternian.

"What?" asked the High Priest.

"Danth, Falling Star's champion is back and he's brought with him an army, an army I'm not sure we can defeat. Daemons fill our skies and—"

Danth interrupted him, finishing his thoughts. "And your team is dead."

"Only Golric, Helios, and Teraxius returned with me."

"Gaernier." Danth looked over at one of his half-orc gate captains.

"Yes sir," he answered. The man wore simple leathers studded with golden plates. His weapon of choice was his glaive. He was a pole-arm fighter. He was certainly coming up through the ranks and fast.

"Get my wife. We have a war to plan."

The bellowing half-orc bolted through the door. Danth looked at Taj. "This was supposed to be over. Something told me it wasn't. We've rebuilt ourselves here. We've rebuilt our civilization. We can't survive another onslaught from that again."

Taj took in Danth's words. He soaked them up, infusing them with his own thoughts and the thoughts of his blades. "It's not what you bring to the fight, Danth. It's the fight your heart brings that counts."

Danth's body turned pale. He forced a half grin. He knew Taj was ready to die for his people. He was ready to die for his people. His people would surely not survive another attack from Falling Star. By the faiths, he hoped, he prayed for Falling Star's concrete banishment.

Chapter 12

In the coming days Taj and the others stood outside their forts, strongholds, cities, and other organized locations opposed to Malagant and his armies. Malagant's armies nearly doubled what Danth had built. Most of Danth's would-be allies were already taken by the time they surrounded the stronghold from which the citadel resided.

Danth wanted to lead the fight but Taj refused to allow it. Danth's military genius was needed to continue the war efforts. Taj, Giovanni, Helios, Teraxius, Lithil, Golric, and his brother Olric would be all that stood against Malagant and his impending first wave.

Malagant's magnificent blackened armor shined with white, silver, and even golden emblems and carvings. Even his black hair glistened with silvery highlights. Malagant was human, though his attributes seemed far superior. His pale white face showed no signs of aging.

Taj's swords stuttered in his mind. It was a first. The stronghold was built around a mountainous terrain scattered by nearby light forests. It was a good spot for the citadel but now, probably not so much. The light forests became dark. The sun was setting. Fighting the shadow at night was suicide. Now even the skies were crying as the incoming daemons drowned out their natural color.

Reforged's structures and strongholds were simply built. They were built for temporary usage and as time progressed, better ones would come to take their place. They hadn't reached that point yet. As of now, it didn't look like they would.

Helios' bow was out. He was ready to draw first blood. Teraxius' falchion was at his side and a pole-arm filled his hands. Lithil's body was weakening. It was surprising he was still alive. His hair flowed. His armor, shield, and sword all polished to perfection. The clerics had told him just the week before, he wouldn't see the weeks' end. Golric and Olric's massive bodies evoked more fiery protection than their allies thought possible.

"You have the sky, right brother?" Golric asked.

"As long as you have my people," Olric answered.

"They're my people to brother," Golric replied.

"These bastards destroyed our home," Olric said.

Taj stood out front. Strategically scattered behind him were the only seven people he had left to count on. There were others in the Hold that could help them but not from the outside of the walls. People like the seven that stood before Malagant and his forces were a dying breed. Thedia was truly a shadow of its former self, calloused over, and thickly skinned.

Malagant approached, leaving all of his army behind him. Taj's frame of six foot and some change was dwarfed by the monster of a man.

"So, monster meets monster, eh?" Taj said, sickly laughing and looking up at the perfectly chiseled face of Malagant.

"Again, so it seems," he answering. "I come with a single offering."

"So offer," Taj said.

"Give us the high priest and you seven will earn your places under me. You seven have shown great courage, perseverance, and most importantly skill. The rest shall burn."

Taj didn't say anything. He responded with the thrust of SOUL, the sword of his left hand. Malagant flashed from existence, shadow stepping back and with his powerful full-blade already drawn. Some shadow people had the ability to shadow step as an eladrin's fey step. Eladrin stepped through using their link to the feywild. Shadow people did the same using their connection to their shadow world.

With a swing of Malagant's sword, Taj's left arm was knocked over to his right side. SOUL and LORE clanged together. Taj instinctively ducked, just barely missing Malagant's killing strike. Helios let loose several arrows all at once, all aimed at the champion of the shadow.

"No, you burn!" Golric screamed, answering his own way to Malagant's words.

The seven found fiery protection all around them. Unfortunately, it was mostly in a form to protect them from the daemons. Olric' fire filled the sky. Collectively, they still managed to bombard the closing in shadow army with masses and masses of napalmic fires. Secretly, when the scouts first warned of the Malagant's coming, Golric and Olric prepared many rituals of devastating qualities. And as soon as Taj pulled his first blade, the goliath brothers rained down upon their enemies.

Taj pulled LORE and rolled underneath yet another swing of Malagant's, just missing it yet again. Another four arrows caught the barrel of a man dead center. Eight arrows now decorated his breastplate. The others moved off, keeping strategic positions as best they could. One ritual Danth started before the fight was centered on Taj and kept a decent radius around him all protected as best he could, mostly from the daemons, magic, and certain missiles.

An overhand swing by Malagant sent Taj to the ground. Taj blocked with both his blades crossed. It was not enough. He scattered, pathetically evading as Malagant strolled about laughing. Every single time he connected swords he'd lose his footing, base, and even his conscious thought. Malagant's force was so great it affected everything, internal and external.

Malagant roared out in anger, nearly stumbling to the point of falling. He turned, giving his back to Taj, who was still trying to regain his footing. Malagant's eyes fell upon Lithil. He dropped his right hand, slightly raising his left. A black entropic force coned out from it. Lithil's shield was not enough. It dropped the shattered paladin to his knees.

"Traitor," he called out.

The battle was full scale. Helios had left Taj's aid to assist the others. Golric and Olric were dual-handedly handling the majority of the situation, with Giovanni and Teraxius taking out the more experienced leaders like shadows as they came into sight. Assistance from within the walls of the stronghold also came. The simple clerics all came together using their rituals to encase the Hold in a massive protection spell, sealing it off from the likes of the infesting daemons.

"We need the priest," he ordered Lithil.

Taj charged forward harder than he'd ever moved before. Just before implanting both his blades into the lower back of the champion, the champion flicked his right wrist backward and upward, spinning with the motion fluidly.

Taj's swords were knocked from their course again. He choke stepped to catch his footing. A series of small blasts then followed, piercing through his back and ripping outward from his chest. Taj fell to the ground weak and badly hurt.

Lithil was already on him. He used a healing spell to reinvigorate Taj and bull-rushed forward, slamming his shield into Malagant. His own momentum ricocheted, forcing the paladin to his back. Malagant shadow stepped yet again, this time reappearing in a half-kneeling position with one knee planted firmly into now dented breastplate of Lithil.

"Look around you traitor. These infidels are falling. They'll all fall. As soon as the priest is mine, the doorway shall be reopened."

Taj utilized the powers of his swords like he hadn't done in a long while. Taj connected his very soul with the swords, forcing rampant bursts of all energies to flow from them. He hurled them both simultaneously at the champion. Malagant stood quickly to defend but this time he was too late.

SOUL pierced his abdomen all the way through and LORE did the same to his upper left torso, directly severing his heart into nearly two pieces. In a thousand years, he'd never really been scratched. Now, he'd been killed.

He stood, slowly mirroring Taj's movements. His entropic blasts melted six holes through his counterpart's torso. Malagant angrily roared out again, sending Taj back with a telekinetic force so strong, even the neighboring fighters flew with it. It even shattered Danth's outside protection spells and rituals. Malagant used a hate to rush forward he hadn't used nor felt in eight hundred years. The tip of his blade found its mark in Taj's heart. He raised the miscreant high and kept running. He wouldn't stop. He didn't feel as if enough punishment had been administered.

Taj's body fell forward on the sword, limp and mortally wounded. A trembling force nearly sent and entire wall of the Hold down. Malagant impaled Taj Odin Xavier on the very wall of wood and stone that protected his people. Malagant fell back as the momentum bounced back tingling into him.

"Now you fool. You think your priest is safe. Those protection spells are exactly what we wanted. We knew what you were doing. These daemons aren't here to infest. They're here to be sacrificed as part of the plan."

Taj's dying face powered its way up to look his killer in the face. His torso had nearly been cut in two. Malagant's unstoppable force and immeasurable power would die with him. It nearly put an entire side of the Hold's wall down but, nonetheless, he was going to die.

"Falling Star isn't here to save you, fiend," Taj gasped, choking on his own blood.

"He will be soon enough," answered the Champion of the Shadow.

"Wha…" Taj muttered, looking up past Malagant's head. The daemons of the sky were molding, forming into something. The protections of Thedia called down by Danth and the others were visually in sight; a giant bluish white tinted bubble of guards and wards covered the Hold. Taj's eyes then fell upon Lithil. He still wasn't up. Outside of the Hold, Teraxius, Giovanni, Helios, Golric, and Olric were still fighting magnificently.

The blood to Taj's head flushed down. Everything momentarily went black. Then, his sight returned. He was dying. He shed a tear for the memories of the man he once was, the man who would never see Adrian, Destiny, Legion, or his newly born children ever again.

"That's right, infidel. Thedia's protections, guards, and wards, along with that priest inside, complete the components needed for our majestic finish."

Taj's eyes fell back to meet Malagant's. Tears of blood poured from his face.

"You see. I've succeeded. I've served my liege well. Your Hold will be my Liege's doorway. Die on that."

With his last bit of life, Taj answered Malagant again. "These aren't my people. This isn't my Hold. I came here to stop the war on my pantheon. You coming here…" Taj spewed blood from his mouth coughing and gagging. His blood splattered Malagant's face. He continued. "You've only helped me rid my world of this forsaken land…" Taj smiled knowing his words cut the champion more than his swords did.

Malagant's face grimaced in fear, pain, and anger. He stepped back, giving himself room. He peeled both SOUL and LORE from Taj's body, wrenching out pain as he did. With the final piece of his quest in place, Malagant crucified Taj, spreading his arms out on wall of the Hold and keeping them in place by the use of his very own swords.

Taj's head fell limp and lifeless. Malagant fell to his knees and rolled to his side. Just as the last bit of life drained from them both, Taj whispered. "You still die kneeling before me, where you belong."

Taj and Malagant died in chorus together. Malagant's body filled with a strange blue glow. In unison, the strange glow filled the sky and the daemons. What was left of the material army also molded into what was coming. Teraxius, Giovanni, Helios, Golric, and Olric all fell back. The brothers' concentrated their powers on the protection of themselves and their three remaining outside allies.

In an instant, a flash and a bang cracked the land and the very foundation of the Corvanian Pantheon. The Hold was gone, shattered, and annihilated upon the massive talons of Falling Star's claw touching the surface once again. This time it was different. He was completely restored and fully powered. His body was surely bigger than before in contrast to the single claw that had made its way through the newly opened portal.

Upon his claw's touch to the surface, a forceful shake shook the entire continent; pieces shattered, fell into the deep, and even broke away from the gigantic continent. Nothing was left to protect Corvana or for that matter Thedia from the coming of Falling Star.

Then, from out of the claw came Thedia's last and only hope. The sorcerer once saved and spared by Taj, who had disappeared some years back, returned. Malakai flew from the grips of the claw with searing powers of purification. The very powers ripped through his own body to use. And they weren't his powers.

In the time he was sealed back in the shadow world, Malakai knew Falling Star and Malagant's plan for a return. He learned Malagant was able to return shortly after being banished back. In the time given, Malakai collected the seven runes of Tyra. Tyra was the name of the Shadow World before Gemini took it. It was the first known world to officially be taken by Gemini and it acted as his homeworld ever since. The runes never changed their name and Malakai had them all. Only an arcane or divine caster of Malakai's ability or greater with the seven runes of Tyra would be able to once again seal off the portal and doorway between the planes. This time, with the runes and Malakai's power, it would be once and for all. Tyra and all of its usurped planes would be sealed from the ancient Tree of Life, which connected all planes.

Giovanni's eyes opened. A falling elf fell from the sky. An explosion/implosion concurrently went off, blinding the rogue once again. The claw was gone, forced back from where it had come. Malakai lay limp and virtually lifeless. The warmth of a goliath's touch soothed his pains.

Malakai's eyes cracked open to once again see the beautiful Thedian sun rising. His body was too wounded and beaten to move. Standing over him was the goliath Golric.

Giovanni's eyes opened. He made it. He was alive and a sense of peace flourished within him. His body was hurt but not unable to move. He was thankful. He quickly rose to his feet. Everything he had, all of his weapons, armor, and belongings had been destroyed. He thought back to the day

Taj's team spared him and allowed he and Aramon to join them. What had come of his life? He wasn't meant for such great things. A thanks was in order. Wait, his eyes fell upon the most ghastly discovery they'd ever seen or felt before. A single piece of stone stood from where the walls of the Hold once were. Behind it, survivors deep down in the citadel began to pour out.

Everyone fell stunned upon seeing the atrocity. Malakai's head tilted toward the travesty. The swords SOUL and LORE glowed so brightly and strongly, emanating such a powerful aura that the area surrounding their wielder's body was still unharmed. Taj Odin Xavier was dead; spread open and crucified using the blade of the Shadow Champion and the blades of his own hands.

Ash, soot, and debris still fell and floated in the sky and drifted downward toward the earth. Teraxius and Helios stood over Lithil's dying body. Giovanni saw the three in the distance. Olric was missing altogether.

"Golric can heal you, friend," Teraxius said.

"No, I'm shattered. The shadow lurks within me. Live well old friend," said Lithil, dying.

Teraxius' body was covered in ash. The former gladiator fell to a knee to grab the hand of his dying friend.

Giovanni, Helios, Teraxius, Golric, and even Malakai came to surround the crucified body of Taj Odin Xavier. Coming from the underground citadel finally, the leader of Reforged emerged. Danth Craven too joined his legendary allies around the body of their fallen friend. Danth was devastated more than most. Golric was at a loss for words. His last brother Olric was gone. His body wasn't among the seen dead. Perhaps, he was still alive just missing in action.

"Where's Alihaedra?" Teraxius asked, seeing Danth.

"She gave her life to protect those in the underground citadel along with our strongest clerics, priests, and shamans. She died well. She served Reforged well," he replied.

Not one of them could hold back their tears for Taj. Giovanni was the lone survivor who knew the truth. Taj succeeded in his mission. He left the Republic of New Magic to stop the war against his known world, or pantheon. He achieved that. Corvana no longer existed. Its continent was all but obliterated.

After Danth spoke of his wife's untimely death, a moment of silence mixed with the natural aura of Thedian peace dawned from the group.

Covered in the ash and debris from the wreckage a single moment of Falling Star's existence in the world caused, the remaining four along with Malakai and Danth stood looking at one another. Not one of them had a single weapon or piece of armor left. It was all gone, all except Malakai who was outfitted with the shimmering and glimmering runes of Tyra.

Beneath the dirt and soil rested an outfit of bracers, leggings, an unusually crafted shirt, a crown, rings, boots, and even a golden scepter for his hands. His outfit sparkled like a dying fire in the middle of the night.

Danth smiled at Malakai. "We thought you were dead."

"How did you—" Giovanni started.

Helios fell to a knee. His hands covered his chest. He was hurting. Golric rushed to his side. For the first time since his unity with Danth, Taj and the others Golric showed signs of emotion. He had just enough healing powers left to keep Helios sustained.

"I collected the seven most powerful artifacts and relics of Tyra, Gemini's homeworld. When I found myself alive after sealing it the first time and on the other side of the portal, on his plane, I dedicated my life and time to recovering whatever I would need in the event I had the opportunity to reseal the next opening. I knew Malagant didn't stay in Tyra for long. I knew another link between the planes would be opening up. I'd just collected the Scourged Scepter of Damnation when Malagant reopened the portal. I didn't think I would survive yet again but somehow I did. Now I'm here with these runes. While in Tyra, I lost my eye in a fight against a demon. I replaced it with a small orb I found on the demon. It helped keep my body and powers full of vigor and power."

One by one, Malakai peeled the runes from his body. With each rune's removal, Malakai's body withered and weakened. When the final piece was taken off and thrown to the ground, the sorcerer stumbled. His hair turned an instant gray. His body matured to an elf of a thousand years. His right eye gleamed green with white speckles.

"What's happened to you? How do you know so much about the Invader God Gemini and his world Tyra?" Helios asked.

"I was there," he coughed out angrily.

"Let those who perished be honored." Teraxius was still completely distraught at the loss of Taj.

"He's not lost, nor is my brother." Golric bolstered.

"Don't try it," yelled the broken sorcerer. "Bring back your brother if you wish but not Taj. He wouldn't want it."

Malakai grabbed one of the rings he'd removed. It quickly glowed and in just a blink, Olric was returned. Golric couldn't believe his eyes. He was ecstatic. Malakai just tossed the ring, falling over to his side and then rolling to his back.

"Break down these heinous things. They've already tarnished and ruined me. They've destroyed what I was and made me what I am. A demonic creation is but the single reason I am able to maintain life. Take the residium and bathe our friend's body in it. Take the water of the bath and pour it upon his coffin. Who will do this for me?"

"I will," Danth, Teraxius, Helious, Golric, Olric, and Giovanni all said at once. Golric and Olric embraced like two young sisters split apart for a long weekend.

"I wasn't dead. I don't know where I was, brother," Olric said.

"You were in the void between the planes. You got caught in it," Malakai answered.

Golric, Olric, and Danth pulled the weapons from Taj's body and carefully took it from the stone. They agreed the stone would be what his coffin was to be made from.

The fight was over, truly over this time. Not a lot was said between the remaining heroes. After the runes were finally broken down by Danth, Golric, and Olric, Taj's body was bathed and cleansed and even purified by the residium of the runes. The residium water turned the stone coffin into a form of astral diamond and sealed it. Taj wasn't confined to the coffin with the swords he wielded but rather the sword that took his life. Malakai knew he wanted the swords returned to his son or brother.

Danth returned to Reforged and the rebuilding of it and the civilizations of the Corvanian Pantheon. Teraxius stuck with him and his child. He hung up his blades and focused on the political sides of things. He took up a wife, Jasmin in the coming years.

Golric and Olric began the rebuilding of their fire people. They kept a strong and tight bond and alliance with Danth and Reforged. Helios disappeared in the wild and unknown. Little is known what happened to him or what came of him.

The day came when the ship was finished. It was Malakai's final request for the people of Corvana and Reforged. Giovanni kept close to the only native of his land that he knew. Taj's body was loaded upon the sohar-style ship. Malakai, upon his own order was charged with the task of returning the body of Taj Odin Xavier to his family and possibly even his home. Giovanni walked with him to the shores of the scarred continent. The ship was in the distance and it was beautiful. The small boats taking the men to the ship were just about finished. Malakai's trip was the final one. The broken sorcerer looked at the rogue.

"His swords have been wrapped. I shall take them to his children, wife, brother, and whatever family is waiting for him in the Republic. Let us go, brother. Our task here is complete. With our actions here on this land, we stopped the invasion of the Republic and our pantheon. We're the reason Corvana is gone and I'm not sorry for it."

"Sorcerer, I fear I do not know you or worse, you no longer no me. The people here are a good people and they're going to need help rebuilding. I can build a life here again as Brick. Its better if Giovanni Vandren is remembered as the man who died burning with all of those Corvanian ships. He died a hero. Why tarnish that?"

"It's not the truth."

"Funny coming from you, you kept more secrets than any of us, even me."

"Then for Taj."

"Taj would want it this way."

"No, he would want the truth to set his family free."

"I wasn't meant for all this. The things I've been a part of, the people I've met, and everything else since I met Taj were all too much for me. They're greater beings than I. I'm a coward, Malakai, and I always have been. Trouble is, I'm loyal."

"Taj succeeded in his mission and the people of the Republic need to know it. His family needs to know it. If something happens to me, then who will tell the tale?"

Giovanni thought about his friend's words long and hard. He looked up at the sorcerer. All he knew was that he was an elven man from Lyneth who later proved to have shadow elven ancestry. Now, he'd spent seven years in the shadow realm. Could he still be trusted? Was he the same person? He certainly looked and acted like it. Was Icis still waiting for him at home?

"These people are a part of your past now, Gio, not your future. Your people are South of here and we've been gone for a long, long time. We need to return and prove to them it was a success. We succeeded and Corvana is no more."

"Mal, these people are not all heinous. Just because to kingdoms go to war and you belong to one doesn't mean every single citizen of the other is evil and wrong. The Corvanian monster is dead. We slew it. Go home and fulfill our friend's unsaid request to be buried beneath the dirt of his own people. Make sure his sons and daughters and brother and wife or whatever is back there for him still get his story and swords."

Giovanni was speaking, but speaking slowly. Malakai took the opportunity to answer him while Giovanni was still looking for the words to continue.

"I will. Will you?"

PART 2

The sohar-style ship, named Blooded directly after its reason for existing, left the Corvanian pantheon carrying with it but a few passengers, enough to safely make the travel back to the Republic. Its orders were simple: drop off the body and belongings of Taj Odin Xavier to his respected family and return.

The journey took months. Malakai's health and powers continued to fade. He knew exactly what was happening to him. Chaotic, Draconic, Storm, Cosmic, were all forms of innate within sorcerers. He was of the rarest kind, Shadow and his innate ability supposedly only existed within the purest of shadow elves.

Clerics were taken to constantly monitor his health. There was no answer as to how and why his body was still alive. There was no answer as to why it suddenly aged so much. Malakai was the only shadow elven sorcerer known to exist. The others had either been killed or disappeared. Before him, Raino Shadowblood, but he was killed when he chose to walk the path of the Forsaken.

Back in the Republic, Legion Cage Xavier, son of Taj Odin Xavier served in the Republic's military proudly. He was just over the age of twenty. He answered directly to General Ector Von Griswald. His unit had been charged with the order of bringing back the leader of the Black Sand Gypsy clan. The Black Sand gypsy clan united several under its banner and pledged a vicious war attacking and killing those from the walls of the Republic.

Since the invader ships of the North, Corvana had ceased years ago, the people of Lotus had scarcely been seen. This erupted the strongest clan of gypsies to terrorize the Republic, somehow hoping to push the inhabitants off their land or to force them to concede. Take down the walls of the Republic; grant a gypsy sanctuary around the legendary Tree that supposedly held the power and life force to all the Plantons, a people native only to the Republic.

Legion was the leader of a small unit of men. He'd worked his way through the ranks like the rest of them. A spitting image of his father, the blond-haired, blue-eyed warrior carried not only his genetic makeup, but his attitude and heart as well. Unlike Taj, he grew up in the Republic so his favored style of fighting was sword and board and his skin looked to be almost natural to the desert, kissed by the sun.

His uncle Adrian Xavier was the Republic's Military strategist for a long time. After the war finally came to an end, he retired and returned home with his beloved wife Destiny and their children. Only Legion remained, Legion and one other. Taj bore twins with Sasha. And Adrian bore himself three children with Destiny as well.

Adrian, Destiny, their three boys Dorian, Simon, and Gideon, along with their sister Dusk and their aging great uncle Cyclor all left the Republic for Eternis. Adrian pleaded with Dauge and legion to go with them. Legion's duty to the Republican military was just about up. Adrian wasn't as worried for him as he was Dauge.

At an early age, Dauge was taken from plain sight while playing with his big brother Legion and his twin sister Dusk. For years, he was considered missing and lost. Many believed the gypsies took him. Others claimed the people of Lotus snatched him.

On his seventeenth birthday, he returned midday. The people of the Republic rejoiced for Adrian's "adopted" son's return. A celebration was held in his honor by order of Commander Agramourne Argoste, a celebration he failed to make it to.

Since his return, Dauge had remained mostly silent and kept to himself. He clung tightly to his big brother and watched closely after his sister. He'd found himself more than once on the wrong side of the law. Time and time again, the people of the Republic just looked the other way out of respect for Adrian and his "lost" brother and family.

It had been just over three years since his return. A series of well-trained and well-skilled marksmen had just journeyed into town, seven to be exact. They'd come from all different walks of life and from all around the world. Somehow, the seven came together through arguments, drinks, food, etc. They agreed to showcase their talents against each other in a bracketed format until the best missile user was crowned champion.

Dauge took up the challenge when one of the men was given a bye in their first round. His adversary was a half-elven man dual wielding crossbows. Dauge's throwing blades found their marks, disabling the weapons and humiliating "The Crossbow King."

The people were surprised Dauge took to the tournament and further won using throwing daggers over crossbows. Apparently, in the tournament, any weapon considered a missile could be used. The six remaining were surprised at Dauge's victory. The others trained and practiced daily. Dauge never trained. The people of the Republic knew his skill. He hunted the native Dune Beasts since his return for coin. He was off on one of his ventures collecting hides so that he could return and collect coin.

Chapter 19

Legion Cage was the spitting image of his father. He stood just a bit taller at six and half feet tall. He kept his flowing blond hair shoulder length, just like his father. Eyes as blue as the ocean penetrate all who looked into them. At just over twenty years of age, Legion was already a scarred mess.

Unlike his father who hailed from Eternis, a city that instinctively instilled the training of two weapons, or dual wielding, Legion took the path of the Republic, the place he called home. He fought well for his age and level of experience with sword and board, though his weapon of choice was the morning star.

Legion was returning from a victorious day against the Black Sands gypsy clan. Malgar, one of the leading forces behind the clan's attacks against the Republic, had been successfully apprehended.

The doors to the city opened as they'd done so many times for him. He loved it. He lived in what he felt was the most protected country in the world. He'd fought for them valiantly, both as a member of the military and currently as a member of an elite hunting party.

Legion and his crew of eight men returned to the city as heroes once again. He loved the attention but posed as if he hated it. His leather garments were pieced with parts of chain and iron, specifically built for him. It was built to maximize protection while minimizing hindrances.

His shield was gone. It'd been lost in the effort against that damned tiefling Malgar. Malgar was also responsible for a member of his team's death. It was the first man he'd ever lost.

Usually, through the crowds of people he could find his brother, Dauge. This time Dauge wasn't to be found. He was probably out hunting the Dunarian, or Dune Beast, a savagely vicious creature of mangy white fur, sharp teeth, and claws, something like a savage looking oversized were-dog.

Dauge couldn't make it in the military. He didn't like people telling him what to do. He couldn't find work anywhere that fit his credentials. Hunting the dune beasts on his own was the only thing he found suitable for his talents. It was all he wanted to do. Being in the wild alone in this day and age was usually suicide, but somehow Dauge managed very well.

He'd recently enrolled in that tournament where the contestants would fight with missiles. To win, one had to either disarm or draw first blood against their opponents to including fatal shots, though those were looked down upon.

"Legion always gets his target."

Legion looked up. As always, he toted the bagged prisoner. Legion had a tendency to bound, bag, and drag his prisoners all the way back. Never once did he ever ask for assistance unless there were numerous bags.

Legion unstrapped the vest that was tied to the ropes that connected to the bag. He was huffing and puffing. He was happy. He wasn't far from his brother when it came to taking orders but Ector was a man he could listen to and appreciate. Ector had been his guide since he was a child, Ector and his Uncle Adrian and great Uncle Cyclor.

Ector was old, nearing his fiftieth birthday. Legion knew his birthday was close. He turned to his men and signaled for them to get the bagged to the proper personnel. They did as instructed.

"I've not yet felt, Sir Ector," he said, happy to see his training mentor.

Ector was knighted not long after Taj left the Republic for the North. It was a title he held in high esteem. He was proud of it and proud to serve to the Republic and his deity Hellwing.

"Just like your father," Ector said.

Legion grimaced. "Not just like my father. My father abandons his people."

"He didn't abandon you." Ector was always trying to help Legion understand why his father left.

"He left and never returned."

"His fate is still uncertain, young one. He could have perished trying to save the Republic, his family, and you. Some time after he left, the war ceased. The ships stopped coming. Didn't you learn that in your schooling?"

"I don't care. It was a suicide mission and he had a child and others on the way."

Ector just smiled and bowed, showing courtesy and friendship to Legion and turned to walk away. In his old age, he'd become wise. He knew walking away from the boy would get him to think more than any words could at the given moment.

Legion thought to himself. He needed a drink and a stout one. Atherton's Golden Wing was sounding pretty good, he thought. He took a one final glance over. All of his people were gone doing their duties. His duties for the moment were done. Finally, he could relax.

He grabbed a taxi boy manning a half carriage, just a soft place to sit big enough for two or three with two wheels and an extension of wooden poles all the way down. The young boy manned the little taxi for Legion. He was too tired to walk and besides, his feet hurt.

The Golden Wing was filled with regulars and people he knew. As luck would have it, Tanya was working. She was his favorite waitress. She was a young woman maybe a year or two his junior. Her dark skin meshed well with her green eyes and auburn hair.

"Legion," she said playfully as walked in the door.

Keeping his usual manners about him, he winked and kept going to a table he knew was in her section. He was becoming a local legend and a true problem for the gypsy clans that threatened war and violence against the Republic.

Before he knew it, his table was littered with people from all walks of Republican life, talking with him, asking him questions about his latest capture, etc. etc.

Tanya finally made it over to his table.

"The usual?" she asked flirtatiously.

"Why not?" he answered, as monotone as humanly possible.

A familiar face was in the room but it wasn't one he could pin a name to. He wasn't drinking and resembled the other tiefling he'd just captured quite well. The red-skinned creature just twirled his knifepoint on the bar and glared at Legion as if he'd known him his whole life. Or worse, was plotting something against him. Legion shook it off. It wasn't a big a deal. It wasn't a big deal at all.

The night was going good. As the night owls came out and Atherton's Golden Wing flourished with the "best the Republic had to offer," Tanya and Legion continued to get better acquainted.

The tiefling made a pass at Legion. Out of instinct, Legion reached out from his table and grabbed his wrist. Tanya was still trying to straddle and kiss him. The tiefling had his attention now.

"I know you friend?" Legion questioned, looking up past Tanya's head to the tie fling's eyes.

The tiefling looked down and cracked a cocky grin. He pulled his hand away and kept walking. Legion's anger nourished his entire body with the man's refusal to answer. Just when Legion was preparing to get out of his chair and call out the tiefling, the tiefling turned.

"I meet your brother tomorrow at noon. Tomorrow the Republic learns he's not the best with a knife. I'm going to draw first blood. I'll probably kill him."

Legion pushed Tanya out of his lap and leaped to his feet. The tiefling just kept walking. Tanya reached for Legion across his chest.

"Let it go," she said.

"Did you hear what he said? That's my brother he's talking about, my little brother!"

"Your brother signed up for that tournament, that challenge of projectile weapons."

"I didn't hear about it."

"There were seven foreigners who agreed to a tournament. The tournament put them each against each other in a bracket format. The entire city of Zzyyx in the Republic knows about it. Your brother just stepped in to make the numbers even. He humiliated the first guy and these guys are supposed to be some of the best in the world. That tiefling, Ekar… he's predicted to win the whole thing and he's got it out for your brother."

"What, why?" Legion was confused but it was coming together for him.

"I don't know. You know your brother. The people here look at Dauge like he's some kind of savior half-devil or something. Everyone's afraid of him and Ekar wants to put an end to that reputation. He's just one of those guys."

"Can he beat Dauge?"

Tanya smiled and kissed Legion's chest. She rubbed on him and took his hand. She was finally off work. Her shift was done. Right behind the tiefling, Tanya and Legion left the Golden Wing as well.

"Can anyone beat your brother? You're my guy and your brother still scares me."

Legion laughed. "Yeah he has that affect on people."

Chapter 14

He was running late. He had that tournament to get to. If he missed it, oh well, he thought. He only offered to enter to even the numbers anyway. His hunting trip turned out to be successful.

Dauge made it back to the city. It was bustling and moving as it always was. He dropped off carcasses and made his coin. Even he couldn't stand his clothing after. It was tattered, cut up, and doused in blood. He always knew how to make an appearance.

Dauge was shorter than his big brother, only about five feet seven inches. His body was lean like his father's but still stockier than Legion's. His hair was as black as a vampire's heart and flowed down, touching the top of his butt. He wore it down usually, unless hunting of course.

Dauge redressed himself with a simple white shirt and black breeches. There wasn't any reason to change his boots. They were still good. Dauge was possibly the most street savvy guy in the Republic. He used his keen senses and vigilant eye to always a keep a step ahead of the rest.

Dauge made it all the way to his destined appointment. There was a small crowd already waiting on him; his next opponent was one of them. A dwarf hailing from Thox was the next in his path to victory. In the crowd he saw his brother Legion. It silently pleased him. His big brother admired his tenacity and ability.

This man's missile of choice was the sling. Typical dwarf, he assumed. Only, this dwarven rock thrower only wore regular clothes, no armor, and carried nothing but a rugged brown sling that matched the color of his bland clothes. His head was full of ratty blond hair and a matching beard flowed down from his face.

The two agreed to the test and the crowd fell silent. The dwarf slowly started playing with the moving of his sling. Sling, Dauge pondered. It was a unique weapon to use these days and one Dauge had never faced.

Just like that, the dwarf fooled the entire crowd. Many believed a dwarf not to be fast enough for a tournament of missiles. Before the crowd could even blink, the frayed ends of the sling were looking Dauge directly in the eye. The dwarf's full throwing posture froze. The holster of the missile and the rock itself both fell softly to the dirt beneath him. Dauge's single throwing dagger cut the very sling in two; sending the missile portion and its holster to the ground, thus leaving its wielder disarmed and Dauge the victor.

The crowd hesitated and then erupted into a big cheer. Dauge turned to walk away. His brother broke through the crowd to join his side. The crowd wasn't as big as was planned or even had been for the previous bouts. Something was going on at the head of the city.

"Dauge, what's going on?" Legion asked his recently victorious little brother. Dauge wasn't one for praise and Legion knew that. So, out of respect he knew better than to comment on his recent humiliation of his latest opponent.

"I don't know," he said coldly. Without elaborating at all, Legion could tell from his body language that he clearly wanted to check it out.

The two brothers walked with Dauge, ignoring the praises of the city. The remaining contestants seemed to be following Dauge. Or perhaps they were just curious as to what was going on at the front of the city. What was going on? All of a sudden, the main gates of the Republic had the people's attention.

A great opening was left with guards keeping the people from passing. Dauge and Legion arrived just as the point of interest seemed to be entering the city. An ancient elf, older than any he'd ever seen, led the way. Completely cloaked in blue robes, only his elven finger and points from his ears sticking from his hood told the people what he was. He was thin and brittle looking. His snow-white hair cried out from the orifice of the cloak. His hands rested comfortably on an archaic-looking silver staff infused with gold, diamonds, and other precious ores and glyphs.

To his immediate left stood another elf, a smaller elf wearing simple green leggings with a matching shirt. Scars covered the elf. His hair was pulled back and rested in a tail down the creature's back. He looked somewhat familiar to Legion, though he couldn't place a name or reason why.

Behind the two followed an arsenal of guardsmen wielding some type of giant diamond-like structure no one present had ever seen before. However, almost all of them knew by sight exactly what it was. It was what was believed to be, Astral Diamond, the most precious form of ore in existence and rarely known to exist.

The people of the Republic were mesmerized. The cloaked head of the staff-wielding elf tilted. A shimmering glare caught both Legion and Dauge by surprise. The two elven men made their way toward the brothers. The convoy carrying the astral diamond continued to march. Now, a closer examination told the brothers and everyone else something was inside; a body rested within the legendary ore coffin.

The hood floated from the withered elf's head. His right eye was missing. It had been replaced with a shimmering green orb with some sort of additional yellow glare.

"Legion?" he stated in the form of a question.

"Who are you?" Legion asked.

"I am a friend of your father's."

"My father is in Eternis… Friend," the elder brother replied. Legion hated the father that left him. His Uncle Adrian, the man who married his mother was his real father.

"No, he is in that box. I've come to return him."

Dauge kept an eye on both of the fragile looking elves. Neither seemed to be threatening in anyway whatsoever; that wasn't stopping Dauge from staying ready.

"Our father left before I was born and when Legion was a boy. He was a coward. We care not for his glamorous return or why he's being honored; to the hells with him." Dauge finally spoke his peace.

"You'll hold your tongue when you speak of Taj Odin Xavier. I don't care who you are." The elf didn't take well to the younger brother's words.

"Mal," started the other elf, placing a hand over his shoulder.

Dauge noticed something about the elder elf's orb eye. Something in it was staring at him, glaring at him; something in it wanted him but he couldn't put his finger on it.

"My father abandoned his duty and his family," started Legion.

The ancient elf's hands dropped the staff and filled with a purple energy. The energy raised the elf's hands, sending a nonlethal blast to the elder brother's chest. The old elf held the power on Legion, forcing him to the ground unable to move.

Dauge jumped to action but a similar bolt from the elf's other hand put him in the dirt in a similar position. The ancient elf, Taj's old friend, had heard enough.

"That's enough! Speak not of what you do not know! Taj died for this country, a land not his own! He did it for the greater good of the entire world. Corvana would have taken the Republic and then the rest of it."

Legion, Dauge, and the rest of the Republic stopped at the ancient elf's angry words. Corvanian ships or troops of any kind hadn't been seen in some amount of years. Where were these people from? Who were they? Why weren't the guards, troops, and soldiers of the Republic helping them?

"You'll hear my story. You'll hear his story," the elf continued, nodding his head at the astral diamond coffin passing by. "Whether you like it, or not."

Soon, Malakai and Giovanni were sharing a congregation hall of the Republic's elite politicians with the most powerful men in the country. Legion and Dauge were also among the crowd.

While at sea, Malakai was ordered to hold and then was boarded by several patrolling ships of the Republic. After Malakai told the story of Taj and older guards, making out Taj's face through the thick reddish diamond coffin, they changed their tune and royally escorted the soldier of the Republic home.

Giovanni was reunited with Icis and their son. She'd waited for him loyally and passionately since he left. She admitted she'd planned to live celibately in honor of her husband's life and to wait for him in the afterlife.

Malakai's passionate story of Taj filled the hearts of everyone. It soon spread throughout the land and Taj was recognized as the greatest warrior and soldier in the Republic's history. Malakai's telling of how Taj Odin Xavier singlehandedly caused the downfall of the mightiest nation of the now two known pantheons, three considering the Broken Lands, made even the sturdiest tough guys shed tears.

Taj's story spread throughout the lands. His legacy surpassed that of even his own father. Taj accomplished almost everything he ever wanted. He just didn't live long enough to see it.

Eventually, Malakai embraced the charge of bringing the body all the way back to Eternis where Taj's family retired to. His final shadow secret was finally going to be at rest. The orb, the relics, the residium, the astral diamond coffin, it was all a shadow ritual used to keep Taj's soul bound to the final piece of the puzzle, the demon orb in Malakai's eye.

Taj watched everything as it happened through Malakai's eyes, respectively. When they reached Eternis, Taj saw the one thing he couldn't have ever possibly prepared for.

Looking through the window of a simple home, Taj's eyes through the doorway of the orb fell upon his own big brother, now christened with age holding his very own Destiny in his hands. Four children showered them with love in a picture-perfect story being told through the glass of the window in their home. Three boys and a girl exchanged gifts with each other and their parents.

Taj's heart sank. He'd accomplished it all. His own legacy was the greatest in all of history. He singlehandedly destroyed the kingdom of Corvana and defeated every enemy he'd ever faced. He was even responsible for the final banishing of Falling Star. Twice. As quickly as he could, he ordered Malakai to release him. And release him he did. With it, the final piece of his shadowy power. Shadow sorcerers were all in one way or another connected to Falling Star and/or Gemini. He was of the most powerful being connected to both.

He knew should he continue to utilize his shadowy abilities, it would recreate the shadow in the world. The scars and damage were of course still there and very plentiful. That shadow stuff was already calculated into Thedia. Calling upon powers native to Falling Star and Gemini could once again strengthen them and possibly even reconnect the planes of existence.

For the greater good of the world, Malakai's shadow sorcery and shadow dragon sorcery would have to never again be seen, heard, or even felt. He would live the rest of his days a broken old man with a dull green orb for an eye.

After Taj's personal mausoleum was completed and Taj was buried. Malakai retired, living in a guest room in the manor of Adrian and Destiny Xavier. Giovanni returned once again to Icis back in the Republic.

Legion and Dauge followed Malakai and Giovanni to Eternis. It was both of their first time to their family's homeland and the Xavier manor, where Adrian and Destiny now lived.

After their father's funeral, the two brothers left the city as well. Legion's mother and Dauge's adopted mother was completely distraught. Dauge's twin, the beautiful Dusk wanted to go with them. He refused. She was stunning. She was slightly shorter, thin, and nimble with weight in all the right places. Her black hair and dark eyes seductively could sell her on any man she wanted.

Dauge couldn't function right with her around. He would always be watching out for her over everything else. He felt the same for Legion and his other siblings but Legion was the only one who could somewhat take care of himself.

Malakai left a gift package for Legion just before he was to depart with Dauge. Legion signed up along with Dauge on a convoy mission. A noblewoman from Thox was looking for an escort back after personal affairs in Eternis left her husband dead. She believed more enemies were after her.

Six were charged with the task of bringing the wealthy Thoxen back to her homeland across the Hangman's Straight. Dauge and Legion were among those six. Dusk, Dauge's twin sister was heartbroken to see her twin home and gone so suddenly, and worse, he refused to allow her to join him.

After the first day on the transport ship and his first guard duty, guard detail went in teams of two and Legion and Dauge were allowed to work together, Legion and Dauge retired to their room.

Legion opened the gift box given to him by Malakai just before leaving Eternis. Removing the top of the box revealed two beautifully crafted swords, possibly the best he'd ever seen. The craftsmanship couldn't be traced or found; lost designs and symbols danced around their magnificent hilts.

The swords had a bit of an aura to them. He remembered Malakai's stories of Taj's legendary swords and how he and Giovanni both told how they were attained. The swords' glow brightened as Legion's hands neared them. He wasn't sure of them at all. His room was bare with nothing more than the walls and their beds to keep the two entertained. Now, the swords lit the room up like a magically infused chandelier.

Back home in Eternis, a sleeping elf with a single eye awoke. Visions came to him of his old friend's swords and the son who was about to grip them. Memories of the myths told to him over and over; if the swords did exist and they were used by a true wielder in unison, then the wielder would be unbeatable in combat.

Taj had seen defeat and near defeat many times. True wielder, Malakai eventually learned through his time with Taj, meant one whom both swords equally chose as its wielder.

Malakai choked and coughed seeing the hands of Legion grip their hilts. Back in the room, Dauge fell back seeing the brightness of the swords as Legion pulled them from the box. Phantasmal ghost chains sprang from their hilts penetrating Legion's soul through his flesh.

"Leej!" Dauge screamed.

"Wait," Legion demanded.

In an instant, the swords forced his arms spread and then clanged together. A flash of light blinded the two. Smoke and ash filled the air and draped the walls of the room. Dauge and Legion stood embracing one another looking down at a very odd and unique scene. The swords were gone. A gorgeous morning star, seemingly sized to perfectly fit Legion, rested where the swords had been. It had a prismatic glow and aura to it. Its chain was magnificent as was its massive ball and hilt.

"What the hell is that?" Dauge asked.

Legion didn't answer. He just grabbed it, taking it in two hands. Two separate and very distinguished voices quickly took over his mind, explaining to them their very origin. LORE was the weapon infused with the ancient king of Esgaria, now known as the Broken Lands, Goddimus Ryven and was merciful and honest. SOUL was the weapon infused with Arakros Awestrike, the great general of Esgaria that singlehandedly sealed the first portal opened by the Shadow World connecting the two planes of existence. It was bloodthirsty, hungry, and eager for battle, victories, and glory.

Since Arakros returned from that portal as Arakros the Chaotic and slew Goddimus, the two had never been civil. Times forged them as weapons, though how was lost. Arakros singlehandedly forced the breaking up and downfall of Esgaria and laid the groundwork for the pantheon to be merged with the primary pantheon, thus resulting in the once fruitful lands of Esgaria becoming broken.

However, their unified respect for Legion's father, their previous wielder brought them together for the first time in eons. Times had changed and Thedia still needed them. Goddimus was still the very same king and leader he'd always been. Arakros was no longer the General that led his armies to so many victories allowing him to conquer the small pantheon, nor was he the Chaotic man who slew him. Arakros remembered dying to the legendary barbarian Mars Mightfist, of the kingdom of Craylanx.

The Mightfist bloodline still ruled the city-state of Craylanx of the Nine Kingdoms. Arakros was now an entity guiding a great weapon. That weapon was once so powerful it fueled an animated dragon carcass mistaken to be a draculich. That carcass was annihilated when it faced Raino Shadowblood there in the Broken Lands.

Taj survived that fight, another reason for the two to honor them.

"Consider us as friends. I will remind you of who you are and what you deserve by right. I will help you see the best in people and help you show mercy when you do not wish to," Goddimus said.

"I will guide you victoriously through your battles. I will help you fight on when you think all is lost. With me at your side there is no battle unwinnable," Arakros added.

Malakai was seeing and hearing everything. He grinned wider than he'd ever grinned before. It all made sense. Never before was a wielder equally chosen by both blades. Then again, until Taj Odin Xavier, no one had ever wielded both blades. Now, the blades were one and no longer swords. They were a massive and magnificent morning star.

"It's talking to me," Legion said.

"What's talking to you?" Dauge knew but he still had to ask to be sure.

"The weapon, Dauge, what else would I be talking about?"

"I figured. I just had to be sure," Dauge replied.

"It's magical," Legion said abruptly.

"Of course it's magical. What's it saying?"

"It's going to guide me. It wants to help me," answered Legion.

"They did belong to Taj, um, I mean Father," said Dauge, calling Taj father for the first time.

One of the voices called out to Legion again. "Raino's actions calloused the world, scarring it indefinitely. Gemini the Invader and Falling Star's invasions forever weakened Thedia. We're nothing like we once were. Maybe, with your help young Legion, we can rebuild and regain our powers. We were forged from Thedian soil and ash. Like Thedia, we're weaker than we once were. With your help, Legion, we can perhaps be restored to our former glories."

Legion looked at Dauge. Dauge didn't know what to think. As the sword continued to talk, Legion continued to relay the messages to Dauge. Eventually, Legion put down the weapon in order to get sleep.

The brothers talked through the next hour of home and why Legion wanted to leave so hastily. Truthfully, he didn't have an answer. How could Uncle Adrian marry his little brother's sweetheart? Dauge's only answer was that Adrian and Destiny both found sanctuary and in each other's arms in dealing with Taj's assumed death.

The team handled their mission and docked at Port Agatha in Thox. Legion spent every waking second away from the mission and sleep with his new weapon, learning about it, learning from it, and training himself with it. Dauge honored his brother's request for privacy, choosing to train privately himself and meditate. Dauge was one with the elements, so to speak, a talent he'd yet to tell even his closest sibling.

The two planted their feet firmly on the ground at Agatha. They'd heard the stories of the country's beauty but seeing it firsthand proved the stories only did an injustice to the country's splendor.

"Well brother, we're here. I'm not sure if that's a good thing or bad. I've heard the people here are smug," Legion said, half laughing. His arrogance was too strong to keep in.

"Good, then you'll fit right in." Dauge let a smirk run across his face. He looked at Legion.

Legion looked back at Dauge. The two brothers laughed and entered the city together. They were young, experienced, sons of a legendary man, and one of them possessed what one might consider the greatest weapon on Thedia.

Chapter 15

In the coming days, the brothers found sanctuary in an upper-class inn called The Dripping Scale. It rested just off the port side and was the biggest and most successful tavern, inn, and gambling hall in Port Agatha.

The Dripping Scale was one of the largest and oldest buildings in all of Thox, consisting of five floors and larger than any two other inns combined. The building was old and in need of some remodeling, especially on the outside. The owners believed its age, wear, and tear was what gave the place character and kept the people coming in from port coming to her.

The innkeepers were usually young and rather nice, mostly humans and half-elves. Dauge and Legion shared a room on the third floor. At first, they offered the two a deal for a room on the first but Dauge wouldn't hear of it.

Dauge was always contemplating strategies. Being on the first floor was a death wish in the event a trained enemy wanted you dead. On the third floor, window access made scaling the wall to the roof or down to the ground extra options. On the first, if said enemy had people waiting outside the window, it would be much more difficult to escape.

Legion admired and appreciated Dauge's intellect and keen strategic mindset. The current goal was simple, to find work. Their family was gone from the Republic, a place they were born and raised only because their father went there to fight. Now, their family was back in their native hometown, Eternis.

The war with the Northern Invaders, Corvana, was over. It'd been over for some time. The new war was the one with the gypsies. Dauge really didn't care for it as his mother was a gypsy, of the Black Sands clan no less.

Eternis was at peace the way it was supposed to be and their family was safe there. Work was everywhere but there was always work in Eternis. Days came and went with offers slamming up against the table all the time. Young adventuring parties were always looking for quality talent to join their ranks. Legion was something between a true warrior and a barbarian and Dauge was, well, just Dauge.

Legion came across the man who would ultimately sell the idea of his team. He'd just finished at the training grounds with his favorite new weapon, the morning star, when a poster advertising two of the city's best gladiators caught his eye.

Dauge was off doing his own thing. A one-on-one gladiatorial battle between champions, he thought, sounds fun. He continued to think and laugh silently to himself. Legion was all the way on the other side of Agatha in a place called The Broken Oar when he saw the poster.

One of the creatures on the poster was a goliath, or half-giant, or creature of giant ancestry. He was bald and stood massively over his dwarven counterpart in the picture.

The Broken Oar was a place primarily for soldiers, adventurers, and the like. That's why Legion chose the place. If he was going to find good work, a place like Broken Oar was going to be the place to give it to him.

"It's going to be a great fight. It's got your interest?"

The Broken Oar was irregularly busy. Legion was just about on his way out. He wanted to return home to see if Dauge wanted to accompany him to the fights. They'd been in Thox for a couple of days now and if something didn't turn up soon, the two agreed returning to Eternis would be in their best interest.

Legion turned around, startled but unmoved. He took a step back to better gauge the man talking to him. It was a half-elf decorated in nice leathers, studded, and enchanted, at least minimally. The man was short, maybe just under five-and-a-half-feet tall and barely weighed a buck and a half, maybe. He wore a white cloak with red designs over his leathers. Bracers, leggings, with this guy everything seemed to match and look perfect.

His eyes were light and his hair was covered. At his side rested two short swords and a sickle, cocked just to the side of his front toward the left. Two blade hilts extended outward from his leather wrist and hand guards.

"Maybe, I know you friend?" Legion answered firstly with a maybe and then followed up with a question of his own.

"You know, the funny thing about this fight, that goliath is fighting for his freedom. He owed another year to the arenas but I paid it off for him. And in the event he survives later, he'll be joining me."

"Joining you?" Legion asked.

"Well hopefully, otherwise it's not going to be money well spent." The gentleman laughed and put his arm around Legion's neck, rubbing the opposite shoulder of the one he was standing near.

Legion brushed away casually and politely from the man.

The half-elf pulled back his cloak's hood extending his hand out to Legion. "The name's Dash."

"And what's your interest in me, Dash? I assure you I have no interest in you." Legion didn't know what to make of it.

"Relax friend. I've seen you at the training grounds with that weapon of yours." Dash stopped to point and appreciate Legion's morning star. "I'm putting something together and I'm thinking you might want to hear what I have to say."

Legion paused. The man was talking about work but what kind of work? Whatever it was, he wanted a well-established gladiator to and was even willing to gamble a lot of money on his winning/surviving and then willingness to join him. Legion didn't know a lot about this Dash character but one thing he did know, he surely didn't lack confidence.

"My brother and I only work together. If you take on one of us you have to take on the both of us, and consequently, we both have to agree to the job."

"So you're saying as long as he agrees, you'll take it?"

"Dash, I haven't heard your proposition yet."

Dash smiled. He knew he was getting ahead of himself but that was part of his game. He laughed turning back to the barkeep to order another round for the two of them.

"Why don't we go and watch the goliath Pitt retire from the arenas victoriously together? Afterward we can go and find your brother and I will be able to explain the whole thing to the lot of you all at one time. Come on, what do you say?"

Legion contemplated. He drove a hard bargain. The guy was courteous and friendly and certainly not pushy. What was the worst that could happen if he chose to just listen to his proposition over some food somewhere, along with his brother?

"I'll meet you there. Let me know where your seating is. I have to get my brother first." Legion said. He couldn't help himself. He had to know. The man touched his curiosity. "So why are you throwing coin down on a gladiator that could still possibly die and might not even join you should he live?"

"He'll join, friend. He'll join. He has nothing, and if not for me, he'd be spending another year gambling daily for his life. I've been saving for quite a while to buy this man's freedom."

"Freedom. You do mean you're not buying a slave but rather a man's freedom."

"Yes, that's correct."

"You said you're putting something together. I take it you mean something that involves leaving the city?"

"Yes, adventuring," he answered.

"You're looking for adventurers?"

"I'm looking for people who are smart enough and brave enough to take up a golden opportunity when presented to them. This world lacks heroes of old. Legends were forged by starting out just like me… and you!" Dash answered becoming more excited as he said the word you to Legion, hoping to sell him even more on the idea.

"My brother and I are looking for work, Dash."

"Ah, then my opportunity might be just what you're looking for." Immediately following the end of his words, Dash's grin lit up like a Draconic festival.

Legion couldn't help it. Something about this man was gentle and smooth. He seemed genuine, honest, and truly excited about the proposition he still had to tell Legion about.

Dash and Legion finally shook hands and left the tavern and inn together. Together, they reunited with Dauge who was at first skeptical. Dauge was just about to walk into the front door of The Dripping Scale when Legion called out to him.

Historically, even the quick-to-anger Legion was quicker to accept a hand in friendship than the elusive and crafty Dauge.

Dash stayed back. Legion walked up. "It's okay little brother, the man offers work."

Dash stood elegant in posture watching the bigger Legion approach his smaller sibling. Looking on, Dauge noticed more than a few people tipping their hats and showing other courtesies to the stranger that just arrived at the scale with his brother.

"It seems you're not the only one that knows him. What kind of work?" Dauge asked, still hesitant of the man. Dauge trusted a handful of people. Other than Legion and Adrian, the others were only known to him.

"I know what you're thinking, little brother. We have to entrust our services to someone or something. I don't know what kind of work. I told him you had to be present in order for me to even hear what he had to say."

Dauge nodded. He liked that. He liked how his brother respected his abilities, intuition, and personal opinions. Dash nodded subserviently to show his compliance with Legion's words.

Dauge felt uneasy about it but Legion was right. He'd have to eventually entrust in someone if he was going to find work. Why not try this Dash character? A closer look told Dauge he had elven blood but wasn't truly a half-elf.

"What's your blood ancestry, Dash?" Dauge asked politely.

"Half eladrin to be precise; I usually answer the question claiming half-elven because the races are so close and to keep it simple, I just say half-elven."

Dauge nodded. The half creature seemed to know what he was talking about. And Dauge knew he was waiting for him to respond.

"Let's make our way to the arenas. We're wasting time, brother," Legion said.

Dauge looked around. Dash's eyes told a calming story; they comforted Dauge. It either meant he was comfortable in his lies or he was being legitimate and honest. Dauge answered in his own way. He began making his way to the arena.

Chapter 16

On the way to the gladiatorial arena of Port Agatha, Dash started his story. Legion listened more closely than Dauge. Dauge's apparent ill concern for Dash's words concerned him. He was Dauge, a man that was not to be figured out or understood. He walked slightly ahead of his brother and Dash.

"What's wrong with your brother? Doesn't he want to know what's going on?" Dash asked. Now, Dauge's actions had him guessing.

"He's always listening, Dash." Legion answered truthfully. He didn't know why Dauge was ignoring the conversation.

"Grogan's Mill," Dash said.

"Grogan's Mill?" Legion repeated.

"Have you heard of it?" asked the half-eladrin.

Secretly, Dauge was listening. Hearing was his greatest sense. He heard every word between the two, even through the waves of people coming and going all throughout the port.

"It's an old farm town on the outskirts of Thox's eastern side, toward the Mogra, right?" Legion answered.

He was correct. Just on the outskirts of Thox's eastern border rested an ancient town as old as any. No one really knew how it survived all those years or why Thox hadn't annexed it. It was a simple town that did most of its trading with the mega-power, Thox.

It was relatively close to Targnok, a kingdom of orcs and such as well as a Mogra. In Thedia, three of these Mogras existed. No one knew exactly what they were or how they got there. One was in the Northern waters. Another was to the far Northeast of the pantheon near the kingdom

Skye. And the last was in the Southeastern part of the pantheon near the kingdoms of Thox and Targnok.

Old tales tell of stories as wild as the fey and worse. The legends of old told of creatures and treasures that existed within the Mogras far beyond the reckoning of mortal understanding. Of course, these were just all tales and nothing more. Even the heroes of legend rarely drifted too far into a Mogras area. And it was even more uncommon for one to return from it.

"Yes of course I've heard of it. It's just an old farm town that hasn't met its end yet. Though it surely will eventually, it's surrounded by too much," Legion replied.

"Precisely, but for some reason it's made it this long," Dash said.

"So what's your point?" Legion knew he was on to something. Come to think of it, he was right. How had Grogan's Mill survived for so long right there in the middle of it all? It came to Legion just as Dash answered him. Simultaneously, Dauge chimed in, saying the same thing as Dash word for word.

"The city holds a secret," said both Dauge and Dash.

Dauge stopped in his tracks, turning to watch Legion and Dash make their way back up to him.

"How did you come to this conclusion, Dash?" asked Dauge.

Dash smiled. He'd finally gotten Dauge's attention. The three marched on toward the arena with Dash revealing puzzle pieces piece by piece to the brothers.

Grogan's Mill was a simple town of agriculture that sold most of its products to Thox. For some reason Thox, even in it's more tyrannical days, never tried to take the city, and not too far away to the west was Targnok, another kingdom that only worked in trade with the town.

Creatures straying too far from the Mogra occasionally gave trouble but that was about it. Usually, Grogan's Mill had the means to hire the appropriate people to engage the problems.

"They've had a serious incursion of shifters ransacking the city and attacking their villagers. People coming and going are being mauled. Several werewolves have also added to the situation."

Legion took over the moment Dash paused, finishing his words for him. "We take care of the situation for Grogan's Mill and we request we'll only do it at the expense of something extraordinary."

"Yes!" Dash said excitedly. "People have helped the town for years, but if you don't ask then you shall not receive. You know what I mean?"

"It just seems too easy, like it should have or could have been done before," said Legion

"Some of the greatest rewards are the simplest to acquire. Usually, they're just overlooked or never asked for." Dash said.

"Either way, it's work for now," Dauge said surprisingly. It wasn't like Dauge to have that kind of attitude and not second and triple guess everything. Legion smiled and agreed. "You have my little brother agreeing to the task. Then you shall have me as well."

Dash pointed to Legion's great weapon, the morning star. "I'm curious, yet excited to see that thing in action."

"So am I," he replied just barely above a whisper.

The three made it to the arena and with Dash's connections they walked past every guard and every barricade in the place. Port Agatha's arena wasn't the fanciest but it did have some of the most colorful history. It was a simple set of bleachers built in an off-circular fashion; originally, it was meant to be oval but the engineers changed it without starting over halfway through. The imperfection of the arena became the thing's singular most popular trait.

A stone wall, maybe eight feet in height, ran around the entire battleground affront the bleachers. The field was simple, just sand, dirt, bones, and weapon and armor remnants. It was big enough for simple battles and small scenarios but mostly in Port Agatha, gladiators faced just singles competitions.

A common misconception of gladiators is the belief that in most if not all fights, a gladiator who lost would die. In truth, gladiators rarely died just for losing. The statistical average was about one in eight. Scenario battles were more dangerous than the single battles.

Today, Dash's prospect, Pitt the Goliath, would be in for a rude awakening. Initially, he was to fight in a singles fight against another gladiatorial champion from another city, presumably the capital city of Xanon. Instead, as Dash and the brothers found their seats directly in the front row just by the wall, it was announced the legendary unbeaten goliath would face five champions in a Dwarves and Giants game.

Dwarves and Giants was a game where one, two, or maybe three combatants would pair off against several smaller adversaries. The smaller combatants would be armed with little to nothing and miniscule pieces of armor while the bigger ones would be just about fully armed and protected.

In this fight, Pitt would be placed against five champions from all around Thox. Pitt alone would be the giant in this game. He was given little armor save a great steel tower shield and a giant executioner's axe that was meant to be wielded with two hands. The shield and axe wouldn't be enough to hold off five champions' attacks. The small nicks and cuts would presumably catch up with him and should the goliath even be victorious, the powers that be wanted to assure his death. Tying up all loose ends of course. The behind-the-scenes dirt on the owners, promoters, and other powers in charge was too much to risk. A man offered to buy out what was left of his contract. Pitt was an indentured servant with twelve hundred gold pieces left on his contract. His owner placed him in the arenas in hopes of making a quick fortune. It worked. Now, a half-elven man offered twice as much as what was left on his contract and offered it up front even if Pitt was to be killed in his last fight. Pitt was going to be in for the surprise of his life.

Dauge, Legion, and Dash made their way to their seats. Turkey legs and ale filled their stomachs. Pitt wasn't even the main attraction of the evening. The three talked about the farm town and its werewolf/shifter problem all throughout the preliminaries.

Then finally, Legion asked when Pitt was up. Dauge kept silent as he did mostly anyway. Dash pointed as the portcullis opposite their seats opened, revealing the biggest humanoid any of them had ever seen. Goliaths, or half-giants were usually around seven to seven and a half feet tall. This one easily broke the eight-foot mark and had a frame to go with it.

Another oddity about the creature was his thick, curly dark hair. Goliath males were always bald on top. They bore no hair of any kind on their heads. It was a genetic makeup of their kind. Yet, this one had dark curly locks down to his neck.

Only a brown piece of loincloth covered his pelvic area. Stains of blood were its only form of decoration. Giant woolen boots, similar in color and painted with bloodstains, covered the beast's feet and lower legs. In his left hand, the creature carried a tower shield as most carried a medium or great shield. It was made of steel but had seen better days. The only glamour of the creature came from his axe. It was exquisite and appeared to be brand new. Its shaft was long and wrapped carefully with dark black fabrics and materials for better grips. Its blade shined like a virgin on her wedding day.

The crowd cheered for their hero of the arena. "We want Pitt! We want Pitt! We want Pitt!" they screamed.

"There he is. What a beast!" Dash said, completely mesmerized by the creature. "I've always heard goliaths didn't have head hair. I guess that makes him just that much more grand." Once Pitt entered the arena, Dash's complete focus became trained at him.

Legion and Dauge looked at each other. Legion laughed. His fancying of the barbarian was borderline homosexual, he thought. Dauge just kept his feelings, personal opinions, and emotions to himself.

Dauge just sat in his seat waiting for the fight to be over. He wanted to watch it to appreciate the fighting and study the fighting styles of both the barbarian and his adversaries but that was the only reason.

Another portcullis built into the stone wall relatively close to the three's left side began to reel open. The iron bars and spiked bottoms heightened the anticipation of the fights even more.

From the second portcullis came five creatures, all of different races, origins, and all with different fighting styles. Pitt stepped back in order to examine the five briefly before the battle would commence.

The first was a dwarven man clad in fully plated armor and wielding a hammer nearly the size of Pitt's axe. The second was a human cloaked in robes with fire in his eyes and ice in his hands. He was frail looking with short black hair and pale skin. The third was a half-elven man outfitted like a warrior chieftain of an ancient Indian war tribe. Furs covered the man's feet, hands, pelvic area, and even his face. He looked more like a shaman than anything with bone necklaces and a bone staff in his grasp. The fourth was a goliath much like Pitt only significantly smaller, yet still over the seven and half foot mark. He was outfitted in the exact same manner as Pitt. And the last was an elven man just about five feet nine inches and truly thin and nimble looking. He wore scale armor with two short swords at his side and a bow in his hand.

This wasn't dwarves and giants, thought Pitt. This was an execution! Who wanted him free? Did she come back to buy his freedom? How did she earn the money? Was she even okay? He was just a nobody from the wilderness that found his way into civilization and then as a slave to that civilization. Now, he was going to die by the hands of that civilization and worse, never touch his beloved Shiva again.

The arena's organizer and promoter gave the signal and the fight was on. Pitt leaped high into the air landing dead center of the five who were truly not ready for the big man's dexterous maneuver. As soon as he landed, he didn't miss a step. He threw himself into a whirlwind, using his shield and his axe as weapons, connecting and clipping every single member of his opposition. One by one, they flew from their feet onto their backs. He'd drawn blood from every one of them.

A second glance told him he missed one. The human wizard teleported from his position to just a few steps back from where he was previously standing; he immediately commenced launching ice-coated missiles toward the barbarian.

Pitt stopped his flurry and threw his shield in front of him in order to shield his body from the missiles. The missile clinked and disappeared from sight. The steel tower shield had remnants of ice all around it afterward.

Pitt's heightened sense told him danger was near. His uncanny reflexes sent his body into another whirling frenzy. Before he knew it, his shield was resting nearly half a foot into the dirt with two arrowhead tips smashed underneath it. The archer tried to take advantage of his focus being elsewhere. Pitt knew the archer and the caster had to go first.

The half-elven man rose back to his feet, as did the elven archer after firing from the ground. He was good with the bow. A chant rang out from the half-elven creature and suddenly, all five of Pitt's adversaries looked cleaner, swifter, and more focused than before. He was a warlord and he was buffing his comrades.

Meanwhile back up top, Dauge found himself overly impressed with the barbarian's amazing agility, fight form, and fight IQ. He was knowledgeable of the fight game, he thought. That meant he would make a great comrade. Legion looked impressed with the archer's ability to fire from just about anywhere. He was one of those kinds of guys. He would always talk and commentate with his friends and the surrounding populace during events and games.

Dash was studying and taking notes. He mumbled something. Legion didn't catch it but Dauge thought he did. It truly shocked him, enough to ask the crafty Dash to repeat himself.

"Come again friend. What was that?" he asked.

"As a gladiator of Thox, Pitt has never even been successfully struck with anything. He's never been nicked, cut, stabbed, slashed, or anything. He's never even been caught by magic. His defense and situation and awareness are the greatest I've ever seen." Dash replied, this time going into more detail than he did originally.

Dauge took offense. His situational awareness and fight IQ and his evasive defense maneuvers were the best he'd ever seen, save those that taught him in the sands of Lotus, in the lands of the Republic of New Magic.

However, it could have possibly been true. Were Pitt's fight ability, awareness and everything else better than Dauge's? They were two different types of fighters, but the situational awareness and fight IQ was the same thing. Was Dauge better at what he did than Pitt as what he did? Dauge shrugged it off for the time being. Rather than contemplate and worry about it, Dauge felt wrapping his head around something more important like the idea of learning from each other was more efficient and effective than the alternative. Dauge watched as three of the "dwarves" in the game all missed the mighty Pitt and a rapping uppercut with his shield hand sent the opposing goliath high into the air and off of his feet, and finally to the flat of his back.

The crowd roared for Pitt. They wanted to see him victorious. The other five were known champions as well but none were nearly as popular, especially in Port Agatha. The dwarf with the hammer and the goliath with the executioner's axe double-teamed Pitt. The archer continued to let loose arrow after arrow to accommodate his teammates. The half-elven warlord continued to chant and buff his allies, boosting their abilities and powers with every chant. He even had divine healing powers to go along with his buffing ones. Lastly, the human wizard sat back sending simple magical attacks from a safe range at the barbarian.

"I think they wanted to get your money and then kill him," said Legion.

"Yes of course. Once they're through with him, why would they want him to be free? I mean, think of the dirt he's got on them. His owner is one of the most notorious in all of Thox. Pitt is out of the House of Nonus, one of the most despised houses in all of Thox." Dash was starting to lose hope for Pitt. It wasn't that Pitt had even been struck but he wasn't really dealing too much damage either. He was just constantly on the defensive. Then again, how else does one fight five truly skilled champions of the arena all while alone? Even if he had one ally, the fight could have been much more balanced but fighting alone against five is just no easy task.

Pitt's plan finally came into fruition. The archer fired his last arrows only to have them both deflected and sent toward his own teammates. One fell astray while the other slashed through the skin of the upper shoulder area of the wizard.

The elf pulled his twin short swords and Pitt simultaneously charged through both the goliath and the dwarf directly at the elf. Two heaping swings, one from the dwarf and one from the goliath both found their way to the barbarian's shield. Bing! Clang! The shield was losing its inner strength. It was bending and folding now, but Pitt made it through again unscathed.

Once out of the way and cleared from his allies, the human wizard saw his opening and released a series of magical boomerangs and exploding spheres all infused with both ice and the sonic elements. Yellow boomerangs halfway visible popped into the atmosphere, disappearing then reappearing, winding and ripping their way toward the barbarian; above his head, several giant blocks of ice flickering in and out of existence due to their sonic nature also fell toward him.

Pitt's momentous force and dexterous leaps kept him from being hit even a single time. He hopped from one foot to the other toward the left side and then back to the right, twisting and twirling like a crafty acrobat in a giant's body.

A few of the forces thrown by the wizard found their way to the shield, just about finishing it off. Finally, he was within striking distance of the elven man who was now holding both of his short swords. Pitt's position was advantageous to him, as the elf's swords couldn't reach him in return.

Pitt reared back and let an overhand swing as hard as he'd ever thrown go. The elf crossed his blades trying to get them underneath the blade of the axe where the head of the weapon and the hilt met; it worked! Unfortunately for the elf, Pitt just yanked it back and downward, disarming the warrior of his last weapons and actually pulling him down and off of his feet as well.

Without a blink of hesitation, Pitt rotated his upper body halfway around to allow his shield to be finished off by the charging goliath's axe. The other goliath had dropped his shield in order to wield his axe with two hands. Neither the opposing goliath's shield nor his axe was near the size of the massive Pitt's.

The shield folded in, crumpling up over and around the blade of his adversary's axe. Pitt was already out of the shield's grip holsters. A forward step put his foot on the back of the downed elf, completely immobilizing him.

With another turn of his body to face the goliath, Pitt thrust his axe forward hard, with both hands landing smoothly and cleanly into the stomach of his kindred. The tips of the axe's top points pierced deeply. The opposing barbarian stepped back. Pitt saw and opening and took it. He stepped from the back of the elf and flew into a whirling motion, catching the neck of the goliath in one clean sweep, beheading the beast instantly, and killing him.

The other stopped momentarily, giving Pitt enough time to grab the fallen goliath's shield. The half-elf started popping off rounds of bolts from a crossbow at him. The shield easily fended off his ranged advances. The dwarf charged forward along with the refooted elf. He'd already made it back to his feet and regained his blades.

Every gaping swing of Pitt's knocked the hammer of the dwarf and the swords of the elf away clean. Following his defensive attacks, he maneuvered his shield as so to protect from the arrows. Every time he cut one, that damned warlord would heal them. That was it, he thought. That buffer would have to go.

Finally, the barbarian from the icy south leaped high and strong, landing just before the warlord. The half-elf dropped his bow and tried to evade the inevitable. Pitt sacrificed innate powers to call upon his natural and supernatural strengths. With his axe now held in both hands and his shield once again dropped beside him, Pitt came down like a storm of rain coming to drown the lower levels of dry land. The half-elven warlord was dead, separated in two by a single swing of his axe.

The remaining three stepped back, stunned at what they'd just seen. It was as if he was more than just a mortal creature. Even for a barbarian, he moved swiftly and with more conviction than most. He was definitely a standout among mortals, among goliaths, and even among barbarians.

The barbarian let go of his axe with his left hand, allowing it to rest softly against the bloody dirt beneath him on its blade. He turned to the other three. It was a standoff. His focus was now on the wizard.

"He's a killer. There's no doubt about that," said Dash, overly pleased with his choice of companion.

"That's not always a good thing, friend," Legion said.

The entire crowd spewed in excitement. Even Dauge stood from his seat. The barbarian quickly knelt down to grab the warlord's crossbow and the crafty wizard used his telekinetic powers to grab the goliath's shield from the ground to shield him from the oncoming bolt.

It worked. However, following the release of the bolt, Pitt lunged forward with a stepping left handed overhand punch, sending the floating metallic piece of protection hard at the wizard.

"He knocked out the damn wizard!" Legion screamed.

The crowd was going crazy. Once a wizard had something mage handed or telekinetically grabbed, it was hard to take it back from them but Pitt did it with ease and knocked it twelve to fifteen feet into the man's face and upper body. The wizard's feet flew high above his head forcing his body into a rough headfirst landing.

Now, the elven swordsman and the dwarven hammer user were back and ready. Together, they simultaneously charged the winning barbarian. Pitt roared out in anger and rage, whirling his axe one, two, and even three times over his head and around his body before letting it go at the advancing obstacles.

The axe's precision nearly cut the dwarf in half. It stuck in his upper left shoulder area right through his left pectoral, penetrating his armor, cutting through it like a hot knife through butter. The still-charging elf took a clotheslining of a shot from the hilt of the axe. The hilt slammed into the elven man's face just under his chin, rendering him unconscious almost instantly.

The dwarf was awake but barely. He was bleeding out. Looking back one final time told the goliath that his caster adversary was still unconscious as well. Pitt gave himself a once over and realized that once again he'd not been struck, not even once.

He made his way to standing over the dwarf.

"Pitt! Pitt! Pitt!"

The barbarian from the icy lands of the frozen ocean just below the southern-most continent looked around at the people cheering his name. His eyes finally made it back down to the dwarf's. He was dying. His peripheral and half glance from the side told him the promoters of the day's events wanted Pitt to finish the gladiators.

Pitt dropped to a knee and placed his hands just over the wound. With one hand, he pulled the axe from the wound and with the other created an empowering blue light that covered his hand. The blue light dripped down into the wound of the dwarf, slowly healing him and sealing the wound. Within seconds, the blue healing power was gone and the dwarf was stabilized.

"He can heal?" Legion asked completely shocked at what he'd just seen.

"I've seen him do it before. I believe he can only do it once or maybe twice in a day," Dash said.

Dauge just continued to watch. His eyes transferred their attention to the promoters sitting high above the arena. He knew the old fat man with white hair calling the shots wanted Pitt dead and he would stop at nothing until he was.

Pitt stood from the wounded dwarf whose eyes were just about opened again and walked toward the portcullis he originally entered through.

"Hold!" yelled one of the white-robed old men from the top; he was clearly one of the senators or arena promoters for the day's events.

Pitt stopped. His head still half focused on the ground but his ears waiting for the man's next words. The crowd fell silent from their chants of his name. Pitt's hair dripped with sweat. The beads of sweat rolled around his twisted locks until finally freeing themselves to fall to the dirt floor below.

Dash sat back in his chair confused. Dauge knew something was up. Legion just wanted the whole thing to be over so they could either get the guy to join them or move on. He wanted to take care of the werewolf problem in Grogan's Mill, get paid and then move on.

"The dwarf and the elf were a team, Pitt. They fight as one. You have but one adversary left standing between you and freedom!" The old man's way of speaking sent the crowd into a crazed frenzy.

Suddenly, both of the iron gates opened pouring in hundreds of gladiators from all walks of life. Races and weapons masters of all types came from the gates filling the void of the arena. The old man smiled with excitement.

Dash and Legion's faces fell blank. This wasn't a spectacle but an execution. The dwarf and the elf from before rolled over, grabbing their nearby weapons. Dauge looked deftly interested in the situation. Pitt turned, grabbing the fallen goliath's axe that lay just a few feet from him. He took it into his hands like a farmer grabbing a tool to go to work. His face and mannerisms were nonchalant like a cotton picker spending the day picking cotton.

"This can't be."

"They've already used and abused him. They made their money and you paid for him. Dash, you're not getting your barbarian today," Dauge said.

Legion kept quiet for the moment, listening to his brother and the half-eladrin talk. In a bizarre turn of events, the wounded dwarf and elf took up their weapons to stand with Pitt.

"Hold! You cannot stand with your adversary! You will be shot down," said the old white-robed man in charge.

Without missing a beat, a dwarven gladiator dropped his pole-arm and shield. Then, one by one the others threw down their weapons to the monster. It wasn't that they were afraid of Pitt, though most probably would have preferred to fight just about anything else, but it was about honor and respect.

Sometimes, death happens in the games of war. The goliath and half-elf were killed but he spared those he could. The dwarf, elf, and human were spared. He'd spared so many before even when he should have killed them. Pitt was a good-hearted man trapped in a monster's body and deftly good with axes.

The wizard awoke to see two of his former allies standing with the reigning arena master. He took his chances, staying down on the dirt like a coward. Gladiators were trained to live, fight, and die with honor. The wizard would have failed in these regards.

Seeing the gladiators uphold the idea of defiance and death rather than fight their reigning hero, the white-robed senator knew he would have to take the idea and run with it.

"The rules are rules and this event was scheduled! There must be a victor among the two sides!" he yelled keeping his tone to a degree to appease the crowd.

"Pitt! Pitt! Pitt!" the crowd started again.

The old senator knew one thing. Pitt became Pitt the arena master by beating the last one. If one was to kill Pitt or even defeat him then they would take and embrace him just the same. Even he had to agree that Pitt's charisma and humble character definitely made him a unique standout of a person.

One man, known in the arenas as the current up-and-comer reacquired his glaive. He was a short red-horned, red-skinned tiefling. His tail always swayed and flickered as he walked. He'd shown powers and abilities both as a warlock and as a mystical swordsman. His black hair was braided and ran long.

The others all stepped out of his way as he made his way to Pitt. When the tiefling finally stood within the glaive's reach of the champion, the crowd fell silent and the gladiators all began taking steps backwards.

The tiefling, known as Kreydose opened his mouth to the champion. The others couldn't hear him. Not the gladiators or the crowd could hear him. Only Pitt and one other could hear his words—Dauge.

In Dauge's time with the Lotus society, he'd keened his senses to specific situations. Among all his senses, hearing was his best.

"The torch must be passed," said Kronus.

"What's he sayin…" Legion whispered to his brother.

"Shhh," Dauge said. "Quiet."

Kronus made his weapon known and seen by all in attendance. Slowly, and cautiously he pressed the edge of his sword onto the giant chest of Pitt. Pitt didn't move an inch. He took the cut with pride. His eyes stayed fixed on Kronus the entire time. Kronus' eyes fell weak. He didn't like what he was doing or why it had to be done but he did respect it. Truth be told, he wanted to face Pitt to see who the greater was. Pitt deserved his freedom and scored a lucky break somehow. So, as the powers that be would have it, Kronus turned the key to his freedom by tearing the weaves of his flesh.

Chapter 19

Just as Dash expected, Pitt took the job and the lot of them made plans to oust the lycanthropic problem for Grogan's Mill. Dash's plan grew into an even more daring dive when he chose to push the team through the problem without even consulting the agricultural farm at all.

Dash couldn't have been more impressed with his team. His bardic trade gave him access to both divine and arcanic powers but only minutely. He was, however, a crack shot with a crossbow and it came in handy more times than ten.

Dash outfitted Pitt with an enormous executioner's axe and the half-giant, also known as a goliath, was a force to be reckoned with while wielding it. Dauge kept hidden and out of the way but always found a way to make his mark in the team's enemies, more so than any of his colleagues.

The team made their way through the arsenal of shifters and lycanthropes of all shapes and races until finally making it to what Dash called, the master's cave. The cave was nothing but an abandoned mansion deep in the light forest, just outside of Thox to the East. Not too far in the distance rested the Golden Sands Desert.

The mansion was filled with traps and hazards at every turn. Mostly, it was being well guarded by the lycanthropes and the shifters following the lead lycanthrope. One thing the brothers could definitely agree on was Dash's ability to gather and dissect information.

The team was about to take down their first enemy leader. The lycanthropes were truly a growing faction in the Thoxen region. Even Targnok and the lycanthropes fell into high tension. The lycanthropes kept too many people all around and neither Thox nor Targnok wanted to deal with them.

Finally, with a heavy storm rolling in and far from anything close to a home nearby, Dash and his crew broke into the main living quarters of the mansion. It was massive and elegant, not like the rest of the mansion, a structure completely worn and beaten by the strains of time.

The room was a giant rectangle and uniquely long and wide even for the size of the mansion. The floor was laced with a red velvet covering and four giant ivory pillars kept the beautifully crafted ivory and stone ceiling from falling in on them all.

Portraits of well dressed and well groomed men and women decorated the walls of the giant room. An additional add-on was clearly built inside the room recently. It was just a long and wide wooden platform with a wooden throne like chair built into it. Several lycanthropes of various races stood around it alongside several shifters. In the chair, the clear master of the cave and leader of the infectious organization, a giant wolfman.

He was a true lycanthrope of worg nature. He wasn't a werewolf. He was a wereworg, or greater wolf. His hair was both white and gray. Immediately upon shattering the twin oak doors that led to the ballroom of the mansion, Pitt and the others fell silent to the beauty of the room and the creatures that dwelled in it. Pitt was even more star struck when he realized the wereworg was not only a wereworg but of his race as well and even more massive than he.

One by one, the others followed Pitt and his executioner's axe through the entrance where the twin doors now lay in splinters. The wereworg was being protected and guarded like a true king of ancient times. There was something more to him, though, something queer to them all. Pieces of his fur and flesh had been replaced by moving metallic parts. His knees were gyronetically formed from moving gadgets and gears. His right eye glowed a strange yellow. His torso was a mixture of metals, bones, flesh, and fur.

"A half-golem," said Dash, completely mesmerized by the creature.

"He's a goliath lycanthropic wereworg," said Pitt completely in shock.

Legion had his morning star out. It was humming with anticipation. Dauge's keen senses told him more were coming; all had not yet been revealed. Then, just as Dauge was about to say something, he stepped up to see several more shifters coming from the back of the room.

The stage-like structure was built dead center of the room and now from the room's rear more lycanthropes were coming. The creatures of the room were all decked out with beautifully crafted and ornamented bone armors and weapons. Residium was clearly used in the forging of the wereworg's soldiers' weapons and gear.

"Whatever he is, let's just kill it and get to Grogan's Mill so we can move on!" Legion was sick and tired of dealing with the lycans. He was ready to return to Thox and to some type of decent home life and living situation. They'd been out on this hunt for weeks, months!

"Easy brother, I'm not sure this is a winnable situation." Dauge gestured first to his brother and then to the others to ease off and take a step back.

Dash was grinning with excitement. This is what he lived for. There was something else to the wereworg.

"He's already wounded! I can see his ribcage!" Legion said.

The smoke hadn't even finished from the busting down of the door. The creatures of the room formally regrouped themselves and finally the wereworg stood from his wooden throne.

"He's not wounded you buffoon, he's dead," said Dash in almost a convinced whisper.

"Dead? Then why do we have to kill him?" asked Pitt as he finally tucked his chest back in. He always wanted to break down the wall or door of something important and make a grand entrance. Now he'd accomplished that goal but it wasn't exactly the picture and moment he had in mind.

"He's un…dead…" Dash said.

"A undead goliath wereworg half-golem?" Legion just restated all the combined information he'd gotten from the lot of the conversations his team was having in all of a few seconds of the door being busted down.

"If he's undead, then why've we not encountered any others? Is he not the master?" Legion asked.

Dauge was still trying to put it together as was their dashing leader, Dash Riproc. Pitt and Legion were just confused and wanted to kill, smash, and get home.

In their travels, Pitt mentioned a personal quest. He mentioned something or someone he'd like to find and reacquaint himself with sooner than later and the sooner he had the funds to do so, then that would be his number one goal.

"This is too much," said Legion, watching his brother toss back the loose ends of his cloak to grab his blades.

Pitt readied his axe and Dash his crossbow. Legion's weapon certainly had the lycanthropes at a distance. Earlier, it had enhanced and enchanted their weapons, giving them all a silver lining. Well, the morning star in tune with Dash's magic and rituals allowed the weapons of the group to become continually laced with silver and residium, a combination which when placed into the flesh of a lycanthrope, could become very deadly.

The Lycan leader saw the source of their power. Legion's weapon was forged from legendary powers. He knew so. He was nowhere near the age of the weapon's but his knowledge dated further back than any other living or unliving creature in the room, minus the spirits of the morning star. Dash, Pitt, Legion, and Dauge all took their respected positions and stood back, hesitantly backtracking from the room.

"Hold your places or be struck down where you stand!" The worg king's voice bellowed out yet sounded as if it were only a whisper from his cords.

As instructed, the team held. More shifters came from the back, dragging several dead bodies from some room the party couldn't quite see into. There was no door, just an entry location into a hallway that immediately cut to the left. It cut off the party's vision from what the entryway and hallway led to.

"You've caused grief for too long, creature," Dash barked.

"You know not of my work. How dare you claim it be the cause of grief? I've warred with horde nations as I've warred with the humanoid ones. Now, you've interrupted my den and slumber. For that, give me the weapon and you shall all go free."

Legion laughed. Dash actually gave the words a second thought and a possible notion to do it. He knew his colleagues wouldn't go for it. He knew he had to kill the creature now or die to him in a valiant effort. This fight would set the tone for him as a leader of a notable team of heroes.

Heroes were gone from Thedia. They no longer existed. Heroes were a thing of the past. Men and women of legend were exactly that, nothing more than a set of stories placed in archaic times in history. Dash wanted to change that. He wanted to prove chivalry, honor, and prestige were not outdated. The powers of the ancient travelers could become the power of the modern ones. Legends weren't made by backing down in the heart of danger or while staring into the eyes of eminent death.

"The power is not in your hands, wolf," said Pitt.

"Worg!" he screamed back.

Dauge whispered so only his allies could hear. "It's undead but it hasn't a single undead follower. Something's peculiar here."

"You know not of my powers I assure you. I'll enslave you all and force you to serve me. Death is much to easy for miscreants like you," the wereworg screamed angrily. "Seize them!" He snapped viciously, pointing at the four.

In seconds, the room's guards charged the four who'd broken down their door and into their master's chamber. Blades dripping with continual silver and residium flew from Dauge before any on either side could even mentally prepare for the upcoming battle. A great swing from Pitt's axe sent three all in a row all in a single swing hurling into the sidewall. All of them were nearly cut in two. Legion fought back and forth with the first shifter that came his way. Luckily, he was able to replace his lost shield with one of theirs and finish the creature off before the others could see it had given him any difficulty at all. Dash fired his crossbow just once to throw off a charging lycan but then fell back to his divine and arcane powers to boost and buff his team as best he could.

He kept them encircled in auras that kept them strong and swift. Should the situation call for it, allow their bodies to heal almost instantaneously. He didn't want to lose anyone. He'd worked hard on acquiring his team. Legion and Dauge were irreplaceable members of his team with a name that went a long way, especially with his mouthpiece. Pitt was magnificent. He could give and take it better than anything he'd ever seen or heard of. He was a monster and one that was on his side. Not to mention, he had quite the faction built up in Thox, a place Dash loved and appreciated so very much.

More than that, he wanted to be a good leader and not a leader known for losing those that followed him. Eventually, if enough people died under your watch, you could be outcast or labeled as something or someone unable to lead and guide people to greatness, the polar opposite of what his goal was.

A necrotic beam shot from the creature's right "unnatural" eye. Its target was none other than Dash himself but the crafty half-eladrin dove and rolled over his own shoulder just in time. The beam hit the giant stones of the wall just behind him melting a heavy piece of it into nothingness. Dash responded with several bolts of his own from his crossbow aimed directly at the wereworg itself.

Even the more advanced and more skilled shifters and lycans fell to the blades and spells of the team. One by one, two by two, three by three, they fell. Just like the arenas of Thox, Pitt walked through their arsenals unscathed. His ferocity grew with every swing. Eventually, the number of lycans and shifters dwindled down to the single, solitary king.

During the entire fight, Dash couldn't help but try to wrap his mind, who could have created a half-golem? The art was thought to have been lost in the dusts of time, much less one from a goliath wereworg.

The creature walked from the recently built staging area of the room where his throne quietly rested. The gentleness of his walk didn't match the cold and vile tone of his booming and demanding voice.

He carried no weapons, nor did his body possess any forms of protective garments, but nonetheless, the creature seemed unshaken by the four's actions against his people and their victories over his followers seemed to mean little at all to the Lycanthropic leader.

"Your den has been taken. Surrender," Pitt ordered, a bit hesitant.

"My undead are bringing war to the proper lands all around the Thoxen region. I have lycans everywhere. I am a growing force with a momentum you cannot hope to stop," he answered.

Legion seized the initiative, charging forward, dropped his newly acquired shield, and rushed forward with both hands around the base of his massive morning star. Both Goddimus and Arakros told him there was something more to the creature that had not yet been revealed. How was he able to have been made and constructed? His body surely should have broken down.

As always, Dauge's blades beat Legion once again. The silvery dripping blades laced with residium found their marks in the creature's body from his waist to his face. As quickly as they pierced his flesh, his flesh just pushed them back out. Not even a single drop of blood spilled from Dauge's throwing daggers and now, he was nearly out. He'd lost so many on this trip. He was about to have to resort to his exotic armblades or short swords.

Legion used his momentum perfectly to duck under the lycan's great claw swing only to leave the chain and ball of his weapon behind him enough to wrap and entangle the creature's right arm as well as having the ball forced through the creature's skull. The attack was monumental in their attempt to finish the creature king off.

A roar echoed aloud and the ball flew from the creature's immediately regrown face. Legion, still having a grip on the base, was ripped from his half kneeling position and launched high into the air. Dash used spell after to spell to keep his friend from hitting the wall behind him too hard or from falling at too dangerous of a speed. Still, by the time Legion hit the ground, the Xavier wasn't feeling to good.

Dauge rebounded by catching his older brother just before he hit the ground, softening his fall but still causing a pile of bodies to slam hard into the velvet covered stone floor below.

Pitt sent an overhand swing with all his might only to have to the creature's left craw grab his blade in prime swing. With one arm, the wereworg played the mercy game with Pitt as he used both his hands to even hope to keep the wereworg to a stalemate.

Even Pitt seemed dwarfed by the creature's immense size. A breath of ice from the wereworg blanketed around Pitt's body, forcing him to lose the grip on his axe and fall to the ground helpless, unable to move at all.

Dash moved and ducked, dodged and rolled until finally he was able to get the beast's attention off his crew. All the while, he still managed to throw a heal spell here and there to make sure they were all still able and hopefully willing. Pitt was hurting the most. The icy breath slowed him down and numbed his body. It was taking over.

Pitt fell back into a deep sleep. When he awoke, it was to warmth and only the cold warmth of his Shiva was present. Trees were plentiful and the fields were flawless. She was there with him! Shiva had returned to spend her days with him. He wasn't just a peon pawn as his peers once told him.

Suddenly, Shiva was gone and he was back in the mansion facing the beast. Was he near death? If so, why didn't they let him die? They didn't know that wherever he went that was exactly what he'd been hoping for, ever since he took that sentence to become a gladiator slave. No, of course not. He never told them about Shiva or why or how he became a gladiator. His mind fell into slow motion and the thoughts reverted back to those times the others laughed at him for opting for his fate. He chose it.

Back to the reality of it all, he was on his back and Dash just nearly took a life-ending blow to cure him of diseases and sicknesses in order to save his life. Once again, the Lycan King was just too slow for the clever and dexterous half-eladrin bard.

A faint voice came from the back, "Use fire!" she said. "His healing is infused with a greater troll's. Magical fire will end it!"

The voice came from the back of the hallway that the party couldn't see.

"Quiet you wretched whore! Ill end you the way your own should have! I'll kill you… you bitch!" The lycan king became flustered and morbidly angry at the faint woman's remarks.

Pitt pulled himself from the ground wrapping his hands the creature's gyronetic right knee. Pitt pulled and pulled with all his might until finally the gears in the creature's knee finally gave way.

The lycan king came crashing down and once again, Pitt took the brunt of it but not before ultimately getting away from the monster before doing too much more damage.

"Ha! Yes, his body can't rebuild that now can it," said Dash excitedly. His barbarian was fighting intelligently and had thought of something the others hadn't. In the meantime, none of them had any fire spells. The ones Dash did have were all expended.

"Move!" Dash ordered to his people.

"Scatter!" Dauge seconded, confirming everyone knew exactly what Dash meant.

Each of them found nooks and exits to the room to escape the mighty lycan-like creation. It picked itself up only able to slightly walk and now forced to move a limping pace. Pitt's actions may have saved the team, Dash thought seeing the creature fight with the concept of walking from a doorway where previously lycans had pulled the dead bodies.

Pitt made his exit directly the same way he made his entrance. He rushed back down the small corridor that led to the door he turned to splinters. Legion found a niche under the staging area and Dauge made it to the back hallway where the faint voice hailed from.

Dauge rushed into the hallway and down a small corridor that opened to a small room where a small band of creatures, odd-looking things, had all been slain. Chained to the wall were several humans, half-elves, eladrin, tieflings, and even dwarves. All were dead save one. One creature looked different from the rest. It wasn't a treant, yet she looked like one, druidic in nature. Her body seemed to be carved carefully from the most beautiful trees, leaves, grasses, and other pieces of nature. It all flowed together so very nicely and beautiful. What the hell was she? Dauge's training and childhood knowledge told him they were very close to the plantons of the Republic of New Magic but they weren't the same. Plantons resemble the race of the creature they were before their hibernation when the continent flipped inside out.

Then, something even more divinely different revealed itself. She was a paradox of existence. As she looked up at him, her autumn colored eyes leaked with a strong yellowish vampiric tent. Dauge knew that color. Something told him it was a female creature.

"What are you?" he asked.

"One of you," she responded.

"I am human."

"I am Thedian."

Dauge smiled. He liked her answer.

"Fire, kill the thing with fire." She quickly abandoned their conversation to remind him the beast had to be killed with fire.

"I have no way to make fire. And you said magical fire."

"I can make such a flame to kill the beast."

"And I should trust you?"

"What choice do you have?"

"The creature's leg has been rendered useless. It can't exactly chase us out of here."

"Do you want to flee or do you want to finish what you started?"

Dauge looked coldly at the girl. She had a point. In her eyes, he felt the calmness of a summer breeze and the warmth of a hot spring on his face. Then he also saw barren valleys and dead trees along with the tornados and hurricanes that go along with nature. What was she other than just a pure oddity? When she spoke her mouth revealed the fangs of a vampire that matched her eyes. Whatever she was, vampiric was part of her makeup.

"Why should I trust you? You're vampire."

"Please! Let me help you. Let me help us!"

Dauge pulled a small device from his trousers and quickly went to work on the chains.

Meanwhile, the other three members of the team found themselves being forced back into the room by the rising numbers of undead. Undead abominations were coming to life at the sound and call of the undead lycan king's newly heard death call. He issues a call to the dead to awake and rise at the sound of his voice and await his commands.

Something empowered the king to be able to stand once again. The room was filled with undead zombies, skeletons, and everything else mostly made from lycan and shifter hosts. The three were surrounded with nowhere to go.

Just then, when all seemed lost, the unique creature came from the back hallway with Dauge at her side. Her very being shattered the undead that felt her presence, all save the king.

He turned infuriated at the bitch's resilience to maintain her life even in its unlife form. She became his prime target, knowing she was the only one that had the means to end him. She was the only one with the abilities needed to kill him.

A black cloud of thunder, sonic, and necrotic energies formed around the wereworg simultaneously to a storm of fire forming around the newly found out creature and Dauge. Dauge was hesitant and scared. He knew not of the creature or her true intentions and none of his teachings, trainings, or abilities helped him read the little girl.

In a clash of powers, the room and all its connecting chambers and rooms went up in a gust of smoke and fluttered to the winds and rains of the heavy storm that had already been setting in for sometime now.

When it was done, Dash, Dauge, Legion, and Pitt stood opposed to the newly found creature none of them had ever seen before or heard of before.

"What are you?" Pitt asked.

"She's a Planton from the Republic but I ain't got the faintest ideas as to what she's doing out here."

"I'm not a Planton," she replied.

Dash knew the best thing to do was change the subject and fast. "That's some kind of power you got there..." He paused waiting for her to fill them in on what she truly was and where her powers truly lay.

Dauge, Legion, and Pitt were still all in complete awe at what she'd just done. The undead, wereworg goliath with mechanical parts was gone. What a combination of things to be a creature king.

"We Wildens have been in your world for some number of years now. Our kin the eladrin have been here since the beginning," she said.

"Right, but what's the story with the Wildens? I remember hearing about them as a kid." Legion said, showing his friendly side.

"Can someone explain what in the dark hells or high heavens just happened. That entire mansion just up and disappeared!" Pitt said in a matter of fact tone.

The Wilden smiled. "I am Kraydia and I am an oddity. I am a paradox of existence."

Dash signaled her to hold her words. He followed up with a series of healing spells to mend the creature's wounds. She was nature's child. Dash remembered growing up, as did Legion and Dauge. Pitt however was ignorant of the creatures. However, growing up around plantons, Legion and Dauge remembered as children when the Wildens first seemed to "wake up."

The story of the Wildens was very similar to that of the very rare race, the shardmind, a creature who was subsequently created after the shattering of "the gate." Shardminds were said to be living remnants of that ancient "gate."

Wildens were said to be nature in humanoid form with origins true to the feywild. Kraydia and the others fled the site of the last battle with the creature king. Eventually and subconsciously, the five found themselves heading back toward Grogan's Mill together, as a team. Well, the four knew where they were heading now that the lycan problem had been resolved and the Wilden Kraydia just seemed to follow along.

The storm kept strong and clouds kept the sun from landing its beams upon her skin. Eventually, the sun did surface and though the vampiric creature was hurting but not completely burning as would have been thought.

Legion pulled a satchel of his belongings higher over his shoulder to make the carrying of it a bit easier. "Unless you're some kind of supreme master, isn't the sun suppose to turn you into dust or something?"

"I have lineage with a vampire. I was never bitten nor turned. The blood of a vampire was mixed with mine. I have a connection to them and their realm of unlife but my blood is very much burning and as alive as yours friend," Kraydia answered.

In the coming days it took to get to Grogan's Mill she became quite the friend and ally. Dauge kept his distance but secretly admired the peculiar pile of nature. He couldn't have his true feelings out in the open. That wasn't him.

Chapter 10

"Grogan's Mill is just over the hill!" Legion said. His face and body expressions poured of his actions. He was filled with joy to see the city just over the horizon. The morning sun was breaking in the day and the team more than a day from the comforts of a bed in an inn somewhere, possibly with a breakfast in bed.

Legion led the way. He usually did. That was his character. Dauge kept his distance from the front but his eyes were always on his big brother. Legion walked with his Star across his left shoulder dangling the chain and spiked ball parallel with his right arm most of the time.

Pitt walked dead center of the group, reassuring himself that in any event he would be ready to protect and react against anything that could or would come at them. He knew they needed more supplies. Even he needed missiles and Dash was all but out of his bolts.

Dash walked just to the left flank of Pitt but kept his eyes fixed upon Legion, the man in the lead. He knew Dauge and Kraydia were to the right flank of the group and the group always walked slightly scattered; this was to prevent traps, ambushes, and/or spells and other attacks from being able to catch them all at once.

Kraydia walked alongside Dauge toward the rear of the group. She mostly kept to herself but made her presence known and appreciated by the group. She wasn't a vampire. Dauge knew that. An undead entity, probably a vampire lord of some degree did something to her. Whatever he did, forced her own kind, new to the world to turn on her. Kraydia 's skin was still weak against the burning sun's magnificent sunlight.

"We're almost there," Dauge said, trying to comfort Kraydia.

"I know. I'm used to the light, Republican. That doesn't mean it doesn't hurt," she replied flirtatiously. "I grew up playing in the sun like everyone else. Just because you found me inside an old mansion doesn't mean I grew up there!" she continued, while flaunting her body and words at Dauge.

Legion looked at Kraydia as just a creature diseased and plagued by the undead but for the moment, still useful. Pitt was indifferent toward her. So far, she proved her worth to the team and that's what meant the most to him. For him, reuniting with Shiva meant everything. And Dash, Dash just wanted to piece together and lead the best team he could. His intentions were true and honest, to himself and his team.

The streets and people of Grogan's Mill were open to the team. Looking around, they found nothing but farmers and crop growers of all kinds. The town was moving with its inhabitants but wasn't exactly busy compared to the average.

"We're looking for the magistrate," Dash whispered to his team.

"And do we know his name?" asked Kraydia.

"Her name is Laena Maerne. She's an elder woman and kind of heavyset. Compliments wouldn't hurt when we get to her either," Dash said.

"Compliments?" asked Legion.

Dash laughed and threw his arm around Legion. Legion moved his morning star as to make it safe for his friend and leader. Dash pulled a little coin from his pocket and dropped it in Legion's hands, finally separating his arm from the Xavier's neck. Legion wrapped and strapped his morning star to his side in its makeshift holster and looked to Dash for instructions. He knew the coin was meant for something.

"Get us a room at a local inn, nothing too fancy, nothing to slummy," he said.

"Got it," answered Legion looking back to his brother. Dauge signaled he was okay with the temporary splitting of the group.

"Dauge, you and Kraydia see what information you can dig up on this town. Pitt, you come with me." Dash gave his orders to everyone, even Kraydia who wasn't an official member of the team just yet.

"Why is Pitt going with you and I am to get information?" Kraydia was confused. She wasn't necessarily against his orders, she was just confused as to how he'd come up with who was doing what.

"Kraydia, you're pretty and different to look at. You can hide your vampiric traits and use your cunning to squeeze every tidbit of useful information out of this town. Dauge will go with you to keep an eye on you, in case you need help. Pitt's coming with me so my tongue can do the talking and his appearance can show Laena we mean business and have the means to get it done."

Dash made his words clear and easy to understand. He was a good man and an even better leader. Something about him was just too good and something about him even stole a bit of Kraydia 's attention from Dauge. Dauge sensed it but couldn't admit whether his feelings for her were real or just in his head. Even if they were real, he would need to remove them and get them gone as soon as he could.

"We meet up here when it's done." Dash pointed to a nearby tavern. It seemed to be the only one in the area and Grogan's Mill wasn't a terribly large town. It was called "The Rotten Tomato." The Rotten Tomato was a simple building that looked like more of a small farmhouse than a tavern. An outside porch and covering deck seemed to be the place where the majority of its patrons sat. It was an outside tavern. The poor town didn't have much, Dash thought. He could change that. He could change that for the better and soon.

Just down a dirt road from The Rotten Tomato Legion found a small inn called Rinkety's Shack. The poor home had seen better days. It was nothing more than an old rundown home turned into a makeshift inn, probably for the owner trying to turn a quick buck. As instructed, Legion entered to get the room.

Inside, Legion found a small Halfling woman working her butt off, cooking, sweating, cleaning, and otherwise tidying up the torn-down place. A pot of good smelling soup was brewing and a few cots were arranged in the main living area of the home. Not much room to walk around, he thought.

"Can I help you?" she asked in quite a rude voice. He could tell she didn't mean to be, she was just busy. The cots weren't made up and there wasn't anyone using them. Then again, they could have all just been out for the day.

"I'm sorry. I didn't mean to disturb you. I'll just be going," Legion said.

"No, no..."

Legion watched the little lady parade around in her white apron, getting soup all over it and everything else. He laughed a little under his breath. She did as well. She knew he wasn't trying to be mean or rude, she was just all over the place and he found it humorous.

"I just wanted to see if you had a place for five guests?"

She took in a deep breath and laughed, throwing her hands at the site of her cots.

"My last guests left just a few hours ago. We don't get too many guests around here other than the officials and trade specialists hailing from Thox.

"Well, I'll gladly pay good coin for a bed and breakfast," Legion said.

"The place is yours," she said playfully, trying to use the conversation to take her away from the all the work she had in front of her.

Legion tossed the lady a sack of coins, the same pouch Dash gave her plus a little from his own purse as well. The little lady's face lit up. Legion tossed his satchel of belongings to the nearest cot and turned to walk out the door. "Thanks, we'll see you tonight."

"Oh my, by the gods, you paid too much."

"Keep it," he said, savoring the moment of feeling important in a stranger's life but knowing more waited for him outside her doors.

Dauge and Kraydia found a spot in The Rotten Tomato and sat down to get a drink. The sun was high in the sky by the time they crossed the threshold of the city's limits. Dauge and Kraydia both knew if there was information to be had, the town tavern was most likely the place to get it.

The Towne Hall was closed. The place of the magistrate's work was shut down. Why, thought Dash? Pitt just walked quietly alongside him. A half-elf with a hook for a right hand approached the two. His brown hair streaked with gray from time told both Dash and Pitt he'd been around. He was a little older and carried himself better than those others of the city.

"How can I help you boys?" he asked.

His simple clothes looked comfortable but bland. His browns and whites matched his walking stick and sandals. Scars covered the man's face and body in every place Dash and Pitt's eyes fell upon. He'd been through quite a bit, the two thought.

"I hail from Thox but do not speak on their behalf my friend. I am looking for the Magistrate Maerne."

"Well you're out of luck. Lady Maerne passed some weeks back," said the half-elf.

Dash fell back a second. Pitt just kept quiet.

"Are you the half-giant goliath gladiator from Thox that grows hair on the top of his head?" The half elf asked as friendly as he could. He was truly a courteous and nice person.

"I am," answered Pitt.

"What are you doing all the way in Grogan's Mill?" he asked.

Dash saw the half elf's interest in Pitt and went with it, allowing Pitt to make small talk with the half elf until he finally found his opening.

"I've solved the lycanthrope problem here in these parts and wanted to assure the people of this town that they were safe once again," Dash said, kindly interrupting.

"Lyanan has been killed?" he said, presumably telling Dash the lycan leader was in fact named Lyanan."

"Yes, my team and I ended him and his small gathering not too far from here. We've come to spread peace to your people and offer our service to the town of Grogan's Mill."

"I too was once an adventurer, old friend. What is it you want and don't be foolish? Be honest with me."

Dash thought about it. Who was this half-elf and why was he hanging around the Towne Hall? Was he just a crazy old man or was he somebody special?

"Oh, how rude of me. I am Quinn. People call me Q," he said.

Dash knew that name and so did Pitt. Quinn ran his own town he founded in the middle of Thoxen territory he called Quinn's Town. What was he doing here?

"From Quinn's Town" Dash asked.

"The same," he answered.

"What are you doing here?" he asked.

"When my good friend Laena passed, I discovered she requested I take over as Magistrate of her city. However, I recently annexed my town to Thox and now plan to do the same with Grogan's Mill. I'd like to disband the town and move the entire population to Quinn's Town if I could. That in fact is what I am working on."

"Well then, we may be able to do business. My information tells me there's something special about this town and it's hiding a secret. I'm looking to make a name for myself as you once did."

Quinn laughed. "I assure you, you don't want to go through what I went through. I was a slave and gladiator like you, Pitt."

The connection between the two was solid enough for Dash to understand. Perhaps luck was on his side. Dash knew Quinn. He and his team made some legendary achievements including several during a stint with the militaries of the Republic early on in the war against Corvana, a country long forgotten since two of his allies' father went over there and forcefully laid down actions to lead to its annihilation.

"We can do business. You're smart. There are secrets of this town I'd love to disclose with you so long as we can come to an agreement on a working relationship."

Dash smiled extending his hand to introduce himself. "I'm Dash. Dash Riproc."

"Absolutely we can," Quinn replied.

"Get your people and meet me back here at this hall tomorrow. There are some secrets to this town, I'd love to hand them off, and clear myself of this place altogether. First I'll need you to take care of something for me."

"As always—" Dash started. He smiled ear to ear. He had more to say but the silence and tone of his voice said it all for him.

"As it always is…" Quinn concluded.

Evening came and Dash entered one of the town's only active taverns, The Dirty Glass. A fitting name, Dash thought. His team, Legion, Dauge, Pitt, and even Kraydia were all there, present and accounted for. Dash smiled. This was the making of everything he ever wanted. He pulled a well-organized team together and together; they were growing every day.

"Legion, Dauge," Dash yelled, seeing his team at the bar. The two turned back to see their leader swinging the door open to the place wildly and proudly. The moon's light beamed in from behind, illuminating him and the floor beneath his feet.

The relatively small building was built like a square with off measurements. There were no tables, just a little bit of standing room for the lot of twenty or thirty to take up. Then, behind the bar stood a young blue-scaled dragonborn. Not too many dragonborn bartenders, thought Dash.

Dash made his way through the crowd of hard-working mudders and farmers and the like reuniting himself with his team finally.

"We got work?" Legion asked.

"We got faction?" asked Dauge, referring to the fact they'd just ousted Grogan's Lycanthropic problem.

"We get paid?" Pitt asked. His saddened tone was expected. It was the way he was. To him, the glass was always just half empty. He was the kind of guy to always expect the worst.

Kraydia just waited and smiled. She didn't say anything. She looked deep into Dash's eyes, knowing he had something good to tell them.

Dash caught her gaze and smiled. He knew she'd caught on to his good news.

"Lord Quinn from Quinn Town runs Grogan's Mill now—" Dash wasn't finished talking before he was cut off.

"What happened to—" Legion started to ask before being cut off almost immediately by Dash who continued with his story.

"Quinn runs this town. That's the fact. We're in his good graces with the lycan's diseasing of the area being cured."

"So, where are we? Where do we stand?" Legion asked.

"We're to meet Quinn tomorrow at the Magistrate's Hall. He has a few things for us to do, or at least something. I'm not sure what all. He said his goal is to move and clear out Grogan's Mill, take what he can from it and move its people to Quinn Town. He admitted to the Mill having secrets and offered them up to us, assuming we take care of whatever business he has for us."

"What about our payment for the lycans?" Pitt asked, concerned about his coin. Coin meant more to him than anything. He needed it to get to her.

"We didn't really touch on it. I'm sure we'll go over it tomorrow, but if we don't, Pitt, think of it as an investment. Now, the good stuff starts coming in and we've made a strong alliance in Quinn, a powerful player in the kingdom of Thox." To Dash, it was all a game and he wanted to get the best players on his side. He was going to build his empire in Thox and Quinn was going to be his way in.

"You them boys that took out that fur freak down thurrrr?" A voice boomed up from behind them.

The crew all jumped and turned. It was an old half-orc, seasoned from the wrinkles time dresses its elderly up with. In farmer's clothes and with grass stains all over him, his pleased expression told the team they had a true fan. To the core, this creature was of the country with a bit of chew in his underbite and a piece of straw hanging from his mouth.

"We are. We are indeed," Legion said, speaking up proudly.

"Them things killed one of my sons. Much obliged, I am plenty obliged to you's all." He took his old worn-out hat off and placed it in both his hands over his chest. A tear fell from his eyes.

At that moment, it was at that moment Legion Cage Xavier realized the importance of his calling. Dauge chalked it up as another casualty of life, predator, and prey so to speak. Kraydia smiled, happy she'd done something to make another smile. Pitt empathized a bit with the man but kept silent. His loss was hard on him, just the same but different. His loss was intimate, not blood.

Dash more than any felt the man's words. He leaned off his barstool and hugged the monstrous farmer. "I'm sorry for your loss and happy to avenge him."

"Oh sirs, vengeance ain't in m'nature. I just didn't wanna see m'friends 'round here lose any'thin or go through any'thin like I had to. Oh, it hurts. It's hurts real bad, y'know? M'other boys is tough and strong and they been helping us through this. Just like you's. You's took care of them mean ol' things fer'us."

Dash separated from the man, pulling a pouch of coins from his side pocket. "Take this and treat your family to a grand meal. Buy your fallen son something from us. We'd like to honor him." The leader of the team overflowed with happiness seeing his actions reflect happily on the faces of those all around him.

"Oh I couldn'ts take you's moneys…" The half-orc was very submissive to the team and the people all around him.

"Please, I'd feel bad if you didn't," Dash replied graciously.

Finally, the half-orc agreed and turned to be on his way. The dark-skinned old man was just grinning and smiling the whole time he walked away and with every step, his smile brightened the night of Dash even more.

Dash and the others took their seats once again with Dash a little taller than he had been.

"So tomorrow, we meet the legendary Quinn?" Dauge asked.

"We heard about him as boys in the Republic. He was said to have traveled with the legendary Atherton Wing. That's where that place comes from, Atherton's Golden Wing." Legion chimed in, explaining Dauge's reason for labeling Quinn as a legend.

"I'm thinking the people of this town have been tried too much. And it's us who are to free them," Dash continued.

"I think you're getting a little ahead of yourself, friend. We helped an elderly farmer and saved them from the lycan problem. Now, Quinn'll be able to get them safely to Quinn Town. And we'll be able to move on, right?" Dauge asked.

Dauge's cold tongue sent chills through Dash, taking him down just a little bit. Even the suave leader's blood ran cold when Dauge's "friendly" reminders came at him. Dauge wanted to remind him they weren't planting themselves anywhere.

"Relax Dauge. I'm just planting our seed sternly here," the half-eladrin bard answered.

"I still say we should get paid for the lycan problem," Pitt said, jumping into the conversation.

"Calm down, relax. We'll get paid soon enough," Dash replied.

"I just need to make sure the coin is there, Dash," said Pitt.

"I know brother. I know." Dash said.

Pitt slammed another drink back.

"I'm sorry. I just have to find her." He finished the last drop of the drink. He spoke aloud but barely. It was as if he was reminding himself of what he was doing.

"You will," Legion said.

Dauge just looked at Pitt and kept his silence. Kraydia looked at Dauge. Something about the human intrigued her. He was different from other humans, as was his brother. One thing was certain; Legion Cage Xavier was the strongest human she'd ever seen. He had a blood boiling temper when angered. Dauge was his polar opposite. He was quiet, observant, and his senses were heightened beyond normality. Something in him changed him from just being a normal human; like her, she'd been changed some time ago and now she'd never just be a regular Wilden again.

What was the key to getting inside Dauge? The rest were as easy to read as a folk story for children. Dash wanted to be known and recognized for what he was, who he was, what he'd done, and all of his other accomplishments. He wanted to build a successful team of heroes more than anything. She'd been with them just a short time and she knew that. Legion was coming into his own and the fame was starting to get to him. Pitt wanted to find something or someone and he kept saying he was going to need coin to do it. Dauge, Dauge was the unique one she couldn't quite figure out and whether she like it or not, it drew her to him. It'd been so long since she'd seen anyone she was truly interested in as she was him.

The night disappeared faster and faster with every drink. Of course for Dash, the night dragged on, and as much as he wanted to just sleep and get on with it, he knew he had to stay away and mingle with the town's people as well as his own.

Dash didn't drink. Pitt drank enough for ten and Legion tried to hold his own with him. Legion could certainly hold his own for a human, Pitt thought. The Xavier boys definitely had something more to their makeup than just the human genetics. The Wilden was getting tired. She thought back to what had happened to her, the vampirism thing. It was such an unusual happening. She wasn't vampiric or undead at all. Yet, she was definitely tied to something not of the mortal world.

Chapter 19

Morning came and the lot of them woke up to a good smelling stew and plates of breakfast lying on the floor next to their beds. Other than Dash, the rest of them couldn't even remember getting back to Rikity's Shack. The little Halfling was moving around vivaciously as ever.

Legion's eyes peeled open to seeing the little woman's bustier just over his face. "Well good morning."

She was topping off his milk and making sure his biscuits, eggs, ham, and sausage were all ready for him. Behind her, Legion saw his leader already up and finished with breakfast. He was just about finished dressing out when Legion's eyes opened. Dauge wasn't known for drinking too much either. He was too unpredictable to say whether he was a drinker or wasn't.

One by one, the crew awoke and dug into the vittles and drink left for them by the young to nearly middle-aged Halfling. Legion's eyes kept straying away from his team and food to the woman moving around the room, still trying to make sure everything was taken care of.

"Eat your breakfast before it gets cold."

Legion smiled. The little Halfling didn't seem to fancy him at all but something told him differently. He did as instructed and the team paid their dues, ate their meals, and dressed out for the day's duties.

"We'd like to keep the place for another day or so my lady?" Dash asked.

"No problem. Your coin is well appreciated here, my lords," she replied to them all.

With that, the team set out to meet back up with Quinn, the former hero of the Republic of New Magic and the current lord of Quinn Town, Thox's newly annexed town.

By mid morning, the team made the last corner between them and the Towne Hall, or the Magistrate's Hall. Quinn was already there, dressed in his white courtier's garments.

"He must have either had court duties this morning or has them this afternoon. Those whites are court-worthy garments," observed Dash.

"Aye," said Dauge, agreeing quickly and whispering.

Pitt grunted in compliance. Legion and Kraydia just kept silent, listening to the others and observing their soon-to-be newfound friend.

"Dash, Pitt!" Quinn yelled.

Legion's eyes fell to Quinn's missing right hand. It'd been replaced with a nasty looking hook. Not very gentrical or noble, thought the Xavier. Then again, he began as his father did, and his grandfather, an adventurer just hoping to change his stars.

That thought brought Legion to an unfamiliar place. His mind fell away from the day, the town, and all of the known reality. His father, his glorious father that he'd hated for so long, he now adored and he didn't even completely understand why.

An old elven wizard and an elven rogue of sorts returned from the New Threat, now the Old Threat also known as Corvana, with his corpse and tales of immeasurable feats and tasks his father accomplished. Should they be believed? He questioned. Were they true? He pondered. Why would they make it up and if so, what really happened to the Corvana?

"Right on time, I like that."

Quinn's voice snapped Legion back into reality. Quinn's brown hair was shorter than Dash originally described to them the night before.

"A haircut?" Dash asked.

"Why yes, I was due," he answered.

The town seemed slow. It wasn't moving as it had been. In the distance, Dauge caught an eyeful of the old half-orc and several little ones that appeared to be his sons plowing a long field and working as if the day was going to be Thedia's last.

Dauge secretly felt for the family. It wasn't the loss of the eldest son that turned his stomach but the idea of a life of nothing more than plowing fields and pulling weeds, vines, fruit, and vegetables. Poor bastards, he thought. By the dead gods, thankfully, he was meant for more.

"Dash, we've got a lot to discuss but I'm glad your whole team is here," Quinn started but stopped prematurely. It wasn't a certainty but the five all knew he had more to say when his voice paused.

"Something on your mind Quinn?" Dash asked, confused.

Pitt shrugged his shoulders and grunted. He looked down at the little Wilden. He thought to himself, if anything would've had his tongue, it would've been the peculiar little creature.

Quinn squinted his eyes and pointed to Kraydia with his good hand.

"What the hell? Is that some kind of Planton?" he asked.

"I'm not a planton!" she screamed. Her anger grew with that question every time someone asked it.

"We don't even really look like those things!"

"Easy lady," Quinn replied. "I've just never seen one of your kind. If I recall correctly, you're a Wilden then, right?"

Kraydia was much more pleased with the half-elf now. She smiled and bowed. "Aye, that I am my lord."

"Well, I've heard of your kind but just never seen one. If my memory serves me right, your kind just somehow awoke and came here from the feywild, right?"

"Yes Lord Quinn, that's right. A few races just awoke and appeared here in Thedia. With Geminus being forced upon Thedia by Gemini the invader, Thedia's probably going to see several new species coming from the Mogras and all other kinds of places. We Wildens have been here for some years now. We're just now becoming noticed though, or so it seems my lord."

"I've seen stranger I guess. No matter. Your race bears no meaning to me lady. Your skills, abilities, and loyalties however, do," answered the Thoxen Lord.

"My abilities, loyalties, and skills might even surprise you and all you've seen... my lord." One thing was for sure. Kraydia was a quick-witted, snappy little thing.

"In my time, young one, I've learned to respect the unexpected."

"You mean expect?" Pitt stated questioningly.

"No, I mean respect. I respect that which I don't know. Therefore, I am expecting of anything and not underestimating anything that might come my way. Believe me, I am always one step ahead of any and everything I come across."

Dauge didn't answer or say anything back at all. He already knew what Quinn was talking about. The well-dressed half-elf had snipers and fighters on point watching out seemingly around every single corner and rooftop. Aside from the younger Xavier, not a single other member of the team noticed even a one of them. They were good. They were elite and served Quinn quietly from the shadows and rooftops while he walked proudly through the towns and cities and of Thox.

Well-played, thought Dauge. Well-played.

"Let us get down to business. In the snuffing out of the lycan werewolf—" Quinn started.

"Worg," Pitt interrupted.

"In the snuffing out of the lycan wereworg," he started again, "you all drew out the creature I was searching for. He was an ally once." Quinn chuckled, thinking back. He pointed to a furry belt underneath his main shirt holding several small pouches.

"Was that a tail?" Kraydia asked.

"It was." He smirked. Quinn apparently had a bit of a sense of humor.

"Tha'Raws is a shifter much like the lot you fought not too far from here. He was an ally of mine for many, many years. He turned during a disagreement of missions and decisions. I knew he was behind it all. His little gnome tinkerer has been captured. His necromancer has been killed. He's a shaman and a damn good one. He means well but sometimes his morals override his common sense. I didn't want anything bad to happen to him but he dabbled in the dark arts, the very stuff he loathed us for allowing in some cases. Anyway, he's been captured and is safely in my prison in Quinn Town. That means more to me than anything. That loon hates me but I love him and want to see him taken care of and looked after. We have barriers to seal off his magic. For that and the taking down of the shifter and lycan problem, you have my gratitude. And with that being said, I have but one more thing I need done."

"And what's that? That's what we've been dying to hear," Legion joked.

Dash threw a stern and quick glare at Legion, telling him without words to keep his mouth shut. Legion was a bit poppy at times but when the time called for it, his dark and sadistic side came out. The others knew that. He was like two different people with two different personalities. His in the city or town personality was much easier to deal with than his on-the-road persona. He was usually joking and fun, but when he wasn't, his dry nature and dark mannerisms rivaled even Dauge's.

"I need a message and some items delivered to a friend of mine there in the Golden Sands Desert. It's not too far from here and a friend of mine, an old friend of mine, just moved there. I got a map that'll tell you how to get there."

"Who is he? What does he look like?" Pitt asked. "No problem." He concluded.

"How do you know it's not a she, big man?" Kraydia flirtingly asked Pitt.

"Uh, I don't know I guess," he replied.

"It's a he and you'll know him when you see him. When you get close to him, he'll find you and when you see him, trust me. He'll stand out."

"We're going to need a little more than that," Dauge said.

"I'm going to get you to his lair. From there, he'll find you. He knows you're coming. Don't worry how but he knows," Quinn finished strongly.

"Lair," Dauge muttered. That term churned him. It ate at him a bit. What kind of friend or ally has a lair in the Golden Sands Desert, he pondered.

The term caught Legion as well. His joking side was gone. The Halfling from the Rikity Shack had his mind at ease. Women did that to him. A pretty and soft piece of something always kept his mind happy and friendlier. Now, thinking of lairs and deserts, Legion's attitude returned to the war in the Republic almost instantly.

Kraydia saw the change in Legion almost as fast as it happened. Her look to Quinn told the Lord his words didn't sooth or comfort them at all.

"What do you mean by lair, Lord Quinn?" Legion asked, his tone a bit more serious and strong now.

"You'll see. I wouldn't send you anywhere I don't think you're ready for," he answered.

"In truth, you don't know too much about us," Legion said cautiously.

"I know the lycans are gone and the mastermind behind creating that beast of a wereworg is in my prison now because of you. I can't tell you who or what he is but just that he is there. The map will guide you to him. And you'll be thankful you took this work." Quinn smiled finishing his words.

The famous adventurer turned lord had them all intrigued. He had Dash's heart racing. These were the things, he thought. These were the things that champions, heroes, and legends were made of.

"What is it we have to bring to his lair and why can't you use magical means, Lord?" Dash's tone carried a bit of arrogance to it this time. His question was honest. There had to be a reason a man with such wealth couldn't afford a single teleport ritual to get whatever he needed to whoever he needed there in the Golden Sands Desert.

"You're smart, Dash, and that is why you're going to be something of legend someday, assuming you don't get killed of course. There aren't too many people left in this world these days strong enough to perform those rituals. Thox has equipment and old items along with learning casters that can get it done but there's just too much paperwork and people in the know going that route, if you know what I mean."

Dash did know what he meant. There were people he was trying to keep out of the know so to speak.

"So what are we transporting?" Kraydia questioned curiously.

"As a rule, you shouldn't ask that question. Either it'll be revealed to you or it won't. Your job isn't to be curious of me but to perform the task given to you." Quinn was smart and his words unfortunately made sense to the lot of them, all except Dauge.

"If we don't know what we're working with, we don't know what we're guarding, and if we don't know what we're guarding, then we can't protect it to our full potential. If we don't ask questions, and we don't know what we're working with, we might be delivering ancient artifacts to a demon lord. How do we know there's not more to you than what meets the eye, my lord?" Dauge spoke up clearing the thickness out of the air for the entire group.

Dash laughed internally. Dauge was smart, very smart, and probably smarter than the rest of them. However, his inability to communicate hindered his connection to the team. When he did speak and communicate it usually dropped the jaws of everyone around him.

"Well played," responded Quinn, impressed with the young Xavier. "Now that Tha'Raws has been captured and his following disabled, I will be able to fully concentrate on my politics here in Thox. With you all as my team, that means quite a bit for you. If you do this for me, if you bring this little ring, this insignia ring to my friend, then I'll forever be in your debt."

"What about those lycans we killed and if we're the reason this Tha'Raws was captured as you say…. Then where's our forthcoming payment?" challenged Pitt.

"Pitt!" Dash yelled at him.

Pitt didn't quiet down. He stood tall and held his ground. He was only in it for the coin and the coin hadn't been brought to him yet. Nothing about payment had been even talked about. He was to the point of walking away and leaving them all.

Quinn smiled. He liked that in Pitt. He connected with Pitt on an unspoken level. He understood where he was coming from and thought back to when he was a gladiator in Corvana before any of the known kingdoms even knew who Corvana was. He remembered traveling with his companions through teleports to and from the different pantheons until eventually becoming enslaved and forced to fight for the once mighty kingdom.

Quinn's mind brought him to the day he earned his freedom at the cost of Tha'Raws' tail. He humiliated his friend but also to prove a point. Now, in a different pantheon in a different kingdom of sorts altogether, Tha'raws was in his prison safely being looked after. Tha'raws was too good and too moral for his own wellbeing. Luke, another colleague of his was gone, lost to the shade and undead. He'd taken up the ancient trade of the Forsaken somehow, during his time fell victim to a vampire, and emerged from it as some kind of monster.

Davion, another ally was lost to the undead as well. A disease took him, but rumors later informed the Thoxen lord of his former ally's undeath. So many of his allies were dead and gone now. Only Oggy his half-orc cohort remained of his former team. Og was too slow to function safely on his own and unfortunately had to be detained in a cell as well. Quinn and Og had been inseparable since childhood. Quinn smiled again, he'd made it through so much and came far. Of all the powers and legendary men and women he'd walked with, he was the only one to come away virtually unscathed and victorious in the never-ending struggles against life.

"Easy Dash, payment is part of the game, isn't it?" he asked, smirking.

Dash turned to look back at Quinn. Barking for payment was a quick way to get shorted coin and further work removed from your plate. Quinn seemed to take heed to it acceptingly. Perhaps it was because he to was an adventurer and traveler at one time.

"Forgive my large friend, Lord Quinn, he—"

Quinn cut off Dash, knowing exactly what excuse he planned to lay before him.

"He just wants what's coming to him. I have a pouch of three hundred and fifty golden coins for the each of you," he finished, smiling.

Pitt's face lit up. The average man made about three to six coins a month. A rich man could make seven to eleven. And in a ten-month calendar that meant an annual income of thirty to sixty coins for a poor to average man and seventy to a hundred and ten for a wealthy one. Here he was, barely freed from the chains of slavery and already, he'd made over three times that of the wealthiest man he knew.

"I can begin my search for Shiva," he said.

Pitt often talked aloud but to no one directly. It was a trait the team had come to appreciate. Dash always assumed he was reminding himself of what he needed to do and what his own goals were.

"Why does your friend have a lair? These are things we need to know, Lord Quinn," Legion said.

"None of your concern," he challenged, hoping no one else popped back at him. "All you need to know is the lair isn't even your destination. All you need to know is you will be heading to an area remotely close to the entrance of the lair. From there, you'll drop off the insignia ring and return to Quinn Town."

"You mean Grogan's Mill?" Legion rechallenged.

"No, I mean Quinn Town. I won't be here a day longer than I have to. The maps will have your shortest routes to the lair and back to Quinn Town."

"So we'll meet again at Quinn Town then?" Dash confirmed.

"Looks like it," the little Wilden said popping up.

"Yes, we shall adjourn again in Quinn Town," Quinn confirmed, pulling a small wooden box from his purse.

"That's the ring I take it?" Dash asked.

"It is," he answered.

Dash grabbed the small box and dropped it in his purse. "It will be done." He locked hands with the lord for the first time.

The two shook hands. To Dash and to Quinn, that meant something. Arm to arm, the two embraced. Dash smiled first. Quinn returned the gesture, then Kraydia and then finally Pitt. Legion's face never cracked nor did Dauge's. The two cold brothers just looked at each other and then to Quinn. Legion didn't care too much for it all but work was work. Dauge felt something more afoul and wasn't sure he truly wanted to be apart of it. Fear wasn't his obstacle but love. His love for his older brother instilled fear into what could happen to them. That was going to happen in the style of life they chose. Something about this Quinn didn't sit well with Dauge. He knew something was wrong. He could feel it.

The team took the maps, coin, and paperwork for Quinn, shook hands and parted ways. Dauge never opened his mouth about all the eyes mounted up on them. This Quinn was someone of importance, so why would he want to hire a group of nobodies to take care of his work for him?

"I don't like it, Dash. I don't this one bit," Dauge had to say. He couldn't hold it in one bit.

"We have the package. We have the routes to get there and back to our guy. Why he wants it dropped off or what's waiting on us there is not our concern," Dash replied.

"Again, we could be working for a serious crime syndicate here. Our freedoms and reputations could be in danger," Dauge pleaded.

"My brother's right," added Legion, looking over his shoulder to seeing Quinn disappear into the small crowds of people walking the streets of Grogan's Mill.

"As of right now Quinn is our in. So far, he's an upstanding member of the Thoxen people. He wants this done not in secrecy but in privacy. Every man has a right to his own privacy. So what, he doesn't want to get the Thoxen government and higher ups involved. Let's do this and make a strong name for ourselves here in Thox." It wasn't so much his words but tone and how he said them. He had a way with words and a way with people. The more he spoke the more sense he made to Pitt, Legion, and even Dauge. Kraydia was neutral either way. She didn't really have a plan and so far, following Dash and his dashing men was working for her.

"Guys, Dash couldn't be more right. And besides, the Golden Sands are said to house some of the oldest places in the Thoxen region," Kraydia said, throwing another useful piece of information out there.

"Maybe so, but first we have to get this ring to this location and see what happens. Quinn's convinced his friend we'll find and know us. Afterward, we have to get back to Quinn. From there, we'll get all the payment we have coming from him and then, the real work begins. The secrets to Gorgan's Mill will be our reward for this." Dash made it sound good, like success was guaranteed. It wasn't. It never was.

"Without risk, what is reward?" Dash said to the crew as one. His words didn't goad any of his teammates to answer or question anything but rather think and ponder in the confines of their own minds.

Legion thought what reward was to him. It would be acquiring wealth, fortune, and fame and a name to go along with the likes of his uncle Cyclor, his father Taj, and possibly even his grandfather Dominick.

Dauge's idea of a perfect outcome was to become the truest to oneself that was possible. He wanted to become the best Dauge he could for him and those around him. Secretly, he wanted to honor those that trained him in his arts; so many tricks and skills from the Lotus belonged to him and not even his brother knew of them. He hoped to one day return to his adopted people and live out the remainder of his days with them.

Pitt wanted Shiva. He didn't care how it happened or what the cost was. He had to have her. She was beautiful. He agreed to a lifetime of slavery in order to save her. She promised to one day return and buy his freedom but she never came. Perhaps the cost was too great or maybe other things came in the way. Whatever the reason, he was free and free to find her now. Coin was coming in and soon he would have her. He could feel it. He just knew it.

Kraydia wanted to return to her people of the Feywild. She wanted to be accepted once again. And the only way for her to be accepted would be to make such a name for herself they'd have no choice but to welcome her back. She wanted the Wildens to not only accept her back but want her back. She wanted to be embraced by her people, all of the creatures of the feywild. The priests of Thedia all claimed all other planes were long detached from Thedia; only in death was one able to reach another plane. The feywild detached when Gemini first appeared for fear that the collateral damage would be too great for them to take. There were still links between the two and those links were precisely how the Wildens first showed up.

Dash's dream was right there before him, at his feet. He had a strong team, growing with every day and waking moment. They were coming together and becoming one with every passing day. He hoped to one day have the team behind him like Starius Duro of Eternis once had. He hoped to have the team behind him like Aliendrad of Lyneth once had. He wanted to be a hero the children pretended to be, a man every woman wanted, and every man wanted to be. He wanted the fame and notoriety as a leader and healer of the land. He wanted to cleanse the world of evil not for the sake of Thedia but the recognition that came with it. His goals were the epitome of the classic adventurer.

Chapter 20

It had been weeks since the team departed from Grogan's Mill to the marked location on Quinn's map somewhere in the Golden Sands. Dash and his team just broke ground taking their first steps on the burning sands of the Thoxen desert.

The desert was said to be beautiful but one of the worst in Thedia. Its days were hotter than any other known desert and its nights colder.

"We made it," Dash said, excited.

"To the desert," Kraydia scoffed. She wasn't happy at all. The trek thus far had been treacherous and scores and scores of Targnok's beasts as well the wild beasts of the area gave it everything they had to end them.

"Relax Kraydia, the mark isn't too far into the desert. On this map, see…" He stopped and pointed the location to the little Wilden. "I told you. It won't be long!" Dash couldn't have been any happier even with dehydration nearly sitting in. He pulled a wineskin from his side, finishing off everything it had.

Dauge and Legion just laughed. They were used to the desert. This one in particular was a little harsher but no matter, they thought. The two brothers were more at home in a desert than they were anywhere else.

After a short stint in the desert, it was finally time for the team to rest. It was dark and the last bit of forest was just out of their sights. The cold was setting in and the wind was picking up. Dauge ordered the team into a deep indention with a large sand wall to protect them.

"We should be fine behind this sand dune. The dip in the dune is deep, should be big enough for the rest of us," said the younger Xavier.

The crew hastily hurled off their gear into the small pit. Pitt was exhausted. He did carry more than the rest and for some reason this trek just had him worn out. He dropped his bags and blades and rolled into the pit. In the same motion, he yanked his bedroll out from a satchel falling from his shoulder.

"Goodnight," he yelled excitedly. He didn't wait to discuss anything. They were good enough friends. They could cover the watch for the night, he thought. It wasn't long before the sand was gone. The hard winds vanished along with the cold of the desert night.

He was back home in wild forests of the Greatland. The trees grew differently there and the wild was a little more dangerous, but only if you didn't know it. He was one with nature in the lands of his people. Even he and his people knew to stay away from the Blue Forest, a segment of something not natural to any prime material world.

However, he was with Shiva! Shiva was with him! She'd finally agreed to put it all behind her and embark on a life of simplicities with him in his own homeland. They would marry and raise children. They would grow old together and one day perish from their material bodies hand in hand as their children watched over them passionately, pleading with them not to take the last step toward the next life just yet.

The fields beneath him were warm and moist, some of the fans, the trees of the Greatland, must have moved to better their positions toward the beaming in sunlight. They always left puddles of warm water and steaming mud when they walked. Then again, the Greatland was a scorching land to live in.

Shiva was cold and it was a perfect mixture. She lay and sometimes even hovered over his body to tease him. She was thin and fragile. Her skin blended with the waters washing ashore his homeland. Her skin was as blue as the ocean's truest water and her eyes like morning frost sickles. Even her hair was the color of the cold. It was mostly blue but with long strands of gray and white.

And she was perfect and flawless to Pitt. Pitt, she'd granted him that name. It wasn't his real name but it was the name she wanted him to have so he kept it. She forced long blonde locks to grow from his head. He kept them. He was an oddity to his own people with hair growing from atop his head.

He didn't care. He was amongst his own and with Shiva. Something about her was dark and unnatural. Again, like everything else about her that was wrong or different, he cared not. He only cared to slam his face between her thighs and pleasure her the way he knew she enjoyed most.

There she was, lying atop him. The more he tried to grab her, the more slippery she got. Eventually, she floated off of him and hovered above him, playfully teasing him with kisses and sexual gestures.

Her warm powers touched the very back of his body even though he lay upon it. The warmth of her massaging powers grew and moved, covering his back and his arms, his pelvis and legs, and finally the soothing powers touched his face and neck. Yes, these were the moments he missed the most with Shiva.

What was she really? She was different. She was not of Thedia, at least in his opinion, though her humanoid figure, even though clouded in the makeup of what she currently was, still resembled an elf or perhaps an eladrin at most. She was only around five feet two inches tall and truly small and fragile. There wasn't much to her but her appearance left a mark on all the eyes that fell upon her.

The ground beneath him was sinking. He was falling deeper into the warm mud and water below. Looking about, his people were carelessly just taking care of their everyday business and none seem to care that the dirt and sand was gagging him and killing him. Shiva floated higher and higher until finally, she was longer in his sights.

"Come back," he gargled.

The desert sand submerged him and moved like a dry quicksand all around him. The more he moved, the more cavities in the underground terrain would fall in and force him deeper into the sand. Sand, where were the trees and the cities of his hometown? Wait, Pitt's eyes opened to a nightmarish reality. Giant centipede like appendages were all over him, holding him, pulling him, grabbing him, choking him to the point that even his behemoth frame couldn't break free.

The appendages were thick, black and slimy. They came to small points from robust beginnings. His hand tried and tried to maneuver its way to his executioner's axe but it was no use. Suddenly, the feelers weakened and a squeal cried out from underneath the sand. Holes and cavities were everywhere around them. When the opportunity presented itself, Pitt leaped from the ground, taking his axe in hand all in one smooth fluent motion.

Coming up from underneath him doused in the guts and insides from something was an already equipped Dauge. He pulled himself from the carcass of the juvenile red worm. Guts and glory were written all over him. Dauge carried a short sword in his right and some claw like weapon in his left.

"Get up!" Dauge yelled.

Most of the crew was already awake and grabbing for their things and moving for their safety. Legion's morning star was out and ready. Dash quickly created a small aura, blessing his friends' weapons with slight enhancements in the event they would need them against anything else.

"Fall back," Dash ordered.

The sand continued to fall in and move about until several red-scaled worms broke ground, revealing their massive bodies.

"One for each of us." Legion laughed.

Kraydia moved into position behind Pitt, blasting one of the five horse-sized worms with a series of sonic energy rays. It's back stiffened, arching back. Two of the creatures lunged simultaneously, knocking Legion from his feet and catching the leader of the group's leg inadvertently with a few scales and legs. The smooth scales left behind a substance numbing Dash's leg. Right behind the substance, a few of the creatures' appendages and feelers gashed him right below his left buttock in his thigh. It was deep.

"Ahhhhh!" he cried out in agonizing pain, losing all feeling in his left leg before falling nearly limp to the ground.

Dauge's newfound weapon found its mark in the same moving worm. Dauge stepped on and leaped from his recently downed brother, thrusting his claw weapon into the creature's body only long enough to hold him in place in order to plant his short sword farther up in its body closer to its head.

Direct hit! He thought. He let go of his open-faced, wrist-sized iron-claw-like weapon to force himself up farther on the menacing creature's body. In seconds, his found his body going numb. He refused to give in. He wasn't going to give up before finishing the creature off. Even with the creature moving at full force, Dauge managed to force himself up from his one hand and plant his short sword into the creature's skull, burying it all the way down to the hilt.

The creature screeched and rolled. The first roll went with Dauge going underneath him, taking the full brunt of his force and weight. The second carried Dauge and its own momentum over, launching Dauge several feet into the air and finally back down to the ground completely numb and useless. His consciousness was all but gone.

The other worm that was moving with the one Dauge just killed pushed and pushed through the sand until it felt it was out of harm's way. Then, with everything a safe distance behind it, it turned back to engage its prey once more.

Meanwhile, Legion was back to his feet, standing with Pitt over Dash, holding off the creatures as best they could. The creatures slowly invaded the two's territory but Kraydia's arcane attacks from behind certainly help keep the three remaining beasts at bay.

Legion's peripheral vision revealed to him his brother's position. One of the beasts was racing toward him. It was the one who fled the engagement initially. Now, three more remained against Pitt, Kraydia, and Dash. The three of them should be able to hold them off, he hoped. He didn't have time to think but only react.

He took his two-handed morning star and started over toward his brother. "Dauge," he yelled defiantly. Legion was defying the idea of the sandworm beating him to his brother.

"Legion," Pitt roared.

Legion left his post in the regrouped stance against the worm, leaving himself wide open for all three of the bastards to have at him. The first turned, ignoring Pitt whom it had been facing head up to snap at the fleeing Legion.

Knowing saving him would leave himself open, Pitt still overhand lopped his axe onto the top of the attempting worm's neck, severing its head from its body. The remaining two snapped at the now-vulnerable Pitt. One was pushed back by Kraydia's ray of frost. She sent a whirling stream of cold into the hot-climate-based creature's abdomen, pushing him back and saving Pitt from another bite and more pain.

Another ray of frost enveloped the face of yet another worm. Kraydia's battle tactics were working and the snaps and bites of the worms still weren't enough to topple the mighty Pitt. Legion was in full pursuit of the other worm still heading for his brother.

Dash came up with a trick of his own, putting one of his many crossbow bolts in the nearest eye of the closest worm. Kraydia's frost blasts kept one back while the now-aggressing Dash kept the other, giving Pitt enough time to regain his thoughts, weapon, and footing.

"Ah, Kraydia get back!" Pitt ordered.

Behind him, Legion heard the arcane assault of Kraydia complimenting the fully capable Pitt and Dash the team's buff caster. These people were friends but they were not his brother. Nothing or no one could replace his Dauge.

"I'm coming brother!" he barked psychotically.

Dauge's eyes were barely open. The creature's mouth finally engulfed his feet and ankles. Dauge's mouth was too numb. He tried to cry for his brother but only slurs emanated.

Legion arrived just in time, bashing the creature's head with the heavily weighted and spiked ball of his morning star, forcing it to regurgitate what it already had in its mouth and belly of his little brother. Like an ironworker hammering pikes, Legion relentlessly attacked his brother's aggressor, all the while hearing the fight of his friends go on behind him.

The worm finally rolled to its back, secreting an acidic spit at Legion. The older Xavier dexterously evaded the attempt and finished the horse-sized thing off with another wild swing, planting the star's ball deep into the lower gut region of the creature.

Legion was tired and out of breathe. After a short break, he planted a boot on the dying worm's body in order to gain leverage for pulling his weapon from its body. Looking back, he saw Kraydia and Dash finishing off the last worm with bolts, blasts, and other arcanic attacks. Pitt finished up, lacerating the other from top to bottom, spilling its guts all over the sand, him, and even partially on the downed Dash.

"You okay?" Legion asked his brother.

"Helenudplfnekwnsdunif."

Legion couldn't make out his words but he knew what he meant. Legion hoisted his little brother over his shoulders and back.

"Come on little brother. Let's get back to the crew and get you healed," he said, pleased. They'd done well he thought.

Legion tossed Dauge down by Dash. Dash's leg was healed. He'd healed it himself since the fight ended. Legion smiled. Their team leader waited until all enemies were gone before worrying about himself and Legion knew Dash was in serious pain. That cut he had was deep.

"Those worms are—" Dash started but Legion cut him off.

"Aren't found in the Republic's desert, I'll tell you that." Legion's finish to the statement wasn't exactly what Dash was going for.

Pitt was cut up pretty good but Kraydia seemed to be okay. Legion and Kraydia darted off without instruction in order to salvage what was left of their gear.

"Ugh, I can feel it wearing off," Dauge popped out. He was still lying in an indention in the sand. Slowly but surely, he was able to get to his feet.

"Where'd the claw thing come from?" Kraydia asked, finishing up the pile of belongings.

"From inside that damn worm that had Pitt all but gone," Dauge said half smiling.

"It didn't have me!" Pitt challenged.

"Oh, take it easy big man. I was there to make sure it didn't get you." He winked.

"I knew it was there! I was fine!" Pitt was becoming hostile.

"Easy Pitt," Dash said, dusting himself off.

"Pitt's not the one that broke rank," Dash continued.

Dauge, the usual cold one with no sense of personality was trying to be lighthearted and now Legion was being cold. In an instant, Legion's face grimaced. He looked bothered and unaccepting of Dash's words.

"What did you say eladrin?" Legion daringly questioned.

"Easy brother," Dauge added.

"What's wrong, Pitt? Who broke rank? What rank?" Kraydia asked.

Dash listened to his people question and talk. It was understood to stay together. In the event of magical or breathing types of attacks against the crew, there were proper procedures in scattering while remaining strategic.

"I didn't break rank," Legion stated.

"No, your brother did," Dash answered.

Now, Dauge was cold. He did what he had to do to save his brother.

"It was a fight, we got split. It happens," Dauge said.

"Separating is an easy way to die out here," Dash reminded.

"It was an accident, eladrin," Legion charged.

"Stop calling me an eladrin. I am only half and that is rude," Dash replied.

"Guys stop! We made it. We're okay. We have a job to do." Kraydia said.

"I wasn't in any danger of any worm," Pitt said, trying to remind everyone and most importantly himself.

"Well, maybe just that first one… he snuck up on you!" Legion said, laughing, trying to lighten the mood.

The crew broke into a series of light jokes. Dauge told the story of how the worm creatures with centipede like appendages made their presence known by moving too close to the sandy surface. More and more, the sand fell into the fresh cavities left behind by the moving worms below. Pitt being the largest possible food choice, he was their first target. Dauge retaliated by going behind and underneath them all before finally coming though losing a short sword but gaining a hand-clawlike weapon in the process only to lose it later in the killing of another worm.

Dauge found one of his short swords but the other one was gone. The claw was also found. Dash and the others confronted Legion about his ability to wield the massive star sometimes with one hand and other times with two. He responded explaining the weapon's ability to learn and grow with him. It since had become unnecessary for him to wield it with two hands. However in doing so, he was able to apply more force. The weapon was slowly adapting to the force thread of his two hands as one, meaning it would strike a target as if Legion wielded it with two hands even though he would only be wielding it with one. His weapon was growing with him.

The team continued through the desert. Days came and went. More red worms attacked the crew and more red worms went down. The desert birthed a variety of worms that attacked Dash and his team. The blue ones seemed to be the most vicious and dangerous but the red worms carried the most potential.

Dauge regularly milked their dead carcasses for poison and carved tools from their bones. Unfortunately for Dauge, his short swords found too much to fend off from the insides of the worms. However, this came to Dauge at a high point during a fight with a massive green worm, a variant that spit and secreted acidic liquids.

Dauge's final melee weapon choice were a pair of shaved-off sickles. Sickles looked like shorter, handheld versions of scythes. He cut the handles down to where they fit tightly and perfectly within his fist. Then, he allowed the top of the blade, the non-sharpened area, to run down outer part of his forearm. The points of the blades extended out just a few inches past his elbows. He used them in a very different manner. He called them armblades.

It was midday in the desert. The team was getting close to their destination. The desert sunk down to a massive valley to their right.

Dash ordered the team away from the ledge. "We should make it to the destination by sundown." He stared at the map.

"These worms are getting on my last nerve," said Legion.

Dauge kept quiet. One of the added bonuses to fighting the worms were the vials of poisonous and flammable liquids he was able to milk.

He coated his throwing knives and Dash's arrow tips primarily with the red worm's debilitating poison. It was to the team's good fortune to learn that the worms were not immune to each others, much less their own, secretions.

Suddenly, a rip roaring sound thundered from the valley to the right. The intense force was so strong it knocked all five of them from their feet. It screeched again. Then, the sound of mortals crying out to each other emanated.

"Spread out!" one of them said.

"It's going to breathe again!" another added.

Dash and crew quickly regained their footing and they all looked at each other confused as to what to do.

"Dash," Pitt started out, executioner's axe already in hand. "We move!"

"Nonsense, we've killed dozens of these worms," Legion challenged.

"None made a screech like that!" Pitt said.

"Remember how we found you?" Dauge asked.

Dauge pulled two throwing daggers. Whether they chose to run, hide, or engage he was ready. He didn't care either way. There were people traveling in the desert but he most likely didn't know them and more importantly they had nothing to do with the mission.

"If it were us, we'd want someone to help," Dash stated. "Legends aren't made by taking the easy road."

"Dash, that thing sounds huge. Legends aren't made by dying recklessly in the desert either!" Pitt pleaded. "They're not our concern."

"Keep your distance, approach the ledge…" Dash stopped. He was at a loss for words. The massive thing extended so high it broke the horizon of the ledge from where the team was standing. Its body was so thick it could've even eaten every other worm they'd faced thus far in a single gulp. Its skin was purple. They'd not seen a purple worm before but the stories of the purple worm were nightmarishly told to them as children growing up.

"A purple worm!" Pitt roared in fear.

"This can't be!" Dash fearfully said, barely loud enough for the others to hear.

Dauge still cautiously but hastily made it to the ledge of the valley and back, signaling for his crew to remain steady the whole time. The thing still hadn't seen them, or him thank the dead gods. Dauge was at a loss for words.

"What's wrong?" Legion asked his brother.

"How big is it?" Dash asked.

"We have to help those people," Kraydia ordered.

"We can't," Dauge said. "We cautiously move and get the hell out of here. There are six of them and there's not too much we can do for them. From the looks of it, they're already just about gone."

"I am a Sylvan and our people survived the Nine Scars War. We did it by knowing when our lost were lost!" Kraydia said. She was serious and sincere.

"Sylvan, thought you were Wilden?" Dauge asked.

"Sylvans and Wildens are the same, human. Some still loyal to the Feywild or those that have just recently come over claim the name Wilden over Sylvan. Thedia's older Sylvans sometimes claim the true elf or eladrin races now." Kraydia said.

"This is no time for a history lesson," Dash said, aiming his crossbow. "Dauge," he started. It was something in his voice when he said Dauge's name in that tone. Sometimes it was to ride ahead and scout and other times it was to start the engagement. At any rate, it proved to mean his decision was final and his mind made up and the others were simply to act according to Dauge's actions.

Moving in, the purple worm was enormous and clearly different from the other worms of the Golden Sands Desert. The majority of the other worm variants had useless appendages extending here and there from their bodies. Not all of them possessed them but some, probably forty or fifty percent of them did. It seemed as though all of the red worms had the appendages, as if they were worms crossed with great centipedes.

This worm was different, firstly in size and secondly in build. Its body was no less than a hundred feet in length and five feet in width. More of its body was still under the desert sands. It's upper top area, all except its underbelly, was thick and armored and colored a deep purple. The soft underbelly was a light yellow and its eyes beamed a black radiance. Its eyes were similar to that of a snake, in the form of slits. The mouth, or rather the end of the beast's body, just turned into a circular hole filled with rows and rows of teeth. The armored top body scales looked just too thick to even attempt to penetrate.

Down in the valley, six humanoids scattered and fled about, frantically rushing off, ignoring the worm and their own allies for the hopes of saving themselves. One, a seventh, actually stood alone against the thing. The rest of them were too far down and away and covered by the storms of dust whirling around for the party to see. This tiefling was clad as a priest of the RiverMortal. Silvery raindrops decorated his armor and weapons. The worm spat at the rushing off humanoids only to have liquids bounce off ethereally apparent walls.

Alas, the angered worm dove straight into the desert, mouth first over the fearless tiefling. The giant worm shot so hard it uprooted its entire body, diving all in and making a new hole in the desert where the tiefling once stood.

"That thing had another fifty feet of body still hidden! Ain't no reason to help them! We can't help them except maybe sending a few prayers and a priest for them. They're done for!" Pitt yelled.

Dash let loose his first bolt, then his second, and finally a third simultaneously to giving Dauge a divine strength boost. "Up!" he screamed.

Dauge leaped high into the air. Right behind him were the three bolts launched by Dash. Pitt and Legion charged down where the tiefling was taken and swallowed whole. Mid air Dauge flung two throwing daggers and gripped his armblades. This time, instead of positioning the blades down his arm he reversed them to extend outward from his fists, as if the blades pointed outward directly from his hands.

One, two, three, four, and five, the three bolts and the two daggers stuck in one of the creature's shell like scales. On its top and on both sides just before the underbelly started, rows of sharpened like, taller, more-pointy scales outlined the creature from its mouth all the way down to its tail.

The creature was already in dive mode by the time Dauge caught it. The sixth missile, Dauge himself, also struck his mark. Both of his blades stuck deep into yet another one of the creature's scale-like body armor pieces. The momentum carried Dauge so hard he nearly lost his grip but luckily, he was able to regroup and reset himself.

Dauge noticed the tip end of the creature's tail. It was a poison stinger! He knew poison stingers when he saw them. And he wasn't sure if anything he knew could take a shot from that thing. The worm was too fast disappearing into the ground with the tiefling before Pitt and Legion could make it to the bottom of the desert valley.

Smoldering fires with traces of lightning and sonic energies surrounded the Wilden elf. Rays of encircling energies shot out from the petite woman's hands. She roared out in flames. For a moment, her entire body was engulfed in her own powers. The rays found their target, the purple worm, just in the nick of time as her rays slammed into the very tip of the worm's massive stinger tail.

Again, it screeched out but this time in agonizing pain. Dash took his position in front of his wizard. Pitt and Legion still charged the ground. Two humans, one a wizard and the other a warrior of some kind, and both appeared to be just about on their last breath. An elven archer broken and busted lay half buried with sand and half drowned in her own blood. Two dwarves, one a priest of the RiverMortal and the other clad in light clothes with staves and amulets around him also lay broken and finished.

The only still moving member of the team was the most unsettling of them. He was short but athletic. His skin gray as a corpse and his hair matched in color. His hair was long and matted. He'd been long without a good bath. Two peculiar devices were attached to his wrists and a short sword and dagger filled his hands. A single black cape covered the rest of the creature's lightly padded armor.

Just as the creature's tail disappeared into the ground, Dauge peeled his weapons from the thick scale and rolled to the desert. He let the momentum of his lunge from the creature carry him over a full forward roll all the way up to his feet.

Dauge turned, arching his upper body back to see the shadow elf staring at him. It didn't know whether they were friend or foe. Coming just behind Dauge were Pitt and his older brother armed and ready for anything the desert might throw at them.

Dauge arched back around, seeing Kraydia and Dash still at the top and just starting their advance downward. "Hurry up. We don't want you to alone up there. Who knows what could come at you!"

"You okay?" Pitt asked the shadow elf.

Dauge turned around, looking at Pitt. Dauge didn't trust shadow elves. Then again, few people did.

Pitt and Legion rushed off, mending and bandaging the wounded until Dash was able to get there and commence his few healing spells. He had enough in him to mend their wounds and stop the bleeding but not enough to bring them to good standings. Kraydia surprised the crew again, proving her worth by complimenting Dash's healing with a bit of her own.

"You can heal?" Dash asked pleasantly surprised.

"I have more than a few tricks up my sleeve you don't know about," she answered.

While Dash and the others regrouped with the others from the other team, Dauge and the shadow elf kept cold stares on one another.

"It's not done," Dauge stated.

The shadow elf pulled a belt of flasks from his body and tossed it to Dauge. "It's dwarf oil. It'll burn for days."

Without further instruction Dauge took off, making sure Dash had plenty of the oil flasks to dip his bolts in.

Only the human warrior of the crew was good enough to fight. Dash and Kraydia hovered over the bodies of those too far wounded to continue. The ground rumbled.

"Spread out. This thing breathes acid like dragon breath," ordered the shadow elf.

The ground below them suddenly gave way. Rock and clay from deep beneath mixed with the sands of the desert blew through the air. The purple worm reemerged, making his presence more than known.

From its location, the crew were directly and perfectly surrounding it, all seven of them, the five of Dash's crew and the two remaining from the other. It flared around, flinging its head back and forth spouting acidic blankets every which way.

Kraydia was on top of her game, casting wonder wall. Wonder wall was a spell in which mini ethereal walls protected the caster and its allies. It could last as long as the caster wasn't interrupted and chose to maintain it. However, maintaining the spell forced casters to go into a deep meditation, ignoring any and everything around them. Dash couldn't believe it. The spit from every direction was batted away or caught and tossed by her simple walls. The walls were only good against simple missile attacks, certain magical ones, but mostly against secretions just like this. Gaseous breaths however negated the walls as they were able to pass over and through them.

Dash dipped his poison-tipped bolts with the dwarf oil and as quickly as he could commit to launching every single one of them at the beast.

"Baby girl, hold those walls until we get enough oil on that body to engulf him in your fire." The others around Dash heard him but Kraydia was too far gone in her trance to hear a thing.

Pitt got the beast's attention, hacking into its softer underbelly roaring out as he did it. Pitt called from the spirits within him and the powers of his ancients to come forth with him and they did just that. Following his attack, the spiked ball of Legion's morning star slipped in through the newly carved slit in the worm's underbelly.

Legion pushed it in deeper with the top of its shaft. Both entities within the star came together, releasing a catastrophic current of electricity through the creature's body. It didn't quite extend all the way through it but it certainly made its presence count.

The purple worm flicked its body forward at Legion after the lightning's stunning attack was over. Legion kept grips on his weapon and the spiked ball ripped out of the creature, delivering even more hurt and pain to the sand monster.

Pitt managed to get out of the way just in time and get another cut in on the underbelly before ultimately having to disengage and move out away from the creature. Dauge let go of his final four throwing daggers, now completely doused with dwarf oil. One by one, the shadow elf's flasks of oil found their marks on the purple worm.

Dash's final bolts marked their spots alongside the underbelly when they could. It just seemed nothing the team had could penetrate the thick hide of the armored topside of the worm. The shadow elf danced and moved around the worm at its impact point of the ground. Right where its body extended outward from the desert ground, the shadow elf moved and danced about, cutting and gashing alongside Pitt and Legion.

More and more acidic blankets flung but to no avail for the creature. Finally, it wised up, peeling its tail from underground and aiming it directly at Kraydia.

"From behind my lady!" The still downed human said barely conscious enough to speak at all. He raised himself in order to fend off the tail attack. He was too hurt. He was too wounded and slow. His movements were barely above a baby's crawl.

The tail pierced him dead in his stomach. The man whispered a cry and spat blood across and down his short brown beard. With a final act he defended his new-found friends and his old ones by swiping the very tip of the creature's tail, lacerating it so badly it would either rot off on its own or just break off by the day's end. Most of it fell off and lay with the dying man who just gave his life for Kraydia.

Dash turned. "No!" he cried.

The wounded tail still trudged on, bleeding and squirting acid everywhere. Dash dropped his crossbow. A bit of acid caught Kraydia, burning her back and shoulders. She cried faintly as her knees buckled from the surprise and mental break from her meditation.

Dash wrapped up the tail fighting it off, holding it off, taking the leaking acid damage while Kraydia moved the others and herself to safety. Alas, the tail whipped too hard and Dash was thrown. He hit the ground hard. The hard ground knocked the air out of him.

"Get back!" Dauge ordered.

In unison, the seven able bodies fighting the thing backed off.

"Now Kraydia now!" Dash ordered.

The hurting Wilden mustered up her strength and conjured her fires with all she had. Her favorite spell would come in handy, she thought. Fireball. It was a spell as old as magic and rarely did people use them in deserts, she sadistically thought, laughing to herself. This time was going to be one of those times where it was needed more than anything else. Fireball was classified as an area of effect spell meaning it hit large areas, usually hitting multiple targets. This thing was so big and the oiled areas were so scattered, it would be like she was hitting multiple targets. Her target wasn't even the worm itself anymore but the various locations of splattered and dwarven oil.

"AHHHHHHARRARGHH! LAEN DIRE RACH EN KRIEG ASSYRIECH!" Her elven heritage coming out, she yelled words to incite the flames in her ancient language.

Sparks trickled through her fingers. Two drops of fire dripped from her eyes. And then, all of a sudden, a fiery combustion of fire encircled a massive area of the purple worm. And as hoped, the dwarven fire caught and the magical core of the fire immediately turned to burn hotter. More blue flames popped up after the initial blast was gone.

Again the creature cried out. Scattered oil fires plagued its body. The shadow elf laughed in excitement.

"It's working it's working!" Dash yelled, hysterically happy.

The worm writhed about in pain finally slamming its body into the hot sands, using the course beads of the desert to oust the fires on its body.

"It's not working! It's putting the fires out!" Legion yelled.

The worm recoiled itself. Only a small segment of his body was burned or even damaged. If they could finish off that segment it would still kill the body, and thus, the head as well.

Legion waved his morning star around. The ball and chain began to glow a light yellowish green. He replanted his feet as if he were tossing the ball like a rock in a sling. The magical weapon created a phantasmal ghostlike ball and chain that flew from his weapon. The weapon then lost its glow.

The worm completely submerged itself in sand only to pop out its head in time to catch the magical bombardment from Legion. The ghost ball penetrated the creature's right eye as its right side was to them. It writhed and rolled again and finally burrowed back down into the desert ground below.

"I cannot believe we survived a purple worm that big! It must have been an elder worm or something!" Dash said excitedly.

"Everyone okay?" Pitt asked.

"It was just a large adult. We've hunted many worms here," the shadow elf answered.

Looking around. The human wizard was dead. The elven archer, the two dwarves, the human warrior clad in full plated armor, and the shadow elf were all that remained of the team.

"Gratitude," said the shadow elf.

"I am Dash Riproc. And gratitude is not needed. We hope you would've done the same for us."

The shadow elf didn't reply.

The human warrior stood, using his greatsword to assist him. "We certainly would have."

The shadow elf didn't seem too friendly but at the same time he did seem thankful.

The warrior peeled his dented helmet from his face. He was a handsome man and young, maybe in his early twenties. His hair was strawberry blond with shades of a darker tint mixed in. His eyes were dark. He was a tall man, possibly over six and a half feet tall. His body was lean but looked bigger due to his armor. His white armor had seen better days. On his breastplate rested the beautiful portrait of a platinum colored dragon head with seven canaries dancing encircling it.

"You serve a faith?" Dauge asked the human.

"Don't you?" he replied pleasantly.

"Everyone okay?" Dash asked this time.

One by one, the elven archer, the two dwarves, the human, and the shadow elf admitted to being okay. Dash's party followed up by stating their injuries as well. Remarkably, none were too badly injured. Only Kraydia who'd been burned severely on her back and shoulders from the creature's acid.

Pitt's legs were hurt. Somewhere in the mix of it all, the creature's body secreted and spewed acid on them.

"Who are you all?" Dash asked.

Legion quickly reunited with his brother. Dauge was out of throwing daggers and now Dash was out of bolts. The purple worm was gone for now he thought.

The human stood tall, answering first and proudly. He was obviously the leader. "I am Storm Stars, son of Evan Stars, son of Stasius Stars, descendant of legendary Thoxen General Storm Stars the First."

The Stars family had been ousted by Thox for Stasius' actions. Legion and Dauge both heard the man speak. They heard the story from Malakai and Giovanni about Starius killing Evan.

"Small world," Dauge whispered.

"I am Legion Cage Xavier, of Taj Odin Xavier, of Dominick Xavier of Eternis." Legion turned, countering the human's introduction with his own.

The human smiled. "I've heard so much about you, Legion, and your family. My family has fallen from grace here in Thox and I hope to someday return it to its rightful place."

"You serve a dragon god?" Kraydia asked.

"Typherion of course, of the eldest tier of dragons," he answered.

"My liege, Trizz of Eastham is dead," the shadow elf chimed in, approaching Storm from behind.

Storm dropped his head. "Forgive me my new friends. I've lost too many friends these past few days. This behind me is Krazaikaei, we call him Krazy for short. My elven friend here is Alanis Tan." Alanis stepped forward. She didn't wear much but basic leathers over her upper body, shoulders, and left arm. Her lower body was completely revealing, minus the short breeches that barely covered her pelvic area. Her stomach was also bare and pleasant to look at. Her dark hair and eyes matched the color of her skin.

The two dwarves stepped forward together. One was clad in plate-based armor but unique and customized to his body. It was gold in color and also carried the platinum dragon symbol that actually represented the gold dragon of honor and loyalty, Typherion. On his back rested a great warhammer. His head was bare of hair but carried a golden beard, though short and neatly trimmed, quite uncommon for a dwarf.

His dwarven kindred looked like a witch of some sort. His black hair was long and clean and unlike most dwarves, he didn't have any beard at all. His skin was pale and his body was covered in dark colored clothes complete with rosaries, chains, necklaces, rings, wristbands, and other forms of exotic jewelry. Amulets, nasty and of dark origin hung from his neck. He was certainly the oddity of the group. He introduced the two of them.

"I am Felzen, a warlock if you will. You're probably asking how a warlock such as myself is traveling with a party so noble as this one. I serve the risen devil Retris respectively and utilize my infernal pact to serve both Retris and Typherion as honorably as I can. This is Dargon Reihak, another priest of Typherion."

Storm looked back and listened while Felzen introduced himself and Dargon. When, he turned back to Kraizaikaei and then placed his eyes back on Dash, the leader of the team that just saved them.

"I'm not sure how we just got through that," Legion said, smiling and halfway laughing. His laughter told those present something wasn't normal with him. In fact, he may even be quasi-insane.

"And you didn't want to help these good people?" Legion laughed to Pitt, mocking his early words. In truth, Legion didn't care to help them either and his words only mocked the decision of the team's leader.

"Still think it was foolish, Legion. We don't know these people," Pitt answered quickly.

"Gratitude," Krazy said again.

Pitt finally nodded, showing acceptance to the dark elf for his words of appreciation.

"What are you boys doing out here anyhow?" Legion asked, aiming his words mostly at Storm.

"Forgive me. Trizz of Eastham was my oldest and most dear friend," Storm said, his voice calm yet stern. He dropped his head to hide his tears.

"It's okay to mourn the loss of a loved one," Kraydia said.

Alanis nodded in compliance to Kraydia's words, placing her hand upon her liege's shoulder. The two dwarves turned and started together, along with Krazaikaei, in digging a grave for the recently slain wizard.

"I started my quest with nine. Of the nine, only Alanis, Trizz, and Dargon were my crew. The others were enlisted in the name of Thox. Felzen came hearing my name and Kraizakaei hoped to earn his freedom. Ekemon was also a priest of Typherion." The human champion of Typherion signaled to the area where the tiefling went down. "He was a good man. I am a paladin and champion of my faith. I had hopes to one day build a team and shatter evils throughout my realm. I've only discovered I'm nothing of a leader and I let myself and my people down."

Dash listened to the others' leader. He was down on his luck and hard on himself. "Relax friend, we all know what choices we make can all have consequences. These men that are left look to you to guide them home."

"Trizz was a magnificent soul," Storm said.

"And so are you... friend," Dash said smiling.

Storm threw his hand upon Dash's shoulder and Dash complimented the gesture right back.

Legion looked off with his brother, reassuring themselves for the sake of everyone that the purple worm threat was gone and no more were coming,

"So I ask you, what brought you to the desert? What brought you specifically here?" Pitt asked.

Storm, Alanis, Dash, Pitt, and Kraydia all sat down next to one another. Kraizaikaei, Felzen, and Dargon were busy burying Trizz and Legion and Dauge were out scouting the perimeter, making sure everything was soft, simple, and unmoving; meaning the ground beneath them wasn't preparing to let loose any more worms.

"So far so good, brother," Dauge said.

Legion let his little brother do the scouting. He only came along to keep a close eye and hand ready just in case his brother fell into trouble.

Alanis unhooked several pieces of Storm's armor. The midday sun was falling slowly into the horizon. Finally. Storm managed to get the breastplate off. Like a huge weight was taken from his shoulders, he leaned back into the arms and lap of Alanis.

"Feel better baby?" she asked her apparent lover.

"I do," he answered, looking up at her.

"So where do you go from here?" Dash asked him.

Storm looked away from Alanis and back to the relaxing Dash. It was a hard fight. Purple worms were notorious for slaughtering travelers, adventurers, and heroes of all kinds. They deserved at least a short break.

"I came here by charge of Lord Decimus Sextus of the Thoxen city Omina. We were ordered to vanquish the undead incursion and retrieve the Virgin Circlet of Dragonkind. We failed at both. We underestimated the level of threat the undead presented. And Trizz and the others died for it."

Dash listened. He was still being too hard on himself, he thought. "Storm, what do you mean by undead incursion. Could we be of service to you?" he asked.

Pitt gave Dash a ridiculous look, revealing his mental anguish with his crew's "leader." Dash looked back at Pitt. "What? Pitt, we have to help these people. We're already here. They need our help!"

"They don't need our help, Dash. They need a priest or someone to fix their insane minds. We find Quinn's friend, deliver the ring and go from there," Pitt said plain and simple.

"Lord Quinn?" Storm asked.

"The same," Dash answered, turning back away from Pitt to Storm.

"He's a good man," Storm replied.

"I got that impression. That's why we're here. I hope to prove worthy to him so that he may guide our names to the ears of those others in Thox who could one day perhaps use our assistance." Dash said.

"He will. He will. And so will I," said Storm, smiling. He tossed his arm out for Dash to catch. The latter obliged and the two engaged in an honest man's shake.

"I cannot thank you enough, Dash," Storm said.

The surviving members of his team slowly but reassuringly claimed the same to Dash and his people. The two crews dug into deep conversation with one another. Dash couldn't help but notice Alanis gazing at him the way a wife stares her husband. As a bard, he was trained in the art of disguise, charm, illusion, and seduction; or at least this bard was anyway. He was a ladies man and he knew when a lady liked him. And Storm's lady friend kept a thick eye on him.

He did very little other than smile back, maybe a hair too much. He didn't want the wrong idea to inspire in the paladin's mind. Finally, after a little more than a short rest, the two teams arose and regrouped themselves.

Like Pitt, Kraizaikaei was hesitant to shake with the others. Well, after Pitt's words and actions. Legion and Dauge stayed away for the majority of the conversation. Finally, it was coming to an end and the two groups were preparing to finally part and Legion and Dauge were finally back reunited with their team.

"All's clear," Dauge said.

Legion stood, brash with his morning star hung over his shoulders and neck. Storm and the others were impressed with his weapon. Its abilities clearly aided in their survival.

"That's some weapon, sir," Storm said.

"My father gave them to me," Legion answered.

"Them?" Kraydia said.

"Them?" Kraizaikaei asked.

Kraydia smiled. Krazy kept his focus on her just for a bit but chose not to let his feelings out. He did fancy her but he was a shadow elf and she was Wilden, or Sylvan elf. Of all the races, those were by far two of the most polar opposites.

"He carried the swords SOUL and LORE and when I was granted ownership of them they came together to form this," he said.

"Impressive," Storm replied.

"I guess. I consider it more of a mourning star than a morning star. It reminds me of all the hatred I had built up for my father until it revealed the ugly truth about it all." Legion stopped himself. Why was he telling these complete strangers about his story and personal beliefs?

"That's admirable, friend," Storm said. "I'm glad you found solace through your pains and hardships."

"Mourning Star huh?" Dash questioned.

"That's what I've come to call it," said the older Xavier.

Dash's lips nearly cracked he smiled so wide. More and more, his people were becoming things heroes and legends were made of. Magical weapons forging for specific owners and new names became their titles.

"Let us journey together. This desert is far too dangerous and neither of us are in any condition to take it on alone," Dash suggested.

"I agree," Legion added.

"I thank you but we've lost too many. We must be getting back!" Storm said. "I suggest you turn with us. As a Holy Knight of Typherion 'tis hard for me to say this but the undead is too much for any one crew these days; the heroes of Thedia aren't what they one were. Nor shall they ever be again.

"I trust you won't make it back at all if you don't come with us. We're better off uniting here Paladin of Typherion, the good dragon." Legion knew his faith well. He'd learned of the good dragon as a child.

Storm looked back at his people. He didn't want to admit defeat. His team was hurt, tired, wounded, and had suffered heavy casualties. Dash and Legion were right. They would not survive the desert alone. "That undead incursion my friend, I don't believe even collectively we could hope to survive it. It's the damnedest thing. They're even fighting each other here!"

Dash's crew listened to Storm. Storm's entire group fell back to the sands, relaxing while they could. They were hurt, all except Krazy. He was only somewhat wounded. Dargon, the only priest of the two groups left, was hurt and out of healing powers. Dash and Kraydia's healings were used up as well. Storm explained his healing capabilities were strong as was his bloodline but during the battle he utilized everything he could to keep his people breathing.

"So this incursion, this Virgin Circlet of Dragonkind, what's it all for?" Legion asked.

From behind Dash, his crew, and Storm, Alanis spoke up. "Decimus explained he fears it truly exists and was potentially found by the wrong hands. He hopes to keep it safeguarded under the watchful eyes of Thox."

"Then it is agreed. You will come with us and we will join you just the same. Together, we will deliver Lord Quinn's gift to his friend, find the virgin circlet, and deliver a devastating blow to the undead who think they belong here," confirmed Dash.

"HERE HERE!" Legion roared out. And quickly, the remaining members of both teams did just the same. Legion secretly encouraged them to agree with Dash even if more questions still mustered in their heads. Dash was thankful. His strong-blooded Eternian warrior brought up to the Republic was already coming into his own. He was truly pleased.

Chapter 21

T he company of ten fought ferociously, against the desert's worms mainly, and together the ten were quite successful. Fortunately, no more purple worms attacked the company. The deeper they got into the desert, the less worms came at them.

Storm started to tell his companions they'd reached the undead occupied territory of the desert. Just then, Not Dash, Storm, nor any of the others could have prepared for what came at them. Two large adult worms, one red and the other pink led a slithering set of eight smaller multicolored worms and possibly twice as many juvenile ones.

As if queer colored worm, the pink wasn't enough to throw them off, both adult worms carried riders. And these riders weren't mortal. The adult worms were possibly twenty to thirty feet in length but scarier. These wild beasts were being ridden by riders wearing pieced-together chain, ring, and plate. Their faces were open from their helms, revealing a power glowing from their eyes, red in color, and skinless faces with rickety weapons weakened with age at their sides. Both riders wore golden circlets but Dash, Kraydia, Dargon, and Felzen all knew they weren't of magical ancestry.

Coming from behind the advancing worms and riders, a small disciplined army of old humanoids, skinless mostly, and dressed similar to the riders of the worms. Each of the skinless beings wore a red splotch of paint on their breast coverings. The riders carried swords at their sides but the units marching behind all seemed to carry pole-arms of different types.

More startling yet, dozens more tore out from the sandy ground below. These ground dwellers didn't carry the pole-arms of their undead kindred but short swords, bucklers, and some even held falchions in their grasps.

In a matter of moments, Storm of the legendary Stars bloodline along with Dash Riproc were surrounded. The eight following them were also surrounded. Though both teams brought five along. Storm's team suffered casualties and Dash's team was without a true healer. It was clear, in order for Dash's team to continue successfully, they would from here on out have to stay overstocked with healing potions or perhaps hire a healer to travel with them. Fortunately, it was a lesson learned while their numbers were temporarily doubled.

Dash pulled his short sword and pierced the rotting skull of the nearest creature climbing out from the ground. Pitt's axe swiped just once in a complete circle, severing several of the creatures' heads nearly in half. Legion put his spiked ball through the upper torso of another that was nearly fully surfaced. Dauge was out of throwing daggers. All of his missiles and weapons were gone. All he had were his twin armblades. He turned them around holding the weapons as pointed weapons extending outward from his hands. The blade parts were gripped to be on the inside closer to his body but extending outward rather than reversed and running upside his forearm. He poked, stabbed, slashed, and cut through eight of the undead bastards before they even knew what hit them. Kraydia created a zone of fires and radiant energies behind them, taking care of probably ten or more of the climbing out creatures.

The paladin called forth his divine might, smiting several more of the arising undead. Krazy focused more on the juvenile worms, sending dart after dart from his wrist bows at several, trying to halt their progress. The goal wasn't to kill them but to hold them off as long as possible. Hopefully, until the nearby climbing undead were finished. Alanis saw her comrade and accommodated him as best she could. Dauge carved her a dozen bone arrows made from the things they'd faced. Alanis was beautiful in her movements and in the way she flung her bow. She released her arrows almost sexually. It was so beautiful and erotic the way she moved. Even Dauge got distracted by the Amazonian beauty.

Meanwhile, Dargon kept a keen eye on things and kept zones of protection up and about for the crews. "Stay in the zones! Stay in my zones! You can feel them!" he screamed.

Felzen looked excited for the most part. He pulled a jeweled wand of black marble and ivory from his black suede cloak. He methodically and harmoniously danced it around. One by one, the oncoming worms bounced back. Lightning bits struck them again and again. Tidbits of lightning bolts sparked every so often from the wand. A powerful charge went off, popping one of the larger small worms like a balloon. Dauge noticed the warlock. He was talented, good at what he did.

The crew kept up their tactics and the undead of the ground were gone before too long. The remaining worms scurried off, seeing the lightning of Felzen dance about them, injuring and killing them lazily with ease.

The adult worms, red and pink were steadfast with their riders and their undead units behind them. Storm was the first to walk through the debris of the slain undead and worms. Krazy walked behind him first to his left flank. To his right, as always was Alanis and as always, her bow was readied and aimed. This time, she kept it trained on one of the riders, particularly the rider of the pink worm. Felzen and Dargon fell in behind them.

"I have three arrows left, love," she said, keeping her eye and bow trained on the pink worm rider.

Dash too was out of bolts from the journey. This journey was definitely going to be a learning experience, he thought. He made his way next to Dargon, immediately sending his magic to the buffing of the parties.

Dauge and Legion stood tall and strong, with Pitt now ahead of them all. Pitt placed the head of his axe on the sand beneath him, keeping the shaft of the weapon vertical and placing both of his hands one atop the other on the end of the shaft.

Kraydia readied the most powerful fire spell she had left, conflagration. "I can hit them all and let them know we're here or I can really hurt those two bastards up front."

There were two ways to cast the spell. One was to spark a little fire to them all hoping something would catch aflame in order to deliver more damage. The other was to really melt a body with every ounce the planes of fire had to offer. It usually resulted in the dissolving of most equipment caught in the blast as well.

"Careful, one of those things might have the circlet, Kraydia," Felzen reminded.

"I doubt it would come out here if it did. Hell, we don't even know what it does," Legion said, uncaring.

"Does it matter? Weapons, armor, or anything imbued with magic is so rare these days friend, so something labeled with the title dragon certainly has my attention," Felzen responded.

"Agreed," said Dash.

"And if it's not in the possession of one of mine, then I care not if it gets destroyed," Kraydia added.

"Wait, no, it cannot be destroyed. We need it! We promised Lord Decimus!" Krazy cried.

"Better it be destroyed then in the hands of an enemy, or in the hands of evil, friend," Storm reminded.

The two worms entwined in one another, lowering their heads and arching their bodies. The two riders' impressions on the teams changed. Their appearance was much more than first thought. Crown jewels and gold decorated their headdresses, armor pieces, and clothing. Giant rings hung from their bony fingers. The rider of the red worm had teeth of steel. His teeth literally made and carved from iron and steel. Their eyes gleamed a reddish green.

The steel-toothed character pulled a sword radiating a dark power from his side. The rider of the pink worm stepped secondly after him with a long staff embroidered with symbols, coins, gold, and jewels appearing in his hands magically the second his feet touched the sand.

The aura of death forced them all a step back.

"Your forsaken here," the sword wielder said. He peeled a dark black steel shield from his back. Old carvings were all over it. Tattered pieces of leathery coverings flapped in the wind. The sun was setting. It was quite a horrid sight.

The sword wielder took his place affront the staff carrier. The two worms slithered about, unwinding themselves slowly before chomping their way back into the underground below. The small undead army continued its march in the distance while the sun slowly continued to set behind them. It was quite a sight.

"I am Storm Stars of Thox, high champion of Typherion."

"I've known champions of the good dragon, paladin," the sword wielder claimed. "And you're not of their blood."

"Our blood need not be shared to serve the same faith," Storm challenged.

"I meant your blood was not to be compared to the likes of theirs." He laughed, mocking the paladin.

"We are here to find a friend of a friend." Dash stepped forward taking charge.

"We know why you're here. We know what you possess. Give it to us and be spared your lives. Three shall stay as a reminder of your misdeeds this day," the sword wielder said.

"Are you the friend of Lord—" Pitt started to ask.

Legion slapped his chest. "Quiet."

"How do we know you are who we are to give this gift to?" Legion asked. "Who sent us here to bring it to you? The person who sent us said you knew they would have it. Now then fiend, who was it?" Legion asked.

Dash sadistically grinned at the undead creatures. Legion was becoming more and more clever with every passing day.

"We are not. You possess the phylactery of the lich Davion of the North," the sword wielder said. The yellow jewels upon his hilt glimmered and sparkled when he spoke of Davion.

"Impossible!" Storm cried.

"It was worn by the noble knight of Valence Sir Garland Jendragon, doubling as a wedding band until his body expired. His was buried with his true wedding band and the phylactery was returned to Davion's last known living friend, delivered directly by Jendragon's eldest boy. Lord Quinn is his last known living friend of his traveling days. He gave you the ring to return here, to Davion. I assure you, you will not survive the hour should you not hand it over to me now," warned the steel toothed sword wielder.

"How do you know all of this?" Pitt asked, arrogantly taking his axe up.

"Give us the ring, mortal. Give it to us now," he ordered.

"Why is an undead so anxious to destroy another?" Dash asked.

"Davion came here from the north, putrefying our desolate sands. Ours was here first and Davion's essence interrupts the balance," it continued.

"Wait, yours? What do you mean by yours was here first?" questioned Storm.

"Give us the phylactery!" it screamed.

In the same notion the undead finished closing the distance. The worms ripped up from the ground, knocking all ten of them to their backs. They flailed around like a dying fish out of water. The undead charged, pole arms ahead, ready to go. The sword wielder took a defensive posture over the staff carrier.

Dash fell back. This was all too much. They had no chance. They were going to fall in the desert to the undead just like Storm Stars predicted. Storm looked at Dash, giving him a look of accomplishment, telling the other crew's leader through expression that he was right in a silent "I told you so" type of way.

"The red worms are weak against lightning," Felzen reminded.

"Most of these worms are weak against lightning," Daron added.

"We have to do something," said Kraydia nervously.

"Like what, die?" Pitt sarcastically suggested.

"Careful, the worms of the Golden Sands Desert do not flock together. They're very territorial." Alanis whispered. Her words were more for herself than the others. She was reminding herself of something she'd learned long ago. The others could hear her but she was off in her own daze, thinking of a way for the teams to survive.

"What's that got to do with anything," an angry Felzen asked.

"They're obviously being controlled," enlightened Dauge.

"And if they're being controlled, it's by the riders. And if the control can be taken or broken..." Dash said, answering several of the team members' questions all at once.

The two skeletal masters continued their slow advance toward the group. Simultaneously, they stuck out their skinless palms of their left hands toward the group.

"Now, give us the lich's soul," the two demanded.

Dash thought through his bag of tricks, sending a dispel magic at the still entangled worms.

What luck! They were right! They were dead on! Instantly, the worms looked stunned and confused. A hiss echoed from one of the worms.

The red worm and all neighboring worms together flapped and flopped but ultimately were thrown to the air. Each color worm had a different basis, for instance the red worms carried debilitating poisons. Apparently, the pink worm's innate abilities were magical. They weren't natural beasts but magical ones. Pink worms were magical creatures.

The two skeleton war masters jumped and turned. The monstrous pink bodied creature was not like the others at all. Was it also intelligent? Most worms had nil intelligence and were just mortal wrecking machines, as if they were born to only hunt, kill, and eat.

"Now!" Dash yelled.

"Now!" Storm seconded.

Seeing the magical powers embodied in the worm, Dargon disenchanted his immediate area. Felzen sent lightning his way.

"No Felzen!" Kraydia screamed, creating a small area of anti-magic around the worm. The ethereal shell of arcane substance popped like an invisible bubble. Fiery sparks and clouds of smoke erupted from the booming blast.

Felzen's lightning bounced from the worm. The bolt disappeared and reappeared halfway through Felzen's stomach.

"Ugh!" he gasped.

The dwarven warlock fell to a knee. In anger, he raised and took charge at the worm. Another blast from the countered dire lightning put another lightning charge through his chest planting the dwarven warlock flat on his back.

Afterward, the worm stumbled and the skeleton's staff began to glow a nasty yellow. Whites and vibrant pinks followed. A ray of power shot forth into the creature's skull from the staff. It was quickly humbled.

The standing nine backed away. This worm tossed and hurled dozens of worms and select undead into the air like nothing. Some even engulfed in flames and others complete entropy. And this skeletal warlord conquered it with such ease. Again, it was under the control of the warmaster.

Storm's other dwarf rushed forward. The priest of Typherion slammed his hands upon his friend's chest dropping to his knees. He pushed and pushed his healing powers into the chest and heart of Felzen. Dargon felt Felzen's life slipping away. Slowly, and then more rapidly, his heartbeat began to falter, stumble, and stop.

Storm stepped forward assisting Dargon. The help was duly needed. Storm's help got Dargon's heart pumping again. His eyes opened and closed. He blinked hard, trying to wipe away the pain.

The worm took the staff wielding warmaster upon its skull. The sword carrier stood fast while the small army of undead charged in a swarming frenzy at the standing nine and downed dwarf.

Mourning Star grew to the calling. Two more chains born from the weapon's top dangled down, forming into two more spiked balls of iron. Legion whirled his weapon around. His right arm gripped it alone with strength. The weapon made its carrying arm stronger. His left took up his small iron shield. His shield batted away the pole-arms and fended off their attacks. The three-chained morning star, called Mourning Star, followed, smashing into all kinds of areas of the creatures charging them.

In threes they fell. Dauge knew his armblade slasher weapons weren't going to be ideal against the glaive-wielding skeletons. He stood near his older brother, using his arms in due fashion, fending off attacks, knocking back weapons, and occasionally severing skeletal heads. Dauge's feet came into place, sporadically kicking down and crushing off knees and lower legs of the creatures during his defense stints of his brother.

Storm, Dargon, and Felzen regrouped with Krazy and kept steady, holding their ground affront Kraydia and Dash. Dash kept his buffering spells over the two groups and Kraydia's fire consistently ended groups of three to nine at a time.

Pitt launched his axe up and down time and time again, opening a clean hole from the group to the skeletal sword-carrying warmaster. The archaic inscribed armor of the skeleton began to emanate an aura similar to the color the staff wielder's staff began to glow, an off red.

Pitt broke rank and made his way through the skeleton horde, charging his way to the still-grounded warmaster. "AHHHHHGGHHHH!" he screamed, charging with everything he had.

The worm behind Pitt tried something but it fizzled and faded. Even Pitt could feel the residue of the failed magic attempt slam into his skin. A slimy substance bathed his arms and chest, making it all sparkle from the desert sun's rays.

Dash couldn't believe it. He saw the residue melt from thin air on top of Pitt. The skeleton proved too much different than ordinary undead by easily evading Pitt's attack. Undead weren't commonly known for their dexterous ways.

His scimitar-like blade, broken and cracked all over, sliced across the left ribcage of Pitt as the skeletal warmaster sidestepped and dropped to a knee beside him. Almost immediately, a black goo lapped around the thin but deep wound. The black substance mixed with Pitt's blood dripping down from his body.

Pitt took only another few steps before falling to his knees, releasing his axe, and holding his wound.

Again, all pain was gone. The desert was gone. His friends were gone. Only she was there. Shiva was her name and she'd come to him again. If this was his eternity, if this was a dream, then just let it be, he thought. He never wanted to return. How'd she get here with him? How'd she get him here? Where'd he come from? The green fields were back, the beautiful trees provided shade from the warm summer's sun.

Pitt's eyes opened again. A nasty scar lay where the wound once was. His skin was sealed though. His mind caught it last minute. It was Storm. He broke rank and gorged through the undead to heal him. Now, the paladin of Typherion was fighting the undead monster alone.

"Get up Pitt, I need you!" he screamed.

Storm was distant from the rest of the fight. He and the skeleton were dueling off and on their own. The pink worm and staff wielder were turned away from the undead horde and his allies. Something had their attention coming from behind them. How long had he been out?

Now, three fights were taking place. The eight remaining were fighting off the undead horde. Storm was dueling the skeleton warmaster carrying a sword and that ridiculously powerful pink worm and its rider were engaged with something that had come from the other side. Something behind them got their attention enough to get them to turn around and ignore his friends and the rest of the fights.

The undead horde was weakening. Dauge looked at Legion. Legion was doing fantastic against the remaining undead.

"We have to help Storm!" Legion cried.

Dauge was way ahead of him. Seeing Dash lead the remaining members of the teams to a domineering position against the fading undead, Dauge elusively dazzled his way through the fight. He darted toward Storm with Legion breaking skeleton bodies in front of him to quickly follow.

A small group of the undead climbed from the group just in time to perfectly surround the recently acquainted duo. Kraydia's fire once again game to the rescue, engulfing all nine of the sons of bitches, burning them back to the ground from whence they came.

Legion and Dauge both knew who it was. They both smiled at their friends' sweltering style of arcane. They didn't have to say anything and neither did she; both brothers and she more than they were truly happy to have found her that day.

Pitt was back to his feet. His axe was back in his hand. He shook the dreariness off and started toward the worm. Luckily, the worm and staff wielder were still focused on whatever was on the other side of the worm.

Dauge and Legion regrouped with Storm and together they continued Storm's assault on the skeletal warmaster. His defense was impeccable. Storm hadn't touched him once since the fight began. He, however, was bleeding profusely. With Dauge and Legion engaging the creature, Storm was able to step back and utilize the last bit of healing powers he had to keep himself strong enough to keep going.

So Dauge, Storm, and Legion were fighting the skeleton warrior wielding the blade. Pitt was having at the rear end of the worm, which was focused, along with its rider, on something new that entered the fight from behind. Something else was blasting away arcanically at the worm and its rider from the rear. Meanwhile, Dash led the rest of the members against the remaining undead threat. The casters of the crews, of course, continued to pick away at all the enemies using their magic in areas they all thought were best.

At last the undead soldiers were done. Alanis took down the last one with her bow. Dash used the last bit of his healing to send both Storm and Pitt revitalizing charges to keep them going. In an instant, the pink worm popped like soapy bubble. Electricity surrounded the creature missing the rider, however. The staff wielder dimensioned himself to the ground just before the electricity imploded/exploded his steed.

Electricity-filled remnants of the worm fell from the sky, burning like a gel of liquid fire. Alanis took the worst of it as one of her arrows took down the last of the undead horde. Dargon was there to purify her melting skin almost immediately.

"AHHHHGGHH!" she screamed. The rubbery worm pieces filled with electricity engulfed in flames, melding into her skin just as soon it touched her. Krazy took a hard hit of the worm blubber as well. Dargon worked expeditiously to keep his teams up. Dash's final healing spell did just enough to keep Alanis up and moving.

The staff wielder landed and empowered his staff, ready to annihilate whatever would come between him and victory. His arcane desert worm was now dead, completely annihilated. There before them all was a creature unlike any they'd ever seen.

"It's a lich!" Dash roared.

The black-boned skeleton was clad in unique protective coverings outlined with silver imbued with magics. His bones sparkled in the light of the desert day. His coal-colored skull was nearly invisible due to the brightness of the vampiric yellow orbs of his eyes. In the center of his yellow orbs burned a bright purple radiant energy. His armor coverings looked specifically constructed to protect his bones. He looked magnificent. Scarce black fabrics blew in the wind, revealing his silver-lined armor pieces. The wind stopped and the fabrics fell to his side.

Almost instantaneously, Dash's "lich" and the staff-wielding skeleton engaged. Magical bombardments, blasts, booms, zones, auras, rays, and cones rang out from the two. Just before he was engulfed, Dash saw the lich ward him and his allies. What was this thing? What kind of undead were out here and why were they fighting each other? Why would a lich protect mortals against other undead?

The entire field of sand where the battle had waged felt an old being's magic and the staff wielder's aggressive powers as well. One by one, and often in two's, they fell and collapsed as collateral damage to the magical warfare dealt by both staff wielder and lich. Had it not been for the protective guards and wards of the lich, Dash knew that he and everyone he'd come with would have surely been annihilated.

Chapter 22

I t was another beautiful day in Eternis. Like always, Dusk jumped out of bed the minute sunshine broke through her window. She grew up in the Republic with her uncle Adrian as her father but now she was back in her ancestors' true home of Eternis, and somehow, she was more at home there.

She knew Adrian's brother Taj was her true father but Adrian raised her. He was father to her. She loved Taj Odin Xavier. And after hearing all he'd done for Thedia, especially against Corvana, she'd come to love and adore him even more. All of her childhood memories reminded her of Adrian's being there.

Nevertheless, her family moved back to Eternis not too long ago and her life had been perfect ever since. She missed her brothers, Dauge and Legion. They left for Thox some time around when her family left the Republic. Simon, Gideon, and Dorian were still around.

Adrian was most proud of Simon and Gideon. They'd taken to schooling and education. They were going to be politicians one day, hopefully. Dorian joined an elven priest of the Rivermortal named Woodway and took to the wild as his uncle Taj once did so many years ago.

Dusk liked to make breakfast. It was always ready just in time to see her father coming down the stairs of their beautiful manor.

"Good morning my daughter," Father said to her.

She smiled. Her warm smile said it right back to him. The color of his hair had left him. It'd been replaced with a streaking white. His body was a few years shy of fifty, and yet, his face showed signs of wear and age. Adrian hadn't had the easiest life.

Behind him, mother followed. She loved mother dearly. Lady Destiny took her in just like she was her own. Destiny adored Dusk. The two were more like sisters than adopted mother and daughter. She loved her family. Her father was really the brother of her true dad and her mother was the ex girlfriend of her true father. Neither of the people she called parents were blooded parents to her. That didn't matter. Adrian loved and cherished her because she was of Taj, his brother. Destiny did the same even more so because she loved both Taj and Adrian.

The three sat around the wooden breakfast table. Dusk always appreciated the smooth circular shape of it all.

"Daddy, tell me the story of the table again," she asked.

She loved the story of the table. Mother told it to her first. Momma couldn't tell the story like Father could. He was natural storyteller.

"Oh, you've heard that story a thousand times. Pass the bread, baby," he said, smiling. He fell in love with his daughter every time his eyes fell upon her. She was daddy's girl and she always would be.

"Have you heard from Dauge or Legion?" he asked.

"No Father, have you?" she replied.

"Honey, Uncle Cylcor is coming back today. We should greet him at the port," suggested Destiny.

"Ugh, I've got too much to do today. Besides, Dorian's supposed to be coming back in as well. I can't wait to see him. I hope his uncle's dark side has left him in his travels," answered Adrian.

"Father, you've told me the story time and time again about the day Taj left home. You told me how he fled Eternis in the night with Uncle Starius. You speak of how grandfather Dominick loathed the idea and he didn't have the stomach to tell him. I miss Dorian. Why did you let him leave?"

"Because my dear, I learned from that fateful night long ago. And Woodway's a good man. Dorian will be safe with him. Or as safe as he can be I suppose. I don't like it any better than you do. As long as Dorian knows his home is here, he'll return often and hopefully, whatever that dark passion is inside his him will be vanquished from the overseeing of Woodway."

"I know. I just miss my three gone brothers," she said sadly.

"I know you do sweetheart. Now finish your breakfast. You're an amazing cook but it'll get cold." He smiled at his amazingly gorgeous daughter.

She had the tanned skin of a Republican girl, not the pale skin of an Eternian. Her skin was beautifully crafted and woven; the natives of Eternis often claimed it was kissed by the dead gods.

"I think I know why you miss Dorian so much. And I think I know why you're excited he's coming home," Destiny said.

"Mom!" she replied, knowing exactly what she was talking bout.

"What's all this about?" Adrian questioned, laughing.

"Mom…" she gasped, pretty much telling her she wasn't okay with her father now knowing why she was glowing and so excited.

"Oh it's okay dear, your father understands. We weren't always old you know. We were young once too," Destiny said, smiling.

"I know he's the king's son but that Bahaus is too old for you and he gives me the creeps. He's evil, Dusk," Adrian warned.

"Oh honey, she cut it off with the prince weeks ago. She fell for that Dar boy," Destiny answered.

"Dar, his father defied fate. I know Cale was a friend of Taj's and has been good to the community but he died and chose to return to life. What's that tell you about them. Dusk, stay away from that boy." Adrian continued to warn.

"General Cale Dar is a good man. He came back for love, the love of his wife and the love of his home. He's the General of Eternis for Gods' sake," Dusk said, starting to get a little angry.

"I've heard a million stories as to why he came back. All I know is Prince Bahaus is as dark as they come and he and General Dar traveled together and are very close. I don't trust either of them. It sickens me to know with Prince Aiden's death some twenty years ago that now Bahaus is the sole heir to King Gerear's throne."

"Why do you acknowledge the late Prince Aiden as a prince but not Bahaus?" Dusk questioned.

"I honor them both and respect them both. I'm just not sure I trust them. Prince Bahaus is a dark creature. There's no denying that. His loyalty and dedication to Eternis cannot be denied. General Dar the same, I guess. They have Eternis' best interest at heart but what they'll do to attain it may not always be considered honorable," Adrian said.

"I know father. I understand," Dusk replied.

"I'm just worried about you, babe."

Just before her father's words finished. Her mother started in. "Your father's just concerned for you sweetheart."

"I know. Kleiven's different. He's a good man. He's fun. He doesn't want a military life like his father," Dusk said, hesitating. It was too late. She'd already said it. Adrian was a retired war strategist and politician for the Republic of New Magic. He felt like everyone should spend a few years in the military.

"What's wrong with the shaping up with the military of your homeland?" Adrian asked.

"I'm just saying. He has plans to build businesses. Grow. Prosper. He's still an excellent swordsman."

"Dusk, from what I understand this Kleiven Dar takes to two-handed weapons over our dual weapons systems. He's a rebel."

"Dad, you're just being negative because I like him and he likes me. You're not going to like whoever I'm with at first."

"General Dar's going to help him get started huh?" he asked.

"No father, he's going to travel, adventure, dungeon dive and all that stuff. He's going to quest for lost treasures and gold. Then as soon as he has enough money he's going to begin building on to Eternis, expanding our borders!"

"High aspirations for the son of a death defier," Adrian scorned in a whisper.

"Adrian!" Destiny said, finally stepping in. She'd heard enough.

The two engaged in a lengthy conversation with Adrian quickly conceding to his wife, filling her ears with I'm sorry's and apologies until she finally felt like it was enough. He was still happy and cheerful though and the day was still early. When it was finally done. The last bite of his last biscuit and rose from his chair.

"Well ladies, I am out for the day. I love you both but I have business to attend to. You tell Kleiven I'll be watching him," he joked. He hugged Dusk from her sitting position, kissing her atop her forehead. He walked to the other side of the table embracing his love for a goodbye kiss and hug and then turned to make his way toward the manor's front door.

"Honey, Kleiven's a good boy and he'll be something great someday. I agree with your father about Prince Bahaus. I'm glad you're no longer with him."

"Yeah I know. He was really nice but so dark and cold at times."

"Your grandfather cut, carved, and sanded this table to perfection. This house, he built with his own two hands. Dominick was a great man. Taj and Adrian are both great men. Though I don't agree with all of his ways. General Dar is still a great man. Dorian rode off with the third battalion.

Woodway and that whole team joined them in that fight against that monstrous horde incursion to the East. They're supposed to be coming home today and I know Kleiven, whether he admits to wanting to be military or not, is still serving for his father right now. And you're excited because he's coming back today!"

Dusk smiled. She was dead on. Adrian knew Kleiven worked with the military but did not serve. That made him even more disgusted with him. Why not just serve and do your time like everyone else, he used to say.

Dusk made her way out for the day wearing her favorite combination of revealing white garments. The one thing her father couldn't stand about her was her inability to dress conservatively, or like a lady. Her white skirt and boots matched her nearly bare white top. It covered her breasts and upper back with wrapping white fabrics playfully dancing down her arms, covering them partially and ending with partial white gloves as well.

She wore her black hair down and made sure she had her best face on. She must have done her makeup ten times, she thought. There she was at the training grounds watching the young boys fight. She knew Kleiven would make his way there.

"I've searched the moon and stars for a face so beautiful."

She heard his voice. It was Kleiven behind her. She tried not to smile too big but she couldn't keep it in. The bleachers surrounding the training grounds arena areas couldn't contain her. She leaped up from her seat, looking down from nearly the tallest bleacher. There weren't too many watching the training this day.

Her eyes fell upon his beautiful face. His orangey red hair was kept short and his matching beard neatly trimmed. A few more scars ran across his face and arms. He wore no armor, only a simple green shirt and brown leggings and boots. He wasn't the most built man in Eternis. In fact, he stomach was kind of large and cushioning. He was a burly man with a little fat insulating his natural muscle.

His yearning desire for her and to succeed in life somehow captured her. She loved him already but she couldn't let him or anyone really know that. She'd have to make him earn it, of course. Thank the angels Legion, Dauge, and Dorian were all gone for the time; they'd never accept him. Then again, he was the son of General Cale Dar.

"You've returned," she said.

"I have. I've come for you," he answered.

"You're going to lay down your sword. I mean, hang it up." She giggled.

"When I can, one day, and hopefully soon."

"What will come in the years in to come?" she asked.

"I don't know. I'll forge it with these hands, cold steel, and love for you," he stated strongly.

She smiled. She loved his words. He wasn't a poet, just a natural with words who spoke truly and honestly from his heart.

She ran down the wooden bleachers, nearly falling face first into the fence surrounding the arena she was watching. She caught herself, regained her footing, and rushed to her lover's side. The two embraced tightly. Kleiven was back.

"How was your trip?" she asked.

"It was brutal. A lot of casualties. I am thankful to be here in your arms today. I could have very easily been one of them, you know. Your brother, my dear friend Dorian, he chose not to return with us. He and Woodway took their people to Myasuna. He said to tell your family he's looking to make it to Aflydor soon but I know not as to why, my love."

"Aflyndor, what business does Dorian have in Aflyndor?"

"Not a clue," he answered playfully.

"My father will be pleased to see you. Come let us join my family!"

She couldn't help but rub his stomach and side. Her fingers caressed his arms and shoulders. He was a big man, nearly six and half feet tall and weighed somewhere close to two hundred and seventy pounds. He spoke gently, like a bard but wielded his two-handed sword like a half-orc barbarian from Targnok.

"Your family never cared for me. That's what I've come to say."

"What, you're leaving because my family don't accept you?"

"Dusk, I love you. I've always adored you. Let's face it. My father isn't the most well-loved man in Eternis. He's returned from the dead for Gods' sake. And your family looks at me differently. I don't want to see your family and I don't want to spend time with mine. I'm not leaving just yet but I spend most days calculating too much. I want to spend the next few days only with you and enjoying your company. Then I will leave again and then I will decide what to do from there."

Her smile could not be contained. She jumped high wrapping her legs around his waist and her arms around his neck burying her head between the right side of his neck and his shoulder. He wrapped her up right back.

"Oh, how I've missed you," he said.

Chapter 23

egion awoke. His friends were all around him, safe. They were all there, his brother Dauge, Dash, Pitt, and Kraydia. Storm was also there along with Kraizaikaei, Alanis the archer, Dargon, and Felzen. They were all asleep but safe.

A small room of stone and dirt surrounded them. Legion felt he was underground. He could sense the musk of the air. The room wasn't too tall either. If Pitt were awake, he'd probably have trouble standing up straight. The floor was purely dirt mixed with old metals and broken blades. The walls were dark and the stones massive. The ceiling was a mixture of hard clay and stone. Yep, Legion was sure of it. He was underground.

The other nine were all in piles, lying and sleeping atop one another. They were wounded but healed. It was apparent they'd been in a vicious battle but their wounds looked as if magical mends had been placed upon them.

A single wooden door proved to be the only obvious exit from the room. Why was he the only one awake? Were his friends going to be okay? More importantly, was his brother going to be okay? Each and every one of them rested with their armor, weapons, and other belongings all around them. Nothing looked to be missing from the crews' belongings. Even Mourning Star was finely strapped to his side. However, the second and third tails were now gone. He knew Mourning Star changed and evolved to fit the situation. It was very normal for them to be missing.

Legion took the first step toward his brother in order to check on him and confirm he was okay when the door creepily sneaked open.

"Your friends are fine. Your brother is fine," a deep soothing voice said.

Legion jumped, startled. He threw his hand down to his side, ready to take up Mourning Star should the situation call for it. Something came over him. Whatever was here certainly had the drop on him and could have killed them if he really wanted to.

"Who are you?" he questioned to the open air, looking around quickly, waiting anxiously as if something was going to pop up behind him anytime.

"You know who I am, friend," the voice said again.

The door slowly continued to move open. Utter black filled the other side. The skeleton figure from the desert slowly drifted into Legion's sight. It was the lich! Where was he? Where were they? And what were they doing there?

"I do not know who you are," Legion replied, stepping back cautiously from the creature.

"You walked with my soul for a stint," answered the creature.

His black bones were even darker than before. His eyes were gone and the glowing colors from before were also gone. Trails of dried blood visibly oozed from his eyes just moments before, or so it appeared. His appearance was different. This time, he was completely shrouded in dark fabrics, woven thick and strong as to protect from the outside elements.

"Your soul?" Legion asked. "What are you?"

"Lord Quinn handed you all a ring to return to a friend of his. Did he not?" he asked.

Legion nodded in compliance.

The lich extended his right hand holding himself up with his staff in his left. The very same ring was on his finger. This was Lord Quinn's friend? How? Lord Quinn was a standup Thoxen with good morals and a strong background.

"Why me? Why am I the only one awake?" Legion asked.

More questions started to arise in the older Xavier. Why were the rest of them sleeping? How was he the only one not out? What was going on?

"Your connection to the undead. You have one," he answered.

"I do not. I'm just a warm-blooded kid from the Republic," he said.

"For starters, you're soothed around me. The others will not take to me as well at first. It's because of your undead link. It came from your father. I walked with Lord Quinn in my mortal days. My quest for power and the crossing with a mummy led to my untimely end and beginning as something I should've never been able to become. The others will wake but it will take time for them to adjust."

"Adjust?" Legion asked. "Wait a minute. If we were bringing the ring to you, then we've accomplished our quest for Lord Quinn. That being said, we should be free to go."

"Lord Quinn sent you here to bring me my Phylactery. I am much obliged. I have things to be done and I cannot do them on my own. Lord Quinn knew what he was doing when he sent you here. I saved your lives. You will fulfill my tasks before you are to return home."

"What were those things? Why is the undead fighting the undead out here?" Legion asked.

"I just came here. A powerful necrotic force beckoned for me. Eventually, I was able to turn against it. I'm not sure what it is under those sands but its necrotic and powerful. An undead incursion has grown into great forces out here. They've even learned to master the worms of the Golden Sands. My powers aren't what they were here. I've come from the Highlands of Valence. Something, a source of some kind, is empowering the undead here to levels in which simple skeleton warriors give me quite the trouble. They can sense undead. The source can sense undead. I've created a sanctuary here using powers far beyond your years and comprehension. I am safe here. I came here for Quinn and Thox. I am a Lich. I am Davion."

It was hard to tell what exactly he would have been in his mortal days but it was clear he was thin and nimble. He was probably an elf or half-elf of some kind. Davion? That was his name? He'd only heard that name once before.

"If you walked with Lord Quinn, you can't be the same Davion of Dorian and Davion of the Kingdom of Magic?" he asked.

"The wizard's duel that left the Republic a desert and all that between those two mighty beings is a tale of another man. I was named after the very same man," Davion lightheartedly said, laughing.

"Huh, how interesting. I learned about that duel as a child in school," Legion said, slowly becoming more comfortable with the undead entity next to him. He couldn't even explain why he was so comfortable with the undead being.

"It's most likely folklore more than anything but that's beside the point. I need you but what I need you to do is for the Kingdom of Thox and its people."

"Well friend, I returned your ring to you, your soul or whatever it is. I am an Eternian by blood. Thox means very little to me." Legion didn't even believe his own words and he knew the creature probably saw through them as well.

"Even you don't believe that, friend," Davion said.

"So what happened to you?" Legion asked.

"That will come in time. Let us all get better acquainted. They should be waking up soon. It'll be better if you break the news as to what is going on. My aura will weaken and frighten them. It will take some getting used to." Davion left. The door stayed open.

Just moments after he left, the others of the room started waking up. It started with Dauge. His eyes opened. Immediately, he jumped to his ready position, armblades out.

The others came to one at a time but unlike Dauge, they weren't so quick to jump to a defensive position.

"It's okay brother... everybody..." Legion started off talking to his brother but finished off saying the same thing to everyone. Finally, after everyone was awake, Legion started.

"Where are we brother?" Dauge asked anxiously.

"I don't know," he answered

"How long have we been asleep? How long have you been awake?" Dauge continued.

"I uh, don't know, not long... look... just listen to me for a second," he said.

The others mumbled questioned and moved around to get comfortable and back to their feet. They all searched their pouches and purses to make sure their things were still there.

Pitt held his head, rubbing it hard. "Oh, my head," he said, trying to rub it as if the more force he applied the quicker the ache would go away.

"Davion the lich saved us. We're in some kind of sanctuary he built that protects him against another undead force here." Legion looked around finishing his words. The teams were starting to understand.

Finally, everyone was up and ready to go. Legion took the lead. Kraydia peeled several coins from her purse throwing each one of them a single piece. Without a blink, the coins lit up. She'd cast light upon them. It was a spell that illuminated objects in order to help their carriers see more clearly.

A dark and narrow hallway rested on the other side of the door. The lot of them stood out like beacons of light in the darkest of nights. Legion treaded carefully. Old paintings of ancient men hung from the stone walls.

Again, the ceiling wasn't too tall and Pitt had to keep crouched in order to pass through the corridors.

"Keep up," Legion said.

Dauge grunted a compliant sound. One by one they voiced their opinion about the whole thing but made sure to keep pace with the ever faster moving Legion. The corridors twisted left and right until finally it came to an end. The hallway was barely big enough for one and half men to walk abreast. Some of the smaller ones like Alanis and Krazy were able to walk shoulder to shoulder due to the build of the smaller creatures.

A simple wooden door with not a spec of iron blocked their pathway. Save the iron handle and locking mechanism, everything about the door was wooden. Dauge moved to the front to take a peek at it all.

"It's not locked," he said, trying out the handle.

"I'm telling you, Davion opened the door to our room. He saved us in the desert. He wants us here. If he wanted us dead we'd be dead already," Legion reminded them.

The door opened up into a large mead hall. It was archaic but nice. A beautifully crafted table, rectangular in fashion and forged from ivory and bone, took the center stage of the room. At least ten chairs were on each side with a single head chair resting at the far end of the table.

Fresh food laced the plates at every seat. Red wine was in the goblets next to each plate. And there, at the end of the table was the undead half-elf Legion had come to learn was named Davion.

"Just because my heart no longer beats doesn't mean I no longer have a desire for good steak," he chirped lightheartedly.

Legion stood strong even after the aura of the powerful lich fell atop them. It hit them like a blanket in the wind being forcefully pushed and wrapped around them.

The aura was so intense that several members took a knee to regain their composure. Storm stood strong with Legion. Dauge couldn't, though he tried. Dargon was the first to fall to his knees. His true nature counteracted the lich's. Felzen seemed to be okay. Alanis managed as well. Krazy dropped. Pitt stood strong, holding in his previous meal with all he had. The aura was making him sick, truly sick. Dash's magics were enough to keep him partially standing but he was still too weak to talk. Kraydia bent to Davion's aura as well.

"Why are we here?" Legion asked.

"Because if I had left you in the desert with those skeleton champions, you would have surely died, if not by them then by the worms," Davion kindly answered.

"You're a lich!" Alanis said, thinking it was time to ready her bow.

"You needn't try it my dear. I'm far beyond the measure of your powers," he said to her condemning words. It was like he knew what she was thinking.

"Ugh, I... ugh... I..." Dash tried to speak. He wanted to take the lead but he couldn't. He wanted to take charge and speak proudly for the team he'd built. He couldn't. And though he didn't want to admit it, Legion was doing just fine.

"Why did you save us?" Legion said, revamping his last question.

"That's a much better question, human," the lich responded.

"Why call me human?" Legion challenged.

"Why call me lich?" he sarcastically answered, implying the rudeness of Alanis was no longer needed.

"Understood," Legion replied.

"Why are the undead fighting each other? I don't get it." Felzen asked.

"Sir lich..." Storm started.

"My name is Davion," he responded cheerfully.

"Sir Davion...I bear the same question. Why—" Storm started again but was cut off.

"Obliged. Thank you," he said to Storm for acknowledging his name.

"Why so thankful to a man who says your name?" Storm asked.

This time Davion's response was hard and cold. The warm-blooded mortals were beginning to irritate him and they could see it. "Because now I'm no longer an undead. Because now I am no longer a lich, because now, I am Davion the friend who saved you all from the desert and soon to be Davion the friend will save them and send them back home just as soon as the problems have the desert have been resolved."

"If you saved us from the problems of the desert, what can you hope for us to do against them?" Legion asked.

"Enough. Let me talk." He stood from his seat. "My phylactery was once worn by the late legendary Knight of Valence, Sir Garland Jendragon. It was in the form of a ring. It was hidden from all as to keep me safe and in return I protected the people of Valence. Hard times call for desperate measures and Lord Quinn asked for my presence here. It just so happened my presence in Valence was no longer needed. At least not for the time being. Quinn was considered my last remaining true friend and upon Garland's death, he requested the ring be sent to him. I've come here to reclaim it as Quinn has sent you all to bring it to me. Well done. Now then, Quinn fears a necrotic presence here in the desert and I must say I've sensed it and felt it to. It's not pleasant and it's strong. My few followers and companions here have battled the undead horde. They're constantly growing and growing stronger, my friends. Life is what I need to bypass them. Life is something I cannot fake or manipulate. Life is too precious a weave. When this necrotic essence is found and destroyed, then I shall see to it you all make it back to your homes safely. I will reward you all handsomely and Lord Quinn will see to it you all will be given the noble's touch when it comes to work in Thox." Davion looked around at the weakened ones and the others still standing. They were his last hope. He truly hoped Quinn knew what he was doing when he sent these.

"What's it to you? What is Thox to you? Why do you care? You're undead now, Sir Davion, but where is your true home. Is it Thox?" Storm questioned.

"No. My true home is none of your concern. What is your concern is what I am looking for. I am looking to empower myself and take the necrotic essence from this place and harness it. I can sense great power underneath these sands and I am and always have been one who has an eternal quest for power. You can understand that, right?" he asked.

"Aye," Storm answered and then several more ayes came from behind him.

The lich continued. "I will harness the powers of this undead entity and whatever else it's obtained along the way. I will use it to protect Thox and its people and whatever other kingdoms I may come close to in my travels. I am a good man and good friend to Quinn. Help me oust this incursion of undead and find whatever relics it may have. Whatever it's using to amplify his minions I must have. Then, you'll be able to rest easy knowing it's in better hands. That's all no concern to you. What is your concern is your current options. You've brought me my phylactery and for that I am grateful. I can release you all to the desert to return back to Thox on your own. Or, you can help me and be rewarded. And with my say so and powers and Quinn's help, I'll see to it you become the most famous team in Thox! Either way, I shall grant you all one wish for successfully handing over my phylactery and soul."

Dauge broke out standing strong. "My sister," he said.

Legion turned around confused. No one knew what he was talking about and Dash wasn't strong enough to speak or question it.

"Your sister?" Legion asked.

"I beg your pardon?" asked Davion.

"You're a lich. See to it she's forever protected. She lives in Eternis. Her name is Dusk. Be her guardian angel or send her one. Do whatever you can to make sure she's happy and well taken care of." Dauge said.

"I don't have any quarrel with that," Legion said.

No one else really said a word and Storm's team didn't really obtain the phylactery to bring back to him. Legion and Dauge both knew Dash wouldn't be happy with their request but then again they didn't really care. Dauge was closer to Dusk than Legion was but she was still their sister and having a good lich swear an oath of guardianship over her couldn't possibly be a bad thing, could it?"

"Now then, let's get started. What's it going to be?" Davion asked again.

Chapter 24

A year passed. Dash walked ahead of the rest. The ten of them knew their positions, held their posts, and utilized their skills better than anything the lich had seen in a long time. They worked harmoniously together. The two teams had been broken down into three and even four teams at certain points. They were all still alive and all still together. They'd grown close over the last ten months, the last five hundred days.

They were dirty, covered in soot, ash, blood, sweat, and debris. They'd just finished ousting the last of the undead horde. An undead entity in the form of a dragonborn was slain as its head. Legion was carrying that head and Dauge the staff it wielded. It was apparent his powers came from the staff.

Finally, they were out of the cold and windy desert night. They'd made it back to the underground castle infused to the dirt and soil itself where Davion made his home. They were excited. They finally completed Davion's mission. It'd been a year. Would Lord Quinn even remember them? Of course he would. Davion promised them great fame and fortune once the undead incursion was finished.

The hidden door leading to the hidden tunnel that brought them in and out of the castle time and time again opened. Again, Dash took the first steps into the tunnel and started down the slanting stone walled tunnel. Just before the lot of them made it to the entrance to the castle, Davion appeared. In the past five hundred days, they'd seen him out of the castle only once, the day they met him.

"Well, well, well," he said.

The team stopped and bowed to the impressive arcanist.

"You've taught us well, my liege," Kraydia said. She was right. The casters would forever be more potent because of him. The warriors learned a thing or two as well. Davion was great at many things, but he was extraordinary at teaching.

"Sir Davion, we've done what you've asked. You've done more than we've asked. How can we ever repay you?" Dash questioned.

In the past year, Storm grew close to Davion; considering he wanted to oust him from the get go in the beginning. "Sir Davion, I and Thox will forever be in your debt. We all are forever in your debt."

"I promised you, Dash, a year ago something unique and one-of-a-kind." The lich pulled a scroll case from within his ribcage. "This will lead you to the first true Temple of Elemental Water. It's believed the water crafter still thrives there."

"Water crafter?" Legion asked, interrupting the lich.

"You'll find out soon enough. Your work here is done."

"Our final reward for eliminating your enemies is a map to another set of quests and puzzles?" Dauge asked angrily. He was the lone soul of the two teams that still didn't care for the lich.

"In the beginning, the directions to this temple was one of Dash's true goals, was it not, bard?" the lich said, finishing with a question to Dash.

"Aye," he admitted.

"Yeah, Quinn told us something about it." Pitt remembered.

"Your duties in the desert here are finished. You've proven truly worthy, my friends, and should the situation call for it, I will call upon you again."

"And my sister?" Dauge asked irritably.

"Yes, what of our sister?" Legion asked.

"She is more than fine. I have secretly entrusted the beauty with something dear to me. She will surely be fine."

"Sir Davion, I hope to one day restore my family name and instate you as an honorary leader of some degree in Thox."

Davion laughed. "I am an undead, friend paladin. My natural life amongst mortals is forever gone. Only those such as yourselves will ever understand me and even with you all, it took time."

"Where shall we go from here, my liege?" Storm asked.

"I am not your liege, nor I am a knight of any sort. The term Sir does not apply. I am not your liege paladin. I am your friend and perhaps your guide. I take it you all will return to Thox and by my powers and Quinn's position, the lot of you have been glorified under Quinn as the sole reason the undead incursion stopped before it began. You've put Quinn on a pedestal he could've never reached on his own. The Stars name is on its way to being glorified once more. Dash, Legion, Pitt, Kraydia, and you Dauge, you have a choice to make. Storm and the others will return to Thox to glory and thanks for serving as Lord Quinn's right hand. Your names will equally be praised but whether you arrive to accept it and witness it all is up to you."

Davion opened the old iron door leading to an old den in the castle. The den held two glowing powdery looking portals swirling in their own existence. They were purple in color and as dense as a light cloud on a sunny day.

"One of these leads to Xanon, my friends. The other leads to Eternis."

"Why Eternis? What's in Eternis?" Dauge asked.

"Your sister for one," Davion answered quickly

"Your father's last two friends have returned to Eternis to see another buried. King Gerear Uil-Endail has passed. A Sylvan—"

"Like me," Kraydia added.

Davion continued. "Yes Kraydia, like you. A Wilden aged beyond his years has returned with an elven man beaten and battered by the strains of a thousand eons. It is said these two along with—"

"Giovanni and—" Legion started.

"Malakai," Dauge ended.

Once again, Davion continued, "These two along with King Gerear Uil-Endail are the last of your father's true friends."

"Well, I think the king was more a friend of our grandfather's and uncle's than our dad's," Legion suggested.

"Remind your people who you are. Let Storm return on behalf of both your teams. Improve your faction with both Eternis and Thox. Become that bridge of friendship they could never build. See the king laid to rest and be present at the prince's coronation. I will always be here for you all but our journey together has come to its end, at least for now. I will always be closer than I appear to be, remember that." With his final words the lich disappeared like they were nothing. He vanished as if no time or bond was spent or made between them. He was truly a man for the hour as it were.

"I must go to Eternis," Legion said.

"Agreed," Dauge added.

"For the king's burial?" Alanis asked.

"No, for my sister and my family," Dauge answered.

"For our sister, our family, and burial of the king, and the coronation of our prince. Eternis is still our blooded home," Legion continued.

"Not my blooded," Dauge replied.

"It's still our home, brother," said Legion.

"I'll go with you," Storm said. "It's the least I can do."

"You have no business there. Go see to your people in Thox. Reclaim the fame that once belonged to your ancestors. Reclaim the name you so proudly deserve." Dauge placed his hand on his shoulder as a sign of friendship.

"Do us a favor and go to Thox. Tell our story. Keep the lich out of it. And we shall return as soon as we can," Dash chimed in to the other team's leader. Over the course of the past year, Legion more and more took charge. Dash saw it. He knew it. His people were starting to look up to Legion for answers, leadership, and guidance more so than him.

"Dash, why in the world would you go to Eternis? You've wanted fame since the beginning. Here it is. Head to Thox and claim your stakes," Pitt replied to his team's leader.

"What? Why would you ask me that? Why would you say that? Are you going to Eternis?" he asked.

"I see no reason to return to Thox. I feel Legion will get me to Shiva. I will walk with him. I feel your own motives might rob me of my own, Dash. We are friends but I must look out for me," said the goliath.

"I built this team. We stay together," he snapped back quickly.

"I agree with him. We must all stick together and remain close. I feel Legion and Dauge are right. I must return to Thox and assure the people of my kingdom that I, Storm Stars of Thox, helped defend the borders against the undead incursion. I will inform them the Eternian sons of Taj Odin Xavier were also present under the guidance and leadership of their team's leader, Dash Riproc," Storm concluded.

Krazy didn't say anything. He merely walked through the portal leading to his homeland. Storm looked at the figure of the shadow elf as it faded into the purple mist.

"I can't say I am a fan of that one," Alanis said.

"Agreed," Felzen snarled.

"Relax, he knows we're heading to Xanon, the capital of Thox. He didn't want to wait around. Kraizaikaei didn't want to stick around for the conversations. We know where he's going and he's been more than a true ally in the last year, especially to you Felzen. He saved you more than once." The priest Dargon didn't like the shadow elf anymore than the others did but facts were facts and the facts were he saved a few of them more than once.

Kraydia leaned over and kissed Dash on the cheek. "I don't care about all this but I must meet this Giovanni I keep hearing about from Legion and Dauge. He's a Wilden, a true Sylvan like me. I'm with you. I am always with you." S and then frolicked off into the portal leading to Eternis.

"Portals, portals like this aren't easy to come by anymore, not even in Aflyndor these days. That undead is one powerful creature. I can sense the undead empowered equipment gone from my body. He took what he wanted but he helped in defending our borders. The enemy of my enemy is my friend, I guess. We should get going. Who knows how long these portals are going to last?" Dash said enlightening the group.

With that, the lot of them bid each other farewell and rushed toward their respective portals. One by one they disappeared into the mist. Storm and his crew arrived in Thox. Kraydia rushed through the portal first because of her feelings for Krazaikei. She'd developed feelings for Dauge but they were gone. She also developed feelings for Dash and Krazaikei but only Krazy knew of it. She'd bed him night after night. She loved the way he moved between the sheets. She also admired and adored Dash. She hadn't any idea which way to go. She loved the friendship of Pitt, Dauge, and Legion and even Dash. She didn't want to lose it or make a bad decision based on emotion so she rushed through the portal before she could make the mistake of following Krazaikei.

Chapter 25

Legion and the others arrived home bearing witness to the saddened state of Eternis. Their beloved leader for so long was to be buried. Legion and Dauge took their crew to the Xavier manor where he knew there'd be more than enough room for the lot of them to sleep.

Dash knew in Eternis, he hadn't a chance to stand out, considering those he traveled with. Dusk recently returned from her journeys as well. Destiny and Adrian, mother and father to the boys, told them of their sister's desires to travel outward. Dauge nor Legion cared that Dusk chose to love a man like Kleiven Dar but neither cared to hear of their sister's adventurous travels outward either.

The lot of them sat around the table along with the rest of their team and Legion and Dauge's parents. Dash was perhaps the most courteous, especially when Giovanni and Malakai entered. Giovanni looked a lot better since the last time they'd seen him. His hair was cut short and neatly pulled back to a small tail. Malakai's very presence chilled the room with unnatural heat. His right jeweled eye seemed to stare through the very souls of each person it lay upon.

Finally, Destiny, Giovanni, Adrian, Malakai, Dash, Legion, Dauge, Kraydia, and Pitt were all sitting around the giant rectangular dinner table breaking bread once again as a family, plus some, for the first time in quite a long time. Eventually, the brothers Simon and Gideon arrived, leaving only Dorian absent from the family gathering.

"How were your travels, my sons?" Adrian started, breaking a large batch of bread in half.

"They were good. We're becoming something of a known team now in Thox. Our friend Storm Stars has accepted the kingdom's gratitude on our behalf so that we could return here to revisit our family and attend King Gerear's funeral," Legion replied.

"Stars?" Adrian asked, concerned.

"One in the same," Dauge answered.

"What's the deal with Stars?" Dash asked

"That damned family is the reason my brother fled his home to begin with." Adrian said in reply.

"Forgive me. I don't know the whole story," Dash said.

"This food is magnificent." Kraydia sparkled into the conversation, squinting her eyes playfully, speaking mainly to Destiny.

"Well thank you dear," the boys' mother answered.

"My wife's one magnificent cook!" Father's focus and tempo changed immediately. He loved bragging about his wife. He loved her dearly.

The conversation continued with Dash leading the talk on how they'd come to meet Lord Quinn and the lich, Davion. Dash's storytelling was on point. He really caught the attention of his entire audience. Adrian didn't like what he heard. Simon, Gideon or even their mother cared either. They were concerned about their kindred.

"Liches cannot be trusted!" Adrian scolded.

"He led us in defending the borders of Thox. I hope to one day unify and squash this bitter feud between Thoxens and Eternians," said Dash.

"As long as Thox and Eternis both breathe, a bitter feud there shall always be," Destiny said, taking the words right out of her husband's mouth.

"I'm concerned about this city, Adrian." Malakai finally opened up.

"Why, what's with the city?" he asked.

"Bahaus is not exactly going to make a great king here," he answered.

"Father, Grath is waiting for me. May I be excused?" Dusk asked. She'd been completely zoned from the conversation.

Dauge was irritated. The main reason he returned was to see his beloved sister and she was trying to get out of dinner for a something named Grath.

"What's a Grath ?" Dauge asked arrogantly.

Dusk smiled, excited and happy to explain. "I've only met him a few moons ago but already I've forgotten about Kleiven and every other man on earth! He's different, though. I can't wait for you all to meet him!"

"What about that Dar boy, baby?" asked Adrian.

"Kleiven, I love him, Daddy, but I can't help it. I just can't stop thinking about Grath," she answered.

"Kleiven's a good boy. You should try to give him a chance," Destiny added.

"I do love Kleiven but right now, I just can't stop thinking about Grath Dreamspear." Dusk knew her actions were wrong and she knew Kleiven loved her. Another had caught her attention and stolen her heart.

"Kleiven's father may not be the most respectable guy in Eternis but he's still Eternian. That's important in this family. It was important to your father so it should be important to you," Adrian continued.

"Just wait until you meet Grath daddy?" Dusk pleaded. "You'll love him as I do!"

Adrian sighed. Dauge glared at his sister. Malakai's glare to Dauge told him now was not the time. Silently and without the knowing of anyone else, he backed off as Malakai silently instructed.

Legion was trying to be as supportive as he possibly could of his sister and kissed her cheek and wished her well as Adrian granted her permission to leave. Dauge refused.

"She's still your sister, Dauge," Dash chimed in.

"Feel free to keep my family business out of your mouth and thoughts, halfbreed," Dauge snarled.

"Easy Dauge," Legion said.

"Wait a second, we don't need all that. We're all friends here," Pitt suggested.

Dauge quietly apologized and nodded to his friend Dash. The conversations continued and Adrian more and more tried to sway the team, or at least his boys, to remain in Eternis.

"There's a lot going on in Eternis and Eternis could certainly use some boys like you all," Adrian told the group.

"For what?" Dash asked.

"There's a lot going on. I for one could use some help," Adrian said.

"Mr. Xavier, what help might we be able to bring to the table for you?" Pitt asked passively.

"There are all kinds of things to do around Eternis. It's one of the busiest cities in the world. Our trade has picked up immensely these past few months. There are always convoy jobs and things like that everywhere. Plenty of important people looking to be protected, hell, there's even plenty of not so important people thinking they should be protected," Adrian said with a laugh.

"We're not escorts," Dash answered.

"Well, I guess if the money's right we could be, right?" Kraydia asked, hoping for confirmation.

"Too much risk in escort jobs, Kraydia. If you fail, the consequences could be catastrophic," Dash reminded.

"Heroes aren't forged on fear, Dash," said Adrian.

Huh, his words caught Dash's attention. He was right but at the same time intelligence was something a hero needed. They weren't in the position to take on those kinds of jobs, were they? Either way, Adrian Xavier did have a point.

"Actually, I got something you boys could do." Adrian stated.

"Father, I would love to stay in Eternis. Our names I'm sure are continuing to grow in Thox. Thox is not our home." Legion said.

"Thedia is our home, Legion. We must treat every village, every city, and every kingdom as if they were our very own," Dash said.

Adrian appreciated his words. There was so much for them to do. They still had the map from Davion. Was staying in Eternis truly the best thing for them, at least for the time being? Dash had nothing against it but nothing truly for it either. They were most likely becoming quick names on the border towns of Thox. They could build on that. And once they were big enough, take their names and travel elsewhere. As it stood, they were just nipping at the wind in many places instead of building a foundation in a single place.

"Agreed son, but Thox and Eternis have a fated history. They will forever be one in the same. Building your name in Thox will build your name in Eternis and likewise the other way. For we still conduct a great deal of business and believe it or not, the understructure says Thox still protects Eternis." Adrian's words penetrated Dash. Something in them caught the half-eladrin. Something in Adrian drew Dash to him.

He was a born leader. He was a natural. Adrian Paschal Xavier knew how to speak to people. Bahaus did have all the makings of a tyrant. There was a lot brewing in Eternis and perhaps Dash and his crew arrived in the old city just at the right time.

"Mr. Xavier, what is It you'd charge us with?" Dash questioned.

"There's a ship arriving. On that ship, I'm expecting a certain package, from Thox mind you, and I wouldn't mind if you boys made sure it made it to its proper home safe and sound," Adrian said.

"You want us to get a package for you? That's it." Pitt double-checked.

"It's not just any package, boys. And yes, for the record, for starters, I need you to pick up this package. Head to the third dock. The ship's name is The Bloody Queen and the man to ask for is Larimus. He's an old Malynkitian that works for his old homeland of Thox on the waters. He's an old, old friend of my father's."

The conversation continued. Dash agreed to take the job. It wasn't his choice job but it was a start and working for Adrian Paschal Xavier wasn't going to be all that bad anyway. It was a great piece of information for a hero to be able to add to his resume. Sad, the one thing he wanted more than anything was fame and/or recognition but through it all, he truly did want to help people as well.

"Fine, we'll pick up your package but legends aren't made by being errand boys. You've taken us in and shared your manor with us. Therefore, we'll get your package and look for work. If work doesn't come our way, then I'm sure we'll find ourselves back in Thox."

"And legends are forged by hunting dragons in their youth. You must not only start somewhere. You must finish that start intelligently and strategically."

All in company silenced to Adrian's words. He was wise even beyond his own age. He'd been around. He'd seen it all. More than him, there were ears listening even wiser than him. Giovanni had very much been around, even to the northern Corvanian Pantheon. And Malakai as well; the draconic/shadow based sorcerer with lineage spreading both worlds had been to both known pantheons, claimed to have seen from a distance The Broken Lands, and even faced the shadow dragon deity Falling Star.

"What about the funeral and coronation tomorrow?" asked Legion.

"The funeral is early. The coronation follows. Afterward, you'll go the third docks and grab my package and bring it back here. Larimus will be standing at the platform of the third docks when she arrives. He's an old man with Thoxen blood written all over his face." Adrian stopped as his younger son spoke up.

"You said he was from Malynkite," Dauge questioned.

"No, I said he was a Malynkitian. He originally hails from Thox. I said that too," Adrian confirmed.

"I must have missed that part," Dauge responded.

"The funeral and coronation should be finished by early noon tomorrow," Simon Xavier added, breaking back into the conversation.

"Then we should have the package returned to the manor by the end of the day. Third docks are relatively far from here," Legion reminded.

"That sounds about right," Gideon, the other quiet brother finally spoke up. He'd said next to nothing since the conversation began.

"Then it's settled. We retrieve this package for Mr. Xavier. As a rule, we shouldn't ask what it is. Then we can began our campaign as adventurers here in Eternis, Thedia's oldest city." Pitt's intelligence shined through. Every once in awhile, something beyond his own brain slipped out.

"Shouldn't I have concluded for the team?" Dash playfully asked Pitt.

"I was just trying to take care of it for you. If it wasn't for you, I don't know where I'd be? Hell, I might still be fighting, I know I'd still be fighting in the arenas," Pitt finished, correcting himself.

Dash and the others all laughed but it was agreed. Destiny and Adrian saw the guests to their respected rooms. Giovanni and Malakai both decided to take part in a night's rest.

That night, Malakai made his way into Dash's room. Dash was fast asleep. Malakai's tangled white hair knotted up and rolled across and down his shoulders and back. The wrinkles in his face told the story of a thousand years of turmoil. He'd survived too much for his years and his physical body paid the price for it. The sorcerer floated in. The majority of his powers were "sealed" when the last of the shadow was banished and locked away in Geminis, Gemini's homeworld. His draconic side still stood but many believed the main portion of his powers were gone. Most didn't know why however, they just assumed it was something to do with his past encounters with the shadow deities over in Corvana. In truth, with the Shadow truly sealed, his native innate abilities had been rendered useless.

"Dash, wake up," he said, standing over the half-eladrin's bed.

Dash pulled the covers down to see the vintage man clad in reds standing over his bed.

"What the—?" Dash said, waking up.

"I have something for you to do for me, Dash." Malakai said.

Something about the creepy sorcerer tingled the half-eladrin's skin and very soul to the fullest. Malakai stared at the "leader" of the group.

"What is it you'd have me do?" he asked. He was both scared and concerned.

"The boys Legion and Dauge are very dear to me. Dusk, their sister is as well. Their entire bloodline means more to me than my own. Forever keep an eye on them and you shall forever be watched over by me. Take this." Malakai pulled a small stone from his robes. It was a turquoise color and dull to the eye.

"It's a Ioune Stone but I bled some of my own mortality into it. My very essence enhances what this stone can do. It will enhance your magical prowess and all the while keep me close to you and both the boys by proxy. You will see and feel your powers grow. And in time, my sorcery will seep into you."

"I'm not sure I want that," he answered, terrified.

"I mean I will be able to channel powers to you should you need them. You call for them. Call to me and I shall answer but only for the sake of the boys. Your desire to be known and recognized forces me to believe"—Malakai tossed the stone onto his bed—"that you'll accept the stone and my request. For when your powers secretly begin to shine, the people will take note of your abilities and accomplishments and your name will grow. Your name will grow and the boys, I shall see to it are forever protected."

Dash didn't know what to say. Malakai didn't wait for a rebuttal or a challenge. He turned and headed toward the very door he entered through. Dash quickly fell back. He was soon fast asleep. Was it Malakai? Was it the sorcerer who'd come to offer and ask for aid? Or was Dash truly that comfortable or tired?

Chapter 26

The next morning Dusk was up and gone again before anyone else awoke. The night before she didn't get that quality time with Grath as she so hoped. He was busy with his team and getting them situated. While in town, his team had a rule of staying close but keeping distance between themselves. Only one walked alongside Grath.

Dusk was cheerful and Grath's newfound pride and joy. Grath wasn't well liked. Most of his kind weren't. Not even the people of Eternis truly cared for them. He accompanied her to the burial of the king.

It was there Dauge, Legion, and the others first laid their eyes upon him. Grath was a tall and a physically demanding specimen. He quite easily had two to three inches on Legion. He was a shadow elf and fit the description of one to a tee, only he was just a little taller, bulkier, and seemingly more dark.

Valsul was personally sought after and brought back to Eternis upon the king's illness worsening. The two were close and King Gerear Uil-Endail personally requested it be the elven priest of Raielyn speak over his burial.

"From blood we're born to ashes we become... King Gerear Uil-Endail was the greatest king a city-state could have and the greatest Eternis ever saw since Mercius Kordur. His eldest child fell defending another nation's walls. He represented Eternis when the world called for it. Prince Aiden was a fine human being and one of the best I ever had the privilege of knowing. Our city and future falls to his last remaining child, Prince Bahaus Sazos-Uil-Endal."

The five-foot-ten prince was pleased. He truly didn't care for his father's life ending. Death was a very natural part of life and the sooner Gerear could see his finished the sooner Bahaus could begin his campaign as king. He was a manipulator and nearly broke Eternis' finances forcing his estranged father to correct the wrongs done to him using his name, rank, and wealth. The grin from his face was ear to ear and he was the only one present not in tears.

"We must honor the king's wishes. His final words were of peace between our land and Thox." The elven priest went on and on about the king's greatness. He was truly great and a legend in his own right. In the end, all of his hard work and dedication could be finished with the reins of Eternis now being handed to his sadistic bastard child.

Bahaus noticed a latecomer to the funeral. He was an old friend and employee of Eternis. Free Armies General Magnus Black arrived late to see his friend buried. His armies were still slightly west protecting the Crystal Cities. He'd virtually made a home there.

Bahaus considered the mercenary general a coward and traitor to the people of the city. He left for a higher payday in Bahaus' mind. In truth, his true reason for leaving was only known to King Gerear and himself. And what in the world was that gray-skinned shadow thing doing in his city? Well, it wasn't quite his city yet but it would be by day's end.

Bahaus still fancied Dusk but Dusk left him for a more normal warm breathing human much closer to her age, Kleiven. For that, the prince hated Kleiven but still adored and admired his old traveling companion and friend, Cale Dar.

Now, she was with another and a shadow elf for that matter! He was the prince of the greatest city ever to exist, why couldn't she understand how lucky she really was? He would have her back. Kleiven was gone but when he returned Bahaus already knew how to take care of him. And Grath for that matter would be a much easier obstacle, damn gray skins he thought to himself.

Legion couldn't believe his sister was there with a shadow elf. Giovanni and Malakai both spoke of a shadow elf in particular that Taj held in very high esteem even though they didn't spend very much time together. Avalon Darksteel, rightful heir and prince to the throne of the Nine Kingdoms to the West, Legion's true father, gave one his upmost respect, why couldn't he?

Dauge didn't care much that her arm was interlocked with a shadow elf. The race didn't make the man. A name didn't make the man. Only actions should be weighed against the being. Behind the shadow elf, Dauge noticed another keenly looking around, but for what? He was an average looking human, maybe an inch taller than Dauge himself. He wore his wavy brown hair just past his shoulders. His eyes matched his hair. He wore bracers and leggings and rings and leathers but not anything truthfully for protection. In other words, like Dauge, he cared not for the encumbering of armor. Peculiarly though, a large hangar holding a clearly magical blade rested on his back; the weapon's prowess radiated and Dauge clearly felt it.

The old priest of Eternis now residing in Myasuna continued his readings over the fallen royale. Dash kept one eye open just for Malakai. Now he knew the truth too. Grath was not the only shadow elf present. Malakai's blood carried the shadow as well. The sorcerer's gift, the Ioune stone from the night before told him so. Pitt held silent as did the Wilden Kraydia, primitively still known still as Sylvans.

The abnormally pale-skinned human to the left flank of Grath whispered something into the shadow elf's ear and hurried off, disappearing into the crowd. Grath never moved nor did he blink. Dusk didn't know what was going on. Dauge would've bet his life Dusk didn't even know the human was there with the Grath.

Finally, the funeral was over and the coronation began. It took hours, seeping into the wee hours of the evening. Dash was hoping it would end soon because they still had a package to retrieve. Bahaus took his moment and held onto it like it was a dying animal clinging to life. He milked it for everything it was worth.

Night was setting in and Dash and his crew were finally away from the public duties of the day. The king was buried and Bahaus, the man who cast out all those religions so long ago including Vasul's, was now the king of the city-state Eternis.

"We don't have long. Night is setting in," Dash said.

The team was on the move. Dusk vanished again with Grath. Grath didn't make any effort whatsoever to introduce himself to her family. Legion didn't understand that at all but Dauge did. In fact, it made Dauge respect him a little more. He knew that Grath understood Dauge wouldn't feel anyone was good enough for his sister, and thus, it was in his best interest to stay away from them. Eventually, he would have to meet them.

"Let's go," Pitt seconded.

It was a very easy task to grab a chariot and cut their traveling time to Third Dock in half. Just as Adrian said, there was an elderly man sitting at the designated docking area of the previously spoken of ship. He was dressed as a Malynkitian but the features of his face and build said Thoxen.

The old man wore bright colors and his wrinkled face told the team he had to be around sixty or so. His face and attitude told of a happy old man with a great spirit and appreciation for life but his eyes couldn't lie. His eyes told of a man fighting the wrongs done to him even still to the day.

"Good'aye gentlemen. Are you looking for the Bloody Queen? These here are her docks," he said cheerfully.

"Yes, in fact we are," Dash answered.

"We're here by request of Adrian Xavier," Kraydia added.

Dash looked back, not happy but not angry. He felt it was his charge to speak to Larimus.

"My father."

"And mine."

Legion first enlightened the man of his father and Dauge soon followed. Dash wanted to say something but he didn't. Part of the reason he wanted the boys was because of their connections and lineage.

"I knew you boys' grandfather and your father when he was just a boy." The old man smiled.

"Larimus," Dash started, assuring they were speaking to the right person.

"I am," he answered.

"Then you have the package?" Legion questioned.

"I do." Larimus pulled a small pouch from his green cloak. It was a coin purse holding a small square box wrapped in bright silks. Larimus opened the coin purse to unveil its holdings. "I meant to give this to your father months ago."

"Adrian?" Dash asked.

"Yes of course. Their father," he responded.

"Taj is our father. Adrian is our uncle," Dauge added.

"They're both our father, Taj by blood and Adrian by experience," Legion reminded.

"It's all getting much complicated for my old head. You're all my friends' sons," he concluded, still smiling.

"What is it?" the curious Wilden asked.

"As a rule, we don't ask. Remember?" Dash reminded.

"I remember," she said, playfully backing down from her previous question.

Larimus looked hard at Legion. Something about Legion struck his fancy. Legion was the first to notice the old man's stare.

"Something about me you like old man?" Legion asked jokingly.

"Your resemblance to Dominick is fascinating. It reminds me of better times. Your grandfather was a good man. He was of good stock. You're of good stock son, remember that."

Legion smiled. Dauge emotionlessly patted his brother on the back.

"We best be moving then," Dash concluded.

"You boys take care. This is a cruel world and it changes people. Don't ever change, not ever," finished the old man.

"Aye," Pitt said, nodding to the old man and turning away.

The crew couldn't find a horse chariot to take them back so they were forced to trek it. It was a long walk and another way for the team to continue getting to know each other. They were getting as close as companions could get.

"Thank you," Pitt started.

Dash recognized his barbarian's words were for him. Kraydia walked behind, peeling her light brown hair from her face, placing her hand on her leader's back.

"Yes, thank you," she said, knowing where her Barbarian was going with it.

"For what?" he asked, trying not to smile. Recognition, Dash loved and cherished it. That's what his travels were all truly for. He did want to better the world and help those in peril that he could. Saving the damsel in distress and rescuing the princess from the fire breathing dragon were the stories that fueled his burning ambition to become such a hero. He wanted stories like those to be told of him one day. And he knew he wasn't the monstrous barbarian type like Pitt or the fearless hero that Legion could one day be. He could assemble and lead such a team.

"For bringing us together," Kraydia answered.

"Aye, for bringing us together. I truly would die for each and every one of you. I truly feel if you do not carry such a commitment, then you're doing your team an injustice," Pitt said.

"Agreed," said Legion.

"Dying is something that should only happen once and if I am to die then I'd prefer it be in good company," Dauge seconded after his brother.

"You should pray you all die next to me. It's the closest thing you'll ever get to an honorable death," Legion joked to his team.

The crew all laughed and Dash slightly blushed. What a good team he'd built. They were still without a true healer but between his powers and Kraydia's they sufficed okay. More magical healing potions would have to be found before undertaking any sort of serious campaign, such as the Temple of Water, supposedly in the frozen lands just south of Thox. That map given to them by Davion would one day be their claim to fame. He knew it.

Midway to the Xavier manor, the crew was stopped. It was Kleiven. He'd returned? Dusk told Dauge he was supposed to be gone for quite some time but he was there. None of the crew had ever actually met him but they knew him from passing, portraits, and detail.

"Legion, Dauge," he said.

He was a little skinner than the portraits had him and he wore both his face and his head clean shaved. He looked different from the pictures but it was him.

"Kleiven, Kleiven Dar?" Legion asked.

"Aye," he answered.

"You look much smaller than the pictures," Legion said.

"I've not been eating well."

Dash put a hand out to Legion, telling him the half-eladrin wanted him to halt in his conversation at least for the moment.

"Are you okay?" Dash questioned, concerned.

"No."

"Why?" Dash asked.

"I love Dusk very much and Grath is not someone I trust. She just left me all of a sudden for nothing and with no reason."

Dauge immediately stepped up. "I am Dusk's brother. Is she in trouble?" he asked.

"I don't know. I don't trust shadow elves," Kleiven admitted.

"What is it you want from us?" Dash asked.

"I just want you to give Dusk this." He pulled a small wrinkled piece of paper from his pocket. He opened it up and straightened out and then refolded it nice and neat. It was still rough looking and wrinkly but nonetheless it was folded much more neatly after with it.

Dauge approached first and took the paper, silently signaling to the General's son that he would do as requested. Kleiven slightly bowed to the younger Xavier and turned to head off into the darkness. Something in his eyes told them all he was staring off into madness. Something was eating him. Something was definitely getting to him.

When Kleiven was gone from sight. Dauge peeled the paper from his pocket and opened it. Legion asked him not to and the others also put in their two cents about it. Dauge didn't care. He wasn't snooping into her business; he just wanted to make sure his sister was all right.

Dearest Dusk,

Whatever came between us I can live with. You in danger I cannot. You told me it keeps haunting you. It's leading you to its side and now you feel more comfortable with the innately dark. Please do not do this. I wish to wed you. Our families have a history that goes back. Please turn away from whatever that thing is visiting you. Please do not shun me for it. Do not feel you are putting me at risk. My heart is the only thing at risk, my love, and I fear it's lost, shattered, damaged beyond repair. Please, let us reunite and never speak of these days apart again.

Kleiven Dar

Chapter 29

Dusk couldn't sleep. She tossed and turned through the night. He was coming back. She knew it. She new he'd be back. Suddenly, her beautiful room in the Xavier manor was gone. The dark fields he'd always brought her to were back and very present.

Her hair flapped in the wind behind her as did the black gown she always seemed to be wearing but never remembered putting on. Fields of grass and trees were all that surrounded her along with the clear blue sky. And then it, the thing, was also there. His gut-wrenching stench ruined the setting. His disgustingly tattered and stained black and brown robes also flapped about his skeletal body. His eyes gleamed and glowed a radiating purple color.

She stared at him as she always did. Though she hated and feared him, she never could take her eyes off him. His eyes shot straight through her and her eyes let him know she was there and still very mortal.

"You will accept my offering. For I must make good on my word."

Dusk looked at the creature and just stared into his eyes. He'd said this before. He wanted to grant her powers. It would make her a sorcerer. He wanted to grant her the innate of a sorcerer and he had the power to do it.

"I cannot. I am but a human."

"You lack only the inner powers, my child," it said to her.

"My skills are natural and with missiles from range. I am a crossbow practitioner," she replied.

"I've seen your skills and my blessing will increase them ten fold."

"Why me?"

"A bond was made, a pact."

Suddenly, she awoke different than when she first fell asleep. Dauge and Legion were shaking her. They felt his presence in her room, in her body. Davion had come for her. It was Davion! Davion was what Kleiven was speaking of. Perhaps Kleiven was right? What if she sought out darkness like what Davion had put in her?

"I'm awake. He's gone. It's gone," she said, still half asleep.

"Davion," Dauge said.

"Davion," Legion repeated.

"I... I... Don't know... What's Davion? Who's Davion?" She was still out of it. She was probably more out of it than she should have been. Dauge and Legion knew exactly what was going on. Davion planted something in her as his way of "protecting" and "guarding" her from the cruelties of the real world. He was only following through with his promise to keep their sister safe.

"Davion is the lich we befriended and aided in Thox, sweetheart," answered Legion.

"Why is he changing me?" She was starting to get scared.

"He's not. He's making sure you're protected. That was part of our payment, sister, for him to keep you safe and out of harm's way," Dauge enlightened.

"I don't want magic in me. I hate magic. Divine and arcane, it's all evil and gross! I can feel the dead in me now. Ugh!" She wouldn't let it go. She felt as if the dead were crawling in her bones. And rightfully so, Davion was a powerful undead and thus, necromancy was probably his most influenced field.

"I will rebuke it and refuse it! Why did you do this to me? Get out! I hate you! I hate you both!" she screamed, turning back into her pillow letting her tears flow like fountains.

"Dusk," Legion said, emphasizing her name to show sincerity.

"Dusk listen to me. We were far away from you and we did everything we could to make sure you were okay. Davion would never hurt you," Dauge said. Dauge only seemed to allow emotion to slip out when he was around his sister.

They did as requested and they left her room. Dusk cried and cried. Davion was gone. Whatever he was going to do, he already did. Dauge and Legion were gone as well. That creature had come into her dreams and nightmares time and time again. She was always able to turn away from it. The things he told her... Were they true? He said she would turn from her comfort and seek refuge in the darkness. This time, her brothers came and interrupted her dream but it was too late. He'd already done what he'd come to do.

That night, before she fell back into the realm of dreams and nightmares, the half-eladrin passed by her opened door. He looked at her. His face itched. He scratched his smooth cheek. His hair was pulled back into a tight ponytail. He'd been wearing his hair like that for the past few days.

"Are you okay Dusk?" Dash asked.

"I am not," she replied.

He helped himself into her room, shutting the door behind him. She told him to get out to and told him to lock the door on his way. Unlike her brothers, he did not comply. Dash found her beautiful of course and she was. That's not what his fascination was about. He heard their conversation and felt a connection, considering the creepy sorcerer Malakai. Sorcery, innate power, could it really be granted through channeled power? If so, how easy was it?

Malakai had given him a stone and something just planted some of its power into Dusk. Dash was scared too. Seeking refuge in the wrong places wasn't the answer and he was quick to tell her that.

"Dusk, you should seek out those who care for you most. Do not push them away because you think they will not understand."

Dash answered so many questions without her having to say a single word. The tears stopped and the sweet lady Xavier turned from her stomach to her back, taking her face from its buried position in her pillows.

Dash hated seeing his friends' sister cry. He took his thumb and wiped the tears from her eyes. He smiled, comforting her. Something in him made her feel safe and secure. Without saying another word, he let her know everything was going to be all right.

"I do love Kleiven, Dash," she said. "Now, I feel a stronger connection to Grath."

"Neither is right for you if you're seeking them for the wrong reasons. Whatever has happened to you has happened to you out of benevolent thoughts and prayers. You're surrounded by people who care and cherish your every move and word."

Dusk smiled. She didn't think Dash fancied her as Grath and Kleiven but he certainly knew how to make her feel good and better about herself.

"I've only lain with one man Dash, Kleiven. And then I felt it was always going to be us. And then this… Davion starting haunting me in my dreams and his words pushed me into darker waters and thoughts. Then Kleiven and I seemed to have lost our connection and then that same connection came back and felt twice as strong with Grath. I don't know what to do."

"Walk away from them both if you must," said Dash. "This isn't you. Your devotion and feelings cannot be trusted right now. I know this Davion and why he's come. He's the lich your brothers spoke of. He's come to protect you and give you guidance as requested by your brothers."

"Why?" Her fragile look could've broken any man.

"They want to see you safe. They know they will not always be around, Dusk. You must understand."

"Something like that haunting me, trying to infest me with its own evil is not protecting me. Besides, they've not seen my skills with a large crossbow. I can put a large bolt between your toes at five hundred yards with the simplest of bows!"

"No one knew what Davion was going to do or what you could do with a large crossbow. Your brothers just wanted to see you guarded. I'm sorry Davion chose a route that I don't think any of us agree with. Davion is true to his words and can be trusted. He's the last of his kind I'm sure. He's what the old would call an arch lich."

"You barely know the thing and you're saying he's trustworthy?"

"I do know him and he is trustworthy, Dusk. You have to believe me." Dash did feel his words were pure but he was lying to himself to think he didn't have a second agenda, an ulterior motive. Dash wanted to empower the young Dusk to hopefully one day possibly employ her or keep her powerful enough to keep her brothers content even when absent from her.

"Lich's live lifetimes over and over. It may take a hundred years for their plots to unfold. I know from the stories I heard as a little girl and even now. Undead are never to be trusted. With mortal life spans, one's true intentions will come out much sooner. It has to. Time simply wouldn't permit otherwise," Dusk informed Dash. Dash already knew truth were in the words she spoke.

"He's wanting to grant you powers that will guard you from the cruelties of this world. Dusk. Tis part of his payment obligations to your brothers." Dash concluded.

Dusk shook her head and the two embraced. Throughout the night, the two continued to engage in conversation. Dash eventually fell fast asleep on the floor next to Dusk's bed. An extra blanket stuffed near the side of her bed kept the half-eladrin warm. He used his arms and hands as a pillow. Dusk was comfortable and felt much more assured with the presence of Dash.

That night, Dusk accepted the lich's dark gift. Maybe it was Dash's presence that helped her take the step. Somewhere inside she felt it was already there. Maybe it was? Maybe she'd subconsciously already taken the gift or maybe it was already forced up on her. Whatever the case, the following morning when she awoke, she knew she'd never be the same.

The next morning Dash was still fast asleep on the floor. Dusk left early before any other in the manor was awake. She'd planned to meet Grath early at the Silverstar II, the very same three-story tavern and inn that her father once grew up in.

As promised, Grath was waiting for her at the front door of the massive place. Instantaneously, a smile ripped across his face. He was still dressed for battle. He depicted a dark prince charming or a dark knight from a dime novel. His black breastplate and silver lining furthered proved of his description that he hoped to carry that dark knight persona.

"Dusk, welcome, it warms the heart to see you," he said happily, embracing his Xavier woman in a tight hug and kiss. To his dismay, she slightly pulled away from the kiss. He knew something was different. Something was wrong. She'd never acted like this toward him. She was always thrilled for his company and now, she turned from it.

"Hello Grath," she said.

Grath knew the night was not going to turn out well at all. Nonetheless he continued through with his initial plan and took his "woman" inside the aging Silverstar II where her father, Taj Odin Xavier, first ran back into Destiny after she'd returned from her time overseas in Thox.

The two took to a table. Grath quickly drew an audience, as he always did. The Eternian natives and the foreigners alike looked on at the shadow elf. Even so, his kind was not accepted. They still carried condemnation everywhere they went. Most Thedians considered them outsiders still. In truth, they were. They were not native to Thedia but some would ague as generation after generation continued to produce life on Thedian soil.

"I feel my presence is not surely desired?" he said, questioningly.

"I've been doing something thinking is all," she answered.

Grath looked around. Silverstar II was unusually full for the morning but then again, so were the docks. Most of the day's patrons hailed from foreign lands as he did.

"And you feel Kleiven is more your mark?" he continued. Arrogance and jealously slipped from his tongue ever so slightly.

"You're creating thoughts my mind did not give birth to."

"Your demeanor has completely changed."

"It has not. I've only been thinking is all."

"Are you ashamed? Do you shy away now for the reality of my lineage has come drown your face?"

"No," she quickly answered angrily.

"Prove boast," he said, implying he wanted her to prove she still cared for him and not for what others though of him or them together. He leaned in to kiss the Eternian.

Dusk evaded the man's pressing lips and pulled herself from their table. The youngling was overfilled with emotion and confusion. She knew not what was in her best interest and what was not. All she knew what that Kleiven loved her and she loved him but something tore them apart. And now, Dash had her convinced it wasn't anything at all that pulled Kleiven from her or her from Kleiven but the magical manipulations of one undead lich.

"Why don't you find one of your own kind to accept your foul taste? Your odor is a stench I can taste in my gut from here!" Another voice stirred the crowd. This one came from a native and a face the people of Eternis knew. Klevien Dar.

Grath turned, seeing the skinny human. He didn't look like much. Surely this pathetic cretin didn't hope to impress his girl by calling on him in front of her?

"Surely this is not your Kleiven?" he jested.

Kleiven had lost weight. He did not look well at all. nonetheless he was present and ready to do what was charged to him for the love of his Dusk. Grath began to stand. Dusk fell to instincts. She knew Kleiven was no match for Grath. She rushed to use herself as an obstacle to keep Grath from moving forward. Not ten minutes in the Silverstar II and ruckus was already brewing.

"Grath please," she begged.

"This thing thinks he can challenge me in front of you?" The crowd moved back as the shadow elf's words elevated. Still, the simple folks of towns like Eternis looked at shadow elves as monsters and demons.

"No Dusk, let him have at me. I intend to have at him. I will not stand by and watch my girl walk with another man without a fight."

His courageous words were unfortunately meaningless to her. She was confused in her own right. She didn't know whom she wanted. Bahaus was dark and cold and Kleiven was warm and pure. Something was drawing her to the dark prince charming that was Grath.

"Kleiven no. I need to find myself right now. I must. For me, I must have time to find myself. I've had so much happen to me."

"Whatever happens, Grath and I have must settle this."

"Kleiven, this is not the days of the cave man!" Dusk screamed.

Grath smiled. It was his choice of resolving issues as well. Besides, he needed a reason to make an example of someone in Eternis. Mercy, he had to show them mercy to prove to the Eternians he wasn't as dark and as cold as they thought.

"Should the two of you engage in this endeavor, I shall never speak to the either of you again," Dusk screamed, looking back and forth between the two of them. It wasn't but a few minutes into their time at the giant tavern before her problems arose. She couldn't pawn these problems off on others nor could she point fingers. As angry as she was, she brought it on herself and she knew it.

Grath looked at Kleiven and Kleiven's eyes never left his. Kleiven didn't really want the fight but what else was he to do? Now, if he engaged he would/could possibly lose her forever. Grath knew he didn't want to fight after her words. If he antagonized it, it would only prove the folks of Eternis and those others currently in the city right about him.

Dusk stormed out. She was fed up, sick and tired of it all. She just wanted to go away. She could feel Davion digging inside of her. His powers were infesting themselves and attaching to her insides and her inner most parts.

"Dusk… Dusk…"

"Dusk… Wait… Dusk…"

Kleiven was running after her. Grath was not. It was that familiar voice she heard that was comforting her. It wasn't Grath's. The nearing of Kleiven's voice soothed her. It eased her stress and comforted her as it had always done. More and more, her connection to Grath was lessening. With every passing second, her attraction to the shadow elf faded. And with every fleeting moment, her desire for Kleiven was returning.

Dusk ran straight into the colossal torso of Pitt. He and the team were making their way after her. Dauge claimed to have something to give her.

Dash was evidently tired from the night before and straying closer to the back.

"Oh, Pitt," she said. Her hands fell to his abdomen and her forehead plopped up against his chest. She found comfort in the long-haired goliath.

"Dusk, is everything okay?" he asked.

"Sister, I have something for you," Dauge said, pulling Kleiven's note from his pouch.

"Wait, just hear me out," Kleiven said coming up from behind her.

"What's going on?" Legion questioned.

"Why is my sister running from you?" Dauge further questioned.

"She's confused, I think," Kleiven answered.

Dusk turned, grabbing the paper from Dauge and then to face Kleiven. Grath was in the background, casually strolling off as if nothing happened and everything was okay. Dusk's heart fell. Could he really care that little about her? What was it she really wanted? Who was it she really wanted?

"Dusk, has Kleiven harmed you?" Dauge asked nervously. He was curiously angry at what could come if she answered yes to his question.

"No of course not," she answered. "Brother," she started, falling back to Dauge's embrace, "whatever it is you had your thing put in me has turned me against myself. I no longer know what is real and who is me anymore."

"Davion," Legion said, thinking aloud.

"It was not to harm you but to keep you safe. You must believe me," Dauge said.

"What did he do to me?" she asked.

"Ignore it. It will still guard you until you're ready to embrace it," Dauge answered.

"Dauge, we do not want our sister infested with Davion's darkness," Legion reminded.

Dash, Kraydia, and Pitt mostly stayed silent. Dash was still half asleep. He'd slept on Dusk's floor the night before. Secretly, he felt a small crush growing within him. He knew better and work came first. The team came first and a love interest that shared the blood of his two brothers would certainly give cause for problems.

"Where is Grath heading?" Dauge asked.

"Who cares?" Legion answered.

"Let us move forward. Grath is no longer our concern," Dash said, finally breaking his silence.

"Legion, I'm sorry. I'm still groggy. Did you get the package to your father?"

"I did," he answered.

"So you did something for father?" Dusk asked her brothers.

"We did," Dauge answered.

"And we're done now," Legion finished.

"So what are you to do now? Are you leaving me already?" Dusk asked them saddened knowing she already knew the answer.

"We've been in discussion as to what is to come next, sister," Dauge answered.

"And I still say we make our way to the frozen lands south of Thox and put that map to use," Pitt added.

"Pitt, as long as fuel for the fire that burns for our names is here, we shall embrace this city," Dash reminded.

"Sometimes I miss the arena," Pitt's voice softened but the people heard it.

"Where'd that come from?" Dash questioned.

"Nevermind," he replied.

"So you all have met Kleiven then?" Dusk asked.

"Last night, on our way home he made our acquaintance," Kraydia answered, finally breaking her silence.

"Yes Dusk, and forgive me but I must be going. Prince, um, I mean King Bahaus Sazos-Uil-Endail seeks an audience with me this day," responded the General's son.

Dusk fell back to embrace and kiss her former love. She still didn't know if he was the one she wanted again but he was a safety net for her. He was her rock and comfort zone. She knew Kleiven would rip out his right eye before seeing harm done to her. Curiously, Dauge and Legion knew it too and they'd just met the former soldier.

Chapter 20

Days passed and soon became weeks, which then turned into months. The shadow elf Grath was long removed from the city. He'd parted ways soon after Dusk chose to walk away from him. He didn't even put up a fight for the woman he claimed to love.

Dash and his team continued to put coin in the purse of the Xaviers and themselves by fulfilling their duties and missions one after another. They also secretly took care of Malakai's quests as per Dash fooling the others into taking the charge along with him. His hidden agenda to keep Malakai pleased still crept only through his own heart.

Kleiven strengthened his bond again with Dusk and Giovanni finally parted ways to return to his wife in the Republic of New Magic. Things were really moving forward. Word of Storm spreading the word of their victories along with Dash and his team made its way back to Eternis. Dash and the others were pleased to see their name growing.

Bahaus finally took care of what he wanted. He reinstated Kleiven back into the military and ordered him to the naval transport ship "Draconis United." There, he would be forced to be away from Dusk for days, weeks, and occasionally months at a time. Grath took care of departing on his own. Good, he thought, save him the trouble.

The five of them were all taking their usual bath together in the private back room of the Xavier manor when Dusk arrived to fetch them. Kleiven had just left for his first duty on "Draconis United." She was discouraged and down but her brothers knew she'd make it and be okay.

"Dash, I just saw Kleiven off to his new assignment. King Sazos reinstated him into the military and Cale didn't do anything to challenge it. Kleiven gave me this to give to you." Dusk pulled a sealed envelope from her purse and handed it to the relaxing Dash. The lot of them were in the den of the manor resting and relaxing and playing simple games. Pitt and Legion, to be precise, and their game of Skull and Bones was getting pretty heated.

"I thought Kleiven finished his time and was looking to start a career as a traveling adventurer?" Dauge questioned.

"He did. King Bahaus told him he was needed and in order to prove the integrity of the Dar bloodline he was needed direly for the position upon the Draconis United," Dusk answered.

"It's a transport ship that never leaves the Hangman's Straight. It goes from Port Agatha in Thox to here and back. Why would he be in dire need? He wasn't even a navally trained soldier. Was he?" Dash asked himself out loud.

"I don't know," Dusk said.

Legion and Dauge didn't ask why Dash got the sealed envelope. They just assumed he was the first to come to mind when she entered the room. The conversation stopped and Dash opened the letter. A small dagger helped break the red wax seal of the paper. It was the wax stamp of the Uil-Endail Family.

Dash,

Bahaus reinstated me. I feel it is to keep me away from Dusk but also I feel there is more to it. Please see my father. I feel if you do not, something terribly wrong will come to pass in the days to come. Something's going on with the military here in Eternis. I feel Bahaus is using whatever's happening to keep me from my beloved but I also believe there may be some truth to his concern.

Regards,
Kleiven Dar.

Dash took his crew and rushed through town to find the General. General Cale Dar, the Dead General as he was sometimes called for his death and resurrection occurrence was there at the Hawthorne's armory.

Hawthorne's armory was a new armory in Eternis and only dealt with high-end clientele for specially crafted and woven armors and pieces. The Eternian General was just leaving when the team showed up.

"General Dar," Legion loudly spoke to get the man's attention.

"Boys," he said with a smile. His thankfulness to see the growing team was evident in his tone.

"Your son told us you might want to speak with us," Dash said, speaking up again as the leader of the group.

"What?" he questioned curiously.

"Your son sent us a letter from the Draconis United. He said you'd want to see us," Dash continued.

A bright flash stunned the group momentarily. A quick sorry slipped from the lips of the Wilden Kraydia. She was once again playing with her simple cantrips and fusing basic spells.

Dauge angrily looked at the little creature. Now wasn't the time or place for it. Dash turned back his shoulder. An irritable look ran over his face. Kraydia smiled and again apologized.

"Kleiven sent us a letter that said there's something troubling you here in Eternis." Dash lowered his voice to where only he and the General could hear. Cale wasn't wearing his military gear at all. The white-haired man with a wrinkled face and pink scar of death kept his clothing simple for the day. It was a simple pair of brown breeches and a white long sleeved shirt. His footwear still stood out. His brown boots were thick and heavy.

"What did he tell you?" Cale asked. "I mean, is that all he said?"

"It is," answered Dash.

"I have something for you. I know these missions you've been running are copper compared to the gold and platinum you're looking for. A few of our smaller armies and units have been mobilized. The Xavier stamp has been used. The Uil-Endail stamp has also been used. I know Adrian wouldn't make orders like the ones we've intercepted. Nor does he know of our concerns. I'd like to get this finished and put behind us before it comes out."

Dauge kept silent but Legion boasted forward. "Xavier stamp, what the hell do you mean? We have our signet stamp but what use would the Eternian military have with it? My father is retired from the Republic of New Magic."

"Yes, but he's secretly been working with Eternis by request of the former king. Now, our second and third armies are to move on his orders," Cale replied.

"Why, where'd they go and what for?" Dash questioned.

"They're looking to move to the Crystal Cities."

"Crystal Cities," Legion and Dauge said collectively. It didn't make sense to Dash, Pitt, and Kraydia but it did make sense to the brothers.

"Why the Crystal Cities?" Dash asked.

"I know why," Legion answered.

"Is General Black still here in Eternis?" Dauge asked.

"Yes, he's staying at Almerouy's Head Basket."

"What room?" Legion asked.

"Why does it matter?" Cale questioned.

"Yes, I don't get where this is going," Pitt chimed in.

"Are we heading to the Crystal Cities?" Kraydia questioned to the group still quasi-playing with her spells.

"We are but not yet. Well, maybe not. I don't know yet. What room is he in?" Legion asked.

"I believe room three," Cale said.

Legion just looked at his brother. "Dauge," he said. Dauge didn't even respond. And Legion knew he was on it. Dauge immediately took off for the Inn where Mangus was said to be staying.

Legion took the lead of the group, pushing his way to the front. "General," he said to Cale. "General Black has made his home in the Crystal Cities. Bahaus has time and time again proved his disgust toward the man for leaving Eternis. If General Black is here, those independent cities are without a head of defense. His armies won't move without him, nor will they move against him. Those cities produce quite a bit of wealth and they're independent. They paid a great deal of money to Black who in turn doubled and tripled his mercenary army size to keep the cities protected. My father told me this story countless times. Bahaus wants to move in on the Cities but Eternis has never pledged a war in its entire existence!"

Cale Dar's jaw hit the floor. Legion was right. Adrian was right. He remembered those conversations. General Black left Eternis and tripled his military prowess in order to defend the Crystal Cities as their primary standing army. A few cities, each independently owned but united through the protection of one another, was bound to be attacked eventually. Was King Bahaus seriously going to attack the cities?

General Black's armies would stand out and see their leader safely removed from captivity before they'd fight and see him dead. They could always acquire another contract elsewhere. However, the possibility of finding a contract that would pay like the Crystal Cities was highly improbable.

The day had just begun. Kleiven was gone and Grath removed. Why did he leave so abruptly? What was going on? Was there some connection between the shadow elf and King Bahaus?

"General Dar, I'm afraid King Sazos is not the king we believe he could be. The people already fear him and admit they do not understand him from his acts as a prince. Should I dare say it? Should we move to see the newly anointed king removed?" Legion continued.

"King Bahaus sent a crew secretly to Falling Waters," Cale added in reply.

"Falling Waters?" Pitt asked.

"It's an old ruined city mostly overgrown and sunk with a vastly growing swamp in the area. It pretty much fed the swamp. The city's virtually sunken now," the General continued.

"Guess the name fits then," mocked Kraydia.

Again, Dash turned and gave her a look signifying now wasn't the time or the place for her "witty" humor.

"It's northeast of here going toward the Efestewelian Hives. It's just over a thousand miles or so before the deep forest and swamp begins. I can have a map drawn up to help guide you there. Inside this mass of messes is Fallen Swamp, prematurely named for the city it began with. Bahaus sent a team there. I'm thinking whatever he's hiding will come to light in that swamp. Perhaps his team forged the stamps to get things done. Adrian would have never signed off on it."

"As we speak, Bahaus plans to move on the Crystal Cities, capture Magnus Black, and is sending a team to Fallen Swamp for some unknown reason?" Legion said, making sure he had all the facts straight.

"And no reason as to why he'd send the team northeast to the swamp? If it's to get rid of forged signets, why not just destroy them here? What's in the swamps that could possible have King Bahaus' interest?" Dash asked.

General Dar just sighed. It was like he kind of had an idea but wasn't sure and didn't want to disclose. Dash got pushy and imposed trying to force the answer out of him.

"Easy Dash, he's still a General," reminded Pitt.

"If we're going to help, we need to know everything that's going on," Dash said.

Pitt shook his head. Dash was right. The goliath's big thick hand found its mark on the shoulder of the little half-eladrin. General Dar took a step back and turned to look out into the open as to better clear his head.

"Falling Waters sank when two legendary teams were planning to showdown there. Both crews were never seen or heard from again. It's believed Falling waters had a vault of magical weapons and scrolls hidden amongst its elite soldiers, guards, and protectors. It's a city that's been gone for a long time. It disappeared when the world was still wholesome and pure. It disappeared when Thedia's crust wasn't so scarred," General Dar said.

"That's it?" Dash questioned further.

"Kramone's Scepter is said to be among the treasures of Falling Waters." General Dar slowly continued to pour information out to the team.

"Kramone's Scepter?" Dash questioned. Pitt and Legion were just as in the dark as the latter. Kraydia wasn't. Her elven ears quickly pointed to attention. "Kramone's Scepter," she sparked.

"It's said to be there. It was carried by an old wizard named Rancy when Falling Waters sank, or that's how the legend tells it anyway." Secretly, Dar knew it was Grath heading to Falling Waters for King Bahaus and the magic there was the reason.

The magic of Falling Waters gave Dash his own notion. It would be enough to elevate his team above the others. It would make them further stand out and grant them capabilities that would otherwise be beyond their reach. Quests that would have been far beyond their reach could now be within their grasp.

"We head to Falling Waters." Dash changed the subject and made a very important decision all at the same time.

"Wait, what about the Crystal Cities and Magnus Black?" Kraydia asked.

"My brother's heading to Magnus as we speak. We should do the same. We should accompany him," Legion added.

"We should. We will," Dash agreed.

"I'm not sure if sending you all to Falling Waters is the best for Eternis, especially if King Bahaus looks to move on the Crystal Cities," General Dar questioned.

"We can only go one place at a time. We have to hope we get Magnus out of there. Even if he gets captured, we can break him out. We have time on that road. If he gets his hands on those weapons and armors and that scepter of Falling Waters, well, it's going to be a lot more difficult getting that a way from him." What Dash said was true but it was also his way of assuring Dar and his own crew that his hidden agenda was still the best idea.

"We must depart for Falling Waters immediately. First, we must assure General Black and my brother are both safe," Legion seconded.

Dauge arrived at Almerouy's Head Basket just in time to see their fears come alive; a plethora of Eternis' finest guards escorting a shackled General Magnus Black from the inn. He was too late. They caught on and got to Black just a little to late. Dauge stepped from sight.

Magnus Black was once a feared and well-respected warrior. He was old and his bones more fragile than they once were. He was wise with age and completely alone in Eternis, one of the few places he felt he could walk as such.

Dash, Legion, Kraydia, and Pitt were coming up fast behind Dauge. Dauge's anger grew. Magnus Black was an honorable man his father spoke highly of on more than one occasion.

Legion knew what his brother planned. Dash and the others stopped, seeing the younger Xavier casually blending in. They knew his colors and his fainted blue cape and robe. Dash, Pitt, and Kraydia slowed to a walk, seeing the General in chains and Dauge hiding in the crowds of people.

Magnus was honorable but vain. His ego was perhaps his strongest weakness. And to be shackled and dragged in front of hordes of townsfolk in a city he considered a home would not go forgotten. It would not go unpunished. Fortunately, his face was absent marks. There didn't appear to be a struggle.

"Dauge no!" Legion cried just before his brother burst out.

The robes and cape came off. Dauge was in full sprint at the guards escorting the mercenary general. Dash and the others came to a stop. They were in complete surprise. Adrian spoke of Magnus' importance to him, his brother Taj, and their father Dominick. And Magnus was a fated hero to Eternis who left on good terms. He was not deserving of this treatment.

Dauge pulled his short swords, piercing one, two, and then a third torso of ill-readied guards. The others of the squad immediately commenced pulling their weapons. A sword hummed at Dauge's ducking head. The younger Xavier maneuvered his head and dropped his shoulder, rising strong again with the same shoulder planted deep into the waist of yet another guardsman. Dauge rose, lifting the man from his feet sending him head first over his shoulder to the ground and the flat of his back.

Soon, Legion's little brother was surrounded by the guards in charge of capturing General Black. Black never moved. He held his shackled body high and watched as his would-be savior fought off the engaging unit of men sent to take him back by the last remaining son of one of his dearest friends, King Gerear Uil-Endail.

"Legion stop!" Dash yelled.

The others were still at a slight stroll knowing there was nothing they could do to stop the situation. It was already happening before their eyes. The mighty guardsmen weren't impressive at all. The evading, rolling, and dodging Dauge continued flawlessly gutting and cutting everything from ankles to throats.

Finally, one of the guards ripped his freedom, restraining him from behind. The little rogue's swords fell from his grasp but another elven guard coming to finish him found the acrobatic Dauge still too much. He lifted his body from the earth, forcing his boots into the face of the guard, knocking the aggressor unconscious. Dauge kept his boots moving, walking up the elf's body, flipping over his capturer and forcing the latter to end his grip. Dauge followed up immediately with a punch to the back of the man's head, stumbling him forward enough to allow him to regain his weapons.

When Legion closed the final bits of distance between them, he knew to stop as the backing-up guards instructed. Dauge stood alone next to the shackled Magnus in the surrounded opening of the people. Eight guards were down, either wounded or killed. Dauge slew members of the Eternian Guard and nothing could take it back. He was a villain of Eternis and an enemy to the people, furthering the cause of Bahaus by his actions.

"Noble effort, stand down, son." General Black's voice was calm and soothing.

Dauge was crouched and readied, his bloody swords prepared for purpose. The remaining able guards continued to back away. Most still able were either cut, wounded, or bruised. Dauge looked back at Black.

Two guards blocked Legion's path. "Dauge stand down!" he screamed, terrified for his brother's life and safety.

"Black's done nothing to deserve this and is a friend of my father. I will not stand by and watch this!" Dauge roared back.

"Please!" Legion screamed.

The others called to their friend as well, begging and pleading for him to stand down and drop his swords. Finally, from out of nowhere Legion's little brother fainted. He fell to ground fast asleep. The guards, Black, and Legion had no idea of what happened to him. The guard leader quickly ordered two of his men to shackle the downed adversary, which they quickly obliged.

Legion turned back to his friends. It was Dash! His magical residue and movements after casting were still visible. "Dash!" he screamed.

The rest of Legion's crew caught up to him. In whispers they argued. Legion broke away only to be caught and grabbed by his people again. Dauge was now being dragged by two guards underhooking his arms. His feet trailed lifelessly as they walked him behind Magnus.

"Dauge!" Legion screamed.

More guards carried off their wounded and dying. The crowd slowly began to disperse.

"Now what?" Pitt asked, concerned.

"What were you thinking Dash? They could have killed him!" Legion screamed at his team's leader.

"Had I not protected him with that spell, they would have killed him or he would have done further damage to our city! And they surely would have had his life!"

Legion listened to Dash's words. Perhaps he was right, then again maybe not? The crew calmed Legion.

"We'll fix this somehow." Something about Dash gave him the ability to comfort people. Maybe that was why he took up the bardic trade? He was good at what he did, a natural leader, someone others could follow and see their stars change before their eyes.

"How can we fix this Dash? My brother killed and wounded Eternian guardsmen, several of them!" Legion's pouring concern was clear from his first word.

"We will," he replied. "We will."

Dauge finally awoke. The sand and ground once beneath his feet was now cold stone. The fresh Eternian air gone from his nostrils replaced with the musty air of a cavernous underground. It was a dungeon. Two guards were still dragging him but now down a long hallway of stone. The ground, roof, and walls were all stone. His vision blacked out and came again. It came and went again and again.

Pain, stinging pain, rolled across his body. He'd been thrown into a cell. He didn't hear the cell door open but he heard it shut. Dauge rolled to his back, forcing his eyes to remain open. Magic, was it magic that got him? It had to be? Who pressed magic upon though? Eternis wasn't overly filled with casters and his keen sense would have noticed if there were any threatening ones nearby.

Dauge pulled himself to the corner of the cell. There was another in the cell. His vision was too blurry to make him out. The cell wasn't very wide but had a decent length to it. Stone surrounded Dauge on five sides, above and below him and to his left and right. Wrought Iron bars plagued his sight from the front. The two guards that took him there were gone and two half-elven guards dressed differently, of course, than the street guardsmen kept watch over their cell.

"What gotchu down here?" the cellmate asked.

Dauge heard him but still moved to collect his thoughts. His heard hurt like he'd been drinking all night. Was it from the magic or the rough treatment? He tried to stand but fell to his butt once again. Dauge finally, comfortable in a corner, plopped his head up again the wall to once again embrace the sweet serenity of sleep.

Chapter 29

By the day's end Dash finally made arrangements to see the King. However, King Bahaus' only request was that he speak to Legion and Legion alone. Dash agreed to speak to Adrian while Kraydia and Pitt went to Dauge about keeping his cool in the meantime.

Getting the audience with King Bahaus wasn't too terribly difficult for Dash as members of his closest order were actively searching for the half-eladrin moments after the guards killing took place. Kraydia and Pitt got the information they needed. Dauge was being held in the underground dungeon on the South side of Eternis, Tam's Dungeon as it was called.

Kraydia and Pitt made their way to the small building built around the singular trap door that gave entrance to Dauge's captivity spot. A single dragonborn guard held the door. After proper papers were shown, given to Kraydia and Pitt by Dash, the guard let them in. The one-room square barrack building didn't have much but a few cots and a desk. Three more guards leisurely passed the time playing bones on the floor. Two were human and the other a half-orc.

Pitt wasn't a smart man but he knew Eternis favored humans natively. Not too many half-orcs were around. He whispered, "A dragonborn at the door and now a half-orc in here. Seems like I'm seeing more non-humans than I remember working for this city?"

"Keep it down. Eternis is a melting pot and mercenaries always find employment here."

"Aye," he concluded.

"We must get to Dauge," she said.

"You there, why are you here?" the half-orc questioned, standing quickly back to attention.

"We are here for Dauge Gray. We come with papers signed by the King himself," Kraydia answered.

The two humans stood as well. They were tired and lazy looking. The half-orc, clearly in charge of the crew, stamped the papers and opened the trap door by unlocking the lock and removing the thick chain around it.

"Go straight down. Take your first left and then an immediate right. There, Gray's cell will be on the...."—he paused and went back to his blueprints and name and cell coordination papers—"...he'll be the first cell on the right."

Kraydia and Pitt started to head downward.

"Wait!" one of the human guards exclaimed.

"Yes?" she questioned.

"No blades, bows, or weapons of any kind. Going to need to search you," he said.

Dauge's companions complied. Their weapons were taken and stashed to the side. Their clothes and armor were removed to assure nothing of any kind was going to be taken down that could possibly be snuck in for the prisoners.

Satisfied, the two were finally allowed their clothes back and to push forward into the depths of Tam's Dungeon. Kraydia and Pitt walked in accordance to the half-orc's instructions. Two guards stood midway down the hallway. They worked in unison, patrolling the single hallway.

Kraydia announced loudly with papers in hand they were there for Dauge Gray. One guard pointed toward the area that the half-orc previously said. The two rushed to the front of his cell. Dauge was curled up in a corner with his head plopped up against the stone wall. A cellmate stood close to the iron bars, looking to the left or right as if he had someone coming or was waiting on something.

"Dauge," Pitt said sternly.

His voice awoke the human prisoner. He shook his head around and asked "where am I" more than once before finally coming to. The spell that hit him was hard and ran deep into him. He was still groggy but finally made it back to his feet and walked over to touch flesh with his comrades that had come to see him.

"My brother, why is my brother not here?" he asked angrily.

"In order to get what we needed to move to purpose, he had to give audience to King Bahaus. Dash is going to see your father and calm him down and explain everything. And we've come to tell you what's coming to pass," she answered methodically.

"Ah I see," he said calmly. "That rat bastard,", anger growing in his words. "What are the charges against Magnus? I don't understand? How can he do this?" Dauge continued to question. "Even a king in a place such as Eternis would need severe charges to keep a man like Black imprisoned and the people of Eternis accepting of it."

"I know not of his plans. Perhaps they'll lurk from the shadows, but you're right, Dauge. And I'm sure your brother and Dash are taking care of that as we speak. Just sit still until we're clear of this."

"We?" he asked Kraydia, uncaring of whether she'd finished her words or not.

"Yes Dauge, we are a team. We're in this together," Pitt added.

Dauge was finally able to move and walk around. He rubbed his head like he'd been clobbered with a club but he was still dreary from the spell. He extended his hands and straightened his legs, arching his body as best he could, stretching out the kinks that were still there. "I'll remain still but move with haste. Remaining caged or silent, or even still, has never been my purpose."

The two quickly agreed and unified their hands with Dauge through the cell bars.

Dash's talk with Adrian didn't take long. Adrian immediately left with one mission in his mind, to clear his son of this mess. Dash agreed to follow the retired military tactician through his duties. Dash took it as an advantage to grow closer to the noble Eternian.

Legion waited, staring at the manmade moat carved around the manor of the Uil-Endail House. A single white bridge breached the gap between his makeshift island and the rest of Eternis. The moat wasn't very deep and was filled with exotic colorful fish. Legion smiled. It was a pleasant scene.

A single guard wearing full knight attire with a newer looking black tunic with a demonic red dragon symbol in the center walked forward. These weren't traditional outfits of any Eternians his father ever spoke of nor was it anything he'd ever seen. The man's helm was full, covering his face and laced with small spikes all across, including two devil-like horns extending from the crown. That getup must have cost a fortune, he thought.

"Papers," the knight said, looking strong.

He presented the papers and the man walked across the bridge to take them. After a brief glance, the guard gave the okay nod and signaled for Legion to follow him. Legion obliged. Where was all this money coming from? The war in the Republic set Eternis and several other kingdoms and city-states back. What did this new king already have up his sleeve?

The King's manor was magnificent, twice the size of the Xavier manor. The single guard walked Legion through a patch of soft grass and gardens filled with exotic flowers and exquisitely built waterfalls, never taking a step off the stone tile of course.

The guard passed directly by the main entrance to the manor. What? He wrapped around the side to a beautiful opening. There, in a small field of dreams and gardens, King Bahaus Sazos-Uil-Endail stood with four more guards outfitted exactly like the one he followed. Another man, dark complected and certainly not native to Eternis stood. His garb was colorful and loose fitting. His head was bald. His skin was of those who'd been kissed by the sun. He wore mostly yellows and purples with his circular wool woven hat being made out of several reds and blacks.

Some Thoxens had sun-kissed skin but this man wasn't Thoxen. He was of the Republic, native to the desert. He wasn't anyone Legion knew. The man carried a guard with him as well. A tiefling lightly armored but heavily armed. Several weapons lay ready across the being's dark amber-tinted skin.

On their knees, about thirty young human boys all from different walks of life. None looked Eternian but were human through and through. Legion's keen senses told him something wasn't right. Bahaus handed the man a small pouch barely filled with coin. No way it was enough to pay for all those kids? Were they slaves? Was this man a slaver? Slavery was only respected in Eternis, not allowed. Eternian law prohibited the selling or buying of slaves personally. However, it was a tricky law. If non natives were purchasing or selling non-native Eternians or walking with them in Eternis, then the law would accept it. Bahaus was breaking his own land's laws? And traditionally, most knew to keep the buying and selling out of the Eternian walls.

The king turned and saw Legion and smiled. Not a bit of worry came from his face. The dark man bowed graciously and thanked the king before making his exit. The man's eye caught Legion's attention. He gleamed at him hard. Legion ignored it and took to Bahaus' hand-waving signal. The king was inviting him in. He waved the guards off, pointing to the kids.

"See to the children. Make sure they're organized correctly."

"Yes my king."

"Yes my king," one after another the dark clad guards said in compliance, bowing as they spoke.

King Bahaus took Legion through the main doors to a room very close to the main entrance. It wasn't too large but it held several trophy animals, medals, awards, and other fancy memorabilia. Legion looked around. Curious, he wasn't even patted. He was allowed in without a single weapon being taken from him.

"My king, I've come to beg for the life of my brother."

Bahaus didn't say a word. He waved the Eternian silent and strolled around the room of his father's trophies and his father's father's trophies. Bahaus wore the fanciest getup money could by. Unlike Gerear, a humble king, Bahaus wanted everyone to know just how much his clothing cost. He was dressed in all whites ornamented with residium-laced gold threading. Golden designs lay across his ornamental bracers and leggings. Yet, his shirt carried the same red demonic dragon as the guards.

"I knew you'd come," he said.

"Of course you did, my king. My brother—"

King Bahaus cut him off, finishing the sentence not quite like Legion had planned but nonetheless, it. "Is an enemy of the state!" His words heightened and filled with anger.

"I'm not asking for his actions to be excused. I'm begging for his life, offering mine in exchange. Is there anything I can do, anything at all to wipe this clean?"

"The only wrong thing is to do nothing. My father told me that once," Bahaus said scratching the back of his neck while turning to face Legion.

Legion went to kneel, as he'd not done so yet.

Bahaus laughed at the jest and ordered Legion to remain standing. "You're among Eternians here." "You wonder what prompted me to imprison Black, don't you?"

"I do, my king."

"Black is a traitor. He left Eternis."

"I understand his contract with our city was finished."

"He left for money. I take him for money." Bahaus' tone was becoming more volatile once again.

"I don't understand."

"He tripled his armies and his coin by leaving us for the Crystal Cities. They don't really have a true standing army anymore. The monsters beat them down until Black arrived."

"And Black made his home there, right?"

"He did. He is here in my possession and his mobile armies are they're protecting some of the wealthiest cities in the world."

"My king, apologies. I care not for Black and I know not why Dauge did what he did. I'm only here to ask forgiveness and offer whatever services I can in exchange for his pardon."

Bahaus smiled. "Relax, patience. We're getting there."

"Yes, my king."

"I've announced reason to the public today that I've got word that Black was looking to move against us."

"He'd never do that."

"Yes, but I need Eternis to believe he would. And I need an act to say he did."

"Why are you telling me this?" Legion stopped immediately. Finishing his words, he knew. He knew exactly what Bahaus wanted.

"I'm willing to say he escaped. Eternis will not buy a pardon, especially when they see Black is guilty.

"You want me to act as a member of the Free Armies and do what to incriminate him?"

"I have a transport ship outfitted with fake cargo and hired hands to sail to Port Agatha. I need you to burn it to the bottom of the Hangman's Straight. Kill everyone on board and destroy the barrels filled with dirt."

"My king, that's…treason," Legion pleaded.

"An act your brother already committed, along with murdering and wounding several of my royal and noble guards. Do this and your brother shall have escaped my prison."

"Why? Why Black?"

"His armies will concede to get him back and remove themselves from the cities, allowing me full access to them. I've spent hidden treasuries my father had on mercenaries, armies, outfitting them, and the like. If we don't do this, Eternis is bankrupt. The Crystal Cities will fill our pockets and bring Eternis to a place it long deserved to be. It begins with you burning the Bloody Queen to the bottom of the Straight or killing each and every member of her crew systematically without being seen."

"Release my brother. That's something he's more keen to doing successfully. Hold me in his place."

"No need. I know where your father and mother reside. I'll do what it takes to see this through."

"You'd threaten my mother and father."

"I do what I must to see Eternis restored to former glory. We're the oldest city in the world and I'm going to see to it we get what we deserve."

"My king, I don't thing Dauge will do this honestly. I can get it done. I will do what I must for my brother."

"Then put words to purpose and see it done."

Legion knew the conversation was finished. Bahaus was already walking out of the room. Legion followed the king and made his exit. The king wanted to blackmail Magnus Black, get his armies to retreat from their location, seize the Crystal Cities, and take the money to begin an empire. And the money of Eternis' treasuries was all but gone anyway. Damned if you do, damned if you don't.

Chapter 30

The next morning the crew was up early and gathered for breakfast at the old Silverstar II. Kraydia wasn't a woman by any sense of the word when it came to food. She gorged herself every chance she got. Kraydia took to the meats over the bread.

Pitt got a mouthful of everything he could get his hands on. He and Kraydia were just alike when it came to eating. Pitt chased down every mouthful with a glass of hard wine.

Dash, of course, even ate with elegance. He kept his manners, sipping his drink and quietly breaking his bread. The big old tavern was packed for the early morning. Lots of ships were coming in. Business was good.

Legion sat cold with absolutely no appetite. He couldn't eat a thing and only sipped enough to keep his mouth from turning dry. His look was cold. Pitt and Kraydia didn't pay attention and didn't catch it but Dash did. He looked Legion in his eyes and his eyes couldn't lie. He knew something was wrong with the older Xavier.

Finally, Dash quieted them by starting the conversation they all knew was coming. "I spoke with Adrian yesterday."

"Nom... Nom... Nom..." Pitt gorged it down, plate after plate of bread and meats.

Kraydia followed his lead, adding fresh vegetables to her plates.

"Wait, stop...listen to me." Dash tried again and this time it worked. Kraydia and Pitt stopped momentarily and then, after seeing the look on Dash's face, gently put down their bread quietly, as if it were going to ease things by doing so.

"Adrian went to see Seth Redd about Dauge. Apparently there's an old clause Seth can utilize due to his time in service to get Dauge potentially cleared by a set sum of money. Of course, your father, Legion, will have it and will be willing to spend it."

"Clause?" Kraydia asked.

"It's an old law from the Eternian First Scrolls. It states a Senior Captain or higher ranking officer of the Eternian guard or military with fifteen years of service can request the crimes of one man to be paid in full with a reasonable sum of money," Dash answered.

Legion's heart lifted. He hadn't done anything quite yet but he remembered Bahaus telling him as he walked out the door, he had until morning to fulfill his duties to the crown. Was this an out for him? Otherwise he'd have to leave his hometown. If he followed Bahaus' orders, Dauge would still be an enemy of Eternis and if he didn't Bahaus would have it out for them. Bahaus treasured the Xavier House, why would he do this to them? No, it wasn't him. He was but an opportunist. Bahaus was but seizing the opportunity his little brother gave to him.

"Do you think Redd will use his political prowess in Dauge's favor?" Kraydia questioned with sauce from her steak still dripping from her lips and chin.

"He's going to have to," Legion answered abruptly.

"Why's that?" Pitt questioned.

"Because the alternative isn't pleasant, I assure you," Legion said.

The others quieted down, listening to his tone and words. "We have to remain absent ill thoughts. We have to remain with sound mind and body," Dash slowly reminded, keeping his eyes fixed upon his nobly blooded ally.

"I will do whatever it takes to retrieve Dauge from the pits of Tam's Dungeon and save him from execution or whatever his fate has in store," Legion answered strongly.

"What are you talking about, Legion?" Kraydia asked, concerned. Her arcanic nature had her interest anxiously burning for answers.

"I spoke with the king."

"And?" Dash quickly questioned.

"What'd he say?" Kraydia said.

"Is the king's blessing upon us, upon Dauge?" Pitt asked.

"We are—" Legion stopped. The swinging doors to the Silverstar II flew open. Legion's eyes fell upon his beautiful sister. She wore her father's favorite satin dress of greens.

"Brother, brother!" she cried, running immediately to his table.

"What is it, sister? Calm yourself," Legion said.

Dusk was trembling terribly. She had the entire table disturbed. Legion pulled her tight, forcing her butt upon his lap. She was his sister but sometimes outsiders looked upon them queer of their unique bond. She rubbed his face and half smiled for her brother. Dusk then dropped her head into her brother's shoulder, crying obviously for Dauge.

"You bring word of father's words with General Redd I presume?" he asked.

"He used his circumvention clause for Cale Dar when Cale arose from the dead. Eternis was to have him removed but General Redd believed so much in him he used his power for the rising soldier of the time! There's no use. There's nothing we can do for my dearest twin, ugh," she cried.

"My oath to you sister, no harm from the hands of Eternis shall come to our brother."

She raised her head and looked her brother in the eyes, ever thankful for his presence and courage.

"What will you do?" she asked.

"Legion, we must stay within the laws of the land," Dash reminded, almost in an ordering tone.

"My brother goes where I go and I follow him. If he is to die, then I die with him. If me assuring my brother's safety removes me from this team then so be it."

"What would the king have us do?" Dash sarcastically asked his friend.

"The Bloody Queen Transport ship is to be burned or otherwise destroyed tonight. As I left his home, he explained it's been finely prepped for a burning. Or, kill every man on board and make it look like thieves under Black's employ did it. It's his way of keeping Black imprisoned and earning the right to march on the Crystal Cities. It matters not. For should we discover a way to oust his plans, the Eternian treasury is bankrupt. He's already sent coin to purchase armies, men, supplies, ornaments, decorations, and everything else. Only the money of the Crystal Cities could save Eternis now." Legion spilled Bahaus' plans all over the table for the lot of them to hear.

For a moment, the table fell silent and the loud outbreaks and scores of people crowding the large tavern were nothing but background noises, like the buzzing of a bee in a forest filled with creatures rarely sitting still.

"Bahaus is an Eternian supremist, a human supremist. Why would he want you to kill Eternians and destroy Eternian property? Especially with Bahaus at its helm, Eternis hasn't the money to purchase more ships," Dash questioned. "I get wanting to frame Black, but why at such a cost?"

"Pitt and I have seen more and more mercenaries taking up the Eternian colors," Kraydia began. Legion cut her off before she could finish.

"She's right. The ship's laced with mercs." Dusk's eyes fell watery yet again. She was exhilarated at her brother's devotion to their other brother but something yet again had her heart sinking with despair.

"Wait," Legion said to the group, halting them with his hand. He looked at his sister now with only her concern on his mind. "What is it?"

"Bahaus ordered Kleiven to The Bloody Queen." Her tears began to pour fiercely yet again. And once again Legion was there to embrace her and hold her from her fears. She wasn't the weakling little sister she once was and something dark was now in her, but that didn't stop her from wanting her older brother to be her older brother, especially in times like these.

Dash laughed and smiled. It came to him just as she said it. Legion didn't know what he found funny. Pitt wondered the same. Kraydia however beat Dash to the punch, explaining to the rest of them just what Bahaus had planned.

"He sent Grath to the northeast and plans to have you kill Kleiven, all the while framing Magnus for a heinous crime in order to get his plan to unfold. Grath and Kleiven have what in common?" Kraydia asked, smiling cleverly. She thumped the tip of her pointer finger to her temple.

Everyone but Dash looked on waiting for the answer. Dusk looked back finally from Legion, knowing the answer herself after thinking about it. "Me."

"You." Dusk and Kraydia answered simultaneously.

"He still longs for your love, Dusk." Kraydia continued.

"Why? It was so short lived," she questioned.

"Who knows, but love can make men do mysterious things," Dash answered.

"It's something we have on our side," Pitt said sternly.

"I won't use his desire to manipulate him!" she roared.

"Why not? He's manipulated everyone else and threatens the life of your brother," Dash reminded.

Dusk dropped her head. He was right. She didn't like being around Bahaus. He was sick and dark. Something about him was twisted and he often spoke of the darker powers. She cared not for the darker powers and loathed that one lurked within her very breasts.

"We must expose the king," said Dusk.

"Impossible," Dash answered.

"Not necessarily. He hasn't been with crown for very long and he's nearly wiped out businesses. The treasury is bankrupt. The people see his hiring of guards and changing their outfits, buying suits of armor far beyond our measures. He's organizing a small personal guard just for him and these men are outfitted each like royal watchers of a wealthy king of a thousand cities. We employ another to do the bidding and then give warning to the Bloody Queen. Dash uses his charm to force the man to admit his employer," Legion spoke with influencing voice and tone.

"Us?" Dash questioned.

"We mimic one of his high guards and—"

"No Legion, we cannot trust this with another's ears. We cannot use an innocent man to save a guilty one. Even if that guilty man is your brother." Dash was holding his ground respectfully.

Legion shook his head, taking in Dash's every word. He didn't accept them, nor would he. Dauge would not die at the hands of Eternis' law whether he was right or wrong.

"We burn the ship. We kill everyone on board. Dusk informs Kleiven to sneak off and stay with her the night of. She informs him of the plan. He makes it to the docks in time to see it fall. He dives in the water and we pull him out. The culprit was a man in the name of the king. Kleiven Dar, son of General Dar will have strong sway against the king," Legion offered.

Legion's offer was bold but tempting. It could work. Truthfully, it would be easier just to replace Dauge, but his skill set and name were quite possibly irreplaceable. He was trained by the Lotus people from birth and raised with them. He also carried the Xavier name and honor. His willingness to die in order succeed was not something typical of most living beings.

"Or... We take the high road, as we always should," Legion added in reply as an addendum to his previous words.

This time, his words moved Dash. The phrase high road got to him. Yes, it was those two words that paused Dash from the conversation. For a moment, time stopped. This was what it was all about. This was what the making of heroes was made of. The stuff of their lives presently was exactly how heroes were forged. It made Dash ponder about Thox and Storm and what of their names there in that part of the world.

"We take the high road. Dauge's actions were unjust but only as an answer to unjust orders made by the king," Dash said, smiling greedily.

The smile was contagious. Legion succumbed and mimicked the smile himself. The others looked at the two of them. They were onto something. Dusk was especially curious. The thrill of plotting against her newly anointed king excited her. She was changing. She knew it. She wasn't the young and innocent girl she once was.

Then something happened that hadn't happened in so very long. A voice came to Legion. It echoed through the halls of his mind. Could the others hear it? No. It didn't seem as if they'd heard it at all. The outside drowned out and the voice in his mind took complete control. He couldn't hear a word the others were saying, but the voice started strong. It sounded like multiple entities in one, a dual sounding voice echoing through the stirs of his thoughts.

The ship was prepped to burn. Our keen senses heard the unseen in Sazos' manor watching over you speaking of a false quest and the charge of another to do the same bidding for the king. Warn Kleiven of the coming attack tonight. Stand ready to ambush the ambushers of the Bloody Queen. Stand as heroes. My magic is returning. It's growing with everyday. Use me to force truth from tongue and use it to bring justice to Bahaus and Eternis. I know you can feel us, Legion. Our presence is growing once again. Once again we are one. Once again we are strong. Not since the days of Esgaria have we felt such a strength. Goddimus and Arakros walk with you always. SOUL and LORE walk with you always. You are the one who brought us together and created peace between us. We are, as you named us... The Mourning Star.

"Legion... Legion... Legion... Are you listening?" Dash asked.

"Sorry," he said, snapping back to.

"There's more to my story. I just remembered. Bahaus spoke of another team charged with the same task as me." Legion took the words of Mourning Star and manipulated the truth, for he felt it would set easier with a bent version. He didn't want to talk or speak of Mourning Star's words in his head to anyone save perhaps Dauge or Dusk.

"I personally believe Grath not to have left to the northeast. I feel he has been set for the same cause. The story sending him eastward just doesn't add up. If it's not Grath, it's someone else. It's another group. We allow the attempt on the Bloody Queen. Dusk informs Kleiven of what's to come…" He paused.

"Grath is still here?" Dusk questioned.

"Go and see to Kleiven. Tell him to keep your words to himself, but we believe an attack to be coming to the transport Bloody Queen tonight."

"Brother—" she tried.

"Go!" he ordered.

Dusk quickly bounced from his lap to her feet. The younger sibling kissed her older brother's cheek and walked with haste from the tavern to her lover's home.

"Legion, we've not agreed upon set tactics," Dash stammered.

"Trust me, Dash. Just this once, trust me," he replied.

"When the ship is attacked. We attack the other crew Bahaus has sent, whether it is Grath or another. And with help of the pouring down crew to defeat the ambushers, we will not only have witnesses to our actions but also hosts to bear us the truth. We shall use your magic, Dash, and whatever magic we must to rip the truth from their stomachs as to who sent them. When Bahaus is revealed, we'll have enough evidence to arrest him and dethrone him for high treason. Magnus shall then be released and with good favor toward us."

"And what of the treasury, Legion?" Kraydia asked.

"I've not got that far," he answered honestly.

"Magnus perhaps will help keep Eternis afloat as a token of good friendship for our hand in saving him?" Pitt suggested.

"Perhaps. If not, we'll find a way to keep going and without asking for handouts. First, we must stop Bahaus," Legion finished.

"Agreed."

"Agreed."

"Aye."

Kraydia and Dash's words came out identically. Pitt followed up at the same time, proving he was onboard with his comrades to oust the king and save the mercenary general. They all agreed to prep themselves for the coming night and to meet at the gates of the first docks come early evening. It was going to be a long night, staking and waiting for the others to come, if they came. It was a gamble and one Legion suddenly managed to convince everyone else to take.

"I'll map the docks for possible entries from the other team. Remember Legion, I'm agreeing because this is for your brother. You should have say in how we do things. If we fail, also remember we set a pact for you, with you, to retrieve your brother and stand against a king in your honor and for the life of your brother. Remember who was at this table today." Pitt didn't speak much but when he did his words were poetic. Dash really was coming to enjoy what was coming of his team. The threat was real but the thrill was still exhilarating.

Chapter 31

Every day since his return to Thox Storm Stars walked higher. His companions walked with their heads held high. He was on the very road to bring his name from the ashes of shame back to a reinstated respected house among all Thoxens.

"How much for that one there?" Storm asked. He branched away from the rest of his team giving little details to what he had to do. He was merely looking for a day of leisure. He wore no armor this hot day and chose, surprisingly enough, to not even carry a sword.

Down an alleyway, Storm's eyes fell upon a half-orc slaver walking several slaves down the alley. Each was chained and linked together. Only a single one was human and for some reason the human stood out to Storm. He had an idea. He wanted to try something. He was going to try it.

"Not for sale," said the dirty old half orc.

The leathers and weapons of the half-orc were worn and beaten. To an ill-trained eye one would suspect a weakly or poorly armed man. The bloodstains and tears in the armor, the wearing of his sword's hilts told Storm the man had seen his fair share of combat.

Storm stopped. He was wearing his favorite yellow shirt and white breeches. He was a charming son of a bitch. Earlier in the day, the happy and thankful paladin purchased an apple. A simple bite would do him for the time he thought. Storm pulled the ripe green apple and plunged his teeth in. The juices were better than expected, he thought. "Sure he is. Everyone's for sale," Storm challenged happily.

"That one's a good fighter." The half-orc was stubborn and not wanting to give up.

"Coin is coin just the same. Quality calls for more coin. I take your word that he is what you say he is," Storm said.

"He's a renowned gladiator. Shows promise. He's even fought here in Thox a few times. I own this one personally. Two hundred and fifty pieces of that precious metal they call gold and he's yours," said the half-orc.

"Done," said the paladin. Coin was something he had in plenty since his return from the desert and his time with the lich Davion.

The exchange was made and the half-orc ordered a few of his underling guards to sever the ties between the binds of the human and the remaining slaves. He was resituated and bound, with the reins being brought to Storm by the half-orc who'd taken them from his underling.

When the slaver and his company and slaves walked from his sights, Storm handed the key to the slave's freedom to the slave. The human was thick and large. His chest was wide and strong. His frame stood just under six and three quarters tall. His hair was short and black, the very same color of his eyes. He had a few nicks here and there that festered into scars but only two that truly stood out. The two scars were across his right shoulder and right upper leg, overgrown like thick welts.

"What is this?" he asked curiously thankful but unsure what to be thankful to or for.

"I am Storm Stars of the legendary War General Storm Stars' family. You are free. There are no tricks or mysteries to solve your good fortune."

"I've been a slave for half my life," the man said. He was probably nearing middle age, somewhere around his thirtieth year of life.

"And now you're free," Storm continued.

"What is it you'd have me do? I owe you my life."

"Take this coin," Storm handed the man a hefty purse, "and build a life worth saving. Take a wife, build a family, and love your kin. I would have you under the Stars House sail to Eternis and render your services to the guard. There, you'll make coin to continue living. You'll build a life there. And seek out a man named Dash Riproc and Legion Cage Xavier of the House of Xavier and tell them their friend Storm is waiting for their return to Thox. Tell them he misses them dearly and looks forward to their reunion. If you have others, please, mine can wait." Storm finished with a smile.

By mid words, the two were shaking hands with opposing hands upon each other's shoulders. "I am Vektro Hal'gharn of Skye, a place I've long been removed from. I feel too long removed to return."

"Well Vektro Hal'gharn of Eternis, or Thox," Storm said smiling and pausing, "find yourself in the world now, a free man, and with one hundred golden coins to do with as you please to begin your new life."

The two embraced and talked a bit more before Storm ultimately ended the conversation stating he had places to be. The strong former gladiator walked from the alley curious as to why the faiths had suddenly shined their lights upon him after so long being removed from it.

Vektro walked in the loins of his former master's choosing through the streets of Omina, a smaller city built between several bigger cities. His first order of business would be to purchase a new set of clothes to begin his new life with. Soldier for Eternis, huh, not a bad idea; he really didn't know much. He was taken and sold at such an early age. All he knew was backbreaking labor and swordplay.

Storm continued through the town until he stopped at a local Sacred Gathering Temple where he knew at least Dargon would be. Sacred Gathering Temples were places built for private worship. Angelical, Draconic, Spiritual, Rivermortal, and everything else were welcome in these non-denominational temples.

Lord Decimus sought their company yet again. He had a charge for them. Not everything was going so perfectly for Storm. Alanis fell ill. Felzen abandoned the party with his newfound wealth, hoping to properly invest it, and Krazy left him some days ago, promising to return soon. Krazy's exploits quickly grew out of proportion and he became perhaps the most popular of Storm's once growing team. Truly, only Dargon remained loyal with him.

What was he going to tell Decimus? He hadn't a team ready for whatever the Lord would ask? He could perhaps set up fliers around town, hoping to attract some new members of good stock. Storm cared not so much about the team keeping its same members as he did reinstating his name. Besides, he thought, Felzen and Krazy weren't truly his kind of people but Krazy was a good friend to him and loyal. Hopefully, he'll return, Storm continued to think. Poor Alanis, something strong got to her. At first, she looked to beat it early but it relapsed. She was sick. She was really, really sick. After Dargon, visiting Alanis would be his first priority.

"Dargon, old friend," Storm said, walking into the simple wooden structure. An old fence surrounded a small piece of land where a decently sized large square building stood. It was technically considered a temple but was more like a single-story home renovated for the religious needs of its followers and supporters.

Dargon was kneeling to a small shrine dedicated to the Draconic Order. The Temple was absent bodies save Dargon's and now Storm's. Dargon raised and made the religious sign of Typherion, finishing his prayers.

"Storm, you're early. I just visited Alanis. She seems to be doing better."

Storm smiled. Dargon was the only real member of his team he considered a friend, next to Alanis. Krazy was a friend but in a different way. You could only trust those in his profession with so much. He'd always been loyal to Storm and the cause and Storm had nothing but good things to stay about the man, even if he was a shadow elf. In fact, Storm was raised to be somewhat racist against them. Krazy proved they could be made into decent people and friends; curiously enough, Krazy's exploits would not label him good or decent by any stretch of the imagination.

"Good, good, that's good to hear," Storm said. "Nonetheless, we must give Decimus the audience he seeks with us. The team we once were is gone but our name still stands. Our notoriety is still climbing. We have to build a team. We have to. We have to get started on getting through that audience with Lord Decimus just as soon as possible."

"I'll see to getting the word around town that we're looking to replace lost members and others who've moved on from us. Decimus is going to want to speak to you. You see to Decimus, I'll see to getting our team together. And by Typherion, your house will be reinstated as a recognized House of Thox. You'll become a hero your ancestors would be proud to call their own. And I'll be there to call you my lord," Dargon said cheerfully, trying to brighten Storm's day.

Storm kept the smile and happy appearance up mostly for his sake. He wanted to always carry a positive image. His team falling apart was certainly beginning to get to him. Storm nodded. Dargon made sense. "I'll see it done."

"You'll rise like a phoenix from the ashes, and one day your deeds will earn you the title lord. I swear it," Dargon said seeing Storm turn back toward the door.

Storm smiled again. Dargon always made him feel better and generally was the only one to know when something was wrong or when he was down. And shortly after meeting, the two parted ways to attend business.

Dargon knew immediately of an old friend. He was a bastard child, a half-breed. His mother was a drunk once promised to the Angelical Order's Glastys, the Locked Angel. She gave herself to the one she called to for life and the elven man disappeared soon after. She was human but the father was not.

Her son worked the taverns and, though a priest, Dargon never opened his mouth to any, not even him, about his kleptic nature. He was always taking things, even if they weren't worth anything at all. Dargon practically raised the boy during his youth. He was older than Storm but still not too much older than the boy.

On the cheap side of town, Dargon pushed his way through, handing gold and vittles to beggars and the homeless until finally he came to the small one-room home of the woman and her child. What was the name? It slipped his mind. He knocked the old rundown door anyway.

The door creaked open. It wasn't all the way shut or perhaps the door was broken. Either way, Dargon made his way slightly into the home. It was trashy and dirty. A young boy, half-elven in nature, the very same he remembered, knelt by a small pot cooking over a fire. The boys hair wasn't long but grown out and slightly shaggy. Its dirty blond color was mostly camouflaged by the dirt and soot the coal mines had covered him with. He'd decided upon a life in the mines? Dargon questioned to himself. Surely not, such a life was known to be horrific.

"Hey, what brings you here?" said the boy, looking up from the pot of food he was stirring.

"I've come to ask for your employ," Dargon replied, smiling.

"My employ? You've never said a word and you've seen me take things not my own. Why would you want me to work for you? What would you have me do?"

Dargon moved through the rubbish of the small shack. The food smelled good. He took in a second voluntary whiff and paused a moment to gather his thoughts. "I knew your mother from town. I know your mother's had a hard life. And you do what you must to help her now. I'll have her sent to a monastery in Xanon. I carry such clout. You may never see her again, but she'll be taken care of. And you can join me and change your stars. For we walk with one such star, Storm Stars." Dargon compared the stars of the sky to the Stars House, hoping the link caught the boys attention.

"I am but a thief and will not leave my mother."

"Right now you're just a thief, but you can become so much more, Siberon. I will send her to a draconic monastery and pay for her permanent stay there until you are able. Do this: Prove your runaway father wrong and make your mother proud. She was a respected priestess of Glastys once."

"I know my own mother priest."

"She'll have the best care Thox can offer. You must travel and work to give it to her. Perhaps one day you'll go to Xanon and see her again. We have an opening boy. I suggest you take it. I'm not much older than you, but I've seen things. And I can guide you and in time we can become a strong and united team under Storm Stars of House Stars. He's the Phoenix of Thox, I swear it, and great things will come to those who walk with him."

Siberon stood up. He wasn't very tall, maybe a few inches over five feet at best. His frame was thin looking and weak. There wasn't much to him at all. Siberon felt a sense of honor in Dargon's words. He had nothing going for him and knew no trade. The mines weren't making him stronger, they were making him weaker. They were killing him and he soon wouldn't be around to care for his mother. "What would you have me do?" he asked.

"Hone your skills. Defend Thox, build you name and fame, explore this world with me and find treasures beyond your wildest dreams. And become something your father would have been disgusted to know he left behind."

Siberon thought about the priest's words. He didn't even really know the priest. He knew the Typherion follower always ignored his sleight of hand moves even when he noticed them. He knew the priest felt sorry for him and this was his one chance to get out of the mines and out of Thox possibly and start a new life. Even if he perished, his mother would be looked after.

Meanwhile, Storm found himself sitting across from Lord Decimus Sextus. Decimus was some years past middle age. His neck-length brown hair was turning white with age. The wrinkles on his face deepened with every day. He was human and his best days were behind him. Decimus invited Storm quickly into the barracks. Decimus was always working. After the proper introductions were made, Storm was escorted downstairs to the basement of the barracks where Lord Sextus worked. He sat across from the Lord at his table making small talk before Lord Decimus finally pushed his papers to the side.

Storm fell curious. The basement was of rock and stone. Why would he choose to work in such a depressing and dark environment? Barrels and boxes were stored in the basement, leaving very little room for anyone to move around or do anything. Oddly enough, that's just how Sextus liked it.

"I understand you wanted to see me?" Storm asked.

"I did. I did," he answered, still grabbing at the papers he'd just pushed to the side. He couldn't let his work go, not even seemingly for a moment.

"I apologize to have kept you waiting, my lord," Storm said. "I've had some unfortunate dealings myself,"

"Lord Quinn of Quinn's Town is here in Omina. He needs a private escort to Daneth."

"Daneth, the city-state capital of the Nine Kingdoms?"

"The same. Do you know of another city with such a name?" Sextus joked.

Storm laughed. "I don't. That's quite a trek, my lord. It will put me away from Thox for quite some time. I'm not sure if I'm ready for that. I am looking to reestablish my family House here in Thox."

"Lord Quinn rose from nothing to get where he is. Having is favor would certainly help your cause."

"Yes my lord. Alanis is ill. Felzen has left to begin a life as a Lanista. He wants to house and train gladiators, build his own Ludus. That leaves only myself and Dargon. Kraikaikaei has left on a personal endeavor. His estimated return time is just within days."

"Lord Quinn isn't leaving for another four days. Will that suffice?"

"It will, your majesty. I only fear my team is not in the condition to execute a proper escort for such a man."

"It will have to work. In these times, men of your caliber are rare. Heroes walk like myths, especially since the day of the last Forsaken. It's been twenty-three years since the beginning of the new calendar, Storm. It's been twenty-three years since the Sundering began. And with every passing year, men made of stuff like you become fewer. These are the days to reinstate a House, good Storm. You were born in good times. These are hard times but good times still."

"Fine. As your hand I shall execute your will. Lord Quinn shall safely be brought to Daneth, even if it's me and me alone who does it."

"Well said," Decimus said, raising a hand and eye to his friend's words. He liked them. Having Decimus secure a strong escort for someone Like Lord Quinn could potentially elevate both his status and Storm's.

Chapter 32

Everyone was gone, doing their own thing, getting ready for the night to come. Kraydia and Dash walked toward the northwestern side of town, a side of town they generally didn't stray to. There was a peaceful waterway built with random simple fountains and gadgets just before the colonized wards of Eternis' outer areas began and the Eternis core ended.

"We've kept our relationship a secret. I still think it's for the best, at least for the time being," Dash said, keeping a friendly distance between the two. Couples were all around them, holding hands, kissing, and embracing one another.

They did the same when not around others. They were a growing name and people would talk. Especially the simple people, farmers, laborers, miners, all these people had nothing else to talk about. Did it matter if they were together? No, but Dash didn't want potential enemies to see her as a way to get to him personally.

And when feelings were involved, decisions could sometimes be manipulated. Dash didn't want his companions to think he could be manipulated, but he knew he could. He was growing strong feelings for Kraydia and wanted to tell her something.

She walked and listened as he talked, speaking sweet nothings into the open air for her carefree ears to take in. She smiled. She adored him. She appreciated him. She loved what he was and what he stood for. Looking around and seeing the other couples and seeing what she was missing didn't seem fair to her. She told him time and time again they would deal with whatever others brought their way. He didn't want to risk it. He didn't want to risk her. She didn't feel they were that big of a name.

They weren't by actions, but they did still walk with the sons of the legendary Taj Odin Xavier. And they still did have a few accomplishments under their belts.

"I told you. I wanted to stand and tell the world and our friends about us. Silver novels…" she started. Silver novels were simple novels written and sold for a few silver. "…Silver novels were made from the stuff of our beginning. We could build a name and a team together."

"I built this team, Kraydia. I found you," he said, getting on the defense.

"That's what I'm talking about. Your image, your persona, everything about you and your accomplishments mean more to you than anything else. They certainly mean more to you than I ever did."

"Kraydia, that's just not true. Where did all of this stem from?" he asked. They'd never fought or argued before.

"It's just. I don't know anymore, Dash."

Dash stopped and turned. He thought he knew what it was about. He didn't. He was wrong. He had to be. She didn't know.

"Is this about my fancying Dusk? I think she's pretty but she's courting a friend and I'm with you."

"I didn't even know. I knew it wouldn't work. My feelings have strayed. You wanted to keep it hidden and bottled up and I felt lonely, Dash. I still love you. I cannot be here with you anymore. Besides, my hot temper doesn't mesh with the group."

"Are you kidding? You fit right in with us all. You know that! Why would you say such a thing?" Dash took her hands into his own. He stared deep into her eyes, hoping to rekindle the flame and remove whatever doubt she may have still carried.

"It's over. At least for now," she said, turning away.

She turned and started away from him. He called out to her. She denied his efforts. Again, she shut him down as he tried one last ditch effort after another. Finally, he said something that stopped her. Her feet couldn't carry her any further.

"What about the team? What about Legion and Dauge? What about Pitt?" he asked.

Kraydia's eyes fell closed. Tears streamed down. Legion and Dauge were mercenaries with a strong family name and background. She was close to them, but not as close as she was to Dash. Probably even more than the half-eladrin, Kraydia and Pitt forged a bond between them. They were close. They were real close.

At night, Pitt was whom she'd go to, to talk about her problems and thoughts. He was a good listener and truly appreciated and cared about everything she said. Pitt loved her and she loved him. The overall benefit of the team was compromised. She would not be able to act right should she see Dash fall and she knew Dash was the same. As strong of a leader as he was, he would not be able to keep a clear head in the event something happened to her.

Dash watched his love walk away. Not even the names of her friends would stop her. She was gone and the team was absent a mage. As a bard, Dash had minimal arcane and divine casting abilities but nothing like they would need to become the team he wanted them to be. It was just another problem to have and one he did not want to deal with at the moment.

"Did you tell him?" he asked.

Kraydia leaned over the side railing of the ship. She'd already booked passage with an old friend back to Port Agatha in Thox. Dash didn't see her board the ship. And thankfully, he didn't see who she boarded the ship with.

Kraydia spent the majority of her time at sea in her rented bunk with her old…new friend. Unlike before, she wasn't lonely. Her loneliness had faded and was replaced by waves of happiness. When alone, he was really a good man. He was looked at as a different one or a foreign one and as a killer and dark. The man who sailed to her, refusing to let her go was a good man and she was going to see it through.

The day came and the ship stopped. It was a small enough ship so that it could actually dock in the local docks of Agatha and not out at sea where rowboats would have to be taken in order to get to land.

Kraydia and Kraizaikaei walked off the gangway together, passing Storm, Dargon, and a young and weak-looking half-elf, and a well dressed eloquent half-elf followed. His right hand was missing, replaced by a small hook-like contraption. From the description, Kraizaikaei knew it was Lord Quinn of Quinn's Town, a legend of Thox.

"Krazy!" Storm said, relieved.

"Storm," Krazy said, mentally biting at him to explain what was going on.

Storm fell back in his own skin as did Dargon.

"Kraydia, so good to see you. What brings you to Agatha?" Dargon questioned.

"It's better Dash and I no longer travel together. Krazy offered me to join him with you," she replied.

Storm didn't know Dash and Kraydia were an item but he did know she once traveled with him and Dash was a friend. Parties did have members come and go all the time. Perhaps it was just her time to move on.

"Besides, I always fancied her," Krazy said, making her smile.

"Whoa, the good elf does carry emotions in his chest," Storm said, smiling.

"Well done, you two. We get a wizard and you get a beautiful lady. Everyone wins," said Dargon. "Oh, I almost forgot, with Felzen gone and Alanis ill, we've taken up the boy Siberon."

Krazy just moved to acknowledge his presence. Kraydia gave him a formal curtsy. The boy pleasantly but shyly responded. He was young, really young. Storm had the boy cleaned and clothed properly. The boy was good with a sling and short bow. Storm also gave him a few daggers in case he was caught up close but melee would never be this child's chosen field. Well, Dargon had him cleaned and clothed and tested his skills before introducing him to Storm. Storm just formally invited him to the team, trusting in Dargon's faith in the boy.

"Eh hem." Quinn intentionally cleared his throat, reminding the friends of his presence.

"Oh forgive me," said Kraydia bowing... "My lord," she acknowledged.

Krazy bowed, showing his respect to the lord.

"Storm, the team is shattered. What are we doing? Were you not going to wait for me?" asked Krazy.

"Apologies. There was no time. Lord Quinn had to be moved. We've taken the charge of seeing him to Daneth," Storm answered.

"Daneth, to the far west... The Nine Kingdoms?" Krazy questioned.

"The same," responded the jolly old dwarf.

"We leave without Felzen and Alanis. We've taken on a boy. Kraydia lifts the group. Fine. So be it." Krazy wasn't happy with the lack of information he had on the subject. Like Storm said, there was no time.

"Felzen is gone for good, at least for now. Alanis is terribly ill. The boy has skills, Krazy, and he could use your guidance."

Quinn saw the conversation being drawn out. He was growing weary and wanted to get to his cabin on the ship.

"Let us move. I'm paying and I want to get to my room," He said walking forward. And one by one, Storm, Dargon, Siberon, Krazy, and Kraydia fell in place behind him.

As much as he didn't like it, luck was on his side. Krazy returned just in time to reunite with his team before they left on a quest that was going to see them gone for many months. Bringing Kraydia back with the team in shambles and a charge such as the one of Quinn's offering lay perfect for him. He was pleased. Things worked out better than he expected.

Chapter 33

Night came. Everything was in place. Someone was missing. Where was Dash? Where was Kraydia? Where was Pitt? Legion was the only one present. They betrayed him. Their decision to stand against the king was too much of him to ask even though the king was a man who needed to be ousted.

Legion ducked behind a few old barrels near the single path where Pitt said he'd bet his life the ambushers would come from. Just down the way was the third dock where the Bloody Queen rested. Dusk did her job. He was sure of it.

That meant his only backing would be the crew of the Bloody Queen. He trusted Kleiven. He trusted Kleiven because Dusk trusted him and his father was a man his own father honored and respected. At this point, he had to trust Kleiven.

Movement came. The docks were pretty bare. The smell of the ocean was in the air. Smaller ships moved silently down the way in the straight. Few guards were scattered, walking. Luckily, King Bahaus' maniacal actions had them in a little disarray.

Legion would've missed it. Mourning Star's senses were too keen. Coming up behind an old run-down fishing shop a hundred feet or so from where Legion hid, a small fire sparked up. It wasn't on the ground or even near the ground but rather hanging from the ledge of the roof. The fishing shop was long abandoned.

There, on the roof of the old fishing shop.

Legion looked up. A heavy crossbow lay mounted. It was dark. Usually, he wouldn't have been able to see something so far away in the dark. He knew it was the magic of the Star that aided him. His vision saw a humanoid figure lying next to a mounted heavy crossbow with an unnaturally large arrow fully readied with a burning tip.

"There," Legion said, talking to no one. In his own mind he was speaking to Mourning Star in the same manner he'd have spoken to Dauge or Dash.

Legion stood and crept to the back alleyways behind the buildings lining parallel with the wooden platforms and docks of Eternis. He moved fast. He wasn't making as much noise as he thought he'd make. His weapon blessed him with more protections and guidance spells, clearing his feet from noise.

Finally, he was behind the old fishing shop. Legion hadn't a way to the top. He had to think fast. WHEW! He heard the thunk of the heavy crossbow and the fling of the arrow. The whoosh sound dug into his anxiety.

He had to think fast. Quickly, he rushed between the shop and the building adjacent to it. Luckily they were close. He planted his feet on one wall and his hands on the other with his head facing downward.

Inch by inch he scaled the building to the top. Another whooshing sound followed what sounded like something igniting. Legion's hands finally gripped the edge of the roof. He let the pressure off of his feet, dropping down to the side of the fishing shop, holding on to the edge of roof only. It would be up to his upper body strength to get him up the rest of the way.

He started up. It was rather easy for the Xavier. His eyes cleared the roof. He nearly let go altogether. Just as his eyes peered over the horizon of the roof he heard the unsheathing of a short blade and the movement of silent steps heading toward him. He ducked his head just in the nick of time. The thrust at his crown was nearly a success. Legion released the roof with his right hand.

The stranger, shrouded in dark apparel, stepped on his left immediately after missing the attack.

"AHHH!" Legion belched out, reaching up.

Legion grabbed the man by his loose-fitting black breeches close to the groin. It took most of his strength to pull his body up with one arm to make the grab but after letting his body down easy and straightening his left arm back out, the weight of his body forced the stranger to lose his balance and fall between the buildings from the roof.

The man's momentum carried him all the way, sending his body over his hand, landing him on the ground face up and spread eagle. Legion let go seconds later from the grinding pain the stranger put on his hand before the fall.

Legion fell safely to his feet. It wasn't too bad of a drop for him. "Ugh," he let out.

The stranger was already up to his feet with yet another short dagger pulled. Legion had yet to pull a weapon and the alley was too narrow for him to try and use Mourning Star.

A fiercely engulfing heat wave swept through the alley. The night sky lit up like an honored event or holiday filled with fireworks and mages. Legion turned from the stranger to run to the edge of the alleyway where the docks began.

The Bloody Queen's right side was completely submerged in flames. How did one man with a few burning arrows do that to such a massive ship so quickly? Wait a minute, it was prepped! Goddamn you Bahaus, he thought.

Men were assembling to the side railing to work on the ship's burning problem. The local guard was also coming. There was even a traveling wizard close by who'd come to lend his hand. A full-sized transport ship was not something that could be destroyed easily. It must have taken quite a bit of preparation for Bahaus to have it engulfed so easily. The flames burned too hot and the local guard stood helpless against it.

Legion's aided advanced senses zoomed in on a few soaking-wet figures pulling themselves from the waters just down the way behind another ship. They were using the local step ladders built into the docks for those trying to get in or out of the water with ease.

Legion had a problem to deal with and another getting away. With everyone's focus on the flames nobody saw the other culprits trying to get away. Suddenly, a familiar voice and a fresh clanging of steel; Legion turned, looking over his shoulder.

"Go Legion. I'm here!" Kleiven said. He was dressed in full gear. His long sword and light armor were freshly shined and sharpened. Legion turned following the first exchange from the stranger's knife and Kleiven's sword.

The stranger split his sights turning his back to the wall, leaving Kleiven on his right and Legion to his left. Legion hesitated. He turned back to help Kleiven engage the stranger.

"I said go!" Kleiven screamed.

Legion turned and rushed the men sneaking out of the water behind the ship directly behind the Bloody Queen. The heat was bad but the with the help of the wizard and mechanical devices brought and used by the guard, the ship's flames seemed to be getting weaker and more manageable. The members of her crew had all but abandoned her, leaping from the opposite side rails, trying to escape the flame.

The ones climbing up were too close to the docks and were already getting out of the water by the time anyone onboard the Queen would have known what was going on. No, they weren't members of her crew. They were the team Mourning Star told him about. They were the team Mourning Star overheard while in Bahaus' manor.

Three pulled themselves from the docks' waters. Not seeing Legion rushing them from all the ruckus going on, they leisurely threw off their dark, wet clothes. Legion neared them, closing the distance faster and faster with every step he took. He pulled Mourning Star. The spiked ball fell freely as he took the shaft of the weapon into his right hand.

Hearing the chain and the spiked ball scrape across the rock and then wood of the docks, the three turned to face their would be aggressor. Legion couldn't believe it. He was right. The first was Grath. He was the thickest and largest of the three. A second was a woman, bulky and fierce. She wore little to cover her lower and upper women parts. Her choice of clothing color was red. She was built as if she hailed from the same land as Pitt, only a human though and not a goliath. Resting on her back was a hangar that extended above her head. She carried a bastard sword. Her wet strawberry blonde hair lay flat against her head.

Like the other two, Grath wore no armor. He carried his lone weapon in his right hand. Black silken clothes clung to his wet body defining every ripple and indention the man had. A small yellow glow emanated from around Grath's left hand. Something was different about Grath, the glow in his eye perhaps? He was supposedly a champion of Raielyn, the angel of freedom. So why would he be endangering mercenaries' lives in support of the king?

The third member of their crew was short and small. He was a gnome or some sort of Halfling creature. A hood still covered his face. A sling came from nowhere and glowing pellets and rocks found their way en route to Legion's face.

Legion evaded the attack, hurling the spiked end of his weapon with an underhand lunging motion. The ball caught the tiny creature as Grath turned to flee. The ball stuck and then Legion's momentum carried it upward, ripping it through the man's upper torso and right shoulder area.

It was a hard hit and the little man fell, severely wounded. The bastard sword of the warrior woman nicked Legion's face just inches away from what would have been a kill shot. Blood oozed from the mark on Legion's left cheek. He leaped back to regroup.

The little man was going for something. His hands began to glow. He wasn't out and now the warrior woman had moved up to defend her friend. If he engaged, he would have to leave himself open for something. What to do?

Then, Mourning Star did something it had never done since its forming. It split back into both SOUL and LORE. It forced Legion forward without thinking. SOUL's tip found itself piercing through the same damaged flesh Mourning Star already opened. Legion hurled LORE upward, fighting in a different style than he'd ever fought. He was still in the process of looking for a new shield because he in truth was a sword and board fighter.

The warrior woman's mighty blade was knocked back. The glow from the now visible gnome's hands faded and SOUL usurped the power, channeling it through its host, releasing it through its comrade, its ally, its friend of over three thousand years; Arakros Awestrike, the entity of SOUL sent the power through Legion and into LORE, the sword carrying Goddimus Ryven. From there, Legion pointed the tip of LORE to the woman and the power now infused with multiple energies spewed out like liquid lightning.

The lightning shot into her eyes, nose, and mouth, sending thousands of volts from the clouds through her body, cooking her from the inside. Either that gnome was powerful or LORE and SOUL were growing strong again like they said they were. The woman turned. Her sword dropped.

Her skin became withered and greenish gray. Her eyes became a dull unknown color. The gnome on the ground changed too. His skin and eyes did the same. Both of their hair became a stringy gray and white. The gnome grew in size, maybe another foot, after dying.

What was going on? "Grath!" Legion yelled. There was no time to investigate. The older Xavier had to catch the last culprit. The swords forced his hands to cling them together, returning them to their allied state of Mourning Star.

There were still no spectators watching them. They were too tied up in the curing of the ship. Slowly, people were starting to see Legion charge after something. People were starting to notice the two dead corpses Legion left behind.

Grath rushed away, through the alleyways away from the docks. The simple style of mostly wooden buildings was different for him. Some buildings were of stone but Eternis prided itself on the old ways of mostly wood with a simple stone foundation. Alas, many buildings were constantly being torn down and rebuilt, not helping the Eternian budget at all.

The clever sniper was good with a dagger, keeping the longer blade of Kleiven at bay. Every thrust of Kleiven's blade saw the spinning and quick maneuvering of the stranger. Finally, first blood was drawn and it was Kleiven's. Knowing his dagger skill would not measure up against the swordsmanship of Kleiven, the stranger knew he had to make a sacrifice in order to attack.

The sniper sneakily faked an attack only to drop to a knee, bringing up his left arm to withstand the blow he knew was coming from Kleiven's blade. His sole area of protection was his hands and forearms, guarded by covers and bracers. The stranger's dagger found itself deep in the left side of Kleiven's belly. Kleiven's sword dug deep and through the bracer, cutting into the stranger's armor.

The stranger called himself, arising back to his feet, holding his left arm forward with the blade still in it. Kleiven was now using the stuck blade to hold himself up. He was hurt and the cut was deep. Kleiven covered the wound with his free hand as if catching the blood and holding it was going to make him better.

The stranger commenced walking forward, forcing the weakening Kleiven to backpedal, still holding onto the sword that was now stuck in the bracer and bone of the stranger. Another wound ripped open across Kleiven's right ear. He heard the force and felt the wind of a moving missile.

The stranger in front of him, his aggressor and would-be killer stopped. A small bolt now stuck through his skull and into his brain ceased his movements. He once again fell. This time to both knees and not intentionally. He was dead. And like the others, his body twisted and reformed into something not human. Its skin was green and this one had absolutely no hair. Its eyes were a sleek black and now closed.

Kleiven fell, losing the balance of the standing stranger and the sword. Someone caught him from behind. Kleiven's eyes closed. He was weak and losing blood fast. Something came over him. Something soothed him and eased his pain. Was he dead? Was he where the Rivermortal wanted him to be? When would he see his eternity?

Legion watched as a massive branch being swung by an old friend stepping out from behind a building clotheslined the running shadow elf. Grath felt gravity zero out. His feet flew up clear over his head, dropping the runner head first onto the loose rock and soil below.

Blood oozed from his face. Pitt dropped the branch and grabbed the thing by his throat. As if nothing happened, he nonchalantly began his walk toward Legion, all the while dragging the unconscious paladin helplessly.

Kleiven and Dash came up from the other end. Kleiven was healed. Dash's magic was in time to save him. Otherwise, the creature's critical shot to his abdomen could have been fatal. The fire was finally driven out.

It seemed like an eternity but only minutes passed. Dash, Legion, and Pitt stood over a now bound and helpless shadow elf. Legion wasn't happy and he certainly didn't want to talk about what Mourning Star did either.

Guards were beginning to approach them. Dash told Pitt to grab the other three dead ones and pull them to the side. He initially asked Legion to help.

"I think I've done enough, Dash. I think I did my part here tonight pretty well. Don't you think?"

Dash felt bad. He let him down. His heart was broken and bleeding. He felt a sense of being unwelcome within himself and everyone else. It was no excuse. Legion was angry and he had every right to be.

"I don't know what to say Legion," he started.

"And where the hell is Kraydia?"

Pitt returned just as Legion asked the question. Dropping the other remaining dead bodies in a pile. The one Dash and Kleiven killed was a little ways away. It took a second to get to him.

"Kraydia is no longer with us," Dash replied.

"She's dead. That bastard king," Legion angrily said.

"No, no, she left. She's no longer with the group," he better explained.

"I don't understand," said Legion.

"I couldn't find her either. We were supposed to meet and prepare for tonight. I went searching for Dash and you and couldn't find either of you," Pitt explained.

"You knew where I'd be come nightfall, Pitt," Legion replied.

"I know. No one else was where they were supposed to be."

"Kraydia and I shared a few differences and she felt it would be better if we no longer traveled together." Dash explained.

"No real explanation as to why and she just did this, confusing you and Pitt causing me to do all of this on my own? I'll kill that bitch." Legion's anger was reaching new heights.

"No Legion. Blame me. Sometimes my expectations of people and what they can take and withstand may be a little high. I'm truly sorry, friend, and it will never happen again. Forgive me. Today, or tonight I should say, I let my personal life and problems interfere with the greater good of the team. For that, I cannot repay you but only promise it will never happen again," he said.

"Remember who sat with you at the table, Legion," Pitt reminded.

"Yes, but you weren't here," he snapped back.

"We are now and still just as guilty when this is over."

Kleiven liked what Pitt was saying to him. He was kind of biased toward Dash as Dash did just save his life. He wanted to stay and talk and get to the bottom of this with them but his orders called. "Guys I'm sorry. I must go and see to the ship," he said, darting off.

"What made you pick up an old tree branch, Pitt? And where in the hell did you get that?" Dash asked, laughing, trying to lighten the mood.

"From an old burn pile near a few places they just tore down. Legion said we had to keep one of them alive. I was going to make sure at least one of them lived," he said casually as ever.

That made Legion smile. Legion did kill his and Kleiven and Dash killed the other one. Had it not been for Pitt they wouldn't be able to continue with the execution of their plan.

"Now, we make him it talk," Legion hatefully reminded.

"What is it?" asked Dash.

"It doesn't matter. It's captured," Legion replied.

"It's a doppelganger. I ran into a few before my time as a gladiator. I even walked with some not knowing it. I was completely unaware. You've heard the stories. You know what they can do."

"Why look like Grath though?" Dash questioned.

"To blatantly incriminate someone the town already had a bias against," Legion answered.

"Hmmm, good answer," Dash said.

"Guards, take him," Legion yelled to a few passing by. They stopped to listen to the son of Taj.

Dash grabbed his hand. "Wait. We cannot risk imprisoning him. We question him now. We question him here, in front of the people. When they hear his answer. All will be undone," Dash suggested.

Legion yelled for those around to come and gather. Those with rank and power should move to the front. Citizens, soldiers, guardsmen, everyone was welcome, even those not native to Eternis. When the creature finally came to, Kleiven was already back, along with a few of the mercs that'd made it off the ship.

"What is your name, creature? Tell me who sent you and why. Tell me who sent you and you shall walk free of this town never to return, ever!" Legion ordered.

The creature slowly came to. Dash's magic hastened the process. He heard the question, especially after Legion repeated it several times.

"I was sent by Magnus Black, Mercenary General of the Free Armies," it replied.

"Then why appear as Grath?" Dash questioned.

"Because no one..." it stopped and gasped for air. "No one likes a shadow elf," It finished, blood splashing up and draining down from his mouth.

The crowd gasped. Ooh's and ah's filled the air. This is exactly what Bahaus would have hoped he would say, thought Legion. His answer infuriated Pitt but luckily Dash was there to calm him. The crowd whispered and talked amongst itself about Bahaus' claim of Magnus Black and how the aggressors of the Bloody Queen were now admitting it. At least the sole surviving one was anyway.

Dash began casting something else again. The older wizard that was present smiled. He spoke aloud, claiming clever trick to the bard. He turned to his peers explaining what Dash was doing. Apparently, he could read magic well.

Dash was using his magic to charm the thing. With the unintended help of the wizard, his hopes were accomplished.

"Now creature, what is your name?" he asked.

"Slar," it replied.

"Slar, you came here and I've already promised to allow you to walk freely even after the severe damage you've caused. You trust I am your friend, right?" he asked, making sure the spell worked.

The spell could do much, from asking a host to perform simple tasks to answering questions. Dash's magic in this field was strong. It was his main focal point. The creature shook his head in compliance.

One man cried out, "Who would have brought things like these to Eternis?" Another cried out, "It's a doppelganger!" The crowd was getting restless and Dash needed his answers, not for himself but for the unnerving crowd.

"Slar, tell me. Who sent you to attack the Bloody Queen and why?" Dash questioned.

"My master," Slar replied casually, as if it were common knowledge.

"Your master, and who is your master?" Dash questioned.

"Bahaus Sazos," he answered.

The crowd erupted. They were nervous, scared, upset, angry, roaring with answers. Dash quickly forced them, with Pitt's help, to settle down.

"Why would Bahaus send you to do such a thing?" he furthered.

"To incriminate our enemies, the Free Armies."

It couldn't have been written out for a play any better. Bahaus Sazos Uil-Endail was being exposed for the monster he was right there on the docks of his own city while he slept on his perfectly made bed and satin sheets. He probably had four girls fanning him as they spoke.

"Why are the Free Armies our enemies?" Dash continued.

At this point, Legion and Pitt were walking around keeping a circle of open space for Dash and Slar. They talked quickly with random members of the crowd, explaining everything and acting as "shocked" as they could possibly act.

"Why do you serve Bahaus? Is it because he is your king? How long have you been in Eternis? Do you call Eternis your home?"

The creature nodded, signifying he did call Eternis his home. Legion smiled. Dash and Pitt shared a grin as well.

"And why do you serve King Bahaus? Is it because he's your king? Did you serve him before?" Dash probed.

"I serve Bahaus, Servant of the High Priest of Asmodai, Lord of the Devils, Magus"

The crowd fell feint. They didn't know what to think. Then, the spell snapped and the creature knew what he'd done. He cringed and crawled in his own skin. He shook his head, trying and pleading with reality itself to tell him or to let him know what really just happened didn't truly happen.

Dash smiled looking around to the crowd using his commanding presence to gain their attention. His magic forced the truth from its lungs.

"Kleiven, take some of your best men and bring this man to your father. Have your father's closest arcanists use their charming powers to force the truth from his lungs again. It'll confirm what these good people here tonight have seen and heard is true. Bahaus is the true enemy of the state. His faith lies with the devil lord Asmodai and follows one of his foul priest's Magus," Dash announced.

"Is Magus a true a threat? A threat that Eternis should fear?" Legion asked.

"Where is Magus? Is Magus in town? Is he close by? Is there a cult or organization?" The town's people started to talk and ask questions. Question after question came. This was exactly what Dash wanted. Once Cale Dar heard this for himself, the people of Eternis and the leader of its militaries would both be and stand against Bahaus and his newly formed small group of guards.

"We must be careful. This thing calls Eternis home. How many more does Bahaus have under his employ?" Dash suggestively questioned.

"Bahaus must be infesting our city, his own home with these things. Who knows what else this Magus has Bahaus doing? A priest controls Bahaus, last son of Gerear. He follows the manipulative god of the devils. This is not good. He must be stopped. This is my home and the home of my father. It's the home of his father. I will not let my blooded home descend into a world of hell," Legion commanded.

Chapter 34

Legion, Dash, and Pitt watched Kleiven take the last of the doppelgangers away. Legion still wasn't pleased with his comrades' actions. The crowd erupted. There would be no keeping them quiet. Dash hoped to make it to at least the next morning before confronting the king.

An angry crowd can be a difficult mob to stop. The more they spoke, the more voices joined in. And the more voices that joined, the louder they became. And their constantly elevating volume constantly increased their own anger.

"I don't like this. This won't end pretty," Legion said sadly.

"Why down? We've been successful thus far." Dash questioned.

"He's sad, Dash, because this is still his home," Pitt reminded.

"Ah yes, I know. We're doing your home a justice and building our name in the process," Dash said, smiling.

"I don't care about your damn name, Dash. I want Eternis free and peaceful for my family, my sister and my mother more than most," Legion replied.

"I know. I'm sorry. You should be pleased with your work tonight," Dash suggested.

"I'm not pleased. The man who took me from my home abandoned me at a most needed time. I'm not pleased that something you said or did probably sent Kraydia away. You spoke to her last and she disappeared mysteriously. And lastly, I took care of this…" talking bout the doppelganger incident and the saving of the Bloody Queen, "and I was the lone member of our crew to do what we said we were going to do…" he paused, "…from beginning to end!"

"I said apologies," Dash stated boldly.

"It's over now. And so far, we are victorious. Let us embrace one another and see this through for Dauge's sake. We can determine our paths and if they still run together after." Pitt hoped his words would sooth his friends' souls. He wanted them calm and friendly. He'd come to love them both dearly.

Kleiven and several of the mercenaries from the ship dragged the no-longer-charmed doppelganger to the doorstep of General Cale Dar. Eternis was especially dark at this time of night. The creature moaned and cried in pain and fear. Cale Dar's home was simple basic, a small single room home made mostly of stone and wood.

Kleiven banged on his father's door, looking back after to assure himself the captive was still being held. Six guards accompanied him to his father's home not too far from the docks and where the fight took place.

He banged on the door yet again and still, no answer. "Father," he cried out.

Finally, the door cracked open. His father leaned his head barely out the crack of the door he made by gently opening it, just barely. His eyes squinted, still adjusting to being awake again. He wore only a pair of legging under garments and nothing more. "What is it and why have you brought all of these people to my home?"

"Father, King Bahaus Sazos-Uil-Endail has committed high treason. He secretly ordered the burning of the Bloody Queen. He aims to double-cross the Free Armies and Magnus Black in order to prove righteous move against the Crystal Cities."

"Why would he do that, son?" Now his father was awake and curious. Not only curious, but concerned; the General of Eternis was now all ears.

"He moves with strong purpose, father. He moves to conquer the cities without shedding a single drop of blood. He's hoping the Free Armies stand down in hopes of regaining their captured leader, General Black."

"Why would he want to take the Crystal Cities or imprison General Black? General Black's been a devoted man and friend to us of Eternis for nearly two decades, maybe longer. What proof do you have?" Cale leaned out a little more to free his hand a bit to scratch his genitals.

"Father! This creature confessed it all! Please, Father, fetch one of your trusted charmers and test him yourself. You're the General of Eternis; your expertise was in the field of pulling information from prisoners! Please Father! You have to believe me. Legion, Dash, and Pitt stopped them in time. The Bloody Queen is burned badly, though. Some of the mercs didn't make it. The rest of them are with us! They're going to stand against this devil-worshiping tyrant with us!" Kleiven pleaded.

His father nodded, agreeing quietly to work with the prisoner and see if there was any truth in Kleiven's words. Cale disappeared back into the darkness encompassing the entire scene behind the door. He called the names of several men and within moments, scores of men trotted from around the house and three even came from the front door itself.

Cale was a simple man but he was a General and required constant supervision and protection. The guards looked different than Kleiven remembered them. They didn't match the description of any league or unit of men currently employed or trained by the Eternian city-state.

The guards all wore blackened robes with red underbellies and lapels over their very delicately placed armor pieces. Cale preferred his guards to wear light armor. Few Eternians were trained with heavy armor anyway. Eternis wasn't a rich city and couldn't truly afford too many suites of plate armor. Hence, Eternians were mostly trained to fight light-footed and with dual weaponry.

"We'll take it from here," one of them said, walking out of the front door.

Kleiven and the mercenaries and town guards didn't know what to do. Kleiven quickly got his wits about him and ordered the men with him to stand down. His father's personal guards seized their captured prisoner and quickly brought him in for questioning. Something was fishy about it. However, though it didn't sit well with him he knew he'd done what he could. His father was acting curiously odd and he wanted to know why.

"Kleiven, I want vengeance on that bastard and this fucking king! Those rat bastards are responsible for my brother. He burned on the Queen," said one of the merc standing behind Kleiven. He looked back over his shoulder to see who it was. It was Peren, a forest dwelling ranger and one of the elite amongst the crew of his ship.

Legion, Dash, and Pitt knew they couldn't return to their quarters until this was done. They decided the Xavier Manor would be a safe choice but they still didn't like it. Legion especially didn't approve; he felt it would be putting his family at unnecessary risk.

"Wait!" Legion yelled.

Pitt and Dash stopped in their paths. Both looked at Legion curious as to what he wanted. "What is it?" Pitt asked.

The crowd was growing more restless and violent. The rioting of Eternis was growing with every passing second. The mob would soon get to Bahaus and with Kleiven taking care of his part, the military would accompany them. Tonight, the military and the other guards would do their duty and tone it down and neutralize it until General Cale Dar confirmed everything Kleiven told him was true.

The three finally made it back to the Xavier Manor. The rest of his family was fast asleep. Dusk waited for her brother outside patiently. Kleiven rendezvoused with them at the manor as well. He went for Dusk. Dusk wanted him there for safety. She felt he was safer with Legion, Dash, and Pitt around.

Kleiven made it back to the manor last, quickly wrapping and picking up his one and only, swinging her about like a happily newlywed couple.

"We did it," he said, looking into her eyes.

She loved him but it wasn't the same as before. It wasn't him. She wasn't the same as before. There was something growing inside her and it was making her change. Now she knew what it was and she would fight it. She would fight it because she loved him and because he stood with her brother for the honor of both brothers against the very king he swore to serve.

The five finally retired to their beds for the night. It was getting late. Kleiven kept Dusk company. Legion, Pitt, and Dash slept in the same room in the manor's basement. Just in case the worst was to come, they wanted to make sure they wouldn't be separated. Early the next morning, Dash awoke first and quickly got the others up and ready. They didn't allow their bodies to succumb to sleep until the crowds were finally quieted down the night before.

Today Cale Dar would stand for the people of Eternis with the military backing him against the treacherous king, Bahaus Sazos-Uil-Endail. Today, a new beginning for Eternis, Legion thought. The four, including Kleiven, talked about it and knew they needed to find Cale immediately.

When they left the manor, the four saw a large gathering at the town square. The familiar voice of the General was pouring over the crowd. A beautiful archaic fountain sprang from the middle of the square surrounded by well crafted and outlined single story structures, mostly businesses. This was the finest area of Eternis. The roads were carefully paved and stoned, almost to perfection. It was readily kept up more so than any other area of the city.

"And let no man stand free against us."

The words were Cale's. Kleiven confirmed it aloud. The four filled with excitement. They rushed to the open square to hear Cale speak on the newly removed King of Eternis. The square was filled with a variety of races and breeds of folk. The General stood upon an old wooden platform near the back of the square built off of an old warehouse looking building. Elite guards, perfectly dressed and strategically placed, completed the appearance to the crowd of the General's speech. Some were his black-robed guards and others were Bahaus' elite black armored guards. All of them stood as if giving the faiths their attention.

Cale looked magnificent. He wore an outfit not even Kleiven had seen him wear. It was General Redd's red suited armor. It was fully plated armor complete with full helm. The helm rested at his feet. On his side, retired General Redd's famous Bloodstone Sword. The Bloodstone Sword was a master crafted broad sword General Redd had given to him during his time of service.

Cale continued, "When we unite and move with purpose, we cut the fat from out bones. We are of the oldest blood of the world. We wash away the wound carved by our own hand to better our coming days. We cut ourselves to bleed out bad blood. Today we do the same." Cale stopped gazing his eyes upon his son.

Kleiven smiled and gave his father the nod telling him without a word he was standing by him to hear him officially remove King Bahaus and label him an enemy and threat to the throne. And to also release General Black and Dauge for the actions of his own son and his friends of Legion's crew.

Cale pointed to the four. "Seize them."

"What?" Legion questioned.

"There must be some mistake," Kleiven suggested. "I delivered the traitor to my father with my own two hands."

Legion, Dash and Pitt all looked at Kleiven prepared to ready themselves at a moment's notice. Had the son of the General betrayed them all? Why was Cale pointing and using the word seize with his own son?

"Are you sure?" Dash asked.

"The enemies of the crown present themselves to you all!" he declared, still keeping his finger pointed at the lot of them. The crowd turned and moved to position themselves against them. The guards and militaries rushed to charge the four.

"Move!" Dash ordered whirling his fingers floating them back and forth.

Three of the rushing guards fell to the ground. They were asleep and fell jumbled and tangled together. Pitt roared out in anger, pulling his large weapon from its hangar. The simple townsfolk panicked. They weren't used to a monster like Pitt. Legion called to his weapon, firing bolts of sleeping energy toward several more guards coming from the same direction of the three. Like Dash's choices, they all fell fast asleep. Now, to their left through the town square and up through back alleyways heading northwest they had a retreat plan.

Dash led the flee with Legion, Pitt, and Kleiven following closely behind. The alleyways were narrow and the four stutter stepped to stop and break; sometimes they turned left and sometimes they turned right. Shortly after the escape, the town's military and people were all after them. And shortly after the fleeing began Kleiven took over.

He knew the streets of Eternis better than any of them. He took them through every nick and natch until finally, they were right back toward the southeastern docks.

"One more long stretch," Kleiven uttered, running as hard as he could.

The four ran through the alley. Buildings three times their size on both sides of them. The smell of the sea touched their senses. Harder and harder they pushed themselves until finally the alleyway was cleared. A few feet of paved rock and stone and at last, their feet were amongst the planks that made the docks. They ran across the entire city from the center to the northwest, and then back down all the way to the southeastern part of the docks. They'd been running for hours. They were tired.

"How'd we evade everything?" Pitt asked.

"Kleiven knows his city!" Dash said proudly.

"Not everything," another voice said, signifying they hadn't evaded just everything.

A black-robed humanoid guard revealed himself, opening the back door to one of the old buildings that stood dockside. His hands began to glow. The yellow of his hands matched the color the old stories said belonged to vampires. He resembled one of Cale's men but looked much older. His hair and eyes were darker than a devil's dreams. The look on his face was charming and pretty. His skin was fair and well kept.

"You'll not leave this city, ever," he said charmingly.

"Says who?" Legion asked with arrogance.

Legion was already angry. And he hadn't brought it up, but he wasn't leaving without his brother. And he wasn't sure that when this was over he would stay with these people anyway. Dash more and more was becoming something of a problem to him. The dissention between them was ever growing.

"Eternis is your home. You'll stay here, forever," the man said again. He looked human but there was definitely something not human about him.

"I'll not leave without my brother and my sister." Legion turned back to stand against the man.

The man waved his hand. Legion walked strongly toward him. He stopped. His chest began to hurt. It was early and the crew didn't take the majority of their belongings from the manor. In fact, other than Dash, not one of them put on a single piece of armor.

Pitt charged forward, seeing his friend fall to a knee. His rage grew with every cough Legion let out. Dash called forth powers in a language not known to any of them. Pitt felt his power grow. His strength took to the hilt digging into it even more.

A mighty swing from the behemoth and nothing; Dash couldn't believe it. Pitt stood in awe at what had just taken place. His massive weapon fragmented upon impact with the robe of the creature. What was this thing and what kind of magic did he possess?

Legion regained his focus and pulled the big man back. "Dash, get them out of here. I got this bastard!"

There was no talking to him and Dash knew it was about Dauge. He knew he wouldn't leave without his brother. He wanted to say something. Pitt wasn't moving back either. Dash rushed up to grab him.

"Come on let's go!" Dash said.

Kleiven seconded Dash. "Let's get out of here! Let's move!" he screamed.

The humanoid with nightmarish eyes and deadly good looks just smiled. Dash finally got Pitt to turn tail with them. Legion stood alone against the creature.

Mourning Star began to glow. The glow frightened the magic user. He stepped back. Legion started his furious movements twirling the ball at the end of the chain around almost majestically.

"Where'd you find power like that? Power like that's not been seen in a thousand years?" he said.

"You're wrong and tonight I'll drink to your bones." Legion smirked back.

The priest coughed and his hands danced about. Only the name Asmodai could be made out and somewhere in the lost language Legion heard him speak the name Magus. He felt striking pains hit his vital organs. The Star told him it was eating the caster's magic for him. Legion smiled, feeling the magic being ripped from his body and taken in by his very weapon.

The caster smiled.

"Legion let's go!" Dash begged.

"Legion!" Pitt screamed.

Legion elevated his voice but wasn't screaming. His voice was as focused as his eyes and goal, "Not without my brother and sister," he answered.

Legion worked his way forward, moving and twirling to avoid possible missiles from whoever and wherever. His movements gained him momentum. The caster summoned all that he had to muster. It was a race now. A light blue oval light encircled the caster. Violently ricocheting colors bloomed from within the circle.

Legion felt his father's weapons, now his weapon, building from the power it'd usurped. He let out the most violent war cry he had in his lungs and with two hands upon the shaft of Mourning Star, he pierced the caster's magic with his own in the form of his weapon.

Dash, Kleiven, or Pitt could be heard and to Legion their whereabouts were unknown. The prismatic orbs held within the blue oval of energy were released prematurely. Some dissipated. Others attacked the caster and some even flew out at Legion and the city itself.

An explosion of divine power left Legion again on a knee and the caster face down in the rubble of his own causing. Half of an old building came down with the explosion, landing mostly on the dark priest. He coughed and regurgitated blood and some food he'd eaten earlier in the day. A slight push up from the priest brought him back to an almost upright position. Hurt, Legion brought himself back to a standing position as well. He was down but not out. What were those prismatic energies and the blue oval light of protection?

The blast was strong and devastatingly powerful. Small lacerations dripped out Legion's blood all over his body. The wooden planks of the nearby docks had been charred to ash or splintered. The priest wasn't out and neither was Legion.

Finally, Legion turned back. Dash, Kleiven, and Pitt were still there but getting ready to turn and run soon. He knew it. Legion wanted to finish him. The uniform steps of the guards coming were getting closer, heavier and heavier with every minute. The townsfolk formed a mob. They were coming too. How? At least some of them heard the doppelganger beast speak about Bahaus the night prior, right? Why was Cale against them?

Cale was for the city? Or was he? Was he for the king? The king was dark and evil and willing to annihilate everything Eternis was for, an ideal and dream only he could see. Was Cale Dar really going to double cross his own son for the king? Had he double-crossed his own son for the king?

Dash, Pitt, and Kleiven were finally able to force Legion to flee with them. He limped as he ran until Pitt grabbed him from behind and tossed him over his shoulder.

"I'm not leaving without my brother!" he said forcing himself off of Pitt's back and onto his feet once again.

"No, Legion we've got to go!" Dash pleaded seeing the priestly thing standing back upright once again.

The smoke cleared and the priest walked from the debris. The goal was to stowaway on one of the ships in the harbor, or better, make it to a moving ship out in the straight.

"Legion," a voice said, coming from the water.

They all looked down to both Magnus Black and Dauge floating away in a rowboat. How had he escaped? How did he getaway and how did he do with it Magnus Black? One by one, they turned and gave themselves to the water.

The guards and mob doused the docks with their presence, firing arrows and bolts at the Eternian fugitives. One bolt struck Pitt's left shoulder from behind. He roared out angrily. Another caught Dash in the lower back, a much more severe injury. The four made it and were pulled into the rowboat by their allies. The boat was a small one and with the six of them, especially Pitt, the boat was really being weighed down.

Legion and Dauge embraced. Both were bleeding and hurt. Dash used his bardic spells to mend both his wounds and Pitt's.

"Brother, how did you escape?" Legion asked thankfully.

"I was tired of waiting for you," he answered.

"How?" he asked again.

"Let's get to that moving sohar and the perhaps, I shall tell you," he said, joking.

It was dangerous but the six made the attempt. Their boat met its end crushed underneath the massive sohar as the suction of water pulled it beneath. It wasn't a quiet attempt either. They didn't have to be quiet. They scaled the side of the ship. The guards of Eternis were under smart leaders. It would not be in their interest to attack this ship just to get the fugitives. They weren't ready for that, not yet.

The ship hailed from the Nine Kingdoms. Its crew didn't want to take them on, not even with the celebrity General. A familiar face came from the shadows of the deck. The six looked around. About two half-elven crewmen surrounded them. Another fifteen never stopped working, scrubbing the decks, changing out belaying pins, locking down the sails, etc.

"Eternis has gone mad! The new king is mad!" Dash preached, hoping someone would listen.

These people didn't seem to care either way. One spoke, "Why did you come here if you're enemies of Eternis? We stop there often. You've brought trouble to us."

"Don't scare them. We care not for Eternis," another half-elf said.

"We take care of our own business," another said.

"What are you doing here? Why are they after you?" yet, another half-elf said.

"Hold your tongues. I know this boy. I knew your father." A man both dark and light with traits of human and elf walked forward. His skin was dark like the faerie stories of the Mogras. His black hair flowed freely down past his shoulders. He wore ornate armors and clothes, very exotic and unique to the times.

It was Avalon Darksteel and they knew him by name, the legendary Prince of the Nine Kingdoms with ancestry both the human and shadow elven races. What was he doing here and why? Either way, what luck! Legion thought.

Legion, Dauge, Dash, Kleiven, and even Pitt froze. Avalon Darksteel had that affect on people.

He smiled and gave the party a once over. "Your father was a good man. I see him in you. You are your father's image."

Avalon looked decorated but his armors were old and mended. They'd been mended a hundred times from the looks of it. Father, or Adrian rather, told them of Avalon Darksteel and Taj's adventures with him.

"Your father once saved me in the desert not too far from Valence. Perhaps I can finally repay the debt," he finished, smiling.

Legion stepped back. Dauge resembled his mother more than his father but Taj was his father too. His trainings and teachings taught him to carry himself a different way. Legion walked like Taj from what his family told him. He walked, talked, and his mannerisms were even like Taj's. Dauge was a different animal altogether. Most didn't know how to take him. Then again, he was raised of the Lotus people.

Dash smiled confidently. He knew the boys would come in handy. Legion was proving his worth every day. They still weren't on the best of terms, but Dauge was here, Magnus was safe, and they'd escaped.

"There'll be plenty of time to talk later. We're stopping in at Porta Agatha soon. From there, we return home to the Nine Kingdoms. You're welcome to stay as long as you'd like. This is my payment to your father for saving me in the desert." He spoke with a sense of charm, a dark charm. He still looked gorgeous, even with tattered capes and clothes. His ornamented armor had all but seen its better days. His hair was long and his face aged. Scars from lessons learned plagued his face and body. Each of his two swords were dark and vile to the eye.

"I can sense the darkness in you, boy. My lineage has waged its war against the undead and the blood of the dead runs through you. See to your rooms. Pelkwyn here"—he pointed over to one of the working elves—"will show you to your quarters. You'll all share a room. Quarters are tight here."

A young elven cabin boy rushed forward. His clothes were soaked and dirty. He'd been working hard on the decks all morning.

"Right this way, sirs," he said humbly.

The five followed closely behind the hardworking cabin boy through the corridors of the lower decks of the ship. It was evident the ship was old and had seen its best days long ago. The ship was sturdy, though water leaked from every wall. Three decks down, the cabin boy finally came to a door on the left.

"This is the largest free room we have. It holds a few cots and plenty of blankets. Welcome aboard, my lords." He bowed graciously and left.

The room wasn't much at all. It was a storage room or was being used as one. It was fairly large and carried enough cots for the lot of them. That was a good thing. A few barrels with clothes and dried rations cluttered the big square room. Most of the ship from what they'd seen was just corridors. Nonetheless, they were away from Eternis and the dark king.

They'd survived and escaped. Legion and Dauge were concerned for their family but Dash reassured them they were fine.

"Well, here we are," Dash said, trying to keep the spirits up.

"So I guess we go back to Thox where our names should still be intact?" Pitt asked.

"It's either Thox or the Nine Kingdoms," Dash said.

"We go to Thox, simple as that," Dauge added, slightly annoyed.

"I guess we're here," Legion said.

"What'd he mean he could sense the darkness in you? He talked about you having undead blood?" Pitt questioned.

"Your guess is as good as mine," Dauge answered.

"Let's get some sleep and figure all of this out in the morning," Kleiven suggested, throwing his body into the first available cot. Kleiven was quick to undress and ready himself for bed.

"You're right," Pitt seconded, taking the next one, following his lead.

Dash laughed, waving for Legion and Dauge to take their picks next.

Finally, Dash took the last good cot. A few more were left unattended but most of them were broken or just too old for comfort. He even helped himself to a few of the dried rations. Raisins, he thought. Raisins were his favorite. He was tired. They all were. It was time to sleep. Where they'd go from there would all be figured out and determined tomorrow, he thought. His team was coming together greatly, even with the loss of Kraydia. Dash smiled. His dream was coming to fruition.

Dauge was just about asleep. Fatigue was slowly taking him. A voice broke the silence of the room. The sound of the ocean beneath them and beating the walls beside them was still soothing in its own way.

"So Dauge, how did you make it out and manage to get Magnus out as well?" Kleiven asked.

"Another time Kleiven, another time," he answered, trying to remain in the drift of sleep.

Chapter 35

Dauge was the first awake. He was plenty rested. How long had he been down there? The others still slept soundly. What really happened to Kraydia? Why'd she leave? It wasn't a personal thing against Kleiven but the team needed someone with more knowledge in arcane than steel to be complete and Dash's bardic knowledge could only take them so far.

"The water wake you?" Kleiven's voice broke the silence.

Dauge looked over to him. His eyes were just barely open, a grim half smile of acceptance and success peeled across his face. He was happy to have escaped and to be alive. The grim set in though and Dauge knew it. He'd been double crossed by his own father.

"I don't know. Sleep's not something I've done much of my whole life," he responded.

Kleiven's situation struck a soft spot for Dauge. He felt for the General's son. His life and family were gone. General Cale Dar turned for the now-rising and evil king of the city-state Eternis, his home. For Dauge, it was a problem he'd never have. He didn't really have a home. Those that raised him were phantoms to the world. Those that raised him would most likely never lay eyes upon him again.

"So, when are you going to tell me how you did it? I know those dungeons. It's next to impossible to get out of those things, especially Tam's. How the hell did you do it?"

"Some things are better left unsaid, Kleiven," he answered.

"Yes, and some things, like my father betraying his only son... are better left unknown. Not every question earns an answer but this one does."

Dauge listened to the man. Kleiven's sincerity was real. Why did he care? They were willing to leave him behind and were trying to convince his brother to do the same.

"We all got away. We're all out of there. Whatever business you may have left there is done. Or, it should be done. We grow from the lessons we learn in life. Remember that, soldier," Dauge said.

"I guess you're right. If you're pondering as to why I'm curious, Dauge, I have several friends working the dungeons as guards, some as close to me as any and I just want clarity they're okay. And I won't have clarity until you give it to me. We both know what you're capable of," he replied.

"Blood was spilled," Dauge said strongly, hoping it was enough to end the conversation.

"Tell me, a young human, his name is Geoff. Please tell me you didn't hurt him," Kleiven pled.

"I certainly didn't acquire any of their names."

"Dauge, he's young. He carries the blond-haired, blue-eyed traits of most Eternians. His hair is short and holds a red tint. A straight, line scar defines his lower lip right in the middle. He's strong and bulky."

Dauge knew the man. He knew him well. It was the last person he encountered before getting out. Poor kid, he couldn't have been more than twenty years of age. He forced the fight with Dauge when Dauge wanted to flee. Before Dauge could say a word. Kleiven continued.

"Dalwart Stonenose, son of Gart Stonenose is my mentor. He served as the dungeon's liaison. Tell me, he would have been the only redheaded dwarf with a black and white beard to his belly in there. Tell me, did you see him? Tell me, did you hurt them? Did you hurt either of them? Dauge, please commit the truth to my ears," Kleiven begged his ally.

Dauge knew the answers. He leaned forward, planting his feet on the wooden floor beneath him. Sitting up, he saw Kleiven hanging on his every movement. Dalwart and Geoff were both engaged. Magnus was even slightly wounded by one and too weak from a lack of nourishment to do anything back.

"Breath still feeds them life. The taste of defeat was put upon their lips but they'll live to lick their wounds."

Magnus' ears perked but his eyes lay still. He was awake to but none knew it. He'd only heard remnants of their conversation. Was Dauge lying to Kleiven? Why? Dauge curiously didn't understand it either. He did in fact engage both of the men Kleiven spoke of. Why was he sparing of his feelings? It wasn't like him. Perhaps his time away from the Republic and the people of his true home were weakening him.

"We've all left a lot behind us to take to this road, Kleiven. You'll see them again I'm sure, in this life or the next."

Dauge's words were comforting but his voice wasn't. The man was dark. And he wasn't quick to release the secrets of his escape to them either. Maybe he was right. Perhaps them escaping alive and together was the most important thing.

Magnus chose to keep his mouth shut and to roll over as if nothing happened. The talking amongst friends continued and eventually the lot of them were up. Legion couldn't sleep either. He was mostly concerned for his sister and family. Dauge knew Dusk would be fine. Bahaus fancied her. Though her soul's safety was a different story altogether. Dauge tried to focus the conversation on his sister and her safety and keep it away from his escape.

"I know what you're saying, Dauge. Dusk and others are gone to us now. How are we to know if they're safe?" Legion questioned, following several soothing words from his little brother.

"We'll have to keep faith in the meantime," Dauge replied.

"Our old friend, Davion the lich is connected to your sister. She told me. We should move with purpose to the lich as quickly as possible. Or even send word to him in hopes he could keep us informed of her status," Dash said.

Yes, the lich was a splendid idea. She did tell her brothers and Dash about her dreams and her connection to the lich. If nothing else, Davion the Lich of Thox would know of their sister. As their conversations continued, it poured onto Dauge more and more on just how he escaped. Despite their best efforts, the dark scoundrel kept his secrets to himself.

"Come on Magnus, you were with him. How did he do it?" Kleiven asked.

"I only know he got me out of there. I was barely of sober mind. He fed me to keep me alive. If my savior wishes for it to remain within him and us, then so be it. I'm bound by my own codes to honor his wishes," he replied, smiling.

"Okay, you've won. I concede and tell you all." The voices and bickering were beginning to bother him. Why not just tell them or dress up the real truth for them and get it over with? He thought.

Suddenly, the boat rocked. Kleiven and Legion both were thrown from their cots. Barrels fell over and sheets and drapes and mounds of laundry tossed about like a hurricane rose from underneath them.

Mourning Star glimmered. Legion could feel its presence once again. It was growing stronger, especially while in the face of danger. He could feel the presence of both SOUL and LORE in him. Arakros Awestrike and Goddimus Ryven were the driving forces behind the two blades that he now held as one, Mourning Star, a weapon that was no longer even a blade.

The crew gathered themselves and equipped themselves as quickly as they could. It seemed like with every other minute, a thunderous crash slammed into the ship knocking it about. Finally, they were ready.

"Sure wish Kraydia was here," Dauge said, still angered about her departure.

"So do I," Dash added, rushing out the door first and as fast as his half-eladrin feet would carry him. "I mean whatever's out there, well, we could use the arcane!"

The ship was caving in from every angle. They were barely able to make it to the top deck without succumbing to the fiery throws and encasing walls of the ship's hallways and stairwells. Dash, Pitt, Kleiven, Dauge, Magnus, and finally Legion finally made it to the top.

Another ship had cross hooks linking the two ships together. By the time Dash and his crew made it to the top deck, the opposing ship's crew were already boarding and engaging Avalon's. Avalon's ship didn't have many experienced warriors but they were trained and willing to die for their liege. Where was Avalon? He was nowhere to be found. Surely, he hadn't fallen. Avalon Darksteel was a legend.

The other ship was similar in size, though slightly larger. It was a Drakkar by design. Drakkar's were a foreign design originally forged by the Kingdom of Steele. Thox had built their own Drakkars, a much fancier and much more sturdy version of the same ship. This Drakkar was one of theirs. The Drakkar was a specific type of longship. Avalon's Sohar was probably more seaworthy but the Drakkar seemed to be in much better condition, especially since being bombarded by the Drakkar.

The wood beneath Pitt gave way, collapsing at his feet. He had no time. He fell fast and hard. The artillery of the enemy ship continued. Burning mounds of old debris relentlessly broke through the walls of ship.

"Pitt!" Legion cried.

"Pitt," Dash yelled simultaneously.

"Pitt no!" Kleiven screamed.

It was too late. The goliath fell to the lower levels of the ship with burning wood and soot all around him. Dash and the others knew nothing could be done at the moment. The enemy at hand had to be dealt with.

"Nothing can be done for him!" Dash screamed.

"He can't help us now," Dauge added, preparing his weapons.

The coldness in his voice even at a time like this surprised his crew. Pitt could be dead. He very easily could have fallen to his death. Mourning Star glimmered again. Its power was coming back to it. It was soon to be fully restored. Legion could feel its essence bleeding through into him.

Countless buccaneers rushed the team along with everyone else on the top deck. Legion waved his flail with bad intentions. The pirates of the Drakkar longship were all humanoid. Most were either half-orc or mul. Mul's were a race of creatures bore from the mixing of the human and dwarven races. Some were tall and thick others short and stout. A skinny mul was about as common as a short giant.

The pirates weren't armed too well and obviously kept their protective gearing light, as so not to sink should they fall into the waters below. Small simple weapons and ranged missiles were the primary assault styles of the aggressors. The muls wielded mostly one-handed weapons with either off-hand weapons or small shields in their opposing hands. The half-orcs were the bigger threats keeping larger one-handed weapons and two-handed weapons at their backs should they choose to grab them.

Muls were a common race and there were plenty on this enemy longship. Kleiven and Dauge fought side by side in perfect unison with one another. One would think they'd fought together like this before. No, it was Dauge and his ability to adapt and overcome that made their dual strikes appear and feel so devastating.

The head of Legion's flail, Mourning Star, crushed in the face of the first advancing half-orc with a two-handed weapon readied.

"Magnus get out of here!" Legion ordered.

Magnus' blade was out. He'd come to fight. "I can fight like the rest of you!" he argued.

"You have to take back my home. Now get out of here or I'll kill you myself!" Legion commanded.

Like the others, Avalon's absence worried him. He admired the young boy's courage. For the first time since he could remember, he did as he was told and fled the flight. His reason for following the order was not what Legion thought. Magnus fled in order to either find or learn the whereabouts of Avalon Darksteel.

Dash sent several charging bucs to sleep, forcing them to collide with each other mid stride. More spells confused the aggressors. Dash used his magic wisely to slow the assault and weaken their aggressors, giving Avalon's crew enough time to reequip, rally back, and win the fight.

Legion let loose his flail again, this time wrapping it around the ankles of his next would-be killer. Another half-orc, Legion jerked back on the shaft of the weapon forcing the monster to his back. His greatsword left his hands as did the air from his lungs.

"No," he cried just before Legion majestically worked the spiked ball of his weapon into yet the face of another half-orc enemy.

Dauge was once again equipped with his armblades. The hilts were palm's length allowing the top of the blades to run all the way down his forearms and just past them. At the end, the point marked the beginning of the blades' curving nature, forming the blade on the opposite side of his forearms and following the rest of the metal all the way back to the handheld shafts.

Dozens attacked him at a time. He whirled and danced, fending off each and every attack while Kleiven cut through them in the process. Dauge noticed Kleiven was nicked pretty good and blood poured from more than just a few spots on the Eternian soldier.

Dauge dropped his body, arching it and spinning, working his way back up to a standing position. Abdomens of muls and torsos of muls fell open, spilling out their insides, making it look like Dauge was killing them effortlessly. He was.

Out of the corner of his eye Dauge saw a caster across the ships toward the Drakkar's far end. The heat of the spell gave way and Dauge planted himself for what was to come. Dash roared out in pain, using what was left of his own magic to deflect the spell and finally to cancel it out completely. The maneuver dropped the bard to his knees.

"Brother," Dauge called.

"Brother," Legion answered.

Dauge left Kleiven behind to finish off the four remaining. A bolt pierced the chest of one of them, dropping him lifelessly to the deck. Dash was down but he wasn't out just yet. He was out of magic and his body riveted with pain. He still had a few bolts to assist his crew with.

"I'm going to see to it everyone of you die for what you did to Pitt," Kleiven roared.

The first one came at him with an overhanded swing. Kleiven caught the arm and wrapped his around it, catching the aggressor's arm and trapping it beneath his shoulder. His bicep and torso squeezed together to keep the sword hand held. Before the others could move, the aggressor's chest slid open for the soldier's weapon. Kleiven forced his sword completely through the pirate.

He grabbed the pirate around his waist and spun the dying corpse to the ground, ripping his sword out to slash the next one that came to him. "Go!" Kleiven screamed to his allies. Pitt was down and unaccounted for. Dash was hurt. He knew how to fend off and deflect spells, but it hurt him. From the looks of it, it hurt him badly. Magnus fled to safety. Hopefully, he was still safe. Avalon's ship was in trouble and soon would be beyond repair if it wasn't already.

Dauge and Legion leaped from the railing of their ship to the top deck of the other. A massive mul, the biggest they'd seen thus far, charged the two.

"I got him," Legion yelled, turning to prepare himself for a fight with the half-human, half-dwarven bald pirate with a massive falchion in his grasp.

The pirate was hesitant, seeing Legion's flailing spiked ball and chain. Mourning Star was an intimidating weapon and it didn't hide its magical nature either. Dauge pushed on to the caster. The caster was the greatest threat at the moment.

Another came from the smoke and flames of the enemy ship's artillery, charging Dauge with everything she had. The lady half-orc kept a simple broadsword in her grasp. She roared as she ran toward him.

Dauge rotated the blades around from aiming backwards with the points toward his elbows to extending out like a typical blade. Now, they were nothing more than sickles with exceptionally short shafts. Dauge effortlessly pushed both blades through the chest and abdomen of the half-orc and rolled with her momentum, spinning around, letting loose his favorite weapons as she crashed lifelessly onto the deck below.

Another explosion obviously sent by the caster forced Dauge to cringe. Were his people okay? The spell left the caster vulnerable just for a second. Without missing a beat, two small bolts fired off from Dauge's wrists. One caught the caster in the left eye and the other split his windpipe nearly perfectly.

The caster grabbed his own throat, falling to his knees. Blood oozed through his fingers and down his hands and forearms. Blood rolled down his face from his eye as well. Dauge could hear the man gagging on his own blood. He was dead just that easy. Dauge was breathing heavily. He'd been working and moving hard.

Dauge looked behind him. His people were coming back. Avalon was still nowhere to be found. The pirates were retreating and conceding. The caster was clearly one of their higher-ranking members and he was dead. Avalon's sohar ship was busted. The pirate ship still seemed to be okay and was outfitted quite nicely.

Toward the bottom of the burning and busted ship, Magnus found Avalon Darksteel working like a slave. He wore no armor, nor did he have a single weapon at his side. He was mending holes in the hull with a select crew of strong lads.

"Avalon," Magnus said, curious.

Avalon's job was just about finished. He looked tired and so did his men. A simple bardic caster assisted in the wood mending and crack sealing but Avalon's back did most of the work. "Magnus Black," he said, wiping his hands off together.

Avalon was drenched. His workers were drenched and the hull compartment was just about knee deep in water. "General Black," he said, turning to face the man. He breathed deeply. He was tired and worn from the heavy lifting and mending of the ship.

"Where've you been? We're fighting a damned war for your ship out there! The underlings can do this!" Magnus was pleased to see Avalon but enraged he wasn't out helping. He was among the greatest swordsmen alive.

"Of all men, I was sure you'd understand. I have faith in my people and yours. Our ship was soon to sink, friend," he said in retaliation. At first Avalon was happy to see Magnus but the General's words turned him away from the man.

"Forgive me, Lord Avalon, my saviors and your people are out there dying. We were ambushed and outnumbered. If it wasn't for—"

Avalon cut Magnus off starting the sentence the same way but finishing it with his own thoughts. "If it wasn't for my assistance down here, we'd have already sunk!"

"Pitt fell," Magnus said changing the subject. Now, with no more to go on with his first disgruntlement, Magnus changed to the next most important thing on his mind, Pitt's life and health.

"We've recovered the goliath. He's alive but not well," Avalon said.

"He is alive?" Magnus asked.

"Yes, though I'm not sure if there's enough magic in the world to heal him," he answered.

"What's the matter with him?"

"He's burned and debris pierced him a thousand times."

"Where is he now?" Magnus asked. Pitt wasn't anything to him really but a friend of the man who saved him, but it was in his blood and in his nature to treat the men all like soldiers, his soldiers.

"In my chambers, the safest place aboard my ship, General. Now, this is finished. I must see to my people. Stay here," Avalon said.

Back on the top deck, Legion and Dauge waded through their opposition, ending life after life viciously. The others of the ship took note of their ferocity. Legion noticed something about his brother, lines on his skin lit up all over his body, like ancient magical markings or glyphs of some sort. His eyes lit up and glowed with designs of a fiery storm coming about.

Dozens of small spikes pierced into his flesh and skull digging deeper with a vengeful driving force behind it. His brother's uniqueness stunned him, like a man caught with a hold person spell. He'd never seen anything like that, especially not from his brother.

Legion fell to the deck. Blood oozed out of the many holes of his head. One of the half-orc's thick clubs had chains and spikes melded into it. The half-orc successfully dropped the elder Xavier. Darkness called to him. It was a direct hit and a hard one. The water, the ships, the fire, and smell of death and the roaring of men faded from his sight and fell absent to his ears. Legion Cage Xavier was out.

Dauge rushed to his brother's aid. A handful of bolts and arrows flew his way. Another caster created roots and vines to entangle Dauge, but again Dauge moved differently toward the aggressors. He simply vanished from sight only to reappear with a dagger through the back of the last caster, a Halfling, interlocking the blade in the creature's internal bone structure.

The rest of Avalon's men continued their charge only to see the remaining pirates fall to their knees and concede. They were out of casters.

They no longer had the jump and they'd lost a lot of men, including all of their leaders.

Avalon witnessed the whole thing. Dauge wasn't human after all. He'd seen his kind before. He was a Xavier and the brother of Legion. No, he was the half brother of Legion but still a Xavier.

"Take what's good from our ship and burn her. She's done for. Imprison what's left of them. If there's no room, lock them on our ship. They'll just burn for their crimes. Never leave behind you an enemy to return. Dauge, take your brother to my quarters. Lay him next to Pitt." Avalon pointed to a few of his men. "You there, and you, take this one to my quarters as well. Nurse them, and I do mean my new quarters on the new ship!"

That meant, take Pitt from the old quarters and put him in the captain's new quarters of the new ship. Then, bring Legion and Dash and do the same. Kleiven was also hurt and ordered to the captain's new quarters. Avalon made it clear Magnus would go there as well. He was putting his guests all in the same room, the best room in the house.

When the work was over and Avalon's old ship was burning, he and Dauge watched it from the rear of his new ship. It was a beautiful sight. Burning embers lighting up the night sky. It was beautiful and Avalon was impressed with his "guests" now more than ever.

"Is it true you were present for the battle of twenty five?" Dauge asked, referring to the battle where Taj and twenty-four others stood against the unending forces of Corvana.

"It is," he replied.

"There's more to those Lotus people than myth spells out, isn't there?"

"There is," he answered.

"Your mother was a gypsy."

"She was," Dauge answered.

"Was she special or did Genasi run in her clan?" he asked.

He knew. Dauge had been so good his whole life, this entire time with the others, and every other moment in his life at keeping his origins secret. He loathed the idea of being a halfbreed. He wasn't a halfbreed. He was a Genasi with human ancestry.

Genasai were creatures with several different manifestations. The most common or core Genasi were claimed to descend from the Elemental Chaos. They mostly appeared as humans but each manifestation carried their own uniqueness. Dauge's human side hid most of his physical Genasi traits. Unfortunately, Dauge held on to two manifestations tightly. Not only were there manifestations, there were also abyssal manifestations, mutated, distorted, and twisted manifests of the core kinds. Earth, fire, wind, and water were the core manifests. He was not generally of the core. He never knew his mother so he knew not of his blood, only what his Lotus family could tell him and teach him. He was what was called a Voidsoul but carried the manifest of Plaguesoul as well. Of the core, he was a Stormsoul.

"I don't know. I wanted it not to get out. It'll be known to my family, my brother, and everyone else that I'm a disgusting halfbreed."

"My father is as human as yours, Dauge. My mother is as dark as any. Like you, I never knew her. I am a halfbreed. There's no shame in it. You cannot pick your parents or family. You are as important as the company you keep. You're as you as you allow yourself to be. Your blood cannot be chosen but those you bleed with and for can. Only concern yourself with the things you have the power to change."

"Kind words from the shadow huh?" Dauge said, smirking. Avalon's attempt to comfort him humored him a bit. He was concerned about mixed blood and the Eternian beliefs on purity. He was more concerned with his desire to lean more into his mother's side than his father's. And though he didn't show it, above all he didn't want to disappoint his brother, the one true person he could count on no matter what.

Chapter 36

Vektro arrived. He'd landed. Eternis was not what he thought. From the looks of it, it was going through some critical changes. Alas, he gave his word he'd serve the city-state Eternis and he would.

A sense of overwhelming evil suffocated him. The people of the city walked in fear. This was not the Eternis he'd heard about as a child. What was going on and why would a holy knight, a paladin of Typherion the Good Dragon send him here. Something was not right but he'd fulfill his duty.

It took a few days but finally Vektro got in front of the right man, General Cale Dar. Many lords and captains were being taken and removed and replaced; those that could not be trusted by the new king were either executed or enslaved.

On the south side of town, toward the southeastern docks a small tavern called the Broken Blades had caught his attention. While standing and facing Cale eye to eye, he recalled the moment.

The Broken Blades was foreign owned, a rarity in Eternis. It wasn't much more than a hole in the wall dive run by an old human lady probably in her seventies. Her white hair was matted and not well kept. The wrinkles and scars of her face told of a life not pleasant at all.

"Might I help you son? You don't look like you're from around here," she said.

The place wasn't packed but it wasn't dead either. It was a rectangular building with vintage tables and stools. Ornamental designs were woven into the sheets and drapes of the place and in some places, even the very wood. To say the least, the place looked very out of place.

"I am here seeking work as a soldier," he said, looking around.

There were a few soldiers and sailors about this night. A few patrons of both foreign and native descent scattered the main area of the Broken Blades. He ordered a drink and before he knew it, he'd taken a few too many.

"There's no lords or captains to talk to right now, son. You're going to have to find General Cale Dar yourself. You can usually catch him early in his quarters to the west of here past the cheap side wards on the left."

She was giving him directions. Eternis was a city made of several wards and smaller towns all built into one. It was massive but spread thin and, truthfully, there wasn't much to it. Most of its buildings were too old and outdated. It hadn't had a true standing army in three hundred years or so.

"Thank you, my lady. Your kindness has not gone unnoticed." He flipped a few coins her way. Maybe to her it wasn't much but to him it was. He was a free man for the first time in years and for the first time as a grown man. He had little money but little use for it. His servitude wasn't over yet. He'd need to spend at least a few years under the Eternian banner if he was to fulfill his duty to the man who freed him.

Something about the look in that lady's eyes and the conversations of the others in the tavern that night still haunted him. They spoke of the halfbreed, the half-shadow-blooded Prince of the Nine Kingdoms to the west

Vektro didn't like it but he'd given his word and he never broke his word, not for anything. And now he stood before the stern elderly General of the city-state. His quarters were decorated with a gothic scent in mind. His office was in one of the many barracks of the soldiers. Things curiously evil and unsettling walked the streets of Eternis and were being housed in the very barracks where Vektro caught up to General Dar.

The barracks were spotless and hundreds of young guards were present; some cleaned while others stood guard, and still, there were more performing scores of other duties. The General sat at his wooden desk. His slightly grown-out hair was slicked black. Waves of both red and white painted the man's hair. His face was wrinkled with age and scars.

"You've come suddenly to join the ranks of the Eternian Guard have you?" he asked arrogantly.

Vektro knew the General didn't believe him for some reason.

"Yes, my lord," he answered humbly.

"Why? Why now?" Cale asked.

The former slave noticed the General's mark of death. It didn't frighten him. This place was magically painted with evil and darkness. Darkness and light were not his concern, keeping his word was. Why did a good man and paladin of Typherion send him to such a wretched place?

"I've only recently been released," he explained.

"Released?" Cale questioned.

"I was a slave in Thox. Storm Stars of the House Stars freed me. He said an old friend resided here in Eternis. He suggested and asked me to come here for work. He hoped I could serve as a soldier or guard to the city."

"Why did Lord Stars send you here? You say he claimed to have friends here?"

"Yes my lord. Legion and Dauge Xavier of the House Xavier and Dash Riproc, the wizardess Kraydia, and the barbarian Pitt were the names he gave me."

"The man who freed you sent you here to serve under King Bahaus out of respect for his traitorous friends?" Cale asked, angered.

"I'm afraid I do not understand, sir."

"Kraydia I do not know. Legion, Dauge, Pitt, and Dash, along with my own son Kleiven, are enemies to the crown here., We could still use you. I warn you. If I discover a plot against Eternis, death will be the least of your worries."

"My lord, if I may," He started, waiting for Cale to give him the sign to continue. Afterward, he did. "I care not for Eternis nor its rulers or enemies. I care not for its friends or wealth. I gave an oath, my word to a man that I would do something in exchange for the kindness shown to me. I'm simply here to keep my word. If I am of no use, tell me. I shall find another means to hold honor to my words."

Cale smiled. He admired the honesty of the man. Not to mention, he was thick and strong looking for a human, especially for a human. Something in his eyes entrenched Cale. It left him wanting more but there would be time for that.

"What's your name?"

"Vektro, Vektro Hal'gharn," he answered.

"Pleased to make your acquaintance Vektro," Cale replied, smiling.

"I am here at your bidding for what you deem a fair charge."

"You're truly free and going to surrender it to my will based on words to a foreign man not present here?" Cale thought hard on the man's words and ideals. He could do a lot with a man such as this. Cale wanted more information on the man and soon he'd have it.

"Let's get a rundown of your skills, son, and from there I will guide you to your most efficient stations and posts." Cale couldn't help but grin deeply.

At first, he was just another foreigner looking for work. Then, he became something of a question but happenstance had him landing in Eternis following the deep change in leadership. Eternis was becoming a harvesting ground for the dark powers that be. Cale swore an allegiance to them once to be returned to life. Thinking back, he should have just stayed dead as his wife left him and his world fell apart, nonetheless. Bahaus was destroying the oldest city in the known world and Cale was forced to follow him. His soul belonged to a dark entity indefinitely and in order to not suffer upon death, he would have to be of substantial use while alive.

Vektro didn't like Cale. Nothing about Cale Dar seemed to be on the up and up. Then again, Eternis wasn't anything at all like it was supposed to be. Further conversation did prove generosity wasn't out of Cale's reach.

"You've been a slave and gladiator and everything in between from what you've told me," Cale confirmed.

Vektro nodded in compliance.

"I'll not have you waste your talents as a soldier or guard. You deserve your freedom but should keep your oath and word strong and trustworthy. I will grant you the money to hire the mercenaries you'll need. I want you to build and organize a team to find and return Dauge and Legion Xavier to me here in Eternis."

"You want me to bring the friends of the man who saved me back to you?"

"That's your charge. That's your sole charge given to you by Eternis. Now Vektro Hal'gharn, will you hold your word?" Cale asked.

When Vektro left the man's building. He had a lot to think about. Cale offered him a single day to contemplate the order. He had but a single day to think over his honor and his word versus the man who gave him his freedom's friends. They weren't his friends and how did he know if Storm hadn't heard what they'd done that he wouldn't bring them to justice?

Cale told Vektro everything to include his own point in the story. He told him why they were wanted and what they did against the city. He even admitted to not fully believing in Bahaus in his ways but bought into it upon his first death in order to be revived. Of all the people who feared Bahaus, Cale was not among them.

Cale knew Bahaus was smart enough to know he needed him. Cale also knew Bahaus realized the General would not betray his oath to his deity, not for his city, not for his own personal goal, not even for his family. He ordered his own son's capture, claiming the boy'd committed high treason against the crown of the oldest city-state.

Vektro was now under the order of General Cale Dar of Eternis and charged with the task of bringing in the fugitives Dauge and Legion Xavier, Dash Riproc, Kleiven Dar, and Pitt. What would Storm Stars think of this? He could just leave and forget the whole thing. There were times when keeping your word wasn't in the best interest of all those involved. And he was thinking this was one of those times.

Chapter 39

Dusk awoke. She'd been confined to her new "private" quarters in the new king's manor. Her family, every single one of them was imprisoned and placed under the manor in its own private dungeon. Adrian, her adopted mother, and the rest of her siblings were all taken. Only Dorian, Dauge, and Legion escaped.

She told the king she would agree to marry him only if he spared her family and kept them close to her. He honored her wishes by placing them in private cells built into his own manor below ground. Dusk's room was immaculate and beautiful, yet still she wept. Whatever was in her was trying to come out. Every day was a fight to keep it from the world. On top of it all, she would now be forced to marry Bahaus in order to spare her family.

She hated him. He was fat and disgusting. Horrifying pictures decorated nearly every piece of visible flesh she'd ever seen of him. The inks in his flesh were flamboyant and bright. When he ate, he did so without a single manner. He was everything she loathed in a mortal being. She thought of Grath and then of Kleiven Dar.

She'd gotten bored of Kleiven and searched for something more. She found Grath. Grath was different and unique. He wasn't like anything she'd ever met before. Then again, he was a shadow elf. Maybe that's why she was attracted to him? In the end, she belonged with Kleiven and she knew it. And he knew it. Now, her husband-to-be was out for him, hoping to find and execute him. She was going to marry a man who hoped to kill her one true love. How could she do it? How could she go through with it? Would he understand? He'd have to. She was doing it all for the safety and lives of her family.

The twin ivory doors to her room crept opened. Her husband-to-be was being lit up by the morning light coming from her window. He stood their gazing at her beauty. There was more to her that he appreciated than she knew.

"You and I are alike more than you think, girl," he said with a sick grin across his face.

For the first time since being relocated to his castle, she noticed he hadn't a single guard near him. Cale Dar wasn't near him either. He was getting cocky and arrogant, even more so than he already was. What was he thinking? Given the opportunity, she'd kill him, and perhaps one day she would and restore Eternis to its former glory.

"I'm nothing like you," she replied, condemning his words.

In a twist, he didn't retaliate. He casually entered and strolled through her room. Her clothes were all either hanging in her closets or folded nicely in her wooden drawers. He slowly went through them, touching them, feeling them, mostly by a single touch of his finger. He looked away from her as the tips of his fingers caressed her clothes. "You are an Eternian first and foremost," he answered.

"I was born of an Eternian father and gypsy mother. I was born in the Republic of New Magic. It's more my home than this place will ever be, especially with you king, Bahaus. How could you throw my family in prison for nothing?"

"Nothing? I can no longer trust the Xavier House. Your brothers actively stand against me. I am the rightful heir to Eternis."

"You might be the rightful heir but that doesn't make you the right one. I'll never love you, Bahaus Sazos Uil-Endail. I love Kleiven Dar."

"Even his own father condemned him as a traitor. After we're wed, it won't matter who you love, my dear. Fear not, the Infernal Blood Moon is not expected for another three months. On our wedding day my pretty, I shall give Asmodai what he so desires most. And in return, he will bless me with enough power and forces to conquer the known world. It's a shame really, we could have been great together," he said as the meanest nice guy he could be. After finishing, she tried to talk, but Bahaus waved her mouth shut, refusing to listen as he walked from her room and locked the door from the outside.

Dusk fell back to tears. What was she to do? Even if she were able to flee, that would mean Bahaus now had absolutely no reason to keep her family alive. Would Dauge and Legion be able to save her in time? Were they even coming back? They had to be. And if not, Kleiven certainly would. She was his world and she knew it. Her situation made her think more and more of her time away from him and how wrong she'd done him.

She closed her eyes as tight as she could. Tears kept streaming from them. She wanted to get to sleep. She had to get to sleep. In the world of dreams, none of this was real. In the world of dreams, Bahaus did not have her or her family captive.

Bahaus arose early the next morning. His first order of business was a military strategy discussion with the General. It was early. The sun had barely cracked the horizon when Cale and Bahaus sat across from each other at Bahaus' table in the den of his manor.

The den was unique with furry green carpet and brown walls. It looked nothing at all like the rest of his place. The round wooden table used for eating was the only piece of furniture in the den. A few ancestral swords and weapons hung on the wall, including his brother's twin priceless long swords. Both men were dressed elegantly and Cale was clean shaved. It was understood Bahaus wanted any present for his meetings, any place where there would be an audience of his to be dressed with elegance and shaved clean.

"Top of the morning to you, my king," General Cale Dar started.

"And to you, my friend," Bahaus answered.

"My king, the chosen armies and regiments are enroute to the Crystal Cities. To my understanding, they've not been warned of our coming."

"We must get there before they figure out Magnus has escaped."

"Understood. My captains know to push them. I ordered the trek to be made under harsh conditions, little rest and lots of work. Our finest men were chosen to lead. Only the day before their arrival are they to rest fully."

"Good, if Magnus makes it back before our armies get there, our plan will be ruined and they will have the jump on us."

"We cannot let that happen."

"Stop."

"Sir?" Cale asked, confused as to why Bahaus stopped the conversation.

Both men paused silently and looked at each other. The maids came and brought the morning's meal. Warm oats, hot butter rum, water, milk, juices, breads, eggs, bacon, and sausage. What an exquisite breakfast, Cale thought.

"You speak to me about our plans as if they're our plans and not my own. Why? You only follow because you have to."

"My king, I sold my soul for the better of the city. I returned to life to return to this city. And in turn I learned I've made a terrible mistake, one I cannot undo. Now, now that my soul belongs to the liege of dark powers, I do what I must to please the dark bastard that carries my soul. This city is still my home and you are the rightful heir. If it is to be Thedia's newest damnation, then so be it. I will do what I must to serve Asmodai, for he is the reason I am here. If I could do it again I would not. It cannot be undone and my soul cannot be saved."

Bahaus smiled. It pleased him to know the pain and anguish his friend Cale was going through. It was sad, but everything the old General said was right. He was even forced to stand against his own son for the good of the city.

"I know you'll stand for the city no matter what. You've proven that. I know your heart isn't where mine is but that's okay. Because our goals still remain the same. I aim to please my Deity as do you. And once the Crystal Cities are mine, the funds to buy ships and armies and wizards and warriors will be there. I will forge the greatest empire the world's ever seen and I will begin my conquest by taking Thox for my own self!"

"Yes my king," Cale simply answered.

"And what of the scouts and assassins?"

"They've narrowed down Magnus' escape routes and paths. He's heading to Port Agatha aboard a foreign ship believed to be led by Prince Avalon Darksteel of the Nine Kingdoms."

"Excellent. And we have our finest on it?"

"Yes, my king. I even hired a few outsiders and none of the assassin crews or solo artists know of the others. There's utterly no chance of failure."

"Tell me, the Wanderer is among the men on your payroll?"

"He is."

Bahaus smiled once again. Everything was in place. Dusk was his to be. The Xaviers were ousted. All of his enemies were gone. The only setback was Magnus escaping. But now it was a race. Soon, all of Thedia would belong to him, or at least, his known pantheon anyway. Then, he could set his sights on that Corvanian place and other pantheons he was sure existed. And the best part was with every kingdom falling, the other deities would lose worshipers and power. More would follow Asmodai, as they would be forced to, and his power would grow and his fondness for Bahaus would become even greater.

"If we can kill Magnus, then we can use our doppelgangers to pose as him if need be long enough to prove our words true and get the Free Armies out from the Crystal Cities."

"We could even order them to attack an enemy somewhere?"

"No Cale, we haven't any true enemies aside from Thox, and the Free Armies would never engage in a battle against a power such as Thox. Hogs get slaughtered and pigs get fat. Let us be pigs for the coming months."

"Aye, sir."

"You understand then?"

"I do," Cale said.

"Good."

"How did you come about the Wanderer?"

"He's been in town for many years. He's old and decrepit. The claims say he can still get it done. I knew a man once who described him to me. I found him but gave an oath not to release his identity. Just put trust in the knowing it shall be done."

"I'd rather not know the darkest parts of your duties. That's why you're the General and I'm the King!" Bahaus said, laughing arrogantly and hysterically. Moments later, he calmed himself down enough to finish his words. "Careful though, General, and choose your words wisely. For I have an understanding Magnus will not make it back to the Crystal Cities. I will hold you to the oath. If you fail me, remember, a slow and painful death will be but the beginning of your eternal quest to learn the most painful forms of torture."

"Yes, my king," said Cale again, this time a bit more hesitant. Bahaus' words made the General think. The Wanderer was actually an old man that claimed to once hold the most powerful sword in the world and claimed the sword one day shied away from him. He claimed his time with the sword brought forth connections that would never go away. And now, Cale would expose the Wanderer for his connections to get to Magnus. Now, everything was expendable, even the old man.

Cale would be sad to see something happen to the old man. He'd been seeing him around town for some time. It took some street smarts to gather who the Wanderer was, but he got it. Ziestian Ruliano was his name. He was old and ugly. He'd been a beggar in Eternis for quite some time. Most of the citizens had grown to like the poor sap. Avalon Darksteel once set up a permanent room in a nearby inn to be his own. The room would be paid for weekly out of his personal account in the local treasury with money made by his tavern, the Broken Blades. The coin his tavern made he never saw anyway. It was being locked away in a personal account

Cale parted afterward. He waited the customary time frame for Bahaus to rise, gather his personal guards, and leave first. Upon leaving the manor, thoughts raced through his head. He once knew an elven man, a friend, Valsul who worshipped the angel Raielyn.

Raielyn represented freedom, or at least the concept of it. Valsul was believed to be somewhere in either Myasuna or Valakuza. He left following Taj's tearing down of all churches not directly related to a draconic faith or the Draconic Order as a whole.

That was neither here nor there for the moment. Right now, he was General Cale Dar of Eternis, direct servant of the city and highest-ranking member answering only to the king himself. Could Raielyn possibly save his soul? Was there someone or something out there that could possibly give him salvation and show him redemption?

Bahaus returned to his private chambers. A map of the southern half of the Runethedian continent, the main landmass of the pantheon, focusing on Eternis and its surrounding areas lay before him. He hovered over it like an owl on a tree branch overlooking a small rat, its next meal.

Small wooden figurines specifically carved to his personal likings and representing every force he had at his command, stood on the map where it was currently posted. So many obstacles and options along the way to the Crystal Cities, he thought.

According to Cale's informants, Magnus was in the Hangman's Straight heading toward Port Agatha, heading away from the one location Bahaus couldn't have him at, at least not yet anyway. The Wanderer claimed great things. Most wrote it off as an old wild man's babbling. Other informants claimed the information to be true. And recently, a strong ally of Bahaus' residing in Thox, serving the massive guild Treeline, admitted further truths behind the man's claims; King Bahaus Sazos-Uil-Endail would put his words to the test.

Dusk awoke once again. It was early but her brain told her eyes she was still sleeping. Her room was thrown to the abyssal background her imagination created. Only flowing black and white stars in the distance existed here. She felt her body standing but there was no longer ground beneath her feet to stand upon. Not too far off in the distant black the thing hovered effortlessly.

"Y…you… you…" she started.

The thing as she called it was the lich with a link to her body and soul. Its black flowing cloaks and robes flapped back behind him as if a wind were pushing the clothes high into the wind. Its eyes glowed a purple tint and its skeletal body was darker than she'd ever seen. Gems and rubies were imbedded in this thing's very black bones. He'd grown stronger since she'd last seen him.

"What do you want with me?" It was clear her body was filled with fear but her tone tried to hide it with every word.

The thing didn't answer; it just stared at her. Its stare was long and deep. Something in her told her he was trying to tell her something. Something was different? What was different this time? Wait, this time she felt more of a connection, an actual connection, something she'd never felt with the lich before.

"You're here to help me," she said, questioningly.

The lich nodded. The power of the undead beast rushed through her veins and soul.

"Why, Davion? Why me?" she asked. Wait, she knew his name. Had she heard it before, ever? If she had, she didn't remember. Why did he want to help her? Did he tell her before? Did he tell her already why they were connected? Her brothers, her brothers were involved.

"I'm inside of you now, Dusk. There's nothing that can be done about it. Your kindred wished for your safety. I must assure it."

"I don't want you in me!" she screamed. "I'm not evil!"

"Take my hand. Accept me into your heart and forget about this wretched place forever. I shall show you things about yourself that will forever change your world. I will personally take you from this place, given the opportunity."

"You've crept into my soul little by little, Davion. There isn't much more I can do. I'd do anything to get out of here."

Davion was without flesh but she knew he was smiling. All he ever wanted her to do was accept him and make things easy for him. She existed far away from him and it made his powers difficult and weak with her. If she'd accept him and accept becoming a channel of his energy and keep him in her very essence, then keeping her safe would be much easier.

"Accept me. I can take you far away from here. I can take you far away from your troubles. I can protect you and put you back in Kleiven's arms. I can surround you with your brothers and those that love you."

She thought hard on the creature's words. They were symphonic to her ears. She could forever be rid of King Bahaus Sazos-Uil-Endail. Once returned to Dauge, Legion, and Kleiven, no one would ever be able to hurt her again.

If she fled Eternis, especially now, she'd leave her family to die. And death would only be the beginning. Bahaus was beginning the corruption of his people. At first, they were against him, in fear of him, worried his delusional mind would get them destroyed or worse.

Days passed into weeks and slowly but surely the people of Eternis began to flock to him. He was big, fat, disgusting, and vile. And aside from being a grown and powerful wizard, Bahaus knew the art of oratory. The more he spoke the more the people of the city flocked to him. More and more, devils and demons could be seen in the streets. Dusk watched from her window as her husband to be spoke to a strong gathering.

Bahaus stood on a newly built wooden podium next to a well fountain close to the center of town. His elite guard was everywhere. So many of them didn't appear as normal mortals would. There was something more to them. And slowly, every passing day brought a new surprise to the people of Eternis. It wasn't his speaking that caught Dusk's attention, it was the sudden change in heart the people of her father's homeland had for him. They cheered! They were cheering the vilest man in all of the world.

Dusk peeked out from her window at the new king addressing his people. Her eyes told her things others couldn't yet see. Yes, it was known outsiders such as demons and devils walked among Eternis now with Bahaus king. And that's what today's speech was all about. The people of the city were scared, but Bahaus was there to appease their fears. Dusk picked up just a few verses into the rightful heir's speech.

"I am an evil, but I am a necessary evil! You walk in fear of what I may bring. My powers, my allies of the underworlds, are here to stand and serve with us all for the purest of cities, the purest of lineages, the purest of hearts to restore Eternis to its former glories and greater!"

The crowd cheered but hesitantly. They didn't know how to take his words. He was openly admitting to walking with demons and devils.

The king continued, "My armies both here and there serve our greatest cause. The kings before me feared our enemies. I stand before you now fearing no man, no army, no legion, no faith." When saying faith, he was referring to the deities of the world. Since the gods were gone, the demons, devils, angels, dragons, elements, the Rivermortal, and spirits saw their mightiest ascend into something of a godhood.

"You fear the dark. I embrace you so you do not have to. I only ask that you walk and stand with me. Our own General Cale Dar returned to life in his youth to serve you and this city. He should not be looked down upon but worshiped and thanked appropriately. Why fear what is here to help? The demons and devils serve me here. They follow my orders. They do my bidding and my orders are to preserve and restore Eternis to its mightiest times, give it greater glories than ever before, and above all..." He paused and looked to the silent crowd. Then,. "...Protect the right and just people of this magnificent, paragon of civilizations, protect the people of Eternis!"

The crowd exploded. It was like a volcanic eruption. She had to admit he was poetic. She loathed him and he nearly convinced her. Looking down, she felt him again. It was looking through her eyes. She already knew what it was doing. She was a gateway, a channel if you will. She was granting the lich free vision upon Bahaus and the happenings of Eternis.

"My king, what of the Xaviers? They're one of the eldest houses here? Why are they imprisoned?" A commoner spoke out toward the king.

King Bahaus was surrounded by guards. Cale Dar was nowhere to be seen. Bahaus smiled, granting the man freedom to speak to him. His question was one he knew he would get. And he answered it majestically. "My friend, my subject, servant of Eternis, son of Eternis, the Xaviers have only not been executed for their treason because of their fallen house members, Taj Odin Xavier and his father Dominick Gabriel Xavier."

It took a moment to get the crowd quiet again. They cheered upon hearing their legends' names. Dominick was one of the most well-known names in all of the world. Taj posthumously grew to fame after his death, after his corpse was returned from Corvana.

"Treason is punishable by death. Because of their noble forefathers, I've decided they'll live secure lives within the basements of my manor. Dauge and Legion, sons of Eternis have turned on their people. They've turned wanting to oust the rightful heir to the throne, me! They want it for themselves. They want it for Thox."

This really got the people angered. Though there wasn't a current dispute between the city-state and the kingdom, the bittersweet rivalry between the two could easily be awoken with simple words. Bahaus knew just how to word them.

"I want the Crystal Cities. The wealth of the cities could finance our entire campaign! We will rise to prominence this age. By my own blood I swear it. I will call forth demons and devils to walk alongside us. There is nothing to fear of them, for they walk for my cause! Praise them. Honor them when you see them. Give them thanks for their duty to Thedia's oldest and greatest city. Why fear hell when hell is on your side? We will walk the lands, sail the seas, and conquer the skies. Eternis means forever. Let us show the world what forever means! Let us show the world what ancient, pure blood of the truest form can do with forged with purpose!"

Dusk wept. The crowd cheered. How could they not see through his deceit? He was vile and dark. The simple people of Eternis were being convinced and manipulated that war was the answer with an enemy non-existent thus far. Create an enemy and go to war with him? What kind of plan was that? Walk with the dark? Walk with the hells? Praise demons and devils? Who could convince anyone this was acceptable and for the good of anything?

She looked down, seeing Bahaus, hearing his words conclude.

"Dusk, an Xavier, in order to show my honor to the house I've abandoned my own desires in order to marry her in honor of her family. I want nothing more than for Eternians to be Eternians and to serve Eternians and Eternis. Dauge and Legion were among the men who ripped Magnus the traitor from his cell. And yet, I still honor his house by wedding his sister. And further, my commitment to the city goes deeper. I've sent word to Thox, where they are headed. Should he return Magnus to Eternis, I will give him my bride to be, my wife, my love."

He made it sound like he didn't want her; He made it all sound like selfless acts on his part. How could they listen to this? It wasn't too long ago the majority of the city's inhabitants hated him and loathed him. Many believed he poisoned his father. After all, he showed little remorse for Prince Aiden when he fell in combat against the Corvanian forces in the war.

Chapter 38

Pitt was still seriously burned and hurt but his wounds were mending. He was stable but moving him could still prove fatal. Avalon ordered his best men to bring Pitt down on their best moving bed. It took eight fully-grown men to get the monster down the gangway.

Dash and Legion recovered nicely. Though, the right side of Legion's face would forever house marks to remind him of the day he saw his brother change. Those marks were scars that magic mended as best they could, but the light pink lines and facial indentions were still there. He was growing. Legion remembered his first real scars as a soldier and these were his first true scars as an adventurer. Adventurers were less common these days and it wasn't a trade he initially chose to take.

The port was busy this day. The Thoxen port of Agatha was always busy. The sea was in the air. Its smell was refreshing to say the least. Avalon liked Thox. He led the crew from the gangway. He looked back, hearing them one by one drop from the plank to the stone ground of the Thoxen city.

Legion, Dauge, Magnus, Kleiven, and Dash followed behind Avalon. Only Avalon and the eight carrying Pitt touched ground from Avalon's crew. Avalon smiled at Legion and Dauge. They'd done well and finding them in the open water of the Hangman's Straight was perhaps one of the luckiest things ever to happen to the half-shadow elf.

"I'm going to miss you all as I missed your father when we parted," he said to the brothers.

"And we shall miss you, Prince Avalon," Dash answered quickly. His team was falling apart. Kraydia was gone. Pitt was hurt and the team and quests were no longer the brothers' main ambitions.

"My lord, where do we put him? Ugh!" one of the eight of Avalon asked, groaning. They were dressed lightly, not wanting to carry anything more than they had to.

"Take him there." Avalon pointed to a nearby inn.

It was called Saceren's Head. It was a fairly large building and from the looks of it doubled as a tavern. It was three stories, long and rectangular. The building structure was old and possibly needed some work. It still looked to be the choice inn for the "betters" of Thox and its visitors.

"Why there?" Dash questioned. He was struggling to take the sack of his belongings. It was filling up and getting heavy.

"It's a good place. Good men stay there. I'm going to pay for your first month here."

"That's a lot of money," Legion interrupted.

"It's okay. I've been around for many decades. I've accumulated enough wealth and wealth is not something I long for."

"It's not?" Dash asked.

"If I wanted wealth I would have remained in the Nine Kingdoms," he replied.

"Fair enough. Thank you," Dash responded.

"I long for glory, honor, contests, and the challenges of life. I look to build bonds with great men and women and leave my mark on Thedia before my time is done."

Dash smiled. It came so natural for him to say.

"I need to send a raven to the Crystal Cities. Let them know Magnus is free." Kleiven didn't want to interrupt the others but he felt it was the most important thing at the moment. Word of Magnus' safety had to reach the Crystal Cities before Bahaus did.

"No," Magnus replied. "No bird message is going to work."

"Why not?" Kleiven questioned.

"They're going to need to see him. Words of such importance must be proven with sight," Legion said. He spoke his mind but in a tone that told Magnus to correct him if he was wrong.

"Yes, and there's a secret to the Free Armies of Magnus Black that most do not know. Bahaus is in for a rude awakening," Magnus replied.

Meanwhile, a separate conversation was taking place. Dauge gave thanks to Avalon.

Avalon warned the younger Xavier not to thank him. "You assisted me after saving you. You and I are even. We are all clean of each others' debts. I am not an enemy to Bahaus Sazos-Uil-Endail, nor was I ever not an ally to your father upon meeting him. This is a dispute I must refrain from entering into. I wish the both you, all sides, the best of luck and hope many hard-fought well-earned victories lie before you all."

What was that? What was that supposed to mean? Dauge did understand. He knew exactly what Avalon was saying. In war, there are always those with things to lose on both sides. Prince Avalon Darksteel fought for the sake of fighting. He was known to many as the Blood Knight for that reason. He wasn't so concerned with right or wrong so much these days since shedding his old life as a samurai as he was the actual art of war and the heart that went into it. He was, however, always more of a just man. The stories continued to diminish with his noble actions and causes.

"I thought you for a hero, Avalon Darksteel?" Dash added.

"Hero, what a vague term," he replied.

Avalon spoke loudly and his words to Dauge were strong enough to pause the other conversations going on. After, during that brief pause, Magnus spoke again back to his own conversation.

"Thank you Avalon. I do not have to return to the Crystal Cities. We, the Free Armies built and forged under my hand and tongue and kept alive by my sword carry the oath, the Oath of Magic and Steele." Magnus turned his attention away from Avalon and toward the rest of the crew around him. "I've known Avalon for a long time. His words blanket his true cause. He's a good man. He's an honorable and just man, but his desire to be tested and challenged by opposition in the world has driven him to make some less than honorable decision." Magnus smiled. He remembered a few battles against an old rival that Prince Avalon assisted him on.

"Your words are spoken with care and truth. I hope you all seek out and find what you're looking for," Avalon responded.

"Oath of Magic and Steele?" Legion asked the group as a whole.

"The Oath of Mag—" Magnus started to explain but Avalon cut him off and finished for him.

"It's the ancient Oath of two of the most powerful kingdoms ever to exist here in Thedia. Due to the nature of their war, it was understood on both sides prisoners were considered lost and killed. In the event you got one back, it was a miraculous happening. The Oath is simple. Those lost will be honored as lost. Those captured will be honored as lost. Those killed will be honored in the ways you honor the dead. Let no one life be the cause of a sacrifice of another."

"So, what you're saying is?" Legion paused trying to think. Out of the corner of his eye he noticed the eight getting help by workers from Saceren's Head. They were getting Pitt inside and most likely to a room. A feeling of relief, they had a place to call home again. Funny, Thox was becoming more and more like the home he and his brother always dreamed of Eternis of being for them while in the Republic.

"If Bahaus approaches the Crystal Cities with word that I am captured or killed, my armies will attack in defense of the cities and retaliation with the understanding that I am already lost. There's another in place as of recently that will lead the charge," Magnus said.

"Who will lead your armies in your absence?" Dash questioned.

"A son, the one I'm most proud of. He grew up in Malynkite City and served them well until he sought me out. Drackice Black, my son has proven himself since joining my ranks and is currently my second in command. He's just another bastard son to me but he's a legendary war strategist. Bahaus will certainly regret his move on the Cities."

"If his armies are going to be fighting the Crystal Cities presumably, then our move should be to attack Eternis. It will be lightly guarded and we'll be able to move in without much of a fight. Meanwhile, the Free Armies will be giving a true thrashing to Bahaus' troops," Legion suggested.

"They're still our father's people. Not necessarily my people. I don't want to see them killed," Dauge replied.

"If they follow Bahaus, then for the greater good of the world they must be stopped no matter what," Kleiven added.

"You're a soldier of Eternis," Dauge reminded.

"I'm a son of Eternis, first," he replied.

"We must get moving," Avalon said, interrupting.

The others stopped their conversations to wish the foreign prince a happy and safe trip to the Nine Kingdoms. They thanked him repeatedly for his help and for offering to remain out of the dispute though he was friends with Bahaus and considered him the rightful heir.

Avalon left when the eight that carried Pitt returned from Saceren's Head. He refrained from allowing any more emotional goodbyes. He simply turned and walked back to his ship, leaving those he brought to Port Agatha in Port Agatha, leaving them like they were nothing to him.

After he was gone, Magnus turned and regrouped the others. "There is something we can do, someone we can inform. He will help us," Magnus said. "We can send a carrier pigeon to him. He's in Valakuza. He's a lord with a decent number of men who could probably take Eternis divided or at full strength."

"And who is this?" Dash asked.

"Not too long ago Seth Redd retired to Valakuza. He's got men behind him. Experienced soldiers long retired would take up arms again to walk with him."

"Magnus, I didn't know Seth left Eternis," Legion said.

"Not many did. He sent a pigeon to me just before he left. He didn't give his reasons. If I call for him, he'll answer. I'm sure of it. He'll answer."

"Magnus, you're sure the retired Eternian General will return with men to fight with you against the rightful heir?" Dash questioned. He restated every single thing Magnus had just said but in a questioning tone. He wanted to make sure he was asking every single thing to confirm when Magnus answered, he would know exactly where they all stood.

"Yes, he will," he answered, smiling.

"I now swear my oath of allegiance to you, sir. I'll send the pigeon," Kleiven said.

"Yes, good. There's no need to swear an oath. We serve the same purpose. Our cause is the same, yours and mine. I will see to rallying men here in Thox to further the cause. Dauge, Legion, Dash, and if you would tell Pitt, thank you all for your help, especially you, Dauge. Without you, I don't know where I would be or if I would even still be alive. I would swear to keep your secret safe, but it seems to have come out," Magnus said smiling. "Leave the removal of Bahaus to me, my armies and my allies. Please, entrust I will take care of it. Entrust I will have someone righteous holding the throne before long. Go about your lives and know you've done enough."

"Eternis is our home, Dauge and mine. Bahaus has my sister and the rest of my family. I cannot sit back and watch while others act in my place," Legion replied.

"Understood. And when the time is right, you will be called upon. Kleiven and I will begin building another force here. There are always those out of work who can become a quick force of irregulars. I have a personal treasury here in Thox. I will rent land, weapons, and armor and train whoever I can get my hands on who will fight. Those with nothing here can be promised something elsewhere. It's going to take time though. You must work with me. I must know you will not do anything until we are ready. Otherwise, you'll compromise the entire campaign."

"You have my word," Legion answered.

"And mine," Dauge seconded, but he waited to answer. It took him a second.

"Dauge, do I have your full support on this?" Magnus asked.

"Yes," he unpleasantly responded.

"I speak for Pitt and myself when I say we will follow your lead on this one," Dash answered. Secretly, Dash was thankful. Trying to oust the rightful king in the world's oldest city was not something he truly wanted to be a part of. Their whole expedition to see the former king buried just got too far out of hand. It could be corrected and with a few changes and replacements he was sure he could make to replace the absence of Kraydia, for example, and the crew could get on with becoming great. They could get on with finding riches, magic, and other legendary artifacts the worlds of old had left behind.

"Very well. Let us move with purpose to see our causes through. I will see you again with cup in hand celebrating our victory in restoring Eternis to its peaceful state," Magnus said to them all.

Afterward, he and Kleiven said their goodbyes and gave their hugs and departed from the team. Only Dauge, Legion, and Dash remained out front by the docks. Pitt was inside. Before Avalon left, one of the eight that carried Pitt handed a small piece of parchment to Dash, giving him the details of Pitt and the room he was in.

"It's just us again," Legion started.

"Yes, we are but three with another bedridden," Dash seconded.

"We've done all we can for Eternis. Our family is at risk, brother. It is time to move with a different purpose and let generals and kings deal with generals and kings," Dauge said.

"And what of your twin, brother? What of our father? What of our mother and family?" Legion continued.

Dash snarled inside. Legion was going to a ruckus in what he was trying and it was really beginning to get to him. Soon, Pitt would be healed. He would have a new arcanist of some sort, he was sure of it. And he would have the names of Taj Odin Xavier's boys following under him! Now, if he could just get them to bypass the Eternian problem.

"I'll fetch healers to look after Pitt and keep fresh bandages and ointments on his body. Let us begin here and see what comes our way. If we're going to tangle with the likes of kings, even of places like Eternis, we're going to need wealth and weapons far greater than what we carry now," Dash said.

"He's right," Dauge agreed.

"Yes, you are right," Legion started. ", I'm going to send a pigeon to the Republic and ask for help. Magnus said he would have carrier pigeons sent to both, the Crystal Cities and Valakuza. Let us take care of our dealings and reunite here in Pitt's room this evening," Legion suggested.

"Done," Dauge said.

"Agreed," Dash confirmed. He was happy. He'd gotten their minds of Eternis and the suicidal thoughts of taking it from Bahaus. Bahaus was a powerful wizard with a strong following and the will to bankrupt his city to get what he wanted. He had connections to the divine aspects of the infernal world due to his stature with Asmodai. Whatever Bahaus wanted, he was going to have. Whoever he wanted dead, would be dead. If he took the Crystal Cities, there would be nothing left to stop him on his conquest. Dash wanted fame and fortune and an early death would give him neither.

Chapter 39

Months passed. Magnus Black was on his way out of Thox with a strong set of followers at his side. Kleiven Dar led the new followers. Magnus spent months using his name to attract more warriors to fight for him. With the money in his personal Thoxen treasury, he bought enslaved and freed condemned men. He spoke publically to gain notoriety. And now he was heading out of Thox to begin his quest to defend the Crystal Cities, the lands he swore to protect and to free Eternis from a tyrant. Eternis was not his contract. They were not his people. They were now a threat to his people and rescuing the oldest city from a vile tyrant would do nothing but boost his name and recognition even further. It wasn't about his name and recognition anymore. It was about ousting an old allied city's new tyrannical king, even if it was the rightful king and true son of his dead friend, the late King Gerear Uil-Endail.

Bahaus' last coins were used arming the new soldiers for hire that had recently made it to Eternis to fight for its new king. Bahaus was now all but bankrupt, the Crystal Cities were his only out. He'd have to take them or Eternis would surely fall.

Bahaus chose to march with the armies to the Crystal Cities. He ordered his bride to be to be bound and taken among other things. He wanted to be present for the start of Eternis' newfound glory.

It was just over the horizon. The first city was within their sights. It looked like Emerald Greene if he wasn't mistaken. He'd journeyed there in his youth. What a fantastic day for a war. How long had it been since an army walked alongside fiends from the hells below. Low ranking fiends, demons and even a few devils were granted to Bahaus' forces to help in the taking of the Crystal Cities. Asmodai was going to be greatly pleased, he thought.

Bahaus had three doppelgangers left. One stayed back in Eternis. One was at his side, walking and talking just like the real Magnus Black. And the third walked alongside the new bounty hunter, Vektro Hal'gharn. It was Cale Dar's idea and one Bahaus quickly agreed to.

Bahaus boldly marched on his largest horse toward the gates of Emerald Greene. The smell of Great Mystic Lake's pure water was still in the air. The mountain chain and water in the horizon impressed even Dusk with its beauty. Still far away but now in the horizon, the Mystic Forest; it was slowly forming to and through what their eyes could see.

"The gates of the first Crystal City are upon us," Bahaus said, riding high on his largest black horse. Cale Dar was at his side against his better judgment. Cale wanted at least one of them to stay back in the event of a counter attack by any of their new list of growing enemies. Bahaus was convinced he had it taken care of. The solidity of Eternis' protection against foreign enemies is beyond your comprehension, Bahaus said to Cale the day they left.

"They are indeed, my lord," Cale said confidently.

"After today, coin will no longer be an issue for us. We will have all we need to build what is necessary to forge an empire greater than any the world has ever seen," Bahaus continued.

"My lord, something doesn't sit well with me," Cale said, scanning the surrounding areas.

"What? I've doubled my forces over night. Half the men that walk with me are fiends in sheep's clothing. Follow me?" Bahaus finished asking, making sure Cale understood.

"Aye sir, I do," Cale answered.

Suddenly, men stood from behind nearby rocks. Men walked out from behind the scattered trees of the open planes. Looking up, now both Cale and Bahaus saw archers mounted in the scattered treetops as well.

The gates to Emerald Greene opened and a readied army of the Free Armies walked out in perfect unison. Most were armed with decent metallic armors over leathers, a good medium-sized circular shield, a pole-arm, and a sword gripped and held behind the shield.

A second legion of warriors made their appearance, ripping out from the very earth, aiming their spears at the nearest enemies they could find.

Leading the armies on foot, a young half-elven man with short black hair sticky and spikey, purple eyes, and a muscular build to be half human and half elven.

He wore little armor and all black clothes. A sheath rested on both sides of his waist. On his back, he kept a longbow and quiver full of arrows. He was fairly young with pale skin. His skin's tint was nearly yellowish. He walked with a sense of confidence and security that scared Bahaus.

"Damn the fallen!" Bahaus said. "They must have gotten a carrier pigeon here first."

"They wouldn't have sent a carrier pigeon, my lord. They could have but it's too questionable. Any one of Magnus' enemies could have forged that if they'd heard he was taken, hoping the Free Armies would fight anyway, assuming he was safe. That way, his captors, us, would kill him."

"Move the men," Bahaus ordered.

Cale started waving signals to the men who began moving with haste to position. The young half-elven man walked alone and confidently toward the advancing army.

"What does this bastard think he's doing?" Bahaus asked.

"He's certain of his advantages over us, my lord," Cale replied.

The half elf crossed his arms and stared at the two and then to the advancing armies all around. He looked back to the city, Emerald Greene. He was ready to defend it to the death for that's how the contract read.

"King Bahaus Sazos-Uil-Endail of Eternis... My lord," he started gracefully.

Bahaus smiled. "I see you're not without manners. You at least know how to address your betters."

Cale slipped his hand down, touching his fingertips to the hilt of his blade. Looking around, there were too many of them but on the other hand, they did have fiends on their side. They had the jump on them and they knew the fields better. They had the protection of the city and time to put whatever they wanted in place. This was not a battle they could win and even if they somehow did, it would not be without severe casualties. Bahaus brought damn near everything with him. Even if he lost Eternis, he mentioned he'd be able to get it back with the wealth of the Crystal Cities.

"General Cale Dar of the legendary city Eternis I presume," the half elf continued.

"I am," he answered.

"I am willing to set reasonable terms of surrender."

Bahaus smiled. Cale knew what the half-elf was speaking of and he knew the moment Bahaus caught on, all hell would break loose.

"I am not even asking for surrender. Simply walk away from the Crystal Cities, all of them, call off your men, or I will begin this war by executing your general, Magnus Black." Bahaus stopped then yelled to the back toward his men. "Bring up the prisoner!"

The doppelganger was bound and gagged and made to look identical to Magnus and it worked. Two large half-orcs walked up with the reins to the creature's shackles in their hands. The half-orcs were big and outfitted slightly better than most, wearing nearly full plated armor and wielding well-crafted master worked full-blades.

The half-elf smiled. "I am Drackice Black, and like you I was a bastard for many years, Bahaus Sazos-Uil-Endail. And I think you mistook my words. I will offer this only once…" he paused and locked his eyes to Cale's. Then, he continued. "Bahaus Sazos-Uil-Endail stays here as a prisoner. If my father allowed himself to be captured, then by the Oath of Magic and Steel he is lost…" He paused again.

An arrow sung from the treetops piercing the doppelganger's chest directly through the heart, killing him instantly. And instantly, he began to change while Drackice continued to speak.

"In the event of my capture, in order to spare me a more agonizing death I hope my own would do the same for…" he looked at the creature transforming back to its original state.

The arrow made Bahaus and Cale both jump. This man was young and ambitious. That single arrow could have easily started a war and it didn't seem like the young man cared at all. It was almost as if he wanted it to begin.

"You've come here with tricks devil worshiper? Fool, until my father returns, or if he returns at all, I am the commanding force behind the Free Armies. I am the Free Armies General Drackice Black. Cale Dar, take your men and go home. Bahaus stays with me. He will be held accountable for his actions. He will stand trial for his war crimes against the Crystal Cities in his futile attempt to take them.

Cale was broken now. This was his chance. He could hear the Angel of Freedom calling out to him. How many got that chance? How many got to hear something like that from a Deity? Perhaps it was all, just in his head? He looked over to Bahaus. His king's words were drowned out from his ears but he knew what he said. Attack was his only word.

375

This was Cale's chance. What if he died and failed? He would suffer immeasurably for Eternity. His son, however, didn't deserve to have his father turn on him. He knew he was a bad person. He knew he wasn't the man he once was. Perhaps immeasurable torture from now until the end of days was exactly what he needed and exactly what he deserved.

It was less than a second before no less than four dozen of Bahaus' men lay lifeless from arrow and spear strikes. They continued the charge. Drackice beautifully and evasively retreated, though he was still scratched and cut by the scores of missiles flying through the air.

Ballistic weapons fired off from behind the gates of Emerald Greene. Burning balls of wood and other debris aimed at the rear forces of Bahaus' soldiers, so as not to hit their own, slammed into the invading armies hard. Several fiends cast away their "sheep's clothing" and ascended back into their true forms.

The catapults' ammunition consisted of rolled up wood with metallic debris, chains, broken swords, shields, and pieces of armor all dipped in Malynkitian oil and set ablaze. Malynkitian oil was some of the hottest and most potent oil in all of Thedia.

The roaring screams of dying men filled the air. Bahaus' forces arrogantly approached and were in the open when they did so. Drackice was strategically placed with every advantageous point he could have on his side. However, the fiends of Bahaus' army fought fiercely and quickly began to even the numbers. There were maybe half a dozen demonic fiends and but one devilish one.

The demonic fiends appeared like blackened bugbears, twice the normal size and glowing red eyes. They wore armor of bones but it deflected aggression better than plate armor. They all carried gigantic double-bladed axes firing off fire-based missiles from its other end. Their black-and-gray dull colored fur quickly brightened with the fresh splatter of blood across it. Now, the screams of the dying echoed on both sides. Luckily, two of the six fell to the burning ballistic weapons.

The devil was different. His flesh was green with black horns sticking out from thousands of parts of his body. His face was long and pointy, his eyes black as the horns; he wasn't very big at all, nor did he carry a single weapon or piece of armor. This devil was different. He was once a mighty demonic servant who transcended into devil form when swearing a new oath of allegiance to the devil Orden the Binder.

The devil never stayed in one spot very long. He waved his hands and explosions erupted. The ground beneath their adversaries began swallowing men by the dozens. Each time something neared him, he disappeared from existence only to reappear seconds later just a few feet from where he was.

"Fall back!" Drackice ordered harshly. He'd never faced anything like this. He wasn't even sure the Free Armies had faced something like this before. Demons and Devils walked alongside a mortal army? Was Bahaus truly that powerful?

"My lord, we must fall back. The casualties will be too severe!" Cale begged.

"Advance, ADVANCE!" Each time he said it he became more excited and demanding with it. Bahaus was determined to take the city. He had to. Otherwise, there was nothing to go home to. Eternis would be bankrupt. Asmodai would be furious with his defeat and he wouldn't have the funds or the name to rebuild his army.

"We'll lose everything!" Cale declared, for the first time giving true sincerity behind his words

"We'll be able to replenish all lost a thousand fold!" Bahaus screamed back.

"The men we're losing are Eternians. We cannot replace them with foreign mercs, Bahaus! We're going to trade the lives of our own people for hired swords! I can't allow this!" Cale declared.

"Stop it and do your duty to your king and country!" Bahaus ordered. He didn't think Cale could do anything or would do anything against him due to his damning situation.

Bahaus formed a wall completely of whirling air just above the city's gates, extending outward in both the left and right directions. Bahaus alone nullified the Crystal Cities' missile and ballistic attacks against his army. Burning arrows and the burning balls of wood, metal, and oil were all caught in the windfall and riveted about like balls being beaten pack and forth with paddles.

Cale leaped from his horse, pulling his massive broadsword and taking the shield from his back. He heard the king yell at him "that a boy" while preparing another spell to probably further incapacitate his enemies. Just like that, he had the tide of the battle turned back toward him and that devil wasn't helping matters.

Cale looked ahead and then behind him where the devil was coming up. He silently prayed to the Angel of Freedom, Raielyn for the first time in his life. "Faith of freedom give me strength, give me courage, and give me the imbued powers necessary to end these bastards. Forge my life in the pact, granting Bahaus defeat in his attempt to seize the cities. Grant my enemies passage through my allied forces and see the hells and their minions cast back down to where they belong!"

The devil grew in size, shifting into something much worse than its initial form. Cale felt its presence nearing his own. He could hear the king's orders of kill, kill, over and over. The devil grew to nearly ten feet. A whipping tail with eight cattails spawned as well. His green skin turned a tarnished bronze. His claws emanated auras of flames that extended out and over his newly created burning sword. The thing pointed toward the gates and ordered the armies of Bahaus to charge with absolution and without any regard for their own lives or the lives of their fellow men.

Leading the charge were the remaining demons, while Bahaus continued to rain down bombarding spells filled with sonic energies. His sonic powers let loose boomerangs full on the energy, and each time one hit the wall or the gate doors, it shredded through it like a giant's teeth through bones.

Four precision arrows sang out with Drackice as their target. Drackice cut through his adversaries quickly and efficiently, never spending too much time on any one target. Since his initial retreat, he'd yet to take another step backward. Unlike his father, Drackice refused to retreat no matter the circumstance. Here, there was nowhere to retreat to. Magnus rarely fell back, but when he did, it was due to dire need. Drackice was still young and stubborn. With Bahaus' sonic blades flying through the air whirling around to look like sonic boomerangs, Drackice knew he couldn't have his men fall back.

The devil focused its attention on the current leader of the Free Armies. It swiped its sword, cutting through Cale's old steed. Cale was sad to see the horse killed. He'd had it for a long time. The swipe opened the devil up and the powers from a source unknown to him ran through his veins and sword, sparking every single hair on his body to stand.

He turned and put the sword directly through the piece of the creature that was eye level to him, it's lower abdomen. Its torso was thick and sturdy, damn near impossible to push through. The sword caught fire, enveloping both itself and its wielder in a blue colored burning power.

The creature roared out in pain. Bahaus was screaming something, but Cale couldn't hear a thing. He couldn't feel a thing. For the moment, even while at war, he was at peace. The devil dropped its own burning blade to grip the mortal by the throat. Its hand and claws wrapped Cale up like nothing. Soon, the fire of his old sword died out. The fire around him died out. There was still no pain, but his body was dying. It was being crushed and cooked all at the same time.

There, in the distance, a man wearing flowing blues and yellows and ornamented with whites brighter than anything this world had shown him before stood before him with a gleaming tunnel of light behind him. The devil was no longer around. The war was gone. The city was gone. Bahaus was gone. He was gone.

"NOOOOOOO!" Bahaus screamed seeing his devil fall.

Upon its flesh hitting the dirt beneath its feet it combusted into a thousand beetles and locusts spreading out to a thousand directions; by the time Bahaus peered back up, Drackice and elite special group of his men were killing all but one of his demons. Only a single demon remained in his army. Several soldiers were still with powers due to possession. Thank the Dark One for that, the king thought.

The hill of defeat found it ways beneath Bahaus' boots and the harder he tried to command and climb, the steeper his hill became. Eventually, the last of the demons fell but not before sending over a hundred men to their graves. It singlehandedly kept Bahaus alive, along with his own arcane skills and powers. Then, something happened and the remaining soldiers on his side native to Eternis stopped and dropped their blades. The mercenaries continued to fight on. Then, seeing their allies virtually surrender all of a sudden stopped them in their tracks.

Lucky for Drackice, he'd taken on a few too many. His entire personal group had been killed. He was down and just about out. Blood oozed from a number of different wounds all across his body. Spears, pikes, and swords were all pointed at him in every direction. He hadn't anywhere to go and death was eminent. And then, the Eternians surrendered, stopping the mercenaries in their paths.

Drackice breathed in deeply. He'd been defeated. His men were victorious. He'd never lost a fight and this was his first battle in charge of the Free Armies solely. His head lifted, staring down the line of his battered body. General Cale Dar was dead. Insects of a thousand types were feasting upon his flesh. Poor bastard, he thought.

Drackice was helped to his feet but the Free Armies General couldn't walk on his own. His former enemies hoisted him and carried him back to a small unit of his allies. He was bandaged and mended with the best his people had.

The mercenaries raised their hands and made sure all of their weapons were dropped. Drackice devilishly grinned. He couldn't help it. The son of Magnus Black, the leader of the Free Armies defeated the advancing King of Eternis!

The Eternians' weapons were all dropped first. The higher-ranking soldiers and captains walked forward to Drackice. Drackice sat on a nearby tree stump, breathing heavily while the healers mended and stitched his wounds. One of the older human captains walked the closest to him.

Drackice's men gathered around, readied for anything, but Drackice waved them off. He looked up to the wrinkle-faced old man. His short white hair hadn't much to it left. Balding spots were everywhere. Scars and war wounds of all kinds plagued the man's body.

"I am Ron Tye. I've served Eternis all my life, my lord," he said.

Drackice breathed in and moaned deeply. The stitches went deep around his knee. He wasn't sure what was more painful, being defeated on the battlefield or the wounds that came after surviving. He personally was defeated. His personal band of warriors were all killed. Only he survived. His men fought valiantly against possessed souls. His heart sank for his personal friends and those that wouldn't make it home to their wives and loved ones.

"Where'd that get you?" he asked, arrogantly trying to get the most out of his victory. In truth, he was still hurting inside for the friends he fought alongside and lost. He was also still hurting from the defeat he personally suffered on the battlefield.

"Bahaus did something to us," Ron said, ignoring the king's previous comment.

"Yes, he sent you on a quest you couldn't complete. He tasked you with an impossible mission. The Free Armies haven't seen defeat in some years," Drackice replied.

"If you must make an example of someone. Allow me the honor to die for my people. Let these people go home. Too many died absent a good cause today," he begged.

As he spoke, Drackice noticed a younger man behind him move his hand to his blades. Drackice pointed to him. The young boy stopped, startled.

"You there," Drackice said.

"Yes, my lord," he replied.

"You moved the moment this man offered his life for your people," Drackice stated. "Why?"

"That man is my father. Forgive me, I cannot stand by and watch him die," he replied. He stood up taller as he spoke, sticking his nose to the air and pressing his chin out straight, hoping to stand as tall as humanly possible.

The boy was young, maybe in his late teens. The old man was frail and weak looking but then again he was old. The young one was taller and bulky. Light brown hair flowed from his head just behind his ears and touched the top of his neck.

"And your name boy?" Drackice asked.

"Zoole, Zoole Tye," he answered.

"Your father's a good man. He was willing to die for every one of you. Learn from him. Take in everything he says and take not a moment of your father's time for granted. Am I understood?"

"Yes, my lord," Zoole replied confused.

"Sir Tye, you will die here today but not in the way you think. Your time as a soldier of Eternis has come to its end," Drackice furthered.

Ron's head lowered. He looked back at his son, worried and scared as any would be preparing for some form of execution.

"Kneel," Drackice said to Ron.

Ron Tye of Eternis obliged him.

"Renounce your allegiance to Eternis for its greater good. You hereby serve me under good name and word. You look to be an honorable man. We're going to trust that honor. Your mercenaries can go home. You can go home. Lead your men home. You will serve the Free Armies as a Lieutenant General under my personal command. And your orders are to return to Eternis and set order to the chaos that it's become. Remove Bahaus and any who would follow him. Kill them, execute them, and torture them. You will stand as active lord of all Eternis until a new king or Eternian General is instated. Am I understood?"

"Yes, my lord." He didn't know what to say. He was too excited and thankful. Eternis was a peaceful place and Bahaus nearly ruined it. He wasn't under Eternian order any longer. He was under the orders of the Free Armies by command of General Drackice Black.

"You will keep Zoole highly trained and his skills will remain sharpened. Teach him your ways and make him and all of Eternis more like you. You're a good man, Ron Tye. Do not let it all die with you."

"Yes, my lord," he said, smiling, silently thanking him all at the same time.

The armies collected their dead and began regrouping to either return to the city Emerald Greene or back to the city of Eternis. Drackice was helped inside the city and was nearing a wagon that planned to take him to his personal quarters when a Free Armies Captain stopped him.

It was an elven warrior, a little high on the ranking system for his age, but he was talented and good at what he did. He strategic skills and skills with swords were well met. His name, what was the little blond haired elf's name. He had skin the color of moonlight and was as tall as a human. He wore flamboyantly dyed leathers and had a knack for personally crafting and making his own hilts for his swords.

"Sir," he started.

"What is it?" he asked, climbing butt first into the wagon and laying his body across the hay inside.

"As ordered, we searched for Bahaus but to no avail. He's nowhere to be found but we did find his personal concubine. I assume that's what she is," the elf said.

"Bind and gag her and bring her to me. Lay her here in the wagon," he ordered.

"She was already bound and gagged, sir," the elf replied confused.

"Huh, we've just taken a prisoner that was a prisoner of our defeated allies," Drackice replied laughing. "Yes, bring her here."

"Yes, my lord."

A few low-ranking soldiers brought forth a bound and gagged dark-haired Eternian woman. Drackice couldn't help but notice she was beautiful. Her skin was fair and here eyes radiantly blue with green tints. Her hair was dark and flowing. Her clothes were tattered and torn.

The lot of them tossed her aboard the wagon where Drackice personally assisted her to a comfortable position over a more dense area of the hay. "Ugh," she moaned as she was finally put in place.

"Hi there, I'm Drackice Black of the Free Armies."

"I know who you are. Our families go way back. Your father and mine fought together."

"What?" He'd never met her. What was she speaking of.

"I am Dusk Xavier of Taj Odin Xavier, of Dominick Gabriel Xavier of the Xavier House of Eternis." Her attitude and tone wasn't a thankful one for just being rescued. Then again, she was still bound.

"Dearest Dusk, I heard my father speak of your father many times. I'm grateful to have been able to get you away from that monster. Let me cut your binds." Drackice pulled a knife to free the girl.

Her attitude changed a bit. "Thank you," she said, smiling but still a bit irritated. After all, she'd been bound for the better half of two months while on the trek to the Crystal Cities. "I'm grateful your father spoke of us, I guess."

"I am too. As soon as you're well and able, we will get you an escort to take you back to your city," he said.

"Gratitude, love and gratitude," she said. "I'm not sure what's left of my city."

"The cancer's been cut from it, my dear," he said, trying to hide the fact that he fancied her.

"Was Bahaus captured or confirmed to be dead?"

"No." Drackice hesitated to answer. It was the lone failure of the battle. Where would he go, especially alone?

"What to do in the meantime?" she asked, not exactly to him but more as a suggestive question to herself.

"In the meantime, my dear, I shall show you the Crystal Cities. There's not much here. We mostly have mines and miners but the ore, especially after being worked on, refined, and finished can be breathtaking," he replied smiling.

"You've got my attention." She smiled.

Chapter 40

Pitt, Dauge, Legion, and Dash were once again hailed for their duties to the kingdom of Thox. Still, in Port Agatha, an old friend had recently been paying them visits in the form of a typical mortal. It was Davion the lich coming to warn them of their sister's situation.

On the day of the Infernal Blood moon, Davion sent word of Bahaus' defeat and her rescuing at the hands of one Drackice Black. Dauge and Legion rejoiced to see victory once again on their side. Miniscule quests kept them busy and gold in the pocket and Saceren's Head was still their temporary home.

The four were out fishing just off the port decks, relaxing and enjoying their time together as friends and watching the ships come in and leave. Pitt's wounds from the fire onboard the ship were healed but the scars remained to remind him of a near disastrous time. Goliaths generally didn't carry hair atop their heads and his was put in place by the old caster he constantly spoke of, Shiva.

"I cannot believe you cut your golden locks off. You were the only goliath in the world to have hair on his head. Well, the only male goliath, right?" Dash started. "That made you different. It helped us stand out." Laughing but was still quasi-serious.

"The locks didn't regrow. Most of them burned off in the fire. I cut the rest of them off. I shaved them off. It's time for me to get on with my life. When I reunite with her, if I reunite with her, then she can give them back to me," he replied.

"Pitt, who is she? What is she? And why can you not let her go. There are beautiful girls all around us, my friend. And we're becoming famous here in Thox," Dash asked.

"Devotion is not something that comes equipped in all of us. You should be thankful he's one of us," Legion added.

"Agreed, I've seen what you can do with an axe and a sword," Dauge said.

Gold put new armblades on Dauge along with a few vestments added to his minimal armor. Legion recently purchased a gorgeous circular shield of iron and then plated with a beautiful bronze. Dash spent most of his money on scrolls and the like. He added a few rituals to his ritual book as well. Pitt now kept a fullblade on his back and a gigantic axe at his side. It was said to once belong to a massive giant to the east toward the Mogras.

"We cannot pick up bigger charges until we have more arcane on our side. I've been able to do most of our healing or get us the proper potions and ointments to keep us moving, but we're going to need more arcane power if we're going to take on jobs with better paydays and more name recognition," Dash added.

"Arcane casters aren't exactly the easiest things to come by, Dash," Pitt said.

"We're just fine the way we are. Besides, you ran Kraydia off anyway. You'll just run the next one off as well," Dauge said, slightly aggravated at thinking about what Dash had done. He still blamed him for Kraydia's departure from the team.

"Easy Dauge, every mortal being is responsible for their own actions and paths. We forge our own destinies. She chose her own path and felt ours were no longer heading in the right direction."

"I'm still curious as to what you told her that made her leave so hastily," Dauge shot back.

"Dauge, why do you question and challenge me at every turn? Our chosen paths are enough to prove we'll not always walk in the same direction. I do hope the four of us remain together always. I took you all from the Republic. I found Pitt and freed him. I want us to rejoice in fame, fortune, whilst forging our names and legends with the land," Dash promptly responded.

"I just feel that perhaps your agenda does not always carry everyone's best interest. That is all," Dauge replied.

Dash laughed. "You think my desires to have a team with a reputation that matches the dead gods could come between your own wellbeing. Well my friend, without that team, where would I be? If I let something happened to you? Where would I be? I know we need more arcane power. I think our abilities to mend wounds are hurting more. Magic is rare these days and weaker than ever. We've done fine with the four of us. We'll continue our success and our names, wealth, and fortunes will all grow together."

"What happens when the day comes when your name and reputation is held against the lives of those you walk with?" Dauge asked quickly, as if he already had the question planned out.

Before Dash could answer, hard steps slamming into the wooden planks caught the four's attention. Dash was the first to turn around, mainly using it as a scapegoat to get off the touchy subject with Dauge.

A young lad, wearing off-red colored leggings and black boots made his way. His shirt and coat matched his leggings. He was nicely dressed with a matching hat and a silk white under shirt to finish it off. He was a young human no older than Legion probably. His face was clean and smooth. His brown eyes were thick but light.

"Sirs Dash, Legion, Dauge, and Pitt..." he started.

The four all stood and turned to the young man none of them knew. He clearly worked for the port system here in Agatha. He was a member of some guard somewhere belonging to Thox.

Dash stepped forward, seizing the opportunity to appear as the face of the group before the others could think. "We are. Who is in question of us?" Dash answered nobly.

"I was asked to bring you these. The carrier pigeons arrived this morning. Looks like you all are popular more than just in Thox." He smiled and pulled three rolled up scrolls from his side purse.

Dash met him and took the scrolls. The nicely dressed man showed courtesy, quickly bowed and turned to be on his way.

The first scroll was from Retired Eternian General Seth Redd.

"It's from General Redd," Dash started before reading ahead. "It's directed to you, Legion." Dash went ahead and read it. The others peered over his shoulder, doing the same.

Legion,

Magnus informed me of Bahaus' true purpose. My men have moved to end him. He informed you would be the one to take up the letter as he was heading this way. I've risen even more irregulars for the movement against the Eternian Tyrant and shall see this through. You, Magnus, The Free Armies, and your compatriots have an ally in Seth Redd. I will make it my personal duty to see your sister returned to safety.

Warmest Regards,
General Seth Redd.

"Huh," Dash started.

Legion smiled. It was good to know General Redd believed in the old motto, once an Eternian always an Eternian.

Legion went for the scroll from Dash's hands. Dash let loose the paper to open the next one in line. The second scroll carried a much heavier significance to the team. It was addressed to the Xavier boys, Dauge and Legion. Dash squinted his eyes trying to pry open the words that spelled their names, hoping behind them rested the characters that spelled out his own. They didn't. Though time and time he tried, the second scroll like the first was addressed to the Xavier boys. This one in particular carried Legion's little brother's name as well.

To the brothers Dauge and Legion of Taj Odin Xavier

It is I Davion. The warring has begun. Bahaus and his men were defeated at the gates of Emerald Greene. Drackice Black carries the responsibilities alone for the victorious day. He alone secured your sister's safety. This is a defeat Bahaus cannot recover from. Alas, his body was never found. He escaped. I know General Redd plans to move on Eternis. Eternis has nothing left. His movement is to protect against an enemy that, as we speak, is being ousted. This letter comes from an old friend. I am to protect your sister and I shall and forever keep you informed of her situations and whereabouts. I will call upon you soon. For your skills are needed still here on the outer lines of Thox.

Davion

Like the scroll before, the others peered over to see the words that had been put to it. Dauge took this scroll. Emotion came from him. Tears streamed from his eyes. Word came of his sister and she was better than when he thought last. He certainly owed a debt to Drackice Black and the Free Armies and possibly a noted thanks with donation to General Seth Redd.

"So it appears Dusk is safe with Drackice," Dash said.

"The lich knows we're here," Pitt reminded.

"Davion did claim his powers stretched across the entire Thoxen realm. He imbued my sister with something she didn't want and more importantly, she never asked for. Now, those powers are proving to be even more useful than first thought. Davion says she's alive and at Emerald Greene. We must prepare for the journey back to Emerald Greene immediately," Dauge countered to the group.

"Easy little brother," Legion said.

"We've only just got here. What can returning to the Crystal Cities do for us? Dusk is safe and secure with Drackice." Dash finished what Legion was thinking.

"Brother, what would returning back to the other side of the lands where the Crystal Cities lie do for any of us? Right now, we are in Thox. Our homeland is torn. We are welcomed here from past actions. Let us rejoice in our names here in Thox. Perhaps, we can earn a bit of coin while here," Legion said.

Dauge thought about Legion's words. His own brother, he thought. Would his own brother risk ill will against his sister? She was Dauge's twin, not Legion's. Legion was still her big brother and Dauge knew better.

Dash pulled the last scroll and opened it. He grinned. This was more like it. Seth Redd and Davion gave the two brothers the words they needed to move on without anymore backtracking. Dash didn't want the hype behind their names to die down anymore than it already had by going off to Eternis to see the late King Gerear buried. And all that ended in a ruckus and one he didn't want to be a part of. This scroll was perfect. It was exactly what he was looking for and it was the perfect thing to get them back on track. They'd been veering off too far. Now, it was time to get back to doing what they did best!

This letter was finally addressed properly, he thought.

Dash Riproc,

You do not know me. I am Stannor Augustus of the city Vorrellon. I've recently acquired the small Thoxen town and originally hail from our glorious capital, Xanon. I've come to ask you all to take up a charge for me. If you're interested, send a pigeon to Vorrellon informing me of your time arriving here. Everywhere I go within this new town's simple walls I hear the praise of your names. I ask now to put faces to those names and remove all doubt that the songs I've heard sung in your honor were not a drunken bard's attempt to make a few extra coins. This mission is dire and the reward shall fit you well. I trust I'll be hearing from you soon.

Lord Stannor Augustus of Vorrellon, Thox

"Legion, Pitt, Dauge… It seems our names have earned us proper recognition," Dash said, allowing his smile to revel in its own relentlessness.

"What is it?" Pitt asked, breaking away from the previous conversation. They were still trying to decipher which was the best plan of action based on the first two scrolls.

The four of them went over it all. Stannor Augustus spoke like a young man coming into power and coming into age all at the same time. It would be a good man to listen to especially when trying to re-begin their quests in Thox.

"So it's settled. We make our way to Vorrellon," Dash suggested, confirming his team was all on board.

"It seems to be the best move for us all," Pitt said.

"Dusk is safe. I yearn to expand my knowledge and power. I truly care not for Eternis or its people. If Bahaus has been defeated then my family will be freed," Dauge said. "I just assume return to the Republic. After all, I did fight for that kingdom's freedom."

"Right now, we are Thoxens now, at least for the moment. The Republic is a world away. Eternis has its own feuds to settle. With Magnus on our side, the Free Armies and Drackice are on our side. That means my sister is safe. Eternis will be safe soon enough," Legion said. "We are here and possess skills far beyond the common man. Let us earn our riches, test our skills, sharpen our wits, and become even greater names in Eternis. I hope to one day have men look at me the way they looked at my father." He sounded different. Reputation was never his reason before but then again, he was growing into his own just like the rest of them.

Chapter 41

Emerald Greene was beautiful. Well, at least parts of it were. The other parts were dirty and dark. It wasn't dark like the creature that came to see her nor was it dark like the innate things inside of her. It was just a dungy city. Then again, the city was built on mines.

Some of the ores were precious and beautiful. Others were rough and in need of refining. And then still, there were the Crystal Ores, which really threw the cities loads of coin. Money poured in after the Crystal Ores were discovered, the towns flourished and Drackice was good enough to personally show Dauge's twin and Legion's younger sister Dusk around the city full of history.

Dusk and Drackice spent most days together. Something about the man reminded her of her own lover, Kleiven Dar. Kleiven's own father redeemed himself in the fight against Bahaus by betraying his friend and slaying one of the hellish creatures that fought alongside him. What did happen to Bahaus? How was he able to escape? Where was Kleiven? Was he still alive? Was he okay?

The sun was setting. The moon was high and full. The night's weather was carefully woven to perfection. Drackice Black and Dusk Xavier walked the streets of Emerald Greene together talking of what was to come and who was to be where.

Drackice wore his favorite dark leggings and matching shirt and boots. They were his Ice Gator skin boots straight from the Frozen Sea south of Thox. His dark shirt was from the sewing talents of Korvina in the Republic. His dress was immaculate.

Dusk wore a simple white dress, nothing more. Her shoes were a woman's simple, small black boots. Her dark hair was pulled back revealing her sharp Eternian features yet her skin told the story of a desert kissed flower.

The streets were dying down. The shift workers made their switch and the night workers were already in place for the most part. Drackice took Dusk to a place in Emerald Greene she'd not seen yet, the Market Street; lined for two solid miles on both sides were businesses of all kinds. The streets were lit magnificently with strategically places torches and candle burning staves.

"So your Kleiven is with my father somewhere with your brothers?" Drackice asked. He fancied her. How could he not? She was beautiful and of good stock, like him.

"When Cale turned on his own son for the new king, Kleiven fled with my brothers. Will you see my family safely removed from the cells in Eternis?" she asked. She continued on with the conversation but her heart was slowly slipping deeper into the awe of the city's nighttime Market Street.

"Of course, my dear. I long for my father's return. I bet you'd have never believed the mining cities of Crystal to have such beautiful areas, did you?" he asked, smiling and gazing upon the tall and short structures himself.

Dusk was beautiful and hailed from good stock. Taj Odin Xavier, Dominick Gabriel Xavier, Adrian Xavier, her brothers, and the ancient pirate Darion Drake of the sea were all in her blood. She came from a powerful bloodline with strong times to the world's oldest city. His father always spoke of the brilliance of the city and its ability to always survive. And, she was beautiful. That made it all the more easy. She would bear his children and link the Black and Xavier houses.

"I never thought I'd see myself here. I never wanted any of this," she said. "I never wanted to leave the Republic." The dark thing inside her was staying dormant for the time, thank the faiths. She wished it gone and thought by ignoring it, it would leave her be.

"You never wanted to meet me or the Free Armies or see the splendor of Emerald Greene? I'm confused," Drackice replied, laughing.

"No," she said, lightly laughing as well. "I meant I just wanted a simple life, nothing more. I wanted to find a husband with a regular income and live peacefully without politics and risks and danger."

"Politics, risk, and danger run the world, little dove. It's better to have people like my father and yours leading the way than people like Bahaus," he responded.

"You're older than I first thought. Aren't you?" she asked.

"I'm a bit older, sweet child," he replied.

"I'm guessing you're close to your thirtieth birthday?" she asked.

"Aye, that is right. I will make thirty this year," he answered. "Do the lines and wrinkles of my face betray me so much?"

"No, I can see it in your eyes and your hands. Hands never lie. The wear on them, they've been worn and your eyes tell the story your hands lay down before those that see you," she answered.

"The stories they could tell. I served my father here in the Free Armies for three years before knowing he was such. He wasn't well pleased when he learned the truth of it, either," he continued.

"What do you mean?" she asked.

"He believed it to be a lie by my mother. Soon enough, my actions and mannerisms proved her words to be truthful. He embraced me after seeing my ferocity in combat. Now, I've become a proud trophy to him. With the defeat of the Eternian's rightful heir, I'm sure he'll embrace me even more." Drackice was middle-aged and ready to be acknowledged formally by his father.

"You won a great victory here. You defeated Bahaus."

"I defeated Eternis. Eternis isn't exactly known for its militant formality."

"You defeated Bahaus Sazos-Uil-Endail, King of Eternis, accomplished wizard and adventurer. Bahaus was present when Agromordeus was slain in the Red Mystic Mountains. He came against you with armies not all native to this world. He brought forth the powers of the hells and you fended him off! You saved me." She paused, smiling.

Drackice smiled back. He tried to fight it but she was playing to his noble and "knight in shining armor" side.

"You'll be responsible for freeing my family and getting me back to Thedia's oldest city," s.

"Let us not forget I'm the hand that started the piecing of Eternis' soul back together. I'm going to see to it Eternis is restored to its former glory," Drackice said. He wasn't patting his own back. He was reminding himself and her what he aimed to accomplish in the months to come.

Dusk interlocked her arm around Drackice's hulking bicep. He wasn't a monstrous man but he was deceptively built and strong. He wore clothes hiding his true physique, not for any real reason other than the man just liked loose-fitting clothes. They kept walking. Dusk didn't mean anything intimate by the act, she just felt safe and thankful to be with such an iron-willed man with an intellect to match his fighting prowess.

Drackice walked Dusk to Coal's Keep. It was once a massive inn and tavern for migrated workers, slaves, and the like to stay in until more permanent housing arrangements could be made. Coal's Keep had recently been purchased by a local gentry and for the last year its entire reputation began to change. It was also the place Dusk fell for the most as the night came on. Before, she stayed in Drackice's personal home but admitted to not feeling comfortable with it all. And it was never meant to be permanent but only to hold her over until her own personal room could be made ready.

Drackice already personally selected four elite guards from his most elite regiments. They were to watch and patrol her room and stay with her at all times. He liked the girl, but more importantly, returning her to Eternis would do wonders to his name, especially in the eyes of his compatriots and most importantly his father.

Dusk's room was pleasant. It wasn't exquisite. It wasn't flamboyant, either, but it was homey. It reminded her of a home, not necessarily her home but a happy home from a fairytale somewhere she remembered hearing about as a child.

It wasn't too large and held only one window for her to look out from her second-story room. It was just a single bedded room with drawers and closets for clothes and belongings. A small kitchen in the back with plenty of bowls, pots, and pans for her to make whatever she'd like. Right now, this was her life. Kleiven was gone and no matter how hard she wished nothing would get them closer for the moment. Her brothers were gone but thankfully for Drackice and the Free Armies, Bahaus was defeated, and thus, the accusations against her brothers should be dropped and dismissed. They would be free to return to Eternis if they so chose.

Dusk fell atop the feather top bed. She sank into the soft mattress. The quilts and sheets and blankets made it that much more comfortable. In the blackness behind her eyelids she saw the thing coming to her. He hadn't come for her in some time but now he was coming again. She tried to reopen her eyes but suddenly her body was just too tired and her eyes were forced to remain closed.

The darkness surrounded her, consuming her room and her life. There was nowhere to go and the beast within was near and getting nearer every minute. No, she said. No she begged again and again but the blackened skeleton doused with dark robes continued to hover closer and closer.

"You wish to be free," it said. "You feel something's lost or missing. You love Kleiven but stray every so often. You're looking for something. What you're looking for can't be found, it's you, the real you, the true and honest you."

The skeleton was closer now. Gems and rubies were still embedded in his bones. She knew the creature better now. She felt closer to him, connected to some degree. She was. Wasn't she? This thing swore it was honest and true. It forced her to reconsider her thoughts on it. It was necrotically alive. It was undead. How could it not be vile? It was vile but meant well. Was that possible?

"Angel, in human chains," he continued.

An angel in human chains, was it calling her an angel? Was it saying she was bound by human chains from an angelic existence? What was it trying to say? What did it want with her?

"What do you want with me?" she asked again. She felt she'd asked the question before.

"Your kindred sent me here. Now, I've only come to help release what's been caged throughout your entire life." The skeleton's voice soothed her. It made sense. She felt something else within her trying to come out, and for the first time since the connection to the creature, it wasn't him. It wasn't the inner powers he forced inside her. There was something more to her than she even knew. She started to accept it. It started to make sense. Whatever this was, it wanted nothing but for her to first embrace the powers he linked to her from within and to accept whatever it was he believed was lying dormant inside of her. She could do it, right? She could do this for him? She did want to, didn't she?

"What is it inside of me you want out so badly, skeleton? What is it you put inside me?" Her daring was increasing. The link between them was forming a bond even she could no longer deny.

"I am forever with you, child. You long for something you feel is missing between yourself and Kleiven. It's not Kleiven that's missing anything. Grath didn't have what you were looking for and Magnus' son Drackice won't either. You yourself do not even know. You will ruin what you have with those that love you if you deny what you are, my child."

She leaped up. The blackness was gone. The bleakness and aura of the dark creature was no longer around her but it still lurked about her room at Coal's Inn. She was awake. Sunlight leaked into her room from the room's single window. The warmth of the rays eased her mind and soothed the uncomfortable aura. Was it a nightmare? No, it was real and it was coming for her again.

Where was Kleiven? How she missed her favorite soldier. The creature was right. She'd done her lover wrong. She drifted away more than once in search of something she didn't even know she was looking for. If all of this came together and everything panned out, she would never disrespect the son of General Dar again. She loved him. She adored him. And she loved and adored how he cherished her every fiber.

There was a knock at her door. It was most certainly the guards watching over her at Drackice's command. She was awake. The day was at her feet. The darkness was behind her, or at least within her. The creature spoke of her letting out what's truly inside of her and on more than one occasion cleared with her it wasn't speaking of what it had brought to the table but what was already in her.

"My lady," a voice echoed through the door.

"I'm here. I'll be ready soon," she replied.

"Just checking on you," it responded.

Dusk smiled. She felt comfortable and safe. She made it to the window where the sun's rays lay across her face. The warmth of the rays soothed her mind even more. The day was ahead of her and it was a beautiful one. The man in charge of everything was a friend now and legitimately wanted to rescue her family and return her to her home. Kleiven was out there somewhere, she thought, looking down at the awakening city.

Below her, she saw workers carrying water and others walking the streets to their designated jobs and locations. Merchants and traders were setting up their mobile shops and the miners were loading carriages and buggies preparing for the long day that lay, ahead of them.

She couldn't get rid of her smile. She was excited to see Drackice Black, son of Magnus and current leader of the Free Armies. She was excited to see the rest of the city or at least some parts she'd not yet seen before. Bahaus was defeated. Eternis was to be restored. The faiths were behind her, she just knew it.

Chapter 42

Somehow by the dark faiths, Bahaus fled and survived all the way to the Red Mystic Mountains. He'd been there before. He, Cale Dar, and a band of others carved their path to the domain of Agromordeus, a Thoxen Necromancer with unrivaled skills and powers. There, Cale fell and Bahaus convinced his soul to turn to Asmodai for help. Agromordeus was killed and the bastard son of the King was among those rewarded for their bravery.

Now, the same city that he once acknowledged even when the King didn't acknowledge him had turned against him. Cale Dar turned against him! And what did it get him, killed! Bahaus recklessly rushed his body up and down mountains, grabbing carelessly at various points to help his body along. He regularly pulled rocks loose from their holding points and nearly found himself falling to his death on several occasions.

Finally he was free and in the open valleys the lower levels of the mountains had to offer. He was far from home and far from anything or anyone he knew, except the old stronghold that once belonged to Agromordeus and the Red Mystics before that.

Bahaus wandered the mountains alone. Wizards were frail creatures typically and he was no different. Alone, he knew he wouldn't last long at all. He failed Asmodai, the Arch Devil of the Hells. He was all out of roads to take for help. Bahaus was looking for miracle. He thought for a moment, even if he died here in the mountains, even if his body was ripped to shreds by one of the many wyverns that frequented these mountains, at least not one of his enemies could claim to have killed him. And those that defied him would have to forever wonder his true status amidst the world.

Again darkness was setting in. It would be cold soon. The rightful heir had enough magic to keep himself warm and fed. Bahaus was among the world's remaining elite wizards. Few had the powers he still possessed. Those that did mostly resided in Aflyndor. And Aflyndor wasn't too far away but it wasn't exactly close by either.

A small cave, perfect, he thought. It wasn't too deep, just like an indention in the mountains and it was low and the deepening dropped even lower into the cave. He would be safe there, for the time being.

Bahaus created fires and manipulated his magics to create simple foods to keep himself stuffed. Even though he knew better than to eat so much, the cocky and arrogant prince wasn't going to change his lifestyle. He wanted to gorge himself as he always did, and so he did.

He fell fast asleep. The warmth of the fire kept him as comfortable as could be. He disregarded the one major thought. Bahaus failed to realize with fires come smoke and with smoke comes the luring of others.

The rightful heir awoke. The fire was out. He yawned and stretched as if he were in the royal manor back in Eternis. He looked around and grabbed his things. It was time to move. He couldn't stay in one place for too long. What if the Free Armies sent hunters after him? They certainly had people that could track his trail. Was it worth it to them?

Bahaus pulled himself from the small cave and rose to his feet once again. Eternis' rightful heir dusted himself off and prepped his gear and belongings for the long journey ahead. Where would he go? Where was he going? The reality of it all crept in, though he tried to keep it out. He was Bahaus Sazos-Uil-Endail, the rightful heir of Eternis and the man who marched on the Crystal Cities by way of Eternis against the Free Armies.

He had a decision to make; either get as far away from the south as possible or find a way to regain his good graces with Asmodai and organize another army to reclaim what was rightfully his. Eternis always had allies. And he was the rightful heir. If he sent word, they would come for him. Banner men would flock to serve him; they'd have to. It was the way it had always been for Eternians and he was of the highest rank amongst them. Then again, it was the way it had always been and what of the place that sent war to the entire pantheon, Corvana? He'd not be known there. If he could somehow make it to Corvana, then he could start his life over again! He could begin again with nothing against him and no one hunting for him. He would have to leave Eternis in the hands of something or someone not deserving. And he couldn't live with that. Corvana would be a new start. However, Asmodai would still be angered with him; perhaps he could start again in Corvana and please the Archdevil.

Bahaus wandered for the coming days and nights in the mountains, remaining cleverly quiet when needed but never taking the cold option of a night without fire. His warmth and comfort while sleeping meant too much to him and something inside him told him if he were to compromise his comfort, he would be compromising who he was.

Finally, his arrogance caught up to him. He awoke one morning especially tired. The trek through the mountains was starting to get to him and the reality that he hadn't a clue as to where he was going. He knew the mountainous ways enough to guide him to Agromordeus' old hold, but to get there could kill him, he thought.

This time, when he arose from atop a small bed of flat rocks just off the main path and a few feet up on a mountainside, he noticed dozens of small furry green and brown creatures standing strong with their lizard like heads all fixated on him and their mini-pole-arms held high with their weapons' butts all placed firmly on the ground vertically.

They were a mix of goblinoid and reptile and even uglier in person. It'd been some years since Bahaus faced those vile things. He compared them to the likes of cockroaches and other unpleasant creatures. They wore next to nothing in regards to armor and either armed themselves with broken javelins, pikes, mini-pole-arms, daggers, knives, and even some carried short swords. And to top it off, there were dozens of them all scattered strategically throughout the path Bahaus had been following upward that led even deeper into the mountains.

"Perfect," he said.

The creatures didn't respond verbally but rather jumped back in fear, startled with the man's words.

"Fetch me a bit of good ale, decent vittles, and some more comfortable clothes," Bahaus said ever so arrogantly.

This time the more intelligent ones became angered, raising their weapons and pointing them all in his direction.

The creatures ranged from two and half to four feet in height. Their hides were scaly yet hairless and their reptilian heads were their only fear-imposing quality. The heaviest ones might have weighed around forty pounds.

Finally, one of the creatures spoke aloud. "Surrender!" it ordered.

Bahaus laughed. And then barked back at the creatures. "I gave you an order!"

The creatures hesitantly backed up again, but this time took a ground-standing position. Bahaus raised his fingers and sparks flew from his eyes and fingertips. The creatures backed up even further. They refused to completely cower down but their fear was evident.

One yelled, "Attack," loudly and forcefully.

Long and narrow was Bahaus' chosen grounds. The grounds beneath the kobolds turned black, shadowed like the sun was overcast. The flames on Bahaus' fingertips and eyes turned black with hatred and darkness. The fires flew up from his body and where there were shadows on the mountain's path, black flames mimicked their summoner.

Necrotic flames hot from the fires of the hells and imbued with the pains of necromancy flew up, engulfing and burning most of the dozens of kobolds. Those that survived the flames' heat seemed to rot necrotically away almost instantly. A single kobold was spared, the one that ordered the attack. When it was over, and it was over in just a matter of seconds, the lone kobold fell to the ground trembling in fear; it'd never seen such magical prowess in all its life.

"I am King Bahaus Sazos-Uil-Endail and I've faced your kind here in these mountains before. You miscreants are servants. Whom do you serve?"

Bahaus made it clear he knew kobolds weren't typically leaders and generally if groups were around, then those groups most likely were in the service of another. Bahaus wanted to learn just who these particular kobolds served.

The surviving kobold crawled back, trembling still. Screams of dying kobolds both from the heat of the fires and the necrotic powers infused in them embedded even more fear into him. The agonizing deaths of his kindred made his aggressor smile. He enjoyed the might of it. Bahaus relished in the fact that he alone just annihilated an entire kobold regiment. He remembered hearing as a younger man that even heroes can't walk alone in today's savage world. Even the mightiest of men need walk together to survive the wild of Thedia. And here he was in the Red Mystic Mountains standing alone, even if it was just against a few kobolds.

"We serve Erebrus, the awoken Titan of Darkness and Nyx his wife, the Titan of the Night. They're here in the mountains, sleeping. Aristophane is overseeing them. Aristophane will see them back to life!"

"What is Aristophane?" Bahaus asked, instead of asking who is, to be even more condescending, speaking of the creature's leader as a thing rather than a person.

"Aristophane is the Uniter of the Defeated, Keeper of the Beaten, Ruler of the Lost," the kobold explained.

"What is he?" Bahaus asked.

"She is… She is…" The Kobold tried to explain but it wouldn't come out.

"Well, spit it out!" Bahaus demanded.

"She's of outer blood," the kobold explained.

The outer blood, that term was used to describe Wargoyles, an ancient race of beings related to the gargoyles but far more fierce, logical, and larger in size. Unlike their cousins, wargoyles stood mostly like regular humanoids, reaching the heights of seven and eight feet sometimes.

"So, she's of the outer blood is she?" Bahaus asked.

"Yes, my lord." The kobold quickly turned to addressing the rightful heir in a way he knew would please him.

"My lord huh, well, I see you've come to terms with reality and understand your place among god men," Bahaus bellowed.

"Yes, my lord," he said again to Bahaus' pleasure.

"Do you know why wargoyles are said to be of outer blood? Do you understand what outer blood means?" he asked with the most arrogance he'd spoken with since meeting the little guy.

"N, no my lord," the kobold replied.

"Of course not, you're just a piss ant miscreant servant aren't you?" Bahaus' arrogance instilled yet even more fear into the little creature.

"Y, yes my lord," he answered.

"They're called outer blood because they're not Thedian natives. They're like shadow elves, not of this world. Their true origins come from places no longer linked to our perfect planes. You're probably lost in my words, speaking of planes and such. You've no clue of the planes."

"I do my lord," he said, happily smiling. His dialect was broken and quickly spoken but Bahaus easily made out his goblinoid tongue.

"Ah, I care not for this conversation any further. Take me to your domain. Take me to those you serve, your higher ups," Bahaus ordered.

The once "fierce" kobold smiled thankfully for the mercy the mighty wizard had just shown him. He quickly agreed to oblige the arcane caster. He explained his name was "Gold Piece" and the reasoning behind his name was certainly worth hearing. Bahaus agreed to entertain the little guy as the two walked alongside one another in route to Gold Piece's superiors.

Chapter 43

Dash and the team made it rather safely to Vorrellon. The smell of freshly cut timbers and the taste of sawdust in the air really quenched the team's thirst. It gave them all a feeling of satisfactory to some degree.

The four walked proudly through the town that was still in the building phase. The slamming of hammers and the grinding of saws filled the air. They all looked around, wondering how their names could have made it this far already.

"This town's going to be beautiful one day," Pitt said.

"It most certainly will," Dash seconded.

"How do you think our names made it this far so quickly? I'm curious as to how this Lord Stannor acquired our names?" Pitt replied.

"Our names are growing here in Thox and they're going to continue to grow. Serving things like Davion, or creatures or, well, whatever you want to call them... Serving things like it on the frontlines will either boost your reputations or destroy it quickly," Legion added.

Dauge kept silent, keeping a keen eye on things a few feet behind the other three. His gear was good now. His armor was good and a fresh set of armblades amongst other things, were at his side. He had the opportunity to fashion them whilst traveling to Vorrellon.

"You know, Dauge, most people have their gear prepared before taking up to the wild." Dauge listened to his older brother speak to him from affront.

He knew his older brother was right. His old armblades were damaged and they needed to be replaced. He purchased the gear and had the knowhow to get it done. Besides, it didn't take him too long to make this specific pair and they were the best pair he'd ever fashioned.

"That time with the Lotus people really changed you, brother, you know that." Legion continued.

Dauge looked up at his brother ahead of him and then turned his eyes back to the "city in building" all around him. Of course he knew the Lotus people changed him. He was who he was because of the Lotus colonies. Who knows who or what he'd have become without them.

"We must find Stannor," Dash reminded the group.

"We're still an arcanist short. Our wizard is gone. And we've traveled all this way on a whim that whatever Stannor has to tell us was worth our time." Legion didn't like the situation at all. Then again, he was just taken from his true homeland after only returning to see the late king put to rest.

"We'll be fine. I have enough in me to keep us strong. We're a strong a team, so strong that lords are calling on us here in Thox, one of Thedia's mightiest kingdoms!" Dash said, reminding Legion just why someone like Stannor would call upon them.

"It's still early. Midday has yet to even break. Let us find a place to rest. Once done, we can spend the rest of the day relaxing and regrouping and discuss how we'll approach Lord Stannor tomorrow," Legion suggested.

"It's not even midday, the trek to get here is behind us. Let us find him now. I'm eager to find out what provoked the future lord into calling on us," Dash replied.

"I'm with Legion, Dash," Pitt chimed in.

Dash's face fluttered with grimace. His mind numbed with mental pains hearing the barbarian speak out. He was the leader of the party. The team was assembled because of him. If not for him, the two brothers would still probably be serving the Republic of New Magic and Pitt would be killing for the entertainment of the crowds.

"Pitt—" Dash started.

"Dash is right," Dauge interrupted.

Dauge speaking caught the rest of the team off guard. They all stopped in their tracks. Looking around, it was a perfect place to stop. They were near a giant hole in the dirt in the ground. This would surely be the place where the town well would be. They all wondered, why were the well diggers not working? After all it wasn't even midday yet.

The three turned around and looked at Dauge. He was still casually strolling with his keen eye on everything. The three others of the team waited and allowed Legion's little brother to catch up.

"Dauge, what makes you side with Dash this day?" his older brother asked.

"He's right, brother," Dauge answered.

"I would think it would be better on a good rest after we've had the day to scope the city and learn of our surroundings," Legion challenged.

Dash sat back and watched the two brothers' discussion. He couldn't help but grin. He was the leader and finally, it was working out to his advantage.

"Normally I would only be able to agree with your words, brother. We are in Thox in the soon-to-be-new city of Vorrellon. Whatever caused Stannor to call upon us could be dire. If so, we should not waste any more time," Dauge said. "Dash and I will seek out Stannor. You and Pitt fetch us all a few rooms somewhere."

"I don't like the idea of splitting up. I don't care if we're in town or not. We don't now these parts," Pitt suggested.

"Right now and since the beginning, we've all been bumbling and stumbling over each other, arguing over what to do and whose in charge. Right now, as I see it. We're all free to act in any way we choose. Our history speaks for itself. We've held off an undead incursion and served Lord Quinn and Davion the Lich, of Thox. Our names have grown. Let us not have our reputation exceed us in the flesh. Not one of us here is better than Dash in speaking diplomatically. I simply agreed to walk with him so not one of us was alone. It would appear better for us all if Dash was to clean up a bit from the trek and speak to Stannor with the notion his team was in town taking care of business and prepping rooms and the like for an extended stay here in Vorrellon."

The other three were silenced. Dash's grin was too much to keep in. He was right. Dash could appear before Stannor with his "men" behind him prepping the team for their stay in Vorrellon. It would make them all look a bit more sturdy and together while in Stannor's presence. Of them all, Dauge was the only to point out they surely didn't act like a team.

Legion and Pitt silenced themselves and dropped their heads. They had nothing to say to the youngest Xavier. He was right. Even with the learning of his blood not being fully human, Dauge kept his composure and seemed to excel mentally far above and beyond the others. He regularly seconded Dash's decisions but in truth, he felt the half-eladrin was nothing more than a puppet anyway.

"Fine," Legion replied. "I'll listen to my brother. Pitt, you should as well. Dash, I guess its up to you to find Stannor and discuss his charge with him on all of our behalves."

Legion slapped the back of the hulking goliath's arm. Dauge further signaled that he'd just go with his brother and Pitt and leave Dash to take care of his "leader" duties. Dash smiled, finally happy and thankful that his team was complying. It didn't make him feel any better that they were listening to Dauge instead of him. Nonetheless, he was still getting it all taken care of accordingly.

He looked back at the three remaining of his team. He thought of Kraydia and how he wished she was still there. Where was she and why did she truly go? Would he ever see her again? In truth, he knew why she left. He knew exactly why she left. Knowing everything, he smiled. He knew their paths would cross again. He just hoped the time in which it did was sooner than later.

Dash was alone in the town of Vorrellon now. His team was taking care of everything else while he prepared to speak to the lord of Vorrellon on his own, on behalf of the team.

Meanwhile, Pitt, Dauge, and Legion found a room in a nearby inn that had not even been named. The building wasn't fully erect; however several rooms were capable of housing guests and the local lead man over the project confessed the town could use the extra coin.

The team took but one room, a large one. They paid handsomely for it. The room was not yet outfitted for a stay. However, the men's bedrolls and personal belongs would suit just fine in the meantime.

After dropping off their belongings and slipping into more comfortable clothes, Legion decided it was time for a stroll through town, alone. He wanted time to clear his head and think about everything currently at hand.

A large patch of grass, a clear opening not yet tainted by the ideas of man caught his attention first. Strangely, the only belonging he kept at his side was Mourning Star. He kept it tied neatly at his side as he walked through the high grass.

Legion fell to his knees and rolled to his back. The comfort of the untamed wild, he thought. It was beautiful and releasing all at the same time. How did he come to be here? How did he come to meet Dash Riproc and the goliath Pitt? Somehow, through everything he was to find employment with Stannor Augustus of Xanon, now of Vorrellon.

Legion closed his eyes. He wasn't tired but the soothing rays of the midday sun caressed his face and skin. He wore simple clothes of basic color. His breeches went just past the knee and his shirt was cut out at the shoulders. He almost looked like a beggar but the style and fabric of the clothes would've proved otherwise.

"Are you lost, my lord?" A voice came over him simultaneous to something interfering with his sun.

"You're in my way... voice... You're blocking my sunlight," he replied to the voice.

The voice belonged to a woman. There was a sensual taste to it. Legion wanted to open his eyes but his own personality told him not to. He didn't know the woman. Though he wanted to open his eyes, his persona told him to keep them closed. He didn't know the voice or the woman it belonged to but her voice was pure like a dampened leaf in the rain. He wanted to open his eyes but he was Legion Cage Xavier of Taj Xavier, of Dominick Xavier, of the House Xavier and he had a reputation to uphold.

"Forgive me my lord, but your lying in my grass," she replied, eloquently smiling.

Legion opened an eye and glared at the woman. She was Thoxen through and through. Her hair was thick and flowing just past her shoulders. Its brown color soaked up the sun's rays better than most. Her eyes matched one of his own. In the growing times, Legion's eyes transcended; his right eye colored deeper and deeper blue while his left was silver, the ancestral color of his mother's side. Uniquely enough, his brother Dauge's eyes did exactly the same.

Her own eyes matched his left one. Though hers were a bit brighter and more purifying than his own. She was tall for a woman, maybe five feet, eight inches or so. She wasn't thin, nor was she thick. She was perfect, with weight all in the right places.

"Your grass?" he asked with his one silver eye open.

She smiled. "It's where I take my breaks from work during the day and I always lie just there." She pointed to Legion's lying body.

Her face's beauty burned through it. It was covered in soot and ash. Her clothes were disgustingly tattered. She'd been working hard, manually. And yet, she was ever so cheerful. What gives? He questioned to himself.

"Forgive me. What is it you do here in Vorrellon? You look a little dirty. Have you found your ways in the fields of mining?" he asked, standing up to greet the woman formally.

She smiled and laughed again. "Oh, by the heavens no! I assist in the unloading of carriages. Sometimes, it can be physically demanding but I'm nowhere near a mine working. I'm just dirty like this because I had to unload a few wagons in the mines here earlier today."

Legion stood and looked the woman in her eyes. She was beautiful and didn't belong anywhere near the life she was making for herself.

"How did you find your way to such a life?"

"There just wasn't a lot of opportunity where I grew up, thief," she said, still smirking.

"Thief?" Legion questioned, confused.

"Yes, I said thief. You did steal my patch of grass," she replied playfully.

Legion laughed and before he could move or say a word, she launched herself past him, diving and rolling to her back in the very spot he just moved from.

Legion turned to look down on the crazy girl. She was human, toothsome and voluptuous. She moved with a sense that could catch a sly man's attention. Something about her said simple and cozy but something else said guilt-stricken pleasure and beauty. She was certainly meant for more than what she was doing.

"What is your name girl?" he asked.

"Your name first," she barked back playfully.

"I am Legion Cage Xavier of the House Xavier, my lady," he said, standing strongly and proudly.

She was taken back. She knew the name and the house. And more importantly, she knew his name. She hailed from one of Thox's cheapest villages. Where she came from, there wasn't much to offer. Her family had nothing and she set out on her own to make it for herself. She was young, younger than Legion, but her eyes told a story of a strong woman who'd worked hard every second of her life to acquire just half of what anyone else would expect.

"I know the name," she said confidently. Her laugh was gone. Her jokes were gone. It was known in Thox he walked with the lich Davion at one time. He fought off the undead incursion for favor in the kingdom. Then, before he could get it, he left for Eternis.

"You helped fight the undead incursion in the southeast didn't you?" she asked.

"I did," he answered.

She smiled but her smile wasn't real. She was painting it across her face. Something about the man was bothering her. Legion didn't ask, nor did he care. What he did care about was her name.

"Now, your name, little dove?" he asked.

She stretched her body and kept her eyes fixed on him. Something about him terrified her and he knew it. She wasn't hiding it at all. She wasn't offering the information either. He was curious. Why was she so scared of his name?

"Why are you afraid, girl? And tell me your name," he asked again with a kindness.

"I've heard stories of your father," she replied quickly.

"What's that got to do with anything? My father was a legendary man and the cause for Corvana's fall."

"He called forth dragons and summoned hordes of undead in the war. Do you possess those same powers, lord Legion?"

"My father's histories and exploits have long been exaggerated. I'm not certain which ones are true and which ones aren't. I know he summoned dragons and I know he raised the dead to fight for him. How he did it, I've not a clue. I'm just a simple man with a flail, my lady. I carry a chained morning star I call Mourning Star," he replied honestly.

She laughed from her stretched out, lying position. "I'm sure you believe that."

"Of course I believe it. It's the honest truth," he said.

She arose from the ground and grabbed the warrior's hands and took them into her own. She locked her eyes onto his, searching deep within them. He'd never had a girl or anyone do anything like this to him before.

"What are you doing?" he asked.

"You're becoming something special. You come from a special blood. Look at me. Look into my eyes."

Legion stared deeply into the woman's eyes. She was flawless, he thought. Yet, she was born of simple blood. She was born to the cheap side of society. The dead gods had robbed her of a noble birthright but countered with a physical blessing beyond measure, at least to Legion's eyes.

"You're fearless. You hope to one day make your House as proud of you as they are you ancestors. You love your brothers and sisters dearly," she guessed.

"Sister," he said, correcting her.

"Sister?" she asked.

"I have but one sister. Other than that, you are flawlessly correct," he replied.

She smiled again.

"I love my brother Dauge and my sister Dusk the most. I am closest to them. I love my entire family deeply. I do yearn to exceed my father's name and his father's name and so on. I want to become my own man as my father once did." He spilled out his true ambitions to a woman whose name he still didn't even know.

"You tell me all of this and you know not my name," she said, tracing her tongue across her top lip.

"You did pretty good work with my desires already. I assumed I'd just clarify and clear up all the rest."

"I am Kattya," she said.

"Kattya, do you have a sir name?"

"I do not. Where I am from, people born of our status rarely carry them," she replied, this time with a little less life than before. Her brightness and verve was vivaciously powerful but speaking of her origins certainly got to her.

"Well, Kattya of ordinary origins, I'd like to employ you myself," Legion suggested playfully, yet truthfully, back to her.

"Employ me, I have work," she responded.

"It's not fitting of you," he said.

"And what is?" she asked.

"I have maybe a little over two hundred golden coins in my purse. I'll pay a year in advance at five gold a month for you to watch my belongings, tend to my clothes, and cook for me while I'm present here. When I need you, I'll send pigeons here to the room of my inn."

Kattya didn't know what to say. Fortune never favored her. She'd worked hard her whole life to get where she was. She didn't have much but she could afford decent food and a roof over her head and that was enough. How did she know he wasn't lying? She had a steady income, but from her standpoint, she'd never have anything more than what she had right now. Wait, he said he'd pay her in advance? How did he know she wouldn't just take the money and go once he left?

"How do you know you can trust me?" she asked, her playful side coming back.

"Ten months in the year, five gold a month, fifty golden coins handed to you by a man you just met from the legendary House Xavier. That's a quarter of my wealth. As a traveling man, a man who never sits too long in one place, it's in my best interest to keep wealth. I need a great deal of it to continue onward. And if you trust in my success in what I do, then you can trust you'll be paid even more handsomely when I return from whatever it is Lord Stannor wants us to do."

Legion pulled out his purse and secondary sack to place the fifty coins into. Kattya couldn't believe her eyes. Part of her didn't want to take it. Elite soldiers and guards who risk their lives every day don't make five gold a month. A good income lay somewhere between two and three gold a month and most didn't make that.

"Why would you do this, Legion Cage Xavier of the House Xavier?" she asked thankfully.

""You're too pretty to be doing what you're doing. I'm going to need someone to watch my belongings here. Maybe not for a year, but I will need someone to take care of my business in town while I'm away. And when I return, should you decide to travel with me, I would keep you under my employ."

"Wow, I don't know what to say," she replied, stunned. "Why so much and why me? How do you know you can trust me? I just don't get it."

"Because my dear, I know you're not happy with your life and you know you're meant for more, but you're stuck in a place that won't let you move forward and you can't get back to. You know I will return and you'll be paid again even before the year's finished."

"Now who's the face reader?" she replied playfully.

"Come, let us introduce you to my brother and friends. You'll come to like them as I have. And you'll come to love my dear brother as I have. Let us have a fine meal with fine wine to celebrate the starting of a new life for us both," he said, smiling.

She entwined her arm with his and gave the okay. The two walked off together. Legion thought to himself, was this truly a wise idea? If not, he was out fifty gold pieces and that was it. His way of life would surely bring him more and from the pigeons' letters; soon his family would be reinstated as well.

Meanwhile, Dash found his way to the construction site of a great steeple. It was to be dedicated to both the Draconic and Angelic Orders collectively. The town didn't have enough money to erect two and the majority of its followers were split. Stannor made a wise decision, he thought.

Finally, Dash met Stannor through the advising of a few guards. He was lightly guarded, keeping two lightly armored soldiers around him at all times. For scare tactics maybe, both of his guards were red-scaled dragonborns.

Stannor was an average-sized man just under six feet tall by a few inches. His brown hair was thick and wavy, extending down just past his neck. It wasn't trimmed or well kept at all and neither was his full-length beard. He looked older than first described. He was a bigger man with a solid gut. Unlike some overweight, their weight just flopped as loose skin and fat, Stannor's was solid to the touch. He was just a thick and hearty man.

When Dash approached, Stannor was screaming and yelling at the workers building the steeple. Some of the foremen looked terrified, Dash thought. A few guards stood around as well, but they were probably just keeping their posts manned, he thought. Lord Stannor was easy to pick out after the locals described him.

"Lord Stannor," Dash started. He was still dirty and the grit and grime of the trek to Vorrellon still reeked from him.

The burly man turned and smiled but looked a bit confused. "Hello my boy, I'm afraid I don't know you." He walked over to greet him.

"I am Dash Riproc. You sent for me," Dash answered.

Stannor's clothes were brown and dirty. He looked like the kind of guy that would get his hands dirty on a daily basis, someone who didn't truly understand the concept of being a "noble" lord. He was the kind of man that wanted to get his hands dirty and feel like he was a part of something.

"You've already made it here, haven't you. Well, look at you," he said with a smile. "Look at me. I'm filthy. I wasn't born into lordhood you know? They say we lords that came from nothing make the best lords because we know both sides of it."

Lord Stannor took off like he'd known Dash for ages. He spoke of how coming from nothing made him understand both the leadership and servings sides of the spectrum. Perhaps he was right.

"My lord, forgive my dress. I came as fast as I could as I didn't know the severity of your calling."

"It's more personal than anything, Dash."

"Is someone in trouble?"

"No, no, nothing like that at all, young friend. I hear you're a good lad. Are you?"

Dash smiled. "I try to be, my lord."

"Here, hold a sec..." Stannor started. The future Lord of Vorrellon turned to the workers of the steeple and yelled. "Keep Quigg's Prints and run with it. It shouldn't prove to be too difficult!" After, he turned back and threw an arm over Dash's neck and slapped him in the belly with his other hand. "Come on, let's get a drink in you and discuss just why I called you here."

Dash went along with it and walked with the lord. For some reason, Dash pictured a man much different in his head, but Stannor was here and he was real. Stannor admitted the job was real, thus proving no one had sent the team a false message through a pigeon. What would Lord Stannor Augustus have in store for them now?

Lord Stannor brought Dash back to his temporary private residence. It was a small hut built strong for the future lord. There wasn't much to it and it was built just next to a flowing stream on the backside of the city. The walls were made mostly of stone, with straw and wood making up the roof of the place. It was pretty nice for the situation and would probably serve as someone's permanent home eventually, but not a lord.

Dash entered the man's temporary quarters right behind him. There were papers and scrolls scattered everywhere. There were a few swords and scabbards and other weapons here and there as well. Stannor walked to a small chest in the back and opened it. Dash watched on as the future Lord of Vorrellon pulled out a very special looking wineskin.

"This here's Nine Wines." He poured himself a small cup.

"Nine Wines, my lord?" Dash asked.

Stannor walked back through the mess of his place and handed Dash a freshly poured cup. Dash obliged the big man and took it. Stannor quickly went to pouring himself another.

"Drink warm, it goes down better. I prefer colder poisons usually but this... This Nine Wines is my favorite," he said.

Dash took a swallow. It was inimitably tasty and refreshing. He had to take another and before he knew it, the entire cup was empty.

"Good, eh?" Stannor asked, smiling.

"Nine Wines, where did you get it? I'd never heard of it before," Dash questioned.

"From the Nine Kingdoms boy, where else. And it's the finest in the world by my account," Stannor replied.

"It's a mighty fine drink, my lord," said Dash.

"Now, I'm sure your concerned as to why I brought you here."

Finally, Dash thought. The drink did catch his attention. So far, they'd fended off an undead incursion, aided Davion the Lich, assisted Lord Quinn, and now Lord Stannor. Their names in Thox would grow above all others soon. Soon, lords would be lining up to hire his team and they would all have to go through him. His name would grow. His fame would grow. His pockets would grow. He would become as household as a sword to a swordsman.

"I've brought you here to help establish myself and Vorrellon," Stannor said.

Dash said nothing. Stannor offered to fill his cup and Dash silently accepted.

"The nobles, royals, and politicians won't give me the coin to get this place going. I wasn't supposed to be the lord, you know. I'm going to have to do it on my own. You'd think Thox would help it own to become stronger but Vorrellon only broke ground by happenstance. It's too much detail and politics to get into, my boy." Another big gulp, this time straight from the wineskin itself, stopped the man from speaking. He sighed gratified with its taste and started again.

"I've come across an old map to a city lost in time. My informants and scholars have told me a thousand tales of what was down there. I know this: it's the last known place Alcarus was ever seen. The tales of his journeys end here in this city I've discovered."

"Alcarus, I've heard the name, the fallen paladin right, the blackguard?"

"Correct eladrin," Stannor replied, not fully taking note that Dash was but only half eladrin. Then again, he probably didn't care either way what Dash's blood lineage was.

"How do you know so much about Alcarus? From what I understand, he disappeared in the ancient citadel of his god Asmodai, the Arch Devil. Azra Goetia has never been searched or plundered. It's never been discovered. Only recently have my years of searching brought forth the necessary maps to navigate a body to its old destination."

"They're tales of Azra Goetia sending waves of wars across the lands and even severing a few kingdoms' lifelines. Are you sure you've found Azra Goetia?"

"I am my boy. And you'll be the first to set foot in there. Think of what that'll do for your reputation."

"And what is it you want?"

"I need three thousand more pieces of gold to finish outfitting this city the way I'd like.

Rumors claim Alcarus had three gold bars. It tells how he acquired them and where they came from but never tells whether he spent them or not. Golden bars generally run about"

Dash simultaneously finished his words with him, "Two thousand gold apiece."

"Right," Stannor said.

"What about everything else?"

"My boy, I fought in wars and even plundered a few crypts myself. Those days are long behind me. I care not for all of that and I live by the rule..." He paused to let Dash brace for it. "Pigs get fat and hogs get slaughtered."

"So, you want us to bring back three thousand gold for you and what of anymore we may find, if we indeed even find the three thousand?"

"If your full take isn't three thousand, then you keep sixty percent of the take yourself and I'll make do with what you bring me. If you do manage to bring me the three thousand, well then my boy, whatever else you find is yours free and clear."

Dash laughed. "I'm not sure how to take this. I got to tell you, I didn't think you'd be sending me after riches for you."

"You're young lad. Take this opportunity to put a little coin in your pocket and outfit your boys as best you can. You'll also have faction with me you'll never need to strengthen. Before you leave, I'll have a look at your boys. I want to see who they are, learn their crafts, and see what they carry. And when you're done, we'll take a second look, eh?" he suggested, laughing.

"Agreed. I think I may be able to convince them. If you truly found the city Azra Goetia, Asmodai's lost citadel, I'm sure we'll find more than enough to keep all of our purses filled. I remember hearing the tales of Alcarus the Anti-Paladin as a child. He once served Fluvius, High Knight of Praetheon, Arch Angel of Wrath. The stories say he turned against both Fluvius and Praetheon, right?"

"Aye, they do. I can't promise you Azra Goetia is what the tales say it is. If even a fraction of it is true, then it should be worth the dive," Stannor added, suggesting that diving into and searching through the old city would most certainly be worth it.

"In my teachings of legend and lore as a child, I've come to learn the differences between folklore and historical accuracies. The documents of Azra Goetia are too spot on to not be real, Lord Stannor. I am honored you've requested my team for this charge. It will be an honor to see Vorrellon built to its true potential, under your watch."

Stannor grinned, pouring Dash one last glass of Nine Wine and finishing the rest of the wineskin off himself.

"I feel the same way. I feel Azra Goetia is real and the graphic stories of Alcarus are too vividly detailed from eye witness accounts to be false, agreed?" Stannor asked of Dash.

"Agreed, my lord."

"Well then, it is settled. Fetch your team and tomorrow evening we shall all feast. I shall have a look at them. And when its finished, I shall have yet another look at them," Stannor said.

"Yes, my lord."

"The Xavier boys of Eternis, Taj's sons, Dominick the Duelist's grandsons walk with you, do they not?"

Dash gritted and smiled. At one time, that was precisely the reason he recruited them. He wanted them to walk with his team, not only because of their skill and unique back-stories and training, but because he knew their names would certainly enhance the credibility of the team and potentially get them places they otherwise wouldn't be able to get to, at least in the beginning anyway.

Now Legion was getting so much attention that some people were forgetting whose team it was and who built them. People were forgetting it was he who forged them and he who led them and it should be he who got the recognition.

"Aye, yes my lord, they do walk with me."

"Storm Stars of the broken House of Stars spoke very highly of you after the undead incursion. The lot of you disappeared before you could be rightfully honored."

"I know the man."

"He's a good lad."

"He is."

"Some of the boys that follow him I don't trust too much but he's just like Typherion himself. If I didn't know better I'd say he was the good dragon incarnate."

"I am honored to know him, my lord. I got word that he left for the Nine Kingdoms."

"I wouldn't know, my boy."

Stannor walked out from his temporary village hut and Dash followed him. He began making his way back toward a side of town Dash hadn't been to yet. Dash walked closely behind the lord. Everything was going perfectly, he thought. This was going to be the quest that put them on the map. Not only was he going to discover the city and be the first to step foot in Azra Goetia in a thousand years, he would also have a hand in Vorrellon becoming one of the wealthiest of Thoxen cities. The way Dash saw it, the more gold he gave to Stannor the bigger his investment.

This would be a strong investment. He hoped to double what Stannor asked for. And when Vorrellon flourished, the people would know it was he and those that followed him that made it happen. To further the genius of it all, Dash apparently knew something Stannor did not. Or if Stannor did know, he truly was a kind soul.

Alcarus was said to wield a powerful shield, one that made him nearly untouchable in combat. The stories of his demise are foggy. None claim he wielded his shield when it happened. Most stories talk of legendary warriors or wizards with legendary staves or swords or weapons. Alcarus was a fallen paladin of Praetheon, the Arch Angel of Wrath, and yet was known for the shield that protected him.

Dash knew more. Dash knew there were those that followed him with gold and fortunes of their own. One of which was said to be a dragonborn sorcerer with a staff so powerful it leveled half a city on its own. Hagaldre Corwarya was said to be his name. The things that could be found and sold could retire them all a dozen times. Still, there were things there that could set them apart from the rest of today's world. Azra Goetia would be the thing that brought them to the next level in the eyes of their peers, thanks to their part in the undead incursion, Storm Stars and his kind words, and now Stannor Augustus, Lord of Vorrellon.

Chapter 44

Dusk awoke. Her dreams were getting worse. Each night she awoke to feel herself in a deeper sleep. As the days passed, her friendship with Drackice felt strained. It was becoming too difficult to face the coming days.

Drackice tried to appease her and comfort her as best he could. It was to no avail. Finally, at least word came in that Former General Seth Redd was preparing for his march on Eternis from Valakuza.

Dusk walked the Crystal City of Emerald Greenee trying to find her way. She tried to understand the dark entity haunting her. It was coming to her. Not only were his powers imbedded in her slowly trying to come out, there were more powers, powers in her that he also tugged on, and soon she'd learn of those powers herself as well.

She dreamed of non-existence and re-existence over and over. What did it all mean? The world suddenly fell different to her eyes and tastes. Nothing was what it seemed. Now, when her eyes fell upon a complete stranger, her mind raced to dig into his psyche. She'd see a fisherman and feel his pain. She'd feel his struggle with the sea and the challenge of chasing the game. She'd systematically understand the sorrow he brought his family by never being there and the sadness his wife and children felt. Everything was becoming linked to her. The atmosphere, the ground, the elements, the world, life, death, it was all becoming too connected with her.

Then, the night came when the creature would once again answer her questions. Some were ones he'd answered a hundred times and others were new. She awoke and rose from her bed. This time the creature was standing and not hovering. The room was still present and the eternal black all around them was absent this time.

His crystallized bone imbedded with gorgeous gems and stones mesmerized her. This time, she could feel the magic radiate from within them. His eyes bled a glowing magma-like substance but it wasn't hot. And it only leaked down to the bottom of his jawbone. As it fell from its face, it dissipated into thin air.

He was more real than he'd ever been and she knew his name, Davion the Arch Lich. He wasn't scary and vile anymore. He was beautiful and the craftsmanship of his body was flawless. Yes, the craftsmanship, the body in which he stood with before her was not his own. It was something created, perhaps by him?

This time, his cloaks weren't dark and dirty. They were bright and flamboyant; he wore a red king's robe with golden designs dancing across it all the way down. Beneath the red were whites to offset his cold wrought iron black bones perfectly.

"Davion, Davion the Arch Lich of Thox. Davion of Aflyndor. Davion the Defender of Lost Magics?"

"I am," he replied.

She looked around. Her room was still in the same position she left it before falling asleep. This time, for the first time, she was awake. She felt the powers he spoke of so often to her more than she'd ever felt. And she knew he knew it.

"You've come to free me. Free me from my own self and release my being to its true state."

"You understand now," Davion replied solemnly.

"I do," she said.

"Do you know what you are, my child?" it asked.

"I am one with this world, am I not?"

"You are. Do you know to what depth your connection lies?" it further questioned.

She thought she knew. She wanted to answer but didn't want to seem foolish in front of her…in front of her…mentor? Yes, he was becoming her mentor and guide through life. She was accepting it. She liked it. She was thankful and truthfully, she loved it. Why did she ever deny him? Why did she ever challenge anything he had to say? She waited. She would let him answer. She would hear what he had to say.

"Your father is Taj Odin Xavier, son of Dominick Gabriel Xavier of the powerful Xavier House of Eternis. Your father was touched by undeath of the most powerful caliber. Xavius Froth, father of the undead and the first of his kind kissed your father. Your father would never be the same; his blood forever changed, churning with the pure undeath of the entity."

"I know my father and the man who raised me," she replied quickly.

"Your lifespan will far exceed your human friends, girl." Davion slowly started up again.

His words had her taken back a step. She didn't know what to say. Was everything inside her from her father?

"Your mother's powers are what's brewing inside you. They're pulling themselves violently out of your brother as we speak, child. In time, your father's touch will come to you to. Your mother comes from a people whose makeup has the blood of elemental creatures from foreign planes mixed in their veins. Your mother was a Genasi."

"My mother was human," She replied in defense, trying not to believe his words.

"There's more," he continued. "Genasi are mainly elemental and generally broken down into air, earth, fire, and water. The common names for them are Earthsoul, Firesoul, Windsoul, Stormsoul, and Watersoul. Your mother's manifestation is not among them. Her connection is to the entropic plane of nothingness, the Endless Void. Your blood is among the countered Genasi, the corrupted manifests, in the inversions of the true. Cindersoul, Causticsoul, Plaguesoul, and then your mother's line, the Voidsoul. You exist from your mother's blood, which comes from the Endless Void of nothingness. Accept it, and your powers will grow. Deny it, and it will punish you endlessly, until you die."

"You're telling me I'm not human?"

"You're not fully human, no. Have you not listened to me at all, child?"

"I have. I'm just not sure I want to believe it."

"You should. The sooner you come to embrace it, the sooner it shall embrace you. One need not fear the darkness when one is the darkness. Do you understand, child?"

"I think so," she said, concerned.

"Why is the blood of a Genasi in your veins bothersome to you?"

"Well, I was born in the Republic of New Magic but I always knew I was Eternian. Eternians of human descent are said to carry some of Thedia's oldest blood."

"That blood is still within you," Davion confirmed.

"Yes, but you see, good lich, I've always known Eternis was my home and Eternians keep their purest bloods in higher esteem. They'll never accept me as I am, as not a true human of Eternis."

"Even if your mother was human, she was not Eternian and your obstacle would remain the same."

He was right. To think she was not a simple human of Eternis still condemned her to some degree, didn't it? Perhaps the truth of her heritage didn't change a thing? Maybe it was nothing? Then again, she was never truly good at lying to herself.

"My father tainted my blood with the purest blood of the undeath. My mother gave me the blood of nothingness. And my father again united it all with the oldest of all human blood, Eternian."

"You're a special soul, child. You should not waste your existence."

"I will not..." She paused thinking for the moment. And then, she addressed him properly, "my lord." If Davion could have smiled he surely would have at that groundbreaking moment.

Chapter 45

It wasn't the next morning but a few days since, but Dash and his crew sat around a circle table with Lord Stannor Augustus. The loud and obnoxious lord was at it again and not one barmaid's rear was safe.

The four were dressed casually and not one of them carried a weapon to the table. They united at a mead hall for the workers. There wasn't much to it really, two large pine doors built into a large rectangular barn-sized building.

Inside the large hall were rows and rows of old, past-their-prime wooden tables. Only a few rounded tables were present inside the hall. Scores of guards and workers dove into the day's meal. Toward the back of the hall was a decent sized kitchen where several halfings and tieflings cooked mass quantity meals for the lot of them all. A few halfling barmaids walked around ravenously refilling the men's drinks.

Near the kitchen Lord Stannor and the four sat and ate meats and breads of mediocre quality. It was evident Stannor thought more of himself and the people of his city than the Thoxens above him. Stannor was quick to grab the legs and thighs of his choice. It was mostly chicken and pork, his two favorite meats.

The other three were already briefed by Dash in the days prior to the meeting with Lord Stannor. The city of Azra Goetia was their destination. Gold for Lord Stannor was the primary mission. And the reward, the gift of being the first in a thousand years or so to break ground in the city and search it for remaining gold or weapons and armor to assist them in further quests. More than that, they were treasure hunters and fame seekers. They would acquire wealth and gems and weapons but more importantly, another strong notch with a growing lord in Thox. They would be the reason Vorrellon became an empowered city of immense wealth and growth. Stannor's status would grow with it and thus, their status in Thox would as well. This would be the first of many stepping-stones they would need to become what they all inertly hoped to become.

"So, Dash, got your boys filled in on everything?" Stannor questioned, taking a heavy bite out of one of the chicken legs.

"Looks that way," Pitt answered.

"Good, good," Stannor responded.

"Magic is as rare as Roc's teeth these days and all you want is the gold. It doesn't add up," Dauge sparked up early. He normally wasn't the one to speak up so early. He was reserved and quiet; Dauge always preferred to listen than talk.

"Any magic that's there is too rich for my blood, son. Powerful magics might lead me to wanting to travel again. My life is here, in Vorrellon and I'll sacrifice everything to see her grow and strengthen," Stannor replied. He paused a second, letting the others take in his words. He looked around to make sure they understood him and then he tore back into his chicken.

"Azra Goetia's successful sieges are said to be mythical tales. The weapons told of in their stories are far beyond any magics we know to exist," Legion said. He didn't know too much about the situation at hand but he remembered hearing stories of the city as a child.

"It's believed Alcarus' personal squire wrote down everything. The fallen paladin once asked him if he was 'writing that down' and his squire wrote that down as well," Stannor added, laughing at his own words.

"A book of the city's sieges in detail could be a worth a nice sum," Legion replied.

"It most certainly could," Dash seconded. "And if found, if it exists, if the sieges of Azra Goetia were truly written and kept, then if we find this city and the book it, will be returned to Vorrellon to further its expansion and growth."

Stannor was pleased. How did he come across such grand men? These men were honorable, noble, and true to the cause. They were legends in the making. "Not since Doriel Von Marr have men like you walked this earth."

The whole lot of them laughed. "I hardly think we deserve to be compared to the likes of Doriel the Saint," Dash joked.

"You men are of good stock. I hope when Vorrellon is built you stay in Thox, preferably in my city."

The four of them paused and listened to Stannor. He was already taking to them more than Dash expected. Dash's dream was coming together all too quickly. It'd taken some time but now the ball was rolling and gaining momentum down the hill.

"I'm not sure if you'll get Legion to accompany us. He's been spending all his time with that girl he hired to"—Pitt stopped and gave quotations with his fingers—"'work for him' while he's away and when he's too busy to do his own errands his damn self!" Pitt could barely hold in his laughter.

The lot of them laughed, even Legion. Pitt joked but he spoke truthfully. Legion had been spending quite a bit of time with Kattya. And what was it he hired her to do? He hired her to watch his room, collect carrier pigeon's information for him and run his errands while he was away or when he didn't feel up to it. The man hired a beautiful woman to be his personal assistant.

"Ha, ha, very amusing, Pitt, but I am very much apart of this team and will very much be apart of this quest. I will see Azra Goetia and be among the first to walk upon its stones in this day and age. I will be the one to find the carcass of Alcarus and retrieve his belongings. The book of Azra Goetia's sieges shall belong to me," he challenged.

"Oh, is that a challenge good friend?" Pitt asked.

"It is. You just make sure your sword is by my side at all times," Legion added.

"And that ball and chained flail of yours by mine," the goliath barked back.

"Mourning Star is as much yours as it is mine, friend," Legion joked.

"So then we depart in the morning. You have the maps, I understand you have the maps?" Dauge questioned.

"Yes Dauge, Lord Stannor has the maps for us. We should depart in the morning. While we're gone this city will continue its building. Hopefully we return in time to have Lord Stannor's financial concerns taken care of," Dash said, answering for the lord.

"I do. I do have the maps. Understand the trust I am putting into you all. I am giving you these maps and trusting you."

"What makes you trust us?" Dauge asked.

"Your actions against the undead incursion, your mannerisms here, and the word of Storm Stars. His father and mine were dear. Our families have forever been close. Storm Stars is an honorable man but he doesn't speak highly of too many. You have my trust. I hope it was not earned in vain," he replied.

"It most certainly was not, my lord. The gold, if real will be in your possession just as soon as possible. You've given us the opportunity of a lifetime. We'll be able to fill our pockets and outfits ourselves for all of our future endeavors. Your grace and actions toward us will not go without proper appreciation. We are in your debt. You most certainly have all of our gratitude," Dash quickly replied. He was a poet. Words flowed from his mouth like water from a spring.

"I cannot tell you how pleased I am to know you boys received me so elegantly and nobly. It will not go unnoticed and when Vorrellon's prowess matches the strongest of Thox's other cities you will stand with me as its father."

Dash couldn't be more pleased. Now they were becoming the heroes he wanted them to be.

"We know you'll treat us just when Vorrellon stands taller than every other," Pitt commented.

"And so, where's your lady friend now?" Stannor asked Legion.

"She's tending to our rooms," he answered.

"Rooms?" Stannor questioned.

"We ended up renting a few more," Pitt said, commenting again seeing his first one go unnoticed.

"Now then, let's have a look at you all. I want to see what you wear and wield before you begin work for me. And when it's done I'll see your progression again. I want to see it a week from now, a month, and after a hundred quests. I want to see the righteousness of honest progress," Stannor continued.

Dash was the first to stand. His light leathers were the cleanest of the four. It held its natural brown colors but the rest of his outfit clashed with the color of the leather. He wore mostly grays and whites. His boots were brown like his leather breeches and breast guard. He kept a crossbow attached to a rope he slung crossways over his shoulder. A small pack of bolts for it stayed at his side. On the opposing side, a short sword rested. A specially crafted pack for three javelins lay upon his back, full.

Stannor gave him more than just a once over. He clenched his lips together up and down and giving him the not-bad nod and look of acceptance. Stannor looked to Pitt next and the behemoth stood, obliging him.

Pitt's long blond hair was gone. Stannor never saw the goliath with hair, a one-of-a-kind trait amongst his people. Pitt's head was shaved clean.

He stood in torn breeches of brown color that extended down just past his knees. Across his massively carved torso, two leather straps wrapped crisscrossed. The hangar to his full-blade was held tightly in its vertical position by the twin straps. The only form of armor Pitt wore was a pair of mismatched brass bracers covering most of his forearms. He kept a wooden buckler tied to his side belt along with a pack holding several javelins.

"You're the gladiator," Stannor said. Pitt's frame and overall appearance were remarkable. Few scars actually laid upon his body, for until recently, he'd rarely been hit at all.

Legion stood next. Pitt once again took his seat. Legion's armor was different. There were mostly pieces of both brown leather and black studded leather to it. Silver studs were the lace of design in his studs. Fragmented pieces of chain and brass were interwoven under and over the leathers all over. Bronze bracers were his forearm protectants of choice. On his back, he kept a large circular shield of steel strapped and at his side the weapon that forged for him from the two blades of his father, SOUL and LORE. Mourning Star shimmered a bit when he stood. Legion wore what a smith would call piece mail or piece armor, meaning it was pieced together by several different styles, types, and forms of armors. Stannor particularly liked how some of the chain came up a bit on his neck before disappearing underneath the lot of it all. He fancied the style.

"I heard you wield a weapon forged from your daddy's, boy?" Stannor said suspectingly.

"I do. I call it, Mourning Star," Legion replied.

"Aren't morning stars just shafts with spiked balls on the end? That's a flail, ain't it boy?" Stannor questioned.

"It's a flail. It's a morning star with a chain linking its end to its stem. I call him Mourning Star. And we will deliver glory to you and ourselves as my father once did when paired with him," answered the eldest Xavier child.

Stannor smiled and nodded, furthering his acceptance. He admired the young men. Their courage, bravery, and nobility seemed to be second to none. He then looked to Dauge.

Against his better judgment or care for doing so, Dauge arose as his comrades did before him. Legion remained standing while Stannor had his look at him.

Dauge's clothes were completely dark. His attire was mostly made of dark blues and blacks. He wore extremely light armor, though not quite as light as the goliath. He opened his clothing in random places to show

Stannor his vestments of protection. Beneath his long sleeves were lightly padded leathers, thin and smoothly crafted. It seemed hidden daggers and weapons were laced and kept all over the youngest Xavier. He wore very few armoring pieces and he wore them mostly scattered across his body. Thin strands of bandings were here and there but nothing too protective. It was evident the man wanted to remain light on his feet. A light sash worn across his torso held eight throwing daggers and the sash was kept tight to his flesh. Dauge didn't want loose garments interrupting his engagements. His armblades were tied neatly together and kept like upright sickles just to the upper left and upper right buttocks at his waistline. Two clean daggers sleeved under his light padded bracers under his long sleeved garments. And lastly at each side, he kept his short swords.

"I am Dauge Gray of the House Xavier. I claim not my house or those in it that came before me. I claim only my brother Legion and my sister Dusk. I want you to know, Stannor, I am here for Legion and his endeavors. Your city, your dreams and goals, they mean nothing to me. I would just assume return to the Republic where we belong. You have my brother's word this shall be done, so it shall be. And I digress, you have my word as well."

Stannor was certainly taken back by the youngest Xavier's words. He wasn't exactly prepared for them. He wasn't prepared for them at all. Dauge's words only made him appreciate the four even more. Dauge was true and honest to his feelings. He couldn't help the way he felt and to keep honesty with the lord even when it wasn't the favored move showed Stannor they were more than just men, they were going to become something great.

"The four of you have enough coin in your purses to retire and live comfortably I'm sure. You all know you were meant for more than that. That's why you're here before me now," Stannor said, speaking to their inner motives.

Curiously, the lord speaking to the men's inner motives proved successful with Dauge. It meant the lord also knew their true reason for being there and accepting his offer to acquire the necessary gold from the lost city Azra Goetia to help build his newly founded city.

"I never thought I'd be charged with the task of finding gold for the man responsible for my employment," Dash said, laughing.

"It's a unique circumstance and I don't feel I'm employing you. I've given you the opportunity to better yourselves and fatten your purses and in exchange, I just ask for a bit of the profit."

When he put it like that, it made even more sense. The four of them were entering into an agreement with the Lord of Vorrellon to bring him three thousand gold and in exchange he'd trust them with the maps to get them to Azra Goetia, a place with the potential to change their status in Thox and Thedia, forever.

"What of horses? Vorrellon's not in an over abundance of steeds, my lord," Legion questioned.

"Steeds will be made ready for each and every one of you. They'll be ready by the morning. This gives you enough time to prepare, does it not?" asked Stannor.

"It more than does," Dash replied, taking a huge gulp from his wine glass following his answer.

"Well boy, then enjoy this city for the day. Take the day to gather your things and secure your places here. I will see to it they're paid for by the city's treasury beginning tomorrow."

"That's not necessary. It's really not necessary," Pitt countered politely.

"A worthy investment, it will pay for itself tenfold when you all return as my champion, heroes of Thox and citizens of Vorrellon. I truly pray to the five faiths above us and below us you call Vorrellon home when this is done." Stannor was referring to the seven forms of primary worship in the world, Angelical, Demonic, Devilish, Draconic, the Rivermortal, the elements, and the spirits.

"You know we will," Dash answered.

"It is time we move," Pitt seconded.

"It is," Stannor agreed.

"We shall clear our calendars and prepare for the journey ahead. Let us take a look at the maps," Dash said.

Stannor pulled the maps from his satchel and scattered them on the table. There were four of them in total. They were rolled up and halfway coming unraveled. Stannor tossed them carelessly. One of the maps was marked the beginning of their journey and a path through the string of rivers down past the mountains and then past the Mogra itself. The Mogra was close to the farthest southeastern part of the main southern continent. It was surrounded by a vicious mountain chain and luckily the path wouldn't send the team through it. Like the other mountains they would pass, they would again ignore these as well.

Then, past the Mogra in the southern most part of the southeastern region of the continental piece where Thox rested, there existed a vile land, frozen and broken from the strains of time and magic. It was rendered unconquerable. It was said to not be passable and the first map opened had a path leading straight to it.

"Now this will take you directly there." Stannor pointed out the significant areas of the map. He then pulled two more open. "These two are both routes that will take you there. One's the high road and one's the low road, so to speak, and I ain't speaking of morality here."

"What do you mean?" Dash asked, eying what he was talking about.

"Well, One will take you over the elevated hills and into some mountainous terrain. The other will take you low and deep into the cold. It's a smoother path but I'd dress warm. You'll be walking a tight line with the frozen coast there and, if you catch it just wrong, you might feel the tide come in, if you know what I mean."

They were all listening at this point and really paying attention. They all wanted to make sure they knew what they were up against. Stannor went over both options and proved how both were viable ways of getting there. The boys went over both maps of the frozen and shattered areas south of the Mogra. Now, it was up for discussion on which way to head.

"Azra Goetia is the destination. Both ways can get us there but the road heading low and near the border will be faster," Pitt stated, reminding them of the facts at hand. And it was evident that would be his way of choice.

"There won't be too much to deal with. It's going to be so cold being that close to the border where the Frozen Sea rests," Dash added.

"There won't be many obstacles because that part of the land won't sustain life. If we run into anything, it's going to be creatures native to the cold. Then, we're in their environment," Legion suggested.

"So you're saying we should take to the high elevations in the mountainous terrain. It's still frozen there too. And all the terrain is going to be bad and tough to get through," Dash said.

"The high road will probably take longer and we'll probably have a few more engagements. I for one am not concerned for the engagements and the temperature will be warmer. You're right, typically the higher you go the colder it gets. We're not going that high, see right here"—he stopped and pointed to a location on the map—"right here, we'll be scaling across some mountainous terrain but not going too high. It'll be rocky and difficult but it won't be too bad. If we go low, we're closer to the water, the frozen water, and if we catch it on the wrong tide, we'd be frozen solid. We could drown," Legion answered.

"We take the high road you ignorant wretch," Dauge popped off to Dash, defending his brother's claim.

Dash turned. "Why such aggression toward me?"

"It's not complicated. You're putting more to it than it is. The low road is an easier path but if circumstances land wrong we're doomed. The high road is still risky but not as risky. The roads mean nothing. They'll both get us to Azra Goetia. One might take a little longer. We're not on a dire mission where lives are at stake. Time is important but not necessarily of the essence, am I correct Lord Stannor August of Vorrellon?" Dauge popped back off to Dash before turning to refocus his attention to the lord, where he spoke to the man in a soft and polite tone.

"You are correct. I'd much prefer you all take your time and lessen your risks than push harshly and something tragic occur. I need the gold but not at that expense. We have plenty of time and there's enough in my treasury to sustain comfortably until you all return."

"You see Dash, there's no reason to take unnecessary risk." Dauge was a bit quieter now. He leaned back; satisfied with the argument he presented and kicked his feet up upon the table. He closed his eyes and leaned his head down. "I'm done. Wake me up when you all figure out what's to come."

"Dauge," Legion said pleadingly to his brother. "Don't be like this. Let us put this together as a team. We need all of us on this."

Dauge's verbal challenge at every turn was starting to weigh on Dash's psyche. His mental state felt weaker than it'd ever felt since he'd been traveling with Dauge. He just didn't have the stomach for it.

"I've already told you all the ins and outs of it. I'm willing to walk either road for the lord here. Brother, you tell me when we're ready. I'll follow you no matter what. You know that," Dauge said picking his chin up from his chest to talk. The distraction once again disturbed him too much to sit by and do nothing. Dauge stood from his seat.

"If you'll excuse me, I'm going to take a nap and prepare for the journey ahead, my lord." He paused of course before saying my lord. "Brother, whatever decision you make I trust, and my vote is behind whatever you decide." With that, Dauge at least waited for Lord Stannor to give his approval to be dismissed. Upon getting the approval, he made short work of the mess hall, exiting the place rather quickly.

"No offense good warrior, friend, but Dash spared me from the arenas and united us. My vote is with him. I too would like to take my leave and better prepare for the journey ahead. From the looks of it, it's going to take at least a month before we get through all the proper channels of Thox and then out into the wild. With terrain obstacles, and engagements, yeah we're looking at least fifty days, or like I said, a month," Pitt said.

Years in Thedia were five hundred days long and broken down into ten long months. Each month consisted of fifty days and each day was thirty hours long. The trek was looking to be anywhere from twenty five to thirty days just to the vile land beneath the Mogra. Then, from that vile area of the continent to the marked destination of Azra Goetia could take anywhere from ten to twenty days with obstacles, weather, and engagement dependent of course.

Lord Stannor excused Pitt, who stood and bowed before the Lord of Vorrellon. Then, only Legion and Dash were left to sit and talk with Lord Stannor. Stannor looked at them both and then down to the single map still left to be unfolded.

"Are you sure you all are up to this?" Lord Stannor asked.

"Of course, my lord," Dash replied quickly and pleasantly.

"I don't care which path you choose or if you even choose it now. I'm just giving you the option to weigh early, you know?" the Lord said.

"We understand my lord. Dissention amongst us is merely verbal. We'll figure the best way whether it be today, tonight, tomorrow, or the day we arrive at the vile land below the Mogra. Rest assured, whenever it's decided, it will be decided and your requested gold will be brought back to you from Azra Goetia." Legion was silenced by Dash's ability to speak. His words flowed smoothly; he couldn't think of a proper analogy to compare them to. He'd never heard anyone speak so beautifully. It wasn't gaudy and fake, nor was it arrogant or cynical. He didn't seem humble or educated. Everything he said was honest, true, and sincere or at least that's the way it sounded.

Legion smiled and then asked to be excused by the lord. Lord Stannor quietly agreed. Legion politely pardoned himself from the table, giving Dash the proper courtesies required, especially in front of lord.

He knew Dash had everything under control. He didn't care about the fourth map or what it entailed. They still had a map that could lead them much farther into the Frozen Sea for a lost temple compliments of the lich Davion. Any quarrel he had with Dash could wait until he was not sitting in front of the Lord of Vorrellon. Legion smiled. He didn't want to admit it. He hated to admit it but Dash Riproc was damn good with his words.

He couldn't help but to crack a strong grin as he left the eatery. And on an even better note, he was free for the rest of the day to embark on whatever silly things Kattya hoped to do.

Their table was silent momentarily while Legion made his way out. Now, just Dash and Stannor remained. The fourth map was still unopened. The first map would get take them there. The second and third were different routes to the same location, Azra Goetia.

"And the last map?" Dash asked. His eyes rolled down and focused on the fourth map before rolling back up to refocus on Stannor.

Stannor smiled. Dash read his body language. There was something to it he was hesitant to release to the rest of the team. Something about that fourth map made Stannor nervous. He didn't have to say anything; Dash could tell by the look in his eyes and by the way he moved.

"The fourth map," Dash once again said.

"Yes, the fourth map," Stannor replied not so confidently.

"I take it the other gauntlet's about to drop?" Dash asked.

"Supposedly, in Azra Goetia exists the Keep of Zhejediah's Hold. An enigmatic prison built to hold the Angelical entity, Zhejediah was said to have been defeated and captured by Alcarus himself."

"What would you have me do? Release the angel and perhaps see a blessing thrown our way whilst in the midst of the hells' most notorious harvesting grounds? Azra Goetia is said to be the first city the hells' turned into a harvesting ground. And by the looks of it, Bahaus is trying to do the same to Eternis."

"Maybe. Right now, Eternis is not my concern, Dash."

"Nor mine," he countered quickly enough to temporarily halt the lord's words. As soon as, Stannor picked right back up.

"Zhejediah was an empowering force in the Angelic Realm before being defeated and captured. Strangely enough, the other angels never came to his aid. He's immortal, of course. He might still be there, or his corpse might still be. Or, whatever an angelical entity would leave behind I guess."

"What's this mean to me?"

"To imprison an angel or something of that caliber, well my research and informants tell me Azra Goetia used Quarene Diamonds. Quarene Diamonds haven't been mined in more than eight centuries. Few have ever been found. If we can find that Quarene Diamond, there would be plenty of coins to make every man in Vorrellon wealthy and to make Vorrellon perhaps the wealthiest city in all the world."

"I don't know if one Quarene's going to do that but it would certainly jumpstart things, my lord," Dash replied.

"You don't have to search for it. There'll probably vicious traps, guards, and wards protecting that prison. I just wanted you to know of its existence and keep the option open for you, should you decide to go for it. After all, how many men can say they freed an angel after…what…an ungodly amount of years?"

That did it. That was what Dash needed to hear. It wasn't about the Quarene anymore. It was about freeing Zhejediah. If he freed Zhejediah from his confines, he would earn his mark in history. None could deny his spot. He would forever be remembered. That's what all this was for, at least for Dash Riproc anyway.

"Guards, what kind of guards would still be there in Azra Goetia?" he asked.

"Not the regular living kind I'd assume," Stannor answered, sort of laughing.

"Yeah, but there'll be something making sure Zhejediah doesn't see freedom. I'm hoping it's mostly broken down. It's been a long time, Lord Stannor."

"Yes it has. I just wanted you to know about it Dash, that's all. You find the Quarene, we renegotiate our split," he said, laughing. "Otherwise, keep everything you find and just give me that three thousand off the top."

"It will be done."

"I know it will," said Stannor. "That's why I hired you."

"You're hoping we push for the Quarene," Dash stated, questioning.

"I would be lying if I said you're wrong. Your lives are the most important thing. Who knows what's in there and the last map may save your life somehow."

"Yes, of course. It might. It'll be good to have in our belongings. I've heard tales told of such stories," Dash responded.

"Go, speak to your team and prepare them for the journey that lies ahead of them," said Stannor.

"Yes, my lord." Dash bowed courteously.

With that, Stannor gave Dash the proper notions, signifying his pardon from the table. Dash left the hall knowing he'd have to mentally and physically prepare for the task that lay ahead of him. He was up to it. His team was up to it. And soon, he'd have recognition comparable to Dominick Gabriel Xavier or the Archmage Esperis Arkanis.

Legion left the mess hall, leaving Dash and Lord Stannor to conclude their meeting for the lot of them. As hoped for, he found Kattya. She was free of her duties and shopping in the market when his eyes fell upon her again.

He froze for a moment in time. The image of her blasted into his skull; he turned the last corner, entering the market street and there she was. She was beautiful, wearing a simple white dress. Her hair was half flowing and half put up. It was even curled a bit. On her left arm rested a small basket where she'd already placed several fruits, vegetable, and other things.

She didn't see him but he saw her and by the gods was she pretty. Her face, her fair skin, the dress she wore, it all melded into his eyes so perfectly. He'd taken many women to his bed but never truly fancied one as he did her. She was beautiful.

"Kattya," he said, calling to her.

He'd just turned the corner to enter the farmer's market and she wasn't far from the outer road. She turned and looked to the man calling her name. Instantly, a smile ran across her face. She couldn't help it and she knew he'd seen it. He smiled too. The two just connected and immediately fell for one another, yet they'd not spoken too much about it.

"Legion," she replied frolicking over to her caller.

She innocently took the distance between them away, coming so close the tip of her nose touched his. Again, he couldn't help himself, he laughed.

"I'm going to be taking my leave soon, dear girl."

"I know," she replied, trying to be strong. He knew the tone in her voice was fake. She was trying to cover up her real feelings. He understood. They wouldn't have the appropriate time needed to properly acquaint themselves with one another. Legion would take what was against him and turn it to his favor.

"I'm leaving and the reality of it is I may never see this place or you again," he said.

Her head dropped. Her eyes closed. He touched his lips to the top of her head. It partially represented his empathy for the situation and partially told of his desire for her.

"I know you're leaving, Legion. There's something I want to tell you." Her head was still down. He wrapped his arms around her to further comfort her. She took to it well and it did appease her thoughts if only for a moment.

"What is it?" he asked.

She paused.

"Well, What is it?" he asked again. He pulled away from her. His hands now rested on her shoulders. He still smiled, as did she. He only pulled away to lock his eyes back into hers. She waited a bit longer. His body language told her he was really curious for her words.

"I'll tell you but only after you do something for me," she said.

"What's that?" he asked playfully.

"Tonight, the Dal'Eruec Carnival. Take me. Their plays are the best in all of Thox. I've not been since I was a little girl. And after, I shall tell you what it is I wish to tell you," she slyly replied, smiling.

Legion sighed a sigh of relief. It told her he agreed to her terms and was pleased to hear them but in truth, he wanted to please her and make her happy. Something in him wanted to do things for her, to make her smile, to make her happy.

"Very well," he started, slightly groaning. The look on her face burned with confusion. Legion couldn't take it anymore. He fell into a burst of laughter. "I merely jest. I would be honored to take you to the Dal'Eruec Carnival to see their famous plays. I heard about them as a child. I'm sure you did as well."

"Yes," she said.

"And after when all is quiet, whatever it is weighing on your heart, you'll spill into mine so that we may carry the burden or whatever it is together."

Kattya's heart melted. She didn't know what to say. There were no words to describe her emotions and feelings toward Legion and it all happened so very quickly. She barely knew him. She'd only met him a few days prior and he already treated her better than any man or person alive or dead ever did. He treated her like she was something special and irreplaceable or at least that's how she felt. She'd never even been formally courted or taught on how to be. Whatever Legion was doing, it was working.

Chapter 46

Prince Bahaus Sazon-Uil-Endail and the kobold Goldpiece walked for nearly two weeks in the mountains until finally coming to a hidden cave entrance. It was protected by a large door of rock that slid open when Goldpiece pulled the secret lever controlling it.

Bahaus smiled at the impressive hideout. He tried to keep his appearance and cleanliness up but the mountains were starting to take their toll on him. He'd been there for just under two weeks, nearly twenty days.

He would have never told the little creature but the bastard was becoming favored by the arrogant wizard. He was sure to tell the little guy "well done" when they entered the cave. Bahaus' clothes were rugged now. They'd been through hell in the wild of the mountains.

He didn't truly want to trust the little kobold but he didn't really have a choice. He knew his options were limited but did the kobold know? The rain came and went, worsening his situation as if it wasn't already bad enough.

The corridors through the sliding rock door opening were roughly carved at first. It certainly wasn't precision work. The deeper the two delved in the tunnels the cleaner the work became. The dirty rock and soil became tiled stone. Finally, the tunnels funneled down to a smaller squaring.

The two continued their path. Each time a second option on the path revealed itself, Goldpiece didn't hesitate, he kept walking like he'd walked the tunnels a thousand times and knew them like an Eternian wife would know her own kitchen.

Finally the tunnels opened up into the first room. Goldpiece opened the old wooden door revealing an old den. Bahaus slowly followed behind the little kobold. Some furniture was still in place but most was broken and busted, rotted and decayed.

"There are many secret passages. We've just entered a Red Mystic's castle. Aristophane makes her home here," Goldpiece advised.

"Well then, take me the safest and quickest way through this place so that I may speak to her, little one," Bahaus said.

With that, the two embarked on a speedy hike through the ancient castle. Like a god overseeing its domain, Goldpiece walked through the castle flawlessly, knowing how to bypass every trap and speed through every room. And finally, after hours of grinding through the castle's tunnels and puzzles, the two friends came to a solid iron door. It didn't look like it was still even operable. It was old and appeared melded to the wall itself.

Tiny blue tiles surrounded them. Soft dirt and rock really set the scene with the tiny blue tiles. The last secret passage brought them back outside the castle and through a half-built escape route. Only, they entered through the exit and were back toward the beginning of it.

"Here we are. Aristophane and her mightiest should be in there. I should warn you, prince, she will not be happy we are here or that I brought you through the secret passages to avoid contact with her followers."

"You leave the wargoyle priestess and her minions to me," Bahaus said boldly. "Thank you little one, thank you for knowing your place beneath me and serving the rightful heir to Thedia's most prime city." Even when Bahaus tried to make his words friendly, they still remained condescending, arrogant, and vain.

The little kobold fell silent and bowed his head. He hated he was a servant and not a leader but fear kept him in his place. It was the nature of his people. Kobolds were cowardly and he was no different. Aristophane butchered so many of his kind to get her point across. He didn't want to be her next victim.

Bahaus used simple magic to peel the door from the wall, revealing to both himself and the kobold the largest of all the rooms they'd seen. It was an ancient throne room and the throne of the Red Mystics still stood.

The room was built strategically odd, not fitting into any known shape category. The room was large and wide and the ceiling was twice the size here of anywhere else in the castle. The floor was made of ivory and bone as were the four pillars that stood symmetrically perfect from one another.

The stone walls looked to have demonic facial expressions painted all around them but not in the usual way. The faces formed from the very brick and stone, like a painter's brush moved the stone and brick like wet paint into the vile faces that rested before them.

To Bahaus and Goldpiece's left, an elevated area connected to eight steps stood. Atop the elevation was the old throne of the Red Mystics. Not only did Goldpiece take him to Aristophane and subsequently save him from the mountains, the little kobold took him to one of the most sought after castles in all of history.

Heavily armored humanoid guards walked and patrolled the area. The armors were dark with shiny yellowish indentions and symbols radiating a power very familiar to Bahaus' senses. The old red carpet was still there, birthing down from the foot of the throne all the way to the foot of the original entrance door. The entrance door had since collapsed. Now, only dirt and rock stood in its place. The castle was below ground and within the very mountains. Time had not been so kind to the ancient wonder.

Several ancient lizards dressed in black robes seemed to be orchestrating the heavily armored and armed guards. Several gargoyles sat on smaller pillars while the sole wargoyle sat on the Throne of Red Magic. It was woven from the very essence of magical existence. To the eye, it was ethereal and she sat on it so carelessly. She obviously didn't appreciate it, nor did she deserve it.

The wargoyle priestess was tall, standing over seven and a half feet when fully erect. Her wings were retracted and in. Her stone style scales were much smoother than the average wargoyle. Besides the guards fully armored in black, the black- and sometimes purple-robed lizards, and the gargoyles in the room, Bahaus and Goldpiece saw halfling-sized creatures with elongated arms and square, triangular, and circular heads walking amongst them all. There were no kobolds?

"I thought Aristophane had kobolds serving her?" Bahaus whispered to Goldpiece.

"She does. We're not allowed her. Our ranking under her rule says we must remain in the undermountain and cave areas, and upon the surface of course," the kobold quickly whispered.

"At least she understands the concept of racial superiority," Bahaus said, laughing.

In the wargoyle's hand rested a scepter fashioned from platinum and rubies. She wore a crown on her head as if she were a king. It was the Crown of the Red Mystics and the scepter could easily be linked to the Throne of Red Magic. Its inability to stay whole and pure gave it away almost instantly. Bahaus knew she would be formidable. He knew her belongings alone made her nearly invincible.

"So, the Throne of Red Magic does exist?" Bahaus said, more arrogant than ever.

The look on the wargoyle priestess' face was priceless, he thought. She couldn't believe what was going on. The little kobold was shaking terribly and humbly sorry for breaking her orders, Bahaus knew it. Bahaus shoved the kobold to get his attention.

"Pull yourself together, kobold. You're under my order now and not an existence here is going to hurt you. You belong to me."

Aristophane said nothing. Bahaus now could see the black armored guards wielding a variety of different weapons were magical constructs and not living at all. The only two purple-robed lizard folk pulled back their hoods, as did the black robed ones. Bahaus was astonished. The purple wearers were actually troglodytes. Troglodytes look somewhat like humanoid reptiles, with thick muscular bodies. They walk erect on their squat legs, trailing a long slender tail. Their heads are lizard like and many are crowned with a frill that extends from the forehead to the base of the neck, or even traveling the entire length of their bodies and tail. Troglodyte skin is a pattern of varying shades of gray and brown.

Bahaus knew troglodytes secreted an oily substance from their bodies when frightened that nearly every living creature found offensive. Troglodytes, even when able to overcome their savage and evil tendencies still would find it difficult to interact socially, as most races find their very existence filthy and disgusting. The stench of a troglodyte is virtually unbearable and when secreting their native oils, the stench becomes almost lethal to the smell.

Troglodytes were rarely seen in modern times. Though they weren't believed to be extinct. Most surviving clans lived in the most savage and vicious parts of the world. This being mainly due their reputation with most of the known world; the troglodyte race was believed to be as primitive as any and one of the oldest with the least amount of adaptations through time. They had pretty much remained the same since the beginning of time.

One of the troglodytes was massive and scarred like a warrior from the front lines. He wore no weapons or armor only keeping a bit of his flesh hidden from a black circlet on his head. And the second kept his purple robe on, save the hood that covered his head. He looked just as vile but the bead in his eyes was much more villainous. This one was with intelligence, thought Bahaus.

The other lizard folk walked and surrounded the entrance/exit where both Bahaus and Goldpiece stood. The kobold fell back and crouched down, once again trembling in fear. He pointed to the barbaric-looking troglodyte. Troglodytes were usually shorter and smaller than humans at least by a few inches. And the intelligent looking one fit the description, however the barbarian was more of an average build when compared to an average humanoid.

The other lizard folk were all bigger. Even than the barbarian-looking one. Not a single one of them was shorter than seven feet. They were huge! Bahaus wasn't even six foot. He stood only ten inches above the five-foot mark.

"The ancient and primitive race of troglodytes. You're no better than Thoxens. You know not that this world has evolved past needing you in it! It's grown past a point where you have a place."

The inhabitants of the room were taken back at Bahaus' remarks. Did he not know of the power that stood before him? Surely, the man was mad. He could not hope to think that he and one kobold could stand to the might of Aristophane, the Throne of Red Magic, and those that followed her.

From the far side of the room, the voice of the wargoyle priestess echoed out. Her voice was booming and strong. It sounded more like a man's voice than a woman's, but alas, it certainly belonged to the woman on the throne.

"You're short and round, not at all with the physique I would have expected for someone to charge in here. That kobold with you shall be disemboweled as an example for those tempting to not follow the order of things."

Goldpiece cringed and balled up even tighter, jumping back through the doorway Bahaus so easily opened. Bahaus once entered a Red Mystic's fortress and was among the members of the team who dethroned Agromordeus.

"Troglodytes, a race as old as the waters of Thedia. Yet, somehow they've regressed. They've failed to evolve and these are the miscreants you have serving you, wargoyle?" Bahaus arrogantly questioned.

"Careful fat man, the monstrous one before you is Garokk. He once served creatures beyond your understanding. When they were finally ousted, he found himself free. Eventually, he came across the men who destroyed his former masters' coven and joined them. His taste for human and elven meat overtook him and now he once again finds himself in the mountains with those greater than him. He found another master to serve. He's blessed with the ability of avoiding death. You should see to it you avoid him. The other is Seskar. Her family's blood served the Red Mystics and she's the last of her name, until she and Garokk copulate, of course. They once protected the artisan stream of the purest water deep beneath the surface. She too finds herself in the servitude of those greater than herself. You should learn from them and bow to me and perhaps I shall grant you a place amongst my slaves."

"Your slave?" Bahaus asked, using his body language to signify is superiority.

"My slave," she confirmed.

"And…" he paused. His eyes stayed fixed on the woman priestess in charge who now inspired him to release everything he had in him, including some things he'd never even see himself. "…If I refuse?"

"You will not. You've got but a single chance to prove the life you possess should be spared."

"I've come here representing a different purpose and when you see what my body channels and you see the force behind my arcane, you will listen to me, otherwise we'll all perish here. I'll personally see to it."

"And what's your purpose?"

"I am King Bahaus Sazos-Uil-Endail of Eternis, the first and last of the Prime Cities. My land was taken from me and I was defeated at Emerald Greene at the hands of Drackice Black, son to Magnus Black and commander of the Free Armies while his father was away. The defeat is critical to me as my own faith has now turned against me. I'm sure of it and now I have nothing to lose. I will regain honor in my faith's eyes and I will see Eternis brought under my rule, or I will see it removed from this plane, forever."

"What does your personal conflict with your own people and the city of Eternis have to do with me?" she asked.

"Goldpiece tells me you yearn for power. I can teach your casters and build their rituals and spellbooks. Unlike most arcane casters, I've memorized the spells of a thousand books and can scribe them as needed, a trait gifted to me from my faith, the ArchDevil Asmodai."

"A devil-worshipping wizard king ousted from his own people seeks an alliance. In no way can you word this advantageously from your position."

"Not an alliance, you piss ant, an agreement!" Bahaus scolded back.

"An agreement, what type of an agreement? What would I have to gain from an agreement with you?" The wargoyle leaned forward on her own lap, still sitting in the throne that once belonged to the Red Mystics.

"I want my city back and from talking with your former pet here…"—Bahaus stopped and reached back with his left hand point his two longest fingers at the hiding kobold—"I understand you're trying to awaken two elder titans, Nyx and Erebrus. From the lore, those two stood with just as much power as any."

"How did that kobold come to learn such knowledge?"

"Nevermind that. I don't even know the answer to that. What I do know is my arcane skills are second to none still living on this plane of existence. You're going to need a caster with my skills and experience. Surely, you knew that already?" The look on Bahaus' face told her and all present in the room he had absolutely no respect for her or anyone else in the room. For that matter, whatever power they could possess didn't seem to strike fear into him either.

"Enough. I've had enough of your tongue. You come into my fortress, capture one of my slaves, have him lead you through the tunnels straight to my throne room where you disrespect me and those closest in my servitude square?" Aristophane stood from the throne. Her scepter glimmered an off white. Then, it transcended into a clear white aura surrounding her and the scepter. The throne itself shared the glimmering properties as well.

And suddenly, the clear aura smothered the priestess, the scepter, and the throne itself. A beam of the clear light shot out lightning in a horrid storm. There, before Bahaus Sazos-Uil-Endail stood a creature freshly made. To her credit, it was magic done differently than Bahaus had ever seen Summoning was one thing. Creating was also relatively understood in the realm of the arcane., She created a being purely from raw magic and it was probably more impressive than her. Yes, he was sure of it. He could hear the little kobold behind him whimpering and crying. Hearing the creature's fear infuriated him even more. He had to send a message to this wretched non-human, non-Eternian, non-royal queen.

The creature stood about half a foot taller than Bahaus and was completely incorporeal. Its armor and clothing seemed to flow purely from its very own ethereal flesh. It appeared to be a ghostly apparition but slightly less phantasmal. Its body formed to a cloudy, slightly off white color complete with an oriental style coolie hat covering most of its face. Ancient symbols systematically turned on glowing red all across the being's body and armor. Toward his waistline, the armor flowed downward differently than expected, becoming something more of a robe at the bottom. At its left and right sides were sheathes for a longer based katana and a shorter one, commonly known in the orient as a wakizashi.

Ethereal residue lingered behind its every movement, temporarily of course, and then it dissipated like smoke in the night from a simple campfire. Bahaus watched the creature move and it moved lightning fast. He was impressed. Before he knew it, all the others fell back, becoming spectators waiting for what was to come. The being drew its blades while Bahaus blinked. It was that quick.

The being bolted forward, moving so fast it looked as if it were an instantaneous teleport. The ethereal residue stretched out behind it proved it wasn't a magical movement but rather just a supremely fast one. The creature cut through Bahaus, slashing from across the right side of his face down through the left pit of his left arm.

Bahaus dissipated. The being looked around. Seven more Bahaus' formed around him just as he finished cutting through the first. In the same moment they birthed they became fuzzy and translucent. It also appeared as if they were fading in and out of the plane. Aristophane knew they were displaced.

First, it was Aristophane, the being, and the rest of her followers that were surprised by the quickness and nonexistent movements and words needed for Bahaus to cast his spells. Then it was Bahaus who was surprised when the ethereally incorporeal residue left behind by the being's flash charge didn't vanish. It fell to the ground forming an oozy liquid thick and now silvery in color. The ooze formed up as the Bahaus' stared at it and the being stared at him.

The silvery ooze formed a body identical in style to the first being, but this one resembled an old foe of Bahaus' to the tee. It looked like the ancient Thoxen Necromancer Agromordeus. No red symbols glowed on its body, though. Its facial features wouldn't be clear to a regular onlooker but Bahaus knew his old foe and this creature was it. However, it was silver in color and becoming incorporeal before his very eyes. Bahaus knew his magic would have to be on point to compete with something the likes of this.

Now, there were two enemies, yet they were one. Which to attack and which to leave alone? The celestial looking samurai was the first to take charge after the momentary pause. He slashed again, relentlessly lashing out against the wizard. This time he would have hit the correct Bahaus, however, the dark wizard's contingency spell, Wizard's Evasion flung him out of the way, mistakenly landing him deep in the exit tunnel he first entered through.

Goldpiece was now ahead of him, looking back at him from behind a small rock slightly large enough for him to hide behind. Goldpiece smiled. He was ecstatic to see his new friend alive. "Master, you're alive! Let's get out of here. We'll survive yet another day!"

His words fueled a look Bahaus rarely gave. He wanted this thing over and done with now. He didn't want to deal with it anymore! He no longer wanted to come to an arrangement or agreement with Aristophane. He wanted her dead.

The celestial warrior walked forward, preparing to enter the tunnel. A series of aggressive bolts, orb, and spun together with blasts met him at the entrance. His powers' presence and aura temporarily blinded several spectators and even blackened flesh and scales in some areas. One gargoyle sitting on a pillar was a legitimate statue. It crumbled like a child stepping on a sandcastle.

The room rumbled and cracked at the foundation. Bahaus walked back through the exit/entry way, smacking his hands together, dusting off the residue of his recent work. Aristophane couldn't believe it. The celestial warrior lay in ruin. Bahaus' magic turned him from ethereal and incorporeal to solid and melting. The same liquid ooze that first formed the second being flowed out as the celestial warrior melted away.

Bahaus walked up to it but not too close. He wasn't that foolish. Blackened orbs that first appeared while he was in the tunnel mixed with green and white orbs hovering around the room. Only a single blue orb floated with them. The creature raised its only remaining arm upward, crying out in pain. The sound emanating from its mouth wasn't anything anyone could make out. The look and sound however was clear. It was hurting and it was in pain.

The Agromordeus-styled being stepped back. Bahaus raised his hand and dropped it back down hard. The blue orb slammed into the melting warrior's essence, freezing it solid. Bahaus' next move was an arrogant one. He walked forward, stepping his right foot on the frozen being's melted-but-frozen body dead center. It took a second heave and push but Bahaus, using all his weight, managed to collapse the frozen thing in, breaking it into pieces like glass.

Bahaus released fires to back up lightning bolts embed with dark energies, all the while adding orbs of various powers, mostly entropic ones, into the mix. His other images still remained in place, yet they moved around as if they were real and casting the spells.

The celestial caster hurled forth his hands, releasing a ray of raw arcane. Bahaus' displacement landed perfectly, allowing the ray to shoot straight through him. A second move by the caster dismissed all of his other images, and unfortunately his displacement. The caster kept he ray going and soon Bahaus was back on the prime material wholly and fully.

His body racked with pain and his voice screeched out, showing it. Luckily, the raw arcane ray was ending just as his displacement was taken from him. Bahaus stumbled. He dropped to a knee momentarily and his hand touched the cold stone beneath him.

The creature raised his palm to the ceiling, raising it slowly. Suddenly, Bahaus could hear the cracking of the structure and debris from above fell, hitting him, rolling off his neck and back. A large chunk of brick, stone, and dirt was peeled by the celestial caster and forced down hard upon Bahaus.

Bahaus thought quickly. Simultaneous to the Dimension Door spell he cast, Bahaus created an iron wall by the spell Wall of Iron. Instead of casting it in a usual manner, Bahaus' magic allowed him to cast it horizontally, beginning just above his back and extending both ways to the far side of the room and the exit/entry tunnel where he first came from.

Standing directly affront him some forty feet away was the rival caster. The caster caught the wall of iron hard in the upper torso. It pushed so violently that when it was over, the far side of the throne room was cracked and now caving in as well. There was no sign of the rival caster, just thick silvery ooze that looked like liquid metal splattered across the opposing wall from where Bahaus was standing.

The wall appeared solid and it didn't look like it was going anywhere. The priestess didn't know what to do, nor did her followers. From behind, Bahaus could hear the mustering of his new friend. Goldpiece came out from behind the wall out of the entry/exit secret tunnel smiling bigger than ever, pleased to be on the winner's side. However, his smile was fake. He knew something was coming and he wasn't sure if Bahaus was going to be ready for it.

Then the wall began to move. It moved around as if it was made of water and encased in glass. It wasn't; it was a magically constructed iron wall! What was going on? Not even Bahaus could explain it. How was something else tampering with his magic in such a way?

Now, Bahaus had rolled out from under the wall and was standing next to it. His body was diagonal to the priestess and Goldpiece on his left-hand side. The far side of the room where the creature was last seen was on his right.

Before Bahaus could do anything, two monstrous hands made of liquid metal emerged from the wall, creating ripples and waves in the "solid" iron wall. The hands were large and got ahold of Bahaus. One even managed to envelop his head and neck.

Bahaus heard the cry of Goldpiece and the pressure of the squeezing creature. He tried to teleport, dimension door again, and various other things to get out from under the grasp but nothing worked. The creature was made of pure magic and managed to infiltrate his own creations, that much he knew.

Bahaus laughed inside. He quickly dismissed the Iron wall cancelling it out completely leaving the celestial caster made up completely of magic stuck inside to be taken out of existence along with it. The wall of iron went back to the arcane weave, he thought. And that damned thing went with it, he concluded smiling.

Aristophane leaped from her throne. The glowing aura was gone. She couldn't believe it. That throne was the instrument needed for controlling the red magic within the castle. And that red magic was going to be the tool she needed to awaken the twin titans and return their powers to them. Something inside her made her believe red magic came from the powers of sleeping titans. Their powers slowly usurped from them, creating new forms of magic, untested and unrivaled by the others. Unlike Forsaken magic, red magic simply empowered and purified magic. It was known to push various other types of powers into originals. For example, a fireball cast may also have sonic, lightning, and ice all blended into one and maximized to full effect. Also, ancient spells long forgotten by the mortal worlds of Thedia could be brought back using red spells to recover lost ones. Did the Red Mystics really find ways to bleed powers from sleeping titans and even elder titans? If so, is that what caused their demise?

"Those powers. They're formed purely from Red Magic. You cannot defeat them," Aristophane said, coughing. Using the throne to call forth the beings and then the beings being destroyed took it out of her. She was weak now. Bahaus saw it and he new if he was going to strike, now was the time.

The wargoyle stutter stepped and lost her footing beside the throne, crashing down right beside it. Bahaus continued walking closer to the throne. Now, Garokk, Seskar, and the others all stepped back from the proven wizard openly in the service of the highest ranked devil, Asmodai.

"Even the greatest powers this world has to offer requires brilliance behind them to steer," implied Bahaus.

"You… You… You defeated raw magic of the Red Mystics. I don't understand," she said, rising back to her feet.

"The magic, if used correctly is said to be unstoppable. Then again, Forsaken magic was said to be unstoppable and an Eternian destroyed the last Forsaken there on the Broken Lands. Taj Xavier saved our world. Now, I will save the world's greatest treasure, Eternis. I will save it from itself or I will die in this dispute destroying you. Either our plans both go fulfilled or neither of us shall see the break of day tomorrow."

The creatures of the room growled and hissed at the wizard. Something startled Bahaus. The wizard with powers unknown to most of the world turned behind him to see the little kobold smothering himself in his legs. Bahaus laughed. He was growing attached to the little guy.

Bahaus turned back around and focused his eyes back to Seskar, Garokk, and then to Aristophane. He paused momentarily while he walked forward. Their growls and howls talked a much bigger game than they were ready to play. Bahaus himself was pleased with how far he pushed the envelope, he stopped to let his adversaries move about and prepare their next move in accordance to his.

"In order to shine like the sun, one must first burn like it. I am not your enemy. Goldpiece says you wish to awaken the mighty titans. Fine, so be it. You will need something of my caliber to execute those rituals properly. That being said, I'm assuming you have the proper rituals? Now then, am I to kill you, Aristophane, and perhaps then die to your people, assuming they're foolish enough to then follow your dead carcass? Or, am I to help for the petty cost of securing the ancient city of Eternis for myself? What path do you choose?"

He was right! She had the legendary rituals only known to exist to the now extinct Red Mystics. She possessed the Red Scepter and sat on the Throne of Red Magic. She owned the lost castle that was believed to have been built symmetrically dividing the two sleeping entities and something in the castle or about the castle was said to hold the key to their awakening or their powers. She would need him and he certainly proved his worth. With Bahaus Sazos-Uil-Endail, ousted King of Eternis, she would awaken her titans and fulfill her quest a thousand fold!

Chapter 49

The outskirts of Thox were now behind them. They'd been traveling for weeks and the only thing Legion could think about was her. Dauge didn't understand it. Dash tried to but the realization of the their time spent together wasn't enough to feel so strong. Pitt understood above all others. For he still longed for Shiva, the beautiful creature of his dreams he in truth would perhaps never see again. And yet, the goliath knew he would never stop looking.

The team mostly took carriages across the roads and through the paths and cities. Now the paved pathways and roads of Thox were behind them. Soon, they would be coming upon the open streams and rivers carved out from the mountains and even the Mogra itself.

The four of them rode upon strong Thoxen steeds. Thoxen horses were believed to be some of the strongest the world had to offer and no one ever doubted their durability. Legion often wandered off in his own mind, thinking back of Vorrellon and Kattya.

Something weighed both on his heart and hers and both bridges were crossed that fateful night. He remembered it like it was yesterday. She told him she thought she'd never see him again. It was a horrible thing to hear. And the thought of being gone for so long away from her wrecked the warrior of Eternian blood.

"She'll be there when you return," Dash said, trotting alongside on his horse.

It was late in the evening and the four had been traveling for quite some time. Every one of their horses was solid black with white socks except for Dash's. Dash's horse was also white and black but virtually spotted all over.

"You don't even know her, Dash. And perhaps she will be. What if I don't return and even if I should, I still dread the time I'm going to have to spend away from her. I've got an affinity for the little lass."

"You're an adventurer. You're going to be a hero world-renowned one day. As a child, when you read short stories and fairytales, didn't the champion always ride away?" Dash asked.

"These aren't short stories or silver piece novels, Dash. This is my own real life you're talking about," he replied.

Silver piece novels were novels written and sold for a few silver mostly done by wives as means to produce additional income for the families. This trade was often practiced during hard times. It became significantly popular during the years of "depression" of certain cities.

"I know but those stories all have similar moral-guiding ideals and typically the hero rides away. You know why?" Dash asked.

Legion didn't ask why back, nor did he answer. He just kept trotting along, knowing Dash would eventually answer his own question. And just as he expected, Dash followed up just as he thought.

"Because if he didn't, he'd be tied down to that town or city. He'd also be putting the little damsel in danger, assuming the hero had unfinished business and enemies lurking about. You don't have too many enemies right now, Legion, but you could in times to come. If you stay romantically linked with her you're going to eventually break away from the team and settle for a life of simplicity somewhere in Thox, possibly in Vorrellon?"

Legion thought about the half-eladrin's words. His words did hit accurately. His career as a sword for sale or mercenary, or even hero was just beginning. Was it truly what he wanted? What else could he do? His conversation with Kattya that night still haunted him.

"You've mentioned a conversation the two of you had just before leaving. What was it about?" Pitt questioned.

Legion just kept riding. He heard the big man and the big man knew it. Not answering wasn't a signal for disrespect from the human. Legion was just still too consumed with the conversation. It replayed to him again and again. More over, Dash's words infested the memory. He paused his thoughts to bounce a question back to Dash.

"Are we all just to remain celibate?" he questioned.

"We are to remain free of romantic chains so that we may pack our things on a moment's notice if need be," Dash replied quickly.

"So then you tell us how to live our lives?" Legion continued.

"I'm telling you that this life path does not leave the proper openings for what you seem to want with her. You're going to find more, tens, dozens, and scores of women lie ahead of you. When you're finished with your travels is when you should see to making one your wife."

The four of them all paused verbally. None said a word. They just kept riding. Dash was completely accurate. He knew what he was talking about. The question wasn't whether he was right or wrong anymore but whether in the short time Legion had to spend with Kattya, did she do enough to convince him this way of life was not as great as a life with her?"

Legion's memories began to play again. There he was. The play was over and they were standing just outside the mobile bleachers temporarily in place for the onlookers of the plays. It was a warm night and the moon shined brightly down upon them.

"Legion," she started, gently placing her hands upon his shoulders. They eased down to his biceps. Only the tips of her fingers touched his shirt. The way her fingertips moved sent chills down his arm and through his spine. Even the way she said his name got to him.

"What is it Kattya?" he asked. "I think we've both got things here to address."

"Yes, and we just met," she replied quickly.

She was shorter than him. He looked down into her eyes. She looked up into his. He waited for what was to come from her lips. He longed for it. He'd just met her yet he was completely infatuated with her. It didn't take long nor was it a beautiful story as to how they met. In fact, it was a boring and sad story. He paid to keep her around and to get her out of that horrible life she'd built for herself. In doing so, he found a way in to talk and get to know her.

"You first," he said.

"You first," she challenged, knowing he wouldn't be able to defeat her pretty smile. She knew she was pretty but it'd been so long since she'd been treated like it. She'd worked hard developing hardened flesh points all over her palms. She was still pretty and her face was to die for and she knew it.

She won, he thought. He'd go first because the silver of her eyes cut through his will like daggers in flesh. The night reflected on her like the sun sparkled water. She was beautiful. Was it lust he felt? He certainly didn't truly know her and she wasn't of noble blood? What was so special about her that he was taken so deeply by her?

"My life," he started, patiently hesitating. He wasn't sure if he could muster the words to tell her what he wanted. His thoughts were just too complex to simply put into words on the spot. For her he would try. "My life is not mine to determine. My brother is my responsibility. I love him dearly. He's all I have who understands me. Without me, I'm not certain what would happen to him. I pray to the faiths everyday to keep my sister and brothers safe. I pray for my father and mother to remain free from harm and suffering. I've come to respect and honor Pitt like a brother. Dash is the flip of a coin. I'm not certain of his motives. I cannot be sure he would not have us all day for some estranged form of immortal glory. All of this I tell you has in one way or another been forced upon me. What has not been forced upon my life is you. You're the sole decision I've made. And now, my life is forcing me to the ruins of Azra Goetia. I will return and feel your embrace again, that I promise you. I hope you wait for me. I hope you entrust in my promise. And I pray these feelings I have are reciprocated. If not, if I am overstepping my boundaries tell me now and I shall still pay you to keep you from those mines. I will still pay you to take care of my things and watch my room while I'm gone. Do not toy with me, Kattya. I am still Legion Cage Xavier of the House Xavier of Eternis and I hereby profess my undying love and loyalty to you. I know I've not known you long enough to formally speak these vows but should I leave and not return, I could not die and rest with these words not said to you."

Kattya smiled and bowed her head, taking in his deep words. She never really had anyone and from the sounds of it, he didn't either.

"All you have is what your family left you," she said. It sounded better in her head than in words but she knew he knew what she meant.

"I'm cursed to this life. I'm not good at anything else anyway," he concluded.

"I'm sure you're good at plenty," she said.

"My grandfather was among the greatest men ever to live. My father singlehandedly unraveled the power of Corvana and set in place their demise. Those are hard steps to follow. They're deep boots to fill, Kattya."

"At least you have something to work toward. I have nothing," she said sadly, still looking down at the ground using her arms to hang from his neck.

"You do now," he said strongly in reply.

"Legion Cage Xavier of the House Xavier of Eternis," as she spoke, she lifted her eyes back to match his gaze, "son of Dominick Gabriel Xavier, son of Taj Odin Xavier, soldier of the Republic and dear brother to Dauge Gray, you've given me the one thing this life has not, a chance. My life has always been lacking a key ingredient and, dearest Legion, I feel you may be it. I will watch your room and protect your things. I will long for you while you're away and prepare for your safe and sound return. I will greet you with open arms and a kiss. I'll learn your favorite meal and have it mastered by the time you're back. I am forever in your debt, a debt I'm glad to be in and I hope it takes me a lifetime to pay it back."

The two both knew it. They were speaking as if they'd been lovers for decades and they'd only just met. They both knew, no matter how strong or determined Legion was, life and fate could have something else in store for him. Kattya leaned in slightly closer, thinking back to both his words and her own.

"A kiss," he mumbled out of nowhere, questioningly.

She was already leaning in when he startled her with the question. She couldn't help but laugh. Legion's sense of humor was generally a bit drier but today it was dead on for her liking. After a short pause, Legion finally got his first kiss. And to the new couple of Vorrellon, the night was only beginning.

"Legion," she said. "Legion," she said again louder.

"LEGION!" Dash screamed.

His memories blasted away by Dash's screaming voice. Legion looked around. Dozens of orcs had them surrounded. Where did they come from? There were random trees and hills, brush, and bushes all around the open plains they traveled on. The open plains could be so deadly sometimes.

Legion looked around. At least two dozen orcs were present. They must have come from over the back hills to their immediate north, he thought. These orcs were Targnoktian through and through. Dash and Pitt had both seen and encountered them before. The brothers had not. They all knew them by their apparel.

The orcs were green and black and nearly every one of them wore a cape made of fur. It was one of Targnok's many symbols. Most of their armor was made of fur, bone, and leathers. The higher ranking ones were a bit taller and carried pieces of chain and plate around their bodies. Three orcs stood to the back. Every single orc carried a spear or pole-arm to some degree. They also carried short swords and daggers either in hand or at their side. Opposite their attacking hand, they carried circular shields of wood and bone. Some even had metal shield. Not a single orc was without massive scars and war wounds. On top of their shields, spears, and short swords, most of the orcs seemed to have short javelins or slings somewhere on their body visible for their adversaries to see.

In the very back, two orcs outfitted in pieced together armor, mostly plated, stood affront another. These orcs had a skin of green darker than the others and their capes looked to have been laced with dried flesh. Barbaric beasts of the most savage ancestry, Dash thought to himself.

The one they all protected was the only one present without a slashing or piercing weapon. His weapon was a bludgeoning one. It was a war hammer, unique and unlike any the four had ever seen. They'd all seen and heard of double-bladed axes and two-sided weapons but this giant of an orc carried a war hammer with a double-bladed axe on its opposing end. And its shaft was much longer than the norm.

Dash signaled for the four to hold. Just over two-dozen orcs surrounded them not counting the three standing proudly in the back. Dauge whispered something to his brother. Legion heard nothing. He was barely back into reality.

Orcs of Targnok, Legion thought. How'd he let these things creep up on them? More importantly, how did Dauge allow it? They were infringing on their land, he reminded himself. They knew the land better than Dash's team did. Dauge was good but a Targnoktian on its own soil would most certainly beat out Dauge outside a desert setting. For Dauge was raised in the desert and the desert was home to him. He was efficient in any setting just not as efficient as he could be in a desert.

The orcs moved about, readying themselves and preparing their weapons. Parlaying was not on the menu and the four knew it. They were on horseback. That could be advantageous or disastrous to them. It all depended on how it panned out and only fate knew how the coins of favor would land in the eye of the storm.

"I don't think they wish to talk," Dash said openly to the crowd, leaning back on his horse a bit to make sure they all heard.

"I'm sure they don't," Pitt agreed.

"I'm going to need to you to quickly remove yourselves from my path..." Dauge paused "...our path."

Legion remained quiet and calm, prepping himself for the enduring fight that lay ahead of them. He looked around. The orcs looked to be just as scared as they were. Then again, it was a fight and anything could happen. In an instant, a wrong move or slip could cost a man his life.

Pitt dismounted first and caressed his horse gently. The others waited. They weren't planning to dismount at all. Pitt's dismounting startled the orcs, but they found their new footing strong and steady. They weren't moving or going anywhere. Of all the races in the world, orcs were some of the proudest and most willing to engage, especially when they felt their territory was insulted or threatened.

From out of nowhere, Dash heard a clinging of metal right before his face. A shuriken whipped from Dauge as he leaped to his feet atop the saddle of his horse. His throwing star caught the head of the arrow that was secretly fired in his direction. The star destroyed the arrow's head and knocked it completely off its course.

Whoever fired the arrow, whichever orc it was, started a fight neither side was sure they wanted. The shuriken clinging with the arrow immediately put Pitt's two-handed fullblade in his hands. Dash readied his crossbow and Mourning Star was out and willing as well. Legion was off his horse, the chained ball of his weapon just praying for the engagement.

The orcs started to charge but a crying order from the one of the orcs in the back stopped their motion. Dash was still on his horse and Dauge stood atop his saddle, preparing to do whatever was necessary to succeed and see at least he and his brother through the ordeal.

Pitt and Legion both had their weapons in hand, Pitt holding his with two hands and Legion flipping his round steel shield off of his back to hold as well. The orcs systematically took a single step back and prepped javelins. The large orc with the massive warhammer/double-bladed axe barked more orders.

Pitt roared out, scaring their own horses enough to flee. Some of them were still caught in the mess of hurled javelins. Dauge launched his body from his horse. His feet flew higher than his head. Shuriken stars filled the air in every direction.

Secretly, Pitt could quasi-speak to horses and certain other animals and ferociously ordered their retreat. Pitt was the first to engage, charging and breaking through several shields of wood and bone held by the orcs.

Four, five, six, and then a seventh javelin bounced from the ever-moving Legion's newly acquired steel shield. He bounced them and bumped them away, using his own moving force to bypass every single missile launched at him. Even a few arrows and bolts found their way to him only to be countered and shunned by Legion's amazing maneuverability with the shield.

Dash tumbled back, flipping in a rolling manner from his horse after Pitt scared them all into fleeing. The half-eladrin bard landed, stumbling, on his feet. It took a second but his footing was regained. Looking up, he quickly noticed two orcs charging with short swords out. He pulled the trigger to his crossbow but it only clicked.

He darted his eyes down quickly for a quick examination. Great, not exactly the perfect time for a string to break on my crossbow, he thought. Dash released the bow and went for his short sword. He was just in time to fend off the two aggressing orcs.

Dash noticed several orcs already wounded and some even slain and from their standing locations it didn't make sense. Wait, he was moving so fast when it all happened. Dash's sword blocked both the engaging orcs, though it pushed him back a bit. Two more shuriken stars flew past him, catching both orcs in their outside legs just above their knees.

The orcs screeched. Dash felt something touch and push off his upper back toward his neck. Dash looked up. Dauge was flying through the air. He'd forced his body into the air, pushing off of Dash's back with his left foot.

Dauge rolled beautifully through the air, pushing and rotating his body into a horizontal position. His body rolled perfectly down the two orcs' backs. His momentum finally stopped when he crashed into the ground. Dust and dirt flew up from where he landed.

Dash couldn't believe his eyes. Dauge's skills were far beyond what he thought. The entrails of both creatures spilled out from their backs, dousing the younger Xavier with blood and guts and everything else.

What was left of their bodies fell lifelessly to the ground. Dash's full vision and peripheral opened up with the dropping of the two orcs and Dauge's body to the ground. Just ahead Legion was felling several orcs on his own, throwing his body around, using his shield just as much as he did Mourning Star.

Dash called forth to his arcane tricks, mixing their own balance and footing with refined arcane powers. Legion was soon to be enveloped in orcs. Dash's quick thinking forced several of Legion's would be killers back and away from him. Dash yelled out words none of the others could make out. He was speaking arcanically; that is, through the powers of the arcane.

"Deis Rach En Krieg Assyriche!" he yelled.

None present could make out what the bard was saying. He was speaking the ancient language, one no longer practiced anywhere in the known realms of Thedia.

Legion let out a frightening growl. Dash gave him just the space he needed to continue with his momentum. His shield beat back the aggressing orcs and Mourning Star sung magically through the air, smashing into and caving in the skulls of several enemies. Legion whirled the ball and chain linked to the shaft he held around relentlessly. He'd mastered the art of rolling with his own momentum and even backpedaling to hide behind his shield for protection when need be. It was surely a sight to see the elder Xavier work with his tools.

A piercing shot opened up the flesh on the outside left thigh of Pitt. The cut dimly told him the location of his next victim. Pitt threw his elbow slamming it hard into the face of his blood spiller. The orc coughed in pain but didn't let out any noise to further prove his anguish.

Its nose crumbled and smashed back into its face. The orc lowered his head and shoulder and pushed forward still. Pitt finished off the one beast affront him before releasing his blade with his right hand. He kept grips with his left and swung overhand, cracking the same orc's helm in two. His blade brushed down, cutting into the side of its head and even its shoulder. Without both hands and full strength, the goliath wasn't able to finish him. Now, with the one-handed backswing of his two-handed weapon, Pitt turned to face the pace-pushing orc.

Dauge was already back up and cutting through rows of the remaining orcs, running past groups of them, slicing each of them open with his arm blades two at a time. The creatures swung back but the younger Xavier made the warriors of Targnok look like simple children. He was on top of his game and no one could stop him.

He danced, leaping ahead from one foot to the next, ducking and dodging while cutting and slashing through the "experienced" soldiers of Targnok like they were statues of flesh. His swiftness made the orcs look as if they were unable to move.

Dash yelled aloud another series of short words that none could make out and Pitt's massive blade burst into flames. Pitt smiled and the heat from his blade finally pushed back the pace-pushing orc.

The broken-nosed orc pulled a javelin from the ground once belonging to one of his comrades. He lunged forward with the javelin only to have Pitt knock it aside. The savvy orc knew Pitt's move and counted on it. He let go of the wooden javelin and forced his entire body forward, putting behind his sword every ounce of weight and energy he had.

The sword found its mark on the flesh of Pitt, tearing through his light armor, splitting the skin between two of his ribs on his left side, the same side as his wounded leg. Pitt swung down violently, screaming out in anger. The orc moved, ducking his head and sidestepping. Pitt's wild and angry swing barely grazed the orc who again attacked, putting the tip of his short weapon into the left bicep of the hulking goliath.

"AGH!" Pitt fell back, dragging the front tip of his sword on the ground, holding his bleeding bicep with his right hand.

Pitt wanted to push the fight further. The cuts and wounds aggravated him but the orc fell back into the horde of still aggressing orcs. Pitt looked to the back of the line. All three of the "leading" orcs were gone from their positions.

Pitt heard a pain-filled screech to his right. He was still positioned closer to the outside of the fighting along with Dash. The brothers Legion and Dauge were in the thickest stints of it. It was Dauge's voice railing out in pain.

Seeing the immediate threat next to him falling back, Pitt took the opportunity and looked over to see the youngest Xavier. Dauge finally found stern footing. He was no longer running through the crowd of orcs spilling flesh, blood, and guts all throughout his path. Pitt saw a nasty opening in his armor and flesh on his right arm. It was javelin made. He'd seen those cuts before.

A massive greatsword came from nowhere, trying to find Dauge's neck. Dauge pulled his armblades back to his face, extending his arms outward and up in front of him. He brought his arms to an upright ninety-degree angle with his fists holding their weapons' grips at eye level. This kept the edge of the swords outward and their points aimed downward.

The twin armblades caught the wrecking greatsword in full swing. The force of the swing lifted Dauge off his feet, launching him several feet back. Dauge had zero chance to keep his footing and allowed his body to roll, using the momentum of the greatsword's swing to drive his body completely over and hopefully back to his feet.

The force of Mourning Star proved too great for the simple weaponry and skills of the orcs. His shield continued to prove to be just as lethal as his weapon. Legion felt the power within his morning star. His weapon's power grew with every swing and every drop of blood. The star talked to him. It ordered warrior to feed it. Feed it blood. "Feed me," it said relentlessly to Legion.

The dry grass now dripped with blood. Heat waves blew across the open plains, hitting select trees in their wake. The weather was turning hot. It should've been getting cold. Perhaps they were still a ways away before the cold would set in. After all, they were heading to the coast nearing the Frozen Sea.

Dash's healing wasn't superb but it would do. He sent magic missiles into the torsos and bodies of half a dozen orcs while still getting off a decent enough heal spell to mend the wound on Pitt's arm and partially close the wound on his ribs.

Legion rushed, seeing his brother in trouble, stepping in to face the orc that put him on his butt. Legion rushed in with a shield rush, making his adversary block with the massive sword. Legion counted on the counter, continuing his momentum, bending his knees to lower his stance. His follow-through saw Mourning Star's chain wrap around the larger orc's leg twice before having its spiked ball end crush into its shin just below the knee.

The creature didn't relinquish one bit of sound following the crushing of his lower leg. He fell to the knee Legion attacked. He didn't have a minute to embrace the pain. By the time he could look up to see the man who defeated him, Legion was already back up to one knee and rising with his shield fluidly in motion.

The shield swipe caught the orc sub leader in the neck, destroying his windpipe and ruining his ability to breathe. The large orc fell over to his back, holding his throat, gagging on his own blood. Legion jumped back to his feet ready to go.

Dauge flipped backward to his knees. He rolled the blades to extend outward from his wrists rather than run down his forearms in the midst of the rolling. He sat back, dropping his weight to his feet. Two orcs were already on the move to get him. Both found their guts impaled by his now outward sticking armblades.

The orcs walked arrogantly, raising their swords high against the downed Dauge. The quick thinking and moving Dauge surprised them with a move of his own. He stood, pulling his short swords, seeing there was no time to retrieve his armblades from the dying and slowly dropping back-impaled orcs.

Dauge stood just as the two impaled collapsed. He cried out angrily but it was too late. Legion, his brother, took a fatal worthy shot from the largest orc wielding the double-sided weapon; on one side was the warhammer and the other the double-bladed axe. It was the hammer that caught him in a downward swing.

The one shot caught the off-guard Legion, felling him, dropping his nearly unconscious body to the bloodstained grassy field below.

"No!" Dauge yelled, launching both of his short swords simultaneously at the behemoth attacking his brother.

Seeing Legion drop, Pitt charged forward too. Dash saw that only a few orcs remained. And of those that did, they were all either bleeding out or otherwise too wounded to continue their fight. Only the titanic orc leader and one of its sub leaders were still combative.

The leader orc rolled his weapon around, hoping for a dramatic finish to the first of his adversaries by splitting his head with the opposing end of his weapon. Legion had enough left to roll to his back and brace himself with the shield. In order to do so, he was forced to let go of his Mourning Star to hold the shield with both hands.

Immediately, he felt the pain of releasing the Star's grip. It hurt. It pained him like losing a loved one. The axe crashed into his shield. Legion maneuvered and rolled with the force, pushing and sliding the shield toward the ground. The momentum of the axe shaved a deep gash in the shield. Legion's body rolled out from under it and away from where the axe end and his shield were.

The warrior was too disoriented to see what was coming. The axe end flew up and back. Now the orc was attacking another. The hammer side swung through the air parallel to the creature's torso level. A soothing sense of warmth drowned his pain covering his body. And in a fleeting moment it was gone. It was gone but Legion felt better. He felt replenished. He'd been healed.

One of Dauge's swords caught the swinging behemoth in its abdomen. The other continued its song, singing past him, just barely missing its right lower torso, from Dauge's perspective. That coincidentally was exactly what Dauge hoped for.

Pitt too was charging forward. Dauge's blade catching his abdomen took quite a huff out of the monster, slowing down his full-frontal swing from the hammer side of his weapon. Pitt showed his true agility, twisting to gain more force, planting his feet perfectly to drive up but under the swinging monster.

The hammer slowing down gave Pitt the time he needed to come up just underneath the orc leader. The creature being struck knocked him completely off balance. Pitt coming up forced the creature's weapon out of its grasp, a difficult thing to do to such a large creature with a two-handed weapon. The orc's arms momentarily hung over the sword, cleaving through him.

Pitt gave out with a triumphant roar. The goliath followed his momentum forward, walking through as needed. When it was done, still raising his sword high and standing back to a tall, upright position, he heard the knees of the orc fall to the dirt below. He gave it his all, hoping to cut the beast in half but only quarterly succeeded.

The tip of his fullblade dropped to the ground. His eyes caught the single thing still in action, a short sword flying. Just as quickly as his eyes fell to it did it find its mark just below the neck where the torso begins in the last remaining sub-leader orc, killing him almost instantly.

Pitt looked back. Dash was up dusting himself off and Dauge was looking around. Several orcs got away. Pitt wondered about the orc that stuck him a few times. He never saw him fall. Did he survive? Several orcs did flee there toward the end.

"Karuuuuuuu Rugh!" Pitt yelled aloud, arching his chest to the sky and leaning back to let it out with all he had.

"What the hell are you doing?" Dash said, laughing, happy they all survived.

Legion crawled over the dead behemoth, reaching for his Star just as quickly as his body would carry him. The moment his palms and fingers made their grip around it, he heard a single, solitary word.

"Glory," it said.

Legion gasped out, still needing more air. He knew it was Dash who healed him and for it he was grateful. His hands upon her hilt one more time, it was a satisfaction unlike anything he could explain.

"You're going to get yourself killed brother," Dauge said, interrupting Legion's momentary trip from reality.

Legion looked back, seeing his brother peel the last armblade from the dead orc. Pitt looked around, pointing out in the distance. The horses were coming back.

"I've called them. I sent them away and now I've called them. My connection to the wild is a bit greater than I've ever told you, old friend," he said, smiling at Dash.

The horses galloped back toward the crew as if he'd summoned them back magically. The goliath's trick impressed even the arcanically and divinely in-tuned Dash. Pitt reached over, grabbing the massive two-handed weapon of the orc.

"I'm not sure I can leave this behind," he joked. "What a weapon. I've not seen one like this before."

"We're lucky to have survived that. Killing Targnok orcs will not ease our passing to the frozen mountains where Azra Goetia is said to exist. Since we're here let's round up any coin and materials we could use from them," Dash ordered.

Dauge walked forward over the dead orcs, grabbing noticeable pouches of gold here and there. He heard the half-eladrin speak out again from behind him.

"We'll divvy it up when it's all done."

Dauge snarled sarcastically, laughing to himself. It was a moment he had something perfect to say to that damned half-breed but he did save his brother with arcane healing. Dauge recovered the rest of his weapons while Pitt, Legion and Dash started gathering gold and materials left behind by the defeated orcs.

Dauge didn't partake in the taking of the dead beasts' gold and things. He looked around, taking the time to reflect while keeping a keen eye on anything that could be coming their way.

"Yep, I'm certain. This weapon is too big and just too good to pass up. I'm keeping it," Pitt said, laughing. He didn't seem fazed at all by the recent conflict.

Soon, the horses were packed. There wasn't too much aside from gold that the party took from the dead orcs, but there were some blankets, dried rations and the like that could prove to be more than useful.

"Should be about a hundred and seventeen a piece," Dash said, counting the last of the coins. Secretly, Dauge never threw in the pouches of gold he found, amassing an extra forty gold privately.

There were silver coins, copper coins, and gold as well, totaling about a hundred and seventeen for each of the four.

"Let's move," Dauge said.

"My brother's right," Legion seconded, finishing up the prep his saddle needed before heading out.

"Staying here any longer than we have to could prove to be fatal. Who knows how many more are out there, around in these parts," Dauge continued.

"You're right," Dash said.

The words hit Dauge, catching him off guard. Dash agreed. More importantly, he knew he had to concede to the mental psyche of Dauge, making him believe he truly cared for his opinions. This would empower him mentally, keeping them all proud and focused on the mission at hand, Azra Goetia.

"That amount of gold Lord Stannor wants just went down a bit," Pitt said, laughing.

The new weapon would've certainly encumbered any normal horse. Thankfully, Pitt's horse was already a superior one, a bit larger in size compared to the norm.

The four leaped atop their horses. Legion made a comment, knowing the goliath could call back horses with relative ease was a skill far better revealed in the beginning of a quest rather than midway through. The four laughed continuing their journey to the Vile Frozen Land south of the Mogra hoping to soon find the mythical city of Azra Goetia.

Chapter 48

It was a long and hard road for Magnus Black and Kleiven Dar but their road finally formed a destination in Valakuza. Word by the gypsies and other travelers they passed along the way was that Bahaus had been stopped and defeated at Emerald Greene, the Crystal City by his own son Drackice Black and his Free Armies.

The aging General and father and the son of another were finally at their destination. Retired General Seth Redd and his recently formed irregulars, as well as many veteran followers, of the General were gone. They'd left to retake Eternis and restore order to its people.

The aging Magnus coughed, his lungs filled with sickness. They'd been plagued with the illness for some days. Magnus was known in Valakuza and the tall iron gates of the southwestern entrance rose with a warm welcoming waiting for the man.

Valakuza was a militant city-state and its soldiers were believed to be two to three times as good as any other known to exist. They trained intensely from birth and every man and woman were ordered to serve at least three years upon entering their fifteenth year of age. Occasionally, when ranks were full, some were allowed to leave the military early.

A midsized wall of brick and stone wrapped around the outskirts of Valakuza. The buildings and structures weren't built very high. Tactical strategies and military minds of the city believed staying lower to the ground was much safer and much more secure against aerial attacks and other ranged attacks.

Several guards of the city quickly jumped to attention saluting the elder General. Kleiven couldn't believe the respect Magnus got everywhere he went. He was like a hero in every city, even in the cities he fought against.

One guard that looked to carry rank rushed to him. Several others did the same seemingly coming out of the woodworks for the Mercenary General. The guard was dragonborn and close to middle age. He wore a suit of fully plated armor with a chain helm. At his side rested a large sheath and on his back he carried a strapped circular shield made completely of steel. And over it all he wore a white tunic with black symbols strategically placed across it. Strange, Kleiven couldn't make out a single one. Typically, kingdoms and city-states and the like used symbols that could easily be identified but apparently not Valakuza. This city-state chose to use symbols and themes queer to any who saw them save those familiar with their city and its customs.

"My lord, you've returned. General Seth Redd has left with his armies. He called for the aid of irregulars. They've left to retake Eternis from King Bahaus." The dragonborn spoke almost like he'd been waiting for General Black's return.

General Black shook his head listening to the man's words. He placed a hand on the soldier's shoulder. "I've run into many travelers on my way to Valakuza. We've traveled a far distance and did so swiftly thanks to the Hangman's Straight and the crafts we used to float through it. I must admit I did not anticipate making it here. Several encounters with travelers tell me Bahaus has been ousted. My son, Drackice Black handed him a sound defeat at Emerald Greene or so it seems."

"He's been killed?" the soldier replied, reassuring the cruel king's death.

"I believe so. The travelers did not say, none of them did," he replied.

Kleiven sat back listening to General Black speak to the man as if they were old friends. He listened as their conversation continued, mesmerized at the way these people looked and spoke to him. Eventually, the soldier finished.

"My lord, I'll have a room prepared for you at once! I'll fetch the healers to cleanse your lungs. Let me take your armor and weapons. Let me get this load from your bones," he said submissively, yet speaking quickly in order to hurry and relieve the sick General.

"General Black, how do you know this dragonborn?" he asked.

"I don't," he replied.

"You two spoke like you'd picked up a conversation you two had a day ago," Kleiven said, confused.

"I'm not sure if you heard the entirety of the conversation. I killed his father at the Battle of Wages."

"I was looking around keeping an eye out and I'm exhausted. Forgive me General but I may have missed some of his words," Kleiven responded.

"It's okay. We're both tired. We've had a long travel. We shouldn't have made it this far so quickly. We'll be safe here and I'll rest easier knowing Seth Redd is retaking the city. Drackice defeated Bahaus at Emerald Greene. Eternis is safe," he said, beginning another series of violent coughs afterward.

"You need to rest, my lord," Kleiven said.

"Aye, I do. The soldier said The Warrior's Burial will have a room prepped for the both of us as long as we'd like. It should be just past Town Square."

"The Warrior's Burial?" Kleiven questioned.

"It's the inn we're going to be living at for a long while, boy. Get used to this town. We're going to be here for a long, long while."

Kleiven did exactly as he was told, bringing the sickly General to the said inn. Kleiven never made it a step inside. The General dismissed him when he was still a few dozen feet away. Kleiven wished his liege well, bowed, and turned to explore the city further. He wasn't really certain what to do. He had no friends here. He knew nothing and no one. It was a city built on military prowess and training. One thing hit his mind he was sure would take the edge off.

Kleiven made his way to the nearest tavern his feet could take him to. The Poisonous Vineyard sounds perfect, he thought. The raunchy and dirty warrior from Eternis walked into the small hole in the wall. There wasn't much to it, not much at all. It was a simple square structure with a few tables, a small bar, and a few old pictures on the wall.

There weren't any barmaids present. An old dragonborn stood behind the small bar, as did an elder dwarf. There were a few matching both of their races scattered here and there in the place. Most of the people were older. Great, fantastic, he sarcastically said bitching to himself in his own mind. He figured he just walked into an old watering hole for the retired.

He ordered a drink from the balding dwarf. Dark ale was his favorite. It wasn't the tastiest or the most expensive. It was all he could afford as a young lad in service to his city. He took a seat at the bar and the moment the cold ale touched his lips he heard the symphonic sounds of an angel. She sang. Her words ricocheted off every wall, glass and other suitable object, piercing his ears, infecting him indefinitely with the longing to hear more.

His head at first slumped into his glass. The singing voice belonging to whatever angel was present now had his attention. He turned his head, pulling his head out of his glass. There, on a small side stage she sat. A young woman not matching his own age with eyes closed and locks of brown hair bleeding down from the top of her head. Blonde and black streaks rolled down from the top of her head as well. With nothing but a backpack at her feet and a dark brown, or perhaps black, dog at her side, she sang. She sang like there was no one watching throwing her cares to the wind.

She sat on a high risen chair, putting the lying dog right at the level of her feet. Her feet were bare of shoes, arched up on the last bottom rung of the wooden stool. She wore a short dress, simple and slightly torn. It was dull and faded from its time in the sun and she was long overdue for a new one.

"And I remember back when I was twenty-two, I'm changing things... my life is new." She'd finished yet another perfect song. This song talked about reflecting on one's life, looking back on past mistakes and making changes for the future. It was angelical.

She picked up immediately following the end of her last one. "Dova kin, var-hymn, dova-kin far." She was speaking in a language queer to at least Kleiven.

"With our blood and our steel, we'll take back our home." Her beautiful song continued. It turned back to the common tongue he could understand, thankfully.

Her words, her songs, it all doped up his memories, filling them all with hints and pieces of Dusk Xavier. Dusk was far away and hopefully safe. How did things get so complicated? The answer was Bahaus Sazos-Uil-Endail, the ousted, yet rightful, heir to the Eternian throne.

Bahaus tried to get him killed, constantly forcing him into harm's way and forcing him to remain in the service of Eternis, putting him in positions he was never qualified for. Then, to make matters worse Dusk fell for another man, Grath. And what did Bahaus do? He sent Grath far, far away in hopes the task would kill him.

In retrospect, he didn't like Grath either but he didn't want the man killed. However, he was a shadow elf and those bastards just didn't belong here. They were remnants and reminders of what an Invading God once did to the beautiful world of Thedia.

The more he thought about it the more he started turning against his love for Dusk. Sure, she was beautiful. And yes, she came from a great family he'd grown up with. She was a traitor. She betrayed him in the most sick and horrid manner. She betrayed his love.

His love wouldn't falter. He worshiped her. He adored everything about her, her strengths and weaknesses and her every little fault. She betrayed him. He would prove to her yet again his love and devotion to her. The beautiful woman's songs brought him back to a place he thought he'd escaped months ago.

The tavern was closing. Kleiven tossed the barkeep a few gold, clearly dropping much more coin than necessary to pay for the drinks. He was drunk. He'd drunk himself into a stupor. Trying to stand up, the stool beneath him fell out, nearly tripping the Eternian soldier as well.

Somehow he made it to the door. He planted his hands all around its frame to keep himself on his feet.

"Here let me help you," a voice said from behind.

Two arms wrapped underneath him. A force took some of the burden off of his feet. He gasped for air. He knew he'd consumed far too much alcohol. The songs, it was the songs that did it. They made him think of times long gone. They reminded him of difficult times, ones he did not want to relive.

Whatever it was grabbing him helped him continuously. She kept talking, trying to guide him in the right direction. She didn't know here he was staying.

"If you don't tell me where you're staying, you're just going to have to stay with me tonight, kind soldier," she said.

That voice, it belonged to the singing angel didn't it? He was drunk but that was a brave notion on her part. She didn't know a thing about him. The streets were dimly lit and few walked on them. Soldiers kept their posts, though. The buildings melted and blurred away. Then the streets went along with everything else.

He awoke the next morning. Kleiven's head ached. The ground was cushioned but nonetheless, he was lying on solid ground. He had sheets pressed under him and a soft wool blanket over his body. A pillow held his head gently.

His blurred vision slowly came back. Looking around, he quickly realized he was in the room of an inn somewhere.

"Where am I?" he mumbled.

Just then, legs crossed over his body belonging to a stunning woman. It was the woman from the night before. It was the woman singing to his heart. Or so, that's how it felt. She was wearing an extraordinary black dress and more pearls than the sea had to offer.

The woman, now nearly fully dressed, walked over to the far side of the room. She interchanged her jewelry taking some off and adding more and then replacing the originals once again. Kleiven's vision still wasn't perfect but it was clearing up with every second.

"Who are you? Why am I here?" He raised his head as high as he could to keep his eyes on the woman.

It was too much. Kleiven's head just fell back into the pillow. The woman giggled. Her giggles flourished into laughter. Kleiven couldn't help it. The laughter was contagious. He was forced to laugh too.

Chuckling, still with an aching head, he asked her again. "Lady, I humbly ask again. Where am I and who are you?" Now his face was cracked from the smile he wore ear to ear.

"I am Malukah," she said, finishing her facial makeup and jewelry adorning.

"I am Kleiven Dar, son of former Commander Cale Dar of Eternis," he said, giving his name and titles simultaneously with her.

Hers was short and sweet. She simply told him her name was Malukah. Kleiven took a second and got a breath. His laughter stopped momentarily. Then, he asked for her to further and titles with him.

"Malukah of?" he asked.

"Just Malukah," she said.

The answer again amplified the smile on Kleiven's face. He couldn't help but laugh and smile around this woman he didn't even know. For a second he fell back in time to a place where Dusk once affected him this same way.

"Just Malukah huh?" he replied.

"Yep, just Malukah," she answered.

"I guess…" he started, pausing momentarily to gather his thought. "I guess thank you. I guess I had more than my share last night?"

"You're doing a lot of guessing," she said, laughing, this time turning her head around to face him.

It was her. This time her hair was just a natural brown color, slightly dark and her eyes were dark like a Thoxen's. She looked like she very well could be from the massive lands of the southern nation of Thox. "The colors in your hair, was I drunk or they all gone now?" he asked.

"They're gone. It's part of the show," she answered.

"That's a beautiful dress, Malukah. The one you wore to sing in last night was tattered and old, torn even."

"Yes, but now I have a date, a middle-of-the-day lunch date. If I wore this to work do you think people would be so quick to tip and do you think they would tip as handsomely?" she said, laughing.

"You're a con," he said.

"No, I'm no con. I don't trick anyone into anything, Kleiven of Eternis. If someone were to ask I would tell them I was just fine. People make their own assumptions, and yes, I can play to those assumptions but its not my fault people aren't more intuitive," she replied, still smiling.

"You're a smart one." He took another deep breath, bringing the low part of his palms to his eyes, hoping by somehow pressing on them, the pain of his head would somehow be alleviated.

"I do what I must. I'm a traveling singer. It's how I survive. I never stay anywhere too long but I never stay gone for too long either. I've mapped out my territory and I rarely stray from it," she said, smiling. "Now, I must be going. You seem nice but I'm afraid I'm going to have to ask you to leave. I must get going and I don't trust perfect strangers in my room while I'm gone."

"You let me stay here last night?" he said.

"I was here," she replied slyly.

"And what if I wanted to do something, even though you were here?" he asked.

"First of all, you were too drunk to do much of anything. Second of all, if I'm here then I can take care of myself," she replied. "Now, it's not up for discussion. You got to go."

Kleiven started to pick himself up off the floor, issuing another mumbled thank you her way again. She didn't seem to mind or need the thank you. She assisted the soldier halfway to his feet, virtually pushing him out of the room, walking right behind him and locking the door behind her.

"Well, it was a pleasure, Kleiven, but I really must be going."

Kleiven found himself out of the woman's door soon after, and soon after that she was far ahead of him, rushing down the halls as if she were going to be late for something important. He knew what to do when drunk or lightheaded. Anytime dizziness or something along those lines affected one's sight, the best thing to do is find a focal point. He did.

Kleiven couldn't help but keep his eyes on her swaying bottom as she walked away. She was gorgeous, having a body to die for. And more than her body, Kleiven had fallen in love with her voice already. Her voice was an enigma.

She was something else and something about her reminded him of Dusk, partially in a good way and partially in a horrible one. He remembered the best times of his life and in each of those moments dusk was present. She also reopened the doorways to hate and anger in regard to her betrayal of him with that non-Eternian, non-human, the shadow elven man named Grath.

Dusk and Kleiven were reunited and everything was behind them, right? Soon, he would once again be in her arms. Soon, all of this would be behind them with only better days lying ahead. He couldn't wait for that time to arrive. He'd longed for it a while now.

The day was new and there was work to be done. First, he had to return to Magnus. He'd most likely have to apologize for completely submitting himself to the toxins of alcohol. Magnus wasn't one he'd consider a forgiving person and this was not the time nor the place for it. He couldn't help it. He needed to let go at least for a night and the alcohol got him to where he needed to be.

Now, the day was new and that was behind him. He was preparing for what was to come and most likely, his return to Eternis. The Free Armies led by Magnus' son defeated Bahaus. Seth Redd was taking his followers and mercenaries to Eternis to reclaim the city. With Bahaus' men gone for the battle at Emerald Greene, now was the time to reclaim it. Even if Bahaus still had loyal forces in Eternis, they wouldn't be at full force, especially considering they'd just tasted defeat. One of the greatest dangers in attacking another land is leaving your own not fully protected. Then again, that was the game of swords, the game of war, knowing what to send and what to hold back.

Chapter 49

The pain in Dusk's body and brain kept her bedridden another week. Drackice looked after her personally. Ingenious, Bahaus thought to himself still connected to the machination's bleeding powers from the sleeping titans, ritual castings, the temple's innate powers, and his own.

Bahaus was now the heart of Aristophane's plan. What she didn't know was that he was also the brain but she would soon find out. Aristophane kept her casters in place. Sacrifices were constantly being brought in. Bahaus further ordered the armies to build and grow, beginning with Seskar and Garokk's outer pushes. This plan got better; knowing his mental attacks on Dusk would keep the current leader of the Free Armies busy while they decimated their ranks.

Seskar would march and lead some of the armies against Emerald Greene, yes Emerald Greene, the city that defeated him. He sold it to Aristophane so perfectly. Aristophane hoped to awaken the titans and in order to do so, very rare and unique things would have to be acquired, and almost every one of them could be acquired through the main Crystal City. Not to mention, with Bahaus recently attacking them, they would already be weak from battle and those that were in tuned to retaliate would be more focused on reclaiming Eternis than joining Drackice, as he'd already "defeated" his enemy anyway. Then, with the armies off fighting Emerald Greene, Garokk could take some of the smaller armies and forcibly recruit right here in the mountains. It was a genius plan, all the while keeping the attention off Bahaus and Aristophane and what they truly aimed to do.

Bahaus' magical prowess was increasing by the day. The entity inside Dusk seemingly fought against him everyday on the Astral. The notion and movement itself, while not directly on Dusk's brain lengths, did still affect her, for Davion was connected to her. He was linked to her very soul at this point and Bahaus knew it. He also knew she wasn't human.

And to think, he was going to grace that feeble bitch with a royal child of his blood. Even so, the offer still stood. He never failed to remind her that she was not only a non-human and non-Eternian, but she was a corrupted Genasi. She was primarily of the voidsoul manifest, a corrupted manifest in its purest form.

"Not this time, fallen crown, this one stays." Bahaus heard the voice of the skeleton constantly sticking thorns in his side.

"Fallen crown?" Bahaus questioned.

He knew what the creature meant. He was referring to his defeat at the hands of Drackice and losing the crown of Eternis. Drackice took it all from him when he crushed him at Emerald Greene. Now, his focus on Dusk would leave Drackice focused on her. He could see through her eyes and see his desire for her. He would use the man's lust for the Xavier girl against him. He would have his vengeance against Drackice and Eternis would soon once again be his.

The world was gone, absent of land and air. Bahaus awoke to the bleakness of the Astral. White speckles of hope appearing as stars flew past him, first at high speeds and then at lower ones. If one did not know how to maneuver through the Astral, it could quickly become hopeless and mad to the said being.

Bahaus' ability to Astral Project was already uncanny and the power of the sleeping titans only enhanced his abilities. How could this have landed so perfectly? Now, all he had to do was wait patiently and implement his will on Dusk ever so carefully to see his bidding done.

This lone creature refusing to accept its fate as dead now stood in his way. By the hells, everything landed perfectly for him and yet the defeat at Emerald Greene and other mishaps continued to quasi-set him back. For every step back, he found a way to move three steps forward.

"I am here to push you back to the prime material forever. I shall make sure you're never able to return to Astral. You have no business in the plane of lost and fallen gods. The gods of Thedia and other planes, both still alive and long forgotten or destroyed, rest here.

"I do not need you or anyone else to tell me of my powers," Bahaus barked back.

Still, the two weren't formed in the Astral yet. Their bodies were still becoming of it, coming over as it were. As their arguing grew, the two watched on as each materialized before the other. Coming up from underneath them, a god-isle.

A god-isle was the remains of a god either dead or long forgotten, or sometimes both now only existent in the Astral Plane, where space, time, and gravity didn't exist. Only on god-isles did things similar to material planes like space, time, and gravity exist at all. And there on god-isles were where creatures like the planar githyanki and githzerai made their homes, building communities and civilizations directly on the fallen gods' remaining essences. Planar creatures used the god-isles to keep them grounded in the Astral and also constantly mined the isles of ore, powers, food, and other things they felt they could use. Hence, some god-isles were considered better than others forcing wars between civilizations.

And then, there were some god-isles that could exist for ten lifetimes and never cross paths with another. Some god-isles were considered greater than others but usually civilizations built upon the backs of those god-isles would never be taken or defeated.

"You've no concept for time here," Davion challenged.

"Nor do you," Bahaus replied. "You've not accepted the fact the world doesn't want you anymore. Its tablets of fate have issued you a warrant of death and you just refuse to turn in."

"This place no longer holds regard as it once did for prime-material-born specimens. Do yourself a favor and return from whence you came."

Bahaus looked on. He knew it was Davion. He'd gotten his name from their first encounter. Davion was a lich once thriving in the Red Mystic Mountains. Now, he made his home somewhere in the realm of Thox.

Davion's skeletal body was purely black and encrusted with diamonds and jewels now. For the first time since meeting him in the Astral, Bahaus saw the creature wearing white robes as opposed to his normal brown and black ones.

His eyes still bled with fire. Fiery drops bled down from the creature's body in several places. The drops dripped down to nothingness below. "You've gotten stronger every time I've faced you," Davion said.

"It's no longer just me you'll be fighting, friend. I've taken powers from sources beyond even your understanding," Bahaus said, rallying back.

"Dying here will leave your material body lifeless, Bahaus," Davion reminded him.

"I don't intend on dying. The girl is mine. I need her to fulfill certain duties. Well, I need her presence too. I've researched and acquired knowledge in specified powers that will leave you speechless, lich." This time, Bahaus finished with the word lich, utilizing it as a direct insult to his adversary.

"I swore an oath. I cannot let you have her." The lich stood strongly behind his words.

"Then luck is on your side. For I will take her, against your will or not!" Bahaus concluded, calling forth to his powers to prepare for the fight.

Feeling and seeing Bahaus' powers, Davion moved to call forth his own. Davion felt Bahaus take a move he wasn't familiar with. Prismatic forces channeled from far away planes opened gates, pushing pure prismatic forces through the Eternian's very veins and blood. Even Davion, a lich and lifelong scholar of the arcane knew not of this art.

Davion was already a lich and was presumably about the same age of Quinn. They'd travelled together even. His natural lifespan would not have ended yet. Though he was a lich, he wasn't an ancient one. However, those that knew him would argue his powers said differently.

In the Astral, many guards and wards spells materialized as transparent walls, making it difficult for others to see what they were up against. There was nothing transparent about the prismatic eyes and now skin tone of Bahaus Sazos-Uil-Endail. He was fighting with powers no longer meant for the mortal world and certainly not by the hands of a cunning wizard.

Davion's immediate move was to counter Bahaus' using defense as his first option. Davion's opening cast was to be a delicate one. He put in place a form of spell turning, meaning, if Bahaus was to cast a spell that focused directly on him, the spell would be turned and cancelled. However, his ability to quicken and shell out spells faster than others allowed him to duplicate the spell, putting in place two spell-turning casts. One was readied for direct aggression and the other for counter spell challenges.

Bahaus was confident, too confident. Then again, the raw energies of two beings once said to rival the gods flowed through him effortlessly. Erebrus, the titan of darkness and Nyx, the female titan of night both flowed through his veins and coolly as his own blood did. Not even the lich Davion could challenge him now.

Greenish energies birthed, wrapping around Bahaus' wrists, extending downward into the deep blackness below. The tentacles of necrotic energies didn't whip at the lich Davion but masses of the same tentacles did. They came from the endless nothing all around them flowing into formation. There must have been at least a hundred. Bahaus was pleased to see them all. Even he didn't believe he could pull off that many.

To his dismay, Davion's spell turning was already in place. The necrotic tentacles growing from the endless black all dissipated. It took the expelling of both spell turnings in place to defend and destroy them all.

Combustions of arcane went off all around the two; every single tentacle exploded infuriating Bahaus even more. Bahaus retaliated, sending hundreds of missiles fueled by strife; Bahaus' rain of missiles was almost completely fashioned from sonic energies.

Davion waved them off like they were nothing. Almost instantaneously, the sonic energies dissipated into the nothingness surrounding them. The lich grinned. It'd been a long time since something of this magnitude challenged him.

Davion's black tentacles, ripped from the nothingness, were next to impossible to see from in contrast to the black all around them. Only four birthed but each of them was larger than ten that Bahaus crafted earlier.

One tentacle wrapped around Bahaus' left wrist, and then another wrapped up his right. The other two came about, locking his legs in place by wrapping up his ankles, spreading him eagle in the vastness of infinite.

Bahaus ignored the gripping tentacles, preferring to fire back with powers of his own. Davion was still focused on maintaining and keeping the tentacles in place, leaving him vulnerable for two massive rays, both blasting outward from his eyes.

The prismatic rays bolted out from his eyes, bleeding energies downward and upward and in all directions. Both rays hit directly, bolstering through the upper torso of the lich. His very bones changed colors. Initially, the change in color was from the assault but Davion tried to counter channeling in the same energies to dupe the power into thinking it was all one in the same. And once the energies were duped, he could dump them from his body without taking too much damage in the process.

What luck! The energy dupe and dump worked. Davion even managed to catch the energy. He rolled and rolled it, forming it into a raw ball of pure prismatic energies of the highest degree. His vision still wasn't reset back to his adversary. His black tentacles were in place holding his adversary and soon his own prismatic energies along with a mix of Davion's would have his enemy destroyed.

Davion turned, unleashing everything he had into the molten ball of prismatic destruction. Bahaus screamed out in pain, feeling his astral flesh tear at the arms and hips from the pulling powers of the monstrous tentacles.

Davion heard his astral flesh tearing. It was also tearing somewhere else, somewhere not targeted. The gigantic ball of whirling colors stopped dead in its tracks just as soon as Davion got it moving. From out of Bahaus' mouth, another ethereal, wraithlike entity pulled itself out.

This creature was no less dark than the endless void beneath them. Like the tentacles, it was hard to see and in the blink of an eye, it changed to a shade of grayish blue so bright it nearly lit up the entire Astral.

Davion never saw the thing hit him. What happened to Bahaus was also still a mystery. The lich looked around, his body was broken and busted and bleeding arcane more than it'd ever done before. That meant Bahaus ripped him out of the Astral and won their fight. Whatever that was that hit him wasn't natural, he thought.

He looked around, seeing a blurred concept of his underground home. The cavern was blurred to his vision. With every passing moment, Bahaus' energies increased. He knew the powers of the mountains flowed through him and now, he no longer possessed the powers to face him on the Astral. The source of his powers would have to be stopped and fast. Bahaus could no longer be tried and tested steel to arcane or arcane to arcane. Something had his power beyond this world's reckoning and that something was somewhere in the Red Mystic Mountains.

His domain slowly came back to him. He knew Bahaus had to be stopped. Who would stop him? Who could stop him? With Davion no longer able, who would defend Dusk Xavier from his forceful advances through the Astral.

Davion's only hope was to lure growing and powerful heroes to the Red Mystic Mountains, where Bahaus Sazos-Uil-Endail now thrived. Had Davion been living, he would have surely been separated from his body and ultimately killed. Fortunately, natural death was not something he needed to fear.

Perhaps somehow connecting to another powerful presence in the world was a viable option? Perhaps another could answer the call. He knew Legion and his brother had their crew and were heading to Azra Goetia.

His link was solely with Legion and even he didn't fully understand it. Legion's blood wasn't purely whole. It wasn't fully warm to say the least. The taint of undeath lurked in the man's verve. He would have to find something or someone to answer the call and soon.

Chapter 50

It had been weeks, well over a month, with only a few more orcish skirmishes and finally the team was making headway. Strings of rivers connected to the same central body of water started flourishing all around them. At one point, the horses even stopped to graze and drink a bit.

"These strings of rivers, they're all connected to the same internal body of water, right?" Dauge asked.

"They are," Pitt replied.

"Yes, the names of these rivers and the bodies they're connected to escape me at the moment. The Vile Frozen badlands are at the deepest, most southern point of the continent, beneath the Mogra. These rivers run in and out in all directions, interweaving between a few different mountain ranges," Dash said.

Dash looked around like he was onto something. Something really had his attention.

"What it is?" Legion asked.

"These orcs are getting worse."

Legion nodded, agreeing with the half-eladrin's words. Dauge moved his horse up ahead of the others, looking around as Dash was. Pitt held steady, petting his steed. He had a particular fondness for the animal. Not like the others, his steed was not just a means of travel but a personal friend.

"I feel we'd be safer on the water of the rivers," Dash said, finally coming to a conclusion.

"What? That's great but how the hell are we supposed to deal with the water? We can't exactly march our horses through the rivers. I'm sure there's some pretty deep points, not to mention they're not going to be able to hold up against the current relentlessly, nonstop," Legion questioned.

"We build a raft," Dash said solemnly, making it clear his mind was already made up.

"We do not know these rivers. That's madness," Pitt said.

"No more than traveling these vicious lands," Dash suggested.

"The river would be much faster," said Legion.

"Yes but could prove to be far more difficult. We know not of the dangers the water presents. The dangers of land we know and can see. We can take them on head to head," Pitt replied.

"Land hasn't been easy for us and we're going to a more hostile territory filled with more creatures of the wild to go along with the Targnok orcs. The water may keep them all away from us," Legion suggested.

"You may be right but I still feel safer and more comfortable right here on my own two feet," Pitt's mind was made up.

"A raft wouldn't take too long to build and I think we have the tools and material between us to get it done rather quickly. The orcs should leave us be on the water. Many of the earth's critters will just leave us be if we're on the water," Dash said.

"The water is a safer bet as long as the raft is built to protect against missiles." Dauge finally spoke up presenting his two cents to the group.

The other three turned and looked at him. He kept a lazy look on his face, signifying his words should be clearly understood and the idea behind them already clear.

"We build wooden shields too. They don't have to be perfect, just something to block against things like arrows and javelins. We reinforce the raft and move quicker. Eventually, this terrain's going to be too difficult for the horses and then what? We're going to have to get rid of our horses and then we're going to move much slower. Moving slower's going to make us easier targets for hungry bastards trying to eat us and mobile orcs used to the land trying to kill or rob us. Targnok's orcs are going to be able to move through this broken piece of earth like we move across plains. Water, water's the same to us all."

Dauge's words shut the rest of the crew up. Even Pitt was convinced. "Maybe water is the way to go, I'll start getting some wood."

"Good, then it is settled. We will move with purpose to get this raft done. Its construction may set us back but in the end it will prove to be the quickest and most efficient means of travel." Dash was pleased. Dauge sided with him, not something he expected from the younger Xavier at all.

"Let's go," Legion seconded.

The four moved fiercely through the day to get the raft complete. Small patches of Bulvine trees would work exquisitely, Dash thought. Dash's arcane spells, Pitt's sheer force, Dauge's attention to detail, and Legion being there to back the other three up proved to be more than functional; they worked together like a well-oiled machine.

Legion's ingenuity came into play carefully going back over all of Dash's plans to constantly improve them if possible. This wasn't going to be some simple watercraft, it needed to be a true work of art. It also had to be big, bigger than the average raft, because Pitt was such an enormous being. He carried the body of two or three men all rolled into one.

By the day's end, it was finished. Dash, above all, was happy with it. The raft was large but dynamic enough to make it through the twists and turns of the river. It would answer her call, the call of the river. When the sun finally set, Pitt lit the fire he made earlier from the leftover materials and wood from the raft.

Legion and Dauge were both exhausted as were Pitt and Dash. The four tied down their horses and fed them handsomely. The night wasn't too cold but it was cold enough to make the warmth of the fire more inviting. They settled, making their camp just a few yards from the riverbed. The humid air from being near the water made the blowing winds even colder on the mainly open plains surrounding them.

Mountains could be seen in the distance; some belonged to various mountain chains and others were part of the chains wrapping around the Mogra itself. They were heading southeast, putting one mountain chain to their left or northeast. Another chain of mountains stood behind it. And then, heading in the same direction they were going, the peaks to another mountain chain separate that of the Mogra existed. Dash informed the party that from where they were planning to go they should be able to bypass all mountains until they split halfway past the Mogra. When they met the middle mark of the Mogra, and the Mogra was to their left when heading south, they might have to conquer a few in their path. The Frozen Vile lands of the Mogra only half imbed the Mogra on the southern side.

"I'm tired but I think I'm going to fish," Pitt said, questioning his own words.

"Fish, aren't you tired?" Legion asked.

"You did do a lot of work today, goliath," Dash said.

"A lot of work," Legion seconded.

"We're close to the water. I grew up near the water, maybe frozen water but water," he said, laughing.

"I think fishing will do you good, friend," Dash suggested.

"Agreed," Dauge added.

Dash looked at him. They kept the raft not too far from the fire but far enough to where the heat wouldn't affect it. What was going on here? What was Dauge doing? Why was he constantly agreeing with him?

Dauge humbly let out a simple, one breath laugh. His head rolled to refocus his eyes on Dash. He knew Dash was curiously wondering why he'd been agreeing with him so much as of late. There was an answer and the answer was a simple one.

"You question why I second your plans and judgments," Dauge stated solemnly.

"I admit it. I do," Dash said.

"I don't agree with you."

Dash nodded, signaling to the voidsoul that he knew what he was saying and understood it.

"Exactly why I'm confused," he admitted.

"It's not that I don't necessarily agree with your tactics and sometimes your plans are nearly flawless. You as a person I simply do not agree with. And lately, your plans have been dead on."

"Me as a person? I brought you and your brother out of the war and took Pitt from the arenas. So far, I feel I've done more than my share for you all," Dash countered.

"You did everything you said. Well, my brother and I left the war for different reasons but that's an argument for a different day. You did what you did to be where you are today. You knew we'd all somehow feel obligated to you. You yearn for a name like my father, Taj Odin Xavier."

"Don't we all?" he asked.

"I only wish for my Shiva to be returned to me safely," Pitt said, breaking into their conversation.

"I wish for the spoils of war and the feeling of victory and conquest in my gut and heart."

"Spoken like a true mercenary, brother," Dauge said, smiling toward his brother after his words.

"I wish to make my mark in this world, Dauge. Is there evil in this desire you see that I do not?" Dash questioned, throwing a few twigs on the fire casually.

"Not if you go about it the right way. I feel you'd let a man fall if victory was still secure and your name still grew." Dauge took a daring step in speaking out so blatantly against Dash.

Dash didn't respond in the expected manner but rather kept his cool, listening to Dauge's words. This was his time to shed away their differences. Pitt took out his blanket and curled up close to Legion. He didn't fancy the man but it was cold and united body warmth was a common way to keep your blood and body from getting too cold.

"If the order called for it, yes I would let a man fall. Captains and Generals do the same every day. You have to know when to make that kind of call, Dauge," Dash said.

"I will never accept a call to see my brother, or Pitt, fall for that matter."

"Thanks Dauge," Pitt said, smiling and drifting off. The younger Xavier's words gave him something warm to sleep on and consequently he needed it this night. Dauge patiently waited till the commotion and Pitt's voice died down and then continued.

"I know Pitt would die in action to save me. He would do the same for my brother. And in that regard I feel obligated to keep the same option open should it come my way for him. You, Dash, I don't see as willing to die for anything but perhaps maybe immortality. Ask yourself this. Would you let one of us fall for this gold Stannor needs? Don't answer the question just think about it. Sleep on it. And then tell me if I am right to have these notions about you.

Dash put his head down staring at the dirt beneath him. The warmth of the fire and the cold of the night and Dauge's words cut deep into the half eladrin. His mind shifted. He wanted to get off the subject.

"The cold, it's starting to hit us now. We're close to the water and that means the Vile Frozen is nearby as well. It's going to continue to get colder."

"Don't drift away from the matter at hand now," Dauge ordered, laughing.

"Dauge, I cannot change your mind of me with mere words. It's going to take time and actions, my friend." Dash knew he wouldn't convince Dauge otherwise with just his words.

"I don't feel this conversation's come to an end," Dauge challenged.

"It has," Dash said.

"Dauge, if he doesn't wish to speak on it, he doesn't have to." Legion finally stepped in.

"It's better for this to come out now and be done than to fester and infect us later," Dauge replied.

"Strong choice of words," Dash said, quickly taking back the reins to the conversation.

"Then they've done their job," he said just as quickly.

"Dauge Xavier, son of Taj, brother of Legion, I will not be able to convince you I am not the monster you presume me to be with words."

"You've said that already," Dauge said, interfering.

And when he finished, Dash patiently picked back up. "I can tell you I am not that person. I can tell you my actions thus far and in the days to come will prove otherwise. They will pinpoint your inaccuracies. What I can tell you is this; we're all already here on a quest to retrieve lots of gold for one Lord Stannor of Vorrellon in the kingdom of Thox. For one reason or another, we've all agreed to take up this quest. I admit I look more for tools that suit us and make us better for future quests. Perhaps you feel the same way or perhaps you're here for the coin. Either way, we're here together and it's in our best interest to keep each other alive. When this is finished, if you do not wish to travel with me, then don't. All I can tell you is that I will do my very best to keep you alive, Dauge. I will see to it Stannor is paid and Vorrellon is built with the gold we retrieve from Azra Goetia. Our names will soar even higher in Thox. And yes, I look to see my name ascend to and even past the clouds in the sky." Dash finished and paused, taking a deep breath. He certainly needed it.

Dauge shook his ahead giving the "not bad" type of response to his bardic ally. Legion and Pitt both chimed in again reminding them it was getting late and that they all needed to get rest. Again and at perfect timing, Dash proved his worth. He had several scrolls of alarm, a spell that would sound if something hostile was getting too close. Of course, there were mishaps when the spell would sound when other things and non-hostiles entered the territory. Still, it was a good spell and a good idea that allowed them each to sleep as much as needed to prepare for the day ahead of them.

Morning came, and nothing happened. Everything was still in place just as it was before they'd fallen fast asleep. It took a bit of time to get the bedrolls rolled up and the horses unpacked. Legion was wary of letting the horses go, even though he knew Pitt could somehow call them back if need be.

"Pitt, you can get us more horses if need be, huh?" Legion asked.

"Yes, as long as some are relatively close. They'll come to me," he answered.

That made Legion feel better about letting the horses go. Legion and Pitt took the raft to the river. Dauge and Dash finished getting the rest of their gear together and off the horses. Now, it was time.

"These rivers can change how they run. They both feed into two large lakes. We can either ride them to the beach and walk the coast to the Vile Frozen, or force our way to the first lake, push through the connecting river to the second lake and from there float downstream all the way straight into the Vile Frozen." Dash spoke as if he knew the lands like a geographical scholar."

"You sure do know these lands," Legion said, helping Pitt push off the raft.

The raft now held all their gear and all four of them. They were off and the river was luckily not too strong. Pitt personally crafted a few paddles to makes sure they'd be able to make it and steer themselves accordingly.

Now, they were off. Would the water prove to be more or less dangerous than the land? They were getting closer to the Vile Frozen where the mythical city of Azra Goetia supposedly existed. It was in all of them to wonder: What if Azra Goetia wasn't truly real? What if didn't really exist here? If it did, why hadn't others found it yet? Well, that answer was easy. No one worth their skin would voluntarily come so close to a Mogra. Whatever was going to happen was going to happen and they couldn't stop it now. They were on their way and respectively there was no turning back.

Chapter 51

Dusk awoke. Her body was in shambles. She could barely make out her room at Coal's Inn but Drackice was still right there by her side. Her headaches were getting worse now to the point where walking was becoming too difficult of a task.

It had been nearly two months since these attacks through her dreams began. It was Bahaus, the ousted king of the Eternis and a former lover of hers. Where was Kleiven? All of this pain and anguish reminded her of her love for Kleiven.

She told Drackice of Bahaus and how he survived the battle at Emerald Greene. She even managed to pinpoint his location in the Red Mystic Mountains. Drackice left her bedside, speaking words she could not make out.

Once again, she was alone in the room and alone in her own mind. She fought ferociously to keep her eyes open, for it was her dreams that haunted her. She knew Drackice was going to act rashly and his decisions would hurt him but she was in no position to challenge his orders.

Drackice had grown fond of the Republic-born Eternian woman. They'd spent many nights walking the streets together. Something about her was so cunning and charming, yet she had a man courting her miles and miles away. She was the perfect sin and he knew she was going to get him into trouble.

He was his father's son and he'd yet to lose a battle while at the helm of the Free Armies. Whether as a soldier, Unit Leader, Gate Captain, High Captain Lieutenant Commander, or Commander he'd not tasted defeat.

It was high noon and Drackice was back in the cities. First things first, he thought; he was the Lieutenant Commander acting as Commander in his father's presence. Next, beneath him were the High Captains. He had to assemble them to put into action his next plan.

With every day that passed, Dusk fell weaker and he knew it. He couldn't risk the entire safety of the Crystal Cities for one woman but it wasn't over one woman, at least it wouldn't be to them. He wanted to save her and secondly, he knew he had to kill Bahaus Sazos-Uil-Endail.

Drackice sent out the orders to the proper messengers commanding all High Captains to report to his quarters by the day's end. He'd not even given them a full day to prepare for the meeting. It wouldn't take long.

Drackice had a lot to do. He checked the numbers of the Free Armies and their individual units. Their numbers looked good. Sheer numbers and vastness was not his taste this day. Drackice searched for something more specific. The son of the true commander of the Free Armies searched for members of the Free Armies that truly stood out.

He spent the first half of the day at Dusk's bedside and the second half of it running the numbers of the armies confined in his quarters. Names of talented recruits he could use. He knew what the High Captains would say and they would surely vote against him. He knew it.

After hours and hours of searching, he found files on seven that would work magnificently. He knew what he had to do. Only the Commander could give the orders to mobilize the army unless all acting High Captains agreed with the Lieutenant Commander's decision.

The dead gods would rise from their Astral graves before all eight agreed to mobilize the armies to engage King Bahaus in the mountains. Drackice knew through Dusk's dreams that Bahaus was gathering an army. He knew another army from the mountains was approaching. That much Dusk did share with him.

He wanted to rescue Dusk simply because he was captivated by her. Bahaus did march on his cities, forcing him to act as Commander and then somehow survived through it all. Too many birds with one stone, he thought to himself on the destroying of Bahaus, not to mention the adding of slaying a king formally to his name! It wasn't about that. He knew Bahaus would grow and in time attack either Eternis or the Crystal Cities again.

The time came and Drackice's quarters quickly filled with the eight High Captains of the Free Armies. The sun was setting and the men were angered. Seven of the eight were humans like Drackice and one was a green scaled dragonborn. The dragonborn was a bardic caster and the highest ranking among them all. Unofficially, though spoken by Magnus himself, his vote could count as two if needed.

"I truly apologize calling some of you on your time off, others while working and even still, I called upon while preparing for the nightshift. Once again, I am sorry," Drackice started.

Drackice's quarters were nice but not anything special by any means. He wanted it that way so the men would think of him as living closer to their means than means traditionally considered to be above them. The eight all wore exquisite armors ranging from chain to fully plated armor.

The dragonborn was the lone High Captain not fully outfitted. In fact, he wore basic red clothing with black boots and a simple cape colored white and black signifying his rank within the Free Armies. Drackice stayed still sitting behind his desk. He'd found the papers he was looking for, assuming his request for their backing to move on he mountains was countered and denied by the High Captains.

"What have you called us together for? The Gate Captains are working double duty for this. You didn't give us preparation, Drackice," said Bolba, the dragonborn bard.

"It's Commander Black, Commander Drackice, or Lieutenant Commander Bolba, you know that. Show your respects to the Free Armies and my father, our Commander," he patiently explained.

"I respect the Free Armies, your rank in them, and your father," Bolba replied. He made his disdain for the Lieutenant Commander clear.

"Why've you called us here?" Lancewold asked. The oldest of the humans present, Lancewold always wore his fully plated armor. He carried a large axe and made sure his beard was always groomed but long. His red hair now plagued with streaks of white due to his age. He constantly kept a mouth of chewing weeds; the natural weeds kept him from being anything but sound. He often said he thought and fought better that way.

"Lancewold, old friend—" Drackice started. Before he could get any further, another from the back interrupted.

"Get on with it," said the rude voice.

"We've come to a crossroads," Drackice started. "My father, the founder and leader of the Free Armies is far away. I have been ordered to hold his position in his stead until his return. Since then, we've battled… And fought well." He closed his sentence with a word he could shake a tightened fist with.

The men cheered, all but Bolba. The dragonborn merely crossed his arms and waited for his current leader to continue. Drackice's eyes fell upon the dragonborn's. He knew the scaled one would be the only one to really give him problems.

"The maniacal fallen king of Eternis, Bahaus Sazos-Uil-Endail marched on our employer's borders and we filled his thirst for war with a taste of defeat!" Once again the men cheered for Drackice, all but Bolba. Drackice stood, turning his back to casually look outside a nearby window. His words kept coming. However, now they spilled out ever so casually.

"I've got knowledge he aims to retaliate. He aims to destroy us and Eternis."

"Eternis does not hold orders to us. They haven't in a long time. The Crystal Cities are our concern," a younger High Captain named Ekath said.

"You're right. the Crystal Cities have more money than any kingdom, except for maybe Malynkite. Per capita, they are the richest cities in the world. He'll want these riches to finance his war campaigns. This I believe to be true. He's growing in power as we speak. The Xavier woman, Dusk, daughter of Taj Odin Xavier, of Eternis has been fending him off through magic for weeks. She believes his power has grown even more as well. We must stop him before it's too late."

"Killing kings is fine, if it's rightfully in our orders. We devastated his armies. He'll not return here," Bolba said.

"Precisely my point, Bolba. As acting commander I do not wish for him to act. I don't want to wait for the punch before throwing one of my own!" Drackice arched his upper torso turning it back to face the men, interlocking his hands behind his back just as his father had always done.

"Our informants told us he fled to the Red Mystic Mountains," Lancewold chided, unsure of how Drackice meant to continue.

"Armies are not forged to chase single thieves. Armies are not built for such a purpose, like searching for a needle in a haystack," Kaltan, another High Captain, said.

"Leave the Crystal Cities unattended? Your father would never agree. To fend off an attack is one thing, but to wage a war, you need all eight of the High Captains to agree, and that young Drackice Black is something you'll not achieve today. I will not live to see the day you ruin what your father's built," Bolba declared.

"I knew you'd say that. And then it means not what the others say and you clearly care not for their decisions," Drackice rallied back, knowing Bolba was falling perfectly into his trap.

The other seven looked indifferently at Bolba. The way Drackice put it, it certainly sounded like he cared not for their opinions.

"It's not that I care not for my fellow High Captains' opinions. I only say my own will not be swayed to plunge any of our numbers into the dangerous mountains of the Red Mystic Mountains, the most puzzling place on earth for the sole purpose of finding one well-groomed wizard," Bolba reaffirmed to save face.

"I only see one way to secure the Free Armies here and now and preserve them for the future." Drackice moved to his table, grabbing several papers, bringing certain files to each of the High Captains. The captains, all of them, looked purely lost, even Bolba whose grim eyes and face proved his anguish toward not knowing Drackice's next move.

"Slate Thundershot is my best man," Bolba said.

"And I've handed you his file. Bring him to me. All of you bring me the man listed on the file given to you," Drackice said.

"What is it you aim to do?" Ekath questioned.

"These are their files, with discharges, effective immediately," Drackice explained.

"These men are mercenaries. They sign on for days, weeks, and months at a time. Some are day-to-day mercenaries," Bolba challenged.

"I've double checked my files. All of these men have been with us for some time and all of these men have at least a few months left on their contracts. Most quit caring about contracts long ago. They stay with us out of loyalty. Now, bring them to me," Drackice ordered.

Against their best wishes, the eight High Captains did exactly as ordered, even Bolba. When they returned, Drackice stood in full gear right outside the quarters. His traveler's cloak flapped in the wind and his white and black cape did the same. His armor glimmered as if recently cleaned and oiled. He looked like a true knight belonging to a kingdom, not a mercenary rebel without a cause. he did have a cause and he was willing to lose everything to see it through.

Each Captain stood by his man. Bolba stood next to a warrior human, a large man, the biggest and by appearance the oldest and most experienced of the bunch. Even a Deva was brought to the party. Devas were a rarity. And to think, one walked within the ranks of the Free Armies.

"When you hear your name, step forward," he said.

"Slate Thundershot," he started.

The barbaric-looking human standing six and half feet tall walked toward him. He wore furs for boots and cloth. A fur wrapped around his head and waistline as well. On his back he carried a hangar that housed a massive bastard sword. His slightly long wavy light red hair was a mess. It almost completely covered his field green eyes. Several wrapped up scrolls stuck out from his boots and a few more were tied into in the furs on his waistline. Most of the furs were matching brown colors but some spotted black and gray here and there.

"Rakka," Drackice said next.

A goblin walked forward wearing nothing but simple loins and holding a sword two sizes too big for himself. The goblin actually wore rings and jewelry as well. To the trained eye, one might think it wasn't non-magical either.

"Sir Westlyn, Dragoon Knight to Zeronaus, Prismatic dragon of Life and Death," he continued.

Westlyn was a large Deva with a sleek, metallic shining skin. Short golden spikes of hair spore from his head shot with black spikes as well. His eyes were purely white with dismal black dots in the dead center of them. He wore fully plated armor with a dragon's head painted on the breastplate. The draconic head was half skeletal, representing the cycle of life ending in death that his faith represented. At his side rested a magnificently crafted warhammer and on his back he carried the tri-shield, meaning three point top arching down to a single bottom point.

Westlyn bowed to Drackice, showing his respect and obedience to the Free Armies, his commander, and the rest of those present this night.

"Alphonse and Shanks," Drackice continued

Alphonse was a basic-looking man wearing simple glasses, covering himself with brown robes and cloaks. He somewhat looked pathetic and his voice as he spoke up proving he was present made him sound like even less of a threat. His light brown hair was short. His skin was fair. He looked very young. It was his younger brother that caught everyone's attention. Shanks was perhaps the standout of the entire mercenary group. He wore mostly scaled armor, said to have been pieced together by his own two hands and refined by his older brother's magic. On his back he carried a jewel-encrusted bow specifically built for his hands and strength. Though many questioned, none could ever answer the mystery as to how Shanks could fire off so many arrows so quickly and from anywhere. More importantly, no one ever understood how he never seemed to run out of bullets. His hair matched his brothers in color but was quite a bit longer and purely straight. It rolled over his left eye. He constantly shook his head and smiled, keeping it from his face. It was just about neck length and his eyes matched the color of his hair. When in hand-to-hand combat, he for some reason always trusted his abilities with daggers over everything else. Some claimed his abilities with daggers were better than the bow. However, Shanks was notorious for pulling the bow in melee combat all the time.

"Keres and Tsin," Drackice said after Shanks and Alphonse approached.

Keres was a beautiful Wilden with traits clearly proving her Sylvan heritage. Tsin was the same. Under the Wilden label, they surely fell into the Sylvan category. Some claimed Sylvan's were the most beautiful but most odd of all elves, having more quirks and peculiarities than any other race known to exist. Keres' strawberry blonde hair was short and curly. She was shorter and firmer than her Sylvan brother. Most of her body lay hidden behind wrought iron armor. The armor almost seemed to be fashioned into her very flesh at some points. However, her armor did not come with a helm. She carried no special weapons or massive ones of any type. She only kept a single weapon with her, a small kukri, a weapon fashioned with a blade of adamantium and with symbols none present could decipher. Her eyes of green resembled fields of plenty to those looking into them, as did her brother's, but his hair was much different both in style and in color.

Tsin's hair was cut very short and was the color of a moonless sky. His skin was also fair, a little more so than the other's. He was tall for a Sylvan, standing almost five feet and eight inches but his weight was thin, even for an elf. He possibly weighed a hundred and thirty pounds soaking wet. A blue traveler's cloak hid most of his body. Not a single weapon was revealed to the open eye. And when he walked, not a sound was made. As he approached, he neared Keres who kissed him gently on his lips.

Then, the quiet moving Sylvan spoke. "I am Tsin and this is the fine lady Keres, Priestess of the Dragon Zeronaus. I too follow Zeronaus, as my wife does. We've served the Free Armies for over a year and we're looking forward to the years to come. Captain Ekath saved my life and spared me from the Inexeris dungeon of Malynkite. My mind and her powers are yours to be commanded." Tsin smiled gently, bowing to Drackice with his closing words.

"Draeden," Drackice said finally.

Another wizard crept slowly forward with the help of his jeweled cane. His skin was blue. His hair black, as were his eyes, his body looked like that of a shriveled man that once stood big, tall, proud. He wore thin clothes and robes to hide his body. His right eye was missing and was covered by an eye patch. Thick scars, nasty and long, covered all parts of his visible body.

"It's believed you're one of our more powerful wizards?" Drackice asked.

"I'm willing to test that challenge," he replied.

"What are you?" Drackice questioned.

"I am a Genasi with primary manifestations in water and storms. Clouds, water, lightning, ice, these are my primaries, but arcane, arcane is where my knowledge truly lies," he said, finishing his hobble to the designated spot near Drackice.

"You're going to discharge our greatest men?" Bolba asked arrogantly. "This is your brilliant plan?"

"Yes, and then I am going to relinquish my duties and titles to you, Bolba. It will be up to you to find your replacement as a High Captain. The list of possible candidates has been made ready for you by my own hand. Now then, the eight of you have been formally discharged without reason from the mercenary ranks of the Free Armies. However, I am personally hiring each of you to join me on my personal quest to finish what we started when we answered the call of aggression on Bahaus Sazos-Uil-Endail. And when we're finished, I'll personally see to it my father raises your wages in the Free Armies once you're all reinstated. Let it be known you only left to see my safe passage to and through this quest."

"I'm with you," Westlyn said without hearing all the dirty details of the mission.

One by one they all agreed. The High Captains couldn't believe it. And the new Lieutenant Commander Bolba couldn't either. He was now the acting commander of the Free Armies and he wasn't Magnus Black or a blooded relative. This was certainly a first time and not expected.

When the smoke cleared and all was settled, Drackice walked to Bolba taking his hand into his own.

"Now then friend, they are yours to command. These are your contracts to protect. My eight friends and I, we're going to take a walk."

"Not even your father will agree to your reinstatement, not you or any of these eight. They're following you because of your name. They question nothing because of who birthed you into this world. They'll learn to regret their decision, should they live long enough to see the day. I pray they do. I pray you all return to see the look on father's disappointed face."

Drackice moved to sock the dragonborn right in his mouth. The dragonborn stepped back, using his hands and mouth to signal warning to the former Commander.

"Remember, I'm the Lieutenant Commander, Acting Commander of the Free Armies of the Crystal Cities now. And you're in the Crystal Cities."

"Come on gentlemen, let's take that walk. I'll discuss everything once we're out of the Free Armies jurisdiction," Drackice said.

Chapter 52

Magnus had his business in Valakuza settled. It was good to know the Retired General Seth Redd was back in Eternis. He too would soon be in the olden city he and his mercenaries once called home. He loved that city. Had it not been for the sheer profit of the Crystal Cities contracts he knew he would've never left.

Kleiven was absent of late. He'd been spending quite a bit of time with that Malukah girl he met. She was pretty but he had a girl, the granddaughter of his late friend, the closest friend he ever had, Dominick Gabriel Xavier.

It didn't matter. They would be leaving this morning and he had Kleiven reassure him nothing would go wrong with their plans to leave. Cale Dar's son was too curious for his own good and even got caught up talking with his former rival, Grath.

Grath had decided to no longer continue his quest to the Wage of Conquerors and other places by charge of King Bahaus Sazos. For one, he was no longer the king and two, he was considered evil among the populace.

Grath announced the plan to scour the countryside and the Red Mystic Mountains, the only place he could have possibly fled to, in order to stop the renegade ousted king and bring the tyrannical maniac to justice.

Kleiven heeded his call and introduced himself formally to the shadow elf. The shadow elf already had a well-trained team but was certainly looking for new recruits to fill the ranks for the forthcoming journey.

Malukah was preparing to leave. She'd had her fill of the militant city. She was planning a trip out of her normal territory. She planned to head all the way to the magical fortress of the Aflyndorian Kingdom.

Kleiven begged her for days to hold. Her travel would be a perilous one and with the brink of so many battles possible and so close by, it could prove to be gravely dangerous. The cheerful and confident Malukah cared not for her new friend's suggestions.

It was obvious Kleiven liked her a lot more than she cared for him. She was so used to being on the go and with meeting so many people, it was becoming too difficult to remember them all. If she had to admit one that stood out, it would certainly be the Eternian soldier Kleiven Dar.

Curiously, Kleiven was promised to another, one he'd fought valiantly to keep; by his own words to her he claimed it. She never told him of her lost love. He probably wouldn't understand. Her lost love was a conflicting one.

Aflyndor was actually home to her. In a way, returning was her way of telling herself it was time to go home and face what you've always run from. Perhaps something about the young soldier brought some truth out in her. It was closing and the final morning of their time together was upon her face.

She opened the curtains to the very same room he once stayed in. For the first time in a long time, she was actually hesitant toward the goodbye with Kleiven. Somehow, he connected with her. He linked himself upon her very essence. And now, she promised she would leave. She had no deadlines to meet and she worked around her own schedule, but it was her time to go and she couldn't break the oath to herself to keep moving when the time was right. Besides, he was leaving this same day anyway.

She knew of the hard news he still had to break to his friend and mentor, Magnus. He was to tell Magnus this morning that he would not be accompanying him on his return trip to Eternis. Magnus was not going to take this lightly based on her man Kleiven's thoughts. Her man, Kleiven, why was she thinking in such a way?

Magnus waited and as expected, Kleiven was promptly on time for their breakfast. The breakfast meeting was to be had at the same local inn Malukah had been staying in. Magnus was dressed for the journey and already packed. Kleiven came fully geared and packed just the same. Magnus fell concerned. Why was he wearing his favored armoring pieces and holding his blades at his side? They were to take an escort to Eternis.

Kleiven's armor was fashioned more perfectly than Magnus had never seen it. His hair was neatly combed and his face shaved clean down to the flesh. Every single piece of his body shined like it was the sun itself on a hot summer day.

Kleiven entered the tavern and inn and quickly took a seat next to his mentor. His cape was new. It was yellow, a bright eye-catching yellow. Magnus didn't understand but he'd been around long enough to know something about what was going on.

"Kleiven," Magnus started formally.

"I almost want to call you father," he replied nervously.

"You most certainly can," Magnus said, letting his guard down.

"Father," he said, pausing afterward.

"Lay it on me, son. It's her isn't it? What about Dusk?" he asked.

"Yes, no," he started, unsure how to answer. "I guess it could be her. It's not. Bahaus sent Grath, the man Dusk left me for out this way and he's in this city now. He gave out a call to those who would dare join him in his cause to ride out to the Red Mystic Mountains, the only place it's believed he could have gone. I answered that call. I'm going to answer that call."

"You know not of Grath or who follows him. You would put your life in the hands of complete strangers?"

"Father, my eye is a keen one and they're trusted and talented. Bahaus would not have used them if they weren't." Kleiven spoke what he thought was the truth but in reality Bahaus just wanted the shadow elf away and/ or dead and thus no longer a threat to his chances of being with Dusk.

"I trust your eye, son. It is decisions at times like this that make us who we are. You know that, right Kleiven?" Magnus asked.

"I do," he answered.

"I must get back to Seth Redd and Eternis and help them prepare for what could be coming and for the future. Even if peace instills across these lands, without a rightful heir and a lost king, they're going to need guidance. My son has the Free Armies and the Crystal Cities under control. If Bahaus were to resurface, he'd surely be able to oust him again."

"And if he does try to resurface, Grath and I, differences aside, will be there to push him down below the water and drown out his devilish desires once again."

The two didn't say another word. They didn't have to. They leaped from their chairs entrenched in their own arms wrapped around each other. Magnus was so very proud of the man Kleiven had become.

"I didn't know you could look so good in armor. I wasn't aware you knew how to shine armor like that," he said, smiling.

Just then, Malukah came strolling down the stairs from above. The tavern was at ground level and the inn part was on the upper level. She wore fantastic ornaments and jewelry to offset her salmon colored dress. The sequins rolling off it were uncannily perfect. She had her hair rolled up and eloquently placed to go with amazing hat.

"Malukah," Kleiven said, not even noticing he uttered her name.

Magnus couldn't believe it. Consequently, he couldn't blame the boy. After all, she was the one to leave him first for something different. Now it was his turn to find his flavor in another. Or would he? Would he have the fortitude to go through with it? He could tell by the sparks in their eyes that something was there but it didn't appear as though either was ready to act on it.

Magnus did what he knew Kleiven couldn't. He knew Kleiven needed his time with the lady but would refuse to just let him walk away. So Magnus gave Kleiven orders through the eyes, as he called it. Kleiven understood and Magnus took his leave finishing the conversation.

"Until that day, kid," he said making his way out of the inn.

Kleiven watched until Magnus was completely gone. He turned back to appreciate the beauty standing before him. She walked delicately and placed her aim toward him. Before he knew it, she was right up to him.

"There's something I must tell you."

"There's something I must tell you," he replied quickly. He took the initiative and placed her hands in his. He knelt down, placing her hands to his lips. Afterward, he rose and stared deep into her eyes, keeping her hands in his own interlocked between their chests.

"You first," they both said simultaneously.

She stopped him, making sure he knew that she would go first. He nodded, preparing to hang on her every word.

"I once loved very deeply and learned a valuable lesson. Love, Kleiven, is like a handful of broken glass. The tighter you squeeze, the deeper it cuts. I loved only once in my life and I'm not sure there's enough left for me to love again. I won't deny the magical bond between us but it's not something I can stay and research with you. I wish I could but I've chosen another life, and in it there's no room for soldiers."

Kleiven dropped his head. Her words weren't exactly like her soothing songs. They were harsh but honest. However, he was pleased she went first. It helped him adapt and alter all the things he hoped to get out.

"We spent a great deal of time together and we bonded quickly, almost instantly," he started.

"We did," she agreed, smiling.

"My heart is promised to another already and though she's broken my heart a hundred times, I am a loyal man. If my loyalty is meaningless to the rest of the world, she knows my loyalty to her. I've strayed allowing this to grow too far. For that I am deeply sorry but I am not apologizing for the friendship and kinship we now have and share. I hope to one day cross your path again and I hope then something between our lives has changed to where this friendship can be more appreciated and more time can be spent grooming it to its masterful perfection."

His words were like a bard's ink on paper. They were perfect, making her only want to tell him her story even more. She couldn't take it anymore. She had to tell him. She had to make him understand.

"Hold on to her with all you have. Let those shattered scars on your heart sit as a reminder of how hard you worked for her. Let her know that. Let her know you'll never let anyone take her away from you. I once had a love and she was taken from me by a young wizard named Alphonse. He once worked in a traveling circus. Zelda left me for the wizard. I came home to nothing. Her things were gone. And I never wanted to come home again. So, I picked up my things, the things I held most dear and began singing for money. I would have done anything not to have to return. I never thought I would have been this successful. I think, with this coin I make now, she would have never left me."

Malukah placed her hands gently upon his jawbones, kissing him more passionately than she'd ever kissed anyone before. It held more affection than he was used to, at least for as long as he could remember. Saliva dripped from their parting lips as she broke away from him now almost in tears. She tucked in her lower lip to better savor his taste.

"Go to her, and never let anything keep you two apart again," Malukah finished turning away.

Kleiven hollered and muttered, screamed and begged but the words just wouldn't come out. And before he knew it, she was gone. She was gone, let loose to the strains of the city, never to be caught again. Watching the kiss from the outside, a miserable and angry looking shadow elf, the warrior Grath, waited with his crew. Kleiven made six and another newcomer made seven. Kleiven wiped his lips and pressed to meet Grath as if nothing happened and nothing was wrong.

"We've no time to lose, I guess," he started to the shadow elf. His words started strong but faltered and fell weak toward the end.

Grath just mumbled. He didn't like Kleiven from the word go but he knew he needed the skill of a swordsman and soldier like Kleiven if he was to be successful in this attempt. Breaking away from one quest to set out on another, not a good way to do business, Grath thought. Then again, this useless quest he now ventured toward was on behalf of the ousted king. Seeing it through would only hurt him, his name, his team, and those he cared about, or so it seemed.

Chapter 53

In the seeming weeks that passed, Storm Stars and his crew met with success finally landing at the Port of the Alliance, a unified city built in the territory of the Nine Kingdoms. Storm and his crew immediately took back to the ship to return. It was then they were caught off guard.

Avalon Darksteel, the half shadow elven Prince of the land asked them to stay, for he had a task for them to take up. Lord Quinn was safely within the walls of the Nine Kingdoms. Their task was finished but Avalon wasn't known for asking favors.

Avalon promised there would be a ship waiting for them upon their completion of the quest. Storm quickly brought up the notion that he was ready and present, why would he not tend to whatever task it was at hand.

Avalon Darksteel sat with Storm, his dwarven priest Dargon, his Wilden wizard Kraydia, his shadow elf Kraizaikaei, and his half elven rogue Siberon. Storm's team had changed quite a bit since it's beginning but the message was always clear. One thing he knew would come up quicker than the business at hand was his relationship with Kraizaikaei, for his name was not unknown in certain lands.

Avalon sat at his favorite tavern right there at the heart of the port city, the Firefly. It was a fairly decent-sized building, built just over the water. Stairs were its only way of entry. An old wrap-around staircase brought you to the old single door. The roof leaked a bit and the tables and chairs were scarred with age. It didn't look like much but Avalon would test its vittles and wine with any in the pantheon.

"We have the best vintages here you know," Avalon said.

"What is it you want us to do, Prince Avalon? You've aided my lands, it is my honor to return the favor, should the quest be deemed honorable by Typherion the Good Dragon of course," said Storm.

A middle-aged waitress, human blooded, brought them each a hot cup of tea and butter rum to start their midday meal off with. It was getting colder in the east but warmer to the west. However, the warmth hadn't taken over quite yet and the hot rum and tea were certainly appreciated by all.

Storm was the first to have his fill. To his delight, it was the best he'd ever tasted. Avalon smiled, knowing he'd proven himself right yet again. Krazy kept a keen eye out, not trusting anything about the building, he never did. In this case, it was the very building falling and collapsing into the water below that frightened him.

"Fine, I'll order the vintage for you. While we wait, yes, again I know you've been asked this before but how is it you've come to be friends and true allies with a reputed assassin and murderer like Kraizaikaei?" Avalon asked.

"To my knowledge, I've never known him to murder or assassinate anyone. He's broken not a single law in Thox. Not to say other lands' laws aren't important, however, I've just known him to be a trusted companion. Should the day come I'm proven wrong, I'll revaluate my friendship with the man then."

Krazy didn't say anything to his paladin's words. He merely raised a glass in cheer before turning up the hot rum sucking it all down in a single attempt. Even Avalon looked impressed with the man's ability to drink.

"Let's have another round!" Avalon said, cheering.

"Wait, Prince Avalon," Storm started, holding down all of the commotion, waving all of them back to their seats.

He looked around. Aside from them, there were but a few weary travelers and locals here and there. The tavern didn't have much in the field of customers. Then again, the place wasn't anything much more than an old structure hung over the water half-assed to give it some kind of glamour. Their were entire towns and cities built in such a way and with more grandeur and caretaking than this old tavern. None had Avalon's perfect approval. None were Avalon's favorite place to sit and eat a meal. None were the Firefly.

"You're right. I'm getting ahead of myself. Due east deep into the Great Forest, there lies an ancient forgotten temple once dedicated to the

Forsaken. In that temple grows a plant so foul it's only known to exist where the Great Forest is deepest and becomes the Blue Forest. Somehow, its come to grow here in this temple. It's called Bhellioa Ivy. I'm going to need it for what I'm planning. Also, the lost seal of Kagekatsuel is said to be buried there. I'll have an artist ink you a rendition of what it should look like. Find me that seal and I'll cleanse all poverty and infractions against your houses personally."

"What's the Bhellioa Ivy for? And what's this seal have to do with anything?" Storm asked.

"Neither is any of your concern. Well, I've learned a great tragedy has fallen upon me. I once considered Bahaus Sazos-Uil-Endail my friend and ally. I learned that during his siege and exploitations, he took what was mine for his own purpose and killed a familiar face that I had working under my care for the last eighty years or so. This Bhellioa Ivy can make plenty of ointments, aids, and cures for the sick, cursed, weak, and dying. Before I have my go at Bahaus, I'll be sure I'm well prepared."

"Bahaus? What's going on with all that?" Storm questioned.

"I'm never uninformed. Whether I am at sea taking carrier pigeons by the day or sitting on the sidelines or taking part in the glories of battle, I know of all things this world has and what becomes of them as well," Avalon added.

"So, you're going to search for Bahaus alone?" Dargon questioned, finally looking up from a small piece of wood he was whittling.

"I will. When the time comes, of course. As for now, I've plenty to keep me busy here in the Nine Kingdoms. First on the order, my brother, the King of Daneth and ruler of the Nine Kingdoms must be met with. Now then, I'll have my squires get you the proper information and maps you'll need should you take this quest."

"We will," Storm said firmly.

The others shot back at the words that came so quickly from his mouth. They would usually have a bit more of a discussion about things first.

"Storm, might we have a word with you first? Might I have a word with you first?" Krazy questioned.

"Sure, absolutely. Just know this, Prince Avalon Darksteel has lent his blade and bow to our causes back in the land we all call home. He's asked a task of us. We shouldn't think twice to answer that call," Storm said, holding to his previous agreement.

That was enough for Dargon. He was convinced. Kraydia was there only for Kraizaikaei. Siberon twirled a small dagger, spinning the tip of it on his finger, only stopping when the finger sprang blood.

"Ouch!" he exclaimed, sucking the tip of his finger.

It was a trick and game he loved to do, to see if he could keep and hold the spin until blood was drawn. The trouble with it was he was always bleeding. He never found himself losing that game. He smiled at the rest of the party. He was a bit scared and Avalon certainly creeped him out. After all, he was the Prince they called monster throughout the lands. He postured up a bit, speaking quickly before going back to sucking on his bleeding finger. "Whatever you say boss. I'm with you. You know that," he said to Storm.

"I'm the only one who's got a problem with this? Fine, I don't like it. It's too rash for my taste. If one of us dies, it's not on my hands," Kraizaikaei finalized.

"Good, it is settled then and with much more ease than I imagined. Your fill is on me. Take what you like. When you're finished, see yourself to the High Temple of Old Light. There, Master Gevan will explain your duties and get you going in the right direction. I have other matters to attend. Thank you," said the Prince, finishing.

Prince Avalon took his leave, leaving the party to finish the meal and discuss amongst themselves.

"Storm, you're offering our services without truly consulting with us first about it. It's slowly becoming a less concerted effort," Dargon said, as friendly as he could.

"Prince Avalon is a good man and he's treated us well. We shall show honor and gratitude by completing these tasks given to us by the Prince himself. This is an opportunity, one we should thank the faiths for bestowing upon us," Storm answered.

The conversation continued minutely after his words. The team was pleased with his thinking and considerations. After all, that's why he was the leader of the team. Storm wanted nothing more than to prove to all of Runethedian, and especially to Thox, that the House of Stars belonged with the elite nobles, honest and true. He wanted nothing to sidetrack him on getting that status placed on his house. The damning labels and political curses placed upon his House would soon find themselves lifted if he had things his way.

The time came and the team embarked on their first mission to find Gevan and the Temple of Old Light. It was soon revealed the Temple of Old Light was an ancient church building still dedicated to the fallen gods of old and, of course, to the modern Rivermortal.

Walking through the city, the team realized just how lucky they had it. The port was said be the most modern of all the Nine Kingdom's city-states. And it wasn't one of the city-states at all. It was built by Malynkite to the northeast of the massive Greatland so the kingdom could routinely send supplies to the weaker kingdom. It also built the port to implant itself on the grounds of the Nine Kingdoms, forcing them to live off of their vast supplies and the like. And as they liked, at their convenience, they took standout pupils from the Nine Kingdoms to go back and serve Malynkite as they saw fit.

The people of the port were very generous and friendly, much more than anywhere any of them had ever been. Most of the people were dirty and worn looking from working so long and hard.

"This isn't a pleasant place," Krazy started.

"These people, the port is their finest city and even it is filled with grief. Just look, these people work their fingers to the bone just to eat decently if they can to provide what they can for their family. These people appreciate everything you do for them, even if it's saying a simple hello. The Greatland has never truly been explored. Malynkite's cities extend purely from the water, some say, dancing around the northeastern coast of the Greatland. This is a harsh land to live on and a dangerous one to explore. That's why it's never truly be done," Storm replied.

"These people appreciate everything. It's a good life. It may be a hard life but I'm not convinced it's not a good life," Kraydia added.

"I'm not understanding why these people wouldn't leave the first chance they got," Siberon questioned, still flicking his little dagger trickily through his two hands and between his fingers.

"Sometimes, it's safer and better to stay with what you know. Or at least there are those that feel that way. Not all people are risk takers," Storm reminded.

"I guess not," Siberon said.

"And it's not all like this. There are some very nice parts of this kingdom. This port is one of the busiest ports in Runethedian," Kraydia said, adding in her two cents.

"You've been here before Wilden?" Storm asked.

"Of course," she replied.

"Why didn't you say so?" Dargon asked.

"You didn't ask," she joked.

"What did make you choose to chase after and join us on a moments notice?" Storm asked her.

"I just…" she stopped. She couldn't finish. They all knew. It was almost as clear as the air they breathed at this point. She fancied Kraizaikaei and he fancied her right back. It was more difficult for Kraizaikaei to admit it than her. Kraizaikaei just kept silent and to himself and the crew kept walking.

After asking a few locals for directions here and there, the crew finally got to the steps of the old single-story temple built purely from fire-hardened brick. The building's color was lost and faded to something different. It could only be described as a building absent of color. It was built with higher walls than ceiling.

Storm beat the doorbell and waited at the top of the small step way. The door was old and made of iron. Within moments, several locks began moving from the inside. It was being unlocked. This Temple of the Old Light was surely built before the time of the new faiths, thought Storm.

The door opened, revealing an aged man nearly expired from his years on the earth. His skin wrinkled and old, tan and leathery and the man carried a big smile and smooth head. He'd not had hair atop his head in decades. It was clearly evident. He was frail and withered.

"Yes, may I help you? We've not gotten many visitors around here as far back as I can remember," he said.

He wore simple clothes, barely covering his body. He was old and harmless. Storm couldn't help but feel for the man. His eyes were filled with honesty and purity. His very being was something special, wasn't it? Storm thought. He'd been around so long and seen and felt so much he'd become immune to the evils of the world.

"We are here to see a Master Gevan," Storm said calmly. "We've come by order and personal request of Prince Avalon Darksteel."

"Avalon, he sent you? Where's the young lad been?" asked the old man.

Young lad, Avalon was said to be pretty old himself. He was surely over the age of a hundred and twenty. Just how old was this man? After all, unless there was more than meets the eye, he was just a simple human being.

"He did sir, is Master Gevan here?" Storm asked.

The rest of Storm's crew sat back at the foot of the steps. They all seemed carefree and calm. All of them except Siberon, he couldn't sit still. He constantly moved and looked around. Something just didn't settle easily with the little rogue.

"I am Master Gevan. Please, come in," he said. The old man crept back, peeling the door back for the team to enter. He signaled and quietly lipped for Storm and those waiting behind him to quickly come in. Each of them, one by one, filed into the old church. Looking around it was evident; this was a temple or church dedicated mainly to the old gods, the Rivermortal, and to the mystical powers of healing.

The old man showed them through a few hallways until finally it opened to a larger square den of sorts. The room was quite large but like the rest of it, even had the old styled brick used for the floor. Bricks were still hardened with fire, of course, but these were done in a primitive manner and these bricks were about three to four times the size of a modern one.

The square room didn't hold much other than a few pieces of artwork on the wall, of course dedicated to the old gods and the old ways. A small wooden alter rested. This place hadn't been kept up to the modern times, thought the members of the team.

"I am Gevan and here we're dedicated to the old gods and the Rivermortal. Here, we focus on the healing bodies of magic and those auras that surround them," said the old man.

"Avalon said we'd get our instructions for the old temple we're heading into from you," Storm said.

"We just need to know what this ivy plant looks like and what this seal looks like, a map to the place and…" he paused, "we're on our way to the temple." Siberon for some reason felt uneasy in Port Alliance and just wanted to get it all finished and taken care of.

"Why's this place got you so worked up for?" Kraydia questioned, looking at the half elf.

"I just want to get home, I guess," he replied.

"Aye, Avalon sent you, did he? I know just what you need. I'll get you taken care of right away. Come this way."

Gevan kept true to his word. Maps, illustrations, and instructions were all already in place for any who'd dare take up the challenge. Apparently, Storm and his team weren't the first to be asked. They wanted that samurai's seal and if that Bhellioa was being desired for some time by Prince Avalon and others, perhaps a plan to move against Bahaus or something similar had been in motion for a while?

Of course, the possibility that the ivy was just simply desired for the anti-venoms and anti-diseases to be made prematurely in case it was needed still thrived as reason enough in itself. Gevan was a fine old man, cured from all of the world's greed and deceit. He was past all of that in his ripe age. He owned a pleasant face, one Storm was honored to meet before leaving the poor country in name of their beloved Prince, the half shadow elven fallen samurai, Avalon Darksteel.

Shortly after their encounter with the old man in the temple dedicated to the fallen gods, Storm, Siberon, Dargon, Kraizaikaei, and Kraydia took their leave from the Nine Kingdoms, heading east in hopes of finding the temple that was said to have not only the Bhellioa Ivy but the old samurai's seal as well.

Chapter 54

The raft turned out to be a phenomenal idea, one that saved their lives more than once. Maybe not necessarily their lives, but the raft's crew was spared from more undesired and unnecessary cuts and bruises.

Dash knew the layout of the rivers better than the others. Finally, he made a decision at a crucial point, sending them down south in the right direction toward the Vile Frozen. The river dumped them early and still far away from the rigid land sitting below the Mogra.

For better or for worse, the river dumped them, bleeding smoothly and straightly into the wild ocean and connecting seas below. They knew better than to chance the raft on the open water. Anything could come after them and nothing was as powerful as an angry sea. The raft had been good to them. Several bands of raiding orcs and monstrous marauders let them be rather than chance the waters on top of what the four possibly had to offer.

They got off right there on the beach as the sun was setting just over the horizon. Dash took a moment to appreciate the beautiful scene.

"I guess we're making camp here huh? Perfect timing for our landing," Pitt said, gathering roots and plants from the edge of the beach where a light forested area began.

"We're almost out of water to. We'll have to boil some of this sea water to refill our water skins," Legion added, wading out into the water to replenish his.

Dauge watched on as Dash stared at the sun. For a moment, he was envious of the creature, the half eladrin now made him jealous. The lone cause of the jealousy was nothing more than his appreciation of the twilight. Dauge longed to find anything as pretty and appreciate anything as Dash appreciated this sunset.

Night fell and the four sat around a small open fire just off the beach shore. The tide rolled in but it wasn't too bad at all. They were far out of the way and in the clear of the rolling water. Dauge caught fish while the others set up camp. He split his bounty and the lot of them roasted meat over the night's open fire.

More stories bled from three of their mouths. Dauge kept his to himself once again. The stories only made him think of home and his time with the Lotus people. It was something he'd never share. He could never share. He would never share. He was bound by an oath to the people that raised him. He was bound by an oath he made to himself, one he could not break for anything.

A light rain set in, inconveniencing the crew slightly. The night was cold. They were close to the Frozen Sea and not too far from the Vile Frozen. They knew they were getting close. They were slowly becoming the tight-knit group Dash knew they could. Without a true healer or arcane caster, Dash knew they would all have to know each others' ins and outs if they were to be successful and see this thing through.

Morning came and Dauge was the first one up. He normally was. The fire was out and the morning dew over the water was beautiful. Alas, it was time to move and time to go. The sun wasn't fully out of the horizon's depths when the team hit the sands of the beach to push closer to their destination.

After nearly another month, thirty-seven more days exactly, Dash, Dauge, Legion, and Pitt broke ground on the Vile Frozen. The smooth ground of the open lands, the soggy areas of marshy grounds, hills, mountains, forests, and everything else suddenly came to an end. The Vile Frozen was clearly named to define it. It was as vile as it was frozen.

The wind blew colder. The rocks breaking through the soil beneath their feet were all frozen and blue, usually smothered in water iced over due to the cold nature of it all. Their trek since hitting the sands pushed first eastward and then down farther south. Once upon a time, high mountains stood tall ahead of them and even helped guide them on their journey. Now, since turning south again following the land trail to the Vile Frozen, the high mountains surrounding the Mogra were to their left.

Almost immediately, fatigue struck the party. Something about the Vile Frozen hit them and hit them hard. Pitt seemed to deal with it the best. The journey almost instantly became impossible. There was no chance to attempt walking bipedal. Weapons were kept sheathed and for safety the four climbed using all fours. The ground wasn't always very steep. It was just the footing. The footing of the Vile Frozen was next to impossible to conquer, even when using all fours. It was Pitt who had the easiest time, even easier than Dauge.

Dauge was troubled. During the thirty-seven day hike to the Vile Frozen, the crew encountered few orcs. The orcs encountered weren't like typical orcs. These had a dark green- and blue-tinted skin. They almost seemed completely iced over themselves and wore clothes fitting to the environment. Nonetheless, they were different than normal orcs and certainly differed from Targnok's orcs.

And the closer they got to the Vile Frozen, the more things unnatural to them encroached on their safety and wellbeing. Bats and worms, some large in size and others not so much, but all imbued with the cold, challenged them for the right to survive and live on. They were challenged to see who had the right to act as predator and who would be forced down as dying prey.

Dauge's trouble fell back to one encounter with several ice bats, as the team called them as well as the frozen orcs that engaged the four with them. A dual engagement left Dauge's back scarred and deeply cut. His underarm on his left side was ripped open horribly with the wound extended downward from the armpit all the way to his upper front thigh.

His wounds were healing and sealed as best as they could be using the best ointments he and Pitt could concoct with what the wild had to offer on top of Dash's healing to finish it off. Most of his wounds came from a swarm of the ice bats and they cut him deep.

Now, they traveled across the Vile Frozen and the wounds of yesterday were becoming the high challenges of today, especially for Dauge. The team was well on its way. The map showed they couldn't be too far from it. Not a single one of them believed the trip was going to be so vicious and heinous. The Vile Frozen was far worse and more horrific than the stories gave it credit for.

The ground was mostly made of badland hills broken up and scattered with jagged rocks and petrified bones and wood. Up and down the crew carefully climbed until finally they found a milestone they'd been looking for.

"The map says this is supposed to be here," Dash said looking straight up.

Before them stood a rounded-off wall. The mountains were still to their left but were slowly bleeding back to their rear flank. The wall was said to be a chiseled design of a sleeping giant. And the wall piece to climb would be the ribs.

"There's his arms curled up under his head," Pitt said, pointing out his finding.

"And that's the loin cloth around his, well loins," Legion added.

Dauge massaged his body, hoping that somehow by rubbing his wounded areas, it would somehow ease out the pain. His wounds were deep and wide, yet still mending. They knew they were in the right place. Now, all they had to do was keep moving and move in the right direction.

"Someone's going to have to get up there first," Dash said with his eyes locked on to the top of the sleeping structure.

"I got it," Dauge said, stretching and still rubbing.

"No little brother. You're not well. We'll get you to the top but let someone else get there first to backup the attempt," Legion sadly pleaded feeling sorry for his hurting brother.

"Who is going to get up there then, huh? I'm the only one that can do it. Let me do it. Link your ropes and hooks to me. I'll bring them to the top. I most certainly can still climb this damned thing," he said.

The anger in Dauge's voice was unsettling. It was clear he was angered from his wounds and hindrances. The others wanted to say something to him but they knew now wasn't the time. They just moved about hesitantly, locking their hooks and ropes to his belt.

"Are you sure?" Dash asked locking his hook into his belt.

Dauge's eyes peered up and just glared at him. The idea behind the look was to make the leader feel foolish for his words. It worked. And not even his big brother was willing to challenge him at this point.

And just moments after getting hooked up, the voidsoul half brother to Legion was on his way. He didn't look hurt at all. The way he moved was unchallenged. Legion wasn't too worried about him making it to the top. He was more concerned about what could be waiting for him once he got there.

Dauge, like a spider, climbed his way to the top with ease. He finally pulled himself over the final hurdle, clearing his body to the elevated ground. The ropes and hooks gave him a slight problem with clearing the ledge but it wasn't too bad. One hook dug into his right buttocks a little but it wasn't anything he couldn't handle or hadn't had to handle already.

Dauge immediately scoured the land around him with his eyes. The land was carved out to look like the backside of a sleeping giant. The badlands and hills rolled out, forming more horrid ground for the crew to cover. He felt several whelps and barely sealed lacerations on his side come open on the climb. He'd extended his body too much, opening his prior wounds.

Steady gusts of wind kept the chill bumps on his body awake. Blood leaked from the wounds, warming him from the challenging elements, a convenience he surely wished he did not have. He looked down at his allies waiting for him to secure the lines. Dauge found a solid rock and platform to lock them all down with.

He gave the lines a final tug after securing them, reassuring himself they were safe and ready to use. They were. He walked back to the ledge, seeing his three companions waiting on him. He gave them the signal, the go ahead to move.

Dash, Pitt, and Legion, with hemp in hand, pulled themselves up the side of the cliff all the way to the top. It wasn't too difficult for any of them. And the four made it. They were at the top of the sleeping dragon milestone. It wasn't the time to stop. They had to keep pushing. They had to keep moving.

Dauge's sixth sense turned on. Without thinking, he dropped down to a knee, ducking his head to miss the oncoming movement his keen senses told him were coming. Ethereal missiles whizzed, just passing over his head. He couldn't see them but he could feel them.

The missiles caused ripples in the air like an invisible gnome running while slowly forming back to his normal self. The ripples caused waves like a child splashing in the pool. Dauge closed his eyes, feeling the vibrations of the missiles pressing hard against him.

"Ugh," a voice thundered out from behind him.

Dauge rose back to his feet, never turning to see who was hit. Legion was already in motion with Mourning Star and that was his primary concern. As long as Legion was safe and with him, he knew there was nothing they couldn't survive.

Coming from the far side of the horizon, a teal-blue-skinned creature came into the picture from nowhere, impinging the four's sights. Dauge and Legion were both fully in motion, charging at the aggressing creature. The creature was tall, probably having a few inches on Pitt and quite easily a size advantage over him. Dauge could feel his covered wounds being stressed and torn open once again. He needed to rest but the team needed to move.

The creature disappeared only to reappear again closer to the four. Its hair was black, thick, and wavy, yet not too long. Its skin blended the colors green and blue. It walked boldly with a falchion in its grasp. A thick green liquid dripped from its blade. The creature wore nothing save a pair of torn black breeches covering everything from the waist to just below its knees.

He stepped forward, still several feet away from the team, with his left foot. His sword stayed high in the air, grasped in his right hand. Pitt roared in anger, mentally preparing himself for what was to come.

Dauge's sixth sense kicked in. The creature extended his hand open palmed toward Dauge. Dauge vanished immediately. Something else rang to him that was more important. The creature's blast of sonic energy missed Dauge, coming down at an angle from the creature's hands. The ground below just behind where Dauge once stood broke apart, erupting into broken fragments of earth and rock. The Vile Frozen spit the earth and rock like a volcano spitting out ash.

Legion turned back momentarily, seeing his brother vanish. Coming up from behind, Pitt still charged forward with him. Dauge reappeared just past the cliff wall where they initially climbed up. It was Dash who was initially struck. Dash fell from the edge of the cliff only to have Dauge appear behind him and push him up and forward and back to his feet on the elevated ground.

Dauge didn't have the momentum to carry them both back over the edge. He fell, catching the ledge with both of his hands. He dropped his short swords in exchange for the ledge. He clung his feet tightly together, snatching both blades contemporaneously with them.

Dauge looked up. Dash was already in place, slamming both the distant Pitt and his brother Legion with enhancing spells to boost their abilities against the Oni. Legion and Pitt were already engaged. Dauge hiked his knees high to his chest and then even higher to where he could kiss them himself, extending his arms just the same pulling his body inches above the elevated ground.

Dauge kicked his legs out in front of him, pushing his body to a horizontal position with the ground, lying now on the flat of his back. His swords were still in place, lying loosely on the ground beneath his feet. Dirt and dust exploded from underneath Dauge, sending it all soaring in the air just above him.

Dauge didn't sit long. He rose to a half upright position, clutching the hilts of his swords once again. His momentum didn't cease there. He pushed the momentum, rolling his body forward and all the way back up to his feet.

Pitt was bigger and stronger because of Dash and Legion was quicker and his light armor now temporarily able to withstand more punishment. Dauge burst into action his feet carrying his body faster than they'd ever done before. He saved Dash and was once again back in the fight.

The oni's giant falchion was no less or more dangerous than his freely cast spells. Luckily for Legion, Mourning Star managed to counter and naturally dispel several of the oni's choice attempts against him.

One swing after another, the oni's falchion clanged against the steel of first Pitt's greatsword and then Legion's flail. With every thrust, the oni let loose dismal blasts of fire and ice. The oni's powers occasionally sang songs of sonic and even radiant energies.

A sonic boom burst into Pitt's stomach, pushing him back. Legion was already in motion, fully rotating around the moment the oni's sword dropped. It only dropped for a second as the oni fought dutifully against the two.

Dauge's charged, pushed his body harder and harder. He wanted this one. He wanted this kill. Pitt fell back. The twirling body of Legion stopped as the chain of his flail wrapped around the beast's neck. The head of the weapon smashed into the side of its head, forcing him down to his knees. Legion felt the abnormal power of his body shift back and forth, landing finally again in his left arm.

The oni felt the power forcing it to his knees. Pitt's footing was again under him. Excitement flushed Dauge's body. His thirst was cut short and taken out from under him. Dash utilized one of his few aggressive spells at a pivotal moment. Shards of ice carved into deadly spikes popped into existence just a few feet from the oni's head. And with the flick of his wrist, he ordered them forward.

Legion was already back to his feet, pulling back on the handle of Mourning Star, choking the beast and holding it in place. Pitt stumbled still, but his footing was again strong. Without thinking much more about it, he sheathed his fullblade to his back.

Dauge slowed to a trot and then to a walk. The oni was dead and the team was safe. They'd won yet another fight. More obstacles and threats were still ahead waiting to be challenged.

"Is everyone all right?" Dash yelled.

"I'll live," Pitt answered, rubbing his stomach where the sonic power hit him.

"It's best we do not rest and keep moving," Dash added, picking up the rear and finally regrouping with the rest of them.

Dauge wasn't happy with Dash but he was appreciative the bard was able to finish off the foe before any real damage was done to them. Dash looked at Dauge and dropped his head down to the ground breathing heavier still. The fight took it out of him and had it not been for Dauge, he most certainly could have died.

"Dauge, thank you. Your quick wit spared me a great deal." The bard spoke hesitantly but knew what he needed to say.

Dauge waved it off, thinking nothing of it. Legion placed Mourning Star at his side, sheathing it properly. He wrapped his arms around his little brother, cradling the back of his head with his hand. Dauge didn't know what to think of it. This was out of the ordinary even for him. Pitt looked off to the far horizon. He knew more were still out there. They were in the savage land of the Vile Frozen. They walked alongside the Mogra, something few were ever known to do.

"This just doesn't make sense," Pitt said.

"What doesn't? We're in the wild here. Who knows what we're going to find or fight in these parts," Legion said.

"No, I speak of the mission at hand. We're in search of a mythical city hoping to find its gold. We were hired to find and retrieve wealth for our employer," furthered the goliath.

"In return, anything over the agreed amount is ours, on top of whatever else we may find to help us in out future travels," Dash concluded. He spoke to end the conversation.

"Let us keep moving. We're too far now to turn back," suggested Legion.

"I long for one far from my grasp. I will have her again, Dash. And perhaps this mission will be the effect put in motion to have it so." Pitt looked at Dash as he spoke, speaking with a half smile and almost laughing happily as he did so.

"I hope you find her," Dash replied.

"We all do," added Legion.

"I hope we find Azra Goetia first," Dauge said, reminding the crew of the task at hand.

Dauge started the trek again first. His crew slowly fell back in line behind him. Once again, they were on the move and they were going to be gone for a long while. It would be weeks, possibly even months before they ever saw or felt civilization again.

The journey was by far more damaging and challenging to the goliath Pitt than any of them. His dreams had returned. In truth, they'd never fully left. Now they were haunting him more violently and dangerously more passionately than ever before. It affected his every fiber.

Other oni's encountered as well as various other wild creatures proved dangerous to the man who once boasted the dead gods themselves, even if revived, were no threat. Dauge felt the barbarian would soon fall in combat. Legion figured whatever was ailing him would soon flee the moment. Dash knew if something wasn't done their goliath ally would die.

Chapter 55

The coming months favored those with the entwining fates. While Dauge, Pitt, Dash, and Legion forced their bodies through the cold and over the Vile Frozen, Kleiven and Grath headed northwest to the Red Mystic Mountains. Drackice Black and his new band of elite mercenaries also took the trek to the Red Mystic Mountains.

The late gods certainly knew how to write ironic fates. Kleiven now traveled away from the woman he felt was his soulmate in hopes of ousting a villain whose eyes were set on his fiancé, a different woman he hoped he would soon be reunited with. And to make things even more unique, the travel would be made with the man she once betrayed him with at his side.

Sometime while on his way back to the Crystal Cities traveling westward, battles engulfed the entire southwestern portion of Runethevara, the main continent in the Runethedian pantheon. Organized monstrous legions poured out from the mountains, waging war on both the Crystal Cities and Eternis simultaneously.

Myasuna, a city filled with fun and the nightlife rested between Eternis and the Red Mystic Mountains but the monstrous armies ignored the city altogether. Myasuna, not a militant city, opted to take the saving grace as a favored omen from the faiths and refrain from assisting either Eternis or the Crystal Cities.

More monstrous legions were still heading southeast. They were planning to walk over Valakuza, the militant sister city of Myasuna, a notion Myasuna was not aware of. Retired General Seth Redd met the southeastern marching armies with an army of elite followers of his own. Men of all ancestry came to his aid and he raised his army fast.

Somehow, through the fighting and destruction, Magnus still managed to make it back safely to the Crystal Cities only to learn his son had marched through the armies in hopes of reaching the Red Mystic Mountains. The monstrous mountain horde were at the walls of the cities and Drackice disowned his duties to fulfill one of his own he thought to be more important.

The nature of that duty was still in favor of the Cities and the Free Armies, as his father knew without having to be told what his son was up to. Free Armies General Magnus Black's now main concern rested with the fate of his son. Would he and his team of specifically chosen recruits be able to slip past the monstrous mountain horde and make it to the mountains? If so, would they then still have enough left to find and oust Eternis' rightful heir?

Back in Emerald Greene, it was those on the seats of power that were infuriated at Drackice's order. Heroic beings were few and far between nowadays and Drackice strategically took some of the best the Free Armies had to offer on a mission far more dangerous than any they'd ever undertaken before.

The Free Armies representatives stood across the councilmen of the Crystal Cities there in Emerald Greene. Dozens of men clad in togas fought, bickered, and argued at the situation at hand. It was dark outside and the clouds were out. The House of Councils was built with stone seating and ivory flooring complete with a half roof and mostly no walls. Pillars and half walls held the room and building in place. It was built to both respect and appreciate the inner workings and outer workings of the day's work while rulings were in progress. Emerald Greene's House of Councils was built by the Thoxens in return for ore mined and refined by the Crystallians.

Native Crystallian leaders wore green togas and Free Armies representatives wore their signature color, black. The highest-ranking Crystallians wore white togas and lightly jeweled crowns, showing off their status among the others in the House of Councils.

The argument was clear. The Crystal Cities were furious that the commanding officer of the Free Armies, Drackice Black took elite members of the mercenary unit away from the Crystal Cities, overall weakening the defense of the cities all the while in a time of war.

Bolba paced back and forth trying to quiet the rioting members of the gathered council. Being in charge wasn't as easy as he thought. He did well to calm the people but it wasn't enough. The people wanted answers.

"Sir Bolba, we pay a heavy toll to have the Free Armies here. General Magnus isn't present to lead those armies. Drackice isn't present to lead those armies and Drackice took with him elite key members and we're in line to be attacked!" a councilman wearing a white toga said.

"Calm yourselves." Bolba tried appeasing them but to no avail. "Never have the Free Armies tasted defeat."

"Never have the Free Armies been held by a non-Black at the helm!" a green toga councilman yelled.

His words incited the crowd of roaring councilmen even more. Bolba was by far the best speaker representing the Free Armies and the current Commander of them all. And even he silently admitted to himself he couldn't win over the angry crowd of councilmen.

"Magnus will return! Drackice still serves the city! He brings forth our best to strike at the heart of he beast! Without his efforts, this battle could prove unwinnable."

Back and forth were the crowds with Bolba and the High Lieutenants of the Free Armies. He verbally fought them off as best he could for as long as he could. It wasn't enough. And by the day's end, nothing was accomplished. Days of formal gatherings to hear both sides continued until, finally, Free Armies General Magnus Black made his appearance.

He'd returned to the city the late the night prior. The hearing was nearly called off as rain set in, pouring across the city and dousing the councilmen. Luckily, there was enough room underneath the partial roof of the structure to keep the inhabitants from being directly poured on.

Bolba was still trying to fend off the verbal attacks from the city's councilmen. He'd never been so pleased to see his true liege, Magnus Black. Magnus sorely walked in, fully geared and already outfitted for war.

"My lord, you've returned," Bolba said, bowing to his mentor and liege.

"I understand the lot of you believe my son taking members of my regiments to the mountains to strike at the heart of the matter has you all a bit shaken. Am I correct?" Magnus asked.

At first, no one said a thing. Obviously, it was his most trusted scouts and informants that secretly brought him up to speed upon reentering the city. He knew what was going on and where the city stood.

"General Black, we're in no position to weaken our forces with that monstrous mountain horde on its way," said one of the green toga men.

"Weaken? I must be confused. I've faced thirty thousand with eight thousand. I've never met an adversary I couldn't defeat; such is why I am here. If that spoiled brat Bahaus is still behind all of this, then I will see him justifiably punished. He attacked my people. He attacked the city. My son Drackice fended off the advance but Bahaus was neither captured or known to be killed."

Magnus' very presence and the look in his eyes chilled the gathering. Even the white togas, the elevated members of the council, were afraid to question or challenge what he said.

"My lord, I do agree with the councilmen. Drackice abandoned his duties to fulfill a task that does purely endanger the city. And for that matter, the other Crystal Cities as well." Bolba turned his attention to now speak against Magnus for the people of the Crystal Cities.

"It's not complicated, dragonborn, what you're wishing to prove here. What you're trying to accomplish I shall see done, at least my part," Magnus said to Bolba.

"How can you agree with us now but stand against our call when alone? I speak of your stance before Magnus' return," said yet another councilman.

"I've only tried to appease you. I do empathize with you all. The city is going to need all of its resources, as our scouts have returned revealing the true size of the horde." Bolba's words certainly weren't helping.

"And you left us, Magnus. And then Drackice left us! And Drackice took with him the mightiest the Free Armies had to offer!" a councilman who'd not yet allowed his voice to be heard stood and added.

"How many times have armies split their forces to gain advantageous positions such as the flank? Does it initially weaken the frontline? Of course, but it's necessary for victory. I'll deal with my son soon enough. In the meantime, Bolba, drop those patches and rings belonging to the Free Armies. I hereby relieve you of all duties to such. Perhaps the councilmen will have a place for you on their council." He turned and looked over the onlooking councilmen and then continued. "This gathering, this meeting, it's all finished. Until you all are prepared to break your contract with me and the Free Armies or until we fail to protect the Crystal Cities, I will hear no such nonsense from toga-wearing councilmen on my Armies' tactics. If I am not at the helm, someone competent will be. I have a battle to prepare for. Good day," he said forcefully before turning and walking away without question or hesitation of what the councilmen might say in retribution.

Those actions, those words, those were all the reasons the Free Armies were so successful with such a solid reputation. It was the very reason the Crystal Cities hired him to begin with. Magnus turned and walked away from the council who in turn had absolutely nothing to say to the General.

The Viking lieutenant as he was often called, Lancewold rushed to Magnus' side shortly after he left the councilmen. Lancewold was a human, big and burly. He wore rough leathers and furs with a cape made of the same thick black fur. His mustache was thick, rolling down his face along with his facial beard. Lancewold's helm covered the top crown of his head with two bone horns curled like a ram's extending out from it. "My lord," he started, catching up to Magnus.

Magnus didn't say anything. He just kept walking. The Free Armies General's peripheral vision caught the attention of a large hangar on the man's back.

"Change to swords finally?" he asked.

"I took to your words in your absence," he answered.

The two walked and talked. Magnus moved like he had somewhere to be. Something was on his mind. "My lord, Drackice not present troubles you." Lancewold knew it.

"He's above such things. He indulges in the wrong things Lancewold. He cannot be replaced."

"He's your son."

"You miss the aim of my words."

"Apologies."

"I've spent more time, effort, money, and others to grant him the gift of a strategist's mind. I've poured everything I have into him and I've not the time to do so again. And yes, he's my son. The Red Mystic Mountains are dangerous and he's not an adventurer. He's not a traveler. He's a soldier. He's a leader, a General."

"Understand, sir."

"Drackice knows better. He should have sent those men without him. I agree with the move he chanced. He should not have been a part of the movement. Whatever's causing this monstrous mountain horde to push against us could be better served with Drackice utilizing his brain and not his brawn."

"Yes sir," Lancewold answered loyally.

"Why are you here?" Magnus asked, turning and stopping finally to face his lieutenant. He looked deep into his Viking's face.

"My lord, the horde nears us. You've relieved Bolba of command. He stormed out of the House of Councils. His skills and morale with the men are still required. We need him."

"I was once pinned down with twelve men. All thirteen survived the onslaught of hundreds of orcs. All thirteen are still alive and well today and within the ranks of the Free Armies. I'll do fine without Bolba. We'll be fine without Bolba."

"Understand, sir."

"You disagree?" Magnus questioned.

"I just feel there is a time and place for everything. And relieving Bolba of his position now may prove to be deadly choice. You're the Free Armies Commander, my lord, and I shall fight for you until all blood and life has spilled from my body."

Magnus grinned, placing a hand on his lieutenant's shoulder. There was too much to say for Lancewold's words. He was a good man and one Magnus was proud to have at his side. The Viking needed no words to see his Commander's approval of him. He knew he was appreciated. He knew Magnus looked at him as a son.

Magnus turned as he always did, looking to walk away, leaving certain things unsaid as was his way. The Viking watched for a moment as the legendary war General walked away back into the city they'd sworn to protect. Then, just as Lancewold took his eyes from Magnus, the man spoke.

"How's your son?" he asked calmly.

"Redwald grows stronger every day, my lord. Soon, he'll be a soldier of the Free Armies. He trains here with us. I have our best teaching him at all prime hours of the day."

"He's safe then."

Lancewold wasn't finished when Magnus spoke. Like most who knew Magnus, Lancewold knew when Magnus spoke it was time to listen.

"Yes my lord, he's safe under your watch and command. He's safe under the protection of the Free Armies."

"That he is, good Lancewold. That he is." Magnus was finished with the conversation and the day altogether.

In the coming days, Magnus saw the state of his late friend's granddaughter, Dusk. Magnus had never seen such vile magic at work. Dusk was in turmoil. She was in true pain. Pain, in its purest form attacked her, biting at her relentlessly. It pained Magnus to see his late friend's granddaughter in such pain but nothing could be done. His favored son Drackice was leading a team to the Red Mystic Mountains in hopes of securing a victory for the people and for her.

Dusk was ill. She was virtually bedridden from the astral attacks of Eternis' rightful heir. The Crystal Cities knew war was coming and it was coming soon. The people of the Crystal Cities praised their mercenary for its defense of the city. The high-ranking officials still stood questioning the band's actions.

Magnus returned to a mess of a world. He wouldn't have Eternis' rightful heir win this. How dare that damned king think himself equal to the Free Armies Mercenary General on the fields of war? Magnus didn't know what was more upsetting, the situation against the cities or the fact his late friend Dominick's granddaughter was in true pain and trouble.

He was the greatest military strategist the world had ever seen and he would prove so again by defeating the Monstrous Mountain Horde for the Crystal Cities, Eternis, and the entire region. Bahaus was a powerful wizard. If not an archmage, he was close. The world had fallen to the time of the Sundering for some time. It'd been over twenty years since the Sundering began.

When Taj Odin Xavier slew the final Forsaken on the Broken Lands in the year forty seven hundred, he ended the Age of Scars. What followed was to become known as the Sundering. Angels, Demons, Devils, Dragons, and the Rivermortal replaced the fallen gods when they sacrificed themselves against Gemini thousands of years prior. Now, with the Sundering's birth, elementals, great spirits, and other unique faiths blossomed into power as well.

Magic was a shattered fragment of what it once was. The world was scarred and calloused. The Rivermortal was even weak from Raino Shadowblood's Forsaken attempt against it. With all this, Magnus knew it only made Bahaus even more dangerous, an even greater threat. Few wizards of any sort could rival Bahaus' power. And with every day, the chances of finding something or someone that could rival him lessened. Bahaus was a force not to be reckoned with. Why didn't Drackice confirm a kill against him during his attack on Emerald Greene?

Chapter 56

Finally, the four for Thox saw it. It was within their sights and now certainly within their grasps. Legion, Dauge, Dash, and Pitt traveled across the Vile Frozen and fought creatures of the frost far beyond their wildest nightmares but at last, it was before them.

They stood just over the ledge of the elevated ground they trekked over. They were high above the grounds below. It was still a safer and sturdier path than the broken ground below. The sun was rising, allowing the structures of the city to glisten in the morning dew.

The four had been facing onis more than anything. Even a few orcish raids chose to stand in their way and challenge them. Rather than take the broken planes of the Vile Frozen's badland, they chose to push onward over a series of giant rocks now broken and frozen and embedded in the earth. They were tired. The ground below would've proved to be too dangerous, especially with the giant encampment recently noted.

"Look, just there. It's Azra Goetia," Dash said excitedly.

The rock they were on would be the last they had to cross. The giant frozen rocks gave them a way around the giant encampment as well as a way around the nearly impassable grounds below. Then, the rocks proved their worth yet again by allowing the four to reach a height giving them full sight of their destination ahead.

Slowly and carefully, they pushed onward until finally the giant rocks that were long frozen over were behind them. The only thing standing between them and the city was approximately a mile.

"Look how the structures look distorted and lean unnaturally. They further prove Azra Goetia is before us!" Dash continued.

Legion nodded. Dash was right. All of the telltale signs were there. That was the city all right and they had made it! Something was lurking about. It was in the shadows or the air. Something was around them.

"Keep your guard up," Dauge said. He felt the uneasiest of the situation.

They'd passed the rock and the impassable terrain was behind them. Now, they were on straight rolling plains. It was still rocky and broken ground and part of the Vile Frozen, but nonetheless, it was the closest thing to a flat plain they'd seen or felt it some time.

Dauge walked ahead and kept both armblades out just in case he'd have to put in work. Legion stalked carefully behind him with Mourning Star gripped in both of his hands. Mourning Star spoke to him a little each day. In the beginning Mourning Star spoke to him often and then suddenly, it stopped. Now, it was coming back to him. He could hear the voices inside Mourning Star calling to him. Was he learning to embrace the weapon better and more proficiently or had the powers of Mourning Star been weakened and somehow, something brought them back to it?

Was it he or Mourning Star that was growing in power, or both? The others couldn't sense the thing's powers but he could. It soon began to warn him that his brother Dauge was right. Things walked around them. Things stalked them through the very air and nothing their eyes could see would give truth to what really existed yet among them.

Legion looked on, keeping his eyes fixed to Dauge. Pitt walked boldly, unworried of what the Vile Frozen could still throw at him. It'd thrown so much already. What else could it possibly have that he'd not already seen or dealt with?

Dash stayed strategically in the center of the other three. "Hold," he said.

Pitt, Legion, and even Dauge stopped, hearing Dash's order. Dauge didn't want to but his senses told him something was coming and it wasn't anything they'd voluntarily deal with. Dauge put up the armblades and equipped his twin short swords, feeling the piercing option to be a better one. In the event of a surprise, he'd be able to move and angle himself out of the way while pushing the points forward aiming for a hit. The slashing armblades would force him to have to get too close to things he wasn't sure of just yet.

Pitt's two-handed fullblade was readied. Mourning Star of course was readied and Dash's short bow was also in hand.

Dash pulled a scroll and rehung his short bow at his side. "Gold flickers and wizards snicker, those hiding and truly blinding those that cannot see, put truth to their form and if they cannot withstand, let them flee!"

Dash's scroll lit up and in a puff of smoke, it was gone. Just ahead of them, not too far from where Dauge was standing, a burst of glittery particles filled the air. Immediate cries of anguish came from nowhere. Humanoid creatures, though monstrous in build, became outlined by the gold particles, and further, seemed to have a bit of trouble with their eyes.

Dauge rushed them with short swords in hand. He was prepared and knew he had to take advantage of the situation Dash had bought for him. His planted his left foot and plunged his right sword straight through the abdomen of the creature. He pulled the sword in an aggressively walking manner, stabbing his left sword, now stepping and planting his right foot through the unknowing neck area of the second creature. Again, he pulled his sword.

The two creatures oozed blood and their true appearances birthed before them. They collapsed, nearly dead. The second one struck was dead and the first one was helpless, bleeding out from the wound Dauge created.

Coming into sight, Dash and the others looked upon two red-skinned humanoids. Great black horns extended outward from their heads. They wore dark black and bright silver pieces and armors. Their skin had a tarnished copper look to it at certain angles. Their eyes were deep and black.

"Fucking half-fiends," Dauge said, looking down at them.

Their swords looked finer than most. They were long and looked arrogant. Smaller bat-like wings fluttered on their backs. The nerves of the dead and dying creatures forced spasms throughout their bodies but they weren't going anywhere.

"They look like tieflings," Pitt said nonchalantly. He shrugged his shoulders, hanging his fullblade over his neck, balancing it by grabbing the hilt in his left hand and the end with his right.

"I don't think they're tieflings but they do resemble the infernal bastards," added Dash.

"Invisible tiefling like sons of whores, what in the hells can possibly be thrown at us?" Pitt asked. "They sure didn't put up much of a fight against you Dauge."

"I got the jump on them thanks to Dash," Dauge said quickly.

"Well done," Legion said, coming up from behind to pat his brother on the back. "I've never seen these things before. They look like tieflings but they're not."

"They're certainly infernal," Dash said.

Then, something prompted Legion to get closer and near the beasts. Their skin was both red and then again the same color as tarnished copper. They both had long black hair, straight and evenly combed back down to their necks. Legion knelt down beside the dying one. A bolt soared just past his arm, finishing the dying beast off, piercing its head perfectly between its eyes.

"No reason to take any chances," Dash said with his short bow in hand.

Mourning Star began to glow. It glimmered radiantly and necrotically and yet neither matched the powers within the creatures. Legion placed his hand upon the forearm of the coiled corpse. It told him! It spoke to him! He knew they were infernal. "They're infernal creatures, native to the hells," he said, still zoned completely out. His eyes were looking about but couldn't find anything they felt worth staring at.

"You don't say?" Pitt said sarcastically.

Mourning star bled information from their dying bodies of their origins. Legion postured back. It was a lot to take in. The others looked on, listening to his gasps for air.

"What is it?" one of them asked.

He couldn't make out which one it was who asked the question. The voice didn't sound anything like any of the ones he was used to. It was muffled. The outside, everything around him was being muffled out. It was only him and Mourning Star.

"Legion, Legion, Legion, are you listening to me?" It was that voice! The voice of Mourning Star and it was becoming even more of a true entity within Legion yet again. Legion thought back, back to the time when both SOUL and LORE were given to him.

Legion remembered the time Mourning Star split to become both SOUL and LORE again, even if it was for a single attack. He remembered seeing and feeling the powers of Mourning Star fade from within. Now the powers of Mourning Star were returning. The entities within both SOUL and LORE and now confined to Mourning Star were all so very present.

Cambions, these things were Cambions, Mourning Star told Legion. Cambions were devils, or at least half devils. Cambions were the product of devils mating with mortals. The males were classified as Cambions while the females, Alu-Fiends. Unlike tieflings, who were forged from devils' casting rituals purging mortals with infernal blood, Cambions came as the product of devils and mortals mating. Tieflings and Cambions have several similarities and often could be confused as each other.

Tieflings were said to come from ancient rituals created and cast by devils infusing mortals, mainly humans, with the blood of the infernal. Cambions and their female counterparts, called Alu-fiends, were said to be the direct product of devils and mortals mating. Curiously, Mourning Star continued, Cambions are far more shunned by both sides than their distant cousins.

This was all too much to take in for Legion and for a moment the Eternian blooded warrior forgot where he was. Mourning Star poured information about these creatures, information that just wasn't all that important. After all, they died just fine, he thought to himself.

"Legion, Legion, LEGION!" Dash's voice finally yelling snapped him back into reality. "What in the Nine-Hells is wrong with you?"

Now seeing the warrior shake his head signifying he was back in reality. "Sorry, how long was I out?" he asked.

"Out, what were you daydreaming or something?" Pitt asked with a laugh.

"Maybe, yeah I guess," Legion said.

"What are these things? That magical piece of metal and chain in your hand's been glowing and glimmering off and on for days now. What's it telling you?" asked Legion's brother.

"Cambions, they're Cambions," he responded, standing back up from his half-knelt position.

"What's a Cambion?" asked Pitt.

"It's a half-fiend. It's a devil blooded half-fiend. These are males, so they're Cambions. Females are called Alu-Fiends," he answered.

"How do you know that?" Dash asked.

"From this magical piece of metal and chain that's been glowing and glimmering in my hands for the past few days," Legion answered, now with his wits back about him and his head back on straight.

Legion, Dash, and Pitt laughed at Legion's sudden comeback remark. Dauge didn't laugh. He didn't find it funny at all. Dauge knew the weapon was speaking to him again. What did it mean? Dauge was educated and he knew the cost of intelligent weapons was high, sometimes too high.

Nothing told him this weapon was going to be anything like what he had in mind, but it was the thought that inspired the fear. He saw in the beginning how the weapon changed for him and then again how it changed him.

"It's not important how we learned what these things are. What's important is the obvious," Dauge said, finally speaking out.

"And what's that?" his brother asked.

"What's right before our eyes, obviously," Dash said, answering first.

"Actually, it's what's not before our eyes. We just encountered two invisible half-fiends," Dauge added.

"We've encountered a great deal of dangerous things since these travels began," Pitt said, finally busting into the conversation with his booming voice.

"What's your end to this?" Legion questioned his brother.

"We've encountered worse," Dash said, trying to lift the team's spirits, not that they were down but still, fighting invisible half-fiends could put a damper on anyone's day.

"That's exactly it Dash. That's the end I seek. You're wrong. We've not been challenged by anything as dangerous as invisible… ugh… Cambions or whatever it was Legion called them." Dauge quickly became infuriated.

Dash's blind attempts to remain heroic and strong fueled his anger even more. Dash was going to get them killed. Dauge knew it was in their best interest to turn back. Something turned these things invisible and he was quick to tell the team that. Even if they did it themselves, it actually made matters even worse; devil blooded creatures with the ability to remain invisible, one could not think of a more devastating situation.

"How many of these things do you think are actually around? These things aren't exactly common," Dash challenged after Dauge spilled his words against the idea of still moving forward.

"We turn back," he said. "We can find the gold for the lord elsewhere or not at all. This is fucking suicide." He was really concerned. He'd never shown so much concern before but it wasn't for himself at all. He was concerned for his older brother.

"We walked through those damned things and you want to turn back?" Pitt asked, not fully understanding.

"We were lucky. Dash cannot outline our entire surroundings with… with…" Dauge stopped trying to think.

"Glitterdust," Dash answered for him.

"With glitterdust," Dauge seconded reconfirming. "There's no way to fight things like this with what we have."

"I can't turn back, Dauge. I stand against you on this one," Pitt said, standing strong behind his words.

His words lightened the load against Dash. Dash silently thanked the goliath for his words of support. Legion was still torn. Right or wrong he stood by his brother but why suddenly did a few invisible creatures strike so much fear into him?

"Brother, you've never shown fear like this," Legion said, confused.

"Invisible creatures with the blood of devils, is something we cannot fight, Legion. We've not the arcane or the divine on our side to do so," Dauge pushed on.

"We cut through them so easily," Legion persisted.

"This time we did. We were lucky Dash put that…" he paused to think of what that spell was called again, "that glitterdust on them.".

"Mourning Star's powers are returning, little brother. It will help us. It will guide us to victory and see us through this, Azra Goetia." Legion's declaration was foolish yet still very strong.

"Fine, but other than you, Legion, I stay back or risk falling for no man or being," Dauge said.

"Agreed," said Pitt.

"I never thought you'd fall for anyone else but Legion anyway," Dash said, laughing. "Heroic efforts such as searching an ancient city that's said to be a harvesting ground for fiends is what gets you remembered." Dash said, after giving it a few seconds of allowing the smoke to settle.

"I need not to be remembered by those I care not for. Time will remember me. Time will remember us dear brother," Dauge barked back arrogantly.

"Let's move," Pitt said to the group, putting the four once again on the move to the fated city of Azra Goetia.

"Let's," Dauge said sarcastically, seconding.

And with Dauge's final efforts to stop the team from moving forward, they did just that against the will of the younger Xavier. Legion threw an arm around his younger brother, trying to reassure him everything was going to be fine.

Dauge wasn't having it. He tossed his brother's arm from his neck and moved forward just a bit faster. He took the lead as he always did. It was his job and duty. "Remember this, should we find an invisible army of these things, the lord shall not see his gold and we shall never see home again," he said finalizing the conversation before advancing to a far lead.

By the day's end the team stood before the ancient gates of cold, wrought iron. Dark stones exquisitely placed without a single flaw built a stone wall around the city. Night lay, upon it majestically, allowing the moon to dimly light choice pieces of the city. Two archway-styled wrought-iron gates locked together were now the only thing between the legendary city of Azra Goetia and the four.

Dauge cased the inside as best he could from just outside the gate. To Dauge, it looked to be nothing more than an old city worn down from the forces of time. It was peculiar, however, how time had minutely affected the city, if even at all.

Something touched Legion. It landed yet again on his flesh, this time at the tip of his nose. Droplets of rain fell from the sky. Darkness finally overtook the night and now rain fell to fulfill the worst possible setting for the team.

"It's getting colder, Dash," Dauge said, still looking through the gated barrier.

"Perhaps we should look for another way in. If those things are out there, we don't want them to know we're here," Dash replied.

"It's too late for that, friend," Dauge said sarcastically. "Whatever's here knows of our presence."

"Are you sure?" Legion asked.

Dauge didn't answer. He took his eyes away from the gate and looked back at his brother, revealing the mental anguish the question gave him. He rolled his eyes and went back to looking through the gate. This time, he placed his grips around two of the wrought-iron poles.

"Is that necessarily a bad thing?" asked Pitt.

"Pitt, in no setting is having invisible fiends know where you are a good thing, especially if you don't know where or how many they are," Dauge replied scornfully.

"We don't know if those things were just caught in passing or if there are more," Dash argued.

"Well we're here. Let us get through this gate," suggested Legion.

"Move!" Pitt ordered, coming forward, preparing to slam his fullblade into the lock keeping the two iron gate doors together.

Dauge sidestepped, quickly getting himself out of the way. Legion was already safe from harm's way as was Dash. With a powerful step and an overhand swing, Pitt sent the blade of his massive sword straight into the heart of the lock, splitting the space between the two gate doors perfectly.

Nothing happened. The lock cracked open and the gates were free to be moved. Dash took a step back. Dauge took a step back. Pitt let the tip of the sword rest on the hardened earth beneath him. He held it steady with one hand while pushing one of the gates open with the other.

"Looks like we're clear to enter," Pitt said, humbly laughing, looking over his shoulder to his friends to see the looks on their face. Perhaps they approved his method, perhaps not.

"Well done," Dash said, not really knowing what else to say.

"Foolish," Dauge snapped.

"Well I didn't see any of you fishing for ways to get in. That's what we're here for, right?" Pitt questioned.

"Lord Stannor wants three thousand golden coins and he said we'd find it here. That's a lot of money. He's going to need it to build up that town he wants. Now then, there's a thousand ways to get money. Why send us here?" Dash asked.

"It's a little late for that," Pitt joked back.

"Stannor wants something more. There's something he's not telling us."

"That's been clear since the beginning," Legion said quickly to his little brother's words.

Pitt walked in first. He hung his blade over his neck, still counterbalancing it with his right hand on the hilt and his left over the blade itself.

"We need to keep moving. Standing out here where that lock was just busted open isn't doing anyone any favors," said the barbarian taking the initiative.

With that, the four made their way across the threshold of Azra Goetia. They'd made it. It was much easier than they'd expected to cross into the city. However, what the city was or how it stood or the options to enter never really came into their minds at all. Surviving the Vile Frozen and making it to the city was the only thing any of them really thought about upon exiting Thox for the quest.

The city was darker than it should have been. Even for the night, the darkness of the city was far deeper than they'd expected. Something neared them. Dauge sensed it. He silently signaled for the group to hold. They did as instructed. In situations like these, Dauge's abilities were impeccably important. All four stood ready.

Dauge's nose never lied to him. He sensed something he'd sensed before. It was those invisible half-fiends. He'd sensed them before. Their eyes were fixed on him. He could feel it. He couldn't see them but he could feel their eyes digging through him. His left armblade and his right short sword were out. He had to be balanced and prepared for anything.

Legion's eyes said he was just as ready and telepathically, Legion knew Mourning Star was as well. Dash's crossbow was cocked and ready to go. He'd brought it up to his face closing one eye to get better focus and braced it with both hands.

Pitt stayed just the way he was. He no longer feared anything and the more time went on, the further his mind fell from the realms of reality. Dash signaled for him to ready himself. He looked down at the soft dirt and rock beneath his feet. The walls of the city were built in circular fashion and the city neared the very edge of the southern land piece. It was strange how no one had found it before.

They were still a ways away from any structure or building of any kind. It was all farther inside. Pitt knelt down and grabbed some dirt, allowing it to trickle down back to the ground from between his fingers.

"Let's keep moving. Whatever's looking at us knows we're here. We need to move," Dauge said.

"What are we looking for?" Pitt asked.

"Gold," Legion answered.

"Places it may be stashed, Pitt. We'll search buildings. We'll search all structures. Who knows what we'll find, perhaps a hidden chamber underground filled with enough riches and weapons to secure us for the rest of our days," Dash added.

"First, we need to see what's in this place," Pitt said, taking his fullblade fully into his hands.

"Agreed," Dauge seconded.

"And I agree as well," said Legion, chiming in.

Dash smiled. "Finally, we've all come to a mutual accord."

"Not yet we haven't. Something's watching us, Dash. I don't like it. I can smell them," Dauge said. His tone was cold. It was a gritty voice angered by his current situation in the world. "I was trained to keep the drop on others, not lose it to things not yet seen."

One, two, three more Cambions appeared before them, all appearing close to their left flank. Each of them had a tarnished skin of copper. Their armor was light. It consisted mainly of torso coverings of metal and leather. Each wore red capes that fluttered in the wind behind them. Their singlehanded swords were longer than the usual and looked to be in better condition and made of a different ore, a metal unknown to the four standing before them.

Each of the three wore its shiny black hair long and straight, extending downward, even with their necks. Most of their under clothes were long sleeved and black, matching their dark clad boots that used chain pieces in place of leather strips for tightening and loosening mechanisms.

"There's going to be a lot of these damned beasts here," Legion said.

Mourning Star was prepared. The two entities inside of it thought in unison. This was Azra Goetia and to see so many half-fiends, to see so many devils, it only made sense. It was SOUL's entity that wanted glory and valiant pursuit of righteousness. LORE wished to help cleanse the world of evil, and these Cambions were just that.

Dash took a step back. He didn't want to but it was instinctive. The creatures made him hesitant. His crossbow stayed readied. The three approached without caution. They carried no fear or respect for the four.

"We're not here for you," Legion yelled, hoping something in his words would spark their interest enough to talk.

The three just kept walking. Dauge mumbled something under his breath to the effect of, the others before weren't so bad. Pitt was more than ready to put three half-fiends in their place. Whether Dash let loose his bolt or the farthest Cambion fired first will forever remain a mystery.

Dash's hand trembled and accidentally set off the crossbow. At the same time, maybe a moment sooner or a moment later, the Cambion standing farther away to the party than the others hurled his hand forward, lashing out a series of thin electric charges, one from each fingertip.

The electrical lines shot forward, one at each of the party members and the fifth acting as a second shot against the monstrous Pitt. One, two, three, four, and five direct hits; it happened so fast, not even Dauge had a chance to move out of the way. All four were blasted from where they stood and hurled to the ground. This was not going to be easy.

The closest Cambion charged. Seeing Pitt as his nearest enemy, he focused on the downed goliath as his target. The last Cambion jumped into the air. His bat-like wings helped carry his body and brought it to a height it otherwise wouldn't have reached. On his way down, he took his beautifully gleaming sword into both hands, planning to come down hard against Legion.

Pitt moved to a half upright position quickly, trying to get himself back to his feet. In order to better maintain his balance, Pitt released his fullblade with one hand and used it to better get himself to his feet. He kept the giant sword out forward and in front of him with his other hand. The notion did nothing to sway the attacking Cambion.

The last Cambion stopped fluttering its wings and fell down back to the earth as fast as its body would carry him. Unfortunately for the aggressive half-fiend, Legion's little brother was there and already prepared for the attack.

Dauge used both his armblade and his short sword to thwart the creature's attack. Dauge sent the handgrip of the armblade to his own pectoral, sending his own elbow over the top and then down again, his armblade still running down his forearm and extending just past his elbow. His short sword came up at an awkward position meeting his own armblade with the camion's sword being caught in between.

Legion rolled over his right shoulder and got out of the way. The casting Cambion was preparing to let something else in its arsenal have its way with the four. Dauge manipulated the creature's sword and own momentum against it. He spun, sending the sword distantly from its wielder. The creature poised back after resetting himself from the landing.

Dauge ducked the creature's claws as it swiped at him over and over. Dauge carefully peddled backwards out of the way, just nearly being missed by the beast. Legion made it back to his feet and the casting Cambion sent Dauge back down to his back.

While backpedaling, a darkened ray of energy blasted out from the casting Cambion in the back. It caught Dauge flush on the chest with enough force to push the voidsoul Genasi to the flat of his back. Dash shot another bolt, catching that same caster in the upper left thigh and certainly hindering his ability to move.

Pitt's sword was loosely being held in front his face and body. It connected and blocked the attempted assault by the other Cambion. Another of Dash's bolts landed successfully in the body of this aggressing half devil. Pitt fending off the attack as well as Dash peppering it with a few more additional bolts did enough to give Pitt the time he needed to once again stand on his own two feet.

Dauge breathed deeply. He was hurt. The second ray from the caster really hurt him. Dauge was in pain. He felt the pain creeping inside of him. It was travelling through his body, forcing its way harshly through his veins. Whatever that creature struck him with found its way inside of him.

The fight pushed on with both sides scoring knockdowns and knock backs. Dauge was still sluggish and partially unconscious for most of it. Finally, his wits were coming back to him. Legion was holding off one and Pitt the other. Dash was standing back firing equally at the both of them. And now, his mental psyche was coming back to him.

Pitt looked to be in more pain than Legion. Pitt was cut and gashed pretty good. His cuts were mostly across his legs and biceps. The cuts were adding up. Legion maneuvered magnificently against the Cambion.

Finally Pitt's fullblade came across at the right time, smashing against the Cambion's blade just where it met the grip of the blade. Pitt pushed with enough force to crack the blade and break it from the half-fiend's grip, dropping it to the ground.

The goliath carried his momentum, making a complete turn while attempting another hack at the creature. This time, he aimed between the monster's head and shoulder. The half-fiend was quick and his claws moved to find their way into Pitt's spinning body. Dash made a well-placed shot, sticking another bolt in the creature's pelvic area, giving Pitt the split second he needed to finish his turning swing.

Legion jumped back, narrowly missing his adversary's attack. He'd focused high the entire combat. The Cambion got used to Legion's high based swings. He stayed back, cautiously watching out for the flinging chain and spiked ball end. Then Legion tricked him. He moved to once again try a high-end attack but turned at the last minute, wrapping the creature's left ankle with the chain and smashing the spiked end of it into its shin just above its foot.

It cried out in pain, dropping its sword due to the immense level of damage it'd just taken. Legion pulled back hard on the shaft of his weapon, pulling the creature's busted leg out from under him and dropping him down hard onto his back. Dark dust exploded like a silent bomb beneath him, sending clouds of dust into the air just above him.

Legion worked the ball and chain free and prepared to swing it again. The final Cambion threw his left hand out and brought it back and then his right, after the right came back his left went out again and he yelled out something in a language none of them understood. The left the opened with the palm facing the sky and he dropped it down toward the ground as if calling something.

Dauge, now finally with his wits about him once again launched a knife, seeing what the Cambion was trying to do. The knife split his brother's legs evenly and another knife came cracking its hilt against his brother's forehead, knocking him back and, though he didn't know it immediately, out of the Cambion's blast.

Dark lightning shot up from the ground and came down from the sky and both chased their way into Dauge's dagger. The one that caught his skull was just in the way and it got caught in the storm as well.

Dauge grounded the first dagger and used the next to knock his brother out of the way. It worked. The wounded Cambion on the ground rolled and grabbed its sword but before it could regroup any further, the already regrouped Legion put Mourning Star's spiked ball through its face, killing it instantly.

The lightning called by the final Cambion finally stopped and one of Dauge's daggers still hung in the air. By fading first out and then back into existence using his voided soul manifestation, Dauge Gray managed to leap and kick the dagger, using the bottom of his boots, hoping it would nullify the electricity from getting to him.

It worked! He reappeared, cutting a front flip midair, placing the back of his heel against the near falling dagger. His maneuver created enough force to send it flying and sticking into the final standing Cambion. It caught it in the upper torso, wounding it. The electrical charge was still fresh and the Cambion caught a taste of his own power.

It stumbled and finally fell to a knee. Dash called out arcanically, forcing a weakness to lightning upon the already lit-up creature. Dash's spell against the final Cambion was enough to maximize the electricity within it enough to fry him from the inside and kill him. At long last, it fell over burnt and cooked and dead.

"Everyone okay?" Dash asked, quickly looking around.

Pitt wiped blood from dripping wounds, dropping his blade in the process to do so. He nodded, telling them all he was fine, hurt but fine. Legion was okay. Dauge was hurting and he could still feel those powers writhing around inside him, but for the most part, he was fine. Dash was still better off than the rest of them and he quickly put his limited healing powers to work, taking both the inner pains from Dauge's body away as well mending the exterior damage to Pitt's lower half. His legs had a tremendous amount of lacerations that needed to be mended.

"I told you. This isn't going to go as you planned," Dauge said, looking to Dash. Dauge had a way of letting Dash know every time something didn't work out in their favor. If it was Dash's mistake, Dauge was sure to let him know and this was no different.

"What are you saying brother?" Legion asked dusting himself off.

"I'm saying whatever it is you think we're going to achieve by getting three thousand gold from this city is not worth the risk. We're not going to make it out of here. We most certainly aren't all going to make it. We can acquire gold a thousand different ways and pulling it from an ancient city that once stood as a harvesting city for demons or devils is not the way to go about it," Dauge replied.

"Relax Dauge. We've defeated the Cambions once again. We'll defeat the next batch and whatever else these things here throw at us. Let's see what this city has to offer," Dash said, starting now to sarcastically respond to Dauge's condescending remarks.

"You're a fool, Dash Riproc, and you're going to get the lot of us killed. Rest easy knowing if my brother dies before me, this place won't take you. I will." Dauge wasn't kidding. He meant every word of it.

The argument continued to rise until Legion finally simmered it down by reminding them all that they were in fact in the ancient city of Azra Goetia. The heated comments finally stopped flying and the team found its way again, trekking through the city of ancient devil origins.

Dauge couldn't let it go even it if was his brother trying to end it. He had to get the last word and remind them all he hated this entire campaign. "I still don't like it. I don't fancy this trek at all," he said while the others finished looting the bodies of their dead adversaries.

Chapter 59

To Bahaus, everything was in order. Aristophane was keeping the armies and their commanders in check while still battling the humanoid cities for totalitarian supremacy over the entire area. Bahaus was already in place too and harvesting the powers of both sleeping titans. Soon, his power would be beyond the mortal world's reckoning.

Bahaus was already one of the last remaining wizards of true prowess and now with the powers of two twin titans coursing through his veins there would be nothing to stop him. He continued to push for Dusk in the Astral. His dominion over her was virtually unbreakable but she wasn't his just yet.

In time he knew all things would fall into place just as he wanted them to. If they didn't, he would force them into place as he saw fit. The Red Mystic Mountains once housed the Red Mystics, a civilization built upon defense. The defense of the mystics had yet to ever be matched. Their fortifications and defense mechanisms were built to weaken and separate invading enemies until they were nearly useless, at which time they began their guerilla tactics to finish them off.

No one knows what happened to the Red Mystics or why they disappeared. One day, the civilization was known to have been thriving in the mountains still making their rounds to the cities they made trade with and the next day they were suddenly gone from the world. The Red Mystics are still one of the greatest mysteries in all of Thedian known history.

Everything in the mountains was exactly as it should be, thought King Bahaus. The wargoyle priestess was fantastic at keeping everything together and in order. And with her on his side, she would be able to hold off any acts of aggression while he milked the two titans for all they were worth. According to Aristophane and the others, he was merely acting as a tool to help in their awakening. Fools, he thought again to himself, laughing.

Morkon was dead. One of the strongest creatures in their arsenal had been slain by General Seth Redd himself. Morkon was abnormally large for a troll but he died just the same. Seth Redd was fighting on the eastern and southern fronts while Bahaus still pushed to the southwest for the Crystal Cities.

There was a time not too long ago, the Crystal Cities were all he wanted. The Crystal Cities were all he desired for they had the wealth he needed to see his campaigns through. Now Bahaus realized the misdirection of his thoughts. He was not thinking on a large enough scale.

He sensed the nearing of his enemies. He was surrounded by enemies and so it was hard to formally tell them apart. Soon, none of it would matter. He was using Aristophane and her horde of followers to keep the Crystal Cities, Eternis, Myasuna, and Valakuza all at bay. While they were all busy fighting off the hordes he hurled at them, he would be soaking up the powers of the sleeping titans. Not even Aristophane knew of his true ambitions.

She was a powerful priestess yet his cunning proved too great for her to understand. He'd not seen her in weeks. She was busy keeping the divine in order for the "awakening" of the twin titans. Bahaus could feel Nyx more than Erebrus but the reason behind why was still a mystery to him.

Bahaus finally planted a powerful force of divination on Aristophane allowing him to finally see through her eyes without her having any knowledge of it. It was working. The wargoyle knew nothing of what he was doing and now he could see her and a freezer burned fire troll kneeling before her famed alter to the titans.

The fire troll was younger than expected to be answering to Aristophane directly. His dark clammy flesh burned by a fiery cold. He was hurt and without treatment he would most certainly not survive the night.

"My grace," he started, still staring at the floor. The creature was still too afraid to look up at the wargoyle priestess.

Shards of petrified ice clung to his body by remaining pierced through his flesh. Fingers and toes were missing and should have already been regenerated. Fire trolls were different. Traditionally, fire trolls had an orange colored skin, a burnt orange with almost a black tint to it. This one was light blue and gray. It'd nearly been frozen to death.

The creature spoke a language Bahaus previously would have not understood. To the others in the massive room, the same room where he once fought the wizard, hundreds of orcs, bugbears, hobgoblins, and trolls stood listening to the fire troll speak his peace to Aristophane with only the trolls and the priestess understanding their kindred's language.

"How goes the war against Seth Redd in the push for Valakuza? How goes the war against Eternis?" she asked.

"We've not reached that far south. At first, Seth Redd spread his armies out like a wall. We tried to break through and the wall broke away. It fought back using guerilla and ambush tactics, my queen. We cannot pinpoint his armies. The harder we try to push on through, the more casualties we take. Redd killed Morkon himself. We need to fall back and retreat, take what little we have and hold until we're strong again. We've moved against too many fronts. The Crystal Cities are still a great threat. The Free Armies are still a great threat." The fire troll feared speaking the truth but he knew he had to or they were dead anyway.

"What happened to you?" she asked, condescending.

"A caster in the ranks, we lost many. A small party of eight carries with it at least two wizards and both put more ice through me than needles to a pincushion. I don't know where they're heading or what they aim to do. They aided Seth Redd and his men against us and I nearly lost my life. Morkon perhaps would have killed Redd had it not been for that blasted archer amongst them." The fire troll continued both angrily and fearfully.

"More are uniting and pressing against us," Aristophane said.

Bahaus listened to her words carefully. She was correct. The entire region now understood the level of power they had to stand up against in the mountains. This was precisely what Bahaus was hoping for. He sat quietly and listened while Aristophane ordered her commanders to circle around her. She and the trolls and orcs and bugbears collaborated and brainstormed on how to fight back against Redd's armies, the Crystal Cities, Valakuza, and Eternis. Redd hailed originally from Eternis but the militant city he now called home had an army of its own.

Everything was once again falling into place and this time Bahaus would have the powers of two sleeping titans to assure nothing would go wrong. Eventually, Bahaus broke his link to the wargoyle priestess and directed his attention to the lovely lass in Emerald Greene, Dusk Xavier.

This time, he utilized newfound powers he'd acquired from Erebrus in conjunction with his own. Soon, he hovered over her sleeping body as he'd always done. He waited patiently. Soon, she would awaken into his dream world. She'd not yet fully left the prime material but when she did, she would enter a dreamscape of his creation. And then he would begin.

Dusk's eyes opened. She didn't even remember falling asleep. Looking around, she didn't see her room the Coal's Inn. Everything around was dark and dead. Dead trees and grass, and dirt that hadn't seen water in years surrounded her to every horizon. Her eyes only granted her the colors of black and gray. Only her bed remained natural. It held its true color. Where was she? Was she dreaming?

"You're very much awake my dear. You're awake in my world."

What was that? Who was that? That voice, it sounded intimately familiar. It was Bahaus! Bahaus Sazos Uil-Endail. She pinched herself hoping she'd awaken. She didn't. She looked into the darkened sky above. Like Davion before, this time it was Bahaus hovering over her. The scene altogether was horrifying and she didn't understand it.

"I've taken color from your sight. When you sleep, you now shall enter my dreamscape. Forever linked are you and I," he said.

She felt another presence trying to break through but it couldn't. It wasn't strong enough. It was Davion and he was giving it everything he could. She couldn't remember the last time she'd felt his presence. She couldn't even remember the last time she'd felt him. Once, she feared the lich and now she begged for him.

Bahaus looked nothing like he did before. His former self was long finished. And with every passing second, Bahaus body mutated further. His skin drifted away, transforming into something deeper and more otherworldly. Shadowy reptilian scales replaced his flesh and even Dusk could see he fought to keep his form physical and together.

Then, the reptilian scales of black forged themselves into something different, something Dusk had never seen. The black turned into bright silver in some places, coloring his body both silver and black. The hair on his head dissipated into nothing as did his favorite facial hair patches. His skin looked like scales of iron. In some places it was as shiny as a knight's in a fairytale and in other places it was darker than the deepest thoughts of a high demon prince.

A clear liquid secreted from the scales, lubricating them. Dusk knew not the purpose but it did make his appearance that much more diabolic. Her only sanctuary came in knowing that Davion would not let her go.

The lich would come for her again. Stories and dreams and conversations with the lich told her it was Dauge who brought him to her. She found herself able to do things she never thought possible since her connection with the undead being began.

"What do you want with me, prince?" Dusk yelled, finally trying to stand up for herself though she kept coiled and arched halfway under the sheets of her bed still.

"It's not what I wish to take from you. It you I wish to take," he replied politely. His polite tone only furthered his arrogance to her. "I've not been a prince for some time now. I am the rightful heir to the Eternian throne. I alone remain with the proper blood needed to hold that throne." His voice was filling with anger once again.

Her calling him prince enraged him. He tried to hold it in but he just couldn't. He was the king of Eternis. Her words reminded him of his place in the world. He'd lost the throne. He'd been defeated. Somehow he survived and found his way to the Red Mystic Mountains where he found new life. He found the kobold Gold Piece and worked his way to and through the creature's leaders. Now, the filthy wargoyle priestess commanded the armies and kept his enemies busy while he used her plans, tools, and powers for his own personal gain.

Why not? After all, he deserved it more than anyone else. He was in fact the true king to the world's oldest city and one day he would restore his land to its former glories. How pathetic were the Eternians of recent, content with living in a simple city only extended by the ancient colonies it once usurped after their war against Thox. During their war against Thox so long ago, hundreds and even thousands came to defend the ancient city. They fortified themselves by building colonies alongside the ancient city. After the war, Eternis expanded its boundaries, taking in the colonies as its own. Now, the different wards of Eternis were based upon the different colonies that were founded to aid the city for that horrific war.

Bahaus shed his physical shell, breaking out of the silver and black scale like pieces of flesh covering and keeping his insides together. His hovering body floated down close to Dusk who, try as she may could do nothing to fend off the king's advance. She couldn't move. She was stuck to the bed and even with her newfound powers she was helpless against the ever growing powers of Eternis.

She could feel Davion. Davion knew he was no match for the powers brewing inside the dreamscape forged by Bahaus. His powers already existed there, for he was the innate that whipped and thrashed throughout her body. She could now feel him trying to break free. Or rather, the champion undead tried to use her to break into Bahaus dreamscape. For he made a promise to Dauge and it was not one he would sit by idly and see broken.

"My child, I've reached stars far beyond the worlds of anything this plane has ever seen. And I choose you to be my queen. You shall serve me privately for the rest of your immortal life. I shall grant you an endless stream of life so that you may never suffer the thought of one day expiring and losing your position to me."

Dusk shivered. She was terrified but she did everything she could to keep her composure. What about her made this thing fight for her so diligently? Why would he not give up? Why could he not have just died against Drackice Black?

Bahaus Sazos-Uil-Endail became nothing more than an apparition, glowing red, outlined in black, with eyes of vampiric yellow. He'd transformed and ascended into something greater than he previously was right before her very eyes.

He descended until he finally sat right next to her there on her bed. He felt her fear. It was too great for her to accept. Her fear was becoming painful. Her fear transcended into something physical. He felt her physical pain. He fed off of it.

Her pain would feed him and his control over her. Her pain would lead to her ultimate submission to him. He possessed the mightiest of all blood and held the proper title as King of Eternis and soon enough, they would once again know his name and feel his might.

Something wasn't right. Bahaus went to speak again but something in his dream reel was off. It was wrong. She and her bed were the only things not created directly by him here, yet he felt the presence of something else. It was a presence he'd felt before. It was that vile presence of the undead. Had he not learned his lesson yet?

From behind, he felt the power growing but it formed from within her breasts. Davion pushed radiant energy through Dusk and pushed it into his dreamscape. That vile sack of cocks, Bahaus thought. Bahaus removed himself temporarily only to return closer to the growing ball of radiant energy.

Bahaus grabbed the ball, filling it with pure darkness from Erebrus himself. Bahaus even went so far as to open a channel directly to the energy and linked it to the orb. It wasn't that the energy level was required but to show Davion just what he chose to stand against.

It wasn't long before the radiant energy put forth by Davion through Dusk evaporated into nothingness. Bahaus stared at Dusk as if telling her his feelings would do some good to Davion.

"Infest my dreamscape will he? What I love the most about undead is that I am able to kill them over and over. This lich will belong to me and die a thousand deaths before real torture is brought to him. I shall see him fully restored through rituals and killed daily with more pain than the abyss dealt in each one."

His words stunned her. She felt connected to the creature though she wasn't. He was linked to her but she'd never really met him. He was something that existed only in her dreams. Yet, vicious words spoken against him angered her all the same.

Bahaus could feel it. More radiant orbs were coming through. How was Davion utilizing radiant energy so easily and with such power? He was in fact undead and yet he forced radiant energy into Bahaus' dreamscape.

Bahaus cried out in rage. He was furious. How was his dreamscape failing him? What was going on? His glowing apparition deepened with color as his anger continued to grow. He opened up, releasing channels of Nyx's dark energies into the dreamscape. The result was chaos with tears and devastation slicing up the temporary realm. The tears and holes gave Davion the opening he needed to slip into the dreamscape and seal it back with powers of his own.

Dusk frantically panicked. She didn't know what to do. An undead being, a lich sworn to protect her in honor to his word to her brother fought for her against an empowering foe with no seeming end to his might.

The reckless wizard with power too great to describe made the simple mistake Davion hoped he would. He used immeasurable force to annihilate that which he did not understand, resulting in tears and holes in his very own dreamscape. Davion could see the tears and holes filled with his own power of the undead, necrotic nature didn't help him much either. It transformed him even further.

Davion looked a bit similar and a bit different. He old cloaks and robes still flowed down, perfectly flawed. Only his blackened skull was visible from the robes. A yellow aura matching Bahaus' tint emanated from the undead being. There was no time for formal introduction. By the time Davion entered the dreamscape, both were preparing for their next move.

Dusk pleaded for both sides to stop. Both sides, why did she not want to see Bahaus now hurt? Davion cared not. His word was to her brother, not her. She knew not of the being in front of her. Bahaus was something far worse than he and a greater threat than any this world had ever seen, save perhaps a Forsaken.

Soon, the entire dreamscape was enveloped in their battle. Necrotic powers mixed with radiant ones battled unknown and dark energy sources, energy sources new to even Davion. He knew not how to combat them but he knew he had to. Finally, the darkness of the dreamscape itself got ahold of Davion and pulled him down to the dirt and rock below.

"Now lich, now you'll die permanently. I will bury you in this place and send it deep into the endless void of the negative plane of existence," Bahaus barked.

In a last ditch effort, Davion used what powers he had left but they worked minimally and Bahaus quickly countered them all without breaking a sweat. He was overwhelmingly powerful, especially in a plane of existence he created from nothing, well from the powers of the sleeping titans.

Bahaus tried to near the creature that was now nearly neck deep in the dirt. Something hit him and hit him hard! It knocked back the creature of raw energy, forcing him far to the edge of the plane. Davion broke free with Bahaus not close by. The powers encasing him weakened with his presence sent to the end of the plane.

Bahaus once again teleported, moving effortlessly through his plane, but Davion had a plan Bahaus was not ready for. The purple diamonds in his eyes gleamed brighter than they'd ever gleamed as he ordered Dusk to run far back behind him.

Another delayed attack ripped Bahaus back into the dreamscape's existence. Bahaus knew what it was and it was such a simple power. Astral destruction, and the worthless being who didn't know how to stay dead chose arcane! The spell temporarily suspended anything he'd be able to do that was tied or otherwise connected to the arcane.

Though it hurt Davion, he wasn't ready for his final trick. The Astral Destruction brought him back to the physical of the dreamscape. The pulling of Bahaus from his teleport back to the material of the dreamscape momentarily stunned him long enough for Davion to wreck his own body by calling forth radiant energies. The energies blasted forward at Bahaus with such force, they too even damaged the already weakened dreamscape.

A hundred bolts of pure holy lightning blasted across the plane of dreams crafted by Bahaus, first tearing into him and then tearing into the plane itself. To Davion's fortunate surprise, tearing holes in the dreamscape seemed to wound Bahaus for some reason.

He was not one to ask questions at this point. His entire direction changed. Dark voids quickly filled the gaps where the radiant energy blasted through. Dusk screamed for Davion to be careful and to just flee.

"Let him have me, dear lich, please!" She wasn't being sincere in wanting to go but she was sincere in wanting him to stop. Davion couldn't understand why.

The platform for their battle was too great and real. It felt no different than any other plane Davion had ever been on. Why did she plead for him to leave? It was too late anyway. He saw or felt no reasonable means of escape. The lich had something on his side the power usurping wizard didn't count on and he would purely use it to gain the advantage.

Bahaus for once used his powers wisely. It must have been the titans in him. With his arcane abilities hindered, he called to his newly discovered divine powers to do the work. A truly impressive conjuration-based spell flew mystically at Davion, coming at him as several snow-white balls followed by tails of bleeding magic.

Davion's previous protections came into effect blocking one after another. One got through, hitting the lich hard. Everything the lich wore vanished but his body remained. His skeletal body held strong. Bahaus couldn't believe it.

"You withstood my power. No matter, my arcane has returned," he said, blinking his eyes as he did so.

The top of his eyelids touched the bottom of his eyes and Davion broke into a hundred pieces and then turned to a cloud of dust. Bahaus laughed. It was a decent fight. He was impressed. Bahaus dropped himself to the ground, reforming closer to what she remembered him as.

Slowly, he walked toward the still shrieking woman. Behind her, he could see the city and her room in Coal's Inn. His dreamscape had taken damage. His little temporary plane would need mending and to do so they would have to leave it.

It took a long while and took much more force than expected but finally he stood over the feeble little girl who curled up in the fetal position, terrified of everything he was. He bathed in the fear. It soothed him.

Closing his eyes and using powers taken from Nyx, he opened a link to her from his own self, taking in her fear and sadness. It fueled him.

Wait, something was wrong. Something hurt terribly. Pain, it'd been quite a while since he felt pain. His body was becoming more physical and natural as it once was in his human state. Something lurked in his veins. It stunned and paralyzed him even in his own plane.

A ghostly apparition arose from Dusk. It flew deep inside him and the things lurking in his veins connected to him. It was Davion! He could feel his wretched existence! The power was temporarily too much. Bahaus separated his essence and reappeared far back from both Dusk and Davion.

It was to no avail! The channels were already open. He opened that new link to Dusk, and Davion was part of that link. How would he stop it now? He couldn't risk Davion tapping into his own resource but if he destroyed the dreamscape, he might lose whatever power and control he had over Dusk. No, he would not lose!

He tried to regroup but instantly Davion was on him again and whatever it was lurking inside of him ate at him. It held him from using his powers and blocked his channels to the titans and his own body back home. Bahaus was stunned he didn't know what to do.

Davion used what was left of his powers to force Dusk physically from the world and finished by ripping his seams from the dreamscape. Blackness surrounded all of them. Bahaus was in a place he'd never seen before, as was Davion. Dusk awoke but not in her bed. She was on the streets of Emerald Greene and the inn where she'd taken refuge was all but burnt to the ground.

Rain poured from the sky, helping the local guards oust the fire. Other guards surrounded her, confusing her as to what really happened. A green scaled dragonborn looked down at her with rain giving his scales that beautiful shimmer. He wore a courtier's outfit; even in the rain the colors of his fabrics matched his scales.

"You wretched witch, you'll burn for this!" Bolba, the Commander of the Free Armies solemnly said with conviction.

She knew nothing of what happened or what she'd done. She did not understand. Before the green-scaled commander could say another word, phantasmal beings appeared, already swinging rancorously at each other with magic and might far beyond those present's understanding.

Bolba quickly ordered everyone back. Dusk remained halfway lying on the city streets, while the two continued to combat. Bahaus felt his connection fading. His astral projection with physical property was dying out. Davion destroyed his links. He hurled everything he had at the bitch Eternian, Dusk. Davion used his teleportation skills, something he was good at even in life, to move in and take the hit for her.

Bahaus vanished before he could see his work complete. He awoke in a painful state, once again feeling the prickles of pain dance harmoniously through his body. His ethereal connections and astral connections to the titans were still in place. It was only the projected links and connections he destroyed. A victory for the lich, he thought. He no longer felt he could connect with Dusk. She was safe from his grasp, for now.

Davion shattered one again into dust. This time, the dreamscape was gone and it was on the prime material that Bahaus annihilated him. Dusk knew better. She felt his presence even still. Davion too was far from her, though. He was regaining strength and power and would soon reform close to his domain and phylactery.

He'd done his job. His duty so far was complete. He successfully fended off something far greater with access to far greater powers than his own for Dauge's sister Dusk. He knew it would take much longer than expected to recuperate. His essence was extremely damaged and perhaps would never be the same.

Bolba looked at Dusk, not sure what to do or what to think. Her nightclothes were tattered and splattered spots of blood stained it in places. She looked up to him for comfort and help. She didn't know what she was, what just happened, or what Bolba planned to do.

His eyes shot a look of animosity her way. It took her back making her no longer comfortable in her own skin. He wouldn't do anything crazy to her. After all, she was still the daughter of Taj Odin Xavier, granddaughter of Dominick Gabriel Xavier. Dusk never felt so alone. She'd never been so confused in all her life.

Chapter 50

Drackice and the other seven pushed diligently toward the Red Mystic Mountains from Emerald Greene; the distance was far. Above them was the Mystic forest and the Red Lake united it all; massive lake surrounded both by a great forest on one side and a mountain chain on the other. Drackice knew he'd be moving east, keeping the lake north of him. The chain began far down the way, fully opposite of where Emerald Greene and the other Crystal Cities resided.

Drackice's push was well worth it. He united his team with General Seth Redd's and even saved the man from utter defeat at the hands of a monstrous troll. Drackice and the other seven knew it was too difficult to push into the mountains.

Retired General Seth Redd ordered the formation of a special unit of soldiers. He handpicked most of them and planned to execute an attack the mountainous horde would never see coming.

Drackice walked alongside Redd often at the encampments.

Fires burned. Tents were up. The smell of oil on steel filled the air. Seth walked this night with his cane. Occasionally, age and old wounds forced the Eternian General to use a cane. Drackice walked right alongside him. Next to his father, Drackice believed General Redd to be the greatest man currently still walking the earth.

"Those with orders to the south pike," Redd said over and over again.

Other soldiers walked through the ranks of tents shouting out the same orders. General Seth Redd always used the three pike rule; it was a rule he'd come up with during one of his early war campaigns.

Soldier encampments could be a cluster. There was always the main tent and then the higher ranking's sleeping area. That went for almost every military. In the event he was ever surprised again, he didn't want the same catastrophe happening again. Everyone, including him, dressed the same while camped, ignored all saluting rituals, and carried the same style tent. To ensure the safety of everyone, all camps were given three points in the form of a triangle. The black pike, the red pike, and then either a south or north pike. It was his rule. If it was a frontal, it would be a northern pike and if not, a southern. The pikes were obviously named for him and his dear friend, Magnus.

Those chosen peeled themselves from their campfires and ate their roasting food, if they had any in the fire. Redd and younger Black walked all the way until they finally reached the southern pike. White breeches, white tankard shirt, and black boots, that was the underdress of all soldiers fighting for Redd. He couldn't believe how well they listened; they were a Rogue Army, fashioned together at the last minute, yet they fought like they'd been fighting together for ages.

The smell of burning wood and oil-christened blades brought Seth back. It also reminded Drackice of when he was a child and his father ordered him to constantly help the troops clean up and prepare for battle. He regularly shined boots, sewed cloth, oiled blades, and built practice fields. And for most of it, his father was never around to see.

Soldiers gathered. Some carried with them blood stained clothes. For some, the blood belonged to others and to others, it was their own. Bandages kept wounds in place and temporarily sealed for the moment. Redd and Black the younger stood at the old pike where they were all ordered to meet.

General Seth Redd looked around at them. These men had come from near and far to fight for him. Some had fought for him hundreds of times. There were those who'd answered his call once or twice. The majority of them came for this particular call. They'd heard his name and probably had never even seen his face before. They answered the call of the people and their voice was Seth Redd.

"Soldiers, mercenaries, warriors, and heroes alike, I'm not here to tell you some little fairytale with an ending we can all sleep soundly to, nor is it the time for moving words to touch the soul. Today I ask a great deal of you, more than I've ever asked. Together some of us have faced many enemies. Galron Moondeep, you dwarven son of bitch," Redd started out stern but a familiar dwarven face pulled laughter from his lungs. He paused finishing up his laugh. "You and I faced the werewolf wizards together at the Wage of Conquerors. Galstaff, our human age catches us but you helped spare Eternis against the lizards with me, remember?" Galstaff was another he remembered fighting alongside. "My dearest and closest friend's son, Drackice Black, of Magnus Black and the Free Armies stands alongside me here." He didn't want to pause but the cheers of the soldiers smothered out his words.

He signaled for them to settle down and asked them kindly over and over until finally, it was quiet again. "We've been fighting these things in the mountains for some time. If we don't strike its heart, who knows how long it will last. We've not the tools to find its heart but Drackice does. We have to open that bastard's chest and use our tools to dig out its fucking heart!" Once again, he was silenced by the roars and cheers of the crowd of warriors.

The General walked a bit, touching the shoulders of those he knew and remembered fighting alongside. He quietly apologized if he passed one that remembered him more so than he did them. After wading through the score of soldiers, General Redd made his way back to the pike.

"Bahaus Sazos-Uil-Endail is behind it all. I believe he caused a stir with something that was already there. It matters not to us who is behind it. The heart must still be removed! It's waging war against everything south of the Mystic Mountains and Red Lake."

"What will you have us do?" a new face asked, interrupting the General's words.

"What would you have us do?" another voice echoed out from the crowd of soldiers.

Again Seth used his hands to keep the commotion of the soldiers down. They were dedicated to him and some didn't even truly know him. They were true to the name and the cause. He was the face and name behind the cause.

"In the end, it's a horde of beasts wanting to tear down the walls to our way of life. The Crystal Cities, Eternis, Myasuna, Valakuza, it's all in danger."

"Didn't the horde ignore Myasuna in its marches?" Galron asked.

"We know not of their intentions or what their moves will be. We know not of what comes next for them. We know our land is in danger. Valukuzans, Myasunians, Eternians, Crystallians, we band together to fight this horde. We've not seen anything like this since the days of Agromordeus! Agromordeus the necromancer was slain by Bahaus, Cale Dar, the dark Prince Avalon Darksteel, and a band hailing from Eternis."

"Bahaus, the prince of Eternis, the rightful heir, our enemy, he aided Eternis in that fight?" a voice bellowed out.

"He did. Cale fell that day but took up the offer of returning to life. Never mind it all, it's a story for a different day. Bahaus is among that horde and he and the horde are enemies to us all. As a collective force, we'll see it driven from these lands!" Seth Redd clenched his fist and raised it high into the air roaring out as he finished his next set of words.

The coming morning proved almost disastrous. They were taken by surprise by legions of kobolds and burning brands. They aimed not to fight but to burn. Days passed and the army of General Seth Redd ventured on. They fought valiantly with Drackice Black and his crew at their side. And then it came. It would never open again the way it opened for them then.

A strong push by Seth Redd and his best men opened a gap for Drackice and the others to move forward. Looking around, thousands of monstrous humanoids swarmed the battlefield and more continuously poured from the down stretch of the mountains. Seth and his army held strong, fighting off the thing as best they could.

Seth and his army were outnumbered and on wide-open grounds were foolhardy for even thinking the fight was viable. The men knew they needed to retreat and fast. Seth's orders were to hold until Drackice and the others were clear and safe in the mountains.

Drackice and his team of seven others moved with more grit and determination than they'd ever done. They fought ferociously through the scattered remnants of the gap to get to the edge of the mountains. Spells rang out, arrows flew, swords were swung, everything blew out from their arsenal and thankfully, it worked.

It worked but not without its casualties. Seth's armies combined would not be enough to hold off another attack. Even with their roguish tactics, Seth's scattered army was all but shattered. He had to fall back. They had to fall back.

Valakuza and the Crystal Cities both had decently standing armies. The Crystal Cities relied mostly on the Free Armies. Myasuna had an army but not one to combat something such as this. And Eternis was in such a civil state, something of this nature could likely implode them.

On the realist side, Seth knew he was the reason some of the smaller villages in between and even the prime cities of the area still stood. His Rogue Army and guerilla tactics were enough to continuously hold them off and occasionally push them back. In order for Drackice to move against the heart of the beast, he needed an opening and Seth was the only one capable of giving it to him.

When Drackice was no longer in sight and his crew absent Seth's eyes as well, Draeden used his arcane ability to send signals back to Seth and the others. Glowing blue orbs danced around in no particular order or pattern. Their presence told Seth what he needed to know.

"Fall back!" Seth screamed at the top of his lungs.

"Fall back!" a backing captain yelled behind him.

The army was too scattered. They couldn't all hear the call and those in place to make the call were either already killed or worse. Seth managed to escape but his body was swathed in wounds. Mostly arrows and small dagger cuts, but nonetheless, the leader of the army was dangerously wounded.

When the smoke cleared on the seventh day, fragmented pieces of the horde rushed back to the safety of the mountain. Seth's scouts informed the slowly recovering leader that Drackice and his team were able to secure a two-day head start. There wasn't much of either side left. The horde had unending numbers and Seth's resources were scarce.

He quickly ordered the camps scattered and quietly placed and well hidden. His advisors disagreed with him, stating that what was left of the forces would work stronger together if need be. Seth reminded them, "If we're needed again anytime soon, we're as good as shattered anyway." He ordered his fastest scout to his side.

He lay nearly motionless in a large hammock hung between two trees. He wore nothing but bare minimal cloth wrapped around his loins. His wounds had been bandaged and mended as best they could. Some could still get infected. There was no guarantee he would survive another week. His body slowly fought off the fever but it relentlessly tried its way back into his body over and over.

A young lad came to him. He was dressed in light armor and carried a short bow with ammunition on one side, a longbow with ammunition on his back, and a small short sword on the other side of his waist. He was a scout. There were probably more weapons than what Seth could see. He was elven and young.

"What's your name boy?" he asked.

"Elekenethal," the boy answered.

"My army tells me you're the fastest of the scouts."

"I just do my job, my lord," he said humbly.

The elf looked very basic with light brown hair and matching eyes. His skin was dark as if he'd lived somewhere where the sun tested the populace. Seth grew curious.

"You're too young to have served me before I think. What brought you to my service?" Redd asked coughing and hacking. Sickness was setting in for the old retired General.

"My father served you at the Push for Power in the east. He died, but not before sending home a slough of letters telling about his experience under your command. Against my mother's wishes, I came and answered the call to arms for you, my lord. I will give my life for your cause, as my father proudly did."

"Are you an only child, son?" The coughing had just about stopped. He'd just about gotten it all out.

"Yes, my lord," he answered.

"You're dismissed," Redd replied.

"Why my lord, if I may ask?"

"I wouldn't feel right if you perished. This isn't exactly going to be an easy task, son. Your mother's going to need you. You're young. You're just too young."

Seth dismissed the boy and the boy turned to leave. Elekenethal couldn't do it. He couldn't make himself leave. He turned back and looked at General Redd once again.

"My lord, if I may," he started.

General Redd's eyes had already closed. He needed rest but he wasn't out just yet. He cracked them open and looked over at the boy, giving him the silent okay to continue with his purpose.

"My father fought and died for you. I want to be remembered. I don't care if I die for this ridiculous battle. I want to be remembered and not just as a soldier who perished, like my father."

"Bold words for a young boy," Seth replied.

"Give me this task. Give me this mission and see it done. If I fail, let me fail doing something the people of Thedia will remember. I shall not. I will see your orders through, my lord. Just give me the opportunity."

Seth looked at the young boy. He was young and his flesh not even thickened with scars yet. His advisors chose him as the fastest and most efficient scout. He didn't want the boy's mother to go without him but many mothers lose their sons to war. He's no different, Seth silently told himself.

"Fine, you're tasked with making it to the Crystal Cities. You are in the gravest danger of us all but have the opportunity to become the safest of us all. General Magnus Black, Commander of the Free Armies should be there. If he's not, someone of proper rank will be. Tell Him General Seth Redd and his Rogue Army calls for aid. We need reinforcements. Ah, hell, it shall be inked on paper and sealed. Your task is to get it to Magnus or man of proper rank. Can you do this? Will you do this?"

"Yes my lord, right away my lord," Elekenethal replied proudly, standing firmly at attention.

"You leave as soon as it's written. You know the land? Do you need a map or can you find your way to Emerald Greene?" Seth asked.

"My lord, my geographical knowledge of this region is well. I know this areas and paths. I can find my way to Emerald Greene faster than anyone else here." Elekenethal spoke proudly and strongly. He was secure and confident, both in his abilities to stay alive and his abilities to find a route to Emerald Greene faster than any currently known.

"Get your things and prepare for the journey. You leave as soon as you're able."

Elekenethal smiled thankfully. Redd was putting his trust in him. He couldn't believe the legendary General Seth Redd was going to put everything the rogue army had and bet it on his shoulders. Elekenethal was going to be the reason the Rogue Army would soon become victorious. The reinforcements were direly needed. Without reinforcements, the scout knew the Rogue Army would soon fall.

The scout took his leave. Seth began thinking. The wheels of his mind rolled fluidly. So far, he'd been pretty successful in fending off the Monstrous Mountain Horde again and again. His guerilla tactics had served him well. Now, with greatly decreased numbers, how would his reprobate fighting style serve him?

It wasn't long before the letter was written and the elven scout was on his way. Seth had an idea. The idea wouldn't last long but it would grant Elekenethal the time he needed to get to where he was going. Sadly, several lieutenants, captains, and even colonels were killed in the last fight. Promotions were in order. Not only to replace the high-ranking dead but for the valor shown on the battlefield.

Often the question was asked. Why consider rank in a temporary army of minutemen and other mercenary style soldiers? In future campaigns, those soldiers will stand higher with ranking ribbons and titles with claims of serving under the legendary General as more than just a soldier. The right to claim Captain under General Seth Redd during any campaign he'd choose to take part in would be exponential to any would-be military driven individuals, especially those looking to a life of mercenary work.

Redd ordered for the packhorses, mules, and horses to all be gathered. The newly anointed captains and greater were too scared and confused to question his motives. The few experienced ranking officers didn't understand it either. The Rogue Army didn't carry with it a standing cavalry, but cavalry was certainly needed. It did have with it several packhorses and mules. Elite mercenaries brought with them horses and other mounts. Redd ordered nearly all of them to be taken too. A few argued that the mount they rode was not just a regular mount but of sentimental value to the man. Those, Redd left alone.

General Redd had many ideas. He scattered the army and had brush tied to the horses and packhorses and mules. Each member of the army was ordered to light three campfires and not too close together. Ancient tricks for an ancient dog, he often said to the men. The brush tied to the horses would stir enough dirt to make it look like more were coming and moving than were actually present. The campfires would make them think the army had grown since the great battle at Mountain's Front.

When the army moved against hording marauders, they fled thinking they were severely outnumbered. At night, from the mountains, Seth knew they saw thousands of campfires where hundreds slept, so to speak. For every three hundred men, there were nearly a thousand campfires. And typically, campfires hosted several men, not just one. His ideas kept the enemy at bay long enough for Elekenethal to finally reach Emerald Greene safely.

Chapter 59

Elekenethal rode hard. His horse collapsed upon making it to Emerald Greene. To his favor, Magnus Black was back in the city and once again in charge of his Free Armies. Elekenethal learned of the recent dissention amongst the ranks but nonetheless got the letter to the General's hands.

He was ordered to Magnus' private quarters where he sat looking over battle strategies and financial plans for the city and the armies. It was a military room decorated with his accomplishments and noble earnings.

"My lord," Elekenethal started.

He'd been ordered to remove his armor and weapons. He wore nothing but clothing long due for a bath and held nothing but the sealed letter he was to give Magnus Black. Magnus ordered the boy in while still writing with his ink and quill. Another was present. A young man played a small harp, remaining silent all the while; it relaxed Magnus and was a fix of his.

"Yes?" Magnus said, stopping his work to look up at the boy.

The boy looked worn and tired. He'd ridden long and hard to make it to him and his eyes showed it. Magnus knew it. He knew the boy must have urgent news or something else of great importance.

"I come with a letter from General Redd of the Rogue Armies standing south of the Mystic Mountains and Red Lake. He says it's of critical concern."

Magnus reached over and waved the boy to him as so take the letter from him. The boy quickly obliged. Magnus made note of the boy's courage to ride alone in these times. The scout stood thankful and proud, especially to be noticed by such a legendary General.

Magnus did not receive the message well. He sat back, rubbing his chin and the sides of his mouth, thinking of what the message said and asked. It was too much but he simply couldn't refuse. The boy waited patiently to be dismissed.

"My lord," he said, barely speaking up. Elekenethal just wanted to know what to do. Was he to leave or wait? Whatever the grand General desired, he would do. He would have to. And he would do it well and right. The look on the old man's face had even the scout, ignorant to the full situation, worried.

"Boy, you served Redd and you serve me now. Find one of my Captains in town and have him bring this to Bolba." Magnus said, inking some lettering of his own on a fresh, new piece of parchment.

The boy bowed to Magnus and took the parchment when he finished. It was an honor to serve such a legendary man.

Elekenethal did as he was told and finding a captain didn't prove to be too difficult. He found one quickly. This one was an older elf and carried scars and white streaks in his dark hair. He'd been around and from the looks of it had spent quite a bit of time with the Free Armies.

"My lord, General Magnus Black wished for me to hand this to one of his Captains," he said with a hint of fear in his voice.

Looking around, the streets were full of people working and ready to work even harder. This was a good city and they worked hard for what they had. The Crystal Cities were working lands. The majority of the people here were poor but worked hard to make ends meet. The other half of the Crystallians were rich and wealthy and most of them had gotten that way by exploiting the lower class workers.

Elekenethal knew of the Crystal Cities. He was intimately familiar with the area and the cities and towns and villages. He'd never really explored the city and he wasn't in a rush to go back. Helping Seth Redd, serving the General was one thing and dying for him honorably was another. rushing back to find an army trying to remain hidden so that it could keep the jump on his adversary was just completely ridiculous.

Finally, the captain finished reading the letter and dismissed the boy. He was done with him. He had no further use for him. Elekenethal was done and he'd survived fighting with the Rogue Army of General Seth Redd and lived to tell the tale and bring the news to Magnus Black's Free Armies.

The captain got the information quickly into the right hands and it wasn't long before the eight High Captains were once again the very same meeting room as last time. This time, General Magnus Black was present. Bolba was present. They all were present. The councilmen of the city were also present as they were equally as important at the captains and the General himself.

Elder Councilmen Eilgeros was present. Eilgeros was an elder half-elven man that had seen his better days long past. What strings of hair he had were frayed and withered. He walked with a simple cane and never dressed too fancy. Only at dinner was he seen wearing lavish outfits. It was a quirk of his.

Eilgeros was a man's man in his youth. He'd worked his way out of the mines. It first started with one idea that made the work easier and more efficient and from there streamed other ideas. It was a long road, but finally he'd made it to the highest chair he could reach. He was a High Councilman of the city of Emerald Greene.

In order to maintain the formal keeping of the day's discussion, Bolba would speak on behalf of all captains and Magnus for the Free Armies as a whole. It was much like an Emperor and a senate. The councilmen of Emerald Greene would also be allowed to speak of course.

Formally, Magnus was the first to take the floor. Coincidentally, it was his favorite day of the year. The weather had been altered and slightly changed in recent times but the last few years, it'd mostly remained consistent with its schedule.

"Today is the first day of Mortalus. We are in a time we've deemed the Sundering. Thedia is in darkness and weakened from its very presence. We need to oust the darkness and relight and rebuild the flames of life. To do so, we must put even ourselves and loved ones at great risk." Magnus walked when he spoke and often used his hands to help intensify his words.

The councilmen listened, in tune with his every word. Even those that defied his requests were still amazed at his infinite glories. After all, he was just a man, wasn't he? Magnus continued carefully cherry picking the councilmen he hoped to sway to his side.

"The scholars of time and the calendars have put us in the twenty-fourth year of the Sundering. Soon, it will be the mark of the twenty-fifth and what have we done for Thedia? What have we done for her? We still pledge our wars and still rip nutrients from her soil. We must pay back the debt to the Rivermortal. We must return what we take or soon the taking well will be dry and we'll have nothing to quench our thirst." Magnus spoke with a passion those that knew him had not seen in at least a decade.

"What's your end here?" Eilgeros asked, knowing he wanted something from the city he'd worked so hard to help build up.

Before Magnus could answer, Bolba, the dragonborn High Captain of the Free Armies spoke up. "Ladies and Gentlemen, my lord here is merely reminding us all of our duty to the earth itself. We are in hard times. We'll not survive if we do not stick together. We still feel the wounds of that great war with the Shadow, to this day."

Magnus waved his High Captain off and the dragonborn immediately stopped his words. After a brief pause, Magnus continued. "I've served this city and all Crystallians well. We are paid a great deal for our services. My deal was struck by the numbers I kept on guard here at Emerald Greene and the other Crystal Cities."

"You are given additional funds for each soldier over a specified number you keep on guard in our cities," a younger councilman said.

"Aye, that is correct. I was also ordered to never go below a certain number and that number I'm afraid I am asking to break. I've never broken a single agreement from our contract and now I am asking for leniency."

"You're asking for permission to breech your contract?" Magnus wasn't sure if the voice attacking his was questioning or stating his motives. It was just another councilman and obviously, Magnus didn't care too much for his words.

Magnus looked up at the middle-aged elven man and stared. His movements stopped. His hands stopped. He just looked at the elf that condescendingly attacked him with words.

"Let us be clear, elf." Calling one by his/her race was a pure sign of disrespect. "I am not asking for your leniency." Magnus meant the elf as a solitary individual. "I am asking for the city to help me partake in the reclaiming of our world, one piece of darkness at a time."

The council erupted in conversation. Magnus couldn't make it out and neither could Bolba. On one side, the council sat and the other, Magnus. Not too far to the back left of the council, Bolba stood. Olden rules said the High Captain speaking as the voice of the lower ranking soldiers not to stand next to the army's commanding General.

"Now hold on just a second. Diaklasis is a respected member of this council. You'll watch your tongue," another elder member said.

Magnus just breathed and sighed deeply. He'd not even got to what he was trying to speak of. More conversations, eruptions, and arguments echoed out and finally, Magnus just had it.

"We have to split the forces and send reinforcements to General Redd on the plains beneath the Mystic Mountains!" His booming voice silenced the entire auditorium.

"Your agreement is to protect the cities of the Crystal, not the world. You're a mercenary and that's what you're paid to do," that arrogant Diaklasis spoke up again.

"And to do so, I need to protect the outer lands. We've seen they can hit us even from behind our walls and forces. Whatever's growing in there, it must be taken out and General Seth Redd has formed an army and has fought against them well but his numbers are weakening. If we don't send reinforcements, trained reinforcements, he'll perish and we very well could be next."

"That renegade retired General fights by ambushing randomly on the battlefield."

"And his tactics have worked!" Magnus said, interrupting yet another elder councilman.

"If they were working, he'd not need us," that same councilman replied.

"Success even can come at a high cost, councilman. He sent a letter to me. My own son has brought forth some of my best with him and because of Seth, were able to make it to the mountains."

"A vested interest, I'm not certain my lord is speaking strategically or emotionally?" Bolba said.

In all of his years, Magnus had never been second-guessed by one of his own. He turned and looked at his own man behind the podium representing his people. He couldn't believe what he'd just heard. It sickened him.

"And what does that mean, Bolba?" Magnus was ready to spear him and cut him down.

"It means, my lord, your son is of emotional importance to you. Would you wish to do the same if it were another's son in there, say Redwald?"

"Of course I would!" he yelled back.

"Drackice walked against us in that move, Magnus. I'm afraid your son's on his own, unless of course you wish to breech your contract with us," Eilgeros said.

"I could have this city as easily as I defend it. What would you do if I were to leave?"

"You have to leave, first, General," Eilgeros added.

"Are you threatening me, old man?" he asked.

"No, I'm responding to the threat of your tongue, sir," he politely and cockily replied.

"I'm merely saying in order to maximize the efficiency and safety of the people of the Crystal Cities it is in our best interest to preserve the Rogue Army and General Seth Redd."

Out of nowhere, a voice of a young councilman spoke up. It was meant to be whispered but with Black's sudden quieting, the auditorium fell silent, just for the moment. And the man spoke and most everyone heard his question.

"I've heard them called Mystic Lake, Red Lake, Red Mystic Mountains, and the Mystic Mountains, is there any connection with that and this General Redd?"

"No," answered several as a collective to the young councilman.

The councilman simply replied with an "oh" and the conversation then immediately picked up as if it'd never been interrupted. Magnus argued with Bolba and then with the council. Bolba argued with the two sets. And the council continued to remind them that they were hired hands and if they wished to be paid and accommodated properly, they would see the contracts agreements fulfilled through and through.

"I feel the Free Armies belong here, where their contracts obligate them," Bolba added, continuing. "I'm sorry, my lord, I don't feel this is our fight."

"Whose side are you on?" Magnus questioned.

"Ours my lord, but—"

"You wish to have another set of soldiers lost at your call, just for you?" One of the councilmen, a middle-aged man asked, standing up to take the floor. He was human and average as average could be.

"We must face this threat. Sometimes, in order to maintain a strong defensive posture, one must engage when the opportunity presents itself," Magnus argued. Now, his words were filled with passion and fire.

"Magnus, you have specific orders to keep the Crystal Cities protected. A portion of your pay is measured on the amount of soldiers kept in each city. The contract orders a specified number at all times. If you're going to breech your contract, you'll owe us money I fear you cannot pay and further, we'll find one to keep their word and honor with us." This time, it was Magoro who spoke. Magoro was a proud dwarven man and believed to be the highest-ranking member of the council.

How the councilmen were ranked was a private affair and one only the highest-ranking officials of the Crystal Cities understood. Nonetheless, everyone knew Magoro and he rarely made meetings or debates for anything. He was virtually retired on all accounts. He'd even cut his long white hair short and kept his beard well-trimmed and groomed, making sure the entire thing was properly braided. His favorite accessories were wooden beads, carved by his own two hands.

Magnus couldn't believe it. They were all against him. Not one it seemed like would listen to reason. Bahaus survived a near-fatal defeat at the hands of his son but regrouped to becoming something stronger and with more backing. And the people of the Crystal Cities were willing to just let it grow until it came to their walls?

"Eilgeros, Magoro…" He paused and turned to Bolba adding his name to the list before returning to the council to cherry pick select members that he'd known better and longer than others. He must have named ten or more, he thought to himself before he began his speech.

"I abandoned Eternis for the glories and gold of my people. My heart still rests there. I had to think of my people and what the greater move for the Free Armies as a living entity was and the resolve lied here, in the Crystal Cities. Now, I ask you to go against your own will and what you feel you know. War is my life. I am war. Strategy has spared my body and secured victory when the odds did not favor us. I am strategy. Will is the stuff a man's constitution is measured by. It can be broken. It can be weakened. Will has kept me alive when the odds were desolate. It has brought back to me battles I thought long lost. I've broken the wills of many great men and armies. And I've seen the wills of my greatest warriors crumble to ashes. I am will. Councilmen, my life has been dedicated to these three ideals. I am war. I am strategy. And I am the will needed to see this through. I am the strategic foundation on which the guide to defeating enemies is written. And I am the force needed to face and endure the hardships of war. For this, you employed me and I've brought your enemies to justice. Fugitives have been captured near and far. Your streets have never been cleaner. And I ask you to not trust in me but in the ideals that make me the man you hired some twenty years ago. Trust in the ideals that have preserved these walls. Trust in the ideals that stand before you now."

His words were indeed moving. Some of the councilmen quickly shook their heads, declining to change anything. Magoro was different.

Eilgeros didn't want to change his opinion at first but their intuition on one another's plans told them both that Magoro had been moved.

Even Bolba felt dissatisfied with his argument against his liege. Magnus kept order and allowed the highest-ranking Captain to speak for the people "beneath" him during audiences and other meetings. Bolba knew Magnus would change this account. He knew he'd done a disservice to his people.

"You move with great purpose," Bolba said, breaking the momentary silence Magnus' words brought on.

"He moves with the purpose of his people," Eilgeros said. Initially, he wasn't going to budge but he knew Magoro had been swayed and he never voluntarily voted against the legendary dwarf.

"Magnus, you know these cities were not founded or kept by honor or just. Wealth, wealth is what drives the Crystal Cities and we've exploited our own to see it done."

Magnus dropped his head, hearing Magoro's words. When the dwarf spoke, the others held faithfully silent in order to better hang on his every word. After another short silence, Bolba tried to start up again but the sound of the commanding voice of the dwarven councilman overtook him.

"Sometimes money cannot buy out your problems. And sometimes, the obstacles in your path don't just go away. We are fortunate in these dark times to have a much such as Magnus Black, General and founder of the Free Armies to stand for us against these rising obstacles. He asks nothing in return but the money we've already spent on them. It's been put to use to train and equip the soldiers that stand ready at our doors. Some lands are scarce resources. Some are starving and need coin. We have resources that bring us far more coin than we need. And we put a heavy load on in this man's purse. You are the greatest tactician and strategist I've ever known. If you feel this to be our most advantageous move then I second it. You, unlike any of us here on this council are a man of honor. I'll hold you to that honor, Magnus Black. I'll sign the parchment and see this thing far removed from our courts. Your honor is what's at stake here, boy. You have the okay. Not one here in the Crystal Cities will challenge my decision. No councilmen, guard, soldiers, citizen, or any other will challenge my words. I'll have your answer by the end of the day. And if you move against these horde forces, know this…" the dwarf stopped and stared deep into Magnus' eyes.

Bolba was waiting for the rest of it to come out. The rest of the councilmen stood in awe. They were going to give their primary defense system the ok to act in any way he so felt so long as he felt it to be the right move, as he was honor bound to do the rightful thing.

"…You have any and all of my resources at your disposal, within reason of course," Magoro said, completely throwing the entire council and Bolba for a loop. None of them could believe it but not even Eilgeros would step up and question the dwarf's motives.

Magnus couldn't believe it either. He'd won them over. Or at least, he'd won Magoro over. He won the man over he needed to get the okay from in order to move in the way he desired. Therein lay the next course of obstacles. Did he really feel this to be the most strategic move for the city? Sitting back idly and allowing Bahaus and whatever else was in those mountains to prosper and grow surely didn't sit well with him.

Was dividing the forces really what he and the Crystal Cities needed? Redd needed men. Redd's need for reinforcements was dire based on his letter. He'd lost too many getting Black's own son into the mountains. That could not be taken into consideration. However, Drackice in the mountains with the people he took from the Crystal Cities was just that. What mattered now was Seth Redd and the Rogue army and their standings with the Crystal Cities and the Free Armies. Mobilizing reinforcements was absolutely going to happen. Strategically, he could send minimal to salvage the elite members of the Rogue army or enough to hold them a little longer. There were so many options and decision to be made. What was he to do? Whatever it was, his honor was on the line. And his honor was something he'd not soon part with.

Chapter 60

"As promised boys, the treasury of Azra Goetia," Dash yelled.

He was more excited than he'd ever been. The treasury was one building not holding up to the tests of time. It'd been beaten down and worn. The ceiling had all but fallen in. It had all caved in. More Cambions came at them and Alu-fiends to but they managed to fight them off.

From what they could tell, the treasury was near the middle of town. All around them, dark town extended far into the horizon. It wasn't precision or science but the dark black square building, tall and torn from time, stood damn near the true center of the city.

The four split up but kept a close eye on one another. Not a single golden coin was found. Not one piece of copper nor was a piece of silver or platinum in the treasury. Maybe some other group had gotten to it first? After all, it'd been here for many, many years.

The four dug through the wreckage and rubble of the collapsing treasury. They didn't even have to enter through a door. It was easier just to walk through the holes in the walls. The four dug relentlessly and carelessly for everything. Their guard was down.

Dash uncovered a trap door hidden beneath the flooring. He quickly grabbed the others and peeled the old thing open. Dust exploded from the old door of iron and wood. It was locked but the lock was so old and rusted, it crumbled to nothingness when Legion yanked on its handle.

The dust and dirt flung into the air combined with the stagnant air held for countless centuries formed an uncomfortable smell and feel in the room. Even the holes throughout the dark treasury didn't help bleed out the stench. It smelled worse than rancid undead.

It was next to impossible to get the smell out. It was thick, thicker than the already thickened air of Azra Goetia. Dash, Legion, and Pitt were forced back from the smell. They had to cover their noses and take breathers. It was Dauge who championed through the smell the easiest. He jumped in the hole, climbing down the short stairway of stone.

Dauge still heard the other three coughing rigorously as he scanned around, unveiling exactly what they were looking for. Still, not a single coin but shelves of golden and silver bars, these things were worth a fortune.

Only high-ranking nobles and entrusted royalty were meant to see such fashionable wealth. Bars of gold and silver were meant for cities that did business with one other. Kingdoms spoke in bars of gold. Kingdoms used bars of silver to do their talking and Dauge just stumbled across more than they could spend in ten lifetimes.

"Boys!" he yelled, ecstatic.

He'd never been so thrilled and truthfully, not one of the other three would have guessed money to be the reason for his excitement. All three were still thankful just the same. Dauge carried a dark personality, one often weighing against the morale of others.

There wasn't enough room for any more of them to get down there with him. And there were simply too many bars to take. The silver bars, some places needed silver more than others and for those places, some silver would have to be taken.

Before the collection chain started, Dauge examined the bars closely, making sure they were legit and worth the taking. The hike back to Vorrellon was going to be a grueling and long one now with all the excess weight.

Just as he expected, the golden bars were approximately worth two thousand gold pieces each, and the silver bars around two thousand silver pieces each. Few kingdoms had the funds to deal in primarily gold bars, much less a single city.

Most city-states and kingdoms less wealthy dealt in silver bars. Those were in the days of old though, today the kingdoms of Targnok, Valence, Thox, Skye, Aflyndor, Malynkite, the Republic of New Magic, the Nine Kingdoms, and even the lesser known or established ones all mostly dealt in gold bars. Even the greatest of heroes typically didn't see gold bars in their lifetime.

It wasn't the same as finding an ancient weapon with true vorpal powers but it was still a worthy task to have accomplished. Seeing a dragon fly over may mean nothing to some, but it many mean everything to another.

It took hours to find the proper carrying bags throughout the treasury and on their bodies to fit the many gold bars. Dash made a jest about how a bag of holding or portable hole would have been handy.

"Look, wait, let's bag the gold up and look for something to make the trip home less painful. We'll be far too encumbered to make it home carrying these ridiculously heavy bars. They were meant to be carried with wagons and horses, not bags and humanoid backs," Legion proposed.

It was a good idea. Dauge popped out and Pitt hopped in. It was going to be a lot easier with Pitt grabbing the bars and tossing them up. Even if the four could somehow find or build a wagon and somehow get horses to pull it, the Vile Frozen would prove far too harsh for wagon and horse.

Bags and bags were filled and tied with gold and silver bars. It was too much money to calculate. There was no way they were going to get all of this money home and what were the chances of this city having the very thing they needed to get it back.

Legion also wanted to send money back to Eternis. They needed it. Eternis was a beautiful city with lush mounds of history and character but wealth was never a strongpoint for the city. Much of its wealth often came from passing travelers and native Eternians donating to the city treasury.

No matter what, donating a load of money like this could further bring his name toward that of his father's and his grandfather's. Dauge cared not for money for the most part but wanted a huge chunk to go to his sister. He loved his sister and not just how a brother loves sibling. There was more to the two of them and only they could explain it. It wasn't an incestuous lust. It was just a devotion the two had for one another.

Dash knew this money could bring to him everything he ever wanted. If this team didn't work out, though, he did want it so he could buy and outfit a team completely and purely dedicated to him and his goals.

And Pitt didn't want anything more than his love back in his arms, wherever she was. Legion believed if someone could prove Shiva to be dead, Pitt would, without hesitation end his own mortal life to search for her in the after one.

This was the find of a lifetime. Few in these dark times could travel and become renowned heroes and survive to tell the tales and of those that did, even in the days of old, not one would claim another find to be greater than this one.

They were rich, rich beyond their wildest dreams. Lord Stannor of Vorrellon would have one of, if not the grandest city in all of Thox and the four of them would have enough left to challenge a king's treasury. Stannor only asked for three thousand golden pieces, stating everything else found would be theirs. It would certainly be in their best interest to hand over a little more to the lord who'd given them the quest and the directions to find the ancient city.

"Counting the silver here, there must be nearly a hundred thousand in gold and silver," Dash said.

"Three thousand to Stannor, let us not forget," Pitt said, laughing.

"We most certainly will have to give more. It will be expected. Traveling back through the harsh Vile Frozen and with the Targnok orcs all over, without the proper magical or aerial means, a successful trip home with all of this on our backs is just an absurd idea," Dauge reminded them.

"I want to bring some to Eternis," Legion added.

"You'll all have your share to do what you wish with," Dash said jumping back in over Legion.

"Foolishness let us think of a way back first. We can build a raft. It's our safest bet." Dauge knew the suggestion wouldn't go over well as the southern waters below them were freezing and partially frozen over but he figured it to be the safest path back.

"Those waters are virtually impassable. Build a raft from the Vile Frozen I take it? Dauge, you are blessed with a keen intellect but I fear you do not always use it," Dash said.

"You idiot, Dash, listen to me. We are in a city full of supplies. If we are going to search this city, we might as well find a safer way home. We tugged on the chain of an angry dog a little too much killing all those orcs on the way here. Assuming we don't find your bag of holding or portable home or some other means of magically carrying these bags, we're going to have to either take what we can and leave the rest here or sail it back to safer grounds."

Between the conviction in his voice and the words that he spoke, the other three had no choice but to quiet down and rethink what he'd just told them. There were over sixty bars there in total and each of the bags found to suffice for carrying could only carry somewhere between six to seven bars. There were nine bags filled with these bars. No way. There was no way the four of them were going to carry them back without any help.

The dreams of getting a hundred thousand in gold back to Lord Stannor and the city of Vorrellon or the kingdom of Thox at all was complete madness unless they found another way to get back. Getting here unencumbered and lightly packed was hard enough.

Something moved. What was that? The crew crept around stalking around the treasury. Something bumped something. The gold was bagged and tied. It was ready to go but they still had no way of getting it back.

"We can always hide it and come back for it," Pitt suggested.

"Are you really willing to come back here, behemoth?" Legion asked, smiling at the barbarian.

"You're right. I guess not," he replied.

"Shhhhh," Dauge said, keeping a keen eye on everything around.

And just like Dauge, Dash stalked and moved through the rubble in the treasury, trying his best not to knock over old desks or disturb old papers. They both kept a keen eye out. Finally, Dash settled his stomach, reassuring himself it was either a natural happening or a coincidence of some sort.

"That wasn't just some strange occurrence. Something moved and more of that ceiling fell in, Dash." Dauge said quietly.

"We're fine," Dash countered.

"I disagree. We need to get the gold and get out of here or better, leave the gold and take what we came for and go. Two gold bars is plenty," Dauge barked.

"I didn't come here for two hundred and fifty gold apiece," Pitt chimed in.

"Where'd you come up with that?" Legion asked.

"Two gold bars are worth around four thousand gold. Three thousand goes to Stannor and one thousand left split four ways," Dash answered.

"Oh, I get it. Well done, Pitt. I didn't know you had it in you," Legion said, trying to make light of the situation.

"Now's not the time for jests," Dauge said with his voice still slightly elevating with each word.

Just as Dauge's words finished, another piece of the ceiling crackled and another large chunk fell in. Thankfully, it wasn't near the four of them at all.

Two of the larger cracks originating from the bottom of the structure and walking up the walls toward the ceiling buckled too. Dust, dirt, and rock fell. Something hidden worked its way in and Dauge knew it.

How many were there? Something was on the roof and more were coming in through the holes and cracks of the wall in the treasury. This wasn't going to be good. There were things much worse than death, and dying to a devil could clearly be one of the darkest ends one could succumb to.

Suddenly, three creatures never before seen by the any of the four popped into existence. One stood on the wreckage of where the ceiling had fallen in. Two more came from the cracks where Dauge saw the disturbance and the flutter of dirt and rock cast up into the air.

The creatures weren't small at all. They stood around nine to nine and a half feet tall. They had to weigh over five hundred pounds, but the leathery coppery skin was pulled so tight it outlined every single bone in the creatures' bodies. Its head looked like a skull with the skin pulled tightly over it and huge eyes pressing out from it.

Once they appeared visually, the smell of the room quickly found its way out. The decaying stench of the bone devil effortlessly overtook it. The dried skin of the creatures ended right where their tails began. The bone devils had tails like scorpions, complete with armoring plates to protect it all the way up to their giant stingers.

"Osyluths," Dash yelled, following the others and bracing himself.

"What?" Legion questioned loudly.

"I know legend and lore, Legion. Those things are Bone Devils! Brace yourselves." Dash pulled his short sword and a javelin, still slightly coughing from the disgust in the air.

"How do you know so much?" Pitt asked, whirling his fullblade around, preparing himself for what was about to take place.

"I just do!" Dash yelled back.

Three bone devils shared the treasury with the four of them. That was almost one bone devil apiece for them to take on. Dash continued reminding them of their chances being dismal. In the commotion of it all, Dauge vanished. He was gone. Now it left three to face three bone devils. They had absolutely no chance to defeat them, according to Dash.

All three looked to Legion. He was their target of choice. They had nothing but complete and total disregard for the others. Legion noticed their eyes. They all fixed themselves to Mourning Star. Mourning Star barely did much for Legion anymore. In the beginning, it spoke to him and performed unique tricks, keeping itself known as something other than normal. No matter what, it was still a highly magical weapon forged and created by the fusing together of two other ancient weapons both held by his father.

"Legion, Legion, can you hear us?" it said. This time its voice was more clear and pure than Legion ever remembered. It said his name twice to get his attention. The bone devils, something about them stirred Mourning Star into waking up.

There was no hiding it this time. Mourning Star even caught Dash and Pitt's attention. Dauge was still nowhere to be found. Surely he didn't abandon them. Mourning Star began to glow. The power it held radiated from its very shaft and chain. The spiked ball at its end pulsed a completely different color.

The treasury cracked and crashed open. Walls opened up and more fragments of ceiling fell in. Three walls of pure ice spewed out from the devils, separating all three of the visibly remaining humanoids.

The treasury took a hit like it was struck by an earthquake. Everything shook and rattled and fell unhinged. The treasury was breaking at the very seams, soon to be completely shattered. In the array of chaos, Dash saw one of the bone devils snag every sack filled with gold and silver they'd stuffed.

The flesh of the creatures was so tight it outlined every single bone in its body. Its claw like fingers were longer than they should have been, making them ill proportioned to its body. This also made it very easy for one devil to grab every sack with one hand.

Dash was the first to strike, launching a javelin and gashing into the very same one that took up the sacks of gold and silver bars. Legion still had a path laid out in front of him against a different one. And Pitt was separated from them all with the walls of ice sporadically and strategically spewed out from the creatures.

Pitt roared out in anger. His own rage took over him. He charged forward, smashing through the icy walls. One of the devils stepped back to better prepare for the oncoming barbarian. With a thousand minutes on its side, the devil wouldn't have been able to prepare for Pitt.

Pitt leaped through the air of falling debris and now exploding ice, pushing his fullblade to a mighty swing with everything he had. Where the hilt met the blade caught the creature right below the ribcage. Pitt waited late to jump.

The blade cut through the bone devil nicely with Pitt's upward swing. It fell back using its tail to catch and balance itself. A nasty laceration from one side of its torso to the other bled out a thick blood more black than red.

The creatures didn't carry weapons, at least not weapons they could see. Pitt landed, replanting his footing preparing for his next go. Legion whirled around Mourning Star and the chain linked to the spiked end grew. The movement of his weapon allowed Legion to keep his distance. Seeing Legion halt in his tracks, the Osyluth sent its coiled tail on a direct path for Legion.

The elder Xavier was by then completely enveloped in his own whirling chain, radiating magic of a yellow color. He sent his chain and ball around the tail of the creature. The head of the weapon smashed through the plated pieces of it natural hide armor, bleeding a poisonous magic into the creature. The chain shortened, tightening itself around the creature's tail, locking it down and immobilizing it.

All three ice walls exploded, taking down half of the treasury's back wall. Dash, Legion, and Pitt felt the force firsthand. The three flew out of the back where the newfound hole in the wall was formed. Each of them fell hard on the ground behind the treasury. The paved road wasn't an easy place to force a fall and looking back up, all three Osyluths were still closing in.

"Dauge!" Legion cried.

"Dauge!" Pitt yelled.

There was still no sign of Legion's younger half-brother. Pitt got up. The three Osyluths were all but out of the treasury. Pitt rushed forward, trying to hold off all three of them. Pitt's fullblade and might echoed out, striving vengeance against the three, while Dash and Legion made their way back to their feet.

Dash screamed and waved his hands. The wounds on Pitt's body mended over and the Osyluths abilities were stricken with weakness. Suddenly, their forceful attacks weren't enough to get through Pitt's defense.

Dash poured on the spells, boosting Pitt's abilities and weakening the devils. It was working, especially since Pitt kept them squeezed at the hole in the treasury's back wall. Legion rushed forward to aid his friend once again with Mourning Star readied and whirling. Its chain was now reduced back to its original length.

Pitt fatally struck one of the bone devils through its pelvic area. The other two wrapped their disgustingly long claws around his blade, locking it in place, making Pitt release it to grab another weapon. Legion wasn't quite up to the front yet with him. All three of the giant scorpion-like tails, even the one of the dying Osyluth came overhead. Pitt's maneuverability was down. He was still trying to reset from the perfect thrust that would soon kill the middle devil.

The bone devils released pain-filled screeches. All three ends of the tails were severed just before they could penetrate Pitt's flesh. They fell to the ground, spraying green substances all over. Legion yelled for Pitt to duck. He did.

Legion took a foot to his back launching himself over all three bone devils. There wasn't much room left between their nine-foot bodies and the top of the hole in the wall but Legion made it. Coming from around the corner was a blood stained Dauge, weapons in hand. He'd just saved Pitt's life. Dash was thrilled and ecstatic.

Part of Legion's body actually caught the top but he grabbed the ball of Mourning Star and threw it one way and used his body to torque another. The chain wrapped tightly around the creature's neck. And with the momentum of his body falling down, it forced the wounded creature off its feet.

Dauge and Pitt double-teamed the last one. One was dying and falling over. Legion was about to pop another's head off. The last one forced its way out of the hole. It raised its hand and pointed a finger. A black stream caught Dash in the upper shoulder, dropping him once again back down to the ground.

Dash still got off his spells but these were meant for Dauge's throwing weapons and he was throwing shuriken. Dauge rushed to Dash's side, continually throwing his now arcanically blessed shuriken.

Four of the six thrown caught the creature and each one stumbled him further. Dauge was covered in blood that did not belong to him. He ran out of shuriken and commenced throwing his throwing daggers. He stood over the downed Dash, agonizingly breathing hard and yelling, agitated.

The Osyluth locked up by Mourning Star still carried the power to throw Legion off but Mourning Star's power to keep the weight to its advantage proved to be too much. Legion hung onto the Osyluth's back, pulling down with everything he had. He knew if he let go, he was dead. Finally, the creature grabbed the chain and spiked ball, hoping to find a way to loosen its grip or stop it from cutting deeper into its flesh and bone.

Legion succeeded. He fell to the ground, hearing a small pop and thump. Seconds later, the crashing sound of a dead carcass falling to the ground soothed his ears. Just before, he heard and saw the evil head of the creature fall to the ground as well.

He breathed a thankful sigh. He rolled over to better defend himself. The last Osyluth had been felled. The three nine-foot-tall bone devils were dead. Dash was hurt. His shoulder was already beginning to swell and scar.

The four regrouped. They still hadn't a way to get the gold back to Vorrellon or Lord Stannor. Pitt picked up Dash and rushed him to the inside of the treasury. Dauge quickly followed.

"What are you doing? We have to get out of here," Dauge ordered.

"How are we to get the gold back?" Dash asked, now inside of the treasury along with the rest of them.

"We leave the gold. While you were fighting those damned wretched things, I was holding off more half-devils. This place wasn't meant to be explored." Dauge pleaded for the others to listen to him.

"We at least have to rest. Pitt's hurt. I'm hurt," Dash convincingly barked back.

"We're going to be dead if we stay here. These things know we're here and know where we're at. They're coming to the treasury. Legion, let's get out of here now!" Dauge was convinced staying in the treasury or in Azra Goetia at all was suicide.

"Let's grab the gold and go!" Pitt said.

"No! That gold belongs here. We cannot disturb it!" Dauge declared.

"We can't get it all anyway!" Legion reminded.

"So what's next?" Dash asked.

"This quest was suicide. There's more to the story than gold. I think Stannor just wanted to know if this place truly exists. It does. And now, with our information, he'll be able to put together a far better plan to get what he really wants from it."

"Dauge, Vorrellon is in need of gold and Thox isn't giving it to Stannor. It makes sense the man wants gold," Legion said, countering his little brother.

"It does. It's not good enough. There's something else here he's looking for. Now, I'm not opposed to searching for it but staying here at the treasury is madness."

Legion quickly spoke up, agreeing with his brother. It made sense. Legion knew Dauge was right and more devils or half devils would soon be there to finish them off. They didn't need to argue any further. They fled the treasury leaving the gold behind.

Dauge gripped the sides of a neighboring building. Slowly, he climbed it, careful to place his feet strategically as so not to fall. The dark bricks and aura of the building made for an unsettling feeling but Dauge was determined to get to the top.

He did. And quickly without even looking around, he locked in a hook and dropped down the rope. One by one, the last three got to the top of the building while Dauge kept a lookout to make sure nothing saw them. They were safe atop the building, at least for now.

Just as Dauge predicted, more Cambions, alu-fiends, and another bone devil came to the aid of the treasury. Azra Goetia was a dark beauty. It was a place that hadn't been touched for hundreds if not thousands of years. The treasury sure didn't last too long. It wasn't a very sturdy building at all.

The bone devil ordered the Cambions to scour the treasury. It threw its hands around pointing and demanding and the Cambions and alu-fiends just listened and minded diligently. They were only seconds away from being outmatched and overwhelmed. Dauge's keen senses and quick thinking saved them again.

"Duck!" Legion quietly shouted to the team.

All four dropped behind the raised wall side of the building they were now stranded on. One by one, the each peered over the side to see the devils and half devils digging and searching, trying to find the heart of the problem.

Then, they saw something they couldn't believe. Their day just got tougher, they thought. The bags of gold were being taken out and transported by the Cambions through orders of the Bone Devil. Other coins and additional treasure pieces were also taken; art of all kinds, other bars of precious metals, and specialty items and gear were all taken and scattered differently by the Cambions carrying them. They scattered militarily like an organized ant colony.

"We only need three thousand gold coins to appease Lord Stannor," Dauge reminded quietly.

"And what about us, why did we come here then?" Legion asked just as quietly.

"Recognition, we are group trying to build our names in this world, Legion," Dash answered slowly as if trying to educate and assure himself the words were sinking in.

"Maybe that's why you came, Dash, but I came for money. I came because I need coin to find my Shiva," Pitt said finally breaking into the conversation.

"This is not the place for this!" Dauge said quietly yelling sharply at the group.

"He's right," Dash agreed.

"Yes, of course you believe he's right. You don't want to address the issue as to why we're truly here," Legion said.

"No, it's too late to discuss all of these things. One thing or another brought us here. Let us make the most of it as a team. We all can agree our best chance for survival and secondly, for success is to stick together. We must if we are to see home again." The argument was getting out control atop the building.

Dauge quietly continued to shush them while still keeping his eye on the creatures down scavenging the treasury. The air was stagnant like the air lying dormant inside a chest for a hundred years here in Azra Goetia. The feeling the city gave wasn't unsettling or evil as it was fear inspiring.

Legion looked over the other side of the wall. It looked clear and gave an opening. The bone devil and the Cambions moved out. Some were staying back to guard and protect in case they were to resurface.

"Guys, they're still moving and relocating the treasury's objects and gold, let's get out of here!" Legion pleaded.

"We're going to have to wait this out. These are devils, Legion. They're beyond our understanding. We know nothing of their tactics. We need to hold out here, at least for a few days," Dash countered.

"He's right brother," Dauge agreed. "We're going to have to hold out. We can't do anything until these things settle down. And we don't know what to expect from the defenses of this place. We hold up."

Even Dauge and Dash could get along if the times called for it. And this time called for it. They were right. Pitt and Legion knew better than to argue. Staying low on top of the building and until an opening birthed was the only logical answer.

Chapter 61

High in the mountains the air was cold. It was harder to breathe in too. Alchemists claimed it was the density of the air. It thickened at higher climates. Drackice Black and his team were high. The Rogue Army blessed them with the opening they needed to push through and it worked.

The midnight fire did little to warm the team Drackice formed out of the Free Armies Elite heroes. Slate and Draeden did well against the cold but the others were beginning to give in. Slate was able to deal with it but Draeden's Genasi nature allowed him to ignore it altogether. Westlyn was another who did well against elements. His Angelic nature strengthened him against Thedia's finest efforts.

The broken ground of rock and root proved tough to sleep on. The team did the best they could. Rain set in the weeks prior. They'd been mountain climbing for nearly three weeks and the weather was only getting worse.

Keres and Tsin stayed close together to keep warm. Alphonse and Shanks did too. After all, they were husband and wife and the two humans were brothers. Slate was stubborn and refused to take aid from any of them. He kept his tent solitary and stayed to himself. All of the tents had to be extra secured. The natural climate of the Red Mystic Mountains was harsh.

"We're going to be dead before we ever make it to Bahaus," Slate said angrily. He was stubborn and bitter. He didn't sign up to fight the elements.

"We're going to be fine. This is the worst of it," Drackice answered.

The fire sputtered. The wind blew it and the rain weakened it. It was dying out and they were running out of firewood fast. The team hadn't seen combat since entering the mountains but the weather was killing them, it was far worse than anything they'd encountered since banding together for the mission.

"Slate, this cretin has to be stopped. I am a servant of Zeronaus, Prismatic Dragon over life and death. His clergy chooses a path to follow. One over the other and I chose death before life; I specialize in the natural order of things and their expirations. Everything expires, Drackice. If we fail and the elements or anything should take us before this campaign is seen through, then it is by Zeronaus' hand and decision. I honor death before life but life is equally as important. I came to this quest to embrace death. This mission will do nothing but postpone Bahaus long enough for the armies to see him finished. We are to die and never leave these mountains," Keres spoke solemnly and collectively. She'd had her wits and mind about her. She truly believed her words, down to her very core.

"If you feel that way, you wretched whore, then why did you come?"

Tsin jumped from his curled state. Weapons birthed from nowhere, filling his hands. Both of his hands held kukris tightly, the same weapon of choice his beloved wife used. Slate merely chuckled at Tsin's attempt.

"You push dangerously to see your life ended early, Wilden," Slate said, tossing the last few pieces of wood they had onto the dying fire.

"Keres is my wife and companion. We are forever one, bound both by blood and soul," Tsin barked back to Slate.

Tsin paused and put down his weapons allowing Slate the honor of believing he'd forced him to back down. In his early years, Tsin barked loudly and fought fiercely. His skill was perfect. His actions, his knowledge, he knew what he had to do to be successful and somehow always found a way. It was his mouth that got him into trouble. It was his mouth that bore him a past he'd never be able to live down.

Keres calmly ordered her husband to sit and relax. He did. Slate continued to bark until Drackice silenced him. Drackice couldn't even believe the man known as the "Doom Guide" would listen to anyone. On the battlefield, Slate was never ordered. He was unleashed.

Draeden told stories of times long past. His stories held tales mostly of the Forsaken and their forbidden magics. His tales told of Goddimus and Arakros' feud over the kingdom of Esgaria in the place now known as the Broken Lands. His stories couldn't fully be proven but they did pass the time and to Draeden, that was enough.

Alphonse was a quirky wizard. He wasn't built very proportionate and just overall didn't have any very threatening qualities. The others looked at him as a weirdo. He was different. He often spoke to himself and kept to himself. In some cases, even his brother Shanks didn't know what to do with him.

While the others argued and bickered and complained about the fire, the cold, the weather, and the situation, the wizard kept himself occupied with simple cantrips and other spells. Shanks watched and kept out of it, christening and oiling his bow and sharpening his arrow tips and sword.

"Shanks, you're a gorgeous man and prodigy of the bow. This is a mission for more experienced and well-trained champions. Why did you come?" Slate asked now, forgetting the whole fiasco with Tsin.

"I serve the Free Armies. I serve Drackice Black. He gave me an opportunity and General Magnuc Black spilled money into my training. I'm far better than I was just six months ago. I knew Drackice needed all the help he could get. I will not dishonor General Magnus Black's contribution to me. He saw something in me and if I die protecting his son, well my friend, then I die. I am just a mercenary to the world, but to the Free Armies I am Shanks, an irreplaceable archer that stands unrivaled."

Slate pushed his lower lip into his upper one, shaking his head, accepting the young teen's answer. Alphonse still just stayed out of it, playing with his magic like nothing was the matter. Eventually, Draeden fell fast asleep. He was first to. Then, Keres and Slate succumbed to slumber and one after another, the team fell with only the two chosen guards for the specified times remaining awake.

It was Slate and Tsin's turn to hold watch. Alphonse at least added fuel for the fire to keep it going before ignoring all and just passing out. It was established; he was an odd one that just couldn't be trusted. It wasn't that he was a bad guy or that his intentions weren't just. He was just the most absent-minded wizard possibly to ever walk the earth.

Tsin couldn't stand it. He sat across from Slate on the opposite most part the encircled encampment would allow. Slate never once looked over to him. He sat on his moss- and stone-made seat tossing what he could onto the fire while relaxing and oiling his favorite two-handed broadsword.

Slate stuck the end of it deep enough into the ground where he could balance it with little effort with one hand while rubbing the blade down with his oil rag in the other. Tsin sat on the cold ground with nothing underneath him. He had a blanket but it was war torn and tattered. He wrapped it around him but it wasn't enough. The fire wasn't going to be enough and the cold was only getting worse.

Tsin had something he knew would help, but he wanted Slate to ask for it. He needed to feel wanted and appreciated. Tsin kept to himself, sneaking peeks at the barbarian every so often to sort of keep his eye on him. Tsin pulled the bright heat rods from his belt. He had four of them. He cracked one and tossed it to the side of him. Immediately, its warmth touched the edge of Slate's skin.

Heat rods were rare and like sun rods, they had a specific purpose. Heat rods were only about a foot long and were perfectly circular rods of metal. When cracked, and heat rods could only be used once, they radiated a low to moderate level of heat.

Tsin strategically and intentionally cracked the weakest of the rods first. He knew even the weakest one was close enough to catch Slate's attention. Shanks and Alphonse were near him to and the heat would warm their freezing bodies.

Slate finally took his eyes from his work in order to scan the area for the newly found heat source. His hair slowly fell back from his face. His eyes perched and fixed themselves to Tsin. Tsin quickly propped himself to look as if it wasn't a big deal or that he wanted Slate's attention at all.

"We're freezing over here, Wilden, and you have heat rods?" Slate asked. His anger was enough to fuel a red dragon's thirst.

Tsin turned around nonchalantly, standing up to stretch and "accidentally" knock back his coat to reveal the remaining heat rods. His actions only infuriated Slate even more. In his sleep, Alphonse thanked absently for the newly found heat.

Rakka rolled over and fought with himself on whether or not to get up. The aura of heat touched at the whims of his pores just the same. Finally, he gave in and laziness lost. He picked himself up wrapped in blankets and dragged it until he was as close as he could be to Tsin. One by one, the single rod brought the team members to close in around the assassin. Even the ones it didn't really affect, the rod still provided comforting warmth they could appreciate.

And slowly, the assassin peeled another rod cracking it and dropping it to the ground. Slate shook his head. Tsin knew he was getting to the big human. The barbarian was soon to crack. He just knew it. Slate stood up, tossing the last piece of fuel he could find to the fire, his seat.

"Why did you crack another one? One was enough to suffice. You know we're going to be here for a long time. You arrogant idiot, I should learn you some sense!"

"Why do you hate me?" Tsin asked, trying to push his words through with an innocent voice.

Everything about Tsin bothered Slate. Everything from his words to his actions to his mannerisms gave Slate itches that nothing short of gutting the damn Sylvan would be able to scratch. Slate kept his cool. As much as he hated Tsin he knew everyone was needed to see this thing through. At the very least, the piss ant could provide a delay for him and act as fodder in the upcoming battles they were sure to have.

"I don't hate you. I loathed the damned words and attitude of your cunt over there. And I told her I hated it. You stepped up to challenge my opinion."

"You disrespect my wife! In what culture is that civil?" Tsin asked.

"The very same where murder is. I know you, Wilden. I've seen your face on posters. I nearly joined a band of hunters to bring in your gang before taking up an accord with the Free Armies."

"Murder?" Tsin questioned.

"I know your past. I know much more about you than you think."

Tsin killed the innocent approach and darted quick and cold words back toward the barbarian. "Words spill from your mouth like shit from my ass. You talk deleteriously against murder. You barbarian, I've seen kill over a scuffle in cards. You've openly called out and killed just as many people if not more."

"The difference, you wretched piss ant, is my adversaries looked me in the eye and I them. They knew I was coming and had the appropriate time to prepare for it. I never stabbed a man in the back first. If my blade found a man's backside, it was because of the combat we were already linked from. You use shadows and trickery to end the lives of those that challenge you. You're a coward."

"Your only gift is might, Slate. Strength, strength can be substituted. Skill cannot."

Tsin jumped. Something touched his backside. He leaped and turned around. Standing behind him, he saw two phantasmal panthers. They looked like ghosts. He heard Slate's laugh cackle like the fire behind him.

"What the..." Tsin started.

"Not every barbarian is foolhardy. Not every barbarian is limited to power and might and a big blade or weapon."

Tsin crouched and carefully backpedaled. Slate laughed again dismissing the phantasmal panthers. Before vanishing, they crept toward the Wilden. Tsin looked over to Slate. He didn't know what to think. They'd been traveling together for a while but tricks were still coming up. And back at the Free Armies, most of them were in different regiments and teams altogether, and thus, they didn't all really know each other.

"I'm just saying you rely on what the faiths have blessed you with. My skills are learned. They evolve. I've tuned them to specifics. You, you were just born with everything you needed."

Tsin jumped back further thinking something else was still around him, sniffing him.

"Relax Wilden, they're gone," Slate said, standing yet relaxed. He was poised and looking around, like he'd heard something.

"What are you looking for?" Tsin asked.

"I just thought I heard something," he replied.

They kept the argument going and soon, whatever it was Slate heard was forgotten. Tsin argued that Slate hadn't the right to disrespect another man's lady. Slate countered saying another mercenary's thoughts or opinions on her shouldn't be a concern. In that regard, there was no such thing as disrespect.

"All I'm saying Tsin, is if you challenge everyone with a loose tongue and foolish mind, you'll be so busy fighting avoidable obstacles that you'll never get to where you're going."

Tsin didn't want to admit it. He still felt the barbarian was wrong but the man's words made sense. He asked Slate to get to the point and he did. And the point was simple. Keep to yourself but do your job. Keep the others around you alive as best you can with the abilities you bring to the table. Any and all internal conflict can be taken care of, later.

A gargling sound caught Tsin's ear. He looked around. Slate curiously asked what he heard but Tsin shushed him. Two seconds ago, it was Slate's hidden abilities that struck Tsin's curiosity and Slate looking around for something he heard. Now, it was something else, having Tsin's attention and Slate being curious.

"Get the others," Tsin whispered as quietly as he could.

Slate nodded and rushed to it. Tsin looped around to the backside of the encampment. It was too late for one of them. Alphonse's feet kicked and his legs twitched. His hands gripped his throat. Blood poured from between the fingers and spouted from his mouth like lava from a volcano.

A mortal body can be a funny thing. It resorts back to its primal, animalistic state when threatened. A man will chew off his own arm if it's trapped and put between life and death. The body of the young, weird human wizard was dying and its instincts were still refusing to let go.

All of the others were moving and grabbing for their things. Slate couldn't tell what caused the laceration on Alphonse's throat but it was enough to kill him. And soon after he saw him, the wizard expired.

Slate looked up. They rested in a small opening surrounded by high walls of the mountain mostly built by large rocks. Draeden was up and right behind Westlyn. He was always right behind Westlyn. The dark spiked hairs on the deva's head sparked glamorously. His body was readying itself with divine powers in the event of attack.

Shanks was up and stationed behind Keres. Tsin wasn't anywhere to be found. Rakka was still sleeping. The team hadn't got to him. Drackice stood amidst them all and gave an order to strategically scatter.

The faces and weapons of a goblin detail surrounded them, peering over the ledge of rocks from overhead. There were a lot of them. The team pulled their weapons. They were a few moments too late. The goblins didn't say anything. Pikes, small pole-arms, and an array of swords came into view from just over the rocks.

"Hold what you got!" Draeden yelled.

"Easy for you to say, wizard," Keres bitched back.

"Fish in a barrel," Drackice said defining their situation.

"Thanks for noticing," Slate said.

"Smart move targeting a wizard, but you targeted the wrong one!" Draeden spoke out seeing the crew of creatures getting ready to fire.

He held his hand up toward the creatures, clenching his fist. Volleys of arrows, javelins, and some non typical missile weapons rained down upon them. The entire team ducked and prepared for the worst. Keres still stood strong. She knew her armor and defenses were a tiptoe higher than most. She was rarely even scratched with that divine plate she wore. However, it looked very average as if it were no different than any other plated armor.

A thunderous boom echoed when Draeden opened and extended his fingers. An ethereal channel of ghostly force flowed up and then out, creating a spherical wall above them. The arrows, javelins, and thrown swords and axes all stopped and clanged like they'd just been dropped to the ground. Draeden's dark laugh echoed out. The challenged excited him.

With the genasi's block, Keres acted next. She now had the time and executed a precision blast extending out from her own body. Shanks was the only one close to her. She touched him. Another ethereal force came out from her. Hers was darker and much more necrotic than Draeden's. Nearly a hundred feet in every direction, every mortal being and creature caught in the forceful blast fell.

Draeden managed to keep his spell by not allowing Keres' divine attempt to break his concentration. He fell to the ground with a violent and aggravated yell. Some of the goblins fell from the rocks. Keres' necrotically charged force knocked them over.

Draeden held them high with his ethereal wall. The weight was becoming a problem. He knew he wouldn't be able to hold them long. Slate saw the look on his face. He was straining to keep it going.

"Go, go fucking get them!" he yelled angrily.

Keres was the only one that could move. Their bodies wouldn't really move. Slate tried but some of Keres' powers were too strong for even her to control. The result, an entire battlefield weakened and stunned.

Keres and Shanks were still good. She was able to touch him before the spell went off, preventing the spell from penetrating his body and mind. The two scattered and rushed in separate directions up toward the higher level.

"Keres!" Drackice yelled.

His vision was failing. Everything was blurred. He was down one man and the rest of his crew couldn't move. Draeden was the only one who could hold off Keres' unrelenting divine force. Too late though, Keres and Shanks were at the top level of the mountain with the rest of their crew in a small pit of an encampment below.

Shanks refused to fire a single arrow. Each time his bowstring was pulled back, it fired off four to five arrows that sang in various directions. Keres kept close to the human, making sure nothing could get to him. The upper area wasn't too flat. It was difficult to move around upon. Keres saw her work. Dozens of goblinoids were struck down by her force, their bodies stunned and dazed and barely able to move.

Keres' kukri was perfect for making bloody smiles out of necks but wasn't quite as fast as Shanks. She momentarily forgot about her crew down below. It was only her and Shanks. They gutted several helpless goblins mercilessly. Shanks covered her flank, making sure there were no surprises. One, two, three, four, five, Shanks again fired off five arrows catching five different already downed targets.

The goblins winced out in pain, some for the last time. Keres and Shanks finished off the entire regiment of soldiers. There was no sign of a leader. No ruling party was present. Not too long after they finished the last few, Keres' spell expired.

The few goblins still being held up by Draeden fell to the ground as his spell expired too. Draeden, Westlyn, Rakka, Drackice, and Slate all stood up slowly and cautiously watching the goblins do the same. There were eight remaining that had fallen off initially and landed atop Draeden's spell wall.

The goblins dropped their weapons and threw their hands up. A voice came from above. It was Tsin. The lot of them all looked up. Tsin stood with one foot on a protruding rock, his body covered in blood. In one hand, he held a blood-doused kukri. In the other, his fist clenched the hair of a dangling hobgoblin head.

From atop, Tsin looked to be okay. He was covered in blood, so it was difficult to decipher if any of it at all belonged to him. Tsin grinned devilishly. He leaped from the top with the head in one hand and the kukri still in the other.

His landing broke his perfect reentrance. His right foot caught a rough piece of ground torqueing it the wrong way. His leg gave way and went limp dropping him to the ground. He let out a light scream. He rolled to his right side and picked up the upper half of his torso to reach his ankle with his hands, hoping that rubbing it would somehow numb the pain. The head and kukri were loose now.

"Are you going to make it?" Slate asked.

"Where'd you find that thing?" Drackice asked.

The goblins slowly tried to sneak back, creating distance between themselves and the party. Draeden caught them, ordering them all to stop. They knew better than to test a feisty wizard with more than enough allies still ready and willing to keep going. They ceased their attempts.

Drackice ordered the team to strip and bind the surviving goblins. They were horribly atrocious. Nonetheless, they were taken care of. Slate stood over Alphonse, staring down at the dead wizard. Draeden eventually came to stand behind him, followed by Keres.

Shanks stalked the perimeter, making sure there was nothing left to be fearful of. Rakka kept a close eye on him from a distance but with a few javelins in hand just to be ready. Westlyn did the same. Tsin didn't care about any of that. He immediately began bragging about his kill of the hobgoblin. He searched and searched the dead creatures for anything that could prove to be useful to him. The selfish Wilden ignored what the others wanted and dug for himself, hoping to sneakily pocket a few coins before the others caught on.

His eyes kept straying over back to Slate. Slate still stood over the fallen wizard. Wizards weren't exactly plentiful in Thedia but seeing comrades fall was a very common thing for a mercenary, Tsin thought. In truth, he didn't even know the wizard and from what he understood, Slate didn't either. Finally, the curiosity got to him.

"Slate," he barked out curiously.

Slate didn't say anything. He stood over the dead human. The cold was setting in. Flakes of snow were actually beginning to fall and mix with the droplets of rain that were also coming and setting in. The bloody scene around his throat was bad but his eyes made him look like it was a completely different picture altogether.

His eyes were peaceful. They were closed but Slate knew they were finally getting to rest. In this world, there was no rest for people like him and he knew that. The Wilden kept calling his name and finally, Slate heard him. It was a muffled out call over and over until finally Slate snapped back to and heard the creature calling him. He didn't say anything. He just looked up and over at the little bastard.

There he stood, standing over one of the dead goblins with the other bound ones tied and gagged behind him just staring at him go through their dead comrades' things. Tsin had that dumb look and smile on his face. Slate knew, he just knew the little son of a bitch was going to say something he didn't like.

"Why are you standing over him? You act like you like him," he said.

"What if I did?" Slate asked.

"You don't like anybody. You made that clear already."

Drackice walked up, kneeling beside the fallen wizard. He raised his head to see Slate staring down at Alphonse and then going back to look at Tsin. Drackice dropped his head and closed his eyes. Another had died on his watch. Another had died on his order.

"Alphonse was a good kid," Drackice sadly acknowledged.

"Real good," Slate added.

"I don't get it! Why are you so concerned with that dead wizard?" Tsin literally had no sympathy for the dead human.

"Perhaps who I have sympathy for and who I do not should not be of any concern to you," Slate suggested.

"His cycle is complete. He was born and now he has died. We will honor him in our memories. We should keep moving," Keres said, jumping into the conversation.

Rakka carefully disappeared from the top where he and Westlyn still kept a close watch on Shanks in the distance. One by one, he ended the surviving goblins. The cold was getting to him. His boots were worn. Holes in the bottom made his feet unbearably cold. Luckily, there were many goblins here who were just his size. It wasn't long before the little creature had a new pair of boots of his own.

"Rakka no!" Drackice stood up, turning back around to quasi-stretch when he noticed Rakka eliminating the remaining goblins. Rakka hissed and barked at the leader quickly.

Westlyn turned and leaped down from the elevated area. His landing was a hard one but he was still fine. His body jolted and old wounded coughed up new pains for the deva but he wasn't about to give in to Rakka's brutality.

Westlyn swung his hammer first but Rakka jumped back, fending it off with a javelin. Drackice and the others ordered them both to stand down over and over but it was no use. The two were locked in. Drackice knew Westlyn wasn't going to accept the goblin just murdering other goblins but Rakka wasn't going to accept another challenging his natural way of life.

Drackice gave the order and signaled for everyone else to stay out of it. Coldness and bitter harshness was setting in and they were only going to be forced higher into the cold mountain. Keres wanted to interfere but Drackice managed to keep her out of it.

While the fight continued. Slate never left his position over Alphonse, eventually dropping to a knee to kneel down beside him.

Tsin moseyed his way back over to the dead body and Slate. "You just tried to give me a life lesson about not concerning yourself with others in the mercenary life. Now you kneel down beside this dead fuck like he was a member of your family? I don't get it, Slate. I just don't."

"Careful assassin, he was a good kid and meant well. It should have been you. I tried to give you a different perspective, not teach you how to ignore the importance of other peoples' lives," Slate countered, this time standing up.

"It just seems like everything I do isn't good enough." Tsin paused. "I'm the one who killed the hobgoblin!" He started off pleasantly enough but ended virtually roaring.

"Then it's you, Wilden. You just don't get it. You never will," Slate said, countering him again as he walked away from the body. After taking a few steps, he spoke again. "We bury the body."

His words got Drackice's attention first. The others perked up to. They all approached the dead carcass of Alphonse, surrounding him. Slate was the lone one not around. He walked on, staring off into the sky with only his thoughts to comfort him. Even Tsin united in the circle around Alphonse.

"We must keep moving. They're going to know we were here. We must keep moving and we must move fast. Every second we spend not killing Bahaus, he grows stronger," declared Drackice.

"We bury him," Slate reconfirmed.

"Time is of the essence," Tsin barked.

"If it were you, you'd want to be buried," Slate replied.

"So funny coming from the man who called my wife a wretched whore and then told me not to worry about what other mercenaries think," Tsin quickly said.

Alphonse combusted; he caught fire and a flash of heat forced the entire party to take a step back, even Rakka. Draeden slowly walked backwards while using his arcane powers to fuel the fire he started on the body of the dead wizard.

"We'll burn him. It won't take long and a strong east wind will take his ashes," said the wizard.

No one said anything. Draeden's answer to the problem seemed to be a fitting one for them all. Soon, Alphonse's body was engulfed in Draeden's fire. Draeden smiled diabolically as the man's body burned.

"Slate, I am in charge here. I am the one that's going to see us through it all." The team was beginning to restart their trek toward Bahaus but Drackice knew he had to make clear who was what and what was who.

"You brought us to these mountains and yet, the Red Mystic fortresses are said to be next to impossible to find. How are we to find Bahaus?" Slate asked.

By now, they were out from under the lower level and back to a strong pace on their path toward Bahaus. Slate's question brought up many good points and the others seconded his question. It was a little late to be asking questions like that, Drackice thought.

Westlyn was the lone being who didn't question it. He was the one who kept quiet through it all. When they all took up the mantle to take down

Bahaus, they believed Drackice would lead them straight to the villain. The believed he knew where he was going and just how to get there.

"You all took up arms and answered my call when asked. You've all served the Free Armies well. Now, outside the rule of the Free Armies in the Crystal Cities, we march through the mountains to Bahaus. Bahaus consistently sends out regiments of his monstrous mountain horde. It shouldn't be too difficult to find him," Drackice said.

"Red Mystic fortresses are believed to not even have a real location. They're said to move within the grounds of the mountains," Rakka said.

"I am a holy knight and I possess the powers needed to guide us to Bahaus. Let us leave it at that," the deva said, chiming in.

"Alphonse is dead." Shanks was the saddest of them all.

He didn't even really know the wizard but the man's death did get to him. He walked with his head down. They didn't even check him or take from him what could still be useful. Draeden burned him and all his things went with him.

"We're going to see this thing through. We have the power of Zeronaus on our side," Westlyn continued.

"You can lead us there?" Rakka asked, still sore and busted from their recent encounter.

"Rakka, great goblin warrior, I should have killed you there. Some things are more important. When this is over, we'll have our duel," Westlyn answered.

"You two nearly killed each other. We all need each other if we're going survive and see victory out of this," Shanks added.

"We have different rules in our civilizations. Both civilizations can agree that leaving enemies behind us in our situation is foolish." Rakka spoke with an intellect that the others never heard from him before.

"There are ways to go about it and your way is wrong and inhumane," Westlyn barked.

"Who are you to make that call? I guess you feel you are right. So then, until that day, paladin, until that day," Rakka said, jesting, as if he didn't take the deva holy warrior seriously.

"The weather isn't getting any better. My feet are getting numb," Drackice mentioned as the team continued their trek.

"The cold will eventually take us. If not on our trip there, perhaps then on our trip back. I was a fool to challenge the good cleric's words earlier," Slate said. Slate sounded like he'd been deflated. He sounded like he'd lost all hope.

"We're not going to die," Drackice quickly snapped back at them.

"I am going to get us to Bahaus and we are going to end him. Which of us sees that through I cannot promise, but Bahaus will not survive the encounter; that I can promise you." Westlyn spoke almost like he wanted to take the lead.

Taking the lead, what did that mean? Westlyn's natural gifts were the only thing leading them to Bahaus. That argument came up but died out quickly before it was finished. Westlyn brought it up again and this time, the others listened as he spoke of his powers. Keres served the same Draconic faith as he did but he chose the path of life, offsetting her choice of death.

By the time the conversation was over, the others admitted they took the assignment off the tables of the Free Armies out of respect and admiration for both Drackice and Magnus. They knew Drackice wouldn't have led them astray. And now they just were hoping for a string of luck to keep them alive and guided properly. They now knew, even without asking, that the son of the Free Armies founder had an ace up his sleeve even before he left the Crystal Cities.

Chapter 62

Legion and the others still clung to life atop the old building. Openings were starting to present themselves. Finally, the four fled from the top of the building, narrowly ducking away at every given opportunity.

Dozens of half devils scoured the city looking for them. It was the bone devils that looked to be in control. How in the nine hells did they kill some of those things? However it happened, it would most certainly not happen again. They didn't have arsenal for it and Pitt was beginning to get sick. The poison of those bone devils wouldn't soon leave him.

"Pitt, I thought you were better?" Dash asked.

"So did I," he said.

The four of them hid between two large buildings, watching as scores of Cambions rushed savagely across the city looking for them. How did they get mixed up in such a violent struggle? Lord Stannor sent them on a suicide mission.

It took hours, nearly a complete day, but the team saw they were just about out of the city. Dauge did what he had to do. And with Dash's help they silently eliminated several half-fiend threats. Cambions and Alu-fiends were both on their lists.

Legion kept Pitt going. Something in the poisons that hit his system restarted themselves. Legion's unnatural strength had bounced back and forth between his arms but found its way to his right arm. Legion's strength in his right arm was that of ten men. He knew it was different and he knew his strength continued to grow.

And without his help, Pitt would have given up. Pitt wanted to submit to the weakness, not wanting to slow his friends down from escaping.

Legion was there to keep him moving and Dauge and Dash took the lead, clearing the path for their weak friend. Something about the fight with the bone devils was hitting him. It wasn't over yet for Pitt and he was starting to realize it.

"We didn't come here for nothing." Pitt coughed, trying to muster the strength to say it cleanly.

"We're going to get of here. Whatever this place is, it's too much for us," Legion replied.

Dauge and Dash were on point, really taking care of the Cambions and alu-fiends stupid enough to fall victim to their path. With Dash's magical influence and Dauge's abilities, they'd perfected their maneuver against the mostly unsuspecting half fiends.

Legion strolled carefully with Pitt's arm hanging over his shoulder. "Come on, big fella, we've got to keep moving."

Finally, they neared the end of the city. They were closing in on a way out. It was the very same entrance they first came through. Dash looked back, making sure their rears were covered. With so much going on around the treasury still, only a light group searched the perimeter and the two alone managed to assassinate several of them.

They'd taken about five hundred gold coins in total from the creatures they'd killed but it still wasn't enough. A door to another building was cracked open. Inside, Dash's peripheral saw a magnificent painting, something more fantastic than he'd ever seen. It was so picture perfect and flawless. That painting would serve as their treasure find in the city.

Without saying a word, Legion, Pitt, and Dauge walked out of the very same entrance they came in through. Dash turned around. The others called for him not to and to stop. Dash rushed to the small structure with a door half opened.

"Dash no!" Legion yelled in a loud whisper.

"Dash!" Pitt coughed his name barely above a whisper.

Dauge turned to go back and help him. Before he could make a move Dash was already on his way out. They all whispered in the loudest voice possible, "let's go" and "let's move" over and over. Finally, Dash returned to the team and the team was safe from the city's walls.

"Ugh," Dash sounded, falling victim to something. More of the creatures came into fruition. Mid stride, Dash was caught across the abdomen, lacerating all the way back to just below his ribs on the left side. He fell almost instantly.

Two more half fiends formed in front of them. Once the ruckus started, the invisible ones formed into picture. One thing about devil-blooded creatures, it was instinctively natural for them to want to instill fear. And seeing numbers of them materialize sporadically around them was a way to get to that fear.

Dauge and Legion readied themselves. Legion had to let Pitt down softly. Pitt barked for the two brothers to run. Dash fell to his knees, coughing like a sickness was about to take him. One of the creatures was male and the other female. That meant they were dealing with one Cambion and one alu-fiend.

These two in particular resembled tieflings more than the others. Perhaps they were tieflings. No, something told the brothers this was a Cambion and alu-fiend just the same. They were just too similar to what they'd been fighting. At least the stir in the city caused the majority of them to remove their invisibility.

The female held a long skinny blade, almost fashioned like a smaller, thinner falchion. The blade curved slightly at the end. It radiated with magic being fed to it by her male counterpart standing close behind her.

Her hair was the typical dark black and her horns and flesh were both a copperish red. His skin was a tarnished color and his hair a brilliant white. His eyes matched and his horns were an odd green. Something told the brothers he was different. He stood out. He held his hands close together, allowing his magic to dance controllably through electrical currents between his fingers. A dark black orb of power slowly began to form.

The alu-fiend's sword suddenly turned black and she charged, taking a swipe at Legion. Legion dropped back, pulling Mourning Star. Dauge turned his body, side kicking her hands where they gripped the sword. It knocked the sword back but not out of her hands.

The sword's radiating powers grew darker as she stepped back toward the two and swung again. This time, her might was matched with the magical prowess of her male counterpart. Black orbs of energy shot forth from the creature in every direction one would use to evade the swipe of the sword. Legion used his strong right arm to knock back Dauge and take the swipe of the sword across the upper torso. It started high on the shoulders and cut down and deep.

Paralyzing powers rushed through his body but Legion's body quickly refuted them. He'd never felt his body strengthen and force out powers like that before. Dauge didn't know what he felt but he knew his brother was cut deeply. In the distance, more creatures were materializing, shedding their invisible cloaks.

Dauge took two leaping steps and then bounced off his sturdy brother's shoulders. The alu-fiend raised her sword to fend off the mobile Dauge, giving Legion the opening he needed to put Mourning Star's spiked end through her stomach. His whipped it around forcing the chain to wrap around her and the spiked ball to catch her hard in the stomach.

Dauge landed. The Cambion stepped back, trying to prepare another spell. It was no use. He managed to send out another array of dark orbs before Dauge's short swords found their way to his heart through both of his collarbones.

There was no time. Dauge dug them in too deep. He turned, grabbing Dash, and ordered Legion to take Pitt. Legion listened and two carrying the other two fled the city with scores of Cambions and alu fiends chasing behind them. One minute, the city was bare and the next, invisible Cambions and alu-fiends popped into sight like there were an unending number of them. The ground was hard and not forgiving whatsoever. They moved. Their adrenaline pushed them harder than the two even thought possible. Legion didn't feel it. His heart didn't race. His blood didn't burn warm. Something was different in him and he knew it. And sooner or late, it would all come to surface.

The half-fiends were gaining on them. With the brothers carrying Pitt and Dash, they would never be able to escape. How far out from the city would they venture? After all, it was the city they were guarding and protecting. The Vile Frozen was just as bad as they remembered.

"We keep going!" Legion screamed.

Dauge didn't answer. He just kept pushing onward. Dauge's body was about to give out. He fell behind Legion and the Cambions gained on him. Just before landing a successful swipe at the younger brother, Dauge dropped Dash and vanished from sight, immediately reappearing behind the creature, planting several of his knives in her back.

Dauge was running out of weapons. The Cambion fell relatively easily to his surprise. There was no time to pull the knives from the falling carcass. Dauge kept running, even planting his feet on the back of they dying, falling carcass.

He stopped. He had to turn back around for Dash, didn't he? He didn't even like Dash. No, he had to turn around. Legion stopped, seeing the half-eladrin fall. He dropped Pitt to the ground as best he could without hurting him. Pitt wasn't out completely. He managed to help Legion drop him where he'd land on his feet.

Pitt softened his fall, allowing his body to drop to its butt. He was feverish and sick. He knew he wouldn't last the trip home. Dash was still cut pretty badly but it didn't look like he was going to bleed out.

The weather was already worse and it hadn't been long at all. To the climate, it seemed to have pushed to the darkest, coldest, and most frigid days of the year. Then again, they were in the Vile Frozen, a place not accountable to holding to weather traditions. In this horrid place of cold, the hottest days of Hammus could go unnoticed.

"Just go!" Pitt yelled.

Dash tried to say something but it faded out. He held his side, keeping his right arm just below his left armpit. That way, he could tighten his entire arm down to his torso, trying to closely match where the cut was. In some way, he thought this would somehow ease his pain. Dash eventually coiled up, holding his own body as tight as he could. The blood still poured, warming the ground beneath him.

Pitt suddenly yelled out for the lot of them to stop and duck. Without thinking twice, Dauge kicked his feet out from under him catching his body with his hands. He laid his body down gently. Legion squatted quickly first before diving face first to the cold ground sprawling out as per Pitt's order.

Volleys of arrows came from everywhere. It seemed like dozens upon dozen filled the air. Some were even filled with magical essences. The stronger of the Cambions were behind them. Dauge could tell. These looked older and carried more scars. The arrows gave them the break they needed to move.

"Move!" he yelled.

Dauge jumped to his feet and grabbed Dash. Legion was right behind him, hoisting Pitt over his shoulders. The two pushed, with their comrades over lifted over their shoulders. The arrows continued. From whom? None of them had a clue as to who was helping them. The arrows consistently fired at standard height level. Most regiments firing arrows or missiles fired them high into the air, hoping the lot of them would come down hard upon their targets. These missiles were firing straight and clean.

"I can tell the Cambions we fought weren't the real ones!" Dauge said, gasping for air while he ran.

"What do you mean?" his older brother asked.

"I knew they were going down too easy. Now it makes sense." He paused again before finishing hoping to catch his breath.

Legion let out a small umph while leaping over a large gap in the ground. He landed strong and kept moving, never losing an ounce of momentum. The arrows were being strategically fired to miss the four and the true Cambions, the older Cambions, the half fiends with experience and wisdom on their side were finally coming out of the city.

What were they protecting? The bone devils, Cambions, and alu-fiends the team had been facing were apparently the weak ones of the clan. Why were the weakest ones protecting that old treasury? Wait, because they were the weakest they were the first line of defense. What else did that city hold? What else were they protecting and guarding? It had more than enough money for more than enough cities.

"We haven't even scratched the surface. We've only fought the weakest ones!" Dauge yelled over to Legion.

"You said the same thing about the orcs in the mountains on the way here!" he yelled back.

"Those damn orcs weren't normal!" Dauge scolded back, lowering his position in order to avoid a few arrows and to make sure they missed Dash.

The way they were running, they were going to be on the frozen beach of the harsh landscape before long. The beach lay purely south of the mogra. They weren't retracing their footsteps to escape. They were making new tracks, taking the easiest path they could to get away. Who was helping them and who was firing the arrows?

In the distance, large frozen and petrified rocks and earth hid the missile launchers. Finally, as the four continued to near them, the things in question revealed themselves. And as they neared them, more ballistic-styled weapons showed themselves.

The creatures were tall. All of them were over six and a half feet tall. Most of them stood over seven feet. They were scaled. Most of them had green scales but the larger, thicker ones carried darker, black scales. They had large heads and rows of vicious teeth. They were reptilian and the archers all leaned back on their tails for balance and support. They were lizardfolk.

None of the four had ever really seen lizardfolk before except for Legion and it was when he was very young. He heard the stories of the great lizard king Katrarak as a boy but that was about it. The few of the lizards had regular style bows. Most of them had extendedly built crossbows.

Their crossbows were significantly different than the average. They were much larger and made of more iron and wood than usual. Even a huskier man would have had problems peeling back the string for one of their crossbows.

"Lizardfolk!" Legion exclaimed, terrified.

"We're surrounded!" Pitt said as loud as he could.

"They're firing at the fucking half fiends, not us!" Dauge yelled.

Looking around, Dauge noticed at least a dozen or so lizard men. Some threw javelins at the Cambions and alu-fiends when they got within their range. The others, just steadily fired their bows. They didn't fight with any kind of real unison, though. They fought like a band of savages just consistently using a hail of missile fire to keep the oncoming Cambions at bay.

When the brothers got within just a few feet of the nearest lizardfolk, the true size of the creatures really came into effect. The average lizard man carried at least two hundred and fifty pounds in weight. These things were big. Why were they helping them?

Dauge dropped Dash and Legion let down Pitt just behind one of the larger petrified rocks where the two black-scaled lizards continued to fire. The creatures didn't say anything. They just kept firing.

All four collapsed to the ground exhausted, Pitt from sickness, Dash from wounds, and the two brothers from that pressing run. The lizards roared out something and then like a second wave, more lizards roared something back. The monstrous beasts began falling back. The Cambions were letting it go.

All of this for a damned painting, Dash thought. "What the hell? These things are helping us?" Dash said, confused.

"I don't get it either but I'm not arguing," Legion answered, with his back propped up against the rock. He breathed in deeply trying to catch his breath.

Legion looked up at the massive black-scaled reptilian. He'd just finished firing his final arrow. He pulled a massive falchion from his back and prepped the downed Dash for a run. Each of the two black-scaled reptilians licked their chops while picking up Dash and Pitt.

He waved the two brothers on. The Cambions were starting to slow their chase. Legion and Dauge now saw the bastards hurling balls of magic at them. Occasionally, a big one would hit, cracking and exploding pieces of the frozen rocks.

The lizards fought savagely and not with any organized form at all but they did still fight as one against a common enemy. Now, Dauge and Legion were following their lead as they rushed to the frozen beach south of the mogra in the Vile Frozen.

The lizards brought them through paths they never would have known existed. Within minutes from fleeing the battle, they were all safe from the Cambions but not necessarily the lizardfolk. The frozen beach was just as they expected, an iced over blanket of sand bleeding downward into the icy waters of the sea.

Dauge and Legion looked around. The ice beneath their feet encasing the sand was cold, really cold. Even the air being breathed in was a difficult ordeal. It was too cold and thick. Dauge couldn't believe how many lizards there actually were. There were a lot more than he expected. Some of them stayed hidden throughout the entire ordeal. Had it not been for them, they would have all surely died.

There were many more green-scaled lizards then black-scaled ones. The black-scaled ones were typically a lot bigger. Finally, one of the green-scaled lizards approached them from a distance. He wasn't too close initially and thus far hadn't given any of them a reason to think he was any different from any of the others.

Dauge stepped back defensively, seeing the creature approach. Legion jumped in front of him. Their two allies were being tended to just a few feet from them, by the lizards. Dauge didn't have to be told or warned; he stood down and suggested to his brother to do the same. Legion quickly obliged his little brother's suggestion.

The green-scaled reptile was a bit smaller than the others. He wore tribal clothing and boned ornaments. He didn't have a single weapon in sight from what they could tell. Dauge gave him more than the initial once over scan to make sure of it, and again, not a single sign of a weapon. Legion bowed thankfully to the creature. Dauge just stood his ground.

"I am Katrarak Kingsblood the Third. I believe your father knew my grandfather," he said with a hissing voice. "Unless I am mistaken and you are not the blood of the Eternian Taj Xavier?"

"Kingsblood, I never heard that name before. How do you know us? How do you our father?" Legion asked.

"Your people knighted and honored my grandfather with an award named after Taj's own father. They felt a kinship amongst themselves. Your father helped my grandfather reclaim and secure his kingdom. I felt the presence of those swords once wielded by your father."

"How do you know of my father's swords and when did you feel their essence?" Legion questioned.

"My father felt them as a young juvenile. Grandfather treated father like any other lizard. That's what made him special. None received special treatment under his watch. My father felt them but never made so much as a comment to your father. However, the presence of the swords touched him forever. My father, the ruler of our people now, touched me with a taste of what those swords radiate. I hadn't tasted such powers since I was a juvenile. He passed the presence onto me. I felt it from deep below the waters. We've come to repay the debt owed to your father."

"Assume nothing's paid. Nothing needs to be paid. Your debt to my father means nothing to me. He means nothing to me," Dauge barked loudly.

"Dauge!" Legion yelled with enough body language to prove he needed to remain quiet.

"I am sorry for his outburst. Your actions today are greatly appreciated," Legion, said bowing again.

"It's okay, young one. I once felt the same of my blood. My father took the dry name Kingsblood in honor of the Eternian people," he said.

"Dry name?" Dauge questioned.

"Tribal creatures take names based on actions. Names such as Baknor the braggart and Eldith the true are based upon a mortal's principles. Tribal peoples' surnames are often earned. The dry lands have common house names such as Xavier, your house name. My father learned of these house names and implemented it in our own realm. He took the name Kingsblood for he possessed the blood of lizard kings. The name honors both his tribal ancestry and the civilized lands of Eternis." The creature smiled as best he could. This was not at all what the two brothers expected from lizardfolk.

"We are far from Eternis. What is your clan doing out here?" Legion asked.

"You are far from home. What are you doing out here?" The creature hissed a bit more in between his words. It was his way of laughing as he spoke.

"I get your point," Dauge said coldly.

"And we are thankful. We'll never make it back. We'd have died if not for you. Now, we are in your debt," Legion replied.

"I can get you close to Thoxen lands. I can you really close safely. From there, you're on your own."

"Pitt's not going to make it, is he?" Dauge asked.

Dauge looked over his shoulder, seeing a few lizards applying ointment all over Pitt's body. Dash was being mended magically by a few healers. It was still going to leave a nasty scar.

Katrarak Kingsblood the Third looked over Dauge's shoulder and then took a few steps past him. "We've fought these things before. I don't know what you were doing so close to Azra Goetia but stay away from it. It's a death warrant. Even we stay away from that place. Everyone does, that's why it's forgotten."

"Lord Stannor of Vorrellon sent us. He needs money to raise his town to the city he hopes it can be. He sent us here saying three thousand gold coins would be easy to find. He was right. It was just difficult to keep," Legion answered.

"He's a fool. Three thousand gold isn't easy to come by but sending you out all this way was foolish. It was purely foolish. He was looking for something else. He wanted proof the city still stood," Katrarak suggested.

"So the money was a spoof. He doesn't really need it?" Legion asked.

"Anyone can use an extra three thousand gold coins but he's more interested in the city and how to get to it and what you saw while you were there. He's going to ask you about the city and not think twice of the gold you return."

Dauge and Legion looked at each other. Vorrellon was a small town, still growing. Thox refused to give him the money he needed to build it the way he wanted. Stannor's logic was to use an old map to a city many believed to be long lost. Dauge and Legion could both understand his logic. It made sense.

"We don't have gold to return. Dash escaped stealing an old painting at the last minute," Dauge said, putting his weapon down as if he was ashamed.

"We will give you the gold you need to remain in good standings with the lord. This will finalize the debt once owed to your people. We will forever be allies."

Dauge and Legion couldn't believe it. Out of nowhere, old allies of their father came and rescued them simply because of Mourning Star's presence. They could feel it. What kind of magic was that? Most lizard casters focused on primal magic. Divine was present amidst their numbers but not as plentiful as primal. Lastly, very few lizard clans had any arcane casters at all. It was mostly forbidden, especially in today's world, for the lizards.

"You're going to give us enough gold to please Lord Stannor? Why?" Dauge questioned.

"I told you. I once felt the presence of those blades by astral stories told to me by my father. Never question the shamans of a great clan. They know things. I must ask to see those weapons," Katrarak asked.

Legion pulled Mourning Star. It wasn't all at what Katrarak was expecting. He heard stories of two blades, not a morning star. The presence to him was overwhelming and even to Dauge and the others; the blade began to glow. Katrarak stepped back. The other lizards bitched that it was time to go. They argued it was time to move and there was no time for this glorious history lesson.

"I can't believe it. My father and my grandfather told of the powers your father once held. They told of the skill of your grandfather." Katrarak was interrupted. The others kept hammering for Katrarak to move. The sound of a regiment of humanoids coming their way was closing in.

"That water's too cold. We'll not survive," Legion said taking back Mourning Star and placing it back at his side.

Katrarak didn't answer. He ran past the two brothers and the two downed allies of them. The others followed with random black-scaled reptilians picking up the two dropped ones. Just past a frozen and petrified patch of trees, an old rowboat rested ashore the frozen beach. It was in no condition to hit the open waters, and further, rowboats couldn't be taken across seas. Maybe they could keep it close to shore but rowboats just weren't meant for such long travels. And the weather just wasn't going to land in their favor either and they knew it.

There was no time to question or argue. The holes in the ship, its rotting sides, nothing said it could be used but the lizards ordered the crew into it. This time they chose not to argue and the two brothers hopped in right as the black-scaled lizards carrying Dash and Pitt dropped them in.

"We'll keep you afloat!" One of the lizards said. His wording was so overtaken by his hissing, it was hard to make out.

Without arguing or saying another word, the crew was in the boat and the boat was in the water thanks to muscle provided by the lizardmen. Water leaked in and it was cold. Dash's body was getting hot. He was running fever. Pitt's body was different. It was weak but cold in temperature. The lizards did the best they could but it still may have not been enough. Neither of them was out of the water yet, so to speak.

"Even with their help, we still might not make it," Dash said, shivering.

"We wouldn't have made it this far without them. If we die, at least the damned hell city didn't take us," Pitt said shivering equally as bad.

The brothers were also cold but not nearly as bad off as the other two. The icy waters and freezing cold atmosphere got to Dauge more than Legion but it still petrified the older Xavier. They were cold and some of them were dying. The lizards were racing to get them to warmth and safety. The frozen sea lay just ahead in the very same direction they were going. Before the sea, the continental piece would rest on their right hand side the entire trip. And before the frozen sea, they would stop back off and hopefully be in Thoxen territory once again.

The boat moved faster than any rowboat was supposed to. Dash cast a series of spells to warm the boat as best he could. He centered them mostly on himself and Pitt. They needed it more than the others. What was this old boat doing out there so far from anything and so close to Azra Goetia? Questions to be answered later, Legion thought. Dauge carried similar questions.

The lizards moved through the water like sharks to prey. They made swimming and maneuvering through the watery dark look easy. Their backs occasionally broke the surface making their presence somehow even more fearful.

The cold, the exhaustion, the damage, it all came into play. Pitt was the first to fall unconscious followed by a drifting Dash. Dauge succumbed to the weakness of his body, welcoming the sweet beauties of slumber. Legion was the last. Mourning Star still glowed, giving him a radiance of heat he'd never felt from it before. It was enough to keep him alive. He pulled the weapon and placed it between himself and his brother, sandwiching the thing between the two of them. They would not freeze to death but their journey would not be a pleasant one. Perhaps, the longest and hardest part of it all was behind them?

Chapter 63

rath awoke. The last thing he remembered they were camped, heading toward the mountains. He and Kleiven were beginning to understand each other. What happened? Something was carrying him. Where were the others? Were they okay? His hands and feet were tied to a strong piece of bamboo-like material. It was a natural material, from the earth.

His body was beaten and bloodied. He couldn't see from his left eye. He felt blood oozing from the socket. Was it still there? His right eye was blurry but good enough to make out another was being carried parallel with him. It was Kleiven. Kleiven was still alive. What of the others, where were the others?

Grath's mind slipped from reality. The prime material was behind him now. He was back at the campsite having a conversation with Kleiven while the others slept. There were seven of them altogether, including Kleiven. The two took turns throwing fuel on the fire, various twigs and logs mostly.

"I never cared for your kind," Kleiven started.

"How many of us have you known?" Grath questioned.

Grath looked down. Kristian was sleeping. Kristian was his favorite ally and most trusted friend. He was a unique one, bordering on the brinks of life and death. He claimed to have descended from both an ancient deity with dominion over death and a powerful vampire. Grath never knew whether to believe him or not but the vampiric traits did come out of the creature more times than not.

"That's not relevant. What is relevant is you proved to me the hatred of your race across Runethedian is a just hate."

"Is it? Because one man did one thing you disagree with, the entire race should be condemned?"

"You knew she was spoken for."

"And if it was a strong enough pact between you two, my time with her never would have happened. I am a shadow elf, yes, but if I were human or elven or dwarven, it wouldn't have mattered. Your connection to Dusk Xavier isn't as strong as you think, or at least it wasn't. I don't know you. I didn't know you at all then. I owed you nothing. I saw a pretty girl and seized the opportunity."

"When this is finished, Grath, you and I shall have our dance."

"You threaten me now while surrounded by my entire party?"

"I fear none of you."

"We are on the same side. My time with her is finished. I've moved on. You should do the same, whether it be with or without her."

Kleiven sat and thought a minute of the man's words. Was he right? Was he at least, half right? It wasn't Grath that betrayed him it was her. Dusk was the woman who swore loyalty to him, and he to her. He kept his word and she didn't. Grath was just the tool used by her to break her word. How could he admit to this man that he was right?

"Bahaus sent us on this quest. We've turned back. New information tells us he is in the mountains and needs to be stopped. If my memory serves me correctly, your father was his closest ally. So, how should that sit with us? You could be an informant for him. After all, we barely know each other and what I do know of you, you do not care for me." Grath spoke with wisdom knowing it was penetrating Kleiven's ears.

Kleiven was just a soldier. He was a simple man from a simple town, the son of a great man. He was the son of General Cale Dar, a legendary warrior and son of Eternis. He wasn't that man and that man was dead.

How did everything get so fucked up? Not long ago, he was chasing Dusk through the streets of Eternis after working long hours. He was tired and all he wanted to do was go to sleep. She was a nightly person, a night owl. She wanted to dance in the rain and picnic at night. And he followed her wishes to the T, hanging on her every word.

Now, he was weeks away, traveling back toward the mountains north of his home with the man she betrayed him for. And the two of them shared similar interests and goals. How was this all going to play out? He still didn't know hardly any of the people he traveled with and he didn't care to know them. It wasn't that he didn't care about them but he was acting as a merc and their travels had just begun.

Enter Malukah. What was she? Other than magical of course, she was something that made him forget of his loyalty to Dusk. No, wait it was her initial betrayal that started the whole thing. Had it not been for her heinous acts against him, his relationship with Malukah never would have blossomed or happened at all. Now Malukah was gone and he hadn't any idea where Dusk truly was or if she was safe at all.

"All I ever wanted to do was be a good man and soldier of Eternis. I wanted to live and die and leave my mark and seed there," he said aloud but to no one directly. Though, it was obvious his words were meant for Grath. He was spacing out.

"Then what are you doing here?" asked the shadow elf.

"I... I..." Kleiven couldn't think or put it together. He couldn't even answer the question.

Why was he there? What was he doing there? Whatever the answer was, however those questions could honestly be answered was just no longer important. What was important was the reason driving the group to head off toward the Red Mystic Mountains.

"Whatever the reason, Eternian, save it. We are heading to the Red Mystic Mountains together. Together, we are going to stop this Bahaus Sazos-Uil-Endail from getting out of control. The true royal son of your city is becoming something vile the entire world should plan to fear, assuming we do not stop him."

Grath's one good eye opened. He was still being carried. He heard the screams of the newcomer to his team horrifying the air behind him. Perhaps it wasn't gone? His left eye was starting to blurrily come into focus. Gnolls, Grath thought, lots and lots of gnolls.

He didn't have to see the bastards, he could smell them. He remembered back, all those times he faced the bastards in the past. He'd helped several towns and villages defend against their ravenous, plunderous attacks. Gnolls stood seven to eight feet tall and weighed sometimes over three hundred and fifty pounds.

They closely resembled a humanoid hyena with reddish-brown fur covering most of their bodies, only thinning out around the head, foot, and claw regions. They wore armor made mostly of horns, metal, and leather. Underneath the fur of the creatures, was a dull gray skin. Their eyes were sometimes yellow, not like a vampires but a different yellow, or black. Their pelts were almost always spotted or mono-colored. Grath knew they were feral beasts that attacked at will, even if they didn't need to. They often served demonic or devilish gods.

Grath faced many gnolls in his time. These got the better of him. He always figured he'd die to one. They owed it to him. He fell back to the black void of sleep, thinking of the village of Dhazhacacha.

The growing city thrived not too far from Valence and the Highlands north of it. It was south of Valence built upon the desert sands that existed just below the kingdom of chivalry.

A determined band of marauding gnolls had been swarming the city for some time before he showed up. They were all but finished. Three previous attacks in two weeks left many of the citizens dead with very few gnolls matching the same fate. Suddenly, he was there again.

The stones and sandbags were in place. None of the walls were over five feet tall. Grath wanted them taller but they didn't have the time or the material. Rocks were being sharpened into valued arrowheads. Everything was being utilized. The city was growing, even in a desert. The other people of the desert, the nomadic people were all flocking to it.

The city was founded by a few wizards who focused on prestidigitation, the creation of food and water. In the desert, it was a highly valued necessity. The gnolls needed their food and water to survive. The people of the city weren't ready to give up.

Magistrate Amaril, an eladrin wizard was the man who hired Grath. He was young but motivated. He apprenticed under Dhazkaban, the man who originally founded the city. When Grath had problems, he went to Amaril. And Grath had a problem. Too many soldiers were afraid. Too many citizens were in fear of their lives, so much that they refused to take up arms.

Clouds of dust stirred by a moving regiment coming in closer caught the attention of the city just down the horizon. The sun was setting. The cold air of a freezing desert blanketed over them. Some soldiers were in place and others were missing. Grath's number one ally, Kristian Boroth followed up with him. He was Grath's informant and confidante.

The people of the desert city looked down on Kristian. They feared him just as much if not more than they did the gnolls. They weren't too fond of the shadow elf either but the vampiric-linked Kristian belonged to a race of creatures known as the Vrylocka, or vampiric descendant.

Grath ordered Kristian to quickly unite the people and order a gathering. The people didn't want to stop working. They knew they had to fortify the place as best they could before the hyena people showed up. Everything they were doing, they did under Grath's command but yet they still didn't want to stop and break to hear what the shadow elf had to say.

Finally, the citizens united under the shadow elf's fist there at the center of Dhazhacacha. Grath jumped up on an old hickory stump next to the Desert Flower, the city's famous tavern. It stood just before the opening at the market square.

The wind was crisp and cold. The setting was beautiful considering the chaos that was coming. All of this for a simple town trying to grow and thrive, Grath thought. Looking down into the populace of people grouping together around the stump where he stood, the shadow elf saw the members of his team strategically scattered, keeping an eye both on him and the people of the city.

"People of the city, listen to me!" he started.

He had to ask them again and again to quiet down and listen to him. After the third try, they finally settled in and began making their way toward the old hickory stump he stood upon. With the wizards of the city, trees and other greens flourished. It's what made the desert location stand out.

Grath looked to the people, seeing his band of heroes looking back at him from the crowd. Something in their eyes blessed him with a confidence he didn't have before. They didn't know it. They would never know it but he looked to them for an inner strength that nothing else could give him. Nothing could replace the stability his team gave him. He would die for them as he knew they would for him.

"To the world, we are just another city, another town and people at risk to what the wild has to offer." Grath paused momentarily collecting the words he just said. He liked them. He could feel a flow of them coming. These were not his people. They were a bag of coins, but nonetheless, they were still a people deserving of life and freedom. Gnolls honored nothing but the strength and power within their own ranks. One of the onlookers called out what he was just thinking.

"You're not even one of us. You're only here for our coin!" His failing human voice yelled. The man was aged and old but Grath knew his concern was for his family and friends, not himself.

"Dhazkaban hired me to assist him in seeing you all through this. It will not be easy and if it's lost I will just move on to the next city, should I survive. The chance of death is greater for me than any of you and as you just said sir, you are not my people! A great man told me once, to die for your cause is the noblest of all deaths, to find one willing to die with you for that same cause is the single greatest accomplishment one can hope for. We will not all see it through this night but we will all be remembered and etched in stone for what we do today. All your lives you were farmers, crop growers, armorers, weaponsmiths, boyers, fletchers, hunters, gatherers, today you are soldiers, defenders of your homeland. Your children will grow, and their children and so on because of your acts tonight. Whether you die in thirty years or three hundred, we all die. It's what we do with the time we have while we're here that counts."

One of his own allies yelled "here, here" and clapped as hard as he could. Soon, others followed. Some were still against the idea and hoped to flee the city. Desert was harsh terrain and with volatile gnolls on their trail, most wouldn't get very far.

Grath raised his hands, pushing the "air" down with them, signaling for the people to settle down and hear further the words he wished to say. It took a few minutes but finally, they quieted down enough to let the shadow elf continue his speech.

"I've been looked down upon my whole life. I am a shadow elf. We are not native to Thedia. Those left behind made it their home. Those people are my ancestors. What comes easily for many of you came to me in a very difficult manner. Trading, bartering, buying, selling, all of it came with much more difficulty than any of you and all because of my blood. And now I stand before you willing to lead you into this fight against these raging gnolls but I need for you to trust me and to stand with me."

A javelin, from nowhere soared through the air like the gods themselves threw it. It was headed straight for Grath. Grath turned to bypass it. His eyes opened. He felt the jolt of the javelin stick him. He wasn't bleeding, at least not from that wound.

He was back still being carried by the gnolls who got him. He was pretty sure that most of his team was dead. At least Kleiven was still alive as far as he knew and maybe one other. The others were most certainly still dead. Grath hurt. He was in pain, a pain he couldn't describe with the help of five devils.

He was fading fast. His consciousness was going to fail him soon. As much as he'd put his body and mind through over the years, there was a certain point one could no longer blame the body for failing at. He was at that point.

A distant wail from Kleiven confirmed for the shadow elf that at least his human ally from Eternis still breathed with him. He had to get away fast if he was going to live this day. How? How was he going to escape these binds while still being completely surrounded by the gnolls? Why were his dreams resorting back to the days of his fight against the gnolls in that desert?

In the distance, he could see clouds encircled around mountaintops. He knew those mountains. They were taking him to the Red Mystic Mountains. He was heading there anyway but he didn't plan to get there as a prisoner to gnolls. One of the gnolls carrying him slipped. Nearly forcing him to lose his grip on the long shaft being used to hold him as he dangled downward from his shackles. It was a very tribal way of traveling with captured people.

Something in one of his metal bindings clicked. Immediately, Grath knew he'd been granted a chance by the faiths above and fate itself. He had to act now. He knew that. Time was of the essence and was certainly not on his side. He had to escape. Those left of his team, if none other than just Kleiven, all depended on him. He depended on himself to assure their survival. Now he had his chance and it was time to take it.

Chapter 64

"We're not far now!" Westlyn said, pointing just overhead.

They'd climbed and scaled to, finally, a flat surface. They were nearing the top flat of the mountain area where they were climbing. The wind was picking up and so cold it could cut like steel.

Westlyn had been leading since that day against the goblinoids. He pointed over the rocky, yet flat, terrain. All around them, the climbing peaks of the mountains still stood, but now they were in a patch where a valley would take them to their next point of cross.

"This rocky valley will take us to an entrance to where Bahaus is," Westlyn said, taking the lead, walking forward, assuming the others were following in behind him.

"And how can you be so sure?" Rakka asked.

"I know," he quickly bit back.

"I feel he is right," Keres said.

"Who asked you?" Rakka questioned.

"Watch it!" Tsin snarled, breaking into the conversation.

"Enough!" Drackice ordered, taking the front alongside Westlyn. "We move. We take care of whatever else it is we must take care of…after Bahaus' demise." The son of Magnus Black paused between the words of and after giving as much emphasis as he could on the necessity of the mission.

"We were allies before this quest. We will be after," Slate said.

"We all get feisty and riled up every once in awhile. It doesn't mean we're not all friends and allies here," Shanks said. He tried to remain strong but the death of his older brother was eating at him hard.

"Are you going to be okay, friend?" Draeden questioned. The Genasi wizard didn't speak much, but when he did, he made sure his words counted and were put to good measure.

"I'm fine. Alphonse was a little different but he was still my brother," Shanks said, dropping his head.

Shanks was the youngest of them all. He didn't want to admit it but his brother's death was killing him inside. He knew Alphonse was unique but he was a gifted wizard and didn't deserve what he got. Keres never stopped offering prayers and divine thanks for his brother. For that, he would be forever grateful.

"You see that large half-buried rock over there, our opening is just past that." The paladin stuttered as he spoke, as if he wasn't sure if what he was saying was right.

"Are you sure powers are leading us accurately?" Tsin asked.

Westlyn turned to look at the Wilden. He paused momentarily just to stare at the man. Tsin was getting on his nerves always second-guessing him. Westlyn didn't verbally respond. He pointed over the half-buried rock again just down the way, signaling where they needed to get to.

The eight remaining kept at it. Tsin steadily kept watch. He constantly ventured ahead, making sure nothing was going to surprise them. Keres kept quiet but still kept a keen eye on Tsin. Rakka walked, straying farther and farther from the group. Drackice pleaded with the goblin barbarian to return to the ranks of the group but he refused to listen. This team was under stress. They'd never fought like that before. The Free Armies soldiers always seemed to get along. Here in the cold wilderness of the mountains, everything was beginning to get to them. Even Drackice had a hard time keeping his attitude in check.

Something screeched from the sky. Tsin ducked his head and moved as fast as he could. Some of the others looked up. For Tsin, there was no need to. He yelled, "Wyvern," as loud as he could before making his move to run for cover.

Drackice's eyes confirmed Tsin's words. Circling overhead, a large wyvern seemingly came from nowhere. This one was big. None of the eight had ever seen a wyvern before but tales of old told stories of the beasts proved to the eight that the stories were spot on.

The wyvern resembled a true dragon but lacked its forelegs. Its crocodile-like head beamed down two beady red eyes. The creature's wingspan was interestingly long, much wider than one might think. Its brownish red scales covered the creature's entire body and at its rear, a long tail floated, extended fully behind the creature. Even from high above, the sharpened stingers at the end of its tail were still easily visible. It roared again.

Drackice and the others hurried as fast as their bodies would carry them. Westlyn yelled, reminding them all that the entrance they sought was just over the large half-buried boulder. The wyvern saw them and after making a final circle darted down, targeting at least one of them to be its next potential meal.

Westlyn stopped and dropped to a knee, turning back to target the creature. Slate followed his lead. Slate ripped a javelin from his back. Westlyn steadied his crossbow. Rakka didn't stop. Tsin didn't stop either. Keres didn't want to leave them and neither did Drackice. Draeden ran faster and harder than any of them, though Tsin still quite easily kept the lead. A few steps after both Westlyn and Slate stopped and turned, the best ranged fighter there stopped and turned to.

Westlyn was still steadying his crossbow and Slate couldn't get a solid aim off with his javelin. Shanks fired off six arrows before either of them did anything. The first four were deflected. Either they stuck but weren't strong enough to penetrate or otherwise just bounced off, none of them found their way through the creature's scales.

The fifth arrow distracted it, allowing the sixth and final arrow to just narrowly miss its eye. It still opened a laceration that started from the side of its eye, running all the way down to the back of its head. It shrieked out in pain. After only a second, it turned its sights to focus directly on the source of its pain. It pushed its talons forward, fully opened, preparing to grab.

Westlyn's shot caught the creature in one of the talons and with Shanks temporarily slowing it down, Slate was able to plant of his last javelins in it. This time it didn't slow down or stop. It just kept coming. Westlyn tucked and rolled as did Slate, both in opposite directions as the creature came in to land.

Shanks was the fastest of all of them. He backpedaled, firing arrow after arrow, keeping the creature's focus solely on him. Westlyn didn't have time to restock his crossbow. Therefore, he just dropped it and pulled his glowing radiant blade from his side. Slate peeled his massive fullblade out from the hangar on his back and rushed toward the rear of the dragonkin.

The wyvern didn't seem to even notice or care about Westlyn or Slate anymore. It was Shanks it wanted. Keres, Tsin, Draeden, Rakka, and Drackice kept going forward toward the rock like Westlyn instructed.

The creature finally stopped to eye Shanks. Shanks turned, running completely out of arrows on the damn thing. A cold blast from Draeden at the last minute once again momentarily halted the creature. It howled again in pain and anger. This time, there was more to it. Rakka and Tsin both froze in their tracks. Draeden grabbed Tsin while Drackice pulled Rakka behind the rock at the last minute.

They dropped to their butts, rolling their bodies up as tightly as they could. The five of them combed through the rock and dirt, not leaving a single root unpulled in hopes of finding the door. Keres didn't help them at all. She held back watching the other four work rigorously to get it done.

"Great, now without that holy bastard, we haven't a chance!" Rakka yelled.

Keres smiled, seeing the goblin fully agitated. The others looked overhead. Drackice was the first to remind them all, that nothing was going to stop the wyvern from getting to them if they didn't find the door. The rock was hiding them from a direct line of sight but that was about it.

In unison, Slate and Westlyn launched themselves atop the back of the monstrous wyvern. Westlyn took the left wing and Slate took the right. When the cold blast from Draeden wore off, Shanks was gone! He'd made it to the others behind the rock. Now the creature felt two more pesky presences atop him. It shook and rattled its body to get shake the morsels but they held on tight.

Slate was about to be thrown when he planted his sword firmly into the back plate of the dragon, right where the wing extended outward from. Westlyn jumped from the creature's back, trying to land on its head. The wyvern moved too much and Westlyn's attempt was a foolish one.

Slate was hanging on for dear life. The wild throwing and moving of the creature's body beat up on him. It made him work every muscle he had to stay alive. He forced down on the hilt of his sword, pushing it deeper into the flesh and muscle of the creature.

Westlyn wielded a warhammer. He couldn't just plug it deep into the wyvern's flesh. He made a jump for it, hoping for the best in a bad situation. Westlyn's feet didn't land on the wild swinging head but he still came down with his hammer as hard as he possibly could. The hammer bounced right off the wyvern's skull just above where Shanks lacerated him.

A bone-crushing crunch echoed out. The hit came with such momentum and force; the vibrations of the warhammer's handle pushed the thing out of Westlyn's grip. The head whipped around, bludgeoning the deva paladin right back though.

Westlyn went flying through the air. He flew far, far to the other side of the valley where he finally landed. His armor was dented in. Westlyn felt broken on every inch of his body. He didn't even have the strength to pull himself back to his feet.

The wyvern kicked off the ground with his feet following Westlyn's hit. He spun, barreling around in the air just seconds after his takeoff. Slate gripped his hilt with both hands and his own weight pulled the sword from the wyvern's body.

The wyvern spun and shook to get Slate off and it worked. He wasn't too high up but it was still a drop. Slate landed hard. His right foot and ankle took the most of it. It was most likely broken or at least fractured to some degree.

As soon as he landed, he took a short pause and then fell to the ground. The others were still hiding behind them rock. Westlyn was hurled far from the group and now, he was broken down. Slate's foot hurt from the twenty-foot drop, but at least he still had his weapon. Not too far from where he landed, he caught a glimpse out of his peripheral vision of Westlyn's warhammer.

Slate limped over toward the warhammer and looked down the valley at the physically destroyed paladin of Zeronaus. He sheathed his blade and took up the warhammer, using it as a crutch to carry himself to Westlyn. He didn't have to look over his shoulder or behind him. The wyvern squealed and squawked, fleeing from the scene. He was done, beaten.

Just for good measure, Draeden sent another icing blast at the wyvern. Not even he waited with his eyes on the beast long enough to see if it hit or if the creature faded too far away before the spell dissipated.

Slate was still walking toward Westlyn. Westlyn was still far from the group. The others were all regrouped. Drackice couldn't take his eyes off of Westlyn. It was that man's selfless act that caused both Shanks and Slate to react as well. Because of those three, the wyvern fled and no one else was dead.

"I'm glad that son of a bitch didn't breathe on us," Slate jested, laughing, still walking toward a groaning and slowly moving Westlyn.

"Wyverns don't have breath weapons, you ignorant wretch!" Draeden barked from behind Slate. His voice proved he was playing and meant nothing by it.

Slate turned around but kept on his track to Westlyn. The others were all still digging and picking around for the entrance door Westlyn told them about. Westlyn was knocked far away. He wasn't there to pinpoint the entrance to Bahaus' location.

Slate took a second to stand over Westlyn. He was breathing but his eyes were closed. It was like he was trying to imagine the pain wasn't real, as if he could just disbelieve and all of it would all just go away. Slate couldn't help it. He just laughed seeing the deva beat up.

Westlyn's right eye squinched down and his left eye came open. It focused directly on Slate. He rolled his body, arching his back left and right as if trying to get kinks out of it. Slate just shook his head. Of them all, Slate respected and admired Westlyn the most.

"That's not going to help. You know that right?" Slate asked, timbering his hammer next to him.

"Makes me feel better though," Westlyn answered.

"I didn't even know you things actually breathed," Slate joked.

"We're very much alive, if that's what you're asking," Westlyn answered.

"That's not what I meant," Slate said, smiling. He lent his hand to the deva, who quickly took him up on the offer.

Slate took a step back heaving the deva up back to his feet. Westlyn bent over and grabbed his hammer. It was hard for him to walk but it wasn't impossible. Slate wasn't a hundred percent either. Together, they made it back to the others.

Of course, it was Tsin to first smart off. "Careful Westlyn, we need you alive to get us to Bahaus."

Westlyn didn't refute his sarcastic request. He just took in a deep breath and nodded in compliance. That wasn't like Westlyn. It wasn't like the paladin of Zeronaus to just take whatever metaphorical slams the Wilden threw at him.

"Why so quiet?" Shanks asked.

Westlyn looked to Keres who gave the angelic fragment a soft smile. He turned and headed down the valley, leaving the half-buried rock behind him. The others formed up and followed him. Drackice remained the closest to his side.

"I thought the entrance to wherever it is Bahaus is holding out of was by that rock?" Rakka questioned.

"I was wrong. It's just a little bit farther down," replied the paladin.

"I cannot believe a wyvern attacked us!" Shanks said, trying to break the tension and ease into something a little easier for the team to talk about and relate to.

"These mountains are plagued with wyverns. It's no surprise we ran into one. We'll probably run into more before it's over with," Draeden replied.

"He's right," Drackice seconded.

"A wyvern is a form of dragon, right?" Slate asked, still following behind Westlyn along with the rest of them.

"No, it's a dragonkin Slate. They're related, like a distant cousin, but they're not dragons. If they were dragons, that one would have killed us all." Draeden enlightened the barbarian.

The eight of them kept walking and talking. Shanks couldn't help it. He couldn't get over the death of his brother. Why did fate have to write his name first? I guess it was the order of things, he thought.

"Here," Westlyn said suddenly.

Underneath a large flat stone, Westlyn and Slate revealed a hidden tunnel. Westlyn first tried to move it by himself. Slate saw he needed help and joined in. Drackice pointed to the high elevations and tips at the mountains surrounding them. Eyes and faces peeked out at them. Scurrying feet elevated the senses in Tsin's ears.

"Goblins, kobolds, gnolls." Drackice named the creatures as he saw them.

"They're everywhere," Shanks whispered. He wasn't whispering so that the creatures couldn't hear him. It was more like he wasn't even sure he believed what he was saying. The number of monstrous creatures kept adding up. They were completely surrounded.

"Go!" Westlyn ordered.

Westlyn and Slate's bodies were both still very hurt. The paladin pulled his shield and did everything he could to prepare for whatever missiles the vile bastards planned to launch their way. Draeden waved his hands, speaking in a tongue queer to the rest of them.

Translucent disk-like spheres and clouds of smoke covered the party just in the nick of time. The creatures from the mountains bombarded the eight of them with more arrows, bolts, javelins, and other throwing weapons than any of them knew what to do with. The sun was set high. It was midday. The blanket of night wouldn't be there to help push their escape along either.

Draeden laughed, seeing and feeling the missiles bounce off of his floating shield-like disks. Drackice knew Draeden wanted to see if his arcane prowess could stand alone against the hordes of the mountains.

"Draeden we have to move!" Westlyn yelled. "Now get in there! I cannot escape until all of you are safe!"

"It is not me you have to protect from them. It is them you'll have to protect from me!" Draeden arrogantly challenged with more arcane flourishing about. With every wave and move, apparitional essences stayed behind. Prismatic colors surrounded the wizard as he danced and flaunted his magic against the oncoming horde.

Now they weren't just launching missiles. They were coming down from the mountains, pouring into the valley like water from a faucet. Rakka was the first one down. Tsin soon followed. Keres was next, followed by Shanks then Slate. Drackice looked at Westlyn. The eye-to-eye signal told the leader of the band it was time for him to go in. He did, leaving just Westlyn and Draeden behind.

"Use your magic for better purposes!" Westlyn yelled, forcefully snagging the wizard and jumping down into the tunnel.

With so much arcane in the works, Draeden distorted and redirected it toward the tunnel itself. His raw arcane power formed together, sealing off the tunnel and their exit, thus creating a solid plug of virtually impenetrable arcane matter.

Draeden planned on plugging the tunnel either way. The arcane was already in the process and the spell already in the works of going off. He just didn't plan to be on the inside when it happened. He wanted to hold off the legions of things while the remaining seven finished off Bahaus.

The eight of them tumbled down a large tunnel. They landed in a cavernous opening, dark and big. In the middle of the thick, clay-walled opening was a deep puddle of dirty water. The walls and ground were damp. A single passageway diving deeper into the earth seemed to be the only path opened to them.

Draeden used his arcane to create a magical fire that burned upon his left hand. It didn't radiate any heat and it wasn't a real fire at all. It was merely an illusionary fire but it still gave light to the team.

"Where in the dead gods are we?" Shanks asked. His fear poured out with every word.

"What were you doing up there Draeden? Killing monstrous hordes is not our objective," Drackice said, looking straight at the wizard. He asked his question cold and hard.

"I was covering your flank so you all could make it to Bahaus. You did say this was a suicide mission, didn't you?" the wizard questioned. The sarcasm in his voice was so thick it could have been cut with a knife.

"We already lost one wizard. You don't think we're going to need your powers against Bahaus?" Magnus' son questioned.

"I think you getting there should be the first priority," Draeden responded.

"We made it and you're still with us." Slate broke into the conversation, siding with Drackice.

"These tunnels should be easy to navigate through. Follow me." Rakka seized the initiative and took the lead.

"Wait, goblin." Westlyn coughed. The damage he took from the wyvern still haunted him.

Rakka turned back around. The gleam in his eyes proved he wasn't happy at all with the paladin's words. "My name is Rakka and yet, you call me goblin. That's not very noble of you, is it?"

Westlyn gave apologies to the small warrior, blaming his weakened state for his negative demeanor. Westlyn still didn't trust the goblin and following him wasn't exactly on his "to do" list. Westlyn reminded the barbaric warrior that it was he who had the innate powers to guide them to Bahaus.

"These passageways, these tunnels, these are the natural homes of my people. Your intuition may get us there, but will it do so in safest manner? I know how these things were created. I know which paths will be new and which paths will be old. I will get us into this old stronghold of the mystics and from there, you may retake the lead." Rakka held strong to his words.

Westlyn looked back to Keres and then conceded to the goblin. He was after all going to take the lead and front role in the passage. He seemed to carry no ill will toward the notion. Once again, they were off. Keres and Draeden dug into a conversation of magic. Keres said she still had many powers to offer the team for the day. Draeden admitted, though he still had quite a bit left, much of his powers had been depleted.

The eight made their way down the descending passageway. They were surrounded by thick dirt and clay. Rocks, petrified wood, and other minerals helped make up the walls of the passageway. The water from the puddle trickled downward, following the crew on their quest for Bahaus' fortress.

Westlyn's body shook. Slate limped. They were both hurt and Draeden openly admitted he was nearly out of spells. It didn't look like much, but blowing spells to create raw arcane energies to make the solid cork that sealed them in took more than the others thought. The shields and smokes that protected them, none of that was easy to cast. Draeden made it look like he was just getting warmed up.

"We should rest," Shanks suggested.

"Rest?" Keres asked, breaking her silence to the team. She often spoke in conversation but when it came to making decisions, she rarely voiced her opinion.

"Yes, even if we get to where we are going, we're in no shape to fight whatever it is Bahaus is going to throw at us," said the man with the fallen brother.

Drackice took a deep breath. They were in a safe spot, believe it or not. They could backtrack to where they first landed. Draeden and Keres could maybe cast a few spells to help hide them or at least their scent. The team argued and bickered over whether or not it was a good idea. Finally, Drackice took the floor and answered for them. He was the leader and it was time he made decisions like one.

Chapter 65

Men from Malynkite were on the way, hired personally by General Magnus Black himself. Magnus sent nearly everything he had to hold over Redd's Rogue Army. He kept the best of the rest, so to speak of each regiment of the Free Armies.

Drackice took the Free Armies' highest standing members with him. Those that stood out above all others were now in the mountains with the General's oldest son. What remained still had quite a bit to offer. Magnus cherry picked the choicest of its remaining members to hold fast within the Crystal Cities.

He was going to protect them all with a skeleton crew, a skeleton crew in each of the cities of course. The rest of the Free Armies would march to meet retired General Seth Redd and the Rogue Army combatting the monstrous mountain horde in the open plains south of the Mystic Mountains.

The Rogue Army had held strong against the hordes of the mountains, but eventually their numbers dwindled and many of those that remained were too hurt or too injured to continue. The Free Armies marched toward them. All eight of the High Captains were at the helms of their regiments. Magnus Black stayed back with what he thought were the most combat-effective troops the Free Armies had left.

The High Captains like Bolba were master tacticians but not always the most combat effective, physically. It was halfway through Stormus and the weather was fine. Thankfully, they wouldn't have to deal with yet another obstacle against the hordes of the mountain. It was bad enough the hordes never seemed to stop coming.

It was the twenty-eighth day of Stormus in the twenty-third year since the Sundering. Today, he would meet with Magoro again. It had been nearly a month since he deployed his troops to the open fields south of the Mystic Mountains.

This time he and the dwarf would meet at the "Raised Glass" winery. It was an upscale winery with only the finest wines and inhabitants a place could ask for. The wealthier side of societies came from all over to experience some of the wines that were exclusive to the Raised Glass.

Magnus pulled himself out of bed. His room was perfect. He never had the maids take care of his room. He felt it was his duty to clean and dust his own room and make his own bed. He did it every morning before leaving. He had his own home in Emerald Greene and he loved it. He still missed Eternis but Emerald Greene was the better place for his people. The Free Armies would have eventually starved in the ancient city of Eternis. Or worse, they would have dwindled in numbers until eventually, only the most loyal remained. Money isn't everything, but those with dependents would have eventually had to find paying work.

He liked the smell of freshly polished wood in the morning. His entire bedroom was made of wood and Magnus loved to keep it freshly polished. His wooden floors got more attention than his boots did on many occasions. His bedroom was on the second floor of his exquisite manor. The Crystal Cities did everything they could to make sure the legendary General felt at home and was happy. Materialistic things meant nothing to the old warrior. It was the "home" feeling and the "know" that his people were taken care of that mattered to him.

His bed always had green cotton sheets and a matching comforter. The shades over his window were an off white color. It was the only color available to him when he got the home but in all of the years he'd been at the Crystal Cities, he'd still not grown accustomed to them.

The furniture was shipped to him from Greystone. The dwarves of the mythical city located in the Nine Kingdoms handcrafted each and every piece of it. He looked around at the room. In all the years he'd been in Emerald Greene, not even a piece of bread made it to the room, not a glass of wine or ale, not even a glass of water. Black wasn't meticulous about everything. His bedroom was a place the problems of the outside world were not permitted.

Magnus awoke and pulled himself out of his bed. Something about his bed made it twice as hard to get up as usual. That was the case for most people, wasn't it? He always slept in his favorite bed-trousers and blouse. They were silver and silk. He peered out the window, looking down at the city he'd watched grow for roughly two decades. Had it been that long since he'd been to Eternis?

It had been that long. One day soon, he would leave the Free Armies to Drackice, the most promising of his children and he would return to the one city he loved enough to call home. He wasn't a native. He wasn't born there, but it was still home to him.

Magnus finally got dressed in his finest green courtier's outfit. It was his finest outfit and green was his favorite color. The predominately green outfit with black lace and lining looked good on him. It especially helped offset his salt-and-peppered hair and growing facial beard. Magnus, before leaving even took the time to trim it down to where it was more of a scruffy, five o'clock shadow.

Magnus pulled his hair back. It was starting to curl in his older age. One last look in the tall mirror hanging from the far sidewall told Magnus he looked better than he expected. This whole thing with the Free Armies got so out of hand. It went so much further than was ever first intended.

The Free Armies General walked out of his home into the streets of Emerald Greene. The people were moving and working just like always. Sometimes the labor of the others plagued him. It ate at him, wearing him down at his knees. Then there were the others that were orchestrating and making everything happen. Emerald Greene was always busy.

The sun's rays tried to penetrate through the sky's clouds but it only partially succeeded. The wind was cool and moving but not so much that it was an inconvenience or any kind of nuisance. It actually felt remarkably good outside. From where the sun was sitting, Magnus knew he had a little bit of time before he would have to meet back up with Councilman Magoro.

Magnus spent the morning walking through the fields of flowers growing in between the streets of the working city. He walked with his hands extended down at his side and his palms opened downward. He walked, letting the tops and tips of the high grass and flowers touch the open palms of his hands and weave in and out of the openings between his fingers.

The fields reminded him of his youth. They reminded him of his days fighting alongside Dominick Gabriel Xavier, Seth Redd, and so many others against the oncoming fearless legions of lizardfolk, refusing to go down or give up. The lizards took to Eternis as their cousins took to the Republic of New Magic. Of all the kingdoms still in existence, none had seen more war than the Republic of New Magic, not even the old war driven kingdom of Thox.

He cracked a smile, thinking back to those days when he and Dominick fought under Seth Redd against Katrarak the lizardman king and his intriguing units of well-trained men. Two armies of small numbers but overwhelming skill were pitted against each other; some still believe it was the greatest war in modern history. Magnus was one who felt that way.

A familiar face, he thought. There, lying in the fields of wildflowers was the granddaughter of Dominick Xavier. Dusk Xavier rolled in the fields of wild grass and flowers like they were blankets of love and comfort. To her, they might have been.

She wore basic brown breeches and a black long-sleeved shirt. She wasn't dressed up at all. Then again, she was rolling around in the dirt and flowers. Her hair was littered by loose grass. She was so playful and carefree in the open field. She was pretty, though, and the inhabitants of the city's streets kept walking, but not without looking and sometimes even pausing to gawk at her even more.

"Enjoying the morning?" Magnus jokingly asked.

Dusk stopped rolling. She was face down in the soft earth. She rolled back over to her back smiling, knowing it was Magnus that stood over her. She nodded, telling Magnus without words that she was enjoying the morning.

Magnus really appreciated the immense smile she cracked from ear to ear. "I heard you've been sick."

"Today's the first day I've been myself in a long time," she said answered. "Where are you going on this fine morning?"

"I'm going to take care of grown folks stuff," he answered like a young daddy to a young daughter.

"I'm old enough. You can tell me what you're doing," she said.

"I'm meeting with Magoro, the councilman," he formally revealed.

She sat half upright, balancing back on her forearms and elbows. Her smile went away. She was curious. Magoro was meeting with Magnus Black and whatever reason he had to accept the meeting sparked her interest.

"Magoro doesn't just meet with anyone," she replied.

"I haven't been just anyone in a long time, Dusk Xavier." He smiled, reminding her of just who he was.

"I know, Magnus Black. I know who you are," she replied.

"Well I am off. I am to meet with Magoro and hopefully put this entire debacle behind us."

"You're sending your armies to fight the thing that haunted my dreams, General Black. He's linked to me, through my dreams. Bahaus's powers grow every day. I feel them. I feel him."

Her words weren't what he was expecting. Magnus did know of her link to Bahaus. He'd heard of it. He'd known about it. "I know. When this is over, Bahaus will be far removed from you and all of Thedia."

He was proud to speak strongly to her. The confidence overflowed through him. He believed wholeheartedly in the Free Armies and with Seth Redd and the Rogue Army united with them, General Black felt his men were unconquerable.

Dusk smiled, pulling herself up from the ground to throw her body at Magnus, wrapping her arms around him as tight as she could. He caught her and returned the hug as best he could. The two kept talking until the conversation came to an end. Dusk, for the first time in a long time was herself again. Magnus couldn't believe it. He heard she was bedridden and from what he understood, she mostly had to be tended to around the clock.

Today was different. Dusk didn't grow up with Magnus but she knew all of the stories and that made him family. She remembered him checking in on her when he first arrived. Flashbacks didn't haunt her this day. Dusk Xavier was Dusk Xavier today and Bahaus Sazos-Uil-Endail, the rightful heir to the ancient city of Eternis did not have a hold of her this day.

Curiously, the undead entity that fought against Bahaus for her, through her dreams and essence hadn't been around either. She was free of both entities. She was free of them all. She'd not been herself in so long. There was still something inside her, something she still couldn't explain. She was coming to embrace it, to understand it; subconsciously she was submerging herself into it.

Magnus made his way through the city to the Raised Glass. He was right on time, rather he was right on Black time; meaning he was approximately fifteen minutes early. This gave him ample time to figure out everything, look around at his surroundings and prep for the obstacle at hand. Today, the obstacle was Magoro, the dwarven councilman.

Magnus took a seat and took the first customary sample wine from the first maid to offer it. The Raised Glass wasn't a very big place at all. One of its many unique qualities was that most of its walls were actually rolled out. The Raised Glass was built out of an old barn and shed but built to be something special.

If the sun was out, the extended awnings had roll-down flaps to keep the sun back. Greens and gardens walked up the back walls on the inside and out. The Raised Glass was actually built to keep its clientele on a shaded outside with a small inside for ordering drinks.

Several well-dressed middle-aged women walked around with trays of various wines. The reason the women were not the typical young age was that this place was built for the aristocratic society of the Crystal Cities. Two of the women, both half elves, carried wines that weren't colored the typical colors.

The women here all wore different full-length dresses and gowns. They didn't wear the traditional "revealing" clothing of most taverns and inns. This was an upscale place built with a pinch of common. It was an ingenious idea for the people of Emerald Greene.

Magnus waved down one of the women. She asked him very politely what he'd like to try. He examined the half elf's tray. He really liked the setting. He'd not been to the Raised Glass Winery too often but the smell of greens and gardens smothering the air did ease the tension of his muscles and relax his mind.

"Do you have an Alderon purple?" he asked.

She smiled and suggested that she did have his preferred choice. She pulled it from his tray and handed it to him. He swirled it just like he would any wine, bringing the glass to his nose for a quick smell before the first taste.

He raised his glass, thanking the waitress, and waited patiently for Magoro to arrive. After four glasses, Magoro finally arrived. It wasn't like Magnus to drink four full glasses of wine before a meeting but he lost track of himself and what he was doing. The aroma and setting overtook him. Then again, that's what it was built for. It did its job.

Magoro walked in and immediately, Magnus stood up calling for the dwarf to come to his table. The elder dwarf smiled and quickly took the first offering made to him before ever making it to Magnus' outside table.

"Magoro," Magnus said, offering the councilman to take a seat.

Magoro sat down and gestured kindly back to the General. This was a meeting he'd been waiting for and also somewhat avoiding. He didn't agree with Magnus' actions but he did agree Magnus was the best man for the job.

"Let's get down to it," Magoro said. "I haven't got all day."

"Very well," Magnus agreed, taking his seat, nodding in compliance.

"You sent out our entire military force, our entire hired military force." He readjusted his sentence, correcting himself. "We have almost nothing here. What if we are attacked? What if we are attacked by something other than this monstrous mountain horde you keep speaking of?"

"When you engage in a duel, you have to accept the fact you may not come out unscathed. If you are to engage in a knife fight, you can't just make up your mind you're not going to get cut. You'll die. We are forcefully being engaged whether we like it or not. We're just seizing the initiative while we still have the chance." Magnus intentionally paused and finished down the last swallow of his current drink. He picked the part of his thoughts to verbally stop at in order to take the swallow. He wanted his words to have the time needed to sink in to Magoro.

"I've seen my fair share of war, General, but that's not the point. The point is the outside world is not our problem, as bad as that is to say. Emerald Greene and the other Crystal Cities, they're our concern. You've left us defenseless." Magoro closed one eye and partially nodded his head at the General, keenly focusing on the man making sure he understood the sincerity of his words.

"I appreciate you concern Councilman. The ones left behind are the best of the best. Each one I'd wager could fell a regiment of well-trained men on his or her own. I sent the tacticians to lead the men. The ones left behind are well-groomed and experienced. They need to guidance. They'll create their own rotations. They know the severity of the situation. We're at war, Magoro. Whether you know it or not, we're at war. Make no mistake about it, whatever's in those mountains is coming down. The natural denizens have ventured farther than the norm as of late. Seth Redd called for men and built an army. They're the only reason we've not seen combat on our own soil yet. I've got plenty of Malynkitians coming. We just have to hold strong until they arrive." General Black shook his head reminding himself that he was making the best decisions he could.

"How do we know that horde would come for us?" Magoro asked.

"They're a horde. It's an incursion. They're coming to conquer what the head of it wants. I have no reason to believe Prince Bahaus of Eternis is not at least among the culprits behind it. Since the Age of Scars ended twenty-six years ago and the Sundering began, Bahaus Sazos Uil-Endail is the greatest wizard still in existence; if not, then at least in all of the

Runethedian Pantheon." General Black was on point. He knew what he was talking about.

"The natural evils and chaos of the world could take us at any time without the proper protection, Magnus. And you left us without." Magoro furthered.

Magnus waited to continue. He waved the same half-elven woman down to bring him another Alderon purple. Magoro took another glass since the woman was already close and the extras were on her tray. She made a suggestion for a new Alderon red but both kept to the newer purple wines of the famous wine city.

"Things have come from the mines themselves and aggressively pushed into our cities. Our own minimal military and your Free Armies kept us safe. What do we have now in order to protect ourselves from such things? A handful of elite veterans perhaps, General, quantity will almost always outweigh quality," Magoro continued.

"I put the focus off of the cities. That mountain horde will attack the men at war with them in the open plains, my men!" Black was smart enough not to yell but he put enough emphasis on it to make the councilman understand. "My men are going to hold them off with the Rogue Army of Seth Redd as long as they can. I have Malynkitians coming from Palomides, one of their mightiest cities. I was once told their strongest warriors hail from there. I hired them with my money. They know I'm good for it. I'm going to pay them upon arrival. They're coming all this way before payment is made because they know I'm good for it. I'm going to go into my personal stash to quadruple the number of men I have. Your Crystal Cities have more money than some kingdoms. I need the pay to continue even though the numbers aren't there. It's going to help keep the Malynkitians under my employ. I can start it but I don't have enough to keep it going."

"That's not the agreement the cities have with you, General."

"Goddamn it Councilman, get ahold of your greed. I'm putting my own lifelong stash of wealth down for this place and Runethedian as a whole. I need your help. Hell, I'm starting to wonder why I came here in the first place."

"Easy now General, you get paid good money when you do right by the Crystal Cities."

"You explained I could do as I felt as long as it was what I believed to be the best for the cities. I feel this is the best move for us."

"One minute you speak as a hired merc and the next you say us, as if you are one of us."

"Magoro, I need you to back me with the cities on this. I need the full pay so I can keep the mercs from Malynkite under my employ. Otherwise, I'll barely have them for a little over a week."

"I just don't think I can get them to go for it. I'm not even sure I want to go for it, General."

General Black dropped his head into his hands using his fingers to scratch and rub his scalp. His mind fell from the world, deep into his own thoughts. How could he get Magoro to agree to his terms? Sure, the Crystal Cities had the money to take care of it but the rich didn't get rich by throwing money away. They weren't throwing money away! How could he get Magoro the high Councilman to see that?

"The Crystal Cities make their money as an independent governing body with stacks of gold waiting for you in the mines you all are built upon. If that's taken from you then you'll have nothing."

"I just cannot assume the Monstrous Mountain Horde, as you call it will be spearheading for us."

"Yes you can Councilman. Bahaus already attacked Emerald Greene once and it was my son who fended off the attack!"

"Can you show proof Bahaus is behind this mountainous horde? He's a prince and truthfully a king of Eternis, Magnus. What proof do you have he's behind these monstrous creatures incurring together?"

"I have proof he's no longer a prince or king of Eternis. He attacked and fled to the mountains. Now, there's a mountainous incursion. I've just put two and two together, Magoro."

"I'm sorry General. I cannot push this forward for you on a hunch."

"What if I abandon the Crystal Cities? What then?"

"We'd address the situation when the proper time is at hand."

"You gave me the right to move in anyway I felt so long as I truly believed it to be the best move for the Cities."

"That I did." Magoro nodded.

"What did that mean?" Magnus asked.

Magoro sighed. He took in another deep breath. He nodded again, signifying to Magnus that he did in fact remember what he said and that he wasn't going to leave him hanging. "Fine."

"Fine?" Magnus said.

"I'll cover you as long as I can. If it begins to be too much for me or the cities, you're done. Full pay is still our accord, until further notice. Do not make me regret this, General. I'm trusting you. I'm trusting you with the Crystal Cities. They're my only concern. If I'm right about this, I'll be able to get you about a month before councils convene and push against me on this one."

Magnus smiled but tried to keep it under wraps. He wanted to keep his professional and stern appearance, even if Magoro knew him better than that. The two didn't talk about anything else.

Magoro was disgusted with himself and he knew when the account treasury was looked over and guards not present were still active on the payroll, the people of the councils would come to see him.

Magnus received so much gold for the amount of soldiers he kept active in the Crystal Cities, to a specified limit of course. Then from that purse, he paid his men. Now, those men were gone and they were still going to have to get paid. Magnus made it sound as if he was going to stop paying them and start paying the mercenaries since they were coming into town. In truth, he was going to continue paying his men and use the profit from the cities along with his own savings to hire the mercenaries. He needed the help of the Crystal Cities to get it all done. This was an investment, both for the lives and freedom of the Crystal Cities and for the Free Armies and his name as well.

A coin toss was coming. On one side, a gifted scheme of tactics would earn him an even greater name across Runethedian. And on the other, a valiant effort gone unkempt would leave the Crystal Cities and most of the southern mainland of Runethedian blasted by the powers and forces of the fallen king, Bahaus Sazos Uil-Endail.

It wasn't the name he was seeking so much as saving the lives of those he cared about in the lands he still called home, the Crystal Cities and Eternis. He also wanted to prove to himself that he still had it. He had to know that he was still the legendary General the world knew him to be. There was also not a single part of him that didn't want to see his son returned home safely.

Chapter 66

Legion's eyelids pulled apart, creating enough space for his eyes to once again lay upon the world. He was warm and the sky smothered his vision. Warm water washed up from under feet up to the lower part of his mid back.

His body was beaten. He rolled his head and saw his brother. He was still out but breathing. The wet sand beneath him entrapped him, trying to keep him from standing up. Oh, how his body hurt. The lizards were gone. Next to him, several large pouches clearly filled with coin.

Dash and Pitt were present and still breathing as well. Legion's vision blurred out and then came back in. The lone lizard still present finished submerging himself just as he fully awoke. Legion got to his feet and awoke the others. They were sick and their bodies weakened from the over exposure to the cold but they were alive and in the warmth of the natural climate now.

Dash looked around getting his wits back under him. He knew right around where they were. The lizards were gone and the money promised was there. They'd paid their debt to Taj Odin Xavier. Legion, as a boy hated his father. He believed him to be a coward and a man who abandoned his people. The time away from the Republic and Eternis proved not only that he was wrong, but that the impact left behind from his father was one not even King Katrarak's lizards would soon forget.

Dash informed them that he knew where they were, somewhere between the bottom southeastern corner and the southwestern end. The Halved Forest flourished there and they were just south of it. He'd been in it many times before. Dash couldn't believe what the lizards did for

Legion and his brother Dauge in honor of their late father. Pitt was equally surprised.

It was early. They'd lost track of time but the weather said the end of the year was close, or so it felt. The first night was routine. They gathered roots and berries and made do over a small fire. The Halved Forest was bypassed and the lightly forested plains took the team right back into Thoxen lands.

Lots of large rocks and fewer trees meant the King's Forest was northwest and the Halved Forest was to the southeast of them. They were tunneled between the two forests in the rocky, lightly forested region that gapped its way between the two forests. Thox was due north and not too far from them either. They'd be there soon enough.

Days turned to weeks and not one of them could kick their sickness. Pitt was the healthiest. Dash was the worst off. Dauge and Legion were about the same. It made sense. They were half brothers after all. Luckily, the encounters were to an all-time low for the team. Minimal bears and other creatures of nature attacked them. This gave the team ample meat for the trip home.

They were not too far, maybe a day's ride from a Thoxen city. One was finally in sight. They were too tired and sick to carry on. The team made camp for the night and roasted roots and heated berries and other goodies from nature's reserve to go with their dried bear meat.

Legion and Dauge coiled up close together. Legion once again started his talks about Kattya, the girl he left behind before they left for Azra Goetia. Dauge questioned what Stannor would do, knowing the ancient deviled city still existed. Pitt often spoke in conjunction to Legion, bringing up his past with a girl he once knew, Shiva.

"Tell me Dash, there's something I never really knew," Pitt asked, pulling the last self-made bowl from the fire. He took the bowl that consisted of melted berries, boiling roots and stuffed a small piece of meat into it.

"What's that?" Dash asked, finishing off the last of his roots.

"I know of the eras and the ages, but when the Age of Scars ended and the Sundering began, well, they don't call it an age. What is it?" he asked.

"The Sundering began thanks to Taj Odin Xavier, Legion and Dauge's father. When the last Forsaken was killed, it ripped and tore at the fabrics of existence. The Rivermortal was never the same. Nothing's been the same. They say the dust has yet to settle since Raino Shadowblood was slain that day. Our world is still trying to heal and mold to what happened to it. Raino sundered our once beautiful world. And all of his damage has yet to be seen by the world. It's been over twenty six years now and all of his ill will's effects have yet to be seen."

Not even Legion or Dauge could say something back to Dash. He spoke with clarity and sincerity. Their father not only slew the last Forsaken and saved Runethedian but singlehandedly caused the downfall of Corvana, the mightiest nation in all the known pantheons ever to exist. He would go down as the greatest and most legendary being ever.

"It's hard to believe my father caused all of that when he killed Raino," Legion added after a brief silence.

"Of all the men that traveled with him, only two survived the journey and he wasn't one of them. Father must have seen and felt perils unnatural to this world more than once," Dauge said.

"Dash just said he took down Corvana or began its destruction singlehandedly," Pitt said

"He accomplished a lot I guess," Legion thought aloud.

"I guess he did," Dauge seconded.

The conversation continued until one by one, they all fell fast asleep. Dash was the last awake. He waited up, fighting fatigue and everything else his body could throw at him for another to awaken first.

Pitt woke first. It was early morning. Dash's body finally gave out. He wasn't even able to utter a word before collapsing.

A few hours later, Dauge and Legion awoke. Dash was still out. Pitt agreed to carry Dash the rest of the way. He was still sick but healthy enough to carry him without being over encumbered. And once again, the four of them were off and just under a day's travel from a nearby Thoxen city. From the looks of it, it was one of the larger ones.

They never bothered to ask Dash if he knew which one it was or if it was a town, village, or city. From their view, nothing told him it was going to be anything less than a metropolis. It looked huge. And it was.

By the day's end they were at the iron gates of a city completely walled in by stones as black as night. From its build, it had to be an outer city, the guys thought. It was fortified well and built to take on an attack head on if need be.

"Welcome to Blackstone," a voice said from the other side of the wall. "What business do you bring?"

"I am," Pitt started. He stopped halfway through his next word when Legion lightly popped him in the chest to quiet down.

"We are under the employ of Lord Stannor of Vorrellon. I am Legion Cage Xavier, son of Dominick Xavier, legendary duelist, son of Taj Odin Xavier, slayer of the Forsaken and downbringer of Corvana. I have with me my brother Dauge and two allies."

Through the gates, the three could see the city streets were still moving but dying down. People were closing down business for the day. A few guards manned the tower, most of them human. The night's cool air blew in. Mucus ran down all three of their noses. Pitt still had Dash dangling across his shoulders. He carried him like he was weightless.

The closer they got to the city, the deeper their boots sank into the earth. The ground was soft and mushy. It especially gave Pitt trouble. He was abnormally large and carrying another full person across his shoulders.

"It rained not too long ago," Legion said.

"From the looks of it, I'd have to agree," Dauge replied.

"It won't matter soon though. Soon enough we'll be in warm blankets lying next to fireplace drinking hot butter rum." Legion laughed excitedly. He couldn't believe it. They were home. They made it home.

"I hope you're right. From the looks of it, we're going to have to walk the Thoxen line all the way down to Vorrellon," Dauge said.

They couldn't see much over the walls except for the higher points of buildings and other structures. The walls were just a bit taller than the goliath. Toward the iron gates, the walls were raised significantly higher in order to build out the guard towers and everything else.

The twin iron gates finally opened. Standing ready on the other side, six veteran Thoxen guards, all of them were humans outfitted in upper-end leathers and chain pieces. They wore the badges and markings of experienced guards.

The three walked in with Pitt still carrying an unconscious Dash. When the guards saw they were exhausted and beaten down from the wild of Thedia, they quickly let their guard down. One guard called for healers for Dash.

"It's okay. He's sick but not wounded. He just needs to rest," Pitt suggested.

One of the guards, the eldest of them, walked close to Legion. He startled the older Xavier. Legion jumped back putting his hand on the shaft of Mourning Star. The guard signaled everything was okay. Legion looked at him. He was old, probably in his fifties. He had a thick gray and brown mustache. The chin was clean-shaven but the mustache started over the top lip and rolled all the way down both sides of his mouth. It even hung down past his face a little. His matching hair was mostly covered by his helm.

"Relax son. I was just going to give you some peace bonds for you and your friends' weapons," he said.

Many kingdoms and cities used them. Peace bonds were long strands of hardened leather used to tie down weapons to their hilts or belts. It was meant to offer any would-be aggressor a few more seconds to think things through while untying the bind. It was also meant to give guards the advantageous position against aggressors, considering their weapons were always free for the pulling.

Legion nodded and took the binds. He immediately started wrapping Mourning Star to the holster on his belt. Dauge took the vest that held most of his daggers and rolled it up to tie it at his side. It was the easiest way to "bind" all of his many daggers.

Each of them now carried two large purses full of coins that they didn't have when they left. The guards saw the coin purses. They couldn't believe how overwhelmingly full they were. Earlier, when they first walked in, another guard that saw Dash signaled for a lower ranking guard to run and get help. They all saw in the distance the guard coming back after several minutes with a few healers running behind him.

"Where are you boys coming from?" another guard asked.

"Azra Goetia," Legion answered.

"Azra Goetia, what's that?" the same guard asked.

"It's not important. We are under the employ of Lord Stannor of Vorrellon. We've returned and we must get back to Vorrellon at once," Legion ordered.

"Quintus, get these men to Falling Rivers Temple," the elder guard barked at one of the younger ones.

"Before we go anywhere, where are we?" Dauge asked.

"Welcome to Blackstone," the elder guard answered, bowing to the son of Taj Odin Xavier.

"Blackstone, I've heard of this city yet I don't believe I've ever been here," Legion said.

"Of course you've not been here," Dauge reminded him. "We've spent our days growing up, fighting for the Republic of New Magic and then a little time in Eternis."

Healers from the temple, physicians, and others with knowledge of the art came back within minutes, following the hurrying guard. Dash was taken away and the others were told he'd be well taken care of.

"From the looks of it, you could all use some rest and herbs. Maybe even a bit of magic to get you back on your way. We'll send a carrier pigeon to Lord Stannor of Vorrellon and let him know his boys returned," one of the elder guards said.

The three agreed and followed the healers back to the temple. All three made sure to peace bind all their weapons on the way. They didn't want anything causing a ruckus. Though they were back in Thoxen territory in the city of Blackstone, they were not home free and victorious yet.

As previously ordered, the guard Quintus brought them to Falling Rivers Temple. The temple was a very odd structure. A clean square wall built evenly in height all the way around the place guarded it. The wall was painted gold and stood five feet even. It wasn't a square run of a wall; parts of it slanted up and down and back again. The temple was built just before a small hill, and the backside of it even ran up on the hill a bit.

It was oval shaped and rounded off at the top. The temple was close to the town square but built far enough away that those inside could get peace and quiet, which often went hand in hand with healing. At the front door of iron and stone, an old bald man covered in ink of the flesh waited. He wore no shoes, only a pair of white breeches without any kind of shirt. He stood like he'd been waiting for them.

He opened the door and cleared the way for the healers that took Dash to enter. He gave the others a soft smile as they walked in behind them. He was human and old, probably in his fifties. The inside of the temple was filled with stained glass and decorated with beautiful pictures of the earth and all of its glorious wonders. This was clearly a temple dedicated to the Rivermortal.

The inside hallways were small and narrow, like the inside of a pyramid. Each room was big, bigger than expected. That was for sure. They took Dash away to one of the first rooms and laid him down on a stone table erect dead center in the room.

Pitt was told to keep going. Dauge was put in the next room, followed quickly by Legion. Legion's room had a soft bed of white feathers on the corner. He wondered why Dash got the room with the table. Perhaps they were going to have to do more work on him than on Dauge or Pitt. They were going to make it.

With Pitt on their side, they would walk just fine through Thox. He was a legend of the arena. Dash set him free. His little brother and Dash didn't get along but they worked well together out in the savage wild. What happened? How'd they get so far from home? What was home? Eternis felt more like home than anywhere. He never felt like he belonged in the Republic of New Magic. He always just did what was expected of him until finally the war came to an end, thanks to his father.

Adrian and mother were still Eternians through and through and his real father's old traveling companion was preparing to live out his final days in their manor, the sorcerer Malakai. Something told him the devils and half fiends of Azra Goetia weren't finished with them. He had a feeling they were being tailed or watched.

Legion breathed in deeply. The fluid in his lungs made it difficult. He took off his arms and protective gear. He stripped to nearly nothing, throwing himself on the bed of feathers. It was comfortable. It was the most comfortable place he'd been in quite awhile. The room's stone surroundings and stained glass hangings engulfed him just before he faded off to sleep.

Dauge went to a room similar to Legion's. He took off his gear much quicker, seeing the bed in the back. He was tired and hurting. He was in much more pain than Legion. Other than Dash, he was the sickest, which didn't make sense. He wasn't even human. He was a Genasi. Through the journey to Azra Goetia and back, he'd slowly come to accept and learn of it. He could change the manifestations of his own self. Something told him he was a corrupted Genasi, not a regular one. Could he still transcend into an elemental manifestation that would allow his body to kick the sickness quicker?

He kept his weapons close and the peace binds that held them were carefully tied. Those ties wouldn't hold a dead man in a coffin. He knew how to pull his blades without being disrupted, even if they were peace bound. Fluids built up in his chest made it difficult to breathe but he knew he wasn't in any threat of dying.

He dozed off, comfortable knowing his brother was safe, Pitt was safe, and even Dash was safe. Thox was a good land. He'd heard both good and bad things about it but in the end, they were a formidable people that would stand eye to eye with you as opposed to staring at your back. At least, that was his take on the people and until proven wrong, he was going to keep it that way.

Pitt walked into one of the rooms farthest from the front. It was small compared to the others but it had a much nicer bed. He felt like he was at a royal inn somewhere. He dropped his weapons and armor pieces and tossed them to the side. He wasn't as sick as the others but he was still worn out and tired. He needed a full day's rest just as bad as the others and he was going to get it.

The last healer to leave the room told Pitt he and others would be checked on regularly and possibly even woken up accidentally. After a full day's rest, they would be examined and checked out for illnesses. Herbs and magic would be applied as needed until they were fully recovered. One thing the man asked was if he was a follower of the Rivermortal. Pitt nonchalantly answered, "yes, of course" as if it were nothing. To him, it wasn't. He may have been the last to find his room, but he was easily the first asleep.

They didn't fully awaken until early the next morning. During the night, random healers and herbalists gave them soups to keep their bodies warm and their minds dreary. Legion was the first awake. A dwarven physician walked into his room, waking him up. The rooms had no doors. The temple just had hallways that ended as rooms.

The old dwarf's gray hair ran long and thick. Unlike most dwarves, this one didn't have a beard at all. His face was clean-shaven. He wore a brown physician's coat and kept all sorts of instruments hanging off of his body.

Legion peeled his body from the white sheets sewn together and filled with feathers. The doctor signaled for him to get up. Legion obliged him. The doctor looked at Mourning Star. He was impressed. Even on the ground amidst bags of coins, armor, and other things it stood out like a shooting star in the night sky.

"That's a fine weapon," he said.

Seeing a dwarf smile without a beard was definitely different, he thought. Legion thanked the man for his words and told him it came from his late father, Taj Xavier. The dwarf was taken back hearing that the man's father was the legendary Taj Odin Xavier, of Eternis.

The dwarf didn't offer his name and Legion didn't ask. Legion allowed the dwarf to examine him. The dwarf suggested some herbal ointment. He turned to head out of the room, telling Legion a few of the understudies would return with bowls of the ointment.

"Make sure you cover your chest, the lower part of your neck below your ears, and your lower back," he said, leaving the room.

Legion and Dauge spent the rest of the day with different students of the healing arts applying the cold ointment all over their bodies. Pitt was actually healthy enough to leave. And he did. It was that evening before Dauge and Legion were released.

Dash was still being kept. Legion dropped a hundred gold to the temple in order to take care of payment for all four of them. It was more than what the temple wanted but Legion made it clear. He wanted the Falling Rivers Temple, Thox, and the people in charge of the temple especially, to know his appreciation and thanks for their work. A little ointment and rest and suddenly, they were nearly better. It didn't even take any magic really, save what was needed to create the ointment.

Dauge and Legion left the place at the same time. The sun was already set. It was dark and in the distance they could see the streets were dying down. It wasn't too late and there was no night's breeze. It was getting warmer. At least, this night was warmer than the last. Perhaps so much time spent in the cold and Vile Frozen threw them off a little bit. The priests of Falling Rivers Temple, a sanctuary dedicated to the Rivermortal, gave them all carrying bags and even purchased new clothing for them to wear around town. Legion more than obliged them with his gift of a hundred gold.

Both of them wore basic brown breeches and long-sleeved white shirts with brown boots. They were both given very thick burlap sacks with a string tied top to put all of their traveling belongings. They were both given a bath before leaving, though it was a quick one.

"We need to find Pitt and get out of here," Dauge told his brother.

"What about Dash?"

"What about him?" Dauge asked.

"He's still part of this team," Legion reminded him.

"To let him tell it, he's the leader of us. No man is the leader of me, brother," Dauge said.

"So, you want to regroup with Pitt and get out here, leaving Dash?"

"I'm not against the idea. He's safe. As far as his cut goes, we can each leave a bit of gold for him and reimburse ourselves with his cut when we get back to Stannor."

"Stannor's not going to pay us with gold, brother. He sent us after gold. We were successful, thanks to the lizards."

"I still have the painting. I don't even remember the lizards claiming they wished for the painting, or did they forget to take it? Either way, it's still in my possession. We can sell it here and leave him his cut. From there, we travel as three to Stannor."

"You and he work well together. I know you've had your differences but at least reconsider. Give it a day."

"It'll take a day at least to sell this painting. We're not going to get anything for it in Vorrellon. The town is too new and hasn't been established. Apparently, the Black cities of Thox are the wealthiest; take Blackstone for example." Dauge waved his hand around as if presenting the city to his brother.

"I'll get us a room. You see what you can do about that painting. If you find Pitt, tell him to meet back here at sunset. I'll reconnect with you here at sunset. From there, I'll take you to the rooms I find. Here, give me your bag." Legion took his abnormally strong left arm and heaved Dauge's sack over his shoulder. He grabbed his with his right hand and tossed it over his other shoulder.

"I have to get the painting first," Dauge said, laughing.

Legion smiled, setting down his little brother's bag. They went on to talk about the success of their mission. At first, Dauge didn't feel it to be successful but Legion reminded him that finding the ancient city opened up doorways for them in Thox that would otherwise forever remain shut. Lord Stannor would preach of their success. No one had to know how they acquired the money. All that needed to be said was that the money he asked for was found and the city of Azra Goetia still remains; mission complete.

Dauge agreed, taking the painting from his bag. His bag wasn't anywhere close to being as full as his brother's. Legion's left arm was monstrously strong, too strong for a typical human. He decided to take his brother's bag up with his left hand and then his brother's went over his right shoulder.

The two embraced in a quick hug. Legion kissed his brother's forehead and the two set off, both turning and reminding each other that at sunset they would meet at Falling Rivers Temple where they would regroup and go back to the rooms Legion would purchase earlier in the day. Dauge made sure Legion knew to get rooms for four. Legion's body flowed with relief. He didn't want to leave Dash behind. He was different but still a good man, nonetheless. And together, they made a pretty good team.

Chapter 69

The wargoyle priestess Aristophane watched over the armies' victories. The Rogue Army was nearly obliterated before the Free Armies of Magnus black interfered. They were winning battles she once thought foolish. Her new ally, equaled leader amongst her horde, Bahaus Sazos Uil-Endail was the reason for it.

As of recent, he'd been infusing powers into the weaker creatures of the horde. Goblins and kobolds fought with arcane energies flowing through their veins. They couldn't even believe what was going on with them. Secretly, when they were close to death, Bahaus would cast spells through them. Not even Aristophane knew of his new abilities to do such things. The act typically killed the creature but what did Bahaus care? So long as the creature took out more than it was supposed to in its dying efforts, Bahaus remained pleased.

Bahaus took himself away from the sleeping titans. He needed a few days to recover. His body was worn thin and, though Aristophane saw his powers and knew what he was capable of, he was in no shape to fight something like her. Davion hurt him. Forcing his body to imbue itself with the raw energies of two sleeping titans was killing him. Hopefully, he would be able to infuse it all and use its magnificent powers before it ultimately took him.

He could feel the energies of the sleeping titans Nyx and Erebrus. Who'd have thought, all he had to do was focus a bit on a creature and he could cast spells through them. That power alone made him unstoppable. Nothing said he could only do it to one at a time? He could walk into any city he wanted and eradicate it.

Eternis, Eternis was the only city he had in mind. They left him. They betrayed him and they didn't come after him when he failed against the Crystal Cities. He failed simply because of a traitor, an Eternian traitor! Now, Asmodai would forever loathe. How does one go about countering the Arch Devil of the world? The answer was simple. All he had to do was become more powerful than such a creature and with two titans like Erebrus and Nyx, he was well on his way.

Why couldn't he become the Arch Devil? Was he going mad? Was the power getting to him? He wanted to test his newfound powers on Aristophane but something told him she was going to be needed. Could they work on such a developed creature? He had so many newfound powers, which to choose from?

His favorite thing to do was blast a creature's killer with immensely empowered magic missiles upon their death strikes. He remembered a powerful knight from the Rogue Army fall. He killed many on that day, but a simple goblin took his life when magic missiles finished him upon being fatally struck.

Another part of the trick he found intriguing. All he had to do was focus and his consciousness bled into theirs. He could see them. He could see through their eyes. On the battlefield, he had ten thousand eyes! How could he be stopped? And the Monstrous Mountain Horde feared him over Aristophane. Aristophane feared him over anything. He would soon be king of Eternis once again and on that day, Eternis would forever be changed. Never again would Thedia's oldest city be the same.

Bahaus found himself free of the sleeping titans finally; it'd been so long since those chains were off of him. Some of the best carving bugbears and orcs helped fashion additional rooms to the old Red Mystic stronghold they held. His personal chambers once belonged to Aristophane. Now, it belonged to them both.

He was rarely there. Mostly, he was strapped to the machinations that kept the powers flowing. Something told him Aristophane was catching on to him. He was so close. She couldn't catch on now. He was too weak to face her. With the damage dealt to him by Davion the lich, he wouldn't be able to fight anything or anyone for some time. Even the powers pushed into him by the sleeping titans couldn't be utilized. He had to keep his body rested and refreshed. Nothing could risk the chance of him dying before the final transformation. He used his own magic to constantly hide his already transforming body. His eyes, without proper concealment, looked like astral stars and the deep space of the night sky. They were like staring into the abyssal forever.

There in his chambers, made of petrified wood, stone, and dirt, he rested on an immaculate bed built for a king. Its sheets were black and the duvet matched. It was tall. The wizard needed a small movable stepping stool to get up there. The room was built with all kinds of odd cuts and angles. Desks with battle plans and other strategies laid out on paper filled one side of the room.

He kept a built-in bookshelf on the opposite side of the door. The bed was large enough for both him and Aristophane, though they'd yet to share it. She was most certainly willing. She moistened at the thought of his powers. Bahaus was the last wizard of the old ways. Even he shouldn't be this powerful and she was starting to notice it.

Just as he spread his weary body across his bed, the black iron door to the room opened. Aristophane revealed herself wearing pink lingerie. She often wore that type of clothing, referring to it as comfortable and free feeling.

Great, he thought. Perfect fucking timing, you wretched whore. He had to be nice. He wasn't quite there yet. He wasn't quite where he wanted to be. He was tired, really tired. He knew Aristophane was going to ask about the progress of it all.

It wasn't that long ago that he was sitting back being hand fed everything by his father, Gerear Uil-Endail. Now, he'd come to become something of a god. He was by far the most powerful thing Runethedian or perhaps even all of Thedia had to offer. No armies could stop him. Soon, the Rogue Armies and the Free Armies would be finished. Fitting end, he thought. The Free Armies abandoned Eternis; they deserved to die. Eternis abandoned and turned on him; they deserved to perish too.

However, Seth Redd was a good man and fought for Eternis during its last decade of beauty. It would be a shame when the man died but all things end. All things end except him! He would go on forever and, kingdom-by-kingdom, he would take until all of Thedia belonged to him.

After Eternis was punished, he would focus on Thox. He wouldn't take Thox either. Thox would be far removed. Every blooded being with roots to the Thoxen kingdom would be cleansed from Thedia. So much of the world would have to be taken back to the ground, leveled, and then built again from the ground up, in his image of course.

"Something isn't right, king wizard," Aristophane started in her sarcastic arrogant voice.

She walked in seductively. Little did she know that since she wasn't a pure blooded Eternian human, nothing she could do would ever entertain Bahaus' cock. The idea was just volatile. More than damn near anything, he hated half-breeds. Non Eternian half-breeds had to be the worst. Then again, since he was royalty to Eternis and she was nothing, that could make her equivalent to a regular Eternian. No, not even his royal blood could fix this monstrous bitch!

She called him king wizard, referring both to his former Eternian title and his trained talents in wizardry. It was an insulting remark. Typically, in full power he would annihilate this cunt for such words. Today was different. Today, he was weak and worn from enduring the infusion of those damn titans. It was high time it was all finished.

"Everything is underway. Are you securing the rituals daily as instructed?" he asked.

"Of course I am. Upon the sun's final strikes of light on the earth each day I feel a surge of divinity. These past few days I've felt nothing of the sort. You've been more and more worn as of late, especially this past week. Your machinations and works are beginning to strike my curiosity. What have you been doing?" By now she was up to the bed, watching him roll back over to his back.

Bahaus smiled back at her, using body language to invite her to the bed. Secretly, she'd wanted him since she'd seen him. Something about his royalty and something about his power just did it for him. His immediate innuendos told her he wanted her just as bad. For the moment, whatever increased his power tenfold mattered not. All that mattered was her offspring would carry the blood of royalty. To the wargoyle race, blood, lineage, and power meant everything.

Bahaus reached for the wargoyle, licking his chops and winking his eye. She stepped back in hopes of making him yearn for her body more. Little did she know, the very thought of her made him sick to his stomach. He had to keep her happy and on his side just long enough to complete the transformation process.

"How do I know you're not conspiring against me to take the power of the sleeping titans for yourself? They must be awakened!" she declared.

Bahaus stopped everything. He raised his body to where he was sitting at the edge of the high bed. His gut fell over his thighs, nearly touching his knees. He was a fat one. Wargoyles didn't look at things like that as humans did. Wargoyles appreciated talent, blood, lineage, and mental fortitude. He glared deep into her eyes. "Look at me. My body is worn and beaten. These rituals and powers have nearly killed me! Why would I do permanent damage to my body only to have you find me out and kill me? These rituals just take everything out of me. They're going to make me appear different, look different, feel and act different, but I am very much the same with the same goals in mind. I want the titans awakened but for different reason. Yet, I do want them awake all the same."

She didn't like it but it made sense. Besides, without him she had nothing. Even the powerful wizard of old didn't have the power to manipulate this attempt, did he? If so, what would he do? The powers of Nyx and Erebrus were far out of even his reach. He was still just a simple human of royal blood from an ancient city. That's it. "Do not let me find anything alternative to what you're saying. I will kill you myself and turn this entire horde against you. Even if you could best me, lover, you stand not a chance in this condition!" She slipped in the word lover to let him know what was coming. She would accept him into her. She started her walk back to him.

He smiled but deep down, he vomited. This was a high price to pay but it was for higher stakes. Somehow, he would have to convince his member to react to her body, though he wasn't sure if he could. The thought literally made him nauseous. Her skin, her scaly skin rubbed against his as her body pushed his back down to the bed. Soon, their tongues interlocked as did their bodies.

Her talons tore at his clothes smoothly. Before long there was nothing left to cover him. She tore at him like a rat to cheese. Her ravenous attitude toward sex did tend to arouse him. He didn't know what was worse, having sex with a non Eternian human or the fact that he was aroused by it. Either way, it would soon be over and if he performed right, he would have ample time to focus his energies back on the sleeping titans. If he performed properly, she would forget all about what exactly was going on, at least for a couple of days. At least for a few days, he would be her favorite person. Now it was up to him to make that happen. Women were like flooring, lay it right the first time and you can walk all over it forever. Now, it was time.

Chapter 60

The remaining eight rested fully. Shanks didn't get a lot of sleep. He stayed awake, mostly thinking of his brother. What was the quest? Was it to thwart Bahaus Sazos Uil-Endail? At the very least, they were pushing to stop this incursion of creatures from continuing their attacks on the Crystal Cities.

The final rest was almost up. Drackice and Tsin took the final watch. In less than an hour the rest of them would be up and they would continue their descent into the deep caverns of the Mystic Mountains. No campfire was needed. Draeden utilized what was left with his spells in conjunction with Keres' to keep the team warm with magical energies.

Drackice kept a strong guard at the beginning of the tunnel with Tsin staying deeper by nearly twelve feet. Tsin giggled every once in awhile when he turned to occasionally look at Drackice. Drackice couldn't figure out what the damn Wilden was laughing about. Finally, he'd had enough.

The air was stagnant but moist. The walls were damp but hard. The ground was nowhere near soft enough to get any kind of decent sleep. Nothing about their location was funny but Tsin just couldn't stop laughing.

"Something funny, Tsin?" he asked.

Tsin didn't respond. He just kept laughing. The leader of the party asked again and again the Sylvan just kept laughing.

"You've struck my curiosity. Now please tell me what is so damn hilarious at a time like this?" he asked slowly starting to laugh himself. He couldn't help it. The man's laugh was contagious.

"In our campfire conversations, you bring up Dusk too often. You fancy her, don't you? You don't even question whether or not you're going to return but if you're going to get to see her again, in this life or the next. Am I right?"

Drackice was stunned. He didn't even know he did it but Tsin was right. Tsin caught on even before he did. He really did fancy Dusk. There was no hiding it from himself but did he really let it out of the bag that easy to everyone else? Apparently so, but then again Tsin was a pretty quick-witted individual.

"Just keep an eye out. Stop looking back here. I got us back here," he said referring to the flank he believed himself to have covered.

Tsin kept his eyes forward on the darkness ahead of him. His natural talents allowed his vision to cut through more of the darkness than any normal Wilden would have been able to. Still, nothing of a threat came toward them.

"Why didn't you seize her when you had the chance? Were you afraid?" he asked, still prying.

"No!" Drackice bitched back.

"You speak of her all the time, why didn't you go after her?"

"It, well, it's just complicated... leave it at that!" Drackice ordered. "Now focus on the task at hand!"

Tsin threw his hands up like it was no big deal at all, throwing out a few okays here and there as he did so. He laughed again but then let it die out. He patiently waited. It didn't take long. Drackice resurrected the conversation.

"It's not easy Tsin. She is the daughter of Taj Odin Xavier, the destroyer of Corvana, the new threat. She is the granddaughter of Dominick Xavier, the greatest warrior the world has ever seen. She is promised to another from her city. She spoke of him often. Who am I to intervene with that?"

"I'm sure his name wasn't the only you heard," Tsin replied now, playing not so eager to speak on it. He was playing of course.

Drackice dove in, sinking up to his eyes in thought. He pleadingly spoke to Tsin, looking for advice on what he should have done versus what he did do. And what to do when he returned, maybe Tsin had an answer to some of his madness?

"Yeah so, she did mention another guy, a shadow elf, named... Grath?" Drackice answered, thinking slowly on, it spitting the sentence out in fragments.

"Of course she did," Tsin answered, laughing.

"What does that mean?" Drackice questioned.

"It means, old friend, that the one she was with isn't the one. If he was, there wouldn't have ever been a second name."

"She claimed it to be a mistake."

"Of course she did. You didn't think she would openly admit to being a lying, cheating whore, did you?"

"Well, no but—" Drackice was cut off.

"She still looks but subconsciously feels obligated to the one she's spent all the time with."

"So what do I do?"

"You become the one she spends the most time with. Aren't you a legendary tactician?" he asked, laughing.

Drackice laughed too. Tsin was making an unbearable ordeal not so bad. He didn't mind taking watch with the Wilden this time. The last time not so much, the last time he wanted to strangle the young elf.

The two continued the conversation and the deeper it went, the further Drackice's mind got from the task at hand. Luckily, nothing came to try them before the final hour was up. And before long, they were all up and ready, prepared for the day's trials.

"Did I miss anything?" Draeden asked with water dripping from his eyes.

"Are you crying?" Slate asked, laughing.

"I am an elemental being. Water drips from my eyes and mouth and ears from time to time," he answered.

"Eyes on the prize," Rakka added, greedily smiling and taking the lead.

The little goblin lit a torch and took the lead. Westlyn followed closely behind. He didn't like the savage barbarian but he was good at what he did and fantastic at this job. There were virtually no possible outcomes of innocent casualties in the near future.

One by one they fell in. Keres and Tsin took closely to each other. Draeden stayed in the middle. Shanks held close to him. Drackice kept himself toward the front but still behind Rakka and Westlyn. This time, with Rakka and Westlyn in the front, Slate took the rear.

And thus, the remaining eight began their descent once again deep into the lower depths of the Mystic Mountains' internal crevices. The opening was barely wide enough for two to walk abreast. It was more like one then another followed closely behind to either the left or the right of the one in front. The passageway narrowed even more as it continued down deeper into the mountains.

The crew heard a clanging of metals back and forth and the bickering of many creatures rushing at them from the deep dark below. The forty-five degree slant suddenly became something the crew didn't feel so safe on. Out of nowhere, they charged. They ranged from two and a half to four feet tall. Their hides were scaly reddish and hairless. Not one of them weighed more than forty pounds. Curiously, several of them had pieces of chain armor covering most of their bodies. Before their reptilian heads and glowing eyes came into sight of the team, the smell of stagnant water and damp dogs hit their nostrils.

"Kobolds!" Rakka screamed.

"He's right!" Westlyn seconded.

"Foolish cretins," Draeden bitched.

Rakka readied his two-handed blade and Westlyn's hammer was more than ready to go. Lightning ripped from throughout the walls, bouncing off one piece of metal to the next. Each time a bolt struck metal, it burst into a cloud of smoke. The first wave of kobolds immediately became smothered in the smoky clouds of Draeden. When the clouds dissipated, their weapons were downed and either sheathed or altogether dropped. Draeden smiled. The kobolds walked peacefully past them.

"Curse of crumbling conviction compels you all," said the Genasi as powerfully as he could.

The kobolds suddenly looked confused and lost. They weren't threatening at all anymore. Draeden laughed. Rakka turned back to look at the wizard, infuriated. He quickly explained why the creatures needed to be killed rather than stopped.

"We can't just leave things behind us," the goblin barbarian explained.

"Now their defenses are down. It will be easier to manipulate them. Just hold a moment," Draeden replied.

Draeden raised his hands while the others encircled around him. Another spell slung by the Genasi and suddenly, golden sparkles and mist wrapped around all of their heads like a fairy weaving in and out all around them, leaving behind sparkling dust.

"They're on our side now," Draeden explained to Rakka.

"I don't trust your magic, wizard," the goblin barked back.

Rakka took one slow step after another, turning his focus from Draeden and the others to the dumbfounded and now befriended kobolds of the tunnel. He worked his way through them in the narrow tunnel way.

"Rakka, don't," Keres pleaded.

"Rakka please," Shanks seconded, hoping Rakka's own fury wouldn't get the better of him.

Rakka didn't do anything. He just passed through them as he was supposed to, taking the lead in order to make sure it was safe for the rest of them. Slowly but surely and one by one, the other seven followed his lead.

"I still don't like leaving these bastards behind us," he said, not being so gentle while pushing through them.

"Relax king of the barbarians. It will prove to be useful. Wizards are intelligent beings. Genasi are intelligent beings. I cannot see a Genasi wizard making foolish decisions too often," Drackice said, trying to calm the goblin.

Shortly after the first wave was passed, another wave of kobolds came at them and just like before, Draeden made quick work of them, utilizing the very same two spells in the same order. And once again, they walked through every single one of them without a sound. Not the swinging of one weapon was needed to bypass the second wave of kobolds. And now they were deep within the veins of the Mystic Mountains.

The down-slanted hallway finally evened out and opened up, not by much but at least two could walk abreast now. Rakka and Westlyn kept the front followed closely by Slate and Draeden. Keres and Drackice covered them with Tsin taking up the rear. It wasn't a true strategic marching order. That was just how it landed when the tunnel finally opened up.

The tunnel finally opened to a massive cavern. The ceiling of the place was nearly forty feet up. All kinds of openings from smaller tunnels to larger caves opened up as options for the eight.

The kobolds were friendly and behind them now, thanks to Draeden. The pitch darkness first bore silhouettes. Outlines of things coming soon became a throng of enemies they did not want to see. Seven-foot tall, feral goblin-like creatures emerged from nearly every hole in the giant cavern, minus the crack that stretched across the ground. They had wedge-shaped ears and greenish white eyes with hairy bodies that looked to be infected with dog mange. Their hides were mostly yellowish but ranged all the way over to a thick brick red.

Green-skinned trolls matching the feral goblins in height emerged from behind them, though not nearly as many in number, the trolls invoked a fear the eight had never felt before. Drackice counted four to be exact. There were at least twenty-five of the other creatures.

Rakka yelled out, "Hobgoblin." Most of the eight already knew what they were anyway.

The trolls didn't carry any weapons. The hobgoblins' weapons and armor were old and rattled. Most were either broken or damaged in one way or another. Their claws weren't long enough to use as weapons but their large swords and mauls would work just fine. Broken armor and busted weapons, this at least gave the team the edge in the gear department but numbers were still not on their side.

One of the hobgoblin's fur wasn't yellow or copper, not even the in-between color; it was truly blue. None of the eight had ever seen or even heard of a blue-furred hobgoblin before. Something about the spiked-maul-wielding creature infuriated Rakka. He started to charge. A roar coming from the largest cave, where only a troll had emerged from previously stopped him in his tracks.

The smell of stale air was hard to swallow. The thick taste of clay was on their lips. Rakka was undisturbed by it. The unified smell of so many under dwellers mixed with the natural smells of under earth did a number on them all, except for Rakka and Draeden. Draeden was an elemental-based mortal. It partially affected him, but the natural smells of the underground did nothing to him.

Slate noticed clear liquids stuck and splattered all over the walls of the underground cavity. He couldn't make out what the liquid was or why it was there. He figured the monsters at hand were far more dangerous and needed to be dealt with first either way.

Something looking like a ten-foot-tall human emerged from behind the troll of the tallest cave opening. Only this human looked aboriginal and wore furs around its pelvic area. Its body was abnormally wide, even for its size. It had two heads, both full of nappy black hair. Both of its hands held giant spiked maces made purely of rock, with only the spikes being different. The spikes of the large maces were made of some kind of animal bone.

Its roar even scared the others that came from the cracks and holes of the cavity. The crack was dead center of where their tunnel stopped. Slate looked down. The crack in the ground of the cavity floor looked deep.

Jagged side edges and moist clay mostly made up the inside mouth of the crack.

"What in the name of the dead gods do we do now?" Keres asked, terrified.

Shanks laughed, perching his bow with four arrows. He was really gifted and talented with that bow. Drackice peeled a short bow himself. The two-headed subterranean giant even stopped Rakka. Hobgoblins, four trolls, and a two headed giant, this was not going to be a good day. Behind them, they still had the kobolds. They were surrounded on all sides and not by things easily taken down.

"How long will your magic hold off the kobolds?" Drackice asked, keeping a vigilant eye on everything around them.

"Long enough. Why, with all of this you're concerned with the kobolds?" Draeden asked.

Drackice didn't reply. There was no time. They needed an out immediately. Drackice looked down at the crack. At first, it scared him. Now, he savored the fact that it was there. The crack was going to be their saving grace. Drackice's eyes went back and forth looking at both sides. On the left side, a two-headed giant, three trolls, and just a few of the hobgoblins. On the right side, the majority of the hobgoblins held strong, including the blue-furred one. One of the trolls stood to the right side as well.

"Move move move! To the right, go... go... go...!" Drackice yelled, pushing his people to avoid the small opening where the crack began at the tip of the tunnel just before it opened up to form the large cavity.

It was easy to see what he was aiming to do. The team charged in. Now, with his footing and intestinal fortitude restored, Rakka left the team, charging straight for the blue-furred hobgoblin. The others couldn't figure it out. They just thought it was a racial disagreement. There was no way Rakka'd seen this creature before, was there? Westlyn wanted to stay up with him but he knew he was hurling himself wildly into danger. The others would need him. Then again, so would Rakka.

"Keep Westlyn alive! He's going to get us to that damned arcanist!" Shanks screamed, firing off all four of those arrows into hobgoblins on the left side.

"What's the game plan?" Keres asked, running as fast as she could.

Westlyn turned and looked at her. He took a second and looked back toward the front. He kept his pace up and then pointed to one of the smaller tunnels on the far side of the cavity, telling them all where to head. His finger pointed toward the left side of the right half of the cavern. The tunnel he chose ran very close to the crack in the center of the cavity.

Rakka charged toward the far right side of the cavern. The blue hobgoblin stood close to the wall of the underground cavern and Rakka was headed straight for him. Drackice gave Rakka the order to return to position with the team but he refused it. He kept going, as if he didn't even hear it.

Rakka drew first blood. He swung his two-handed blade, gashing open the upper torso of one hobgoblin that overshot his attack on him first. Maces and swords cut into the goblin's flesh. The other seven pushed toward the tunnel. They even bypassed the lone troll of the right side. He wouldn't make it to them in time and he was far too big to chase them into the smaller tunnel.

One after another, they dove into the tunnel. Shanks pulled arrow after arrow, firing between three and six every time he pulled his bowstring back. He was the first to get to the tunnel after Westlyn. Westlyn didn't want to enter with everyone not in before him. Shanks demanded it. Westlyn waited until at least Keres was safe.

Shanks pulled flasks of oil and set them neatly on the ground while his people rushed to the tunnel. He dipped every arrow before firing it. He focused at least seven or eight on the troll alone. The crack was too wide on the far side of the cavity. The hobgoblins and trolls on the opposing side had to run all the way from where they stood to where the team originally entered the cavern to make it to the other side. The three trolls and the giant jumped, hoping to clear the crack.

Two trolls fell. One made it easy. The two-head giant nearly lost it but one of its maces stuck in the ledge. It hung there for a second before the other troll and hobgoblins assisted him in making it back to his feet. Thankfully, it lost one of its weapons in the attempt.

When the hobgoblins got close with the troll that originated on that side right behind them, Shanks grabbed the flasks and hurled them into the air, yelling for the wizard to act on his actions. Draeden just recently entered the tunnel. He mumbled a few words and the flasks of oil suddenly combusted.

Fire worked its way through the air of the cavern. It spilled everywhere. Burning oil, liquid fire landed upon several of the creatures that already had oil-dipped arrows in them. The original troll caught fire and screeched in pain. The remaining troll darted for a nearby cave entrance, hoping to hide and avoid the fiery pains caused by the humanoid invaders.

With a half dozen hobgoblins lying either slain or severely wounded, Rakka made it to the blue-furred oddity. His body carried twice the number of lacerations of the six he'd dropped on his way to the target. One particular wound started just below his armpit and sliced down, opening his entire insides up, laying his flesh wide open.

Rakka cut through those six that made it to him first like he was an invincible war machine immune to the steel they threatened him with. Now, he was near death. Drackice yelled something violently passionate at the goblin barbarian and suddenly, he began to fight more fiercely than he did before.

"We can't leave him!" Slate said.

"We have to save him!" Westlyn declared.

"He's lost. He should have listened!" Drackice said, signaling for everyone to push deeper into the tunnel.

Shanks was the last one in after Drackice made the war cry to him. He continued to fire his arrows as the fire continued to burn and the screaming pains of dead and dying creatures continued to blister the air. The tunnel was small, barely four feet tall and equally as wide. The monstrous creatures would certainly have a hard time getting through this small tunnel.

Tsin tried to crawl through them. He wanted to get out and save Rakka. The others tried to stop him but he was too dexterous and slippery for them. He and Shanks shared a sight with Westlyn that the others would only hear. Tsin was completely out of the tunnel and engaged with nearby hobgoblins when it happened. The large cavernous opening lit up more than it should have for a fireball, even one fueled with oil. Tsin looked at Rakka. Rakka was burned and charred. The insides where his skin lay open were blackened. He wasn't bleeding from it and it didn't look like it'd been cauterized with fire.

The troll that caught fire was running around like a chicken with his head cut off. Rakka just killed the last of the six he slew on his way to blue fur. Missiles fired out from the hobgoblins eyes. There were five of them, leaving behind white streaks of raw magic. They missed Rakka and went straight into the dying troll. Thanks to Shanks' intellect, that troll wouldn't cause any of them any grief, Tsin initially thought.

When the last missile struck the aura of fire emanating from the troll, the troll exploded instantly. Prismatic colors shot out in every direction.

Hobgoblins were hit. Some vanished. Some died instantly. And some took horrific poundings from the prismatic powers. Each one that died set off additional combusting spells.

"Draeden get up here quick!" Tsin yelled.

Draeden crawled back to see the fiasco. He couldn't believe his eyes. Rakka was in the middle of it. They wanted to help him but there was just no saving the lad. He was in the middle of a magical shit storm. Every time one of the creatures fell, another spell or two went off and none in the area were safe.

One of the more powerful and more experienced hobgoblins fell and two magical walls erupted. One was nearly invisible to the naked eye. It separated Rakka and blue fur from everything else. It literally enveloped them.

"Wall of force?" Draeden muttered, questioning to himself.

The next one blocked the very same tunnel they were in. It was cold and solid, made of pure ice and snow. Draeden quickly informed them that it was a wall of ice. The others scurried and dug at the wall, trying to get Tsin back. Keres screamed and prayed, begging the others to get her man back.

Draeden froze in fear. He didn't know what to do. Basic things were firing off arcane powers upon dying. What did he get himself into? This couldn't be normal or expected. The team bickered at what to do. One of their allies was either dead or soon to be and the other was still locked out there with the remaining cretins still alive.

They could hear more spells going off as they argued but the giant sheet of ice blocking their tunnel from the cavernous area where both Tsin and Rakka still were blocked them from seeing what was going on. Keres yelled out something in a language queer to them all. It sounded ancient and archaic.

The ice melted and withered down but a vaporous wall of frigid air remained. A large hole opened up in the wall of ice but it wasn't completely gone. She fought to get out there. Westlyn fought for her to stay back. Westlyn took the charge of bringing their allies back.

"He's my husband!" she demanded, trying to get past Westlyn.

Westlyn kicked her back and took her back to the cavern, standing strong and tall with his hammer readied in hand. Tsin was going back and forth, ducking under the wildly and fiercely swinging giant. Every time he swung, he left another hole in the ground where Tsin was standing just before he connected. Tsin looked too fast for him.

Westlyn looked over to Rakka. Somehow, he was still standing. Blue fur looked hurt and charred from the magical debris too. Rakka was on his last leg, fighting with everything he had. Strike for strike, they clanged swords. Rakka couldn't break his defense, nor could the blue-furred creature break Rakka's.

The grotto was burned and ravaged by the multitude of spells that went off by the dying hobgoblins and trolls. It could have been a lot worse. Few hobgoblins remained. None looked able to continue fighting, none except blue fur.

Tsin fought against the two-headed giant alone. It swung its mace with its left hand and tried to pound him with its right. He was quick and maneuvered through and around the giant effortlessly. Westlyn saw the fight as too dangerous to continue. Rakka was more hurt. Tsin wasn't bad off at all. He didn't even look like he'd been hit.

Rakka looked like he'd make it. He looked like he had blue fur taken care of. Tsin was surviving against the two-headed giant but wasn't doing anything to see it fall. Westlyn charged toward Rakka first. Once he was close enough, he channeled his healing powers through his hand, sending a charge of life back inside the goblin.

Wounds stopped bleeding. Flesh mended. A new thin layer of skin and light fur started its formation over the disgusting wound on the left side of Rakka's ribcage. The surge of life only made Rakka fight more fiercely.

Westlyn didn't stick around to see it. He turned his sights to Tsin and the ettin. His peripheral said the others were pouring out of the tunnel. He didn't see Draeden. He could hear Draeden yelling for them all to get back in.

The final troll pulled itself from its hiding position. Tsin was on its mind. They were all out of ideas and the spells going off upon each creature's death actually helped them more than hurt them. Now there was no fodder to be killed in hopes that their deaths would do further damage to their living enemies.

The troll walked slowly, grunting angrily at the food still fighting against its allies. Its long arms extended down but he opened them up, preparing for what was to come. It opened and closed its fists, pumping them. This gave the rightful blood flow to its arms and hands so when it came to tearing its food apart, it would be more than ready.

Rakka finally figured out how to make headway against the creature. Reckless abandon would be his only chance. Rakka swung with everything he had, leaving himself open for counters. At first blue fur just defended lightly and bounced away from him. After the third attempt, blue fur's weapon was knocked from his hands and tossed away.

Rakka swung for the high heavens and low hells with every horizontal hurl of his blade. Blue fur tried to grab another blade from a downed ally of his. Rakka wouldn't have it. His previous swing left him unbalanced. He took a second step forward to regain his footing. That one step gave blue fur the opening he needed to aggressively move against him.

He leaped up at Rakka, picking him up from under his swinging arms. Rakka's arms were fully extended and unable to retract the weapon. Like blue fur's weapon before, his weapon dropped. Rakka's body was picked up as blue fur yelled and charged toward the giant crack in the ground.

Tsin couldn't help but notice his friend in trouble. The second he took his eye off of the ettin, it got him. A hammered fist came crashing down atop him. One shot, one win. Tsin took it straight on the head, full force. His body fell to the ground. In one successful attempt, the ettin felled the Wilden.

"Tsin!" Keres cried.

She spoke in that ancient tongue of hers again ending with the words "La Ta Shing." The Blue furred hobgoblin stopped in place. He was only a few feet from the edge of the crevice. Rakka fell from his grasp. He fell hard to the ground, onto the flat of his back. A brief sigh of pain and relief almost came from the severely wounded goblin. His adrenaline fell and slowed. He still breathed heavily. He was beaten.

Westlyn slammed his hammer onto the ettin's foot seconds after it smashed Tsin to the ground. It roared maniacally. Westlyn spun, missing a dual strike from the creature, planting his hammer now in the back of the same knee of the leg where he'd smashed its foot.

The creature stumbled, dropping the same knee to the ground to comfort it. Westlyn reworked his grip and spun back the opposite direction. He used each successful strike to carry his momentum back and forth. This time, his holy hammer slammed into the side of the ettin's face. "Oooooof" a painful sound leaked out from its mouth. It fell to its back just as Rakka did.

Westlyn didn't stay to finish it. He let go of the hammer with one hand grabbing Tsin, knowing he would have to be dragged. Westlyn started back toward the tunnel with Keres using what few flame- and fire-based spells she had to slow and hinder the troll as best she could. It was still in pursuit.

Slate rushed off and grabbed the beaten Rakka. Blue fur made sounds and grunts, telling those around him he wasn't happy and in fact, very angry. He wanted to finish the goblin but their feud would last yet another day.

All of them were in the tunnel. The troll's lengthy arms penetrated it. Its appendages and body were too long and big to enter it. Draeden used his arcane powers to once again thwart the aggression. He took the dirt out from under the troll dropping the nearly nine-foot creature into the hard clay all the way up to its neck.

Draeden cancelled the spell almost as fast as he cast it. The troll found itself neck deep it hard clay and unable to move. There was just too much weight in hard clay and wet dirt to be moved. Slate bellowed out a calling sound. Ghostly panthers and a floating school of similar piranhas popped into existence. The school of ghostly fish swarmed the creature to a point that not even Slate could see it. The two ghostly panthers were just as vicious in their attacks against the troll's head.

The others kept moving. Draeden forced them to crawl past him. He watched until Slate's ethereal creatures finished off every piece of visible flesh on the creature. Before they vanished, even parts of its skull were missing. When he was satisfied, Draeden turned back to start heading off with the team. The troll's skull caught his attention yet again. It began regrowing skin at a rapid rate. The skull mended itself almost as quickly as Slate's spirits devoured it.

It was coming back. Trolls regenerated, even back from the dead. From behind, Keres hurled a series of fiery combustions at it. The already dead troll had nearly regenerated back to health, but her flame-based spells stopped its regeneration almost instantly.

"Now let's move," Keres declared.

She was right, Draeden thought. The eight were on the move in the narrow four-foot by four-foot tunnel, leaving only the blue furred hobgoblin behind as a living enemy. They reassured each other verbally to keep moving. And they kept moving.

The tunnel finally came to an end, opening up to another giant cavity even deeper than the first one. It was nearly a fifteen-foot drop to the bottom. This cavernous opening was too wide, too long, and too deep. Unlike the other one where Westlyn's innate abilities guided them through toward the direction of their target, only a single cave-like entrance existed from what they all could see.

Keres spent most of her remaining healing powers on Rakka and Tsin. Drackice reminded her not to be biased and that Rakka needed it much more than Tsin did. Tsin was still very hurt. They were all alive.

Rakka didn't awaken until they were at the end of the tunnel. He cried, wailing in pain from the damage dealt to him, in particular the ribcage gash. It was healed but not fully and in its condition would probably still put anything or anyone through excruciating pain.

Tsin was up but dizzy. His body and bones were rattled but Keres kept them in place and going. He was going to make it. And he was up. It was his turn to once again perform for the group. He needed to climb down the side carefully and investigate the ground level with Shanks looking over him with arrows and Draeden looking over him with spells.

"You okay, Tsin, you got this?" Drackice asked with some understanding conviction. His every word and body movement projected his inner faith for the Wilden. It was a subconscious attack to make Tsin want to agree and admit to being fine and up for the task at hand.

Tsin nodded. His body was rattled but his spirit wasn't. And it was he who gave the phrase most expected from someone like Drackice. Tsin took this mission because his wife believed in it. Secretly, his wife believed in the Free Armies and the Black family probably more than them all. She also believed in Tsin. And they'd been together for a long time but Tsin was still like a little boy, always trying to impress her.

"With every heroic tale, there's a tragedy waiting to be told," Tsin said, starting down the side of the wall. "I guess we're that tragedy."

The wall was slippery and made for a difficult time grabbing and setting himself. He dropped the last six feet. It was just easier. The wet clay smeared all over his hands and breeches. It wasn't too big of a deal; he was already dirty.

He looked up to see Shanks and Draeden in place should anything go wrong. Reconnaissance was his duty. He needed to keep a lookout for his surroundings but thankfully he had the archer and the arcane caster to lookout for him. The passed opening was large and flat without a giant crack down the center as an obstacle. This one looked like it was molded out of an underwater stream of powerfully flowing water, and a lot of it.

The ground rose and fell, up and down. It was as hilly as the Bone Marches. There was a place he never wanted to see again. The walls were smooth but not flat. All of it was pure hard clay, dark and wet. The wavy walls, ground, and ceiling made moving over and through the deep underground cavity very difficult.

Tsin crawled on all fours very carefully. Nothing seemed manmade. It was all very natural and all too smooth. To his eyes, nothing had walked through this cavern for a very long time. Nothing seemed to have touched this clay in months.

"It's clear?" Tsin yelled, confused. He wasn't even sure if he believed what he was saying. He kept crawling up and down the clay hills, looking back every so often to assure himself his back was covered. From the looks of it, there was only one way to go, the deep cave entrance on the opposite side from where their tunnel ended.

After he and the others were satisfied, they took to the rolling clay hills of the deep cavern. One by one, they went down. Luckily, it wasn't too far of a climb and no one hurt themselves getting down there. It was hard to get to the other side of the newest cavern in their path on the way to Bahaus but finally they all made it.

The next entrance was a little larger. The mouth to this cave was wider and the throat the crew would have to walk into was also wider. Westlyn paused. He looked back to Keres first. Tsin and Rakka stayed back. They both needed help getting across. Rakka shook his head. He was still hurting and fatigued, but he knew something was wrong with the cave.

Westlyn turned back away from Keres and looked down into the throat of the cave. He paused and squatted down to further look into the mouth of the cave. "I know we're on the right path. This isn't going to lead us where we need to go."

"Where is it we need to go?" Rakka asked from the back, still overfilled with intense pain.

"I—" Westlyn's words were cut short by Keres'. She stated her very essence could sense Bahaus. She silently cast divination spells, some of the most potent from the very sphere, and they told her the open cave would lead to death, not Bahaus.

"I thought it was the holy one that sensed him? I thought it was Westlyn who brought us closer to him, day by day?" Rakka asked, pointing his weapon at the holy knight.

"I am a priestess, Rakka. My divination powers are some of my most powerful. There are times I can see the future, look to the past, and even alter the immediate reality. I'm merely saying I feel that cave is a deathtrap." It took a second but Keres' explanation to Rakka was enough to satisfy him.

Rakka shook off the pain and injuries. He signaled for Drackice to mend him further. The team leader did as he was asked. Drackice was capable of mending wounds almost as well as a priest or priestess but not quite.

Rakka started a deep search through the smooth clay. Several feet from the left of the cave entrance, Rakka stopped. His hands rapidly began touching different areas of the wall and floor. He stopped and took a step back, looking straight at Drackice and smiling evilly. "Your scout missed something."

"That's a wall goblin," Drackice replied, getting angry.

"Something moved through it and not too long ago," the natural cave dweller explained.

"It's solid," Tsin explained, trying to defend his own abilities for missing a possible secret passage.

"Not your fault, Wilden," the goblin said.

"I don't get it," Slate said.

"Neither do I," Keres seconded.

The goblin had enough of the talking and so did Tsin. He was still hurting a great deal and Drackice and Keres' healing powers were enough to stop the body from dying but not enough to stop the body from hurting. Every nerve ending was still filled with intense pain from the clobbering he took at the hands of the ettin.

Rakka pieced away the wall using his fingers to find softer areas in the clay. It took him a second to find them but he did. Once he started, he began shoveling the clay with his hands at a rapid rate. His fingernails bled from the clay being forced underneath them. His body and fur became covered in it all. The thick clay walls and ground were very hard. In just seconds, Rakka made an indention on the wall Draeden's fiery magic against an arcane-vulnerable target would have had trouble rivaling.

"What in the—" Drackice just stopped. No one cut him off. He just didn't know what to say.

"It was an umber hulk," Rakka explained.

"What is that?" Drackice questioned.

"Subterranean…" Tsin waved off the explanation.

"Do you know what an umber hulk is Tsin?" the goblin asked.

Tsin and Rakka immediately got into it. Westlyn yelled for the two to quiet down. They were both hurt and tired. They didn't really have the strength or the desire to continue fighting with each other or Westlyn. In a way, they were happy the holy knight intervened.

"Draeden, use your magic and get us through that soft clay. You have something that'll work?" he asked.

"I have just the thing," he replied with a smirk.

"Good, let's move."

Something about the deva paladin was just strong. Everything about him was just truly powerful. His very presence could be intimidating to the wrong people or crowd. Even to his own allies when he spoke, they stopped and listened.

Chapter 69

It was late in the evening when the brothers regrouped at Falling River's Temple. The holy sanctuary was closed for the day. It was in the twilight of the evening. Dauge couldn't fetch the right price for the painting but Legion got two rooms big enough for two each at the Dreamy Cauldron. The relatively new inn was small but growing. It was trying to expand and would do anything to win potential customers away from its competitors.

Legion secured each room for about a gold piece a week and he paid for two weeks stay on each room. Legion stashed their goods and belongings, hiding them well in one of the rooms. He locked both rooms and left the small inn in hopes of quickly reuniting with his brother.

Legion and Dauge talked about Pitt and contemplated where the barbarian could be. They agreed to give it a couple of days before leaving. Dauge openly admitted to having second thoughts on selling the painting. It could be worth a mint but it was just one those things that was irreplaceable.

On the way from Falling Rivers Temple to the Dreamy Cauldron, the cool breeze of a Thoxen night soothed the two brothers. Through it all, they were still together. They talked of Dash and his insane desires to build magnificent teams on heroic deeds and loyalty. He was willing to sell out damn near anyone for the heroic praises of the deeds. He was a peculiar fellow.

On this particular night, Blackstone was still very busy. It wasn't too late yet and the tailors were still sewing and the smiths still smithing. The smell of hot iron and freshly baked bread caught the two brothers' noses.

"Baking bread at this hour?" Legion wondered aloud.

"Someone out there's always hungry," Dauge answered slyly.

"Ahh, I can smell what you're stepping in," Legion replied.

The walk was an easy one. Between the two of them, there wasn't a single weapon, piece of armor, or anything remotely heavy. Legion kept a little coin on him, as did Dauge, but nothing overwhelmingly heavy. They'd been traveling for quite awhile. They lived for over a month, traveling every day fully encumbered.

"It's not like Pitt to not tell us where he planned to go. I just don't get it," Dauge said.

"Sometimes people just move, I guess," Legion responded.

"We should move. We need to rest and then get back to Stannor in Vorrellon as quickly as possible. Once we get the gold to Stannor and give word from our eyewitness accounts that Azra Goetia is still very much alive, we will have accomplished our mission," Dauge said to remind Legion of what still lay ahead but also to keep himself in check on what step to take next to fulfill their obligation.

"There we are," Legion said, pointing.

They'd walked and talked through the night and now were at the steps of Legion's chosen inn, the Dreamy Cauldron. Just as expected, it had a simple front porch, a few windows and wooden rocking chairs and that was about it. It didn't look like much at all. The front porch's wooden platform was kind of old and busted looking but in time with a little work and coin, it could be fixed up to look nice.

The roof overlapped the porch and the old cantina-styled inn exuded a smell that reminded the boys of home and their mother's cooking. Legion hadn't seen Dauge's face light up like that since they were children.

"Smells like beef tips and casserole," Dauge said.

Legion appreciated the Dreamy Cauldron even more now. His brother was a dark person and not much got the boy to smile anymore. And with every passing year, the things he liked that could make him smile dwindled even more.

The inn was still new enough to where it appreciated every single customer. One large hulking half orc posed as the security while two middle-aged human girls served the entire downstairs den hot beef-tip soup and bread.

The brothers took a place near the window and found themselves reconnecting. Legion even brought up the peculiar change in Dauge. Dauge explained that he knew he was different. He was always different.

Inside, something told him he was always just a different kind of person. The food and smell made them think back to their times growing up in the Republic of New Magic.

"Dash is still hurt but where could Pitt have gone to? It's not like him to disappear and not tell us where he's going."

Dauge agreed. To Dauge, it wasn't his concern. If Pitt wanted to leave, he could leave. Their mission was to get the money back to Lord Stannor and Vorrellon. It was a lot of money and they technically failed their quest. They still had the painting, however. It was their father, their true father Taj, that blessed them with a hint of success. It was his actions with the lizards that allowed them to be successful. The lizards gave them the money they needed to return to Stannor successfully.

"Pitt's a good man. If he wants to leave, he can leave. We've got enough to deal with. We will get what's coming to us from Stannor. We will have recognition in Thox for later opportunities. As for now, I just want to finish this and go home."

"I couldn't agree more," Legion said, laughing.

He blew on a hot spoonful of stew and beef tips. Dauge ate almost with precision and finesse. Legion dipped his bread deep into his bowl and chased it all down with heavy pints of ale and wine. He was relieved to be home and still alive.

"What were we thinking? Why did we ever agree to go search for the mythical city of devils, Azra Goetia?" Dauge asked, laughing.

"I don't know but we're still here and we never have to go back."

"Amen to that," Dauge seconded. "I just want to go home."

"Me too." Legion said.

"We're going to be fine. We just need to get this money to Vorrellon and into Stannor's hands. From there, we can do whatever we wish. We'll have accomplishments done here in Thox and we can return to Eternis with our heads held high."

"Accomplishments and recognition mean nothing to me. I gave him my word and that's what matters, big brother. I want to go to Eternis and forget all about Thox and the Republic of New Magic. Thox wasn't a bad stay but its just not home. I just want to go home. We've been fighting all our lives."

"I miss our other siblings."

"As do I, Legion. Let's go home," Dauge said.

The conversation continued and the boys ate more than their fill of the beef tips and stew before retiring for the night. Everything was as it was supposed to be. Legion showed Dauge where he hid everything in the rooms before leaving. It wasn't long before the brothers were fast asleep.

The next morning, Dash was released. With his natural charisma and talents, it didn't take long for the half-eladrin to find the brothers. He was already waiting for them at one of the few tables offered by the Dreamy Cauldron's den area.

Dauge was less pleased to see him than Legion but he was there and dressed and ready to go. The brothers had their things packed and ready. They planned to pick up a few horses and head to Vorrellon as quickly as possible.

"Dash," Legion said, dropping his sack from his shoulder to the ground.

He knew seeing Dash would mean their leaving would have to be postponed, at least for a bit. Dash sat closer to the center of the smaller building, away from the windows sipping his hot coffee. Dash smiled and waved the two over to have a seat. The brothers hesitantly obliged.

"How are you feeling?" Dauge asked. "Are you still sick at all?"

"I feel fine. The temple did a number on me. I should be good to move quickly," he answered.

"How'd you find us so easily, so quickly? Not that we were hiding, but still," Legion asked.

"It's kind of my talent, Legion," he replied.

"Where do we go from here then? Have you seen Pitt?" Legion asked.

That particular questioned pissed off Dauge just a little. He took his seat last, glaring at Legion. What a stupid question to ask. He knew where they were going next. They were going to head to a nearby stable, pick up some horses and ride to Vorrellon.

"What do you mean, where do we go from here, Legion? We head to the stables, get some horses, and get moving," Dauge snarled.

"Was I going to be brought into this conversation or even asked of my opinion?" Dash questioned.

"No, we're in Thox. We have the money. We have to get it back to Stannor to complete this quest. What other possible viable option is there?" Dauge asked.

Not two minutes after being reunited, Dash and Dauge were already at odds again. Legion laughed, hearing the two bicker back and forth. It was relatively funny even if it wasn't beneficial.

"Perhaps you're right Dauge. I just thought it would have been nice to have my opinion voiced and heard by the guys I consider my team," Dash replied.

His cunning words were meant to stop the Genasi with human blood. They pushed to no avail.

Dauge never missed a beat coming back with sly words of his own. "I assumed your decision would be the best one, to move to Vorrellon to get to Stannor."

Dash just laughed, "Well played," he said still, laughing.

The three spoke of Pitt and where he could have possibly gone to. Dash admitted he'd heard something about a large goliath heading west out of Blackstone. The goliath was said to be looking for something and was joined by a small company of people. The people of Blackstone knew Pitt. He was a gladiatorial champion. It had to be Pitt. How could he just leave and not say anything?

"Whether it's Pitt or not is not important. He shouldn't have just left. We must move to Vorrellon at once. From there, we can all part ways and do as we wish," Dauge ordered.

"Part ways?" Legion asked.

Dauge found Legion's question quite annoying. Without having to spell it out for him, Dauge made every distinct move he could to make clear that fact he wanted to part ways with the half-eladrin. Legion shook his head, seeing the look on Dauge's face. The genasi's face spelled everything out, piece by piece.

"You're right Dauge. We must complete our task," said the eladrin.

Dash wasn't acting like himself. Actually, he was, but it just didn't seem like it. The reason being, everything was already laid out for them to do. There wasn't much else for him to touch on. Dauge dug mentally, looking for some type of ulterior motive for his non-disagreeing act. There wasn't one. Dash was still Dash. He was just a little behind and groggy but he knew what had to be done and what came first, and to Dash, the mission objective was first.

It came first to Dash but for all the wrong reasons. Getting this done for Lord Stannor would help his name ascend through the ranks of the Thoxen people. Even Dash knew his desire to have that name he yearned for so badly would eventually get him or someone else killed.

The three actually stayed another few days before leaving out of Blackstone to the east en route to Vorrellon. Dash made a move that shocked even the other two. He bought them all three places on a caravan haul that was heading toward Vorrellon. It wasn't going directly to the city but close enough to where they could get off and make the final half-day's trek on their own.

They had to wait until the caravan was leaving before they could head out, of course. There were four large carriages filled with workers and crates filled with different types of materials. This way, it would take them a lot longer to get to Vorrellon but it would be a more comfortable journey, as well as safe. This way, they would have a dozen Thoxen guards protecting them as well as all others aboard the caravan.

It took almost two weeks for the caravan to reach the point where Dash, Dauge, and Legion were going to take off from. On Thoxen roads, in Thoxen soil, the caravan and escort was for the most part, safe.

It was a hot mid-afternoon in the month of Krozus when the escorted caravan passed by their desired spot. Dash motioned and hollered at the conductor, and upon request he pulled to a stop, allowing the three to get out.

There wasn't much talk about Pitt after they left Blackstone. What was left to say? He deserted them without even a hint as to why or where he was going. Dash actually took it the hardest. Then again, he was the man who spent coin and effort on the man. He handpicked Pitt and helped purchase his freedom.

With the hot sun beaming down over the beautiful Thoxen fields and hills of enriched grass, and the light Thoxen winds making the day almost perfect, the three set their eyes on Vorrellon's highest buildings and structures from a good distance away.

"Even from here, it looks like it's grown since we've been away," Dash said, smiling. He walked a little ahead of the group, hiking to the top of a nearby hill. The fields were beautiful. The sky was purely blue with not a cloud in sight. The sun was shining magnificently in this month of transitioning weather patterns.

"It's a beautiful day, Dash," Legion said.

"We need to take advantage of what the faiths have touched us with. We must move and make it by nightfall," Dauge said, ruining the moment of comfort with his cold orders and hard taste of reality.

"Relax brother. We're in the realm of Thox. We're safe here," Legion replied.

"If we're safe here, then why did the caravan need an escort?" Dauge asked.

"Touché brother," he said softly, speaking just aloud but not directly to his brother. He waited for a moment and then said it again.

"Come," Dash said, excited to see the city not too terribly far away.

They made it to Vorrellon much quicker than they anticipated. With the weather so perfect and everything just landing right for them, they were able to travel at a much harder pace, putting them in Vorrellon just a few hours before nightfall.

And just as they expected from the distance, the city had come a long ways since they'd seen it last. Leaps and bounds were done and completed by ways of the city, since they last laid eyes on it. It was still a small and growing town but more structures were up and more people were out and moving and working.

They passed the troupe of guards near the entryway to the city with no issue. The guards did ask them to peace-bind their weapons as was a growing custom in Thox. The three obliged. Dash immediately wanted to find Lord Stannor. Dauge reminded him that it was still pretty late in the day and the first thing the next morning was probably a much better move. Legion however had other motives.

He'd been thinking about returning to Vorrellon since the day he left. He thought of returning victorious and Kattya being happy and excited to see him. He couldn't wait to see the little beauty. Not a day had gone by since then that he didn't think of her. He appreciated her story and the way she looked, very easy on the eyes.

"Fine, I must admit Dauge, you are right."

"And besides, Dash, I carry the money," Dauge snarled in a tone that was both arrogant and vicious.

"I carry the money that belongs to Stannor," Legion spoke up calmly but above the other two to remind them both just who had the money for Stannor.

"Deception is key in this world, Legion," Dauge replied at his brother trying to teach him that not everyone should know just who had what and what was who.

"We're all friends here. That's why I never asked for a single coin or to even see it. I never asked who was carrying what. I didn't care. I trusted in the fact that we were a team."

"I'm going get a room somewhere." Legion waited and then pointed to a newly constructed large rectangular building. It was lightly colored and two stories tall. A sign hung overhead that said "The Blue Ox." "I'll go there."

Legion had his room waiting on him. He'd given Kattya more than enough money to take care of everything, including herself while he was gone.

That night Dash disappeared to a room somewhere inside the Blue Ox. Dauge was next door to him in the Dreamy Cauldron.

Kattya was gone from Legion's life. This was to be expected, though still not wanted. Subconsciously, the idea that some random mine girl would take his money and remain loyal to him while he was away for what could have been weeks or months. He'd only just met her. What was he thinking? Perhaps this life would force things like this upon him? Perhaps he should plan for all people in his life to come and go like the passing of the wind?

Sleep set in. He was getting sleepy. The warm comfort of the Dreamy Cauldron took him to the plane of dreams, far away for Vorrellon and Lord Stannor and even Thox. In the morning, he and Dauge would walk with Dash to complete their mission without Pitt who disappeared on them. Without a trace, without anything, the massive goliath was gone. There were rumors and words thrown around about where he could have headed, but in the end he was gone and no longer part of their team. How could he have left so quickly without saying a word to any of them about anything?

When morning came, Legion was the last to rise. He was tired and worn from his travels. He and Dauge regrouped with Dash and the Dreamy Cauldron fed them a warm breakfast before they made off to see Lord Stannor.

They sat around a small circular table and discussed the quest in its entirety. Dash wasn't pleased that a measly painting was all they seemed to gain from the ancient city that allegedly only stood in myth. Dauge was pissed off the Kingsblood lizards gave them the money they needed to appease Stannor and have their quest considered successful. Legion, well Legion just thought about Kattya. She was gone. She left him and she took his money with her. The quest, he thought to himself. Quests would come and go. Money would come and go. His dealings with Kattya, her origins and their time together, it was all done and gone and for nothing.

And finally, they were off to meet Lord Stannor. He wasn't at his own manor or any of his regular places but the people around the growing city helped guide the three toward the lord. A few new colts were being born in the horse fields.

His favorite horse Diamond was giving birth to her first colt. The training grounds for the horses were big. Several wooden posts held up the wood siding for the circular fences that encased the training grounds. Several horse handlers were already inside the grounds breaking horses. It was early. Too early to be breaking horses, thought the three. Just like they were told, Lord Stannor hung over a piece of one of the wooden fences chewing on a piece of hay, watching as a few men helped the colt remove itself from its mother's womb.

Stannor wore thick and rustley dark clothing with a straw hat and thick boots. He wanted to be one of them but only the bottom portion of his boots seemed to touch the mud. Dash knew his kind. He'd seen and met them many times before. Maybe he was different but mud only on his shoes certainly didn't make him any different from any of the others.

"Lord Stannor," Dash started, pissing Legion off.

Legion wanted to be the man to call for him but he lost his chance. Truthfully, Dash waited, giving both the brothers a chance to talk but they didn't. Dauge wasn't a talker and Legion's head was still up his ass about Kattya.

The Lord of Vorrellon turned, hanging his left arm over the fence as if to balance himself. His beard had grown even more since the last time they'd met. He looked over at the three. It took a minute but his memory reminded him of just who the boys were.

He smiled and pulled himself from the fence, opening his arms to welcome them all home. He'd gotten bigger since they'd seen him too.

"Boys, boys," he said, bringing them all in for a tight hug. He looked at the three of them with chewing tobacco still mixed in his beard.

The three quickly pulled away from the man and Legion peeled a large purse from his belt and handed it over to the lord. "That's your three thousand gold."

Stannor couldn't believe his ears. He opened the purse to see the coins. He laughed overfilled with joy. He couldn't help himself. He laughed and laughed until finally asking. "So then, the city's real after all? Or did you boys steal this from good hardworking folks?" he asked seriously, but still with a hint of joke to it.

"The city exists," Legion answered.

"Pitt stormed off somewhere in Blackstone. Thanks for asking," Dauge barked angrily.

Dauge turned and took off from the conversation. The three didn't have time to kneel or show proper courtesies to the lord. He was in a place where they could tell he wanted to fit in and be one of the guys.

"What's wrong with him?" Stannor asked. "I know that trip wasn't a short one or without its danger."

"Forgive him my lord. We are all weary and tired from our travels. Pitt decided to stay back in Blackstone, entrusting this quest to be finished by us, the remaining three. I hope we've done you proud, my lord." Dash bowed and smiled.

Stannor couldn't believe it. The three brought him all the money he needed. Now he could finance what he needed to in order to see his city flourish and prosper. Everything was there. More importantly, the legendary city of myth, Azra Goetia was proved to exist. "The city really does exist," he said.

"It does. And it's not without its dangers. I suggest you take the money, my lord…" Dash stopped, knowing he was overstepping his boundaries. "If I may," he started again very cautiously.

"You may," Stannor answered.

"My lord, that city is filled with things not all of this world. It should be left alone in the Vile Frozen where it belongs. Perhaps the day will come when the right people will step forward to remove it but until then, let it bask only in its own existence."

"The things that city must still hold? It's been untouched for so long!" Stannor excitedly replied.

"My lord, it would be best if left untouched," Dash recommended.

"Did you boys make out with anything for yourselves?" asked Stannor.

"No," Legion said, jumping into the conversation. "Nothing but an old painting."

"That's too bad. I'm sorry boys. And the other one, the fourth, is he okay?" Stannor wasn't being arrogant or cocky. He was legitimately concerned. Legion and Dash could tell he felt bad for the three losing a friend and coming back with nothing.

"He's fine. He's just gone. I'm not sure where he went. None of us have any idea where he went off to." Dash answered strongly, trying to urge Stannor to get back on track with his train of thought.

"Boys, Vorrellon is my city and it's growing. You are more than welcome to live and stay in Vorrellon. I'll get you boys some papers that say you stay here on my coin anytime you want. You eat and drink here on my coin anytime you wish. It's the best I can do for you now. When Vorrellon is the most booming city in all of Thox, it'll mean a lot more than it does now."

Even Legion couldn't help but smile. Dauge had walked off. Dash was next to him and Pitt, the goliath gladiator, was gone. And with all that, Legion still managed to crack a smile. Dash grinned too. He graciously thanked the lord for everything and the opportunity. Stannor made it clear to the both of them that their names would not go unsung to the people of Thox and to the people of Vorrellon.

Dash and Legion followed Lord Stannor to a nearby building still on stilts, and from the looks of it, just recently built. The smell of freshly cut wood still filled the small one room building. A small block of steps helped the three of them into the small building with still no door.

Inside, Dash and Legion saw a very basic building. There were some papers on the floor and a desk toward the back far side of the room.

Stannor rushed right over to it. He sat down, trying to manage his belly and body from knocking everything over, and went to work searching for something. "Ah hah, there we are!" he said proudly.

He pulled three wrapped scrolls from the bottom of the desk sealed with his official seal and green wax. He confirmed that the stamp of his seal was inside and on each of the papers. The papers, he said would prove that everything they did within the boundaries of Vorrellon would be on the city's coin and not their own. All they had to do was present the papers and they would be allowed to do as they wished.

Stannor got up and walked right over to the two. He asked what to do for Pitt. Dash recommended he keep it just in case the goliath ever returned to Vorrellon for any reason. Legion took both his and Dauge's papers and Dash took his own. The two thanked the lord again for hiring and offering the job to them first. He thanked the two back for undergoing such a dangerous quest on such short notice. He apologized he couldn't do more for the two men but they didn't seem to care too much.

"Why were our papers here? Shouldn't they have been in your manor or office?" Legion asked.

"I just recently moved them out here. I've got an affinity for horses and I've been spending a lot of time out here. I didn't want anything to happen to them," he answered.

"Fair enough," Legion said, smiling.

"Where will you go from here, son of Dominick Xavier?" Stannor asked Legion.

"I don't know. Perhaps I should return home."

"And you, Dash?" Stannor extended the question to Dash.

"I'll have to discuss with my team what our next move will be. You will always be informed of our whereabouts, my lord." Dash took a step toward Stannor, placing a hand upon his shoulder.

Stannor liked the motion and nodded in compliance. With that, the two broke away from Lord Stannor, saying their final goodbyes. Dash and Legion walked and for a time; silence smothered them both. Neither said a word to the other. Dash knew what Legion was thinking and visa versa.

Finally, Legion broke the silence. "Dash, I am returning to Eternis with my brother." He wanted to say it and get it out and he knew if Dash interrupted him, he might be swayed in changing his plans.

"Have you talked to Dauge about this?"

"I have," Legion answered.

The two walked slowly and casually through the growing streets and city of Vorrellon. The people moved and worked hard for their lord. The people here seemed to love their lord and love their city. It wasn't grown and full yet, but they all knew what it could be with the right work and right attitude. And these people had it.

"This city's really going to be something," Dash said taking the conversation in a different direction.

Legion laughed. "I know what you're doing, old friend."

"I'm admiring the growing point of a city. Is there something wrong with that?" Dash asked jokingly.

"I'm not a Thoxen," Legion replied sternly.

"Neither am I, but I can appreciate their hospitality."

"I'm not staying here."

"Legion, Vorrellon is growing. Lord Stannor gave us a key to the city, in the form of a scroll of course, but still. You're young and your blood is vivaciously looking for excitement. What will you do in Eternis?"

"Dash, I will be an Xavier. I will work for my uncle and help my mother. I will see my brothers and my sister. Eternis is my home. It is where I belong. I am not saying you cannot come along, but I'm not sure what I want and what you want still run alongside one another."

"You carry the Mourning Star, Legion. Is that for nothing?"

"No, it's still at my side and will be until the day that I am no more. It will forever serve as a defense for Eternis. And when I am dead my children will wield it as the same defense for the same city."

"You were meant for more, Legion. You know that," Dash said. "I won't try and convince you of this. Take your brother and go back to Eternis. My place is here with the name we've started building in Thox. I will find my way building a foundation here in Vorrellon. And if you ever see yourself back these ways, I'll always have a place waiting for you. I'm honored to have shared this time with you Legion Cage Xavier, son of Dominick Xavier, son to Eternis."

Dash stopped Legion so that he could face him when he spoke. Legion listened to the half eladrin's words and took them in deep and carefully. He thanked the man for his words and wisdom and his actions against the creatures of Azra Goetia. And just like that, Legion Cage Xavier walked away from Dash and the last non-blooded member of his team. His plan was simple. He would reacquaint himself with his little brother and the two would embark on a journey back to Eternis. This journey would be different. This journey would be safe and comfortable. They wouldn't have to worry about the evils and the wilds of the world. They would pay for safe passage and arrive wholesome and pure, and fully rested.

Legion walked away, turning his head back every so often to see Dash walking opposite of him in the opposite direction. Every time Legion turned around, he watched the backside of Dash walk deeper toward the crowds of the working class Vorrellonians. He really did like this city and had faith that it would grow. Why did Legion really want to return to Eternis?

Eternis wasn't even really his home. Legion's home was much farther away. He grew up in the Republic of New Magic, behind the massive walls of the kingdom that stood as the forefront against the unending numbers of Corvana. His roots were in Eternis. His family today resided in the old city. He felt obligated to do the same.

Legion found Dauge sitting quietly toward a well near the center of town. His face was wet and his dampened hair slicked back. Legion smiled and walked over to his little brother.

Dauge looked up at him. "I'm not going to leave you, brother. So whatever decision you make is fine with me."

"We're going home, brother," Legion said, surprising him.

Dauge stood almost immediately hearing his brother's words. Legion knew Dauge hated the Thoxens. He never came out and said it, but he did. He didn't have a reason to hate them but he hated them nonetheless. It could have very easily been his blooded nature to hate them, but all the same, he hated them. And without ever saying it, Legion knew it through and through.

"When do we leave?"

"As soon as we're packed and ready," Legion answered.

"What of Stannor?"

Legion handed his brother his scroll to the city. He explained the seal of Stannor kept it wrapped and sealed and inside the same seal would prove they could walk, talk, sleep, drink, and do whatever within reason in the city of Vorrellon and Lord Stannor would pick up the tab for it.

"What good does this do me? I'll never come back to Thox. I just don't feel as if I belong here, brother."

"Dauge, you didn't feel like the Republic was the place you belonged, or even Eternis."

"I never said anything like that about Eternis!" Dauge started before Legion finished and for the first time in a long time, he was smiling.

Legion appreciated that smile and embraced his brother tightly. Much to his surprise, his brother engaged the hug right back and equally as tight.

"Come, let us break bread and have drinks for our last night in Thox."

"I'd like that, Legion."

The two brothers headed back toward the growing town square. They decided to eat somewhere different. They wanted to try something unique. Whatever they ate, they would appreciate it because soon they would be far from Thox across the Hangman's Straight and behind he walls of Eternis.

Chapter 90

Draeden's magic reopened the seamless tunnel the umber hulk left behind. It wasn't long before they were passing back stone walls to their right and just above them. They knew they were scraping the outside perimeter of something.

They would need another day to rest and mend Tsin and Rakka's wounds. Both of them were still really bad off. Especially Rakka, his wounds were still partially opened and now they were beginning to fester. Fever was starting to set in and the others could see a quick change in pace for the busted goblin warrior.

"The wall," Rakka said, rubbing his hands over the stone wall making itself more visible with every pass of the humanoid hands.

The umber hulk tunnel didn't take them too far in before the stone wall of a fortress made itself known. It only made sense that the bludgeoning force of Westlyn's hammer be the instrument that brought them into the place, if this even was the place after all.

Westlyn issued a motion for the others to all step aside. They did just as he asked. It wasn't the most efficient way in but it would prove to be the most effective. The tunnel Draeden opened for the eight of them was one of the largest areas the team had seen since entering the underground. The umber hulk's initial tunnel was easily widened by the genasi's magic.

"Wait," Tsin said, still barely able to move on his own.

Rakka rubbed away more dirt, revealing even more of the stone wall. Finally, he turned, putting his back up against the upper area of the stone wall before falling down to his butt. Fever was setting in on the goblinoid and he was hurting. Not all of his wounds were mended. He and Tsin needed rest and more healing. When the powers came available, Keres utilized them. Unfortunately for the goblin, she favored her husband. He was too weak and tired to question or argue. It was okay. He was still going to make it.

"What is it?" Drackice asked, signaling for Westlyn to hold.

"This is going to send a frenzy toward us. We can't fight that, not fully up and readied. With both Tsin and Rakka in downed conditions, we need to rest until we're all healed and able to move forward at a hundred percent." Slate wanted to press on but he knew the dangers of being too aggressive. He was far older than he looked.

At least some of them were in unison with their thoughts. It was time for the group to rest. They weren't beaten down, but Rakka was hovering on death's door and Tsin was still battered from the slam of the ettin.

No need to set watches. Only Tsin and Rakka needed to rest and heal. Draeden and Keres rested too, just to replenish their spells. That left Drackice, Slate, Shanks, and Westlyn to guard the lot of them. Half of them were down regrouping spells and/or healing while the other four held strong for the whole lot of them.

The tunnel was dark but Keres' fires made it easier to see. It stank horribly but Draeden's cantrips nullified the spells. Each member of the team brought their own tools to the table. Alphonse was gone and his skills would be missed but they still had enough tools to see this through.

Finally, Keres became fully empowered once again. This time, she used nearly every spell she had to heal the two downed men. She transferred them all to healing and mending words for both Rakka and Tsin. The priestess was virtually out of spells but still had her physical weapons and armor to protect her.

"Rakka, these scars will forever be with you. You're going to make it," she said, standing up seeing the goblin's last wounds heal up. Tsin's body felt worlds better but he was still sore from the pounding he'd taken.

The stone wall was kind of at an upward slant from the ground area of the tunnel. From the direction they came from, it was on the right hand side. Westlyn would be heaving his hammer in an upward swing to get through the wall. The stone of the wall hidden behind the clay and mud was thick and hard. It was cold with a dark mortar between it to keep it together and held. Drackice looked around. He knew Westlyn had to get them in and once they entered, there would be no going back.

Drackice thought back to home. He missed Dusk. It wasn't the sexual endeavors he fantasized about daily that he missed. It wasn't her sweet smell or velvet touch either. It was the simple conversations with a simple girl in a complicated town filled with simple people trying to live in it. Westlyn prepared himself. Everything was in order and nothing came around to distract them from the next step in the quest: getting through the wall.

Westlyn leaned over his hammer, resting the head of it on the cold clay ground. Drackice nodded, telling him to go through with it. Westlyn grunted, nodding back in compliance. The others stood back and readied themselves. Anything could happen. They knew that.

Westlyn spit on his two hands and rubbed them hard together. He gripped the shaft of his weapon and fixed his eyes upon the wall. He knew he needed to get through it as fast as possible. From the first hit, whatever was in there would be alerted of their coming.

"Here we go!" Shanks said, preparing.

"River of all creation, take your sound back from this place..." Draeden quietly mumbled. He closed his eyes and bowed his head, making it look more like a prayer than an arcane cast.

"Zeronaus, father of life and bringer of death, split the strong from the stone," Keres added, following Draeden's lead.

Keres wanted to weaken the stones for Westlyn. Draeden took away the sound. No one even asked if there was anything they could do. They didn't know magic so it really wasn't their place to question their arsenal.

Westlyn reared back and the driving force behind the deva, his holy energies, and the hammer shattered the target brick. Cracks streamed out from where the deva's hammer hit and bit-by-bit the hole got bigger. Chunks of stone and mortar continued to fall. First, it was slow but it gained momentum as the crack danced across the stone.

Not a sound was made. Westlyn didn't understand but he didn't care. His face lit up like a night sky set ablaze from siege warfare. The stones crumbled to dust beneath his very feet. He couldn't believe it. Immediately, he along with the others looked over to Draeden and then Keres. They were behind the safety spells.

The hole was made, revealing a relatively large room. It was square and made completely of stone. Westlyn was the first to enter. Shanks and Slate quickly followed. Draeden entered somewhere after them. Keres was the last to leave the dark tunnel. The ceiling was tall, taller than it should be considering its location. Then again, it wasn't that tall. Top to bottom was maybe thirteen or fourteen feet. It was slightly wider than it was tall.

Humanoid remains were scattered. A few tables with adorning chains and hooks filled the room. The entire place was stained with blood. Some spatters were turning yellow, meaning it was as fresh as two or three days.

"A torture chamber," Slate noted.

A single locked door stood to the far right side of the room from where the team entered. It was made of iron and wood and kept that small opening, with the three iron bars, right at the top just below the crescent arch in the wood.

"So you're not dumb. Good to know," Draeden sarcastically said, snickering.

"Careful wizard, here anything can make one a foe. Perhaps your sarcastic thoughts now pour more fluidly due to your possessed state. Remember, I deal in spirits, elemental," Slate strongly answered. He even finished with a slight head nod and pure eye contact in order to make sure the wizard got his point.

"Shhhhh, we're in now. The time for egos and bickering is over," Drackice ordered.

Now, everyone whispered. They were out of the tunnel and Westlyn confirmed they were in the right castle. Old fortifications and constructions of the Red Mystics were typically very difficult to find, especially the more important ones. This one had been found before. It was the stronghold the old Thoxen Necromancer Agromordeus once used.

"We have to get through that door," Shanks said.

"Don't you think I know that, archer?" Tsin answered.

"I didn't say it was your duty or up to you to get us through," Shanks said.

"It falls into the Tsin tool box, so it's my problem," the Wilden challenged.

"Just the same, if it's your tool to pull then, pull it," Shanks replied.

The annoyed Tsin threw a mean stare at Shanks and walked toward the door. The rest of the seven took position and steadied themselves for what could come. Slate held the hole leading back into the tunnel with Drackice. Draeden as always, stood in the center of the room and group to maximize his protection from any and everything that could come at any angle.

The door was locked but didn't have anything else to it. There wasn't much to the door or the lock. Tsin picked it without snapping a single lock pick. It didn't take much at all. The door creaked open. Tsin turned around and lipped a silent "let's go."

Tsin was the first to enter the dark hallway. The hall passages led both right and left. The ceiling came down, now only reaching a height of about seven foot. The hallway was only about four feet across. It was going to be a tight squeeze. The stones that made the hall of the place led in both directions, left and right.

Drackice looked at Westlyn.

Westlyn looked at Keres. Westlyn's eyes were just looking for comfort, weren't they? They were looking for something to land upon while his instincts gave him the answers he needed. Westlyn looked up to Tsin and whispered, "Our destination lies left, but I think a safer, more efficient route lies right."

Tsin threw his body back and forth, making sure it was safe on both sides. To the left side, the passage just bled deeper and deeper into a blackness he couldn't see through, even though he was Wilden. And to the right, another door similar to the one he just picked.

Slowly, one by one the crew fell in, leaving Slate now to guard the door they just exited from. The hallway to the right was long enough for everyone to enter before Tsin would have to pick the lock. Slate now held off the rear where Tsin just opened the last door. After Slate, toward the rear, was Drackice and then Draeden. Tsin took the front followed with Rakka directly behind him and then Keres. Westlyn followed behind the priestess and lastly, toward the middle was Shanks.

So Tsin took the lead, being the trap finder and disarmer. Rakka followed as the setting was perfect for his natural and racial strong points. Keres was strong but her healing needed to be guarded on both sides. Westlyn was also strong but not the most dexterous being. His side style healing and defending nature made the fourth spot perfect for him. Shanks was a ranged attacker. It only made sense for him to stick close to the middle. Draeden the Genasi wizard was fragile to say the least. He urged Westlyn to rotate with him in the marching order. Eventually, Westlyn agreed. Drackice stuck close to the rear, as it was just the point in line where he landed. His abilities to make others fight better would serve efficiently toward the rear unless a rear assault surprisingly charged them. And lastly, the barbarian Slate Thundershot held up the rear. Slate was big and strong. He had tricks and powers that normal barbarians didn't have. This made him an elite rear guardian.

Once again, Tsin picked the lock. This one gave him more trouble than the last. It took three picks to get the damned thing done. Once more the door opened. Tsin turned, arrogantly bragging about his work. From the back, Drackice yelled in a whisper for the Wilden to just continue forward. Rakka poked the proud Wilden with a short javelin he had in hand. The poke was to urge the braggart to move forward. Finally, Tsin conceded and did as he was told.

"He would be really good if he just stayed focused and didn't brag so much," Shanks whispered to Draeden.

Draeden coughed. He tried to keep quiet. He was still quite ill and the sickness was coming back. Keres turned and rubbed the poor wizard's neck and shoulders, though she still tried to keep her eyes forward as best she could.

"His foolishness and childlike arrogance is part of him. A flaw he grants freely upon himself for those that would do him or his people ill will." Draeden barely managed to get the words out before the cough took back over. A prime time for that sickness to come back, he thought. Draeden sneakily peeled a small vile of a thick black liquid infused with some form of ash. Popping the top off, he snorted the whole thing spitting a bit of it out through his mouth.

The whole thing gagged him. It always gagged him but the antidote eased his pain. It should, he thought. It was made from the remains of vampires and lycanthropes. It wasn't the easiest find or cheap for that matter. And come to think of it, he was running short.

The next door opened and to the right was nothing but an immediate wall, but the left opened to an even deeper passage. Drackice questioned Westlyn again. Westlyn reminded the son of the Free Armies' leader that though they were descending farther away from their destination, they were only doing it to bypass more obstacles.

"I believe this is going to wrap us around. It's going to take longer but it'll be a smoother trek," Westlyn said.

"I hope you're right, for all of our sakes," Keres said.

And from there, the eight marched slyly and carefully around. Westlyn was right. The path took them back and all around, leading them back toward where he believed their destination to be. Finally the long hallway turned left again and this time, it opened up. It was wider and taller and the gray stones now only made up the flooring. Beautifully crafted petrified wood and other hardened materials made up the walls and ceilings.

Multiple doors opened up the bland passageway on both sides. And more and more oil paintings decorated the walls. It was as if the passageway itself wasn't part of the fortification but merely led another way around to it all the while staying connected and linked as one.

The team didn't know what to do. Tsin suggested bypassing the rooms. Westlyn agreed and Drackice put the thoughts into motion. One after another, they tiptoed carefully past the doors. Tsin's inner desires made him want to open the doors and see what was behind them, but this time his better half controlled him.

Drackice looked closely at the doors when he passed them. They were smooth and carried a sleek look. They were painted and unlike the other doors that arched at the top. These doors were wider, thicker, and were the typical rectangular shape of a door.

Drackice stopped. Slate stayed held up behind him. Westlyn looked back, feeling the ones behind him slowing down. Westlyn silently signaled to his liege. His body language asked the question his voice couldn't.

Drackice motioned them all to hold. Tsin and most of the others were already past the doors. And just past the doors a stairwell led straight up; the stairs were made of the same petrified wood and hardened materials as the walls. The occasional stone was put here and there in the stairs to act as a solid base for them. The walls and ceiling slanting upward with them returned back to the hard stone that made up the previous passageway.

Drackice touched his fingertips to the middle door on the left hand side. There were three doors on each side, six in total. He looked back at the others on the side he wasn't paying attention to. Part of him wanted to clear out everything and the other part of him said that Bahaus was the target and that taking on any unnecessary battles could prove fatally wrong in the long run. What if random obstacles and encounters damaged his team beyond repair? They were already down a wizard. No, they were down Alphonse, evocation specialist and brother to Shanks. Drackice chanced it and whispered aloud.

"We have to see what's in these doors."

Westlyn couldn't believe it. He never made it a habit to contest his superior's wishes but this was madness. Westlyn reminded them all. They were not here for loot or gems or magical weapons or armor. They were here to see the fallen king and last of the Uil-Endail bloodline vanquished.

"Why are we going back on your first order, sir?" Westlyn asked.

Drackice was distillated on the door the tips of his fingers paraded across. Something about the doors stopped him dead in his tracks.

"What's with you?" Slate whispered.

"The other doors, they looked like doors for a fortress, right?" he asked.

"Yeah, so what? Many castles and strongholds have different architecture running throughout them. Even if the same engineer built the whole thing, dungeon doors aren't the same as bedroom doors," Shanks stated.

Drackice smiled. "Exactly."

Draeden's evil grin was still there. He flailed the word "curiosity" aloud but carefully. Nothing about Draeden was good and Keres knew that. Secretly, she admired and fancied the darkness that surrounded the genasi's heart. Draeden let out one of those evil closed-mouth subtle laughs.

Westlyn looked back to the wizard. He waited for a minute and took a good look at the man. He knew what he wanted to say but wasn't sure how to say it. When the words finally came to him, the door in front of Drackice opened, throwing him off his game yet again.

Drackice didn't feel a threat from the doors or the setting. The whole scene looked safe to him. This was a different passage that led to something most would have turned away from by now. He knew what this was. And just as expected, the six doors one by one proved to house nothing but bedrooms. Each room looked exactly the same, with duvets of white hanging over the beautiful giant beds clad fully in the same color.

Each of the six rooms carried the finest in wooden furniture and not a day of age touched them. They should have rotted away by now, thought Drackice. Red velvet carpets really brought out the white-laced sheets and blankets in the rooms.

The dark cherry brown chest of drawers and armoires really made out the perfectly squared-off rooms. Paintings of young beautiful women in dresses hung in each room. All of the dresses were white and each of the girls looked of the same blood. Some had darker hair and one had purely blonde hair.

"These rooms belonged to important dames," said the son of Magnus Black.

"Dames the holders of this castle wished to keep removed from the rest of its inhabitants," Draeden added.

"I wonder. Many speculations about the Red Mystics have always captured my curiosity but their race or the races of the Red Mystics has never been proven. All of these girls look to be half elven," Westlyn said.

"Aside from Agromordeus, not too many tales exist or have been proven of others finding and utilizing the Red Mystics old strongholds and castles. The ones that have been found have proven too troublesome and dangerous to utilize. The mechanics of the places constantly change," said Draeden.

Rakka mumbled angrily and pointed toward the stairs. He didn't care about the feeble rooms or what they did or didn't hold. He wanted to see this through. Not because ousting Bahaus would set with him morally but because he anxiously thought about the gold and riches behind the fallen king.

Rakka'd been quiet for too long and he was too close to make a bad decision now. It was time to move and something inside told him Bahaus and the riches that would bring his old clan and tribe out of poverty and into the limelight were not too far from his reach.

"This castle sure does have its quirks," Slate said out of nowhere.

"These bedrooms so far away from everything else just prove something or someone wanted these young girls to stay clear and free of the stronghold's normal society. Maybe even a safety precaution, who knows?" Keres stopped. She then started back up about how she'd just reiterated what had already been mentioned.

"These rooms mean nothing. We need to keep moving," Shanks said, deciding to finally throw in his two cents.

"Leaving things behind can sometimes cause too much to lie ahead." Draeden broke away from his cough and sick laugh in order to get his point across to the team. It worked. They knew what he was saying.

Drackice understood but Drackice had a rebuttal to the thought.

"Draeden, what if these rooms had housed things that proved truly difficult for us to overcome? What if they left lasting scars upon our bones? Our prime state would have been weakened and wounded and I believe we need everything we have to take on Bahaus Sazos-Uil Endail." Slate asked.

Drackice apologized to Slate and then to the rest of the team. This wasn't a mission meant to scratch the itch of curiosity. They had a job to do. It was Drackice's fault they stopped and opened the bedrooms. "I feel Slate is right."

"It never hurts to turn every stone, my lord," Tsin said.

"You were the first one to move past," Drackice replied.

"I did as I was ordered. I say we search everything. We should leave nothing behind. And who knows, since we're here we might as well get paid, right?" Tsin said.

Now, once again Tsin's voice became almost annoying to Drackice. He tried to like and appreciate the Wilden but he just couldn't. At some points he was more bearable than others but for the most part, Drackice just couldn't stand him. That didn't mean Drackice didn't appreciate his natural and unnatural talents though. He knew Tsin was key to getting through a place like this.

"Enough, let's move," Drackice said.

"To the stairs?" Tsin asked.

"No, we're backtracking," Shanks said answering before Drackice.

Drackice just laughed. Shanks said what he was thinking. He didn't need to add anything to it. It was enough. The stairs were actually wide enough for them eight of them to walk two by two. And the higher they ascended, the farther the width of the stairs extended. The stairwell opened up nicely after the first twenty feet or so. This looked like a long stairway. They were nearing Bahaus. They were getting close. Soon, it would all be over.

Chapter 91

It took some days but Legion and Dauge were finally gone from Vorrellon. Lord Stannor was behind them. Pitt was a part of their past and now, so was Dash. The two brothers did their duty for Vorrellon and Thox under the banner of Lord Stannor.

Weeks passed. The weeks soon became months before the team reached Blackwall. Port Agatha was too far away and they two would have to venture across all of Thox to get to the port in order to backtrack through the Hangman's Straight to Eternis.

Blackwall was one of Thox's northernmost city's, resting close to the water of the Hangman's Straight. The Black cities of Thox were said to be the strongest and housed the most military and training. Blackstone and Blackwall were but two of Thox's Elite Black cities.

Blackwall was different. It didn't have a lord since the last stepped down from illness. The Wall of Warriors, a stable of four, broke down the duties of the city into quarters, one for the each of them. Blackwall was also close enough that small ferries could be taken from the city across the Straight to Eternis. Blackwall didn't make a habit of the ferries but with the proper coin and/or patents, it could be done.

On their way to Blackwall, Dauge and Legion talked about Dash and why he didn't strike up the old painting and what should have been done with it. He knew they were both now at their wits end with him. He'd brought the team together. He was the reason they were even a team, or accomplishing anything at all. Kraydia left because of him. And it was probably his doing that forced Pitt out. Honestly, what could he have done to force Pitt to leave so abruptly?

They knew Dash considered himself a failure and rightfully so. He couldn't keep the team together that he built. Azra Goetia was a fail! Had it not been for their father, Taj Odin Xavier, and his relationship with the Kingsblood lizards, they would have not had the money to give to Stannor. Not everything pans out the way it's supposed to and the Azra Goetia quest will go down as a victory logged under Lord Stannor and his city of Vorrellon.

Blackwall was a different kind of city than the boys were used to. It was definitely a militarily heavy city. Training and the taking in of new recruits were constant here. The boys even learned of the prison system. Here, prisoners were forced harshly into slave labor. Though this wasn't unheard of in some cities, it seemed to be more coldhearted and dark here.

The walls around the city stood high. The structures inside were all lower than the city walls. Buildings weren't named here. All the taverns looked like mirror images of one another as did the inns and the barracks and the warehouses and the training grounds, etc.

Dauge immediately knew what this was. This way, no one could say this one person of importance hangs out at one particular tavern or inn or another. This way, it all blended in and meshed together. Blackwall was clearly the strongest military town they'd ever seen. Fortunately, or unfortunately, they couldn't stay long.

It took days and lots of work but finally, the two landed spots on a small barge moving some prisoners to Eternis. Outlaws, bandits, killers, rapists, and so many other types were among the head count. Most of them were sub-species but there were a few humans and monstrous humanoids in there as well. They were being taken to Eternis in order to be sold to a warlord who wished to make the exchange there, on neutral ground.

As long as Eternis got their cut, things like that were common in the world's oldest city. And for that, Dauge and Legion didn't mind. And they were told that as long as they didn't mind spending a night or two on the barge with some of Thox's worst criminals, they had a place on the boat—for the right price of course.

The prices were definitely gouged but the two brothers didn't care one bit. This was their last hoorah for Thox. Even Dauge, so young, was ready to return and say goodbye to the crazy life of traveling and uncertainty. Life was meant to be an adventure, he thought. Not like this.

The large barge was made of mostly wood and stacked with giant crates standing over twenty feet tall. Inside the crates were the prisoners.

The top areas of the crates had large enough holes for the people inside to breathe but probably not get out. A gnome would have had trouble getting its head through.

Dauge and Legion were given quarters at the top underneath an area of the deck that would act as cover for them. It wasn't much and for what they paid they certainly deserved more. The thing was almost over. It was all just about behind them.

The trip would take a little over two days and the boys would finally be docking at the home of their old blood. Dauge was more excited than Legion. Legion couldn't figure it out. They were told to stay out of the way of the workers and remain confined to their area underneath one of the decks as much as possible. They were given buckets to take care of their bodily wastes.

It was early on the first day of their travel and the month of Razkus was off to a cold and wet start. Not an hour after their departure from Blackwall the first raindrops slammed into their boat. There was a lower deck for most of the crew but some of them had temporary rooms built on the barge on the top deck.

These ferry barges were more like giant rafts. They were stable and strong but there wasn't much to them. They could carry a fairly decent amount of weight and were thick and strong, but there was just no true definition or dynamics to them. They surely weren't seaworthy and the small trips back and forth across the Straight were about all they were good for.

By the first day's end, a light but steady rain had set in. People still marched up and down the steps from the upper to the lower decks, constantly working and taking care business. Legion and Dauge tried to stay as dry as they could beneath the overhang on the upper deck level. They had a few light blankets and pillows but that was about it.

"For the amount of coin we gave, we should have the captain's suit," Dauge muttered.

"Relax brother. We've dealt with worse and soon we'll be home and all of this will be behind us." Legion tried to reassure his brother.

Every so often, the two would see women walking and shielding themselves with various things from the rain all across the barge. They were constantly going up and down to the decks below. The women looked pretty but like they'd seen better days. What were they doing here?

"They're pleasure after a hard day's work, brother," Dauge informed.

Legion paused and then gave the notion that he understood. "They're whores."

"Yes" Dauge answered.

"Even for a short journey?" Legion asked, wondering, not necessarily to Dauge though.

"I guess. It would do you some good to take one. It would help get your mind off of that girl you thought was going to stick around for you. What was her name?"

"Kattya," Legion quickly replied.

"Yeah that one," Dauge replied, not impressed.

"Maybe, not one from here though. I just want to get home and I don't want anything to disturb that," he said.

The rain started falling harder. The wood beneath them was starting to catch more of the rain. They would either have to sleep in the utter wet and cold or figure something else out. Dauge reminded Legion that he was a Genasi and he'd sleep just fine in the cold and wet. Legion was still purely human. He needed to find something else. He needed to find somewhere else to sleep.

Legion peeled himself from underneath the overhang. He wrapped up tightly, and thankfully he dressed warm, knowing it was already toward the final days of the first week of Razkus, the beginning of the colder months.

The first woman he came to was elven. She was dark and short. Her auburn hair was wet from the storm. She was thicker than he liked but her wet hair matted to her face and the soaking wet common outfit aroused him in a peculiar way. This wasn't anything he'd typically find attractive but maybe Dauge was right and he did need to get over Kattya. And what better time than now, because once he was back in Eternis, she needed to become merely a girl from his past.

Before he could say a word, the young elven girl pulled her hair back and down to one side. She almost embraced the rain and cold as if it were inviting her in somewhere. Something about the whole scene invigorated Legion. This time, he didn't want to be a gentleman. Why should he be? This time, he was going to use this woman the way that miner girl used him.

Her lips were sultry. Something about them made the Eternian want to ravage her even more. He kept his wits about him and began an easy conversation with the girl about the cold and the rain. She quietly explained that she was used to it and that this was going to be her last ferry trip. She planned to stay permanently in Eternis.

Legion didn't want to hear any of that but he made like he did. The two carried the conversation as long as they could. Every so often, Legion turned back to assure himself that Dauge was still under the overhang and fine. He was.

Thunder and lightning began to roll and some of the crew began fearing what lay ahead. At least half of the crew stopped working altogether. More and more of the crewmembers made for the lower decks in hopes of getting out of the rain and storm.

"I would like to hire you, girl, but as you can see I have no quarters here," Legion said, finally realizing that his hopes and plans were useless this day.

"I have a small cabin. Most of the working girls share small rooms. We're usually four to a room but the other three have been taken by men already. The men wanted them for the whole trip, so I got the cabin area all to myself!" She smiled sexually, keeping her mouth open as to amplify the tension.

"Then there would be plenty of room for my brother as well?" Legion asked, immediately thinking of his little brother.

"It will cost more. I will be up front with you," she said.

"Fine, name your price."

"For the night, I will have five gold pieces. For your brother to stay in the room, he'll have to pay just the same." Knowing Legion needed a place to go and feeling that he really wanted her. She tested the boundaries with a high stake just to see if he'd take the bait.

"Ten gold for the night," Legion said laughing. "Take fifty and I'll keep you and the room until the trip is over," Legion arrogantly joked, pulling the coins from his purse.

The girl couldn't believe it. Fifty gold coins would change her entire life. It didn't seem like much for this man, she thought. She asked of course what he did for a living but the evasive Legion just ignored the question. He didn't care. All he wanted was what he paid for and not a thing more.

He signaled to his brother to climb out from underneath the overhang. After explaining to Dauge the situation and where they were going, Dauge reminded Legion that it would still be in his best interest to at least get the girl's name. Legion laughed and finished it off with an "oh right."

"So elf, what is your name?" he asked. He couldn't help but let it come out rudely.

"That's a bit rude, don't you think?" she asked. "Is it common to just talk to people using their race as a means to address them where you're from?"

"I am Eternian," he answered.

"I've been to Eternis and not all are hospitable but none have spoken to me in such a manner as you have."

"And I bet none of them have given you fifty pieces of gold to put into your pockets either," Legion didn't care and the anger built up inside over Kattya was coming out.

Dauge appreciated the anger and the sex that followed would be all he needed to get the miner girl out of his system. Dauge above all wanted the girl out of his mind. He wanted everything from their time in the Republic of New Magic to Thox put behind them once they reached Eternis. For once they reached Eternis this time; everything else that happened prior would all just be a bad dream.

The girl still didn't give Legion her name but with the storm getting worse, she ordered the both of them to follow her down one of the stairways to the lower decks. What luck, he thought. Legion was pleased that their situation was already turning for the better. Now, they had a place to stay for the duration of the trip.

The stairway led down to two different decks before finally ending on a third. The third deck was dark and moist. There wasn't much lighting and with almost everything being made of wood, torches were not really recommended, even with the dampness from the rain.

She knew were she was going, though, and proved to be an effective guide through the dark hallways and corridors of the barge. She managed to guide them through the twists and turns and even told them where the slips and crevices were and to watch out for them. Finally, she pulled a key and made a final left turn. It was a large key, as was customary for certain ships and types.

She opened the old basic wooden door that looked to almost be just apart of the wall until she pointed it out. The door opened to a bland off-white room with nothing on the walls and four large cots spaced out across the large area. The room was actually pretty decent sized. It just didn't have anything except for the four large cots and the appropriate bedding.

"So, this is it?" Legion asked, a bit discouraged.

"I feel it's worlds better than where you were, Eternian," she replied sarcastically.

Dauge ignored the both of them and rushed toward one of the cots. He stripped to his skins and wrapped himself in the blankets offered and made quick work of the cot. Within minutes, he was fast asleep.

"I see you're brother takes to our room well." She walked over to the farthest cot, ushering Legion, making him follow her. Little by little, her clothes came off, revealing an elven woman with quite the body. She had weight and curves in all the right places.

Just before making her way onto the large green cot built for two, Legion grabbed her by the arm and spun her around. He locked his lips to hers. The force between them instantly drove the woman into a frenzy. She'd never felt a force like that or felt wanted like that. Even if it was for pay, she could dream and pretend that this was a man that just couldn't resist it. He had to have her.

Legion ripped the woman's basic blouse down. He grabbed down by her groin with his strongest hand. He gripped the loose area of fabric slowly and tightly. His face eased back from hers but he kept his eyes locked into hers as if to make sure she wasn't going to try anything. In an instant, her leggings tore off as if they were tear-away in the back.

Once the clothes were no longer in the way, he took her ass into his hands, hoisting her up around his waist. His grip was tight. She wrapped her legs around him and her arms around his neck. They didn't make it to the cot. Legion slammed her hard against the wall, penetrating her body. The entire scene was so exhilarating, she didn't even see him come out of his pants.

His lips fell to her neck. She yelled out thrust after thrust, tearing into his back with her elven nails. Even through his shirt, she managed to dig into flesh. The cuts of her nails pushed him to shove his member into her deeper and deeper, harder and harder. It hurt. It hurt her. he didn't care. Her moan said no more but don't stop all at the same time.

Legion's back was to his sleeping brother. her eyes caught a glimpse of Dauge's sneakily prying open. She grinned devilishly, moaning and praying for more. Her mouth invitingly and excitedly came open, partially to tease and taunt the curious Dauge.

Dauge merely opened his eyes just for the moment. The racket his brother was causing awoke him. he'd been trained to sleep through the worst conditions and this was far from what he'd seen, especially considering his time with the Lotus people.

Legion ravaged the poor girl more fiercely than she'd ever felt before. His back bled from her nails. She'd even bitten his neck, drawing more blood. It seemed the more she bit and dug into him, the more fiercely he tore into her body. He repositioned his hands underneath her butt from inside of her legs hoisting her up to where her sweet flower submerged his face. Now, her legs tied themselves around his neck and even more than before, she screamed out, keeping her hands at the top of his head as if to keep him there. Yes, yes, yes, over and over she cried out to the dead gods for the beautiful disaster taking her body.

One after another, she pulsated into his mouth and face. He was covered and dripping. It only made him force his tongue and mouth into her more. To tease, he raised her a little higher to explore the crack of her backside with his tongue. And just as she was getting into it, he'd drop her back down and begin pounding her into the wall, yet again. Who was this creature? She'd never been taken with such authority before.

Finally, even she'd had enough and she felt the madman slowing down. His hands raised up and went around her legs again, catching her buttocks into his hands once again and once again, he pushed and shoved his body into hers with everything he had. He never roared out. He never really made a sound or even breathed heavy. She couldn't figure it out. She didn't understand. She started pleading with Legion to stop but he wouldn't. He didn't. He refused. Her begging only made him force it into her even harder.

Eventually, tears fell from her face. When he knew her body couldn't handle anymore. He let go, allowing her to drop freely to the floor. Her butt hit hard. For a second, she thought it was over but a tight grip from his hand to the top of her told her it wasn't. She'd never been so scared in her life. Slowly, he eased his cock into her mouth. Her back stayed propped against the wall and her legs spread open with her butt on the floor.

Her eyes met his. She didn't like the grin on his face but she did what he wanted, pleasing him in every way possible. And then it started. She'd never done such a thing before but she was terrified to anger him. She closed her eyes opening her throat allowing his juices to flow down smoothly.

When it was done, he pulled himself out of her mouth and turned for a cot not belonging to her. She sat upright against the wall, a sexual mess. She didn't understand. Now, the monster just walked away? Who was this son of a bitch?

She politely offered and then requested the beast of a man to sleep alongside her in her cot. Legion cared not for her request. Part of it was getting back at Kattya. Somehow, hurting the elf both physically and emotionally would help him think he'd gotten back at the miner who'd got to him. In truth, he knew this meant nothing to Kattya but he liked to think he was taking a strike at all women.

Legion fell onto the cot and quickly wrapped up. Even while the woman still sat spread eagle with a cloud of confusion hanging over her, Legion closed his eyes and prepared for dreamland. He was tired and satisfied. His cot and blanket was warm. It'd been a long time since he'd had such a sleep.

Dauge and Legion awoke to rumbling and shaking. The barge was being pushed around. This wasn't a storm or a natural current. Bombardments going off on the surface level shook them both right out of their beds. The elven girl was curled up on her cot, screaming and crying.

Dauge never unsuited but Legion did. The younger one waited for the older while he reequipped everything. "Hurry," he said over and over again.

Legion hurried as fast as he could. Dauge set his armblades to the side of his belt. They hung loosely from their straps. They typically were stocked hidden on his back when he knew they were going to be put to use. He allowed them to hang loosely from specially made frogs at his side.

The second Legion was fully strapped down and ready to go, Dauge burst through the door and charged through the halls like a man on a mission. The barge rocked and every so often, the both of them had to catch themselves. About every thirty seconds, a huge boom went off and the barge shook even more. One of the booms nearly took Dauge off of his feet.

Legion couldn't believe it. He thought back, though, just for a second at the little elven girl he'd ruined the night before. She was safe on the lower decks; at least he hoped she was. He couldn't believe it. He couldn't believe he cared at all. Then again, he wasn't a bad person. He just didn't have a reason to care for her. He hired her for her services and she fulfilled the obligation.

Dauge and Legion reached the top deck. Before the barge ever left, the eight hired mercenaries were pointed out to everyone. And everyone was ordered to stay out of their way. They were only to take orders from the man in charge.

Dauge and Legion got to the top only to see most of it burning and caving in. Luckily, these transport barges were pretty thick. Joined at the hip with hooks and ropes, a relatively large cog-like vessel sat. More and more orcish pirates launched themselves, either from loose swinging ropes or by their own two feet from their boat to the barge. Wooden gangways were being thrown down and utilized as well.

They wore light leathers and clothing. Most wielded large falchions or small crossbows. They'd only take one shot before dropping the crossbow it seemed like. Then from their ship, blackish arrows soared through the air, striking the large crate like-prison that held the prisoners.

Each time an arrow hit, a small piece of the wooden crate disintegrated. Dauge and Legion hit the top deck just in time to see the true strength of the arrows. Most of the girls, workers, and mercenaries were either dead or dying. Some were being taken alive as prisoners. They were most likely the unlucky ones.

Some were literally being taken back onto the other ship kicking and dragging. The orcs carried them and dragged them by their hair. They screamed for help but there was no one around to help them. The fight of the mortal spirit, Legion thought.

Dauge unhinged his armblades and Legion cracked a laugh while pulling Mourning Star. Mourning Star gave a radiant glow of power but nothing that Legion could truly appreciate. It was like the weapon didn't want the fight to take place.

Legion looked at a few nearby orcs that were doing work to their barge. Dauge yelled for his older brother to get back. Legion paused and peered over his shoulder. The rain was still coming. It in no way was trying to let up. Fire, rain, storm, the water below, and burning barge filled with pirates, this was just their luck. They sure could use Dash and Pitt right about now, thought Legion.

The dawning of the day was coming. It was late in the night or early in the morning hours. Within an hour or two, daylight would cut back into the night. Of course something would have to happen in order to ruin his perfect night's sleep, Legion thought.

Dauge pointed to the gangways over toward the ship. Legion didn't understand. There were too many orcs all around them. Why not just go after one of them? Then it hit him. Dauge wanted to target whoever their leader or leaders were.

"Right," Legion said.

They were in sync. They didn't have to speak and spell it out sometimes. Sometimes they were just on. Dauge and Legion rushed for the gangways. The orcs onboard the barge weren't prepped for their attack at all. One orc looked back after finishing off the last of the two would-be mercenaries. He grunted angrily. Nothing prompted any of them to prep for a possible surprise attack.

Seeing more arrows hit lit Dauge's attention up. He'd never seen arrows like that but he'd heard of them. They were extremely rare and only made through truly dark rituals.

"Necrotic arrows!" he yelled.

"We need to get to the source before those fucking prisoners get out!" Legion said.

Dauge was faster. He taunted and screamed, trying to get the missile attention of the orc ship to focus on him and not his brother. And just as expected, it worked. A flurry of arrows and bolts flew his way. At least two or three were of the necrotic nature. The same arrows that were eating through the giant crate, piece by piece.

Dauge vanished and then Mourning Star turned to a complete red. It was dark like the color of fresh spilled blood. The arrows stuck into the ground of the barge. The necrotic ones dismantled several boards and wooden pieces. Dauge reappeared on the gangway several feet from his brother.

He'd vanished and teleported. Legion always grabbed Mourning Star by the shaft and chain when running. Otherwise, the flailing chain could prove to be troublesome. He often utilized it as a one-shafted weapon when running, almost like a bo-staff.

Legion's feet touched the wooden gangplank and Dauge disappeared again. This time it wasn't by teleport. This time, he leaped from the wooden walkway and over the railing of their ship to board it.

"Dauge!" Legion yelled, letting loose the spiked ball and chain of Mourning Star.

One orc came from behind and another pulled himself atop the gangplank from the orcish cog. They both charged simultaneously but Legion's vengeful roar and whirling motion caught both the aggressing orcs off guard. The first one was caught critically on the head as he charged. The force knocked him from the wooden plank and into the cold water below.

The second one was already in mid swing but so was Legion. He dropped to a ducking position, nearly falling to both knees as he carried his momentum around. The chain wrapped around the orc's legs and the orc swiped down with his falchion, missing. Legion jumped back to his standing position, yanking back and upward on the shaft in doing so.

The orc yelled out in pain. The spiked ball dug deep into the back of his lower calf and ankle. Precious tendons ran down in that area. The orc fell hard onto his back. Legion heard the plank crack a little. He reeled back Mourning Star and turned back to head for the orcish ship where his brother chose to recklessly dive into the chaos.

One foot after another, Legion climbed up the gangway until he finally reached the top guard railing. Orcs were everywhere. He looked over his shoulder again. This time, he noticed the giant wooden crate that acted as a prison was all but done. Just a little more and those prisoners would be free.

Down on the deck, his brother effortlessly flowed like wind through the orcs trying to encircle and overbear him. His armblades dripped with their dark blood. Most of his face and torso was already doused as well. Dauge looked up only for a second to see Legion.

Legion jumped down. His eyes told Dauge where to look and what to do. This time, this random time against a random adversary they fell into sync like they'd never been before. Dauge rolled the wooden handles of his blades to stick the blades outward rather than allow them to run down the bone of his forearm.

He twirled one final time, delicately cutting open several throats before finding two final orcs to stick them deep in to. Dauge looked up. Legion charged down to take his brother's position. The cog was actually running out of orcs. There was still a trapdoor leading downward where orcs still poured from. Legion and Dauge would drop them faster than they could pour out. And what about the orcs on the burning barge?

Dauge's eyes fell upon exactly what Legion feared. Up top, there were four orcish archers in the crow's nest. Those were the four firing the necrotic arrows. Dauge looked around the ship. The ship had ballistic mechanisms firing off regular missiles as well. This ship was well-built and designed. That was for sure. Dauge was without weapons. He left the armblades inside the final two orcs he cut down with them. At the front of the ship, two sturdy orcish fellows both wielding massive double-bladed axes stood in guard to another. A Genasi who held the helm strong, even in the horrid storm, he kept the ship steering correctly even with the tied barge half sunk still locked to it.

The Genasi was clearly embodying the stormy elements of his kind. The two orcs wore dark black sleeveless leathers around their bodies. They were big, even for orcs. Legion whirled Mourning Star around, yelling out in anger hoping to keep their attention.

What if the prisoners did get loose? All he had to do was break free of the barge and they would be stuck at sea. That barge was too far gone to go anywhere. It was half sunk but its own build options were keeping it afloat. There were chambers built to keep water in and lock and secure it from other areas. Half of it still broke the surface but the other half stayed completely submerged. It bobbled in the water at a forty-five degree angle.

Dauge pulled and threw faster than he'd ever done before. The remaining orcs didn't know whether to target Dauge or Legion. The ship was big but it wasn't that big. Dauge stayed positioned at first. The mechanisms each got a dagger down their barrels or through some of the ropes and pulleys that made the mechanics of it work properly.

The most amazing part of Dauge's attack was not his precise shots against the missile mechanisms scattered across the ship. After they were taken out and he took a quick glimpse to the side to see his brother fell the last orc guarding the Genasi, Dauge in a single motion leaped to the guardrail throwing four daggers from one hand. His other hand cut the first two of the roped hooks keeping the barge tied to the ship.

One, two, three, four gasps of pain gave way as three of the four orcs fell lifeless back down into the cup of the crow's nest. That shot was nearly impossible to land much less fatally. The fourth fell from the crow's nest all the way down to the top deck below.

Dauge kept a running movement with his final dagger cutting through the ropes ruthlessly fast that still kept the barge linked to the cog. Legion made it to the top deck and the two double-bladed-axe-wielding orcs charged him. The Genasi, in fear of his life, moved away from the helm and headed over toward the very tip of the ship. The ship wasn't big enough for him to get by the three engaged in melee without putting himself in harm's way.

This particular Genasi wore crafty leathers outfitted with pieces of chain and metal. It was a very unique piece of armor to say the least. She wore her snow-white hair up and bunned. At her side, she kept nothing but a short sword and a short bow on her back. Something moved about in the wind behind her. It was like an invisible cloak of some kind. She turned, pulling the short sword. This Genasi was prepared for war.

Legion's blood red ball and chain wrapped around the shaft of the first overhand swinging orc's axe. With his weapon tangled, the orc pulled back, feeling himself to be the greater primate between the two. The other took his shot, seeing Legion locked.

Legion's eyes and body were focused on neither. He tried to keep his back to neither of them and rather one rib cage per adversary. In the distance he could hear his brother telling him to hang on and that he was coming. He could hear screams from the barge. That must mean it's being cut loose, he thought.

Legion didn't want to, but he didn't have a choice. He had to turn and focus his energies on the orc whose axe was tangled up with his weapon. The other axe swung at him horizontally. Legion turned his head just to keep an eye on where the creature stood. He lifted his knee straight up to his chest and then extended his leg out, hitting the orc hard in his stomach. It didn't hurt the creature but it did knock the breath out of him and push him back a step or two.

Legion screamed angrily. Mourning Star decided to help him. Suddenly, the shaft of the axe tangled up with Mourning Star melted and the axe fell in two pieces. The orc managed to catch the lower portion but the upper portion fell flat to the deck of the old wooden ship.

Seeing a tactical advantage, he turned and with an overhand of his own he hurled his flail atop the head of the opposing orc. The orc stepped back again. It raised its double-bladed axe with a hand gripped on both sides. Mourning Star's vertical fall forced it to once again wrap around the shaft and somehow melt the axe of the second orc once again into two.

Both orcs stood back, seeing Legion's ball and chain do hideous work against both their weapons. Now, both pulled what was left of their weapons. Neither seemed fazed to be wielding two one-handed axes as opposed to one doubled-bladed, double-sided axe.

Legion back stepped, trying to get the both of them in front of him. They mirrored and followed, slowing the action down a little. The few steps leading to the helm at the upper most part of the front acted as his guide back down to the main portion of the top deck.

The Genasi dispersed and returned as a puddle of water standing adjacent to Legion. An upward thrust from her short sword cut the torso of the oldest Xavier from bottom to top. Her liquid appearance became glacial before reforming back to its normal state. Legion felt the cut. He could take the wound. Then, something in the wound kept digging at him.

He fell back, losing control of his vitals. His bowels even released. Legion, for the first real time let go of Mourning Star, unable to keep a grip on its hilt. Before the world went black, he noticed something dripping consistently from her blade, a bluish liquid.

Legion's eyes cracked open again. He'd not a clue how long he'd been out. His body was debilitated. He couldn't move but the pain was amplified and he surely still felt it. He hurt. He hurt bad. He gasped out in pain.

He lay completely beaten at the center of the cog's top deck. Dauge's armblades were back. He'd reclaimed them and made it to his enemies already. His brother was something of a prodigy when it came to battle and war. Perhaps it was his years of training with the Lotus. The sky faded away once again. His last image was of Dauge dancing with the armblades against the Genasi and the two orcs.

Again, his eyes opened. The pain was still there, though it was numbing now. Dauge still fought all three. Finally, Dauge vanished and reappeared behind Genasi who once again turned into a liquid immediately. Dauge rolled both armblades as he'd done previously. This time, he caught one of the orcs mid double swing, piercing both blades into its lower right rib cage. Dauge forced the things up as high as they would go before releasing them for his short swords.

The orc fell back, releasing his axes and falling to his knees and then to his hands. One hand came up to hold the wound where the blades still held their mark. He coughed and gagged and blood quickly began to ooze not only from the wounds and down the blades but from its mouth as well.

The second orc came at him from the side with the Genasi now reforming in front of him. Dauge's Genasi power to teleport by vanishing from existence and reforming in a different place were gone for the day. He'd have to rest before those powers were restored. The orc opened his arms wide, extending his blades out as far as he could. He brought them in, trying to scissor Dauge between them.

Dauge dropped lower than he expected, splitting his legs all the way down to his groin. His groin touched the wood of the deck and another weapon of Dauge's was lost. He planted it firmly and deeply into the orc penetrating first through the stem. He worked the short sword in until the top of the hilt was touching the creature's testicles.

He temporarily let go of his other sword and put his hands on the hips of the creature to catch it from falling on him. With a heave and a push, he flipped the orc over him, reclaiming his sword and his footing. Now, it was just him and the Genasi. And still, the air was filled with the screams and pleas of drowning mortals.

Without hesitating, he knew she was stunned by his performance against the two orcs. He charged forward. The woman, like him, carried two embodiments. His short sword would have landed flush on her sternum but her abilities forged her into stone and his sword slid off to her right side.

Instantly, she was flesh again. She slammed her arm down by her side and twisted, using his own momentum against him. His choice was to either lose the sword or have his wrist and possibly forearm snapped.

Dauge stutter stepped wildly to catch himself. He turned back, seeing the woman standing there with her short sword still dripping that same blue liquid. Dauge gave no cares toward the weapon or what it possibly possessed.

The girl rushed him unexpectedly after a short pause and stare. Dauge held his breath, smashed a small glass flask on the ground. Out of fear and hesitation, she utilized her last trick, turning her body into watery vapors to avoid the attack. The flask carried highly toxic vaporous fumes.

Dauge dove and rolled to avoid it all. When he turned back over, she was already materialized again and coughing and choking. She stutter stepped and staggered. There was nothing he could do. That was the last of the flasks given to him by the lotus people. His alchemic powers were still maturing. Hopefully, he'd find and befriend a strong alchemist somewhere in Eternis.

He looked over to his brother and then back to the girl. She fell to her knees holding her throat momentarily, before falling over to her back, lifeless. Dauge walked to his brother seeing the wound across his torso. It raced from the lower stomach area near his left hip and rode all the way to the center of his body, ending somewhere between his pecks. His leathers took a hit.

Legion's eyes fell upon Dauge. The pain was starting to kick in much worse now. Dauge smiled, knowing he would be all right. Dauge peeled a potion from his purse. It was a small one and he refused to tell Legion where he'd got it or how long he had it. All Legion needed to know was that it was going to mend and heal his wounds.

Dauge dragged Legion to a nearby area he deemed safe and looked over toward the trapdoor. First, he thought. He walked over to the dead girl who made one really bad decision that cost her life and took her short sword. This will replace the sword that went into his balls, he thought. He once again reclaimed and stocked his armblades and returned to his waking brother.

"I'm going to clean out the bottom decks. I need you to stay right here while I'm away and don't die on me."

"When will I know of all your tricks, brother?" Legion's words slurred and were sloppy but Dauge got them.

He smiled. "When I am dead and dust, and there's nothing left for me to give."

Legion begged sloppily for Dauge to wait until he was there to go with him. He didn't want his brother going to the lower level without him. What if more of those Genasi were down there, he thought.

"I know what you're thinking, brother, but you'll just get in the way," he said.

When Legion's eyes opened again, he could move, surprisingly. The wound was still there but not bleeding. He still felt slow and Mourning Star was no longer glowing. Dauge was sitting not too far from him. The rain was still coming and Legion could tell, not too much time had passed. The barge however, he could see was now several feet from the boat. That meant they drifted at least a little since he'd been out.

Tied and bound in front of the relaxing Dauge was a tiefling. His skin was more a yellow orange and his horns were a darkened red. He was bright colored fellow, even for a tiefling. Most tieflings were dark in color but still colored. This one's color was a little unique. He lay on his stomach with his hands and feet hog tied together.

"What happened brother?" Legion asked.

"This sword, the one that Genasi cut you with, has an ability to produce blowfish poison every so often throughout the day when activated. That's why you could feel everything but just couldn't move," he answered. "Now for the more important question, who in the fucking dead gods is this and why were we attacked?"

Legion shook his head, pulling himself to a half-upright but spread comfortably position. He took a second but finally, he reequipped Mourning Star and stood looking up into the rain. The rain required Legion to close his eyes but open his mouth. He was a bit thirsty and appreciated the situation. Dauge stood after seeing Legion.

"Now then, tiefling, who are you?" Legion asked.

"Just fucking kill me!" he screamed.

"It's not if you die friend, it's how long it takes," Dauge said, smiling.

"I was the one supposed to buy the prisoners. I figured this to be an easy score. They didn't know I had a ship and I knew they'd barge them over to Eternis," he said.

"Are you wanted anywhere?" Legion asked.

"Why, you looking to collect the reward?" he asked.

"No, I want to make sure we don't cross those people if we have you," he replied.

The tiefling stopped talking. Dauge took a step over his tied body, pulled up his head by his horns and thick black hair. With a single motion, he cut the pirate's throat from ear to ear, giving him a fatally deep smiling face across his neck.

"We're going to need a little luck and a lot of help getting this thing close to port in Eternis," Dauge said.

Legion knew his brother was cold but that was perhaps the coldest act of murder he'd ever seen him do. Just a few feet away, he saw the barge still half sunk and people waving and pleading for their lives. Legion and Dauge knew they would need them, all of them. Or, at least most of them would be needed. "There's an elf in the lower decks, a working girl. Whoever brings her to me will be safe and be granted safe passage!" Legion yelled.

Dauge curiously thought and then asked, "And what if one of those green bastards brings her to you?"

"After seeing what happened here, I don't think they're going to find the will to fight, brother," he replied.

It took nearly an hour but four orcs, some humans and elves, a few dwarves and halflings, and two working girls made their way back to the vessel. With the help of the newly found wash-ups, they refit the damaged sails and made their way back to the busted barge. Had it not been for the rain, the barge would have surely burned to nothing.

Legion, seeing his elven call girl saved, ordered one of the orcs to bring her to the captain's quarters. He quickly agreed. The orcs were then ordered to tear down what was left of the busted crate and shackles and chains were placed upon each and every one of the prisoners. Not a single one gave a single bead of sweat to resistance.

There were nearly fifty of them. This cog was a little bigger than average. Cogs were perfect for this straight but still a little too big to sail into harbor. The orcs explained the ship could house thirty to thirty five men comfortably. With everyone on board, they were having to put people in the cargo areas. The conditions were not safe or convenient. Thankfully, it was only about a day out from being within reach of Eternis.

Everyone on board the ship agreed to listen to Dauge and Legion without question or concern. Those first four orcs carried out their orders to a tee. They liked that. Dauge ordered the ship to anchor as close as it could to Eternis. And with that, the two brothers rejoined their elven working girl in the captain's quarters. It was quite humorous. The orcs had to escort them to the captain's quarters, the place they explained would be their home until they arrived in Eternis.

Chapter 92

When Bahaus awoke everything around him was different. He no longer saw beings of flesh and bone but lines and levels of existence. What were levels of existence? Everything carried definition by weight of their importance to him and his goals.

They still looked very much the same but to him they still appeared different. The ensuing battles took the lives of most of the cretins he could remember. That bitch of gargoyle still had a heartbeat. He hated that scaled cunt.

Bahaus awoke to glorious news. A shadar-kai human named De'Nari engineered a new throne room for him and Aristophane. It was built secretly underneath the main castle and fortress and built precisely to her specifications.

It was beautiful. Every single stone was pulled from the farthest mines where only the purest of bloodstones existed. Bloodstones weren't typically truly expensive gems in the grand scheme of gems, but they were still erotically gorgeous to look at. Each one looked like they were bleeding out from the inside, constantly.

The twin thrones made of iron, swords, spells, and bone rested high upon a mound of mended bones and steel. Spells meshed and hardened it all. The room itself was large, spanning nearly the size of the entire fortress itself and this was one of the Red Mystic's larger works.

Speckles of gold and platinum traced over each stone hundreds of times, and in the dark the room lit up with stars. The golden and platinum was magically infused to do so. And to Aristophane's liking, there were no seams between the stones; it all meshed together, making the room look like it had been carved completely out of one large bloodstone.

Bahaus awoke no longer pinned to the machines and the titans but to sitting on his black and red velvet throne alongside his gargoyle queen. De'Nari was there, kneeling before them, obviously proud of his work. The lines of De'nari, in the eyes of Bahaus, were dim. He meant nothing.

Scores of creatures of a variety of races stood proud in the throne room. Another to come forward and kneel was the gnoll Ankhemao. Ankhemao stood tall and old. He'd been around for some time. He'd followed Aristophane for nearly the entire length of it. Most of his long snout had been crushed in and pieces of his nose and ears were missing.

He wore his armor decorated with the flesh and teeth of his enemies proudly. He stood tall, with halberd in hand, before he fell to a knee to both Bahaus and Aristophane. Again, the newly infused Bahaus saw the creature as dim. He saw them all as dim creatures. He wasn't a mastered product yet but he didn't care. He no longer needed them. He no longer needed any of them.

Behind the highest-ranking gnoll among their horde, two more walked forward with chained prisoners. These gnolls were younger and now to Bahaus they had absolutely no lines at all. They forced the two prisoners to their knees. One was a beaten shadow elf and the other a human whose lines shined brightly. They were thicker than anyone else's in the room. That sole diamond in the rough was perhaps the only reason he didn't vindicate their existence with a proper cleansing.

Without a word, his newly found powers told him. This human carried the same blood as the one who once served him and found his way to the devils before turning back to his old ways. Cale Dar was the single reason he failed in his attempt on Emerald Greene. And now, his son kneeled before him, chained and helpless.

Bahaus only saw his once-ally-turned-enemy kneeling. Next to him was a shadow elf. Shadow elves could always be of some use. His acute attention to detail told him the tongue worn around the neck of Ankhemao belonged to the shadow elf kneeling beside Cale Dar's offspring.

Speak, to speak, why? What did speaking do for anyone? Wasn't verbal communication such an outdated process? And yet, the mortals still did it? How cute? Another heartbeat suddenly caught his attention, though it was one his eyes could not foresee. It wasn't formed yet. It was going to form soon. It would form in the womb of Aristophane. She would bear his child! It could not be! He would have to extinguish her from the world long before that abomination was allowed to be birthed.

The prisoners, what to do with them? His cretins—his people, or whatever they were—they brought him gifts in the form of prisoners. They could have captured any but they were not in the business of capturing their adversaries. These two meant something. One was the son of Cale Dar and the other was a shadow elf. Even he was impressed with their simple minds. If they were going to bring captured beings to his presence, it should be the kind that would fill his heart and spirit with cheer.

"Shadow elf, what is your name and what orders are you on to attempt something against myself and King Bahaus?" Aristophane asked condescendingly down to the beaten shadow elf.

Both the shadow elf and the son of Cale Dar were stripped of everything. They were naked and covered in mud and blood. The monstrous cretins that served them weren't too forgiving, a quality Bahaus considered redeemable amongst his people.

Ankhemao chuckled, standing up from his kneeling position. He once again bowed to show his loyalty before carrying forward with his words. "My liege," he started, not really directing his words to either. He kept his eyes to the floor as he spoke. "His tongue was removed when he chose to remove his handcuffs without permission."

Bahaus never flinched. Ankhemao, the most experienced of all the beings loyal to the horde serving under him and Aristophane popped. It was such an effortless task and the legendary gnoll that had plagued the countryside for decades was no more. Splatters of blood, flesh, and insides saturated the clothes and faces of those nearby, including the shadar-kai engineer De'Nari.

Aristophane couldn't believe what he'd done. The only reason the Rogue Army and its allies had been held off this long was because of the war-torn gnoll and Bahaus obliterated him like he was an ant upon a dying hill.

"Bahaus!" she yelled in desperation. "What do you—"?

Aristophane was cut off. Bahaus forced her from her throne next to him. She vanished from sight. A large mushroom suddenly grew out from the eyes and holes of the skulls and bones mended below. And then, from out of the eyes and mouths of the mound below the thrones came thousands of vermin.

They rushed the gray scaly colored mushroom and even began to eat each other over it. Bahaus gave his old slight grin and chuckle. A fitting end to a scaly bitch who thought she belonged beside me, he thought. A fitting end to the dirty cunt who thought she would bring my child into this world. What fantasy to believe I would allow the birth of a Sazos-Uil-Endail not to be pure.

The overflow of power nearly overtook him after his removal of Aristophane. The others around didn't know what to do. They couldn't resist but they were forged under her, not him. He decimated her without even lifting a finger. All they knew was that they were the elite amongst the horde and now it was the horde that he commanded.

Bahaus' very skin began to change as he sat upon the throne. Something urged De'nari to move forward. Nothing spoke or moved, until De'nari moved and bowed to the new prince of power. Bahaus' skin became transparent. And inside of where his flesh should be, one looking on saw nothing but space and stars; the harder one stared the deeper into the blackness they'd become.

Bahaus became a living embodiment of the Astral Sea, or so he looked. De'nari stood. The others couldn't believe it. He wasn't shaking or nervous at all. Bahaus finally echoed out his voice. To some, it was too potent. Their eardrums burst and blood oozed down their jawlines and necks. Those that could withstand it heard something more arrogant than ever before.

"Tear down these thrones and join them to one. In what world do I have an equal? Such a place does not exist."

One of the highest-ranking members of the horde was splattered to bits. There was nothing left. And what for, anger or frustration; he possibly killed him over boredom. It was evident. Bahaus no longer cared for the horde or what they did. Ankhemao's skills kept them alive against the Rogue Army.

Bahaus emanated a laugh, bringing every last one of them down to their knees. The fallen prince used his own powers to touch De'nari. The others clasped their ears, crying out in pain. His laugh echoed out, driving them all to the brink of their sanity. Fight as they could, the laugh of Bahaus Sazos-Uil-Endail drove all present in the room save himself and De'nari to the point of complete and utter madness.

Bahaus created a new essence and state of being for himself. The others didn't know what to do. He left a thought in the head of De'nari to leave the prisoners as they were but heavily guarded. Bahaus reformed and planted his body back down, connecting it fully to the machinations that continued to bleed the titans of their power and pour it into him.

Wait, his body was on the verge of becoming something even more than what it had already ascended into. His mortal body needed no more but his soul yearned for it all. Greed, greed could cost him everything. It nearly did already. The titans were from a world now long gone. They were from a world that no longer existed. Should he press on, he would become nothing more than a host to the powers they once cultivated.

He wanted something different. He wanted to become something in his own right. Bahaus forced the powers from his body. An ethereal force burst out from his being. Walls caved in and mountaintops collapsed.

Bahaus knew. His enemies knew where he was. Every single one of the creatures under his command or previously Aristophane's, and even some that were unfortunately just in the area became something much more than they ever were.

Their flesh disappeared. Their eyes fell to nothingness, a see-through state, as did their entire bodies. Hands and feet became talons and claws. Hair grew long and thick like the mane of a lion. The creatures grew teeth and all formed into something universal. Humanoids, monstrous creatures, kobolds, elves, hobgoblins, gnolls, they all grew into something resembling a large lycanthropic lion with perhaps the blood of a true fiend. And only by motion could partial lines be made out. By looking directly at one of the creatures, a perceptive eye could tell something existed by the distortion of the existence of things lying behind it.

Aside from De'nari, the shadow elf, and Cale's child, all within a very large vicinity belonged to him and were creatures of his own liking and creation. He wouldn't disrespect his own existence by using things put into place by the lost gods of Thedia.

Razkus was cold and getting colder. The titanic implosion of the mountains, the monumental explosion from Bahaus caused hundreds of mountaintops to fall in and walls and chains of mountains to reform and reshape. Bahaus now made his mark on the world. The ancient chain of mountains once belonging to the Red Mystics had physically been altered.

The titans' bodies were gone, as was everything he remembered about the fortress he was occupying. He knew others were coming for him. He could sense their presence. Were they close enough? Did they feel the wrath of the fallen prince? Wait, no longer was he the fallen prince. Now, he'd risen. He was the prince risen back from the ash of a lost city. Yes, without him Eternis was lost.

Then, everything went away and crashed around him. The things of his imagination dawned for the first time during the collapsing of the fortress he'd occupied. The thought of it tickled Bahaus; he'd literally moved mountains. He found and obtained a power far beyond simple arcane. He'd become something more than he ever thought possible.

Bahaus appeared, hovering just over where the shadow elf and Cale's seed still knelt. His new creations helped keep them in place. They both looked up at him in terror. Terror! Bahaus appreciated the fear he instilled in the two. His lower half still bled down, molding itself into the air, almost as if a ghost. The way his creatures moved, it looked like they meshed and blended in and out of form together; it was like they could share existence and come to and out of form together.

Bahaus cackled his evil laugh. Kleiven kept his eyes and head high. Grath did the same. They were both terrified but they knew come whatever may, there was nothing they could do about it. When the fear left their hearts, Bahaus sensed it. He also sensed life in beings not constructed from Thedian origins and distorted by his imagination.

Kleiven leaned over as best he could, whispering something into the ear of Grath. Blood snuck out through his lips and ran down his chin.

"If I get out of this, make sure Dusk knows I died loving her." His eyes met Grath's. He'd given the shadow elf a fated quest, something to achieve in the wake of his death.

"And you do the same," Grath managed to get across in spite of his tongue.

In that lone second, there was moment where Kleiven's entire world came crashing down like the mountains. He couldn't believe it. How could Grath say such a thing to him? Wait, they weren't friends. They were acquaintances, united under a common goal.

Suddenly, Grath changed. Grath looked like him, human and pure, Eternian through and through. Even though he had pale skin and red hair, he was still a human and native to Eternis. Then Grath's body transformed again and vanished.

He had smooth golden fur all over his gigantic feline body. A darker and more golden color hung down thick and strong, forming the mane behind his neck. He was still a bipedal. He looked like him! He looked like him. Kleiven brought his open hands up to his face. Wait, he was free?

He was set free. When? He saw the same smoothness and claw-like talons. He was Grath and Grath was him. Darkness set in. Blindness overtook his body. Kleiven fell fast asleep, leaving behind everything he ever was, just like Grath.

Chapter 93

Siberon finally made it. He'd returned the samurai's seal and the Bhellioa Ivy to the rightful askers. Storm was going to return to Thox even though he'd begun a name for himself there in the Nine Kingdoms. The rest of his team would stay with him.

Siberon felt differently. He had his money. It was time to move on. Dargon helped him but he felt that as long as he was around Dargon, he'd never reach his full potential. He wanted to make unbiased decisions and not worry about what Dargon thought. He promised to regroup with the others but he wanted to make a stop there in the Crystal Cities.

His ship was docking. He was on a vessel built to be seaworthy and the journey went fine. He had new clothes, new tools, new everything. Siberon's future was looking up. He had connections in the prime port city of Crystalle. Crystalle was a beautiful city but that's not why he was going.

Siberon favored black and white clothing. He wore his new short-sleeved shirt and knee-long pants with pride. He'd even purchased a bit of jewelry from the western lands. The Nine Kingdoms were great but not a place to live, if you asked him. Those damned orcs trained in their ancient samurai art instilled a fear he never wanted to feel again.

His days at sea were coming to an end. He bought a ticket onto a vessel far too large to personally port in Crystalle. Luck was on his side; at least he'd found a ship in the Nine Kingdoms heading back to the place where he wanted to go.

This was The Finest Tusk, and it was a grand sight. Maybe one day he'd return to Thox and rejoin Storm. After all, that was the plan. He pretty much knew that they knew he wasn't going back. The told temple was found and they did everything they set out to do. It was just his time to go. Teams came together and broke apart. That was the reality of it.

Crews that stuck together did often make history more times than the ones that didn't. Oh well, this was the start of his life. This was the beginning. He'd taken part in every luxury the Finest Tusk has to offer.

He especially fancied the working women aboard the ship. He typically favored elves to humans but had an acute fondness for half-bred things. Half elves were at the top of the list as far as Siberon was concerned.

Time drew past and it was finally his time to board the next set of rowboats to the port. He boarded the boat next to around twenty or so other passengers. The smell of salt from the sea really opened up his nostrils. It was just about high noon and the weather offered a cool breeze but nothing too harsh for the half-elf.

The boat ride back got Siberon to thinking. Storm was a good man and honored paladin of Typherion, the good dragon. He had a goal, a personal goal that he would see to over anything and everyone else. Perhaps that's what drove Siberon away.

Kraydia and Krazaikaei were an item. That left Dargon. Dargon was still strong, honest and pure. So was Storm; he was a true-blooded member of the House of Stars and he wanted to see his family reinstated. After the acts of Stasius, that would most likely never come to pass. So then what? Why did Storm actually go all the way to the Nine Kingdoms if he was trying to reinstate his family back into the noble ranks of Thox? No matter what the paladin did, a Stars would never govern a city of Thox again, much less Port Agatha.

Possibly, everything would come to pass more smoothly than he believed was possible and he would return to Thox and rejoin the group. He just didn't believe that to be a viable option. If everything was in place as he thought and everything went as planned, he would have absolutely no reason to return to Thox or rejoin that crew.

Krazaikaei was a bastard son of a bitch anyway. Kraydia was strong willed but her connection to that damned assassin refused to let her speak or think for herself. He nearly died in that temple because of that damned shadow elf.

Krazaikaei was the kind of man loyal to nothing and no one except himself, but Siberon caught a strange vibe from him. Something about Storm Stars kept Krazaikaei in line and honorable. The shadow elf did all of the things behind the doors that Storm couldn't. And Krazy would rather die than reveal those secrets to the paladin. Who would have thought; a shadow elven paladin and a human knight, a holy knight of the good dragon closest friends?

Siberon thought back to that giant pit at the top of the temple. The temple was mostly grown over once they entered, they found themselves going high into it and staying there. They were surrounded by solid stone on every side. The small entombed passageway was all they had. When the passage came to an end and they knew what lay ahead was what they needed, Siberon took it upon himself to dig and pick around for something unseen.

That's when he found a small crevice between the wall blocking their passage and the floor it touched down to. He dropped to his stomach and sprawled out on the floor, reaching under, hoping to try and figure a way to help continue the team's movement.

Something happened. The wall in front was a trap door that had been released some time before they got there and from the looks and feel of it, it'd been down for quite awhile. The wall began to fall, as did the immediate flooring beneath them. Krazaikaei ignored everyone, including his love Kraydia. He stepped and pushed off of Siberon, maximizing his chances of getting to safety.

The wall and floor only fell in about ten feet across. With magic and tools, they all made it across but Siberon fell in because of Krazaikaei. He fell deep into the black pit below. That wall conked him on the head hard. He'd just barely managed to grab the side of that slick stone wall when a piece of that wall socked him.

He could have very easily been put to sleep and let go of the wall and then who knows what would have happened to him? He would have most certainly died! A skill set is important. He knew that in his line of work. He wanted to broaden his horizons even more and continually increase the depth of his toolbox.

He had coin in his pocket, plenty of it. He had to give it to Storm. Storm didn't ask for much but he did make sure his people were taken care of and made sure all of them gave a little something to the churches nearby dedicated to the Draconic ways. It was his way of giving back to the Typherion and the Draconic Order.

Siberon snapped out of it. Light droplets of rain diagonally touched across his body. Wind and rain, he just missed it. Luck was still on his side! He was back. The rowboat came to a stop. He looked up at some wooden docks pushing out in every direction. This was an extensive dock, he thought. He missed Crystalle. It'd been awhile since he'd been there.

Over the immediate horizon, he could see the moving city. Port cities were always busy, especially one like Crystalle. Ships were always coming and going and rowboats were always entering and exiting the place. They had so many minerals and ores, refined and unrefined, that the rest of the world needed, that's why the Crystal Cities were said to be some of the wealthiest cities in the world, if not the wealthiest altogether.

Siberon couldn't help but smile. He was where he would call home for the foreseeable future. The keepers of the rowboat belonging to The Finest Tusk helped the passengers out one by one. Siberon was a traveler. He didn't carry or have much. He did have a thick purse and a grinding mind. He had goals and ambitions this city would easily help feed and quench.

"This way," the boat guide said.

Siberon thanked the middle-aged hardworking human and went on about his business. His feet on the docks of wood belonging to Crystalle were something he didn't think he'd ever feel. Come back, he thought. He'd never actually been to Crystalle but something of his had been here. Something of his was still here! Everything about it excited him. Was he really just a poor child before Dargon snagged him? Work he'd done behind closed doors previously linked him to this city and he swore one day to make a stop here. And today was that day.

His soft moccasins barely picked themselves up. They scraped the rocks and dirt of the streets of Crystalle. Once his feet no longer felt the wood beneath them, he breathed in deeply. Wood had been his only ground for some time and now it was dirt and rock again. There was work to be done, a field to harvest and the city was the bounty.

Chapter 94

The passage all around them collapsed and bent out. Hints of power touched them from Bahaus. Their passages and the walls and caves keeping it place all came crashing down. Draeden's heightened senses and reaction spared all eight of their lives.

Keres was equally responsible for keeping them alive. Draeden forced a bubble of power out from the center knuckle of his hand. He held the hand out just above his heart. A thick jellyfish force of white power encircled them. Keres' eyes closed. Her head fell to bow in prayer.

All eight of them fell with nothing below or around them. Everything vanished and crushed into nothing in the blink of an eye. In that blink, all eight fell to the newly created endless void. Was it really endless? Who knew? All they could see was the black around them and the shattered debris chaotically falling just like them.

Everything they dug into and through was gone. Draeden's powers were enough to group them back together and keep them from falling quickly to their end. Keres' prayer thankfully went answered. Draeden's own powers were reinforced at Keres' request to her faith, Zeronaus the dragon of life and death.

Divine energies channeled through her. The powers were so intense her skin began to glow. Her eyes radiated something unseen to anything in the world before. Draeden tried to keep it together but the pressuring powers of the twin titans being pushed through by the already empowered Bahaus were too much.

"I can't hold it!" he exclaimed, gritting his teeth.

"You have to!" Drackice ordered.

"Come on Draeden," encouraged Keres. She fell back to silent prayer hoping her faith would help her further.

The echoing laughter of something dreadful cried out, surrounding them. The feathery fall suddenly came to a stop. Draeden's magical prowess ended. Keres' divine fueled assistance to the wizard gone as well; the ground beneath them was hard once again.

They were all there, slowly picking themselves up off the ground. The ground was made of a solid clear material constantly intermixing with a light green and teal colored substance. It was like the mixing took place in between two clear shields making a solid piece of mass for the crew to stand upon.

Their eyes scanned the area all around them. And all around them the same colors ran up and down, creating walls and ceilings and rooms. It looked like a mystified castle of someone's dark fairytale coming to life right before their very eyes. And then suddenly, before them, a gigantic throne made of the same stuff materialized. And to a flawless perfection came the thing that was meant to sit upon it, a newly reformed and vested Bahaus Sazos-Uil-Endail.

There was no face but only eyes to look down upon the remaining eight from its seventeen-foot frame. His existence in the room proved the tops of certain rooms were very misleading. This castle or fortress was made completely from his power. Whatever this thing was that once was meant to be the king of Eternis was no more. The true nature of its despicable heart radiated from its presence. Its very essence caused nausea and sickness to the remaining eight.

By now, they were all up and standing ready, though still confused at what it was. Draeden was the lone survivor not to rise. The creature stood over them like a titan made of the same material as the fortress; only the stuff inside him was dark and murky. The green splotches formed unique designs that shined a brightness nothing else around them could hold a candle to. The thing's head was protected by some ancient-looking helm formed from the very same magic its body and fortress hailed from.

"Oh mighty Zeronaus, keeper of heaven and earth, seer of life and death I ask you grant me one last caress.

Touch my body and fuel this hate, secure blessed Thedia and seal his fate.

The usurper of powers and keeper of evil, see to it now he does not prevail.

Only your powers can tame this wild, I ask you to perform and I offer my body as host and child.

Kiss my body and light my soul, secure this life and keep Thedia whole. I beg of you almighty dragon of dragons,

Heed my call and this insurrection!"

"Keres no!" Draeden grumbled from the ground, reaching out to her. He was a pile of near lifelessness. He kept one hand over his face and reached out as if to grab her.

"Keres!" Westlyn yelled.

"No Keres!" Drackice yelled.

Once again, her body began to glow as it had done before. Westlyn silently prayed to the same faith she did. He was considered a Dragoon to the followers of Zeronaus. Dragoon was the highest rank a holy knight could receive from the clergy.

Westlyn roared and the call of a hundred dragons shook the walls of the magical fortress. Bahaus shook too. He charged, whirling his warhammer madly. The creature raised its palm to face downward at Westlyn, but a channel of raw divine might sparked from Keres, shooting up toward the hand in the shape of a thousand draconic heads. Each one screamed and each one bore a different color. Her body opened up as a being called to the mystical light above.

Whips and tentacles shot forth from the creature's giant palm. The ethereal spirits pouring out of Keres met them with an iron will, battling them back and stalemating continuously, thus giving Westlyn the opening he needed to get in close and slam the warhammer into the would-be shin area of the giant creature.

Westlyn's warhammer shattered and so did he. He puffed into a confetti-like a balloon popping from too much air. A giant hole was etched from the attack. Keres armor broke and splintered. On one side came a giant dragon wing gold in color. And on the other side came one of only bone and torn scales. Her body slowly became wrapped up and enveloped by the seeding things coming from both sides.

Drackice stood back. He didn't know what was going on. Upon Westlyn's smash, the fortress itself tinted a darker shade and momentarily faded out. Rakka took it upon himself to seize the opportunity and fled, jumping out of the fortress' area just in the nick of time before it returned. The goblin acted as such a thing, a cowardly creature with loyalty only to itself. Drackice couldn't believe it. Wait, yes he could. Yes, he could believe it.

Draeden stood back up. Slate was now in full advance toward the creature. What on earth or in the high heavens did he think he could do to such a thing? Draeden mustered up what he had left. He saw something he didn't want to see. The two sleeping titans were now dead. Since becoming whatever it was he'd become, he'd taken most of what was left of their powers. This thing could not be stopped and he knew it.

Draeden had a contingency ritual in place. He'd done it before he left. He knew this would come. He couldn't get to them all but he could get to Slate. Tsin, try as he may just couldn't seem to penetrate the raw power of the thing.

Bahaus wasn't really trying to fight them as much as he was trying to complete himself and form once and for all as the being he'd come to be. They just happened to be in the way. Draeden saw through his arcane the invisible armies of indefinite numbers marching to both the Crystal Cities and Eternis.

This battle was a loss, he thought. The creature hadn't finished forming yet, so there was still a chance. There was still a chance, but he needed Keres to channel her divine power with his raw silvery fire. Few wizards today, even those before the Sundering could perform such tasks but Draeden had the ability to break down arcane and channel it as raw energy. With the lifeblood of both him and Keres interlocked with both arcane and divine powers of their caliber, and with Keres' soul still drenched from the residue of her draconic god, it would surely have to be enough to end this Bahaus Sazos-Uil-Endail and break him down.

Something disgusting spewed from its mouth, leaking down like some kind of breath weapon gone wrong and not fully formed. A dull orange liquid dripped down, even staining its own body in its attempt to rain down on the surviving members.

Draeden and Keres universally pulled forth magical shields from their arsenal, shielding themselves and those around them from whatever it was that rained down from the thing's mouth. Slate was too far out of their range of protection but his fast movement got him underneath the creature before the orange liquid could get him.

An invisible shield of raw arcane and divine magic held off whatever it was this creature was trying to hit them with. Then suddenly, beneath them sprang thousands of black tentacles. They all came forth, reaching extraordinary lengths. There was nowhere for them to go now. These black tentacles of Bahaus' would surely be the death of them.

"Keres, can you hold this shield on your own? Good because you're going to have to!" Draeden asked, then ordered.

Draeden let go of his arcane shielding. Keres tried to pick up where he left off but there were holes in her protection. The orange liquid began melting through her guard. Tsin leaped out of the way just in the nick of time. Without the both of them holding it, they were doomed.

"Draeden I can't hold this!" she declared.

"You have to!"

Draeden's most potent spell was one he'd never tried before. With Rakka gone and the collision of the creature's power with Westlyn's turning him into nothing, that left four for Draeden's plan.

"Keres, you hold this thing off of us. Shanks, Tsin, Drackice, follow Slate's lead and get this thing off of me! That's what we're here for!"

Drackice knew Draeden wasn't exactly the heroic type, but his own ego and arrogance would make him fight to the death to prove his own prowess. He knew Draeden was up to something. He wouldn't sacrifice everything and everyone he had left for nothing.

Slate was already behind the creature, digging into the same hole Westlyn started. Keres yelled out, asking how it was that Westlyn was obliterated and Slate was somehow fine. Drackice explained, yelling at the top of his lungs that it was because Bahaus was still unrefined raw energy and each moment he thickens and hardens more.

"He's becoming solidified magic! We have to stop it!" Drackice declared.

Knowing his name and bloodline, Drackice Black turned himself into a martyr, running around away from the shield in a direction very open for the creature to strike him down. Shanks stayed underneath the shield of Keres, firing everything he had faster than he'd ever done at the black tentacles. He picked the ones out nearest his friends to keep them alive as long as he could.

Tsin remained hidden, barely showing himself. What he didn't think of was this whole thing being Bahaus and his creation. Tentacles pulled Tsin from his cover. Slowly but surely, they brought him to the head of Bahaus. He was completely wrapped and helpless to the tentacles that held him. Bahaus laughed and with each push of breath from his bloody, pieces of Tsin fell to nothingness.

A tear in the very essence in the room opened. Everything, even tentacles were sucked into it. It caused a vacuum. Shanks ran dropping his bow in the rush to get away. Bahaus allowed several more tentacles to get pulled from his own ground. Tsin was gone. Several tentacles were to and now an endless void was opened. The void wasn't far from Keres and her magic was fading.

Keres' eyes shut. Her body and life force was fading. She put everything she had into the divine mettle of protection she cast over them all. They didn't know it but she scattered the protection to keep them alive. It'd been minutes that Drackice, Shanks, and Slate scurried around chaotically trying to keep the still forming beast from catching them. Tsin was lost. He was gone. He was lost to the endless void to nothingness created through the fabric of existence by Bahaus himself. Keres' body went limp and her eyes finally shut just seconds after Tsin fell.

"Now!" Simultaneous to Keres falling and Tsin being lost to the void, Draeden replaced Keres' powers with his own.

Draeden knew just how magic worked and the mechanics of it all. It took time but he forced out an ancient ritual that was said to no longer even be possible. Draeden ritually called forth to an ancient power long believed to be gone from the world. The Genasi Draeden sprung an Anti-Magic Field all around inside the fortress made of solid magic.

The result was catastrophic. He wasn't even sure where they were but he knew the still forming Bahaus would feel it and he did. Raw magic from the levels of titans being pushed down and ripped away by a simple mortal caster, but a mortal caster infused and empowered by a deity of his ally made the concoction of powers that much more delicate.

Implosions and explosions erupted! To those still awake, flames of black and blue, green and red filled the air and sky. The northern most piece of the Runethedian Pantheon heard the explosions and the indentions being forged into the land below. More mountains from the Red Mystic Mountains fell from their standing places.

Draeden felt like the magic inside of him was literally torn from him, as if he were a sorcerer or something. Draeden's eyes opened. Slate was down and his body shattered but he was alive nonetheless. He couldn't see Drackice or Shanks. He couldn't see any of them except Slate and Slate was hovering over death's door.

Clouds of ash and debris surrounded them. Every second opened the eyes to better lines of sight. Draeden heard a cough. He heard Drackice's voice yell out "Finish it!"

Keres' armor was splintered. Remnants of it remained. Her body bled and was cut like prime beef. Something was keeping her going. It was fuel. She was fueled by the loss of Tsin. Perhaps she saw him fall? The void was gone. They were all surrounded by earth on every side. The entire cataclysmic event cratered the ground beneath them!

Keres was breathing heaving and in her hand she held a massive blade once belonging to Slate. Her weapons were gone, obliterated by the seismic downpour of powers. On the far side of the crater kneeling alone, she saw a short, overweight human man tattooed from the face down. His long red goatee being interfered with by the white strands of age; his hair was a dark sandy blonde, a complete different color than his beard. He was Eternian though, through and through. She knew this was Bahaus Sazos-Uil-Endail.

Everything in Keres' life brought her to this point. She believed in honor and the balance of life and death. Her raven hair was matted with blood and debris. Ash and soot covered her body and soul. Her lover and lifelong mate Tsin was dead and gone. She was to be left behind on the mortal realm without him. Everything they'd wanted stood in front of her.

Her peripheral vision caught Shanks. Shanks lay lifeless with splattered pieces of stone and debris carved through his body. He did not survive Draeden's concoction. With nothing left to lose, she screamed out with the hatred of a thousand lost souls reeling Slate's blade toward her mark.

Bahaus vanished just before she could reach him. Her eyes went black. Draeden's eyes went black. Drackice lost all sight as well. Slate's vision failed him to. An echoing laugh familiar to them all came over them. It became so loud, their eardrums bled and busted. And soon, looking around, all they could see was each other.

They all looked the same. No more were they different. And with a unified master, they would be able to live and thrive without feud or argument. Now they were one and one within each other! Their master would give them orders and they would fight and kill to see who could succeed with the orders first!

Bahaus survived a near fatal attack but Draeden's maneuver cost him tons of power he'd never get back. He would forever chase the dragon trying to get back that kind of power. He was still beyond the limits and boundaries of anything the mortal realm expected but Draeden stopped him from achieving his ultimate finale!

What a fitting punishment, to become something distorted and mutated to his will and desire. He was nothing more than one of many formed from their creation process of Bahaus' mind. Bahaus grinned with hatred and greed. More titans and sleeping powers of the old world could still be found. Most importantly, there was nothing left to stop him from razing Eternis to ash.

He felt his control on the invisible army of prime fiends failing. What would become of them? They would either return back to their original forms or turn back into something abdominal. Abominations were typically created in such ways. What if they remained as such? What would control them?

He had to think. What should he do? Who cares if he lost control? They were already aimed in the right direction. He had time to find more sleeping powers to replenish what Draeden robbed him of. No, there would be plenty of time for that but first; Eternis had to be far removed from existence. They took his throne from him ignoring his blooded legacy. By ignoring his blood, they disrespected every Uil-Endail that came before him!

It was settled. With a victory in the mountains though at a high cost, Bahaus would make his way, using arcane of course to the city gates of Eternis. There, he would explain slowly and carefully why the world's oldest city had to be removed. After all, every great novel has its end. Every great series has a final story. It was high time that ancient pile of sticks was taken from Thedia!

Chapter 95

The cool wind of the Hangman's Straight reminded the two boys of home more and more. They were almost there. Their ship, the King Dragon was an old warship turned into a transport vessel. It was a magnificent ship, though its time at sea would soon be coming to an end.

"What is the first thing you want to do once back on Eternian soil?" Legion asked.

Both he and Dauge stood at the side railing of the old sea carriage. They leaned over, breathing in the air of the sea, taking in everything the beautiful day had to offer. The trip on the King Dragon wasn't a long one, which made each day under its sails more important to them.

Though they didn't talk about it, neither of them wanted anything to do with the adventuring life ever again; the search of fame and glory killed so many good people. So many lives were ruined from the epic search. Now, they just wanted to go home and be with their family.

"I want to touch my sister. I miss her, brother. We have a connection, a bond that cannot be explained."

Legion nodded, agreeing with Dauge. He knew what he was saying and he understood it. Dusk was his kid sister too, but she was Dauge's fraternal twin.

"I wonder if she learned of her true past as you have?"

"You mean you question whether she's discovered her identity as a Genasi."

"You know what I mean, Dauge. You're still my brother and closest friend, no matter what."

"The high faiths would give bards enough tales to fill a thousand books on their struggle of peeling you from my hand."

"Careful, blasphemy isn't on today's agenda. Let us honor the faiths, for they've granted us safe passage back to Eternis."

"You're right this time, Legion. I have to admit. I never thought I'd see the day past Azra Goetia."

"Nor did I," Legion replied.

A few footsteps came up from behind them. These steps were subtle and smooth. They softly pressed against the wooden planks of the ship. Dauge's keen senses caught on first. He turned back to see one of the few women he frequented while on the ship standing behind him. She was tall and slender with weight in all the right places. She was even slightly taller than him, wearing her favorite skin-tight black skirt and blouse. She looked radiant.

Secretly, she liked her time with Dauge, and though she knew it was coming to an end, she hoped for at least one more visit. Dauge looked back at her and smiled. He was a little on edge seeing the port of Eternis not too far off in the distance just over the waterway.

"Dauge, this ship will sail away and our paths may never cross again. Perhaps a final goodbye visit would do us both some good?" she suggested flirtatiously.

"Not today," he answered, still looking at her, admiring everything about the woman.

He pulled a few coins from his purse, much more than she was used to and leaned back to hand them to her. She couldn't believe it; neither could he. Today was a good day. His family was going to be reunited soon. And the five most prominent faiths combined—the demons, devils, dragons, angels, and the RiverMortal—all together wouldn't stop Eternis from thriving in peace with the Xavier family at its helm.

The lady didn't know what to think. She was thankful for his generosity, but truthfully, she wanted him again. Something about the brothers when they were close made them lose sight of everything else that was near them. With money like his to throw away so randomly, she believed the two could have a beautiful life together, possibly even in Eternis. She was stuck to this kind of life. At first, she loved it and the thrill and coin kept her, but soon the reality of her age would catch up to her. She was a human woman and nearing the quarter of a century mark.

Human women could look pretty for many years, but men seemed to favor the younger and more teenage women. The money was fast. She had nothing saved, and every time she thought of a client as a man potentially wanting and hoping to keep her, she was let down. And this time was no different.

There were so many back in her younger years that would have sacrificed fortunes for her. Now, he was just another beautiful face. She'd lost that hint of extraordinary and innocence she had while still a child. One day, one day her man would come. One day, she would find her knight in shining armor. It just wasn't this day and it wasn't Dauge Grey.

Dauge watched the woman thankfully turn away and head back toward her possible other clients walking and strolling around the ship. It had all but come to a stop. Their things were packed. They didn't have much, and since they took over they made it clear that they would be among the first ones to board the rowboats to Eternis.

"What happened to the elven girl?" Legion asked.

"I don't know. She's been keeping to herself all day."

"That orc telling us the story of the King Dragon made for a good story."

"Yes it did," Dauge replied.

"This ship's sailed under many flags."

"Now it sails only for Eternis." Dauge reminded his brother of what was to come of the once pirate ship.

When the ship finally came to a halt and everything was in place for those leaving to board the small rowboats going ashore, Dauge and Legion put their bodies and things on the first one. They left an orc by the named Grag Wrathborne in charge of the ship. Dauge was pleased to know that the human prostitute made it from the pirate attack as did the elven one. Grag was an experienced sailor and pirate. He would do fine at the helm.

The people aboard the ship couldn't believe what the Eternian brothers did in order to save them. Their names were already flowing through the city like ocean water onto a ship during a violent storm.

Once the ship was anchored, Grag knew it needed many repairs. It probably wouldn't make a single voyage back to Port Agatha. He made sure the brothers knew that. He was still ordered to remain with the ship. They instructed him that the ship still had enough food and water for him and more would come soon. They would return with instructions for the ship or someone with proper authority would.

Grag was so thankful to be alive and treated well. He more than thanked the brothers, reminding them both that he would oblige their every wish. The other orcs were brought in to Eternis and taken prisoner by the local authorities.

Grag was a younger orc but still a veteran. He was probably in his mid twenties. He wasn't very scarred but his eyes and face were wrinkled from years of hard work in the cold and elements of being on the water. He was a child of the water no doubt. Dauge did a superb job in choosing him.

By the time Dauge and Legion got everything put into place and the prisoners from the sea battle taken in, Eternians were already out and singing praises to their names. All they wanted was a warm meal and to see their father, brothers, and sister.

It was still early in the afternoon and the sun was out. There was a cool breeze and being near the water touched the city with a few more degrees of cold. It was still pleasant and by no means unbearable.

Something was the matter with their city and many regiments were missing. Several local barracks that should have been filled with people were vacant, almost abandoned looking. The streets weren't filled with too many people, but it was still a port city and people were moving. The local guard, each and every one of them, looked overworked and tired, like they hadn't been to sleep in days.

What was going on around here? The brothers couldn't figure it out. They'd had a long year thus far and all they wanted was for everything to fall back to place peacefully. The local guard took the orcs and other prisoners and the other free people from the ship embarked on their own quests through the city. Maybe it was just them? Maybe they were just too a little edgy and jumpy?

The local guardsmen and soldiers didn't really have anything to say. Everyone looked pale and overworked. The local markets and trades places were still open for business and business was still going back and forth but something just didn't sit well with the brothers.

"We need to head to Xavier Manor," Legion suggested.

"My thoughts exactly," said Dauge.

"No matter what's going on, it seems as though our family is always in the center of it," Legion joked.

"Well Bahaus is the last of his family and he no longer holds our city's throne. That being said, I stand curious as to who does."

The brothers continued to question each other and think aloud while heading back to their family home. On three different occasions, the two had to stop and ask for directions. After all, this was not the place they grew up in, and though House Xavier was their family and the Xavier Manor was now being sought over by their adopted father, they'd only been to the place a dismal amount of times.

The sun was beginning to set and the twin oak door of the Xavier manor finally stood before them. They were aged with time. The entire place had aged. Candles pushed light through every window. With the sun retreating for the night and candles burning from inside the house, Legion's mind vacated to a pleasant spot.

He thought back to when he was young and the things his father used to do for him. Now, he knew his father to be his uncle. His true father died saving all of Runethedian from Corvana. He alone was the reason the mighty northern kingdom ceased its attacks.

Was it an honor to hail from such a man? Adrian often spoke of Dominick, his grandfather, as if he were a magical myth only to be whispered when none were listening. To this day, it was believed Dominick Gabriel Xavier could not be bested in melee combat.

Legion caught his mind racing and snapped himself back into reality. Dauge assisted. The two looked around. People were staring at them. Most were lit up and gave silent praises and thank yous. Neither of the brothers understood why. Nonetheless, they knocked on the door and waited for what was to come.

As hoped for, Adrian answered. He couldn't believe it. His boys had returned. They'd aged since he'd last seen them, maybe not so much with years as with wisdom and time on the ground. Adrian often spoken to his family about ground time, or time spent traveling the grounds of the world.

"Boys, you're back! Come in! Come in!" he said.

Adrian wore his favorite white flannel robe and turned immediately, showing his backside to his sons. Their mother looked as perfect as ever. She was so beautiful, even in her golden age, the men at market still whistled their catcalls to her. Jokingly of course, as they knew exactly what family she belonged to.

Adrian quickly explained not a single brother was still around. Gideon was expected back any day. Adrian explained Dusk traveled somewhere toward the Crystal Cities and last they heard, she was safe behind the walls guarded by the Free Armies.

There was no time to be angry. Dauge was disgusted with Dusk. She completely obliterated his welcome home party. He would retrieve her from the Crystal Cities, even if it meant his welcome home wasn't going to be a long one.

The family was busy. Finally, the situation with Bahaus was explained over dinner. Mother had made an exquisite dinner. Each person just ate smaller portions that night since she wasn't planning on having guests. They sat at the table, which still stood mostly empty.

"Father, the nest is all but empty," Legion joked.

"They'll return. They always do. I'm just glad you two did. I don't want to get into it about Dusk. She's safe. That's all that matters," he said.

Legion and Dauge pried into their father who finally, after some time, broke down the situation with Bahaus and the mountains. He explained how many mountains literally fell from their standing positions. He explained how the Rogue Army held by Seth Redd took the brunt of it but kept coming and kept stabilizing. Seth Redd was the sole reason Bahaus didn't take the entire southwestern portion of the mainland on the Runethevarian continent. Runethevara was the name of the Runethedian's mainland continent.

General Magnus Black's added backing to the Rogue army and most of everything was explained to the boy, as best Adrian knew. Adrian explained two major families resurfaced, trying to push their way back into the throne. A third arose later but he felt as if they weren't as significant a threat as the other two.

"The oldest house in all of Eternis is the—"

"Ekkehardt House," Legion said, finishing his father's sentence.

The table was set magnificently. It was a new table, freshly fashioned from the finest wood. Dauge noticed the candles and the exceptionally clean house; everything was just flawlessly set. Adrian was planning something special tonight with mother, Dauge thought to himself. He silently laughed, applauding the effort.

"And the Bloodstar House—"

"Has been one of the most prominent in the last hundred years or so," said Dauge. This time it was he who finished his father's sentence. "Recently, they've fallen to the wayside in the public eye."

"Yes, and now there is a new house to Eternis and one I'm sure isn't going to go quietly into the night. The fucking Viktors. House Viktor is a new house. Or rather, they're new to Eternis. Hell, I'm not even sure where they came from. They've been in Eternis for a few years, but only recently, since the removing of Bahaus, have they surfaced as something noticeable," Adrian continued after taking a huge bite of Destiny's freshly baked bread. Normally, he'd have better manners but his sons were back and he was excited.

"Is this House Viktor really a concern when Bahaus is out there?" Legion asked, breaking into another piece of warm bread.

"Precisely my point, these are dark times. The Sundering is truly a testing time for us all. There are too many things out there and Eternis always seems to be in the middle of them," Adrian replied.

"So Dusk is in the Crystal Cities. Dorian has yet to return. Gideon and Simon are now gone, that throws my mind adrift," Legion spoke his thoughts, trying to gather and piece them logically.

"Woodway is a good man. Dorian should be safe. I must allow the truth to spill from these lips. I put Gideon and Simon both on a vessel headed for Valence. I told them not to return until they hear from me. I told them to head for Gaia, the City of Gardens."

The two boys listened to their father. He was a well-educated man. He was very smart and truly crafty. And Legion knew if he sent his boys away, then that meant what was to come was potentially catastrophic.

"Your children have scattered to all corners of Runethedian. I'm starting to think your faith in Eternis' ability to stand and withstand is fading, Father." Dauge gestured up to Adrian.

"I'm sure this city will find a way to make it. It always does. I'm just not sure what condition it may still be in when it finds that way. Between the Bloodstars, Ekkehardts, and the Viktor houses, and with the Uil-Endail family being all but shattered, I'm just not sure what lies ahead for our beloved city. Its sad boys. I grew up here. When I left for the Republic of New Magic, I thought I would always be able to come home and things would be just as I remembered. The sad part is, the only things that stay as you remember are the memories in your own mind." Adrian stopped to finish a bite of food. He smiled at his beautiful wife. She knew his mind was elsewhere, though, still deep in thought.

"Enough about all of this nonsense; tell me Legion, tell me Dauge. Tell me of your travels to Thox. What happened? What kept you there for so long? What finally brought you home?" he asked.

"Legion, what did bring you two home? I prayed to the five faiths that the both of you would be delivered back to my arms. It seems they listened," said Destiny, smiling.

"Our time away had found its end, Mother," Dauge answered.

His words weren't cold. They just weren't filled with warmth, nor did his face carry any expression. The Xaviers were reduced down. Gideon and Simon were gone but still blooded members to the house, as was Dorian.

"I grew up in this house, as I wish every day you two had." Adrian caught himself choking up a bit on his words and thoughts.

Destiny laid down a heavenly smile to Dauge. She always appreciated when he called her mother. She was his mother. He did not come from her womb, but she cared for and nurtured him just the same. She liked to think she didn't treat any of her children differently than the others. If she did, she was biased toward Dusk. The two had a bond that just couldn't be brought out into words.

"It's okay, Father. I don't know why you would send Gideon and Simon so far away from home. I want to reunite our family," Legion said.

His words brought hope and warmth back to Destiny and Adrian. They knew he wanted. It was Destiny who explained Genevieve's fate. She'd recently passed on. Cyclor was old, very old, but he was still making it. Lately, he'd been working in the Grohlm Ward. Grohlm was the old derelict harbor. It had long been out of use. Criminals and outcasts lived and thrived in old half-sunken ships or abandoned buildings or locations.

He'd been working, spending his own money to clean the ward up. The outcasts there looked at him as some kind of hero. Even in his old age, people knew the old man and the tales that followed him. People still feared him like he was in his prime. Honestly, the criminals and outcasts mostly had to help him around. He was nearing his end. He knew it. And he didn't fear it, he embraced it.

"Mother and father, and the five children with an aged uncle, is all that remains of House Xavier?" Dauge asked out loud. It was more of a stated question than one directed.

"We've always been a family of Eternis. We were never truly a house of Eternis Dauge, not like the Ekkehardts and Bloodstars," Adrian replied.

The family was reminiscent of times long past. Legion wanted to go and see his uncle. The tales of his deeds and efforts both as a hero and villain still lit up his eyes. Adrian laughed. Legion maneuvered the conversation back into the direction of his legendary uncle, now long retired. He especially liked the stories of the airship he navigated during the war.

"Legion, sometimes your eyes light up just like your father's. It feels good to be able to call him that to you now," he said, finishing his meal.

Dauge didn't eat much. Legion finished all of his and everything Dauge had left. Destiny ate her fill and even broke her own manners to peel a few extra biscuits from the bowl in the center of the table.

As much as he tried to avoid it, Adrian found himself leading the way, along with Destiny, in stories of Cyclor and Taj before, during, and even after the war. Eventually, story time faded and it was time to get some sleep.

Legion took a room near to the kitchen on the first floor. Dauge walked the stairwell all the way to the top the floor. He would sleep in Taj's old room. There, in the room of his father, Dauge found something he'd fallen in love with.

Two of the most beautifully crafted swords he'd ever seen hung nicely on the mantle just over the bed. The rest of the room was simple and the small twin bed looked archaic. There wasn't much to the room. It didn't seem like much had changed in it since Taj was a boy. It was clean. It'd recently been dusted but everything in the room was from a time now gone.

Those swords, those swords kept his attention. They were beautiful and perfect. They were from a different fashioning than he was used to. He'd seen swords like it before but not with this hint of flavor and land. They were kept in sheathes with only a half inch of blade sticking out from each of the two. There was a wooden mantle built exclusively to hold the two sheathes perfectly.

That night the brothers both slept soundly. Something about those swords comforted Dauge in a way he'd never felt before. He liked that. He appreciated it.

The next morning, the Xavier manor pulled each and every person within its walls out of bed, using the smell of bacon and eggs, and bread. Destiny had breakfast cooked long before daybreak came. Sausages and steaks finished off the superb breakfast.

Her personal favorite was cantaloupe juice. She diced and squeezed the juice out herself. It was fresh from that very morning. Dauge and Legion came from their rooms to see some old familiar faces breaking bread with their parents.

The old elf with shadow elven ancestry sat next to the scarred Sylvan one. Malakai and Giovanni, from the looks of the scene, Adrian had been expecting them. Both had open rooms at the house but apparently chose to embark on their own private quests still.

"Malakai," Legion said, unable to stop from smiling.

The old shadow elf turned back and looked at the young human. Malakai now looked like something out of a horror story. He looked just like the ancient sorcerer fighting against the heroes in silver novels and other tales. He was the epitome of what a bard could use to finish a good tale.

Giovanni was still old and scarred from his past travels. The look of hunger fed his eyes. The desire to do much of anything just wasn't there for him. The rectangular table was filling up. Dauge fell back to his youth. He didn't have much of one, but the smell of Destiny's cooking in his family's old ancestral home really brought him back.

The two boys quickly grabbed a seat. Giovanni seemed to favor Dauge just a bit. Malakai didn't care for anything or anyone there. Malakai actually loved them all. He considered them family, especially since he didn't speak to or even know of a single member of his own still alive.

The stone that replaced Malakai's eye still glowed. It wasn't an actual glow but more of a reflection from the sun's light penetrating in through the place's many high windows. He sat curled over with his head down. Even from a sitting position, he needed his old staff to keep him upright.

Adrian and Malakai were already deep into their own conversation by the time the boys came down. Destiny tried to ease them away but they wouldn't have it. Giovanni slyly tried to do the same, but again, it just wasn't working. The old Giovanni may have been able to do something about it using his slick charisma, but this old one just didn't care enough.

Finally, the uncomfortable silence broke. Adrian broke it. Not a being there had ever seen or heard Adrian plead so hard before. Giovanni was on the fence. He didn't know who to back. He understood Adrian's perspective but Malakai suggested a move was the only logical one where Eternis was left standing in the end.

"Malakai, I'm grateful for everything you've done for this family. We consider you no less blood than anyone else here. What you've done for all of Thedia, not just our pantheon, cannot ever be undone or matched. You said it yourself. And if what you say is true, then the last part of the Shadow's powers lie within you."

"They lie within every shadow elf," he replied, his every word fueled with bitterness and anger.

"Mal, you said it yourself. You are a sorcerer and your innate powers hail from Falling Star, the legendary shadow dragon of Gemini." Destiny tried to add in, getting it out piece by piece in between the verbal war of the other two.

Only those still truly religious even spoke those names anymore. Gemini the invader was long gone from this world. The scars and aftermath he left behind was still an overriding force not soon to be forgotten in any part of Thedia.

"I saw and battled Falling Star, Adrian. I sealed my own powers…"

"If you sealed your own powers, something you worked very hard, then obviously you thought it was for good reason. Malakai you cannot do this! I beg you!" Adrian reached across the table opening his hands palm out, as if the motion would help Malaki better understand.

"I was there when Falling Star was sealed. I am the one that sealed him. You know this, Adrian. The world does not."

"Mal—" Destiny tried to talk but he immediately silenced her.

"Do not speak to my wife—" Malakai silenced Adrian following his order to Destiny.

Another uncomfortable silence fell until Adrian finally broke it. He'd had enough and there was no way in his own home, the home of his blood, would he allow this former criminal to disrespect him and his wife.

"That's enough! Do what you will, but do not speak to her that way. You're a good friend, often misunderstood. My brother saved you from a life of nothingness here in the prisons of Eternis. I only ask for your sake and the sake of all of Thedia now, you said you alone could break the seal. As long as you didn't break the seal, the grip of Gemini's shadow world on Thedia was finished. Falling Star could now only reenter this world through you. And you swore you'd not let that happen. Our beloved world will not survive another War of the Shadow. And another Final War of the Shadow could finish off everything. Look what it did to the Honored Lands. They're now called the Broken Lands, Malakai. History, read your history. History says we'll not survive and this one city is not worth all of Thedia!"

Malakai's matted hair fell back and his neck creaked back. He arched his head back and snagged a mug of warm water from his area of the table. He'd not even touched it thus far. He gulped it down. More than mouthful of it fell down his face and onto his clothing. His hair was long and nappy but his face was still as clean-shaven as ever.

"It's not about the city. I believe the doorway to the shadow realm of Gemini does lie within me. I created it. I could tell you things of my time there and in a thousand years you'd still not understand them. Bahaus is coming here and he will be stopped. I will not guarantee anyone's safety. I cannot promise the city will still remain when it's finished. My whole life has brought me to this moment. I know what I must do."

"Malakai, I will be around if you need me." Giovanni spoke but his tone said something different than his words. He wasn't overly sure of his own sentence.

"Are you sure about that? Taj told me of the time…" Malakai started but Giovanni just waved him off.

"I don't like this anymore now than I did then. I don't feel more honorable and it's not eating at my conscious. I am indebted and now I repay the debt. My first act will be to muster all I can from the city. I will learn who is willing and able to add any form of support against the coming storm."

Malakai eased the cup back down. Giovanni took his leave without saying another word. They'd been at it a long time and they knew each other well. Malakai knew Giovanni's next move just as Giovanni knew his. Malakai knew something else. Something else pushed him one step ahead. Whatever it was that held the horde in check, and whatever it was the led them with that iron fist was not going to be taken down by things from the material world.

Chapter 96

Malakai watched from the shadows and kept his distance from the Xavier house. The coming months that came to close out the twenty-sixth year of The Sundering were dark. Those ghostly lycanthropic felines replaced the hordes that previously charged down from the mountain.

The Rogue Army was caught off guard and mostly slaughtered. Few if any remained. And those that could remained scattered and fled to anything that could be called safety or protection. The things came down in numbers unseen or heard of by the southwest of Runethevara, the mainland in Runethedian.

More of the things pushed toward the Crystal Cities, eradicating nearly everything in their wake. Ghostly armies of unbeatable creatures, how did one fight something such as that? Malakai held fast and just when all was about to be lost, armies of the undead rose from the ground and fought for the ancient city.

What compelled them to act in such a way? What called them? Against their father's orders, Legion and Dauge fell into many different Eterian ranks, trying to do the right thing for their city. Tervel, the human lord of House Ekkehardt and probably the strongest political figure in all of Eternis called out to the world, hoping it would answer as it once did. Or perhaps, maybe it would answer as it did for the Republic of New Magic?

Had it not been for the legions of undead throwing themselves to the ghostly grinder of the enemy forces, the creatures would have easily swept the southwest. Myasuna and all the way to the eastern edge of the southwest to Valakuza felt the wrath of the creatures.

None in the area were safe. Malakai pondered. What would become of the rest of Runethedian once this was finished? It would spread and expand. Things of that caliber were rarely satisfied. It was their ambitions that kept them from being normal or simply, "just above average."

Malakai could sense him. Not too far away, Bahaus rested ethereally. He was everywhere. He'd splattered his essence across the skies of the southwestern region of Runethevara. It was the only way to keep his creatures under his control. He was weakening still. Would it have been more advantageous to leave them absent a master and charge straight for Eternis once those infiltrators got him? No, because then if they turned he would have to fight them, and he poured too much power into them to have to deal with them himself.

Another great power wasn't too far off, either. Malakai saw how Dimmu Craspus Bloodstar ran his family. He wasn't the house lord but he was the acting enforcer and most things went through him. The Bloodstar house was run by Dervan Bloodstar, an old dwarf known for building the best traveling and adventuring teams known to exist. Few had perished under his council.

The dwarf swore off alcohol decades ago, but Malakai knew the trying times had him drinking once again. Pity, a sign of weakness could cost him his political prowess, and like it or not, he was in a political feud with Tervel and the Ekkehardts. It would be hard to beat Tervel or any Ekkehardt politically. They were in fact Eternis' oldest and first family and house.

With Dervan running wildly about on drunken rampages, Dimmu forged teams as his house lord once did. The Bloodstars were once a powerful house of Eternis now recently shamed by just a handful of actions and bad decisions.

Tervel bought armies to throw against the creatures. Eventually, the armies stopped coming. No price was good enough for a man to willingly throw himself to the slaughter. Dimmu's teams began returning slimmer and slimmer. Soon, it was the whole southwest that was beaten down. Anything southwest of the Red Mystic Mountains on Runethevara and stretching so far east as Valakuza was all but beaten.

The creatures surrounded it all. The Crystal Cities, Myasuna, Valakuza, and finally Eternis were all surrounded by the ghostly things nothing could stand against. The undead powers tried to impose their will against them but the imaginary creatures of Bahaus Sazos-Uil-Endail proved to be too dense and simply impenetrable. The people of the region wondered who and what the undead were and where they came from. Malakai knew. Malakai knew exactly where they came from. And deep down, Legion did too.

Legion and Dauge returned one last time to see the smoldering piles of rubble and ash in and all around their beloved city. They fought hard and fought well but the things were just too much. The more powerful undead did a number on them but there were just too many.

Malakai watched it all like a dream from a shadowy place not native to the prime material. He felt the Eternian king reforming. A greater presence than any he'd ever felt from the prime material, save Falling Star of course; and then the presence of the undead came and neared him even closer.

Legion's chest pounded. Survivors would say he fought like a raving lunatic, like a man possessed. Was he? He didn't even remember half of what he'd been through the past few months. The twenty-sixth year of the Sundering was coming to an end and with it either the creatures that came from nowhere or the entire southwest of Runethevara.

Legion and Dauge were covered in a milky white liquid. It was the color of the thing's blood. Mourning Star had its way with them. They even seemed to avoid him at times. Dauge was hurt, though. He needed divinity. Clerical help was an immediate must. Legion helped him through the city.

Malakai gave a final order for everyone within the walls of Eternis to remain indoors until he gave the okay to come out. Once again, Eternis was surrounded. Then, as if nothing, the creatures vanished into thin air. Legion was already inside the Healing Hand fast asleep next to his brother. His brother was being tended to by the best physicians in all of Eternis.

All was lost.

Malakai walked through the busted gates of Vlixx, the northern ward of Eternis. Ash and smoke was mostly all that remained from the ward. Few soldiers or guards were left. Malaki pulled and pulled, bipedaling a crawl to make his way out into the field.

A lone man stood before him. Malaki felt nothingness come over him and pain taken from his body. Soon, his back arched up right. He'd not stood up straight in years. He thought back to his time in the shadow world. It was only seven Thedian years but it was almost ten thousand years back and forth, both ways there.

Back and forth, how to explain that? He lived there and then unlived there. All that was behind him now, as was the greater undead presence he'd been feeling. Malakai didn't need to look back. A conjoined understanding of arcane knowledge told them both who they were to each other.

The creature was something ascended. It was once a lich but now found itself far more powerful than even the undead title it once held. Its name was Davion and it came on behalf of Dusk. Davion was a decrepit old blackened skeleton with gems in its eyes and shrouded in the mysteries of its old cloak of death. It, like Malakai, carried an old staff to keep its body upright.

It was the first day of Mortalus and the weather was perfect. The sun was on its eastern path down. A slight breeze pushed the trees, making them wave just a little. The wild croplands at Eternis' western porch swung in the breeze as well. And Davion's cloak of undeath did the same. Both Malakai and Bahaus knew he carried magic and powers linked to the old ways.

Malakai instinctively knew the undead were on their side, this time. This time, they were called forth to fight on their behalf by the creature Davion, the legendary lich who now for some reason had an affinity for the city.

For a moment, Bahaus looked just like he did in his youth when he watched Starius Duro slay the Thoxen Evan Stars. He was just under six feet tall and very heavyset. Inked pictures and portraits decorated his body and a long red goatee really notched off his facial expression. His Eternian blond hair flowed long and freely and his Eternian blue eyes stared coldly at the two adversaries before him as they did toward the city that rested behind them.

The smell of death and burning flesh clouded most of southwestern region of the mainland. Cracked rocks and broken bricks made up most of the cities and towns in the area. Valakuza and Eternis were still trying to count their dead. It wasn't confirmed but Retired General Seth Redd just had to be among them.

"The city belongs to me, shadow," Bahaus said. Bahaus intentionally toned down his powers. He spoke peacefully but with force. He wanted the others to understand the simplicity of how the standoff could potentially end. Davion moved like a whisper, vanishing into thin air.

"The city belongs to no man. You were cast down by its people," Malakai replied in return. Malakai kept hunched over his old carved staff. It was his favorite staff. This one was fixed with jewels and rubies and carved from a black marble rarely found anywhere in Thedia. It was truly a stone hard staff but also carried hints and pieces of iron that ran throughout it.

"You are old and weak. Your body withers, but your true powers I can sense. This encounter will leave you lifeless and myself forever weakened. Your filth is not even of this world. What could make a shadow cock stand for a city it has no ties to?" Bahaus asked. This time, he let his arrogance out and voice carry. He even finished with a smirk. "Wait, where did your friend go? On a search for his soul?" Seeing the lich disappear caught Bahaus' attention but it didn't instill any type of fear or emotion.

"My own code says I am to honor those I deem worthy of my kingdom's crown. Taj Odin Xavier was my friend. His father died for this city. He died in war representing this city, wizard. All of the old arch mages are gone. I know what you stand for. I know what you stand as. You are the last in a world evolving past your caliber. Things of your power with your mind are no longer fitting to the world we live in. Thedia ill needs something such as you. Your time on this prime material plane is finished."

"What are you saying?" Bahaus questioned. "Do your words move with such force that you aim to tell me, had I not come here, you'd have come to me?" Bahaus tried to finish the question without laughing but he just couldn't.

"I spent more time than you can conceive in a world far beyond your understanding."

The two continued to bicker back and forth, yelling in order to cover the distance. The lich was still gone, but Bahaus could feel the insurgence of its power overwhelming the entire landscape. It bothered him little. He was excited to see the look on Malakai's face after he dismantled the lich as if he were a petty beggar on the cheap side of the streets.

The conversation continued. Then, symmetrically lining up perfectly came four giant white horns of bone from the ground. The horns slowly continued to arise. Bahaus tried to take a step but the horns put him in the perfect center of their unique circle. The horns raised to nearly fifteen feet into the air

The smell of death blanketed the surroundings. Bahaus clenched his fist and swung it back and forth, as if unleashing some kind of invisible attack. The winds of undeath were countered. Streams of whirling creatures all blended together burst out from Bahaus in every, direction.

And they looked just like the creatures he imagined and had the entire region fighting for so long.

Malakai's keen perception and special eye saw through to their true forms. The stronger ones were made of his raw powers but others were distorted and mutated to his liking. There were humanoids in there. Civilized beings were among the hosts of creatures used to fill the ranks of his dark army.

The four horns continued to rise and Bahaus continued to shell out unrelenting powers of immeasurable force. Davion, the true lich, reappeared more ghastly than he did before. His cloak both bled and burned simultaneously. His skeletal mouth opened and the same bleeding flames poured from it as well as his eyes. His blackened bones and gemmed eyes could have instilled fear into even the mightiest of men, but not Bahaus.

The horns continued until the bodies they were attached to were finally unearthed. Each one stood at the center point of the bodies' enormous draconic heads. The heads were shaved clean of skin and scales. They bore no flesh or bleed either. They were old and ancient bodies resurrected through the unending powers of Davion. Liches were known as some of the most powerful undead forces ever to exist. Even liches were beneath undead dragons, or draculiches.

Skeletal bodies of four giant dragons ripped from the earth roaring, phasing their magics, preparing to do as instructed by their master. Davion's black skeletal hands freed themselves from the cloak, revealing an orb dull in color and cracked from age. Nothing of the orb would have anyone believing it possessed any type of power. Combined with the powers of the legendary lich, it called forth the four dragons once attached to it.

Bahaus had to think. Draculiches were just as powerful if not more, than any known titans of the old world. Bahaus still had much of their essence flowing inside him but that damned Genasi caster really did do a number on him.

The old Eternian wizard dropped to his knees and slammed his fists to the ground. He heard the lich calling out to him. The lich spoke in tongues queer to his ear but not to the titans whose powers he usurped.

Bahaus called to his magic just as the lich did his. The titans were either dead or lost to the planes by now. His mechanisms were built to slowly continue the bleeding of their powers and infusing of them into him. Who knows how much damage that damned Genasi caused? He was certainly weaker than he was before he got here. Taking away the army allowed his powers the revitalization they needed to resurge and start again.

He whirled his liquid ghosts of creatures like whips, wrapping them around the four draculiches that were already in flight. The draculiches were still trying to form and gain their full power and potential. He was kneeling with his head to the ground. Four giant whips made of those lycanthropic lion creatures in ghostly form kept the draculiches momentarily at bay. He knew they wouldn't hold for long.

Instantly, Malakai opened his hands to the sky. The rumbling of the earth beneath his feet by the emerging of the draculiches nearly cost him his footing and focus. He was old enough and wise enough to hold his ground.

"Bones of darkness, shadows afar, become the shield I need. Turn this arrogant's words of hate into fields of weakness. Shards of arcane and shields of power, create utter and total weakness from my enemy, this hour. Bleed his bones and drink his blood, overwhelm this thing with thy shadowy flood!"

Hundreds of tiny orbs popped into play. They surrounded all the area around Malakai. Some were ivory white and others stone gray. They hung like stars in the open atmosphere in the field chosen for their battle. Four immediately popped and dissipated, but one of the creatures peeled itself from the ghostly whips of Bahaus.

The creature suddenly fell to the ground, materialized. Once his feet felt the earth, the lycanthropic mutation was gone. She was once again the half orc she was before. Her skin fled from her muscles and her bones sneakily escaped her body. She fell to nothingness, a pile of miserable internals.

Malakai fell back in fear. Could he really do this every time he called forth? His spell was meant to act as a hundred spells at once. The orbs hung in the air like stars in the night sky. The lich was far away from them both, back to Malakai's left flank. Bahaus had four draculiches held in place.

Thedia's days of high magic and power were now long gone. Somehow Bahaus brought them back. And his time spent in the Shadow world made him something far too great for Thedia as well. In order for this prime material plane of existence to survive, great powers such as them would have to die.

His powers were sealed and he was soon to break the seal if he kept up his act. And breaking the seal meant opening the channel back to Falling

Star of the Shadow plane. Gemini's shadow plane could not have access to Thedia. Thedia was no longer strong enough to survive it.

Even though Malakai explained to Adrian and the others of the decision he made, he still cringed at the idea of reopening that channel. Having that channel open on Thedia's prime material was just another catastrophe waiting to happen.

Winds funneled in over Bahaus. The higher they went toward the sky, the wider they became. They circulated, creating a miniature tornado just over his body. Bahaus still kept his face and hands toward the ground.

Holes opened up across his arm and the ground itself took blood from the old wizard. Yes, that's right, Malakai thought. The old tales of Bahaus, even during his heroic days shined light on his ability and willingness to blood cast. Blood casting, more than ever, was considered a vile a despicable act. It seemed as though the more horrid and nightmarish the act, the more desire it gave Bahaus to execute.

Bahaus clenched his teeth in pain. Strands of blood trickled through them and his lips, falling down from his body to the ground as well. The old powers were awakening things meant to long be forgotten. And the earth itself carried a high price for such things.

Tusks emerged. Long brown hair and then eyes; a creature resembling a giant mammoth phased into the picture from within Bahaus' self-brought tornado. Malakai knew just exactly what it was, but he couldn't unravel the mystery behind the wizard's actions.

The lich stepped back. He knew exactly what it was. The thing's presence alone weakened him to almost nothing. His draculiches were just about ready to overbear and shatter the ethereal whips of Bahaus and his creatures and now this thing had to arrive.

"That's a Behemoth! It's the strongest land spirit there is!" This time Davion's words were physical.

Land spirit, Malakai thought. Now it made sense. It made perfect sense why Bahaus would call forth such a thing. Even during the years of heightened magic, Malakai's infinite knowledge on the matter couldn't shed light on any from before or even ever that could ever summon such a thing.

Bahaus' face cracked back. His eyes now fixed on the shadow sorcerer. The skin on his face rose in lines like something was crawling all around it. His lower lip split down the middle and blood dripped down from his eyes and teeth. Yet, the monster wizard grinned with sadistic joy.

Davion barely kept the orb in his clutches. He gripped it and wrapped it up with his arms, bringing it in tight and close to his body. The Behemoth's presence weakened him. He'd not hurt in such a way since his natural life. What now? The draculiches were his mightiest weapon. He put so much into them. This was all he could offer the mighty shadow elven shadow sorcerer.

Malakai's senses zeroed in on the Behemoth land spirit and then the anti-earthly creature. Undead were not natural creatures to any plane. They existed solely out of magical manipulations, necromancy performed darkly, and other vile reasons. That behemoth served as the champion embodiment of creation and life. When a behemoth land spirit made its presence known, most undead shattered. The mere presence of such a spirit was known to decimate even the mightiest undead.

What could summon such a thing? Malakai felt the Behemoth's presence. Draculiches were things the mightiest archmages of old used to fear and now four were being locked up by this damned fallen king. Four Draculiches floated in the air completely entrapped by the powers of this fucking mortal being. Was he still mortal?

"Magus, king of the shadows, come to me and comfort this man's soul with darkness. Bleed yourself from his veins and in turn put soothing and comfort. Take war from his heart and birth doubt and fear. Oh Magus, shadow God of all spirits and purifier of assassins, take this thing from his comfort zone. Take him from what's he's become and return him to what he was!"

Malakai knew to call upon Magus meant closing his eyes and granting darkness to his mind. Would he come? If so, his eyes wouldn't see it. Powerful spirits were being called. Who'd have thought, the greatest spirits in all of Thedia awakened for the final dual of great casters? The survivor, if there was one, would be the most powerful being in the known plane.

Malakai felt the presence of Magus arrive. It pushed back against the behemoth and Bahaus. The warmth of the shadow's cloak eased Malakai's mind. Momentarily, he was surrounded by the power he knew and was part of and not in a fight for his life.

"If you send the Behemoth to attack us, Magus will cut you down," he said, keeping his eyes tightly clenched. And with them clenched, he'd never seen more clearly.

The phantasmal wraps made of the creatures formed from Bahaus' imagination dissipated. The draculiches never got to fully form and burst to dust seconds later. Bahaus kept a full focus on his land spirit that kept Davion at bay. Davion now fell helpless to the ground. As long as the behemoth was present, he would be useless.

Bahaus felt his powers still slipping. He'd have to push hard and finish everything before it was all gone. That damned Genasi wizard really did a number on him, that son of a bitch! If he didn't focus on something as powerful as the behemoth land spirit, anything could happen. If the thing chose to charge and attack on his own with Bahaus' powers not keeping him in place, and it engaged Magus, well, two spirits of that caliber colliding could be catastrophic.

Another smile came across his face. Catastrophes were why he'd come. Eternis needed a catastrophe of its own and he would serve as such a purpose. When this was finished, he would be the one to close the final chapter of Eternis' long book of life.

The shadows around Malakai moved. It was Magus, a spirit long left behind by Diemos, the highest priest of Gemini himself. The whereabouts of Diemos had fallen under deep scrutiny as of late. Magus, his "go to" spirit of the shadows was very much present and in full strength.

At a certain point, truly ascended beings knew better than to fight with what they'd mastered. It was far greater to become something worthy enough to summon such things that only others of their own kind and greater could measure up to. Could Magus, the legendary king of shadows measure up to the Behemoth? The Behemoth was said to be the earth's very own avatar. Thedia in avatar form was the behemothian land spirit and Magus was the only thing standing between the Behemoth and him.

Even with Gemini and Falling Star gone, the presence of his shadow world was still prevalent in the essences of things like Magus, the King of Shadows. The shadow was such a strange thing. Many believed the shadowed undead to be the same as Gemini's shadow. It wasn't. Many thought all shadow came from Gemini. It didn't. In Gemini's presence all shadow of every origin and type kneeled before him. And Magus was the highest spirit of Gemini's shadow. Malakai called to him. There was none other that could help him. And little by little the seal that kept Gemini and Falling Star away and out of Thedia was breaking.

Malakai's seal was to Falling Star directly. And all things considered, that was probably the worst thing to be linked to. Now, the powers of the legendary dragon of the shadow were all that stood between Eternis and eternal damnation.

Bahaus opened the ground just ahead of him. His hands waved around as he stood back up to his bipedal position. Like paper tearing in half, the ground opened. The sky roared with thunder as rocks fell upward from the growing crevice deep into the abyssal atmosphere.

The crack was aligned directly with Eternis. The Behemoth was keeping Davion helpless. Malakai knew Bahaus wanted a catastrophic end for it all. Why not have the Behemoth attack? What was he waiting for?

Malakai knew that they were the things of legends. Davion called forth to creatures strong enough to bring kingdoms to their knees and Bahaus alone with his ethereal powers and imagined creatures destroyed them.

Malakai knew if he moved or offset his standing in any way, he could lose Magus and losing Magus meant losing the fight. They would both have to be careful through this fight. The slightest mistake would cost them the entire thing. As it stood, Magus and the Behemoth kept them at a stalemate.

"What's the matter, you fucking foreigner? Send your shadow king against the soul of Thedia and see what happens?" Bahaus let out his sickening laugh and cracked his fated grin.

"It does not have to be so, king of Eternis," Malakai replied.

There was a strain in his voice. A strain that said the earthquake brought him to his senses. Malakai held his position and prayed to the thing responsible for his powers. The seal was breaking. This would finish it off. What would happen if Falling Star returned? Would Falling Star return?

"Never!" Davion yelled out from nowhere.

Gigantic bones reached out from both sides of the crevice. The earthly walls opened for hands and arms made completely of bone. The hands gripped in the middle and pulled each other together. And slowly, the crevice returned to its original form. The lich let out a screech of horrid pain. Davion was hurt. A nasty scar was but the only thing left behind from the earthquake Bahaus hoped would finish Eternis and possibly the shadow elven sorcerer as well.

Bahaus waved his hand and drips of blood flung out from his tips. Two nails from his right hand dropped from their fingers. The lich was no more. With a wave of his hand and a curse from his lips, the once human wizard from Eternis with blood as royal as any, Davion fell to a pile of ash. And before the ash could even touch ground, gusts of ridiculously hard winds blew him to the four corners of the earth.

"How dare you thwart my attempts!" yelled Bahaus, now thankful the lich was gone.

Bahaus knew what was going on. Legendary archmages of the days of old spoke of such things as unkillable and unfathomable monsters. And he easily decimated four, though they weren't fully powered. Davion's fueling of the creatures ceased when the Behemoth arrived. The more he thought of it, the more he loved it. The people of Eternis watched on as their last hope died before their very eyes.

"Bahaus, I beg you, let the Behemoth go. Put the Behemoth down!" Malakai's words started sincerely but ended in anger.

"Or what? When this is finished, you will be remembered as a shadow elf of few words and even fewer deeds!" Bahaus erupted into laughter spilling out thousands of spells from his body with each one aimed specifically for Malakai.

Offensive spells were easily deflected by the defensive spells and the two casters counterspelled one another as if they were swinging swords. The Behemoth and Magus held steady in place. Malakai knew at any moment, the bastard could release him upon the city and him.

"Gusts of wind, blocks of ice, guard this city and let those that challenge you, make them think twice!" Malakai's robes flew off of his withered body, completely engulfed in frozen flames. A clear, see-through bubble opened up, surrounding the city.

"You think your pathetic magic, magic called upon from a deity far removed from our world can save this place from me? I'll cut you down myself!" An infuriated Bahaus, now weakened and tired from a session of arcane warfare with Malakai, finally let loose the mystical reins of the Behemoth, giving it orders to take any and everything in its path with it back to the Rivermortal.

The Behemoth roared, easily shattering the protection Malakai placed upon the city. At least the protection spell did its job, he thought. He was bare and now cold. The shadow spells froze his blood and soul, weakening him to the point of nothingness. He felt Falling Star. Falling Star was coming and the seal was breaking. He made a promise to forever guard that mysterious seal with his life. He'd never seen the seal nor had anybody else. The seal was somewhere between here and the Shadowrealm. A passage of mystical arcane existed between his soul and the very plane of existence Thedia hoped to tear itself apart from. Between the two worlds, he was one of the points and he solely created a seal that was meant to forever remain.

Bahaus called for the Celestus, or Sword of Celeste. The sword was said to only exist within the Behemoth and could only be pulled by one mighty enough to call upon one. The calling tore open the lower abdomen of the Behemoth. It didn't hurt the creature. In fact, the creature only noticed because a small portion of his power was taken.

Celeste was the last goddess of magic and one of the last true gods of Thedia. The sword was like nothing Malakai had ever seen. It was far too big to be wielded by a mortal human. It looked like it belonged in the hands of a king titan.

Silvery magic radiated from its being. The black void beneath the Behemoth bled a sparkly rain and it charged forward like the ghostly spirit it was. Malakai saw the opening. It was the split second between the tear beginning underneath the Behemoth and Celestus forming.

The blood casting wizard vanished, reappearing just a few feet from Malakai. Magus was gone. The Behemoth cried out. Bahaus felt pain, an immeasurable amount of pain he'd never felt before. It hurt. It truly hurt. His heart fell and stopped beating. Magic reinforced the man's heart but what could have caused such an effect against him?

Tails of shadows whipped around like sheets draped across sticks flapping in a strong wind. Celestus broke through the whipping tails of shadowy protection. The Behemoth angrily took its attention from the city and focused more on the thing internally fighting against it. Malakai looked away. He tried not to see it. The endless void beneath the Behemoth was his chance. He sent Magus deep inside the endless void and now in order for the behemothian spirit to keep its power and stature, it would have to go deep inside its own void and pull out the cancer writhing around inside.

Malakai sent the King of Shadow in against the Behemoth at precisely the right time. And like the world disappearing from two eyes closing, both the spirits left the fight. The shadowy protection left behind for Malakai from his spirit was also gone. Unfortunately, Bahaus still stood before him with Celestus.

Malakai felt the presence of his old friend Giovanni near but he wasn't staying. He had a different agenda on his mind. Malakai thwarted Bahaus for as long as he could. He had a few spells left. Each and every one of his remaining spells he utilized to counter spell. Bahaus wasn't casting but it was the only known way in the world's oldest books that Celestus was ever blocked.

Celestus grew to nearly thirteen feet and shaped itself to look like a massive falchion with katana characteristics. There was no hilt. At the end of the blade where the hilt was supposed to be, fiery chains of black and white ran down toward the caster.

His every movement guided the sword of the lost magical goddess. Malakai stepped back. He was finally done. His resources were finally tapped. There was nothing left but thankfully, the foolish and cocky wizard made the mistake of pulling the sword. All he had to do was use the Behemoth at full power and nothing would have stood in his way.

"Falling Star, I call to you, let my life be your guide and my body your host. Do not let this Thedian claim what's yours!" Malakai cast no spell. He was out of everything. And he knew the only thing left for him to do was find a way to return to the shadow plane. That way, there would be no entrance or passage back for Falling Star. He was end of the mystical portal. And the seal was broken. Falling Star would come. Would he come in time?

The gem in Malakai's eye glistened, feeling such hatred and passion from the shadow elf. He was willing to give his own life and essence to see this other thing defeated. Malakai felt others nearing him. Eternians neared him. Then, a voice called to him for the answer to a question. It was Bahaus. And this time, Bahaus spoke with a strained voice as he did.

"Why are you doing this? This is not your home!" he screamed violently.

Black flames intertwined with red ones shot forth from his body. It was the gem and its origins that saved him. Now, stinging pains shot down from his eye like lightning. He didn't ask for that!

"An Eternian befriended me and gave acceptance when no one else did," Malakai said, trying to yell back but his voice was now fading.

"So you made a friend in Eternis and now you'll die for his city?" Bahaus swung Celestus and the final pieces of shadowy protection faded along with the fires that guarded him as well.

"It's more than that. Yes, yes I'll die for his people!"

"Foolish!" Bahaus yelled but the shadow elf's answer did stop him momentarily.

The sword hovered over his head and Bahaus asked the question "why" to the elf. Malakai fell to the ground. He was naked. One rib was sticking through his beaten body already. His vision faded. Now, all he could see was a blackened tunnel narrowing in around him. He felt the Prime Material fade away from him. He was gone and alone. Though he knew Falling Star wasn't good for Thedia, he still felt more comfortable surrounded in the shadow.

On the far end of the endless tunnel, he could see. And for the first time in a long time, he saw clearly. Falling Star was coming and coming for the thing that challenged his only chance for a return to Thedia. Malakai felt wrathful powers ravage his body. He couldn't see it or see what was happening to him. He could hear the faint laugh of the diabolical wizard in the background. His knee fell. It hit something. Only the darkness and the tunnel surrounded him now. Or, was he dreaming? No, he was still very much on the Prime Material, but his focus was too great and Falling Star sensed it.

Chapter 99

Legion and Dauge never left the wall of Eternis. They were right close to the nearby gate. The gate they neared worked on a pulley system and connected to two giant wooden doors made and reinforced with pieces of iron and stone. Legion and Dauge watched the entire fight.

Malakai finally went down. The entire city was indoors. Not a single man was gone. Giovanni fled the city but why? What was he doing? Only they remained outside and they did it against city orders. Malakai was down. He'd fallen to all fours and that giant sword summoned from the belly of that mammoth spirit thing was cutting through him like a hot knife in butter.

Dauge still seemed fine but something in the Behemoth's direct roar while in sight did something to him. On the front wall, Legion fell into the fetal position. He was beaten and down just from the simple roar. He and Dauge both agreed Malakai needed their help but what could they do against things Thedia no longer even carried. Creatures as powerful as they were long gone from Thedia.

It was Mourning Star who finally grounded Legion and helped him collect his thoughts. Dauge didn't know if it would work but waiting and trying to get the city gate opened would take too long. Dauge grabbed his brother and used his powers to transport the both of them to the foot of the gate on the outside of the town.

Malakai's senses came to. He sensed the two boys and knew he had to do something and fast. What in the dead gods were they fucking doing out here? They were going to fuck him with a cock of the gods! Falling Star was coming! Falling Star surely would leave none behind, especially from the bloodline that helped end his presence here!

Mourning Star cried for blood. It yearned for it. The spiked ball at the end of its chain saturated itself with a wrathful magic unrivaled by most of what Thedia had left. The roar of the Behemoth replayed itself over and over in Legion's head. Something about that roar hit him in places he didn't know he had.

Dauge watched his brother's eyes roll to the back of his head. His body grew. His clothes tore as his muscles ripped through them like they were nothing. His teeth even lengthened and the roar of the Behemoth fell out from his mouth.

Legion saw nothing. He was in his own place, on a rock at the edge of a cliff. Far to the other side of the cavernous opening rested another ledge much too far for him to reach. A green creature resembling something of a goblin but much bigger and with darker, pure black eyes stood. He rested on his hind legs but also on the fore knuckles of his hands. Its arms rested in the frontal, knuckle-down position much like some type of monkey. And its face was the mixture of a goblin and an orc, complete with the underbite and two large teeth sticking up from it.

"Yuri," he said.

Legion knew this thing. This was Yuri, the spirit of anger. How did he know this creature's name, much less its portfolio? Nonetheless, it was Yuri and he was there in his domain. And then suddenly, before he could say another word or ask a single question, he was back. Well, not back but somewhere between Yuri's home and the Prime Material.

Legion's eyes returned and his muscles and body did also. They fell back to their normal size and look. Legion gasped for air. Dauge wanted to keep an eye on him but he knew he had to keep a close watch on Bahaus. An upward swipe sent Malakai's' now lifeless body high into the air. And from the looks of it, it was going to land not too far from where they were standing.

"What happened to you?" Dauge asked while still in a readied position.

"I, I don't know," Legion replied.

Malakai's body was just about to the ground when another ghastly roar came out from him. It didn't belong to him but it came from his body. A ghostly apparition of what looked to be a dragon's head came singing out in roars of hatred from the shadow elf's body. He looked to be deadlocked on Bahaus. The draconic apparition was much bigger than anything else any of them could compare to any dragon they'd heard of before. Its teeth looked like sharpened scythes and its eyes filled with nothing but endless shadows.

It was hard to make out, but as it extended, a neck stayed connected to Malakai and kept him suspended. Dauge and Legion fell frozen in fear to the ground. Not even the spirit of anger or Mourning Star could help them now. They fell to the ground frozen, completely useless. The grass and dirt beneath their bodies warmed and comforted them. They were soothed by the gusty winds of the day.

They wanted to help, and though they tried, their fate rested in the lost shadow elf and whatever it was that pulled itself from the elf's body. Bahaus swung Celestus directly, hitting the ghastly apparition. The sword dissipated and a small burst exploded in his hands.

Bahaus screeched in pain. He looked down, falling to his knees. His hands were done for. Blood and fingers tattered. His hands were ripped and tattered like a beggar's clothes. The face of the dragon disappeared finally, after it pushed itself through the body of the fallen Eternian king.

And suddenly, both Dauge and Legion were free from their frozen prisons. Before them rested the bones of the man they once knew as Malakai. There was no sound and no sight of the dragon thing. Whatever the hell that was, they were glad it was gone. Bahaus was still on his knees. His eyes told a story that his body could barely prove. His eyes had seen things nothing would understand. And though he tried and tried to call forth to magic, the arcane didn't answer him. He was stripped of everything. He felt it leave his body.

What did that thing do to him? Who were these two boys coming up on him? He felt the tip of a sword at his throat and the lower shaft of another weapon pushing into his neck from the other side. They were both human, or looked to be at least. His vision was off. He couldn't make them out. One held a morning star by the chain and far end of the weapon together. The lower end he used to touch the wizard's neck.

Bahaus looked down. His fingers were all there, but not a single one looked usable. The men spoke but he couldn't make out their words. Hands grabbed him and helped him to his feet. Where were they taking him and why were the powers he'd taken not doing anything?

Then, his senses came back to him. General Seth Redd and the Rogue Army were vanquished. He could feel his powers fading, but still, the things he transmutated were around. They were no longer the creatures of his imagination but some of their hosts lived. He sensed the Genasi wizard that delivered problems to him previously. A few others that walked with him were also among the living once again. Some were dead. Some died in the form he gave them. Good, they deserved it. His senses were coming back.

Bahaus walked ahead of the two that got him. His senses were still punchy. He looked down at the bone pile. They weren't even still properly connected. Malakai had been reduced to nothing more than a pile of elven bones. Bahaus stopped and looked down upon him.

"I told you once I'd look down upon your corpse. You could have never beaten me." Bahaus smiled, appreciating his own words.

"You're royalty. You're going to spend the rest of your life in an Eternian prison," said one of the voices behind him.

"At least I'm imprisoned where I belong," he said.

He looked back down at the bones and spit. He kicked at them and stomped them until finally the two boys forced him toward the city gate. The gate was still closed. Bahaus knew he had time. He'd won.

"That thing was a shadow elf. I've never met a shadow elf worth a damn. They're no better than Thoxens. How dare you, Eternian bloods wanting to take me in. You should be helping with my escape. I rid this world of that fucking shadow cunt!" Bahaus continued his insults and laughs. The more he talked the more he laughed.

No one appreciated his humor more than him. Bahaus truly was his own best friend. It took time but finally the gate was opened. The local authorities came and took Bahaus. They took him away shackled. His wounds were tended to and mended. The local physicians and clerics didn't believe he'd lose any fingers or a hand but he'd never be able to use them again either.

After Bahaus was taken away. Dauge walked alongside his brother in the streets of Eternis. Legion knew what was coming. He knew his brother wanted to know what was going on with him. What happened to him? He didn't even know what sent him to Yuri or what tore up his clothes.

The streets were filling up once again and the people of Eternis were ready to celebrate. Dauge and Legion went back to retrieve the bones of their lost friend. They quickly found a proper coffin. Malakai Downing was dead.

Neither could believe how easily people were ready to forget about Malakai. Truthfully, they didn't see any of it. All they knew was what the brothers told them. Only they watched the fight from beginning to end. What happened to that undead thing, that lich Davion? Was he truly dead? Bahaus cursed over and over at how he defeated the both of them and still lived to tell about it.

With Malakai and Davion's deaths and Bahaus' powers somehow being sealed and banished, the last of the great powers of Thedia were done. The Sundering was still here. The Sundering was meant to define a time that the world was getting rid of the old and welcoming the new. Old wounds were mending and becoming new scars. Thedia was full of scars and wounds. Soon those wounds would heal and the time of the Sundering would be over.

Daulphine Grassrunner, an old halfing man and keeper of the Dead City Ward of Eternis took the bones of Malakai by piling them up into a temporary box. Daulphine was an old centurion by age. He passed the one hundred mark some years ago. Little hair remained atop his head and his always loose fitting clothes would often get him stuck in weird predicaments. Daulphine was always wearing clothes that were too big, claiming they're just comfortable. He rarely left the Dead City Ward. That was probably why the kids of the city started calling him "Old Bones."

Legion finally responded to Dauge after he asked the same question ten or twelve times. They walked the city streets, seeing the people of their beloved city overfilled with joy because of what just happened. Legion didn't know what or why the Yuri thing happened to him and he certainly didn't want to talk about it. It was high time he did. He knew his brother all too well and Dauge wasn't going to let this go.

On both sides, the brothers walked, passing businesses and houses. Eternis was a simple city. As of late, it'd been plagued with complications and darkness. Dauge and Legion hadn't been home to see it. As expected, the conversation came and Legion prepared for it as best he could. He looked to the city streets and thought of his father and uncle growing up. He thought of the stories of Cyclor and Dominick he'd been told over the years. By the time it was all over and Malakai's bones were finally set in the Dead City Ward, the night sky had just begun to cast over Eternis. The sun was setting and night was coming.

"I don't know what happened, brother," Legion started, looking up to the sign of the Silverstar II.

"What did you see when you became whatever it was you became?" he asked. "It's important. You're my brother, but if you become a threat or a danger, I need to know what I am up against and how to handle you."

"You mean if you would have to kill me?" Legion asked. He didn't ask as if concerned but shocked by the question.

"No, if I had to stop others from doing so," Dauge answered.

Legion listened to Dauge's words. He was more sincere than he normally was. In fact, Legion couldn't think of a time where he'd been so sincere before. Of all the brothers and the sister, they were the two closest. Simon and Gideon were being sent far away and for good reason. It would be many moons before they saw them again. At least they were together, he thought.

"I don't know. The world was gone. It was like I was in a giant cave with a bottomless pit beneath me. The walls to the cave were too far away for me to even fathom. It was dark. I was standing on the edge of a cliff, and far away on the other side I saw another cliff. I thought to myself. If I jump, I might just make it. I knew it was out of my reach. There, I knew his name. I saw Yuri sitting and smiling with a pleasantness I'd never seen or felt before. He wasn't violent and furious as the old tales make him out to be. I don't know how to describe Yuri, Dauge. He's green like an orc. He's built like an orc with the face crossed with a goblin or something. If I had to guess, I'd say standing straight up, he'd have to be thirteen or fourteen feet or so. I, I, I don't know. It's all so fuzzy to me right now." Legion dropped his head, catching it with one hand.

"It's okay, brother. It had to be something in the magics around you were exposed to. We have to get you to the right clerics," Dauge replied.

"No, I'm fine."

"You're not fine, Legion. You turned into something fierce and something I don't want to deal with. And worse, you don't even fucking remember!" Dauge was starting to become aggravated.

Luckily, a calm east wind blew over them. It eased Dauge's anger. It made him think of the Republic and when he was a child, before he was taken and turned into the monster he currently was. He thought of his mother and how he missed her. Eastern winds had an effect on Dauge.

They both allowed a brief blanket of silence to lay over them. The wind moved the trees and blades of grass with uninterrupted ease. After what they just witnessed, Eternis was finally surrounded by peace.

Legion temporarily changed the subject. "They're going to talk about that for years to come, ages even."

"History is written by the victors and we were the only ones that saw it. We have to make sure it's told correctly, brother. For some reason, it occurred a stone's throw from Eternis, there again signifying its importance to Thedia. Eternis is filled with a fruitful history and itself sits as an archive for Thedia."

"Aye," Legion answered.

"Now, why not see a cleric?" Dauge asked.

Legion chuckled, looking back over to his brother and the down to the ground. He kicked a few rocks but just kept walking. They didn't even know where they were walking to. They knew they were in the Thrayle. They walked and talked so long; they made it to the Thrayle Ward and didn't even notice it. The southern ward of Thrayle was home to most of the Eternian civilians. Simple markets and schools existed here but nothing more. The most unique part of Thrayle was the museum district where some of Eternis' oldest buildings resided.

"I don't know. I can't explain it. For the first time since getting this damned thing," Legion said, pointing down to Mourning Star at his hip, "I feel like something other than this weapon has control over me."

"You want something else to have control over you?" Dauge asked.

"No, I'm sorry. That came out wrong. I'm saying, I've always known of Mourning Star's powers and I feel them grow and I feel them weaken. Sometimes, it's truly euphoric and other time I feel it's less than a stick. In the presence of other magical things, it tends to re-empower itself, maybe it's an ego thing, I don't know. In the presence of Yuri, Mourning Star stood down. It's never done that before. I don't get it. I want to figure this thing out first."

"Why do you care? Why not get rid of this spirit of anger? Listen to the name, Spirit of Anger; I'm going to assume it's not a good thing to invest your life into, Legion."

"Please Dauge, I beg you. Just give me a little time and let us see what transpires."

"If you make me kill you, I'll follow you to the afterlife and fucking kill you again," he said.

His words made Legion laugh. He tried to stay still with it but he couldn't help it. Laughter erupted out of him to and the two brothers fell into each other laughing, half embracing one another from their sides.

Chapter 98

In the coming days, Eternis helped many to safety. Many that were turned into the distorted things of Bahaus' imagination were saved. Drackice Black was among them. Of the entire team that went with him into the mouth of the pit, only the Genasi wizard Draeden and the human Slate Thundershot returned.

Legion's favored weapon, Mourning Star, brought him to Draeden. The wizard was weakened and beaten almost to death. All those found looked as if they'd been through a meat grinder or blender of sorts.

Within weeks, Simon and Gideon managed to make it home. They'd not made it all the way to Valence, and with strategic carrier pigeons, they were summoned back home. Most of the Free Armies were destroyed. What remained did stay in the Crystal Cities.

Drackice and his survivors didn't know much about what happened. They were just thankful the Eternian guard was there to save them. Magnus personally led the escort that brought Dusk back to her family. Magnus didn't want to admit it but he was happy to be back in Eternis.

The days weren't as bright and the night's not as comforting. Something was missing in the world of Thedia. The air wasn't as crisp as it once was. With the death of Malakai Downing, the shadow elven shadow sorcerer of Falling Star, and Bahaus' powers being sealed away by him, and with the Davion lich lost in the fight, the last of the high magics of Thedia were now finally gone.

Bahaus was brought down in the deepest dungeons of Eternis. He was locked away and mostly forgotten. The people of Eternis wanted to forget they bore such a son. His blood was Royal and still had to be treated as such. He couldn't be executed but would now be forced to live out the rest of his days deep beneath the land of Eternis.

Some of Bahaus' creations didn't go away. More monsters stirred in the mix. The Eternian military and guard worked vivaciously to get rid of them. Legion and Dauge headed most of the excursions to do so. The Free Armies began hiring and training new recruits to replace the ones lost in the battle. Retired General Seth Redd's body was never found. His Rogue Army was all but obliterated. The few survivors that did manage to get out sought refuge there in Eternis.

Slate decided to once again make his home in Eternis. He was Eternian with a curious backstory. He claimed to be of the old blood, that is, Eternians from the time it was first built. Something transported him and through a variation of time-manipulating principles, he found himself back in his homeworld and in his homeland.

Slate had been with the Free Armies and he'd already married a woman and left her back in Eternis. So this time, he wasn't coming home for the first time in ages; he'd merely returned to find the woman he left behind. He claimed the old blood and old ways and yet still somehow managed to find the courage to marry a non-Eternian native. And she was an elf, no less.

Slate returned to a simple home, a warm cooked meal and the three children he'd left behind. His days of traveling and fighting were over. Eternis begged and pleaded for the man to continue working toward the bettering of the city, but all he wanted to do was retire and spend the rest of his life in peace.

Draeden was different. He was still young and the dynamism of life still excited him. The infinite thirst for knowledge and the quest for answers to questions unasked drove him to still want and do more. It wasn't long before he met up with Legion and Dauge. That of course led to Drackice meeting up with the lot of them as well.

Kleiven was never found. His body was long amongst the wreckage of the Rogue Army. Drackice didn't want to admit it but after he learned Dusk's longtime lover was considered dead, he felt he'd landed another opportunity with the Eternian beauty.

Legion was too busy dealing with the inner workings of his own being to realize what was going on. Dusk was falling for another. She was falling for the son of Magnus Black. Magnus later discovered the Free Armies actually forced both him and his son from their ranks. The Crystal Cities literally bought the mercenary army and ordered them to be kept at the Crystal cities indefinitely. This wasn't such a huge blow for Magnus, as he actually wanted to return home to Eternis to finish out his days. Bahaus' battles left him nearly a cripple.

Drackice was still hungry for it, though. He'd not done enough yet in his lifetime. Magnus built the Free Armies and always planned for Drackice to take it over one day, but that dream and vision were both now gone. The ship Legion and Dauge captured was taken and refitted right there in Eternis. Most of the orcs were taken into custody. Few were set free. Nonetheless, some were set free. Grag was kept by order of both Legion and Dauge.

Grag was brought in and trained. He began his training to becoming civilized. Grag the orc began his journey into becoming something more than he was. The transitioning process had begun.

The beautiful thing about Eternis was that it was resilient. It was a city that recovered fast. It had to. It always managed to find away to survive. Adrian still led the Xavier Household and Legion and Dauge kept close to him.

Adrian Paschal Xavier, the father of the house, finally got to sit down to a warm cooked meal made by his love Destiny. And at last, every immediate member of his family was there. Dusk sat close to Dauge. They were always a close pair and difficult to separate. Simon and Gideon were back and pleased with the way things were going. Legion, the oldest, sat closest to his mother who headed the opposing side of the table.

Eternis would live. The Xaviers were becoming a very important name in the Eternian realm. Three very old families emerged as high powers.

The oldest family still known to exist in Eternis was the Ekkehardts and the Ekkehardts were the people's choice all along to be king. Time and time again the family turned down the honor. The Uil-Endails led the city-state for many, many years. And now, their time was finished. Legion always appreciated the Ekkehardts and everything he'd ever heard about them. Dauge didn't care for them one way or the other.

Destiny wore her husband's favorite yellow sundress and made his favorite fish and mixed vegetables. She cooked the wild crops and seasoned them just as he liked. The candles were lit. The cloak of night ousted the sun's final rays. It was a cool evening. The local guard was still working as they always were. With their numbers still low, most members of the guard and military still had to continue to pull double duty.

Adrian just purchased a new table. It was still long and rectangular. This one was made of Greatland Oak, the strongest wood from the strongest tree. Greatland forestry was said to be the sturdiest, the finest, and the all around best in all of the pantheon. It was so hard to come by though because the Nine Kingdoms rarely utilized it for export and Malynkite was too busy to do it themselves. And considering they were the only two kingdoms in or around the Greatland, the Greatland forest was still considered just an untapped resource.

The family kept a strong bond to the Draconic Order as well the Rivermortal, offering prayers to appease both sides before breaking bread. Dusk was happy to be home and surrounded by her family again. Gideon and Simon were too. They didn't know what to think when they were ordered to flee the city for their own safety.

Dauge kept close to Dusk. He'd missed her. He always felt he needed to be near her. Being split from her weakened his intestinal fortitude. Legion looked around. His family was complete. He didn't have much in common with Simon and Gideon but they were still family.

"One is still missing," Legion broke the silence saying what everyone else was already thinking.

"Dorian," Adrian answered.

Dorian was named after a legendary arch mage from the Republic of New Magic. Dorian was always the black sheep of the family. The door creaked just as Adrian spoke his name. Dorian's voice echoed out through the halls. He yelled the word Father once and then a second time for good measure.

His voice flattened the atmosphere. Everyone stopped. He hadn't been seen in a long time and with Bahaus nearly conquering the whole southwest region of the Runethevarian continent, it was a safe assumption he was probably dead.

He wasn't dead. Dorian was a dark man with a cold heart and his family knew it. Legion knew it. Unlike the others, he wasn't cleaned and bathed. He still wore most of his black plated armor. It was dented and discolored. Blood from all kinds of things had dried on it at different times and days since he'd last cleaned it.

His thick purple cape looked more like a blanket than a garment. His face hadn't seen a razor in days. His eyes told of a long stretch and trial against his body. His black hair was cut short, but dirty and not fixed. He'd just made it back from an obvious journey. He'd been long to the road and his body screamed for a fresh bath and warm meal.

Destiny leaped from her seat, her body overflowing with excitement. She couldn't believe it. Now her family was finally pieced back together. The family nearly found itself scattered to the four winds but no more. Once again, for the first time in a long time they were all under one roof.

Legion looked over to his father, pausing before taking a bite of his sugar bread. He looked back to Dauge and then to the other two.

"Did you know about this, Father?" he asked.

Adrian smiled. He did know about it. He'd just not told anyone. He wanted it to be a surprise. Not to anyone's surprise, Dorian walked in the way he was. Adrian at least expected the boy to bathe and clean up and maybe even wear decent clothes to the dinner table. "I did. I met Woodway at the market the other day. I saw him and asked of my boy. He said his team was close behind him. He promised Dorian would get the message."

"What message, Father?" Simon asked.

"The message that we're reuniting as a family for the first time in a long time and that I would like all my sons to join myself, my wife, and my daughter." Adrian accidentally gave out a little belch and wiped excess food from his mouth with a handkerchief.

Dorian shook his head, listening to his father answer his brother while walking into the dining room. He missed the Xavier House. He'd been long on the road with Woodway and the others. It was time for his return. Eternis was safe. That was important to him. In the end, Eternis was still his home.

"Well hello, Father," he started.

Soot and dirt still covered most of his body and face. Destiny was wrapped up all around him. He'd gotten bigger. Dorian was a monster now. The road had been good to him. He'd grown in size, at least a few inches, and his muscles tripled in size since the last time they saw him. He was a human but resembled goliathan stock.

"Honey, let our boy have a seat and have his fill," suggested Adrian, opening his palm out to imply an offered seat to his son.

Dorian took the seat and broke into the bread with his brothers and sister immediately. He was hungry. He ate like he was damn near starved. His eyes and body told his family that he was tired and worn down. The others sat in silence for the moment while he ate. Finally, he slowed down to look around. "I am allowed to eat, aren't I?" he asked.

Destiny stood over him from behind the chair. She clung to him, holding his arms and casually rubbing his back. His armor mostly negated it. Eventually, her hands found their focal point to be his neck and the back of his head. Her hands rolled up to play with his ears. He liked that, especially as a young boy. She kissed his forehead over and over while he ate.

"Of course you are, my precious boy. You never have to leave home again!" she pleaded with tears streaming from her eyes, not just because Dorian was home but mainly because the entire family was all back together and under one roof once again.

"It's okay, dear. He's back, and safe," Adrian pled.

"I know. I'm just so…" She paused planting her lips hard upon the crown of his head. She cradled the head of her son and rocked it back and forth, not even paying attention to his trying to eat. He looked up at the wall, almost irritated, but in truth he was more thankful than any to be there. He'd been through a lot, and he was willing to put his travels up against any of theirs.

"I'm just so thankful he's home. I'm grateful you're all here," she said, peeling her mouth from his head and looking up at them all.

Legion and Dauge told their story. Dauge knew some of them didn't believe the whole thing. Every one of their mouths dropped when he pulled out the painting. They couldn't believe it. Even Legion thought it was gone.

"I thought we got rid of that thing?" he asked.

Dauge didn't say a word to answer. He just smiled. Adrian took the painting, claiming it would fit nicely in the family vault. The painting quickly caught Dorian's attention. With a mouth full of food, he stared at Dauge. He was not impressed but he had other ideas for the painting.

"Taking old paintings from cities long forgotten are we? Don't you think you may be disturbing things that shouldn't be disturbed? And then you come here and into my house with it?" Dorian was not friendly at all.

Dauge returned the scorn equally. They never did quite get along. Another awkward silence blanketed the room. Adrian broke the silence first, trying to calm everyone. Dauge didn't reply immediately but he kept the painting out, revealing that he didn't care about Dorion's feelings on the matter.

"Your house, son; this is my house," Adrian reminded.

"Why in hells would you ever return? You were far better off gone," Dauge finally replied.

"We never made our original path's goal. We ventured to the far eastern cities of Runethevara. I've been knee deep in those fucking insects of Efestewel ever since then. The velox truly are an inconvenience." The last part of Dorian's words were turned back and directed to Adrian.

"I've heard nasty things about the velox," Legion said.

"Father, may I be excused?" Dusk asked out of nowhere.

Something didn't set right with Dusk. She wasn't really into it. Her entire family was safe and sound all under the same roof as her and yet she was stuck far away, deep within her own thoughts. She wasn't really there. Her actions caught Dauge's attention.

He turned to look at his beautiful sister. She wore simple clothes and kept her hair neatly tied back. She was dressed for dinner but not necessarily this one. She put little effort into her dress, even knowing that her family was getting ready to be reunited.

"Dusk, is something the matter?" Dauge whispered.

"No, I'm fine. I just favor sleep right now," she answered.

Adrian signaled for Dusk to remove herself from the table. She casually broke away, minimally saying her goodnights to the family. She took a small green apple with her and strolled up the stairs of the manor heading to her room.

"What's wrong with her?" Simon questioned.

"That Dar boy was never found. Kleiven was her best friend," Adrian answered. "I'm sure that has something to do with it."

"That war claimed a lot of people," Simon said.

"Yes it did," said Gideon.

"Velox?" Dauge asked, turning back toward Dorian.

"Yeah son, did you really say velox. I've heard some nasty stories about those things. You stay away from them. You hear?" Adrian couldn't believe his son had been out fighting the velox. The velox were probably some of the vilest things in all of the world.

"Father, I cannot believe you would detest me defending towns and villages that could not defend themselves," said Dorian.

"I've just heard people say that they have fought demons to dragons and that the velox are the things they hate the most," Dorian's father replied.

"Don't confuse what I'm saying. I said they're an inconvenience but I do not hate them. People and creatures aren't the same. I've learned to hate many people in my travels but I do not hate the velox. They're merely acting and moving on instinct. After all, our entire world once belonged to them, the Age of Insects, remember?" Dorian was tired of talking about the insects and he wanted to move on from it.

"Your uncle was not too far from you on that one." Dorian did appreciate it when Adrian spoke of Taj, his uncle. He liked what Taj represented and what he did to get the life he wanted.

"I like the story when he cast down all but the Draconic churches of the city." Dorian smirked. Sometimes he just liked to be a hard man to deal with.

"What pleasures do you get from being such a difficult man?" Finally, Dauge spoke up to his brother.

Dorian's face turned to meet Dauge's. There was a second of a pause. Everyone knew something was about to happen. Dorian was a dark and cold man. Something in him reminded Adrian of Taj—Taj in his later days of course.

Adrian slipped off into thought. His baby girl called him father just before leaving the table. He couldn't help but smile to it. It'd been many moons since she'd called him that.

Dusk walked across the top catwalk toward her room. She came out and walked across again, stealing everyone's attention yet again. Obviously, she didn't mean to. Dauge looked up at his sister. Oh, how he missed her. He cherished her. He savored every moment with her. He took his focus back to Dorian the moment she fell from sight. Something happened, though. Upon her exit back into her room from atop, the mood of the table seemingly changed.

Everyone just went back to eating. They watched for as long as they could. Dusk disappeared into her room. She was lonely. Even in the company of her family, she found her heart still wanting and cold. She'd done Kleiven terribly wrong. Now, Kleiven's father, Cale, and he were both gone from this world.

Who knew what happened to Grath. As far as she knew, he was probably dead too. It's not that she wanted him back but she still did feel for him. He was a good man. Kleiven, Kleiven did not deserve what she did to him and now he was gone. He died defending the city and her. And what of that thing that was once connected to her? What happened to Davion?

She felt Davion's power over her take flight. His presence was still very much there. She felt a connection to him or something that she could not explain. And now, all she wanted to do was get to her bed and fall fast asleep in order to put this miserable world and all of its pains and problems behind her. At last, sleep overtook her and the pains of Thedia no longer plagued her.

Back at the table, the rest of the family continued. Their thoughts and intentions temporarily derailed by Dusk and her actions. Her leaving somehow created a temporary break in the tension somehow relieving it from the room.

"Apologies, Dauge. I'm worn and tired from my travels. I should not be so difficult in dealings with my family," Dorian finally said, breaking the silence.

"I can take a page from that book myself, honestly," Dauge replied.

And soon, the table was merry once again. Even with Dusk's absence, Destiny knowing that she was in her room safe and still, her entire family was together once again gave her a warmth she'd not felt in years.

"I hear that there was a man saved claiming to be an Eternian?" Legion asked.

"Aye, Slate Thundershot. He has all the characteristics of an Eternian. He's got children here already, believe it or not," Adrien said.

"The other's an elemental person," Dauge furthered.

"You mean like a Genasi?" Destiny asked.

"I know what a Genasi is. I'm not sure that's what I am but it would certainly make sense."

"And Dusk is—" Destiny started. Before she could finish Dauge answered with the same.

"Genasi?" Adrian question aloud.

"Father, I am not a true human. The Eternians will look down upon me when the truth is revealed. I care not though. My mother was a racially traitorous whore. I guess that means if Taj isn't my father and you're not my mother, then I do not belong here, nor does Dusk." Dauge was sickened.

He acted as a battle-hardened, cold man but his family was still his soft spot. He would die without thinking twice for any of them, including Dorian. Dorian's face grimaced with his words. Dorian was a proud human of high stock here in Eternis, according to him. He'd not even gotten to the subject of Legion and Dauge bringing in the true king of the place.

Dorian was a very stubborn, dense man with unique beliefs that almost made him sound ignorant at times. In truth, Dorian was well educated and his education and intellect made him a truly dangerous swordsman.

"You are a member of this house. Your blood is mine, I care not whether you believe it to be true or not," Adrian replied.

Secretly, he was scared. He couldn't believe what Dauge was saying or why he was saying it. What could have happened all of a sudden that made him believe he wasn't human. Adrian didn't so much care about the non-human part other than the fact it proved Taj wasn't the father.

"What if your mother was a Genasi herself?" Destiny asked, throwing her own intellectual spin on it.

"I thought of that, Mother but my father, Taj Odin Xavier was not a race traiting piss ant." Dauge was getting upset. With every word, his voice heightened with anger.

"Maybe he didn't know? After all, we didn't know you were Genasi. We would've still been in the dark about it had you not told us." Destiny smiled hoping the warmth of her own smile and words would comfort her son.

Dauge looked down at the food before him. He closed his eyes. He hated not being purely human. He was what he was. In truth, with the time spent with the Lotus people back on the Republic of New Magic's continent, he knew something in him was different but until now, he just refused to accept it. He didn't accept it until another one of his own was at risk.

"What is this heresy you speak?" Dorian asked.

He was just calming down from the previous engagement of hostilities when Dauge had to go and set him off again. Dauge must want to fight, he thought. Dorian glared at him from across the table, slowly, still eating. He took one bit after another from bread and then from the meat and then a spoonful of soup. His eyes never stopped nor blinked. They kept still on Dauge.

Dauge fell back intimidated. He wasn't scared but he actually felt like he was in the wrong.

"Taj was said to have necrotic powers. That weapon Legion's got is supposed to be the true weapon formed from the two most powerful weapons ever to exist here in Runethedian. Some believe them to be the most powerful in all of Thedia, the greatest from any of the pantheons. Perhaps, something from the powers touched you. You're fucking human,

Dauge, whether you like it or not. Taj wasn't a race traitor and he wouldn't put himself inside of any fucking non human!" The last part of his words came out really loud. He was starting to become angry about the idea as well.

"Now, whatever it is that lurks inside of your bones comes from things that once belonged to Taj. Let us see an end to this conversation, brother?" Dorion finished his words more softly than when he began. Finally, they were connecting.

Even Dorian didn't want to see his brother's lineage from the family removed. Many conversations came and went. The topic of his bloodline and lineage steadied itself amongst them. In the end, the family ruled it was either something in Taj or the mother that gave Dauge his unique Genasi-like abilities. And if the same abilities swam around inside Dusk, it was for the same reasons. They were Xaviers, end of it.

The question arose many times about why Dorian returned to Eternis with Woodway. Did they plan on leaving again? Were they looking for others to join them? Dorian did everything he could to avoid the conversation and evade the questions. And he did it well.

Finally, it was high time to turn in. The moon was high and the sun fast asleep. The cloak of night blanketed strongly across the plains. Simon and Gideon were the first two after Dusk. Then, Legion turned in, walking alongside his mother. Adrian stayed a bit longer with his two sons, Dauge and Dorian. And then finally, he kissed both of his boys upon their foreheads and turned in for the night.

Dauge remained with Dorian. Both rose from the table casually and began putting their things in order. They kept looking back at one another, hanging things on the walls and pulling clothes from here and there to prepare for bed.

"I'm not returning with the good elf," Dorian said.

"I didn't ask," Dauge replied.

"I just felt like I needed to tell someone."

"Why?"

"I almost feel guilty for not," Dorian answered.

"Where's he going?"

"Back to the eastern reaches of Runethevara."

"The good elf?" Dauge questioned.

"He's become truly devout in his beliefs. He's a loyal servant to the good dragon, Typherion. He acquired the name along the way."

"Good for him," Dauge joked back.

"I've got more pressing matters, Dauge. Matters I believe you may want to be a part of."

Dorian's words penetrated hard. Did Dorian return for him? How? Why? Who and what told him Dauge was evening coming back to Eternis? He had no idea he was returning, did he?

"I'm sure you're either looking to start your own band or replace fallen or lost members of your crew," Dauge replied nonchalantly.

"I said I'm not going east again with Woodway. He's a good man but not my kind of company."

"Why did you wait until now to speak this to me?"

"Why do you think?"

By now, they were turned to face each other. There was still a bit of space between them but their eyes met with each one looking over their own shoulder, back toward the other. Dauge turned back around first, finishing up his dealings for the night. Dorian finally turned fully around to stand and focus fully on his little brother.

When Dauge finished, he turned to see Dorian standing before him. They never really got along but accepted that they were family. They both truly respected and honored the sacred house from which they both descended. Dauge took a breath and finally answered, knowing he knew what Dorian was getting at.

"Something tells me whatever it is you're doing only select people know about. Why not bring us both, Legion and myself?"

"Legion's weak. He's weak just like father was. That damn weapon's got a control over him we won't be able to break."

"Why would we have to break it? I've been far with him. He works well with Mourning Star. If that thing's got a hold of him, I can't tell."

"It was forged from SOUL and LORE and the stories claim father was so eaten up by them, he didn't know which was what or who to answer to. He carried necromantic abilities unlike anything seen in years, then with SOUL and LORE walking alongside that he was a fucking monster," Dorian said.

"SOUL and LORE formed to make Mourning Star," Dauge replied. "Legion doesn't carry any necromantic traits."

"I believe in you and your ability to keep your problems under wraps. I'm offering you to join me, but only you. That's the end of it. I'll hear no more about it."

"I will not leave Legion. He's my brother."

"I am your brother."

"And you're making the choice, not me."

"Fine, so be it," Dorian said, finishing. He turned away from Dauge like he wasn't even there. He began reequipping his traveling clothes. He was already setting out like he planned to leave that night. A second thought crossed his mind and he bid Dauge a goodnight and headed off to one of the many vacant rooms.

Dauge watched Dorian. He didn't even ask what it was that he planned to do. He didn't know where he planned to go or how long he planned to be there. He was closer to Dusk than any. Maybe because that was his twin sister or maybe because it was his only sister, who knew? Among the brothers, he and Legion were virtually inseparable. And nothing was going to change that. Not even Dorian could change that now.

"Dorian, where is it you plan to go? I may not follow and walk alongside you but perhaps I may still help." The difference between awkward and final silences could only be measured in depths and thickness. Dauge took the chance and once again broke what Dorian meant to be the final silence of the conversation.

"You cannot walk where I am going. You cannot even ride a horse to get there. I'm crossing the high seas, brother."

"You know we captured that ship, the King Dragon. It was to be given to Eternis but if you need a ship, take it. It's yours."

Ships fetched quite a price and the King Dragon, since its refitting, especially could call for a pretty coin. Conversations at the table and prior came up about their capturing of the ship and how Grag was handling everything about his new life.

"In case you're not to return. I'd have knowledge of your whereabouts. Where is it you wish to go?"

"I wish for you to know but I'd rather my location not be chanced to fall upon deaf ears."

"Fine, so be it. Keep it from me."

Dorian laughed. He'd come across an old map and that map was going to lead him to the rest of his life. He had to be careful who he told and who he brought with him. He thought the momentum that carried him back to Eternis would drive even his brother Dauge, whom he'd been at odds with, to join him. It didn't. Secretly he both admired and appreciated the bond between him and Legion and somewhere deep down, he wished he'd bonded with his brothers in such a way.

They all turned in, even Dorian. He chose not to leave that night. Dauge offered him the King Dragon, a ship that was originally meant for Eternis. Would he take it? That was a question he could not answer at the time. He would most certainly have to sleep on it.

Dauge turned in too. He was tired, not just from the day and the long night but from his travels altogether. They were all finally united under one roof. Grandmother Genevieve was gone. She'd passed. That was okay. It was her time. She'd fallen ill toward the end and now she was no longer suffering.

The house would rest this night with all of its people intact. By morning, they would separate once again. If none other than Dorian, they would separate once again. Dauge wanted Dorian to stay and so did Legion. They all did. He felt greater things calling to him. In the end, it was time that would finally tell if his decision to continue moving was a just one or not.

Chapter 99

By morning, Dorian was already gone. He'd left a note for his mother. Dauge sort of figured as much would happen. He further thanked Legion and Dauge for the offer of the King Dragon but felt it belonged with Eternis.

Eternis was in a political cold war. The three major houses of Eternis were feuding over who would take the throne over now with the Uilendail family gone. With Bahaus Sazos-Uil-endail in chains and bound beneath the city and he being the last of the royal family, who would now be responsible for Eternis? Who would take over and lead the city through the Sundering and whatever else was to come?

Dusk got up shortly after Dorian. She was up and in the city early. It was her day, she told herself. She was going to go shopping and buy a whole new wardrobe. This day would begin the rest of her life. Perhaps the grips of that thing Davion were really gone from her? Perhaps it was dead? Or perhaps the freedom she thought she felt was merely a trick being played on her? Either way, today was a day she was going to enjoy.

Gideon and Simon were both up early as well. Gideon was out to watch a morning play and Simon was helping his mother with the kitchen. Adrian was outside picking weeds from the yard. Dauge and Legion were the last two to rise. The push of forced travel across dangerous lands finally caught up with them.

When they did wake up, breakfast or brunch rather, was already made for them. They finished their meats and breads and even the cake their mother made to welcome the two of them home and headed out to the city.

Finally, they were home. The two nonchalantly spoke of Pitt and Dash and wondered where the two could be. Legion was concerned for them both. Dauge truly did not care for Dash. Even though Dash was the reason for everything they'd done, he still cared very little for the half-eladrin.

By the day's end, Dauge finalized the paperwork with Gilbert Psalmblade. Gilbert was a goliath, or half giant just like Pitt. Unlike most warriors of Eternis, Gilbert clad heavy armor and wielded a massive two-handed executioner's axe. He wasn't native to the city. Still, the man managed to work his way through the ranks to become the second highest-ranking military member of the city, just under Novar "Numbskull" Caelegate.

Novar is a dwarven man and native to the kingdom. When King Gerear passed, he slipped through several ranks immediately becoming not only the head the local guard but also, the General of the Eternian military. He was also the Keeper of the Newport, one of Eternis' eight different wards. Novar often claimed to have more duties to the city than the entire political brand altogether.

Newport was the main harbor area used of Eternis. And because of Eternis' unusually deep waters, many ships that typically were not able to dock next to the harbor were often able to do so; of course this was contingent on the water levels and tide at the time. Most of Eternis' business took place there in the Newport ward. This area of business had been open now for nearly fifty years.

Gilbert did not like the idea of Dauge just handing over the reins to the ship. He felt like he needed to get something back for his troubles. In the end, they finally agreed that the ship would stand as a commissioned ship of Eternis under the orders of Dauge Gray of the House Xavier. If and when the ship made money, Dauge would receive thirty percent profit, as would his brother Legion.

Dauge made sure Legion was put on the paperwork as well. Dauge furthered that the money would be placed in an account at the local treasury. It would be placed there under the House Xavier title. Dauge liked how it came to be. He now had a ship, and after refitting and repairs and everything else, whatever profit was made from the ship he and his brother would receive sixty percent in total.

Legion on the other hand took the day to walk the streets of his beloved city. The people of the city more or less recognized him and fairly spoke his name. He wondered. Were they in awe of him because of who he was or because of the family he was a part of. The Xaviers weren't a very strong house in Eternis but they were respected and always recognized.

Legion walked the streets a tiptoe higher, thinking back on everything his family had done in such little time. He couldn't believe he'd made it to the mythical city of Azra Goetia and lived to tell about it. He was back in the city where he belonged. He didn't grow up here but nonetheless it was home. He might as well have grown up here. He didn't know the city like he did the city Zzyx back behind the walls of the Republic of New Magic but he was getting to learn it.

Eternis was a widely spread out city broken down into eight different wards. Something about the city kept peace in his heart. Everything seemed to be at work here, behind the scenes if you will in order to keep everything perfect and peaceful. He wasn't even concerned that Dorian was already gone. Something told him Dorian wasn't going to stay long anyway.

Throughout the course of the day, Legion spoke to many people. He felt it was his duty to get to know the city. It didn't take long to realize the city was mourning the death of retired General Seth Redd. Legion managed to scrounge conversations out of Gilbert and Slate Thundershot.

Slate was an older man that had been working alongside the Free Armies for some years now. He was happy to have finally been returned to the city he'd called home for so many years. Against Eternian tradition though, he married an elven woman that gave him three kids. Titus was the oldest, followed by William and then Stephina.

Even with the racial disagreements amongst Eternis on interbreeding, his children were immune to the negative treatment. They smiled to their faces but talked behind their backs. Slate explained to Legion he knew the truth of it but there was just nothing more he could do. He hoped to one day rid Eternis of its primitive flaw but felt his time would expire before he saw that day.

Finally, sitting in the Broken Swords having a strong brew sat the old dwarven General of the city. He was born and raised here and highly admired. He was Novar Caelegate, often called Numbskull. He acquired the name Numbskull for being such a hardheaded man, even for a dwarf. Other dwarves didn't even seem to get along with him sometimes.

Novar, now looking to be in his early thirties, sat without weapon or armor; he wore his clothes loose fitting as to remain truly comfortable. His common brown clothes made him appear average, nothing of the sorts a

General should be wearing. His auburn hair was receding at the top of his head but nonetheless long and braided with wooden beads toward the back and all the way down. His beard was still thick and broken down into two braided and beaded halves.

Seeing Novar there alone, Legion thought of it as a chance to get to know the true Eternian General. His street credit got him the information he needed to find the General. It wasn't difficult. There he was, sitting quietly and alone at a table close to the front nearing a window. The young dwarf looked out the window sipping his hot cup of tea. He always had a hot cup of tea to go with his cold brews.

"Sir Caelegate," Legion said. He knew it was him but he still wanted to ask aloud just to be sure.

Ever since the changing, he knew something was different inside of him. He knew there was a rage within him he'd never felt before. And he didn't know how to deal with it. Now, while walking in the city, he'd never felt calmer. Would it return? If so, then how? What would come of it, if anything came of it at all?

The dwarf looked up at him without verbally responding. His eyes told Legion he wasn't expecting company this day. Legion would change his plans and meet him anyway. He wanted to get to know Eternis and in order to do that, he had to meet the men and women behind the machinations of it.

The dwarf opened his hand, silently offering the neighboring seat to Legion. Legion politely thanked the man and took it. A waitress, tall and a little thick for Legion's liking came over to refill the dwarf's ale and to take Legion's order. Her hair was a light auburn and her eyes dark. Her body was slender but her butt was thick and big. She was pretty though, but for a human she carried several elven qualities. Perhaps her blood carried elven lineage?

The dwarf just fixed his eyes to Legion's face. He intertwined his fingers and placed his thumbs underneath his chin, resting the rest of his united fist right on his mouth. Legion appreciated the little moment of silence. The dwarf's eyes to a second to drift away from Legion to stare down at the large glass of ale sitting before him, but Legion watched them just shoot back up and rehook themselves right into him.

"You have my attention, son of Taj," the dwarf said.

Wow, the way he spoke really threw Legion for a loop. He addressed him as the son of Taj, his father. He addressed him so formally and professionally. This dwarf's face was still thick with hair but that hair was cleaned and trimmed. He spoke with elegance, a true difference from typical dwarves.

"I've returned. My father fought and saved us from the northern threat, Corvana. I grew up in the Republic of New Magic but Eternis is my home and finally, we've returned to make it such," he said.

"We?" Caelegate questioned.

"We, my brother, well, my brothers and my sister, my mother and father, we've all returned to Eternis finally. Dorian will not stay but as for the rest of us, we're staying. We're rooted here," he answered.

"I see. And what does any of this have to do with me?" Caelegate asked.

"You're the highest ranking military man of Eternis and with the Uil-Endail family gone and the houses politically feuding over the throne, this all makes you the most important man in the city," Legion replied, finally summoning up the essence of it.

"Do you see any high guards around me? I wear no cape, crown, or wield any scepter. I am just a man in a simple town that's so old it still believes in having kings and queens. Eternis is barely worthy of one. We're a simple town rich only with history, son. The local magistrates of each ward should have someone collectively to answer to, yes, I agree. Eternis is in need of a restructure." Novar wasn't good at making friends and he hated being treated like someone of importance.

Novar was important whether he liked to admit it or not. He was important to all of the people of Eternis and though he'd not thought of it before, Legion was right. The Ekkehardt house, the Bloodstar family, and the Blackwind house were all battling politically, along with several guilds most likely already, and all for the sacred key to the kingdom.

"I am Legion Cage Xavier of the Xavier house. And I am here to render my services to you and the city in anyway you deem necessary."

"Good to know," Novar replied carelessly.

Legion pushed the issue and continued to push the conversation for as long as he could. There was no use. Novar wasn't saying much. Legion did get one thing out of it. Novar was a diehard for the city and felt it was his responsibility to keep the city alive and well. Eventually, Novar opened up to him.

"I hear your grandfather was the greatest fighter the world had ever seen?" Upon finishing his words, he threw back the last half of his big mug of ale.

Legion smiled and laughed a bit. Now he was getting somewhere. Finally, after nearly an hour of pointless conversation, Novar wanted to talk. Why did Legion really want to talk to him in the first place? What was the point in all of this? His goal was to learn of Eternis and to do that, he had to know the people in charge of it. He knew that. It was good to consistently remind himself.

Legion immediately became joking and haughty. "I may be a little biased but I'd have to agree." Legion slammed a fist playfully and not too hard onto the table after answering.

Novar smiled, pleased with Legion's mannerisms. He cut the conversation back to the battle of Malakai and Bahaus. Legion explained what happened from what he knew and how he and Dauge were the ones who got Bahaus and brought him to the Eternian prison.

"And so it is then, the legendary Dominick Xavier's boy is the one who stopped the northern threat and his grandson is the one who brings in the rebel prince? You house was destined for greatness, boy. You remember that." Novar's words were sincere and them with a strong left eyewink, as if to reconfirm what he was saying.

"Thank you sir, tell me please, what will Eternis do with no monarch to guide the people?"

"Eternis has always faired well. The lessers will work as they've always done. Those middleclass folk will do as they've always done. And the upper class will work hard to pull more clout their way. Some will fail. Others will succeed. The high houses will feud and eventually, the Ekkehardts will claim what is theirs by right."

"By right?" Legion questioned.

"The Blackwinds won't get it, not on my watch. The Bloodstars have lost face with the people. It only makes sense for the Ekkehardts to get it. Tervel is a great man and he comes from the strongest and purest blood. And so long as no one in the family does something foul, they'll elect Tervel to the throne in no time."

"And if this is to be, would it have the backing of Novar Caelegate?"

"Of course, but Tervel taking the throne would not be my first choice."

"Then what would be your resolve to a city, such as Eternis absent a king?"

"As I said, boy, Eternis is in need of restructure. Times have changed. Thedia has changed. Runethedian has changed. Eternis is the only thing that stays the same." Novar excited himself thinking of his own words as he spoke them.

"Maybe that's what the world needs? Eternis is looked at for its age and grandeur structures that have stood the test of time. Maybe the world needs something like Eternis, something that'll never change?"

Novar glared a curious stare at Legion. What was he up to? The boy made perfect sense, but who was he to be so smart at such a young age? Then again, he did descend from two legendary men. Even his uncle Adrian was recognized as a legend in his own right for his tactics put into use for the Republic of New Magic against Corvana.

"You're a clever boy. Don't ever lose that."

"I'll try not to," Legion jokingly replied.

"That's an honorable series of words, boy, but the fact remains that Eternis needs to change with the times."

Legion nodded. Perhaps he was right. After all, who was he to question? He'd only just returned to Eternis. Novar was serving the city long before he got here. Legion didn't want Novar to think of him as cocky or arrogant. So, he replied in the only manner he knew how. "My words were merely a suggestion sir, and all ears should be open to second opinions. You've run this city for quite a spell, long before I got here. Novar Caelegate, I'm not challenging your ways but rather just hoping to be useful."

Novar couldn't help but like the boy. He was a kid in his prime. He was probably somewhere in his mid to late twenties and carried the attitude needed to succeed in the world. He was a Xavier, the house most widely known and recognized from Eternis. The two continued to talk but eventually the conversation died down to nearly nothing. And finally, when Legion knew it was done, he bid the dwarf farewell and took back to the city.

Legion still felt a coldness in him he'd never felt before. Something from the fight between the two legacy casters, Bahaus and Malakai, did something to him that he couldn't explain. Walking and talking with the good people of Eternis made him happier than he'd been in a long time.

Legion couldn't help but ponder. What if the roar that possessed him allowed him to be both darker and happier when in the appropriate surroundings? The people of Eternis were all around him. He'd already spoken to so many great people of the city. Looking around, the ancient structures from a time long past soothed him. Thinking about it, he actually walked along the same streets as those from a thousand years before him. What was the city like back then? What were the people like? How would he fair in such a place? Again, Legion smiled, knowing there still so much of the city left to explore. He furthered the grin, knowing that there was still so much of him left to explore.

Epilogue

The next three years and change were spent rebuilding the foundation of the great city. On the thirtieth year of the Sundering, the time era finally came to an end. Eternis officially called an end to the era when a blanket of darkness swept across all of Thedia, dimming out what little magic the world had left.

The dawning of the Darkening's first year marked the twenty-seventh birthday for Legion and the twenty-fifth birthday for both, Dauge and Dusk. The last few years of the Sundering were actually rather peaceful for the ancient city and most of Runethedian, as no significant wars or battles were known to have taken place.

To give themselves a proper backing here, Legion signed up for the local guard shortly after he talked with Novar. He served a three-year term, getting released just months before the Sundering came to an official end.

Aflyndor, the magnificent kingdom of magic was said to now be the heart of all magic in Thedia, or at least Runethedian. Some believed their powers kept the world sustained in its darkened state. Arcane still, more than ever, became something that was heavily looked down upon. Divine casters weren't looked down upon as arcane casters but even they were losing their respected grounds in the cities. Only those martially trained and adept to the primal kept their standings throughout the world. If anything, for some reason they gained a following unlike anything they had ever seen before.

The world's brightest places dimmed and its darkest places got darker. The northern pantheon, Corvana, called the new age, the Age of Darkness. Runethedian gave it the name, The Darkening. Kingdoms were far less likely to war. Cities were less likely to bring feuds to battle. Everything had a heavy price now. Thedia was a mere shell of its former self. And though the Eternian Taj Odin Xavier defeated the last Forsaken there in the Broken Lands, Raino Shadowblood's efforts would never be forgotten; for he'd left his mark upon the world. It was a mark the world would never be able to forget.

Eternis was still Eternis though, and the people of the city still walked a tiptoe higher because of their ancestry. Shortly after the dawning of the Darkening, a new threat of an old lineage came about. Legion and Dauge knew they were going to have to partake in its annihilation, or at least felt obligated to render their services. Dorian was nowhere around. He'd not been seen since the day he'd left. His former team, led by the good elf Woodway, was killed by the threat and hung on nearby pikes as warning to the city should they decide against proper negotiations.

It began along time ago, when the Kingdom of Magic was still around. The highly empowered kingdom organized a new breed of people. Somewhere already around and seeing the unique beings and their abilities really amplified the kingdom's desire to see a breeding done right for it. The strongest human slaves and dwarven slaves were put together. A new race came from the procedure. The race took the name, Mul.

The muls were a different people. They became tall as humans and kept the stockiness and sturdiness of a dwarf. They could work for days at a time in some cases. They were an elite slave worker to say the least. The nickname mule came early but calling a mul a mule was a quick way to get punched and beaten.

Eventually, a mul slave rebelled against the mighty Kingdom of Magic and many claim that his rebellion was instrumental in bringing the kingdom down, following further rebellions. The survivors fled after many wars, south to the edge of the continent. It was there they discovered a city they'd not ever known or heard of before. That city was called Eternis. The muls took the city and burned it, killing those who chose to fight honorably and enslaving all else that remained.

Their new city was called Raielios, in honor of the angelic deity they chose to worship, Raielyn. Raielyn was the angel with a portfolio over freedom and thus, the enslaving of others really didn't make sense, but again, the muls were a new, different people.

Unfortunately, the muls found the city of Eternis under heavy pressure. Neighboring lizardfolk, troglodytes, and everything else came and swarmed the walls of the city, hoping to break them down. The muls fought back with a ferocity never before seen by the original natives of the city. It was then that an angelical being, Mercius Kordur, returned.

He was a deva, a fragmentation of an angel. He reclaimed the city, attacking the muls from the inside when the mul people were at their weakest. The muls were driven out and once again. The city of Raielios became the city of Eternis, belonging to the rightful first men of Runethedian once again.

During those final three years and some months of the Sundering, Legion was not without difficulty. That roaring sound haunted him. It never left him. And as the day's passed it only got worse. The people of Eternis bore witness to things no man should be forced to see. They watched him change and grow and fight with a force even the muls would stand in awe of. He was sent on missions deep in the ground and far away from the city. The people of Eternis began to wonder about him, especially toward the end. Were they safe with his presence upon them?

Most berserkers were barred from cities, far removed once discovered. Even with Legion's history and lineage, it was coming time for him to be taken from the city as well. At one point, he spent nearly four months in an underground circular prison pit. He was forced to remain there until the berserking spirit within him was gone.

Now was the new age, The Darkening. The city was still going to thrive. Legion was thinking deeply about leaving his beloved city. With every passing day, his condition got worse. On many occasions he was able to control it, but what was to come of the city or him on the day he couldn't?

Then, with the coming of The Darkening dawned yet another threat to the peaceful city; on the day of an Ekkehardt wedding a band of muls entered the city. For the past few weeks prior, traveling caravans, carriages, and other travelers had been attacked relentlessly, many never making it home or to their destinations. The Eternians knew it was the recent incursion of the muls.

The city gates were breached easily on the western front. They rode into the city, disregarding the old law of not riding horses past and into the city. All five looked battle-hardened and war torn. Their armor was dirty and covered, dented and opened by scars from battle. Soot and blood stained their bodies and clothes. Their weapons bathed in the same soot and blood.

They rode deep into town square where Sir Elekar Ekkehardt was preparing to wed his lovely fiancé. They steadied their horses, seeing Tervel Ekkehardt not too far from them. Not a single mul had a strand of hair on his head. One did keep a long ponytail birthing from the very back of his head, extending all the way down his back. For the rest, their heads were shaved down to the skin.

Legion wasn't too far from Tervel in the frontlines of the crowd. Dauge neared his side. The one time Tervel was left unprotected, he thought. Two of the muls had very distinct and different facial features, thought Legion. He didn't know what to do, whether to act or whether to hold. Tervel was the closest thing to a leader the city still had.

The lead mul first pulled back the reins to his horse. The four muls backing him secondarily followed. Two muls held large crossbows of a unique design in one hand and a large javelin in the other. One mul outlined his body with heavy armor. He kept it decorated with insignias of Raielyn, the Angel of Freedom. Another was covered in tattoos and dark robes. They fluttered in the winds. The one with Raielyn-inscribed armor kept a great hammer by his side. The hooded mul's eyes glowed from beneath its hood. And the final one wore no armor but elegant clothing, finely woven. They were bright and got even brighter at the seams. On his back rested a large hangar. Blood stained the back of his clothes.

Tervel walked forward, even against the suggestions of the men and people. He took center stage while the others of the city backed away. The horses were unsteady but their riders managed to steady them. Tervel was old. His hair was a deep black and streaked with blue and gray colors. It lay tightly upon his head and combed back. His outfit was pure white and tightened at the center of his chest line. Tervel walked forward. The people of the open city encircled the lead mul and the current liege of the Ekkehardt house. The circle ended a mess, scattering chaotically around the other four horses,

"What are you doing here, riding horses into town? Why do you come here weapons ablazing?" Tervel asked fairly.

The old man's tone was true and sincere. His questions brought forth so many more to the people of Eternis. He slowly approached the horse carrying what appeared to be the lead mul. He placed his hand upon the mane of it. He stroked the fine hair of the horse, looking up at its rider. "It's a fine steed."

"I've not come here for your compliments to my horse, though Liza is a fine steed if I must say. I've come here to offer message from Suzerain, Lugo Zjhaste."

"Apologies, I'm not familiar with the man," Tervel answered.

"He is our liege. This city rightfully belongs to Suzerain Zjhaste. Allow the Ekkehardts most beautiful daughter with the strongest lineage to wed his youngest son Amaryl. This will forge a pact between the two families and together they shall rule Eternis. Eternis is in need of a true monarch. Eternis is in need of a confirmed ruling house. Eternis is in need of protection, a real army not a hired one. All wealth runs dry. Eternis one day will run out of luck and chances and then who will pay for the armies? The army we offer is of the finest quality. It is one that has never seen defeat on the battlefield. No simpletons, every single weapon wielder wields their chosen instruments with such talent and experience that no basic infantryman could ever stand its equal."

"Eternis belongs to the people, my friend. Whatever was here before or whatever comes after is of no concern to us. We are here now. You are right. We are absent a true ruler. The last of our royal line sits in our own prisons, mainly for his own safety. The Ekkehardts are old in blood and in tradition, but we have never forced any of our own daughters to the arms of unworthy husbands." Tervel spoke with a kindness that almost became derisive.

The lead mul pulled back the reins again, raising his horse high into the air. The horse's front two legs kicked about chaotically. He was outraged. He couldn't believe what he'd heard. "How dare you speak of Suzerain's youngest like that!" The others were moved as well but not nearly as much as the lead mul. He was truly sickened by Tervel's words. He was at the brink of war, even with just five surrounded by the city.

"Forgive me, sir, I meant not that he was unworthy. Our daughters choose their own husbands, men that have actively proven worthy in each of their own eyes."

The mul's horse dropped down. He was still shaking his head with disgust, believing Tervel to only be reshaping his words in hopes of hiding their initial intent. The lead mul pulled a decorated scepter from the side of his horse and pointed it at the old man. Then suddenly, he looked back over to Legion and Dauge. He'd known they were there all along.

He turned back and headed for the gates. The crowds of Eternis scrambled to break away, giving them the clear opening they needed to escape the city. The city didn't give chase. The people immediately began to surround Tervel. Tervel was a good man but one not known to walk alongside the simple folk. He typically helped from afar. Today would be different. Today, he would walk alongside them and cheer them. He would do whatever it took to boost his people's morale. After all, soon he would be king, wouldn't he?

Legion looked at Dauge. Dauge thought back to all of the close calls they had with Legion's "situation" over the past couple of years. He looked back on how many people fell that didn't have to, how many times he covered for him. His brother was a berserker, truly possessed by some raging spirit. He couldn't keep it in. He couldn't control it; and worse, he didn't know what actually set it off.

"So it looks like we're going to be engaging muls next. Will you be able to keep that thing in you under control?" It'd been some time since the berserker had last come out so Dauge asked the question, but truth be told he knew the answer to it already.

"I don't need to control it little brother. I just need to unleash it," he replied with a smile.

The muls left Eternis. In the coming days, many raids took place against travelers both coming and going from the city. They were all blamed upon the muls. A small battle took place, which claimed the life of one of the old residents, Slate Thundershot. Slate was among the men who first attempted to go after Bahaus with Drackice.

Legion was a good warrior and equipped well, especially with Mourning Star at his side. Dauge was fast and could hit a dozen targets in half as many seconds. He wasn't as sturdy as his brother but he didn't have to be. And with Legion's new affliction and Dauge's natural knack for hating people, neither were fit to lead anything.

There was one who was. Drackice Black, son of the legendary Free Armies General Magnus Black. Drackice spent his days rallying the people and the troops to do their duty to their city and the people of the entire pantheon. When it came to inspiring courage, none were better than Drackice Black.

Drackice already had at least one ally still walking with him, the wizard Draeden. Draeden was a Genasi, an elemental being and a hard one at that. He'd become Drackice's right hand man. They were the last two together of the nine that originally set out from the Free Armies. Over the course of many days, Dauge listened to the man speak. Legion lost his ability to understand feelings or emotions. All he carried now was a sense for logic and order.

Legion initially hoped to find a cure for his affliction, but through time, he'd gotten colder and became less interested. Dauge listened continuously to Drackice's words. Drackice also frequented their home for Destiny. And even there, Dauge listened to his every word and paid attention to his every move.

Dauge wasn't overly enchanted by his awe-inspiring words of wisdom and bravery. He wasn't charmed into believing everything Drackice said. It was between the lines that Dauge focused. Drackice had a plan Dauge believed could work. And Drackice also had a well-suited wizard. In this day and age, such things weren't so easily acquired. Dauge didn't truly care for the son of Magnus but he did respect him. He liked the wizard. The wizard was cold, quiet, methodical, and most importantly, he kept to himself.

Dauge knew Legion would listen to him. Once he broke it down for him, he would understand. Rumor around town was that with all of the major tragedies and battlefield skirmishes leading to so many unnecessary deaths, Tervel was beginning to reconsider his decision. None had come this time for Eternis. Who would come and what would they fight? The feud was still early. By the time anyone else knew about it, it could all be over. The muls were of nowhere. They had no home. At least, this band of muls didn't. They might as well have come from the mountains.

Just fifteen days from the day they originally tore through the city, Dauge sat down with Legion explaining everything. It was an easy conversation. Legion jumped on board rather quickly. He wasn't excited about it. The logic and reason as to why made sense; he had the strongest weapon in town and was probably among the top one percent in skill.

The next and final step would be to meet with Drackice Black. Drackice hadn't requested for anyone to join him. He probably didn't plan on entering the mouth of the beast head on as he'd done before. After Dauge was through with him, that's exactly what he was going to do.

It was early dawn on the sixteenth day. The temperature was moderate but clouds filled the sky and drops of rain began to drizzle out of them like water from a lightly squeezed sponge. Legion and Dauge left the Broken Swords with full stomachs and clear heads. Today was a good day. Even Dusk's peculiar activities and personality wasn't going to ruin it for Dauge. She kept claiming something happened to her. Dauge knew she was right. He kept hoping that if he ignored it, it would go away. He knew this wasn't so. And the more he thought about it, the more he couldn't decide. Was she going to be okay? What was she doing this day? What was it that the damned undead thing did to her?

No, Drackice was the target today. He had to speak to Drackice. Dauge wanted to unite and cut the heads off the muls, leaving the body of the beast without any direction. Somehow, he knew Drackice wouldn't agree but he needed Drackice, and more importantly, he needed that wizard.

The muls, where did they come from? How did they get here? What was it they truly wanted? How could they barge into the city so easily? Did they watch the movements and seek holes in the defenses or did they just chaotically charge in? Slate Thundershot, a powerful man from the city of Eternis and loyal soldier to the Free Armies was dead already. How many more would die before peace would yet again find and cloak the city of Eternis?

CPSIA information can be obtained at www.ICGtesting.com
Printed in the USA
LVOW10s1954300116

472583LV00001B/3/P